REVERSE

KATE STEWART

First Line Editor
Donna Cooksley Sanderson
Second Line Editor
Grey Ditto
Cover by Amy Q- Q Design

For my dear friend, Autumn Gantz. I can't imagine what life would be like if you hadn't picked up the phone five years ago and taken a chance on a writer who was struggling to realize her dream. A frank conversation about a music-based book I had yet to release started our inevitable 11:11 journey, and I'm so incredibly grateful for every step.

And for all those creatives who we declared heroes before we spotlighted their flaws and exploited their demons. Forgive us, for we know not what we did.
You were only human.

REVERSE FORWARD

HA! See what happened there? I can't take pun credit, it occurred naturally.

Welcome to my first forward. I'm pretty sure I will be terrible at this, but alas, I must because I need to preface the setting for this book.

Picture this, Sicily, 2035, wait…this isn't a Golden Girl's episode.

Let's try this then…

Two households, both alike in dignity, in fair Verona, where we lay our scene—year, 2035…Nope, that doesn't really work either.

Okay, so here goes. Years ago, I decided Drive would never, ever, ever, ever, have a sequel and swore as much vehemently over the years that followed.

In January of this year, I made myself a liar.

So, nearly five years of "I'm not doing it" later, inspiration hit. I would love to apologize for the direction this one took, bearing in mind the requests from readers for a different take, but alas, I cannot because I fell passionately in love with this story and the characters.

Why all this gibberish, Kate? This book takes place thirteen years into the future, in the year 2035, which gave me a few liberties, that I did not take to the crazy extent. There are no flying cars in this book, nor do the characters materialize in a "Beam me up, Scotty" way. This isn't that kind of book.

That said, I spruced up a few things technologically to suit this story—and I mean very few—to the point they'll probably go unnoticed by some or many. Other things noted in the book have been aged well beyond our current year of 2022.

While I did my absolute best to keep up with the timeline from the previous book, the age progressions, and the love story timelines of all characters, I may have fumbled a little with the ball. I'm not saying I did, but it happens.

So, my request to you, dear reader, is…*go with it* and just enjoy this tale of woe from that of Juliet and her Romeo. Kind of. No spoilers here.

Clears throat.

As was the case with DRIVE, book #1, the chapter headings in REVERSE are clickable, so you can listen while you read to further enhance your experience. If nothing else, I implore you to listen to the songs during the most crucial chapters as they really do elevate the story. Music is both the muse and basis for this series.

If you have not read *Drive*, I strongly urge you to stop and grab it before proceeding to this story. Is it necessary? Absolutely. If you want to experience and feel this book as I intended while writing, it's a must.

Once again, I must thank you, dear reader, for giving my books a try with all my heart. I hope you enjoy it.

XO
Kate

NOTE TO READER

To experience this book in its entirety, like *Drive,* we have made this an interactive e-book. Each chapter heading is a clickable link to the song so you can listen while you read. And because this duet is my personal ode to my driving force—music—I couldn't resist incorporating the soundtrack through Spotify.

Download Spotify for free.

Listen to the Reverse Playlist.

Listen to The Bittersweet Symphony Duet Playlist

PART I

"With the lights out, it's less dangerous
Here we are now, entertain us"
Nirvana
"Smells Like Teen Spirit"

ONE

Someone Like You
Adele

Natalie

Glancing over my monitor to his office across the bustling newsroom, I see him typing a mile a minute. Rolling my chair closer to my desk, I duck out of his line of sight in an effort to shield my guilty conscience.

Nate Butler
Subject: Decisions
June 7, 2005, 2:23 a.m.

Salutations post countless beers,

I find it amusing that you work at a place called The Plate Bar. Did those idiot owners even research the name? I'm sitting on the patio at my best friend's place, staring at the city lights, and I'm wondering where you are. I swore I wouldn't bother you after beer one, and then decided on a formal email after beer three. But I still can't afford you. It's sad, really. So, the countdown begins, Miss Emerson. And though it's just a few short months away, I find myself wanting to make one last effort to persuade you to go out with me (for research purposes of course). I have two tickets for the Ritz this Saturday.

GET. IN. MY. TAHOE.

Nate Butler
Editor in Chief, Austin Speak
Sent via Blackberry

"Natalie, line four," Elena, our office receptionist, chimes in as I damn near jump out of my skin. "It's Jack with The Dallas Morning News."

Nerves firing off as they have for the last half hour, I stand abruptly and think better of it, easing back into my chair. A closed door may pique Dad's interest. I press the intercom to reception. "Tell him I'll call him back, and Elena, I need an hour without interruption, okay?"

"Sure, hon," she replies with the maternal tone she's always used with me. I don't take offense to it—even in this professional setting—because she watched me grow up at this paper. To her, I'll always be the ginger-headed, twin-braid sporting little girl that considered the office furniture a part of my playground. Turning down the volume on my phone while my conscience screams at me, I glance around quickly before scanning the first few emails again.

Nate Butler
Subject: Courtesy
June 7, 2005, 5:01 p.m.

It is my understanding that a drunken man extended a concert invitation to you last night. And while I do not condone that behavior, especially from a future employer to employee, I find it extremely rude that said invitation has not been acknowledged. Teamwork is key here at Austin Speak, Miss Emerson. I can only assume you take your position seriously and are against the feminist lyrics of Sheryl Crow. My apologies. Moving forward, I will refrain from extracurricular emails, but will settle for a second interview, in my office, by 6:00 p.m. today.

Nate Butler
Editor in Chief, Austin Speak
Sent Via Blackberry

Nate Butler
Subject: Oversight
June 8, 2005, 11:13 a.m.

It occurred to me that you may not be receiving these emails, but I think we both know, Miss Emerson, that is not the case. And since I have no proof of this, I have no choice but to believe you remain steadfast in your decision not to mix business with research, however disconcerting that may be due to the nature of your profession. But for the sake of office morale, I may be so inclined to have a beer at our place around 6:00 p.m. this evening to discuss this issue.

Nate Butler
Editor in Chief, Austin Speak
Sent via Blackberry

"Geez, Dad, laying it on thick," I whisper with a budding grin, popping up once more from behind my screen before zeroing in.

Stella Emerson
Subject: Deadlines
June 10, 2005, 9:42 p.m.

Dear Mr. Butler,

I am flattered by your correspondence and excited about the chance of working with you. Due to my current situation, I am unable to receive emails in a timely manner because of connection issues. I will be remedying this situation within the coming weeks. While all invitations are appreciated, I prefer to do my research alone. I am happy to report that things are rapidly progressing with my articles, and they will be delivered to you in two months' time.

Best Wishes,
Stella Emerson
Future Entertainment Columnist, Austin Speak
Sent via The Plate Bar

"Ewww, best wishes?" I wince. "Burn. You struck out hard." I can't help my laugh at her witty, dry humor, especially in her email signature 'sent via The Plate Bar.' The web wasn't nearly as accessible back then as it is now. Thirty years ago, the world was just on the precipice of the digital age. I recently did a story about advanced technology versus the gadgets of the eighties, nineties, and even the early 2000s. Most born past the millennium—including me—couldn't identify what many of them were, let alone figure out how to use them. At this stage, I can't imagine what little to no access life was like.

These thirty-year-old emails are proof of just how advanced we've become. That life existed without one-touch convenience.

Fascinated but hesitant, I briefly battle the churning in my gut, a sure sign that what I'm doing is wrong in more ways than one. Unease bubbling, I consider closing out the window and returning to the task my father charged me with.

I'm supposed to be searching the paper's archives for excerpts from articles for Speak's thirtieth anniversary edition printing this fall. Years ago, Dad hired a tech team to transfer everything Austin Speak to our current mainframe, including every article circulated. Apparently, the transfer also extracted everything from his dinosaur laptop—including ancient Austin Speak email chains. He didn't oversee the project himself. His priority was the stories of *today* rather than yesteryear. I'm not sure he's aware his email chains were included in the transfer, tucked away in a marked file in the archives. A file I stumbled into minutes ago and haven't been able to click out of, while morally warring with myself to move on. But it's the subject line of the following email that has me prying further—an email dating back to November, twenty-nine years ago.

Nate Butler
Subject: Trick? or Treat?
November 1, 2005, 10:00 a.m.

Miss Emerson,

Did I dream last night? Images keep flitting through my mind of a dark-haired, curvy temptress rolling around my office to "Xanadu" in white roller skates.

Nate Butler
Editor in Chief, Austin Speak

I pause, a dangerous inkling coursing through me while a bold line comes into clear view in my mind. Just as I acknowledge it, my curiosity blurs it, and I step over, unable to stop myself.

Stella Emerson
Subject: Trick? or Treat?
November 1, 2005, 10:01 a.m.

Sir,

I'm going to keep your psychotic break in confidence as I need this job and the platform it provides me as a budding journalist. I assure you that I have no idea (buffs roller skates) about what you're referring to. Now, if you'll excuse me, I have a deadline and a very anal editor to report to. I can't afford to entertain your delusions any further.

Stella
Xanadu Enthusiast, Austin Speak

Nate Butler
Subject: Trick? or Treat?
November 1, 2005, 10:03 a.m.

In my office now, *Right Girl*, and lock the fucking door behind you.

Nate Butler
Editor in Chief, Austin Speak

"Oh my God, oh my God, oh my God," I exhale in a barely audible whisper as I briefly kick back in my seat.

They were involved.

Gaping at the revelation, I again glance up to see Dad still occupied in his chair.

My dad and Stella Emerson, now Stella Emerson Crowne, wife to one of the biggest rock legends in history, were involved romantically.

Shock vibrates through me as I scroll through endless emails between them. There are hundreds—if not thousands—of emails spanning over four years from my father to a woman who isn't my mother. Years of emails from one of my heroes to another. Years of his life where he was clearly infatuated and crazy in love with Stella Emerson Crowne.

Not Addison Warner Hearst, my *mother*, his *wife*.

It's no secret amongst us who work at Austin Speak that Stella was one of the foundational blocks who aided the paper in becoming a reputable and well-respected local news source. In fact, whenever Stella's been mentioned, Dad's been completely transparent about *that aspect* of her time here and her contributions. Thinking back, not *once* has he ever mentioned he was involved with her personally.

Not once.

I would have remembered that, considering I've idolized her career as one to aspire to, along with any other ambitious journalist. But back when they were involved, the social media revolution hadn't yet begun, and there were no online pictures, nor was there a digital footprint of the progression of their relationship. At that time, there was a considerable amount of control on what surfaced on the web, on access itself. Dad never had a Facebook for anything other than the paper, and apps like Insta didn't exist yet. The two of them weren't newsworthy then...but Reid Crowne *was*.

Even so, Dad has purposefully kept their involvement under wraps, but why? Dad and I share everything. He's been an open book to me my whole life. Granted, relationships are different, but he's been pretty candid about those, or at least I thought so. Thinking back now, I can't really remember him referencing a specific ex.

Feeling a little betrayed—knowing I really don't have much of a right to be due to the personal nature—I decide not to torture myself and respect his privacy enough to scroll to the last few emails. If anything, I need to know *how* and *why* it ended and, more specifically, *who* ended it. I skip forward nearly five years to read the last few.

Stella Emerson
Subject: I'm Here
September 11, 2010, 6:02 p.m.

Nate,

I'm almost embarrassed to admit I'm scared, but I've never been able to hide the truth from you. Even if I didn't admit it, you'd be able to read between these lines somehow. I've strayed halfway across the country from everything I've ever known and everyone who truly knows me.

But I guess the meaning of home is subjective now, isn't it?

When the wheels touched down in Seattle, it sort of felt like walking into a warm embrace. Nothing was familiar, and yet being here feels like déjà vu. Like my life here, my chapters were already written, and the city was just waiting for me to begin to live them. Even the overgrown elm tree next to my apartment building is oddly recognizable. Or maybe I'm romanticizing myself in my new life here. I'm sure you're thinking that right now as you read this, though I'm more the cosmic believer of the two of us. As crazy as it may seem to the rationalist you are, I can sense I'm starting the life I was meant to. Though I have to admit, certain parts of me are still trying to make peace with leaving.

During the flight, I drew upon memories that made Texas feel most like home. One of them was the day we spent at the farmer's market beneath the sun, sharing food and smiles while switching papers. A day that remains one of my favorites. I already miss Texas, and I'm nervous about starting the job at Seattle Waves because I have a feeling that I'll hate my new editor. My last one is irreplaceable. I miss him every single day. But I feel…safe here.

Love,
Stella

Nate Butler
RE: Subject: I'm Here
September 12, 2010, 8:04 a.m.

Go with your gut; know it's a good one to trust because it brought you where you are. If you get overwhelmed, just remember how far you've come from that day you waltzed in here wearing a *Pulp Fiction*, Samuel Jackson "Tasty Burger" T-shirt and demanding that I take you seriously. I was just at the market yesterday and thought of that day too. It's definitely a Stella thing.

What have I told you about starting sentences with the word but?

I can't be sure, but I feel your old editor really doesn't miss your bullshit, or your defense of Stellisms, you know, the words you bent and tried to pass for English that don't exist in the dictionary. Nor does he miss schooling you on proper news etiquette. Or maybe he does. One thing is certain.

Texas misses you.
I fucking miss you.

Always,
Nate Butler
Editor in Chief, Austin Speak

Nate Butler
Subject: Making Waves
October 3, 2010, 6:03 p.m.

Subject Line pun intended. I'm so proud of you. You're turning that no-name paper into a fuel source for shaky subscribers. I have zero doubt Seattle Waves will be a reputable 'rag' in no time. While you were a force to be reckoned with here in Austin, you're a fucking hurricane now, Stella. You outgrew this paper and Texas far before you left it. I regret not giving you more leeway. Please, don't hold back now. Not for anything or anyone. As much as I hate admitting

this, seeing your growth there makes it even more apparent you made the right decision to go. You're thriving. I'm proud.
Always,
Nate Butler
Editor in Chief, Austin Speak

Stella Emerson
RE: Subject: Making Waves
October 4, 2010, 4:34 p.m.

Nate,

I haven't been taken seriously as a journalist all damned day due to your email. It was the first thing I saw this morning, and coming from my harshest critic, you know how much it means to me. So, because of that, I've been smiling like a lunatic and getting odd looks. You would think I would be used to that by now. I'll be honest, I'm more in love now with this place than ever because I feel I'm on the precipice of something I can't explain. I don't love how much the fit feels right for reasons you're aware of. At the same time, I'm embracing Seattle. I'm hugging her back, hard. So much so that I'm about to start house hunting. I know, right? Can you fucking believe it? I'm laying roots for the first time ever, and ironically, I'm not scared. It's like I can picture it, and I'm already there, but Texas is always with me.

Love,
Stella

Stella Emerson
Subject: I'm Sorry
November 9, 2010, 9:00 p.m.

I know why you didn't answer. I'm so sorry for anything those headlines might have made you feel. Running into Reid was completely unexpected. I don't know if you want a single detail. I know

I wouldn't, but please know it wasn't planned. I'm sure you will tell me not to feel guilty, but I fucking do. It hurts me so much to know you were probably blindsided by that picture. Please believe I don't want any tension or resentment between us, but the sinking feeling inside me tells me it's unavoidable. Nate, this is the first time in my life that I hate my profession and journalism as a whole. I never wanted to become any part of a headline, let alone one that could damage the two of us.

I'm sorry. I miss hearing from you and wish you would or felt like you could still talk to me.

Love,
Stella

Scrambling, I look up the headlines for November 9, 2010, and see a candid picture of Stella and Reid, tucked away and kissing on a side street in Seattle—and it's no PG kiss. Not even close. Obviously, they thought they were hidden from view. The article goes on to identify Stella and speculate what this could mean for the Dead Sergeants' notoriously single drummer. My heart sinks as I read my father's reply.

Nate Butler
Re: Subject: I'm sorry
November 10, 2010, 3:00 a.m.

Don't be. Texas is no longer your home, and it's evident. You're making another life. I think we've always known what that would eventually include. Please don't let your worry for me overshadow your happiness.

Always
Nate Butler
Editor in Chief, Austin Speak

According to the time stamp, he replied to her at three a.m. from his office. A vision of my dad sitting alone behind his desk while staring at the picture pops into my head as a burn begins in my throat. I can only imagine what he must have felt as he tried to devise the right response for her. In the end, even though I'm sure he felt destroyed, he took the high road and, not only that, attempted to relieve her of the burden.

Stella Emerson
Subject: Headlines
December 13, 2010, 7:00 p.m.

Nate,

We're engaged, and it's going to print tomorrow. I didn't want you to hear it from anyone else but me. I wish things were different. I wish I still felt like I have the right to know you—and a large part of me is breaking right now knowing I've lost that right. I'm still going to make the case that I loathe that it's happening and always will.

Love,
Stella

Nate Butler
RE: Subject: Headlines
December 14, 2010, 1:02 a.m.

Stella,

Have you forgotten all I've taught you? Any worthy newsman is aware of a national headline before the ink is laid. All I've ever wanted or will ever want for you is your happiness. Your engagement is already scheduled to print on page one in Austin Speak tomorrow. Congratulations.

Out of respect for your choice and for myself, this is goodbye, Stella. Be happy.

Always,
Nate Butler
Editor in Chief, Austin Speak

Eyes misting, I catch sight of my father pacing his office, his phone to his ear. A million questions flit through my mind as I resist the urge to go back and probe into his past to quench my growing curiosity.

A few years before I was born, Stella Emerson Crowne left Texas and, from what I've gathered thus far, broke my father's heart in the process. Mere months later, she married a rock star in a very publicized winter wedding, leaving my dad a casualty of her happiness. A casualty who's been my rock throughout the whole of my life. A man who's shaped me into the woman and writer I've become.

As a journalist himself, Dad not only had to endure reading the headlines but had a duty to report them as well. I have no doubt he assigned someone to cover her wedding day, owing to her association with the paper. Dragging my mouse over the file, I dig through the archives to see that's the truth of it. A reporter named JJ, who left Speak years ago, covered the fairytale wedding in its entirety.

He had an obligation to his readers to report the stories they wanted, and because Stella held a desk at Speak, it cemented his fate as both spectator and reporter.

"Daddy," I whisper hoarsely as my heart breaks for him trying to imagine how he was forced to endure that aspect of it.

Is that why he's kept this hidden?

Was it humiliating for him?

My eyes remained fixed on him as he bends from where he stands and taps a few keys, squinting as he does so. I can't even muster a smile as he practically presses his nose to the screen in an effort to read the words. Mom's been on him for years to use his readers and even bought them in bulk and put them within reach in every imaginable space he occupies.

He's as stubborn as they come, an inherited trait passed down to me.

Annoyed by whatever task he's working on, Dad collapses into his chair, squeezing his worn stress ball. I scan for any more correspondence between him and Stella after his goodbye email—and I come up empty.

Was that the last time they spoke? Saw each other?

More questions flit through my mind as I grapple with the heaviness circulating through me. How long had they been broken up before she left for Seattle? How long after did he meet Mom? Pulling up my cell phone, I shoot off a text.

When exactly did you and Daddy start dating?

Her reply comes less than a minute later.

Mom: A hundred years ago.

What was the exact date?

Mom: February 2011. We met at a media party, and you know this. Don't ask me when we got serious. He's still my longest one-night stand.

They met mere months after Stella and Dad stopped communicating, but how long after they broke up?

I look up Stella's last article for Austin Speak and see it was printed almost eight months before she left Austin, which indicates she might have quit the paper when they broke up. My phone buzzes again.

Mom: Why? Afraid you're illegitimate? (tongue emoji)

Not funny.

Mom: What is this about exactly?

Just curious.

Mom: I'm at the store. Can you grill me later? If you come home tonight, I'll cook.

Feeling oddly displaced, my current headspace won't allow me to face either parent right now. My curiosity is fueling my need for more answers.

I can't tonight. Tomorrow ok?

Mom: Sure. Love you. If I'm off the cooking hook, please tell your father to pick up Chinese on the way home.

Will do. X

I message her again as amplifying guilt continues to surround my heart.

I love you, Mom.

Mom: Love you too. By the way, if you're curious, you were well worth the hellacious sixteen-hour labor but it's also the reason why you're an only child.

My heart warms as I recall the story of Mom's nightmare in delivering me, her finish to the story the best part. As many times as I've heard and memorized what she refers to every year as "our day," I'm not as versed in the story of my parents' coupling. I've never really paid much attention in the *adult* way. Whenever it was brought up in the past, I always did the typical fake gag routine. Now I wish I had paid closer attention. As it is now, any outsider within a few feet of them can see they love and respect each other, *deeply.* It's obvious.

So why is this revelation affecting *me* so profoundly?

Why did my instincts tell me to lie to her—other than the fact it's not a subject to broach via text message.

Even so, why am I so afraid to outright ask my father, who just so happens to be the best source?

As I try to reason with myself, I'm terrified of what my gut is saying—my dad wouldn't have kept their relationship hidden unless he *wanted* it that way.

It's one thing to have an ex. It's another thing entirely to have an ex who went on to marry a world-famous rock star.

Mom has to know. She has to. There's no way they didn't have the ex-talk. All couples do at some point, *right?*

Dad is painfully frank, which some may consider a character flaw, but one which I proudly inherited. Regardless of that, every part of the journalist he cultivated in me is dying to walk across the hall for answers. But this isn't someone else's story. It's fact-checking his personal past that has me chickening out.

Not to mention the fact that the ancient emails have me questioning the authenticity of my parents' start so soon after his heartbreak and scrutinizing the timeline.

By my quick calculation, my parents married a year after they met. Just a few months ago, they celebrated their twenty-third anniversary. The question of my legitimacy is asinine because I came into the picture months after they wed, a souvenir they created on their month-long honeymoon.

The alarming part is that I deeply felt Stella and my father's connection while reading. I'm positive if I read more—especially during the thick of their relationship—I would feel it on an even more visceral level. I fear it may haunt me if I don't get the full story.

Just ask him, Natalie. He's feet away!

But something about the lingering ache I feel as a spectator after simply reading a dozen or so emails keep me from doing so.

I just inadvertently opened Pandora's box—a box that doesn't belong to me, a box I had no right to open.

Far too tempted to go back in, I drag my finger along the screen with the file and linger over the trash, flicking my focus back to Dad as I do so. Confusion, anger for him, and curiosity war in my head as I drag the file away from the trash and opt to hide the email chain in a desktop file before closing out the window.

Nervous energy coursing through me, stomach roiling, I glance around the bustling and recently renovated warehouse Dad converted into a newsroom when he started the paper. A u-shape of executive offices outlines the floor of the small warehouse, one of which I've occupied since graduating last spring.

In the center of the floor that Dad nicknamed 'the pit' sits rows upon rows of columnists' desks. Scanning the desks, my eyes land on Herb, an Austin Speak staple who was one of Dad's first hires. Herb is in his late sixties now and comes in on a part-time basis. At this point, it's safe to say he's more of a fixture than an integral part of the paper. Though that's the case now, he was present *then* and undoubtedly laid witness to Stella and my father's relationship.

Standing abruptly—without a clue as to how I'll approach it—I take a step toward my office door when my dad pauses across the pit, sensing my movement in his peripheral. He glances over at me, his lips lifting and forming his signature smile. Unable to school myself in time, his brows draw when he reads my expression.

Stay cool, Natalie.

Doing my best to ease the conflict inside, I muster a reassuring smile, but I can already tell it's too late. Dad's features etch in concern as he mouths an "Okay?"

Nodding repeatedly, I wave my hand dismissively before grabbing my coffee cup and making a beeline for the breakroom. Acting plays a small part in being a journalist, if only as an exercise in composure. People are less inclined to give you what you need if you seem too eager. At the same time, too much confidence can cause a similar issue—dissuading trust.

It's a balance and consistent exercise in composure until you reach the level where your name is more valuable and you have enough accolades as a journalist to be sought after, like Oprah, Diane Sawyer, or Stella Emerson Crowne.

Leaving college wet behind the ears as the daughter of one of the most highly respected editors in journalism, I have a lot to prove to myself and those in my field. Even though I write under my mother's maiden name as Natalie Hearst, my work for anyone in the field will always be synonymous with Nate Butler and his well-established and credible paper. I have so much to live up to, considering my father took the magazine from an ad-dependent paper to a next-level publication. And when he retires, which he insists will be sooner rather than later, it's up to me to help maintain its integrity.

Though I grew up in the newsroom, Dad's never pressured me to take it on but is responsible for so much of my love for the written word. Like Dad, my favorite news to report consists mainly of human-interest stories. His own writing journey began with a touching story during a time stamp no one ever forgets—9/11.

Challenged with dyslexia, he pressed on and figured out a way to work around it and carry out his dream to run a newspaper—which is more than admirable. My father is my hero and has been since I was young enough to recognize it. So it was only natural I spent my childhood sitting next to his desk, imitating his every move, typing on one of his old laptops before I could speak. Thanks to Mom, Dad has a dozen or so pride-filled videos of me doing just that to prove it.

My character traits and love for journalism aren't the only things I inherited from him. My strawberry blonde hair and indigo-colored eyes make our relationship unmistakable when we're within feet of each other and even when we're not.

Additionally, Dad has shared so much of himself with me that I know I could recite the milestones in his life in chronological order without much thought. Maybe that's why I'm so rattled because apparently, there are gaps in his history I was purposely not made privy to. The sudden shift of viewing my dad as a twenty-plus man in love rather than my Little League coach has me reeling.

Of course, my parents had histories before they met and married. Of course, there are parts of their lives they don't share with their daughter—secrets they plan on taking to their graves—but there's just something about this particular secret that isn't settling well with me. At all.

"Natalie?" Alex, our sports columnist prompts, staring up at me from his desk. Empty coffee cup in hand, I gape back at him, confused as to how I ended up lurking above him. "Can I help you with something?"

"J-just wanted to see if you wanted some coffee?" I mumble in shit excuse, lifting my mug as though he's never seen one.

"It's after two," he says curtly, just as confused by the gesture as I am. "I don't drink coffee after two."

"Okay." I bob my head, eyes again on the office now feet away, just as Dad hangs up the phone and starts to make his way toward us. Guilt and panic mix, prompting me to flee before he can reach me with his probing eyes. By the time flight kicks in, he's already striding toward me, seemingly as confused as Alex.

"What's up?" Dad asks as he joins me at Alex's desk.

"Kid was just asking me if I wanted some coffee."

"You can fetch your own, asshole," Dad snarks, giving me a wink.

"Well, as everyone knows," Alex fires back, "I don't drink coffee after *two*."

"No one knows, Alex," Dad taunts dryly, "nor cares."

"I want no special treatment," I remind him. "I have no issue getting coffee."

"Well, you don't have to play gopher or clean toilets. You've paid those dues already. This is a family-owned business, so there should be advantages to being a *Butler,* even if you write under *Hearst.*"

I nod, not in agreement, but because I'm staring at him with an altered perception while trying to forget what I just read, the gnawing in my gut constant.

He loved Stella. He *really* loved her. It was so evident.

An image of my smiling mother, riding next to me on Daisy, her favorite Haflinger, flashes through my mind as new pain sears through my chest.

"Well?" Dad chuckles.

"Well, what?" I ask.

"Your coffee," he nods toward my forgotten cup.

"Right. Want some?"

"No thanks, baby, I'm good."

"Oh!" I say loudly, startling him. "Mom wants you to pick up Chinese on the way home."

"'K," he nods before frowning. "You aren't coming over?"

"Tomorrow," I back away slowly, my eyes plastered to his. "I'm going to go get coffee." I toss a thumb over my shoulder, turn, and practically sprint to the breakroom to fill my cup. Mid-brew, I begin panicking about the fact I might have left a window open on my desktop. Discarding my cup in the sink, I haul ass back toward my office to see Dad's still standing at Alex's desk, making small talk. It's when he sees me empty-handed that he follows me into my office.

Fuck. Fuck. Fuck. Fuck. Fuck.

"Okay," he sounds behind me in his distinct dad tone, "time to tell me what's going on."

Relief washes over me briefly as he takes a seat opposite my desk before I round it to see I did close it all out.

"Nothing, I'm just thinking. I got a line on something, but I don't know if the source is credible."

He dips his chin in understanding. "So then, what are the rules?"

"According to my expensive education, or my dad?"

"Dad," he smirks. "Better choice."

"Don't run it unless it's *concrete.*"

"There you go," he says with a grin. "Or?"

"Find a better source."

"That's my girl." He stands as I look him over. He's well into his fifties but doesn't look a day over forty-five. Women have been fawning over him my whole life, especially my teachers when I attended grade school. It was embarrassing.

He tosses a glance over his shoulder as he heads toward the door. "You sure that's all?"

"How many times have you been in love, Daddy?" I ask, as casually as I can manage.

"Ah, so this *is* about a guy? That explains it." He frowns. "You didn't tell me you were dating again."

I broke up with my college ex, Carson, just after graduating from UT last May. Carson took a job in New York, knowing I wouldn't leave Texas. He made his decision—and it wasn't me. It's been surprisingly easy to live with. Dating afterward felt like a chore, so I've been opting out and concentrating on the paper instead.

"You didn't answer my question."

One side of his mouth quirks up as he squeezes the stress ball forever attached to his hand. "First and foremost, a journalist."

"Always. So, really, Dad, how many times have you been in love?"

I study his expression carefully, his relaxed posture as he answers easily.

"A few times."

"So, more than once?"

His grin grows. "Yes, a few generally constitutes more than *one*."

"Was...did you..." I bite my lip, "were any of them...I-I—"

"Okay, is this something you *want* to talk to me about? Because it doesn't seem like it."

"Maybe another time." I match his smile, genuinely thankful for the out I so obviously need. "After a few beers. Sorry, I'm just in my head today."

He pauses before he rounds the desk and presses a kiss to my temple. "All right then, rain check. But for you, I'm an open book. You know that, so just ask."

Ask him, Natalie, or it will eat you alive.

I open my mouth to ask and curse the coward within refusing to speak up. "Some other time."

"Deal. Love you," he whispers.

"Love you too, Daddy," I croak, hearing the shake in my voice. A shake he doesn't miss.

Shit.

He pauses at the doorway. "Natalie, you do know you can tell me anything, right?"

Tears threaten as I gaze on at him. Biased as I might be, Nate Butler is the greatest man I've ever known. No man has ever held a candle to him, and I doubt one ever will. It's not just who he is as a journalist or his accomplishments, but it's how he is personally as well. His warmth, his instilled empathy, and the way he treats people, namely me and my mother.

How could Stella walk away from him?

From their emails, it's clear it was her choice to leave Texas—to leave my father—only to marry Reid mere months after they ran into each other in Seattle. There's a story there, but I'm not sure I can stomach any more, yet everything inside me refuses to let it go.

Was Reid a choice? Was the choice made easier for Stella because

Reid is a rock star? As the thought occurs, some of my hero worship for Stella Emerson Crowne dims.

I should be thankful she did what she did. If she hadn't, I wouldn't exist.

"Would you believe I'm oddly sentimental today?" I lie to my father a second time—a rarity—knowing that the anxiety etched on his face is because visible signs of emotion are an anomaly for me.

Though his expression calls bullshit, he heads toward my office door anyway, giving me the space I need to come to him, if and when I'm ready. That's our relationship. He stops at the threshold and glances over his shoulder one last time. "Give it some more time, if you need it."

He thinks I'm still mourning my breakup with Carson when, oddly, I'm mourning *his*.

"Heals all wounds, right?" I prod as subtly as I can manage.

The crease between his brows deepens. "Right."

"But in your experience, does it really?"

He pauses briefly and grins. "The only truth about time is that it *flies*. Just yesterday, you were bitching about the way I was braiding your hair because you," he lifts his fingers in air quotes, "'want them to be as pretty as Macey Mc Callister's.'"

"Was I that much of a brat?"

"You were and *are* the perfect child. That's why you're an *only*." He taps the frame of the door. "I'm taking off. See you tomorrow."

"Night, Daddy."

Taking his leave, he walks over to his office, grabs his jacket from the back of his chair, and turns out the light. The second he disappears into the lobby, I divert my attention back to the screen housing the pinned folder that holds more details of my father's personal past.

The battle begins as unanswered questions begin rotating in my head.

What the hell happened between my father and Stella Emerson Crowne?

My gut tells me that even if I did ask him outright, he still wouldn't be the credible source in finding the whole of the story. If I want the whole truth, I'll have to open the file and further invade his privacy or find another source.

Twenty minutes later, I stop the debate and reopen the archives, dangerously assuring myself before I do. "Just a few more."

TWO

Anytime
Brian McKnight

Natalie

Tossing away my blanket in irritation, I click off the flatscreen as the credits roll on *Drive*, a screenplay Stella wrote over two decades ago about her start and evolution as a journalist. The movie also includes her husband, Reid's coinciding journey as the drummer of the Dead Sergeants and the band's history leading up to the height of their stardom.

While Stella and Reid's love story played a large part in the movie, my father wasn't mentioned, and the paper was thoroughly glossed over. Though one thing remains certain—Reid and Stella met around or close to the time Stella started working for Austin Speak.

In fact, it was Stella's feature in Speak about the Dead Sergeants that drew a Sony executive's attention, eventually getting them signed. Ironically, just before that twist of fate, Reid left Stella holding the bag of their budding relationship to move home and provide for his alcoholic parents. Thus, portraying him every bit the desperate, starving artist who was giving up on his dreams.

Even as Reid broke her heart, Stella made him promise not to give up. She even went so far as to have an expensive drum kit she won by chance delivered to where he fled to encourage him to keep believing. A few months after their breakup, the Sony exec attended a show, and the Sergeants, Reid included, were signed. Just after, Reid went on tour with the band, which led to years of separation between him and Stella. Years I conclude that she dated my father.

At the end of the movie, Stella and Reid reunite after the most incredible of coincidences in Seattle—half a country away from where their story began here, in Austin. Stella was house hunting—as she'd reported to Dad via email—when she stumbled upon Reid at an open house. Reid just so happened to be accompanying his lead guitar player, Rye Wheeler, who was interested in the now-famous A-frame Stella and Reid became cemented at.

Shortly after the mind-boggling, seemingly fated reunion, Stella and Reid got engaged, and Dad cut all ties with her.

The movie highly romanticizes Stella's belief in fate and destiny and the part they played in Stella and Reid's relationship throughout without a single hint of the fallout—my father and his broken heart.

On a mission for more, I grab my phone to start a Google search, and my heart skips a beat when I catch the time displayed in large numbers on my home screen.

11:11

Momentarily stunned by the sight of the time frequently mentioned in the movie—a time where superstitious Stella made wishes within those sixty seconds—I do my best to pass off the strange notion that arises.

Maybe it's a sign for *me*.

Perhaps one of encouragement?

"You're doing a shitty thing, Nat. Own it," I utter dryly, batting the idiocy off. At this point, I'm grasping at all moral straws in an attempt to keep on with my investigation while combating the guilt.

Standing on the patio of my apartment—just a few streets over from the heavy traffic of Sixth—I decide downtown Austin remains alive and well with the ever-present varied lights and the level of street noise in the distance.

Dipping my gaze, I sweep my quieter road, which is riddled with a few potholes, and even fewer passersby. I imagine Stella three decades ago, nearly three years my junior, as she trekked her way through these very streets. Streets she frequented, determined to forge her future in journalism.

More curious than ever, I Google Stella Emerson Crowne. A list quickly populates of images and articles, many written by her. I take a seat in my lone chair—which takes up the whole of my four cubic feet of balcony—and began sorting through them. She's given several interviews over the years, most of them in the last decade, due to her success. As I pick through the endless barrage of information, I become more and more frustrated when I don't find mention of my father, especially in the earlier articles.

Unless Stella is a borderline sociopath who could lie her way through any test, my father meant far more to her than she's allowed the world to know.

I know, and sadly, I may be one of a very few which leaves an acidic taste lingering on my tongue.

For the past twenty-five years, it seems they've both lived their separate lives pretending that the other doesn't exist, but why?

It has to be purposeful, has to be. And if so, that means she's buried their relationship history too. They seemed to be on amicable terms when they split.

Why did they break up in the first place? In the film, Stella was already in Seattle when she reunited with Reid.

Even though a lot of pieces are clicking together, I know I'm missing the most vital parts. Too many to feel real satisfaction, especially for someone in my field.

Did she leave my father out of that script to spare him? Was he hurt by it?

Can I let this go?

A resounding *no* thrums through my psyche as I try to grapple with the fact that everyone has a dating history, including my parents. But it's the intimacy of the emails I've read so far, the underlying love, affection, and devotion between them that keeps me calling 'bullshit' on the movie and pacing my apartment until sunrise.

"There's always an angle, Natalie," I mutter beneath my breath for the umpteenth time as I set my tray atop the wiry metal table on the patio of the small bistro, which sits only a few blocks from Speak.

"It's been a while," Rosie, our gossip columnist prods as I take a sip of my lemonade, and she takes the seat across from me.

Per usual, she's a cheap lunch date—her lithe figure taking precedence over hunger. Her plate is covered in mixed greens topped with a teaspoon of dressing—rabbit food. "What's new, or should I say news?" I ask before taking a hearty bite of my brisket sandwich.

"Not a lot," she says, glancing around the patio. A habit she no doubt formed back in L.A. where she stemmed from.

The sun collectively starts to beat down on us as she exaggeratedly pats her forehead with a napkin. I grin behind my sandwich in anticipation of what's coming.

"I can't believe I gave up California temperatures for *this*."

Early spring in Texas is a toss-up in weather, though it's mildly comfortable today—at least for me, which gave me the perfect excuse to get Rosie out of the office so our conversation didn't drift into the wrong ears.

What Rosie Knows is one of the most celebrated and most-read columns at Austin Speak. With her connections in entertainment and media and her expertise in unearthing celebrity gossip, we got a considerable circulation boost when she started at the paper. She has a penchant, if not a God-given talent, for sniffing out news before any other source. She's rarely, if ever, scooped.

In college, I followed her gossip blog and podcast like religion and brought her talent up to Dad on multiple occasions in an attempt to get her to Austin. So, when Dad finally made the call to recruit her, we sweetened the deal by offering to sponsor her podcast nationally through my mother's media company.

Even with that bait, it surprised the hell out of us both when she accepted and traded in California weather for the sweltering Texas sun six months out of the year.

A perk of when she's here is that she's one less testosterone-driven man to take up Austin Speak office space, for which I'm thankful. Because of my admiration for her work—and our closeness in age—we took up easily together as friends, so my lunch invitation isn't out of the ordinary. However, my motive for extending the invite is far from innocent.

"What are you working on?" she asks, forking a bite with a manicured hand, her blonde locks pulled into a high ponytail. Though she's got a little of that California-bred Barbie look going on, she's down-to-earth and can quickly shift to a split-tongued devil when provoked. These traits made her an instant ally. She can drive the most ego-driven man to his knees on any given day of her choosing. Another reason to love Rosie today is that she's prompting me with the right questions out of the gate. Bless her.

I shrug nonchalantly. "Just going through the archives and pulling old columns for the thirtieth edition. We're going to highlight the headlines that got the paper where it is today. I just finished year one."

"Damn, that's a task."

"I'm up for it and have months to prepare, so I'm determined to do it justice." I sip my lemonade and decide it's go time. "I'm sorting through some of Stella's old articles now."

Rosie's eyes widen, letting me know she's already on the hook. Despite her age and the fact that she's brushed elbows with countless A-list celebrities, she is a die-hard fan of all things Crowne family.

"Oh," she jumps in her seat as if in afterthought. "Speaking of," she palms her forehead dramatically as I hold in my chuckle. "I totally forgot. I just got a line on something *big*."

"Oh, yeah?" I ask, keeping my tone even and proud of my acting skills for the moment. "What's that?"

"Well, according to my source," she starts as we share a smile, "young Crowne is releasing a debut album very soon."

"Young Crowne? You mean—"

"Elliot Easton Crowne." She fans herself as I try to conceal my victory smile behind my sandwich. *Here we go.*

"Did you know Easton was named after The Cars guitarist; you know, the band who wrote the song—"

"Drive," I finish for her, clear hearts flashing in her eyes.

"Technically, a man named Ben wrote that song and sang it, but Ben was obviously taken because Ben First is the Sergeants' lead singer. He and Lexi made Benji, who is fire hot as fuck now, by the way."

"Really?"

"Oh yeah, at least the last time he was pictured. I'm guessing Easton's namesake was Stella's idea, and she didn't like Rick."

"Rick?"

"The lead singer of The Cars."

"Ah."

"So, I'm assuming they grabbed Easton's name because you know Stella believes in all that cosmic stuff," she waves her hand around animatedly, "and that song helped bring them back together, so no doubt that's where he got his namesake."

Recalling the movie, I place the part where Stella walked into a club she used to frequent with Reid and discovered him singing her favorite song as if willing her back to him. I'd teared up watching it as she sobbed at the edge of the stage while Reid sang, oblivious that she was standing there. That scene took place just before the end of the movie, a few scenes before they found each other in Seattle.

"I watched the movie last night," I declare, knowing it will earn me points.

"Really?"

"Yeah, I mean, I've been reading her articles, so I got curious."

Rosie sighs dreamily. "It's still my favorite."

As subtly as I can, I lead her back to the point. "So, Easton's releasing a debut album? I didn't even know he was a musician."

"Honey, have you seen a recent picture of Easton Crowne?" She admonishes, pulling up her phone and tapping furiously.

While I do genuinely love Rosie and her company, this behavior is precisely why I dragged her out of the office to dig around. If there's any dirt—good or bad—on the Crownes, she's the one to go to. Reid and Stella's story is one she considers a modern-day Elvis and Priscilla. Though it's old news, it happens to be her favorite news, especially since King and Queen Crowne had a prince. A prince that's rarely ever mentioned in the media.

I must admit, as much as my father's relationship with Stella intrigues me, so does the other half of the story. Stella's half. Maybe if I get closer to that half, I'll find some of the answers I seek.

I'm just not sure what the questions are…yet.

It's when Rosie lifts the phone that I'm struck by just how much of the *other side* exists. Hazel eyes glare back at me—or rather at the camera—as I take her phone and study the picture, cupping shade over it with my hand.

"Yeah, honey, take your time and drink that man in. Mm Mm Mm."

Grinning due to her reaction, I do. From the top of his six-plus frame lays thick unruly, jet-black hair which juts out beneath a beanie. In this particular shot, he's dressed in a form-fitting, faded grey thermal, dark, snug-fitting jeans, a plastic bag of takeout in one hand, the other grips the handle of an ancient, black box Chevy Truck. His posture next to it insinuates protection as if the truck has sentimental value while he scowls at the pap taking the picture. Everything in his demeanor screams, 'fuck off.'

"It's clear he hates the camera," I note.

"That's why he's releasing it without promoting it."

"What?"

"Yes, girl, no PR, no press announcement, no warning at all, and from what I was told, he's not planning on granting a single interview. Which is crazy considering—"

"Stella is a journalist," I interject.

"Exactly, Easton Crowne either doesn't give a shit if it sells a single copy, or he *hates* the media so much he's not willing to help *himself* get the word out. If the photos are any indication—"

"It's definitely the latter," I finish for her.

"Right. He's been almost impossible to photograph over the years—along with all the Sergeants' other kids—which has, of course, made his photos worth a shitload and the paps more relentless." She finally bites into her salad, but that doesn't stop her gushing. "The whole damned band has done a good job keeping their kids out of the spotlight over the years to the point they're hardly recognizable now. But daaaaammmmn, just look at him." She sighs. "I'm willing to bet his father is helping him produce, and he doesn't want that out."

And that's your in, Natalie.

I jump on it. "Keep that out of it. We don't want legal breathing down our necks."

"Sure?" she asks. "It's just speculation."

"Even so, as protective as they are, we don't need the headache. Trust me. The fact that he's releasing an album will be enough."

"Agreed," she says quickly when I hand the phone back, and she again admires the picture. "Damn, he's gorgeous."

"And a raging asshole from the looks of it," I say through a mouthful.

"Hard to believe Stella worked at Speak and then went on to marry a rock star," she sighs wistfully.

"She helped make him a rock star," I remind her. And my father helped make *her*. That part I leave out as the movie replays in my head, and the underlying resentment again begins to simmer.

"I think that might be why I took the job at Speak," she says, swatting a fly away from her lettuce. "Damn sure isn't the weather here."

I nod, my thoughts beginning to wander back to the emails.

"Lucky bitch," Rosie adds. "Can you even imagine what it's like to have the attention of a man like that?"

I shake my head as her eyes light, and dread courses through me as I anticipate Rosie's next words. She again delivers.

"You know, maybe you could contact her. Stella is down to earth, seems like a *remember your roots* and pay homage type of gal. I bet she would give you a quote or a few paragraphs about her time during the startup of the paper. It could really boost circulation."

"Not a bad idea." I lie, wiping my mouth with a napkin. "I'll bring it up with Dad."

Never.

Never will I ever bring up Stella in front of my father again. "When are you planning on publishing the article about Easton?"

"I'm still digging around," she says, "but I'll have it up by Monday."

It's Wednesday, and if I decide to use this angle, I'll have to work fast.

Casually, I pick up my lemonade as my head swims with possible scenarios. "So, what else is going on?"

THREE

Runaway Train
Soul Asylum

Natalie

The clock is ticking. That truth continues to bounce through my racing mind as I do my best to psych myself up, still trying to justify the reasoning behind the act I'm about to commit.

So, maybe part of the job of an investigative reporter involves a little bit of calculating as well. No budding journalist worth their salt can skirt the fact that it takes some manipulation—along with a set of brass balls—to get in where you can fit in, at least during the formative years.

Facts are, unless you've established a name for yourself as a journalist, few will pay you a bit of attention unless the *subject* of the story is newsworthy. It's a dog-eat-dog world in media, always has been, and unfortunately, due to the increasingly cutthroat nature of instant news—as in reporting a full-fledged story within hours before you're scooped—it appears it always will be. Rosie is confident in her position that no one else has a clue on the line she's landed on Easton; because of that, I have the luxury of the window that I do.

Typically, Rosie would hit publish on such a worthy headline within hours. She's holding back due to confidence in her source, and maybe due to her slight obsession with the subject and her need to get it just right—which buys me time. The downside? It also gives me time to go to war with myself morally, and that's where I'm at.

Before today, I prided myself in not becoming the type of dog to go cannibal. In fact, I want to be just the opposite. Every story I've penned so far, I've also stamped with a level of integrity I haven't wavered from. If I do this, if I manipulate this situation out of curiosity, I may not be able to sleep as heavily as I have thus far.

Am I really willing to cross a line I've refused to every day of my short career for answers that won't help my current position? I'm not scooping Rosie, and this isn't my story. What harm could it do just to dig a little, to get a glimpse of the other side?

"Just fucking do it," I scold myself. Eyes fixed on the most recent shot of Easton—which Rosie pulled up at lunch—I keep my peripheral vision sharp, mainly on my father as he sits at his desk.

Aside from his open hostility toward the media, the rest of Easton Crowne remains a mystery. There's so little about him on the web it's ridiculous, especially in this day and age. It's absolutely astounding to me that there are literally crumbs and nothing more. Rosie is right. The entire band did everything to protect the identity and privacy of their children, and now that they are all grown, they seem to be keeping it that way by choice. It's plausible they hired someone or a team of someones to help them with that task over the years—which has proved money well spent.

Even more staggering is that the entire Sergeants' family seems to have an impenetrable circle of people they trust who haven't sold them out to the media—until *now*—which is another astonishing rarity indeed. Rosie has never, nor will ever, reveal a source who wishes to remain anonymous. If I want to know the who, as far as her source is concerned, I'll have to figure it out on my own.

But that's not my intention.

What is your intention, Natalie?

The answer is becoming as clear as the line that appeared yesterday—the need *to know* that's ingrained in my psyche.

Not just a part of a story but the whole of it. A need that's been embedded in my bones ever since I was a child.

All I do know at this point—especially after reading a few more emails between Stella and Dad—is that I'm becoming more and more curious about the other side. As I war with myself, I decide to make rules, new rules, and create a new uncrossable line that will allow me to get close enough to the fire to see what it consists of, but remain far enough away not to get burned.

I'll draw the line at any point to spare my father because of the line I've already crossed by invading his privacy. Come what may, I'll take the heat upon myself to protect him from a single degree of it.

Gazing at the picture while gathering more courage, I surmise that the only thing evident about Easton Crowne is that he's good-looking. Yet, there's a bit of depth to his angry stare. His evident aversion to the press is slightly surprising because of his mother's position as one of the world's leading music journalists. At the same time, it isn't surprising he hates the media. Being a child of a celebrity, *two* celebrities, couldn't have been easy.

As I study the beautiful byproduct of my father's heartbreak, a few things become clear.

One, I'll have to tread lightly with him. Easton is, no doubt, well versed in how to handle the press and does so mainly with blatant hostility.

Two, he'll probably fall under one of two categories. He's either an entitled celebutante or mature beyond his years and smug because of it. From his expression, I'm guessing it's the latter.

Inhaling a calming breath, I muster the courage to dial the number. My window is closing, and I've only got four and a half days to pull this off. Not only that, I'll have to do it completely off my parents' radar. Guilt surfaces again as I hang up the phone before the end of the first ring and groan in frustration.

Dad hid the facts from me. Therefore, I'm safe in playing ignorant. But if I'm not careful, I could hurt him. It's deceptive as hell, but because of Rosie, I'm covered regardless. Summoning my confidence, I dial again and brace myself for the inevitable backlash. Phone to my ear, I kick back in my office, crossing the expensive Choo pumps Mom gifted me for graduation on my desktop.

"'Lo?"

"Hi, Easton, I—"

The line goes silent due to disconnect.

I bark out a laugh, knowing he thinks I'm some groupie who became privy to his personal cell number. Deciding to go all in, I type up and take a screenshot of the beginning of a mock article before shooting it off with an accompanying text.

I'm not a groupie. Feel free to dial me back.

Three minutes later, my phone rattles in my hand, and I can't help the victorious lift of my lips. Without uttering a word, Easton just confirmed Rosie's source is legitimate.

"Let's try this again, shall we? Hi, Easton."

"Who the fuck are you?"

"If you give me a chance to tell you—"

"Cut the shit. How did you get the information?"

"It's my job."

"Fucking press." Though he's speaking low, his timbre reeks of mildly reserved disgust, like he's holding himself back from doing real damage to me. "I'm not talking to you unless you tell me who the fuck you are."

"My name is Natalie Hearst. I work for Austin Speak."

I'm met by another telltale silence, which only confirms he's aware his mother used to work here. It's then I cling to the hope that he may know something that might help me fill in the *why* of the secrecy. Intuition tells me to follow my gut, just as fresh venom snakes over the line.

"What the hell do you want?"

"My father and your mother used to date. I didn't know if you were aware of that—"

"If this is some ploy to get to my parents—"

"If I wanted your mother's audience, I'm pretty sure I could get it considering… Look, I'll be frank since that seems to be your love language, and I'm fluent. I'm only interested in interviewing *you* on your upcoming debut album." *Lie.* "I have to say, in the spirit of full disclosure, I'm a huge fan of your mother's work and the Sergeants." *Truth.* "But I'd love to get an exclusive with you before you release."

"You have no basis—"

"You've already confirmed it's true by calling me back." I go all in. "Maybe we can even do a sidebar with you and your dad and his involvement in producing it."

More silence, and it's damning.

"None of this is public fucking information."

"Look, I know you don't want it out, but it's happening, and it's my job to fish out the details. Although help from your father isn't exactly newsworthy, considering it would be expected support. But if you're so adamant about it, we can leave that part out. Either way, we're reporting you're releasing a debut album because apparently, you won't, and I think it's only fair that we hear from you, especially regarding your reasoning behind—"

"This is blackmail."

"Hardly. It's a chance to get your view in print."

"It's fucking blackmail to grant an interview."

"Tomato, toe-mah-toe."

"Tell me this, how is an exclusive in a regional fucking paper going to help promote my album?"

"First of all, your mother's illustrious career started with this *regional paper*, and it's about to celebrate thirty years in print, so a modicum of respect would be appreciated. A paper, by the way, which was ad-based and is now owned by a major media company that reports *nationally* and makes your point even more moot. I'm assuming the reason for your silence is that you don't want the media's help, but—"

"Doesn't seem I have a fucking choice in the matter anymore, does it?" he snaps furiously.

"No. This is going to print with or without your say, so it would probably be in your best interest to put yourself on record with a viewpoint for your reasoning—speaking of which, we have a common goal. While you're adamant about keeping your own father's involvement with your career out of the story, I feel the same way. So, if you agree not to breathe a word of this to your parents, I'll leave your father's involvement in producing out of it altogether."

"Pretty ridiculous, considering your fucking name will be on it."

"That's my cross to bear and my issue to deal with after the fact. However, this is my offer, and it expires in exactly one minute."

This is where it gets tricky. If Easton disagrees, the lead ends here because if Dad catches wind, I'll have to explain to him I was fact-checking for Rosie—after I found the emails. He won't be happy, but he'll be far less furious with me. I eye Dad over my monitor, hating myself briefly for the deception before pushing all my chips in.

"Easton, I really don't want—"

Easton's resigned sigh cuts me off before I can get any assuring sentiment out. "How soon can you get to Seattle?"

"How about tomorrow?"

"Don't expect a fucking warm reception."

My victorious smile is only dimmed by the pit growing in my stomach.

"Wouldn't dream of it. I'll text you once I lan—"

The line goes dead as I kick back in my seat, listing and mentally ticking off all the ways this can go horribly wrong.

If my father figures out that I am using his paper's credibility or his past relationship with Stella to gain a false interview, he could very well fire me. Not to mention the damage it will cause to our relationship. My only cover for this is Rosie and will remain Rosie. But my advantage with Easton is I'm the only one who knows it.

But is it worth it?

Easton could be and probably is just as clueless about our parents' past relationship as I am. The pregnant pause when I mentioned the paper tells me he may know enough to lead me to a missing piece. Do I really want to go this far for it?

Why can't I just let it go?

Fed up with questions I could already have answers to, I do the unforgivable thing I shouldn't. I open the emails and again begin to read.

"Explain this to me again," Dad says as he thrusts a wooden bowl of my mother's pasta salad toward me in offering as she lines my plate with garlic Texas Toast. Tonight, Mom has laid out a spread of my favorites on the large oak patio table on the back deck of our expansive ranch home. The patio borders endless acres of perfectly manicured grass. Though I moved out my second year attending UT, I dine with them twice a week. My gaze flicks past my doting parents, who continually fill my plate as I eye the stable full of our horses we never neglect to ride. Though Dad opts out most days, Mom and I share a deep bond in all things equestrian. Nostalgia kicks in as I scan the grounds with appreciation.

When I was young, I knew I was lucky to have the wide-open space in which I acted out my imagination. An imagination that kept me company until my diapers-to-adult best friends Holly and Damon came along, becoming staples in our family. My parents worked long hours to create their combined empire. The tradeoff was that their collective best friends gave me the siblings they didn't provide. While Mom was born into inheriting her media company from my grandparents, my father worked his way in from the ground up with Austin

Speak, becoming editor in chief at only twenty-six. After marrying, they collectively came together and became a reckoning force. Even with the resources, Dad has always kept the paper on a smaller scale. As I stated to Easton, it's become a nationally recognized news source.

"Earth to Natalie," Mom muses, drawing me back to them both.

"I'll only be gone for three, four days tops," I reiterate, pulling my attention back to and between them. Guilt and a lingering ache in my chest combine, taking my appetite as I push my food around. I've already come this far, so I decide to lay out more of my rehearsed excuses.

"I've already hit my deadlines," I report to Dad as he studies me closely, "and honestly, I'm in need of a little R & R. I'm thinking I'll take a little road trip."

"Holly can't go with you?" Mom asks as I sip my beer and shake my head.

"No, she's got finals coming up." *Truth*. But I didn't ask her. This is a secret I plan to take to my grave. As close as Holly and I are, there's not a chance in hell she'll understand why I'm going. Truth be known, I don't really understand it myself.

"Alone," Dad repeats, his suspicion and concern dueling.

"Journalists do it all the time," I admonish.

"For *work*," he drags out as he calls bullshit. "Does this have anything to do with our conversation yesterday?"

"What conversation?" Mom asks, looking between us just as warily.

Shit.

"I think our daughter is seeing someone," Dad speculates.

Thank God.

"No, I'm not," I correct defensively, which sadly only makes me look more guilty. "I'm just steps ahead of everything at the office right now, and I want some *me* time. I haven't taken any off since graduating," I point out.

"True," Mom says.

"I'm already narrowing down my articles for the thirtieth anniversary," I turn to Dad as he mulls over my words.

"You seem confident."

"It's inherited." That remark earns me a dazzling grin from him. "Besides, I've been reading *Speak* since I was five. Memory alone has served me well in picking out the majority of articles to highlight already, and we still have months before it goes to print."

"Something's up," Mom weighs in, aiding Dad's suspicions as I make peace with the fact there's no chance of an acting career in my future. I'll have to up my game tomorrow when I come face-to-face with Easton, or I'll be screwed.

"Nothing is up. I'm just a little burnt out. I need…*something*." Dumping more pasta onto my plate to keep my hands busy, I let a little fake annoyance through. "I don't see anything wrong with that."

"All right, baby, if that's what you need," Dad acquiesces as he and Mom do that freaky silent communication thing and collectively decide to drop it.

Considering my emotions are all over the place from the latest emails I inhaled before I arrived, I decide I'm doing an okay job because inwardly, I'm freaking out. I'm set to board a red-eye halfway across the country in a few hours and feel relieved they haven't grilled me so much on the where but mainly on the why. Thankful I pay my own AmEx bill, I look over to my father as he pops a beer and reaffirms my decision that he'll never know. Even if I have been granted the first and only interview with Easton Crowne—which would no doubt boost circulation—I'll never use a word of it. That's the only way I'll ever live with myself for doing something so deceptive.

With a raw heart and hellfire gnawing my conscience, I drain my beer and look between my parents, only to catch more of their conspiratorial expressions. Though they're still in silent communication mode, there's a pride in their eyes as they both turn to look back at me.

"What?" I roll my eyes. "It's freaky when you do that, you know."

"What?" Dad asks, his grin growing.

"Talk without speaking."

Dad gives Mom a smug smirk. "When you're married to someone nearly a quarter of a century—or the *right* person—it comes naturally, trust me."

My parents have always been considered the 'it' couple amongst their friends, not that they care. Mom was right in saying I knew the details of how they met—a media conference in Chicago. The way Mom tells it, she took one look at my dad and lost the sense God gave her.

Mom always jokingly calls him her longest one-night stand.

Dad calls her the one that will never get away.

Sadly, I get that part of it now and no longer find it romantic.

After a whirlwind romance, they married just shy of a year of dating, and neither looked back.

Or have they?

There's been maybe one month of my life where I wasn't sure if I'd become another statistic of divorce. I was seven. During that time, Mom took me to stay with my grandparents for a week. When we got home, something had changed. They put on a good front for me, but more weeks passed before things truly got back to normal. There was a second shift, and they've been fine ever since. I've never spent much time thinking about it, but now I'm curious as to why.

"Where is your head tonight, daughter of mine?" Mom asks, a grin on her face as she glances back at my dad with bulging quizzical eyes. With the lift of a shoulder, he pops the top of another beer before reaching down to scratch the ears of our ancient basset hound, Sparky. Forcing myself back into the moment, I scrutinize the two of them.

"Who made the first move?" I ask, tipping my own beer to start a dangerous line of questioning.

They each point their bottles at the other with a smile, like it's some inside joke.

"Seriously," I ask. "Who started it?" Inside I pray for satisfaction. Everything inside me wants it to be my father. Much to my dismay, he points the neck of his bottle toward Mom.

"The hell *I did,* Butler. I couldn't get away from you fast enough," she sasses with an exaggerated eyeroll. "Smug, arrogant," she ticks off before turning to me, "your father was a true jackass."

"We didn't like each other much," Dad adds, "at *first*, but I damn sure liked what I saw at that party."

"Until I shot him down," Mom quips, tabling her empty beer and snatching his for a sip.

"We went toe to toe for weeks until I shut her up," Dad continues.

Mom smiles in reply. "Not a bad way to be silenced."

"This stays PG-13," I remind them both through a forced grin.

"Let's just say Nate didn't like answering to *me*."

My smile grows authentic as I grin between them. "So, Daddy, you didn't know she was your new boss when you met at the party?"

"When he hit on *me* at the party," Mom corrects. "Only to get shot down and shown up by his new boss the next day."

"You knew?" I ask Mom.

"Oh yeah, once he introduced himself. So, I just let him run his game."

"Let's get this straight," Dad spouts, taking his beer back, "you were never my boss. You only had me by the balls because the ad company you purchased bankrolled the controlling interest in my paper *at that time*."

"Either way, you were completely misogynistic." Mom widens her eyes at me. "Yep, baby. Hate to break it to you, but your father was a *pig*."

"Horseshit," he grins. "I just loved seeing you riled up. Especially in that red dress—which you only wore twice in two weeks because you saw my eyes dropping inappropriately when you did."

"So, it was hate to love?" I ask between them.

"Not at first," Mom says softly. "I had just jumped out of fresh hell with an ex, and your father had just endured the same not long before we met."

Whipping my attention back and forth, I do my best to gauge their expressions for any bitterness, lingering sadness, or resentment—especially in my father's eyes. Thankfully, I come up empty.

Be satisfied, Natalie. Be satisfied. Cancel your trip and move on with your life.

"So, you didn't like each other, and then?"

"Then we did," Mom says, her eyes meeting Dad's for a loaded pause.

"Who broke first?"

"Baby, you're rather inquisitive tonight," Mom says, her brows drawing as she breaks her stare off with Dad. "Why such an interest?"

"You were getting to the sex part, weren't you?" I divert, palming my forehead.

"Well, you weren't immaculately conceived," Dad delivers bluntly.

"No shit," I say as Mom narrows her eyes. She doesn't like me cursing but allows it because my father has the foulest of mouths. Not that I didn't taste my fair share of soap or get grounded for PMS-induced emotional lash-outs by both.

"When did you know, Daddy? That it was Mom?"

He tilts his head, studying my mother, who stares back at him unabashedly. The answer settled somewhere in her chest. She knows it, and I'm the only clueless one. Dad grips my mother's left hand, her large diamond glittering due to the candle burning at the center of the table as he slides his thumb along the back of it.

"I can't wait until you get to figure that out for yourself," Dad replies softly before turning to me, his blue eyes glowing with sentiment, "because it's one of the best parts of living."

"You aren't going to tell me?"

"No," Mom answers in reply, getting lost in the moment with my father.

They love each other, still, and it's clear. They've spent my entire existence loving each other, so why am I so determined to dig into my father's past?

Be satisfied, Natalie!

But I can't, especially after living the first year of Dad's old relationship—line by line—until I was forced away from my desk by Mom's summons to dinner. I spent the entire ride to my childhood home in stunned silence, the truth evident. My father might have been madly in love with Stella Emerson, but Stella Emerson reciprocated that love fully, in black and white.

Even so, I've already gone too far.

This has to stop here.

One day I'll summon the courage to ask, but for now, I need to let it go. If I back out of my half-baked plan now, good karma might give me a break for warning Easton that his secret was coming out. At least now he can prepare himself for the media shitstorm the announcement is sure to toss his way. I'll just shoot him a text and cancel, assuring him of my word to keep Reid out of it, which will buy his silence.

Just as I reach for my cell to shoot him a text and refund my ticket, my phone lights up with an incoming text…from Easton.

EC: 415 Cedar Street @3

Guilt batters me as my parents begin to clear the table, their eyes lingering a bit longer on the other, no doubt from the reminiscence I drew out of them both with my prompting. Hands full of plates, Dad pauses behind Mom as she opens the sliding door. He leans in and kisses her shoulder, the look in his eye when he withdraws clearly not meant for me to see. Feeling sick, I avert my attention back to the Texas sun just as it dips below the horizon, coloring the sky a violent red.

What the hell are you doing, Natalie?

Just as I bring the question up, my phone lights up with a gate change announcement for my flight leaving for Washington in a few hours, and I'm not sure I'll be on it.

FOUR

Bette Davis Eyes
Kim Carnes

Easton

Sitting in the last booth—which runs adjacent to the bar—I dart my gaze out the windows between my truck parked a few spaces to the right of the entrance and those outside scurrying along the crosswalk. Others congregate at a small cluster of tables next to the front door, soaking up what little warmth they can get from the afternoon sun.

Flipping my cardboard coaster on the tabletop, I sink farther into the heavily worn seat, hating the fact that I'm early. I should have made her wait, questioning if *I* would show. One thing I do know is she's not getting a single fucking quotable syllable from me until I feel her out.

I'm educated enough in what Mom calls her 'past life' in Texas to know there may be some truth to her claim our parents dated. Although why she mentioned it remains a mystery, especially since she made it clear she wants them kept out of this. If anything, that useless information was a display in poor taste, the definition of classless.

If she'd shown a little of that, I might not be sitting here ready to rip into her. With respect to my mother's profession, there's a big difference between hungry mass media and good journalism. There's also a fine line in how to approach someone with a request to pry into their personal life—and she crossed a dozen lines in minute one. Her father might own Speak, and her mother might have inherited a media empire, but it's obvious growing up surrounded by seasoned professionals has done fuck all for her. I'm willing to bet she's newly graduated and hungry to make worthy headlines to compete with her parents' legacy. If so, she's going about it all wrong. Especially if I'm her first stop in making a real effort.

Anger resurfaces as I mentally run through the list of those who could have sold me out—my suspects limited to a few. Even with that list, I can't think of one who would benefit by uttering a word about me releasing my album. It's that she mentioned Dad playing the role of producer that's really thrown me.

Acidic irritation runs through me as music begins to blare from the digital jukebox in the corner of the bar opposite me, accompanying the background noise of scattered conversations and clinking glasses.

No matter how hellbent Dad is on me seeing this through, he would never compromise my need to do this my way or our relationship in this capacity. Both my parents have spent my entire existence trying to protect me from the information-hungry masses, more so, bloodthirsty predators like Natalie Hearst. I'm positive Dad would never do so much to shield me, only to toss me straight into the lion's den—even with us at odds about how I chose to go about this. This source—whoever the fuck they are—can't possibly be on my shortlist. Sadly, the only way I'll find out *who* is, is by getting it from her. This means, temporarily, I'll have to play amicable enough while keeping my temper at bay. This is an ask that, at the moment, is too fucking much.

I've been without the need of my parents' protection for far longer than either of them would admit, but have yet to relinquish their rights in doing so. Their need to believe—especially my mother—has kept me silent, but not for much longer.

Anger simmering close to boiling, I do my best to sink into the easy rhythm of the music, mimicking the pluck of guitar strings with the fingers wrapped around my pint glass.

Glancing up at the plastic, ketchup-splattered clock hanging above the bar, I decide if she's a second late, she gets nothing. As the clock ticks past 2:59, I start to count down the seconds, willing it to run out. I watch it tick down to fifteen and go to get up when I catch sight of her. Strawberry blonde hair whips around her face disrupting the view as she takes confident strides toward the bar. Her long, toned legs are covered in tight-fitting black denim and matching plain Uggs. The rest of her is swallowed in layers of colorful shirts, a sweater, and a thick scarf. It's as if she put everything in her suitcase on. Opening the door, she steps in and searches the bar. Her eyes find me easily as she zeroes in and walks my way. Her lips lift slightly in greeting as her eyes fix on me, her gaze not meeting mine fully until she comes to a stop at the foot of the table.

It's then she lifts them fully to peer down at me as she starts to unwrap her scarf, her plump, glossy lips upturning. The initial hit of indigo eyes feels like the strike of a crowbar being leveraged against my chest. Tightening my grip on my pint, I kick back in the booth, resolved that she's a snake. A beautiful snake, but a snake just the same.

"You've already decided you don't like me," she says, a barely perceptible Texas lilt curling the end of each word. "I can't really say that I blame you right now." She slides into the opposite side of the booth before signaling to the bartender, pointing to my beer before lifting two fingers. I remain silent. It's her shitshow.

She casts her eyes down briefly before lifting them back to mine to thoroughly inspect me. "Look, Easton," she sighs, "I'm sorry. That phone call was," she shakes her head, "to put it bluntly, it was an asshole way to approach this and get an interview, though I'm sure you're used to it."

I give her a dead stare in return.

"I reconsidered coming," she lifts her head to the bartender, who summons her with the flick of his wrist to pick up her own fucking beers.

Yeah, princess, this isn't that kind of place.

If I hadn't researched enough to know that she is an heir to a media empire, I would assume she was a pageant princess of some sort. She's beautiful, polite enough, obviously educated, and proper when speaking as if she's ready for the next spelling question. Nothing about her sticks out as extraordinary, except the eyes. They have a depth I wasn't expecting, probably intelligence. Either way, I flick that aside as she fetches her beer and rejoins me, pushing a fresh dark draft my way. I push it back toward her to decline while tilting my own up. She sits back, taking a large sip of brew while glancing around, no doubt to sum up the place with a few sentences for her article.

"Describe it," I order.

"Sorry?"

"Describe the bar," I lean forward, bracing my forearms on the table. "How would you write it?"

"Sticky," she says with a light laugh, peeling the menu off the side of her palm.

"Fuck this," I say, unable to believe I entertained her in the first place as I move to stand. She grips my arm to stop me, and I sneer at her, my shoulders locking up as my anger spikes. I shouldn't have agreed to this. Showing up gave her too much leverage.

"Jesus, okay." She licks her gloss-slicked lower lip. "Dark and dank, clearly in need of a deep clean…but perfectly necessary. If there were a list of the lost art of bars, this would rank high."

"Why?"

"The jukebox, for one," she adds quickly, "the selection itself is a nostalgic trip down memory lane. I've been here two minutes, and I can feel it already." She sweeps the room with her gaze before bringing it back to me. "This is what bars used to be. Shots and beer, nothing to grind or garnish with an herb. The definition of a classic dive bar…" She keeps her gaze pinned on me as the crowbar digs further into my chest. "Black walls, matching but worn comfortable leather booths, checkered tile floors." She glances to our left and grins. "Bumper sticker slogans plastered at eye level." She clears her throat, projecting her voice in presentation. "Bathed in a symphony of neon light the second you step inside, you can picture the bloody, loose molars from desperation-laced bar fights. The atmosphere alone screams, 'welcome all those who are lost. We offer nothing but spirits to wash your confusion down with.'"

Momentarily settling back in, I sip my beer as her eyes flare in irritation.

"So, did I pass?" She shakes her head, her posture weary but not from our battle. I haven't even given her a tenth of what I had prepared.

"What the hell is with you anyway, Easton? You can't be that jaded already. You haven't been weighed by the *true* critics, *yet*. Is your contempt for the media real, or is this," she gestures between us, "contrived especially for me because of how I approached this?"

I lift a brow.

"I mean, sure, I can only assume paparazzi made life difficult as you grew up. I can't imagine it was easy to maintain privacy with celebrity parents. Still, you're literally repainting a bullseye on your back by releasing a debut album with your father being who he is. If you hate the press, interviews, media in general, you chose the wrong fucking career."

"I didn't choose it," I snap instantly, and she jumps slightly at the aggression in my tone, though I'm surprised a little by her own blunt delivery.

Annoyed I've instilled the wrong fear in her, I rip off my beanie and run my fingers through my hair. She fixes her purplish-blue gaze on their task and my hair before lowering her eyes to my chest, and lower to the beer in my hand before she darts her focus away. "Anything I say to you is off the record until I say so, understood?"

She nods slowly before firing a question anyway. "So, you're claiming it's a blood thing?"

"I'm not claiming shit. That's a fact. I grew up in a whirlwind of notes, tuned by melody, shaped by lyrics. My parents' obsession with music and their love for it was the seed that I stemmed from. There hasn't been a day of my life where I haven't been entangled in the purity of some sort of melody, either someone else's or my own. Music is as necessary for me as the air I breathe." She couldn't possibly understand the extent of it, but she doesn't miss a beat.

"Fair enough. Did it come easily?"

I hesitate because there's no easy answer for that. From the time I was able, I was working on becoming a part of it all. I'm just not sure if my talent is natural or earned, or if it's enough. "I've been playing for as far back as I can remember, so I'm not entirely sure. That would be a question for my parents."

I study her fingers while she keeps them wrapped around her pint. Long, delicate. My eyes flick up to her face—pink-tinged pale skin, a few light, barely-there freckles dart along the side of her nose. Up close, her hair is more blonde than red, slightly on the coppery side. Briefly, I wonder what the rest of her would look like without the layers of clothing she's wrapped in. It's obvious she spent mere minutes on her appearance before she got here. The thin layer of makeup she put on is unable to conceal the pale blue half-moons beneath her eyes. She either isn't trying or is too tired to care. I find myself wondering why I give a fuck as she fires off another question.

"So, would you say you're a prodigy or just a byproduct of your environment?"

I'm unable to guard the surprise in my eyes, but I shut it down quickly.

"That's not for me to decide."

"Can I hear it?"

I give her a firm shake of my head.

"That's going to make this hard."

"Then let's wrap this up. I'm sure there's a return flight to Austin sometime today."

"Jesus." She takes a hearty sip of beer. "I'm not here to stunt your growth."

"Why the fuck are you here, and why did you bring up our parents dating?"

Casting her eyes down, she sets her beer on the table. There's obvious guilt there, and I'm clearly missing something important.

"I shouldn't have mentioned that. Can you just forget I did?"

I remain quiet, my question still demanding an answer.

She traces the rim of her glass. "I'm not expecting to bond over it, if that's what you're insinuating."

"You like to be the one to ask the questions," I say in a blanket statement, knowing it's the truth.

"I do. I *chose* this."

"It's an obvious choice. You're a media princess."

Her eyes narrow. "And you're rock royalty. We both have legacies to try and live up to."

"We won't be bonding over that, either," I state, finishing my beer. She pushes the beer she bought over to my side of the table in offering, and I ignore it.

"So, what's it going to take to get a proper interview with you?"

"I'm here."

"No, you're not."

I give her honesty. "A friendship I'm not offering. Take care, Natalie, and if you print a word of anything I just said, I'll make it hurt."

This time I do stand with every intention to leave, because fuck it, if she carries through with her threat, I'll deal. I always do.

FIVE

Got You (Where I Want You)
The Flys

Natalie

This is a lost cause. It's clear I just wasted eleven hundred dollars on a last-minute plane ticket, maxing out my AmEx for unjustifiable reasons. Nothing could have prepared me for the unsurmountable wrath behind his eyes, or Easton Crowne in general. For a millisecond, I thought his persona might've been contrived, but he's clearly disgusted by anything disingenuous. He also seems to have zero patience for anyone not delivering the truth in the raw. Even if I saw the expression he's given me a thousand times on the web—which, with the amount of research I did, I probably have—nothing could have prepared me for the punch it packs face-to-face. He's already raging against the world. While I was ready to face some major resistance, I wasn't at all prepared for his beauty or his raw presence.

After packing at breakneck speed, I only slept a handful of hours since I landed, and everything about Seattle feels foreign to me. Nothing at all like his mother's experience of being enveloped in warmth. My parents planned expensive trips overseas for our family vacations and did their best to expose me to various cultures and other walks of life. Though we had some stateside adventures, the Pacific Northwest was never included in them. I'm convinced I now know why. To my father, Washington was probably considered Stella and Reid's designated corner of the universe, the rest of the world their playground. I'm sure Dad—much like the rest of the world—was always aware in which grounds the Crowne family were stomping and made sure to steer us clear. The question is, who was he protecting? Himself, my mother, Stella?

Glaring down at me, Easton takes a large swallow of the beer I bought before tossing ten bucks on the table to ensure I know my place with him. Nowhere.

"I don't need to be your friend."

"No danger there. Admit defeat and go home, Natalie. You're not ready for this."

"You don't know me."

"I know you came underprepared, and you're grasping at straws already."

"You don't know shit," I snap, exasperated.

"Then fire away."

He doesn't give me longer than a second to form a response.

"Either come with decent questions or grant me my freedom."

I sit stunned at his audacity as he looms over me, six feet and inches of venomous contempt.

"That's what I thought."

Before I can blink, he's stalking away. He's already on the sidewalk when I catch up to him and keep my voice low. "Why are you so against promoting your album or word getting out that your father is helping produce it?"

"Lame start, and we both know why," he says, clear irritation in his voice as he pulls keys from his pocket, stops at the door of his classic Chevy, and unlocks it. I manage to catch the door before he slams it.

"Look, asshole, I traveled halfway across the country for this interview, and I don't have enough to print a full page."

"Not my problem," he snaps, reaching for the handle to close himself inside the cab just as I wedge myself between his driver's seat and the door he's intent on slamming me out with.

"Yeah, well, I'm making it your problem," I say, gripping the wheel and boxing myself farther in by stepping up into the cab and hovering above him.

He cants his head up at me as my hair is whipped continuously around my face by the freezing wind. Ducking farther into the truck, ass in the air, catcalls sound out around me from the occupied tables outside the bar. Briefly, I swear I see Easton's lips lift, but it's gone before I can properly gauge it as my hair repeatedly slaps my face. "Are you hesitant because you don't want your father's status in any way adding to your possible success, or is it because you're afraid your work won't be viewed as your own?"

"Are you seriously going to try to conduct this interview with your ass hanging out of my truck?"

I inch closer for some reprieve from the wind, hovering above him as he stares up at me, his expression unreadable.

"Yeah, I am. I blame lack of sleep. So, is that it?" He mulls the question over as I study his face. Perfection. His father's perfect bone structure, his mother's dark hair and olive skin tone, which is much deeper in person than pictured. "And if so, why allow him to participate at all?"

He harrumphs, his lips lifting slightly at the corners. "For that answer, you'd have to meet Reid fucking Crowne."

I bite my lip to keep from smiling and fail as the wind whips into the cabin, and I shudder from the chill. I'm rewarded with the sharpening of his hazel return stare, another gift from his father.

Easton Crowne is dangerously attractive, but not in the traditional sense, and appears untouchable. After the reception he gave me, I have zero doubt he views me as some polished princess who exists galaxies out of his realm. I can only imagine the caliber of human beings he's been surrounded by in his lifetime. I assume many of them established musicians, movie stars, gurus of every sort, you name it. He's grown up in a kaleidoscope world, and to him, I'm probably just some southern belle as annoying as a gnat landing in his dark beer.

"Jesus, you don't even consider me worth a minute of your life, do you? You hate the media, but you've gathered conclusions about me in a few minutes, making you the worst kind of hypocrite. It's what I know that's bothering you."

We stare off for silent seconds, and I know I still have his attention for that reason alone.

"What I want to know is how you fucking found out," he bites out bitterly.

"Never reveal a source," I snap. "That's Journalism 101."

Tension rolls off both of us as I stay put, in his space, doing my best to keep what little shred of confidence I have left. He glares at me with a mix of 'you're crazy' while weighing whether or not I'll carry out my threat.

Exhaling, I step down, still blocking him from shutting the door but giving him space to make his decision.

"Look, my father is my editor, so I get it. It's not the same, but I do get it."

The buzz from the hearty sips of beer I took on an empty stomach hits harder as I straighten my posture and come to my senses. It's as if the entirety of my education went out the window when he threatened to walk. When he sees I have the good sense to be a little embarrassed about it, amusement wins with the slight tilt of his lips. That's two almost smiles I've drawn from him. Maybe there's a chance to turn this around.

"Freshly graduated?"

"Shut up," I snap, unable to help my smile. "I'm well aware of my behavior at all times."

"All I'm saying is that I've been singing and playing instruments since I was two. We're not in the same ballpark."

"Again, so quick to condemn. My father didn't read me bedtime stories, Easton. He read me news articles starting with the Roosevelt administration all the way up to Anthrax before I started reading them myself. I wrote my first column when I was seven. It was about my horses. Hi, kettle, nice to meet you. I'm pot."

As to the question of why I'm here? The truth is I really don't know…I maxed out my AmEx, and on a whim, came here for what? To be ridiculed by a beautiful asshole who seems to be able to see right through my ruse.

"Look, I'll admit I'm slightly off my game. I've barely slept in two days. I'm fucking exhausted and running on fumes and misplaced emotions, and definitely didn't plan on—"

On what, Natalie? Being attracted to your father's ex-girlfriend's son?

Heat coats my neck, and I feel the flush traveling up. I'm thankful for the rapid wind stinging my face to disguise it as more catcalls sound from the tables outside the pub.

A smug smirk graces Easton's features, and somehow, I know he recognizes everything I'm not saying. Instead of shying away, I switch gears and palm the top of his truck, my dark beer-bred brass balls on full display.

"My legitimacy as a reporter aside, what's the worst that can happen? Maybe your success can't touch the Sergeants' legacy." Annoyed, I wrestle the hair obstructing my view and secure it inside my fist hoisting it atop my head to see his eyes intent on mine. "But you're not doing it for that, Easton. You said it yourself. You're doing it because you have no choice. Maybe that's why you don't give a damn about promoting it or trying to sell it because we both know your father—no matter who he is—can't make you a success. Either way, your reasons are your own. Just let me relay that one truth to them, so you don't come across as a pretentious douche bag."

Why are you giving him a pep talk while offering him something you can't deliver!? You have a paper to earn and inherit. Go home!

An electric current begins to thrum through my veins from the intensity of his gaze. I exhale harshly as he remains mute, and all hopes of salvaging this trip dissipate while I battle to keep the rest of my sanity.

"Obviously, I'm nowhere near the caliber of reporter of my dad or your mother…*yet*. But I'm too fucking intelligent to let inexperience or shaky confidence be the reason I tap out. It will have to be something far more substantial than that to tear me away from my own aspirations, and from what I've gathered, I think it's the same for you. Stick to that, and good luck," I exhale sincerely. "I wish you well, I really do, and again I'm sorry for the way I approached you. I mean that. I'm not…I haven't been myself lately, and you're right, it's not your problem. Take care, Easton." I step back and palm the door closed for him. He keeps my gaze through the window as he turns the truck over. Defeated but refusing to let him see it, I decide to give him space to make his exit.

His window lowers an inch just as I step back on the curb. "Get in."

Turning, he slides on the bench seat and pulls up the lock, which sits in the window frame of the '80s model truck. As I round the hood, a roar of cheers sounds from the tables. Rolling my eyes, I playfully give them the one-finger salute before sliding onto the bench seat and shutting myself in the truck.

"You have to slam it."

I do, and before I can get a word in, Easton pulls the gearshift next to the large steering wheel down and gasses us out of the parking lot.

SIX

Honest

Kyndal Inskeep, The Song House

Natalie

In a matter of minutes, we're parked just outside a closed storefront. Easton eases his key out of the ignition and reaches into the small space behind the bench seat producing an army-style faded green jacket. He hands it to me before wordlessly exiting the truck. While packing, I hadn't at all prepared for Seattle's spring temperatures versus Texas's. I blame my lack of sleep caused by the spell I've been under since I opened the email chain between our parents. Before I left Austin, I transferred the file to my laptop, and by the time I landed in Seattle, I had read through nearly two and a half years of their relationship—which only drew me further into confusion as to why they split up.

The love between them was so there, so evident, that I found myself tearing up multiple times due to loss alone.

I've been so completely immersed in their world that I barely remember checking into my hotel. Without so much as glancing around my room, I dumped my suitcase and stared up at the ceiling before managing to get a few restless hours of sleep. Feeling as insane as the acts I'm committing, I decided after waking I had no choice but to see my emotionally induced, half-baked scheme through. Just as out of sorts now—jet lag kicking in fully—I slide on the offered jacket with a soft "thank you," meeting Easton at the tailgate of his truck. As we start a silent walk, the material of his jacket blankets me in warmth as an earthy, birchwood scent drifts from the collar. The smell is both divine and comforting.

Allowing Easton to take the lead, I follow him down a small shop-littered street that looks catered to tourists. It's picturesque, almost romantic in feel as the sun peeks through the flowering blooms, christening the large branches of the towering trees that line both sides of the street.

Easton slows his pace slightly as if taking in the scenery for himself before veering towards a sidewalk leading us past the Mural Amphitheater at Seattle Center, which sits to our left. An extensive view of the Space Needle hovers above the cinema screen-sized mural. Stopping, I take a quick picture with my cell as Easton continues to walk with purpose just ahead of me. It's then I'm able to fully admire the outline of his build. I guesstimate his height somewhere around six-foot-two, six-foot-three. The cut of his tight jeans outlines both his thick muscular thighs and ample ass. His simple, form-fitting thermal clings to a trim waist, stretching over his muscular back before straining against the width of broad shoulders and bulging biceps.

The man clearly takes care of himself and seems to be in peak condition. If I'm going by looks alone, his genetic makeup will make him an idyllic and mouthwatering front man.

I was momentarily dizzied by the sight of him when he removed his hat at the tavern, and his dark, thick locks fell to rest just below his ears, enhancing his dark lashes and jawline. His presence is more surreal in motion, his chiseled profile and alluring gaze digging into me as he glances my way before I catch up.

After waking and rushing to get ready, I'd only slapped the bare essentials on my face. While he wears the rumpled 'fresh out of fucks given' look like he was born to do it, I look like I could use a lesson in self-care, a far, far cry from my put-together, everyday look back home. I can't exactly hate that I overslept today because I have no doubt if I had arrived at the bar in any sort of business dress, I would have gotten less than the five minutes he originally gave me.

Within a few hurried steps, we're at the entrance of Chihuly Garden and Glass. Before I have a chance to pull out my card for my ticket, Easton is slipping his wallet back into his jean pocket, two in hand. I mask my confusion as to why we're here but simply follow him without prompt because I lost control of the day the second I slipped into his truck.

Within minutes, we're entering a darkened room centered around an illuminated glass work of art. Easton steps out the way of those entering the room behind us, putting a large amount of space between us and those taking photos as he stares at the sea of multicolored blown glass. Standing near the back of the room, I play along during a few uneasy moments of silence before finally speaking up.

"Okay, you've made your point. You're a man of few words," I whisper. "Why are we here?"

"I haven't been here since I was a kid," he says thoughtfully as if he's speaking first, not answering my question.

"Okay. Why am *I* here?"

"This is your first time in Seattle." Not a question and something he shouldn't know but a fact that I made easy to gather. Right now, I'm a sleep-deprived, directionless, emotional mess due to the revelation of my dad's past life and my deception. Even so, I'm determined to try and take some control back. As the thought occurs to me to do better, I feel my energy waning further.

"Are we going to the Space Needle too? How about Pike's Market?" I quip, well aware of the city's most frequented tourist stops.

He nods toward the glass. "You don't think seeing this is worth the price of admission?" His eyes are lit with appreciation as he darts them over to me.

"I wouldn't know. I didn't pay for it. Thank you for that, by the way...and it's beautiful, but—"

"But?"

"But I'm not writing a puff piece, Easton."

"You're not writing *anything* at the moment, are you?"

I dart my gaze away.

His eyes remain on my profile as I bite my lip and stuff my hands in his jacket pockets. Amongst the contents, I feel a lighter, a safety pin, and pull a package out to see a dual pack of condoms—LELO-HEX-XL.

My eyes fly to his, his expression not changing a fraction as I quickly stuff the package back into my pocket.

"Congratulations," I mutter dryly with an eyeroll before darting my gaze back to the brightly lit piece.

We stand in silence for another few seconds before I speak again.

"You've never given an interview," I whisper.

"No."

"So why wouldn't I want to be the first?"

He shakes his head ironically, a clear call of bullshit. He's sensing an ulterior motive for my visit, and with every passing minute I remain vague, I'm giving him every reason to suspect me. Fleeing his evasive stare, I leave Easton's side and walk to the edge of the installation. Bright red cornstalk-shaped lightning rods surround a small patch of yellow glass resembling lily pads. Just beyond, green spikes surround and accentuate a portion of the fixture before similar stalks in indigo blue sit in a cluster around a large, red-based, twisted pile of glass, the top of it colored neon yellow. It's as if the whole installation is developing, reaching for something higher. The more I take in, the more my appreciation grows for the imagination and thought put into the work and the symphony of colors situated in an array of mind-boggling patterns. All of which are fused together in a way that shouldn't flow but do so effortlessly.

Sensing Easton at my back, I feel a faint tug on the tips of my hair before my whole body erupts in chills.

Did he just touch my hair?

Feeling surrounded by him, I tilt my head toward the collar of his jacket and gather another hit of his scent. It's intoxicating, knowing he's at my back, and maybe, he's just as curious about me as I am about him.

I blow out a breath, feeling a sort of intimate shift between us, the need to explain myself a little more pushing front and center. Hopefully, in doing so, I'll be able to lower an inch of his seemingly impenetrable guard. His love language seems to consist of honesty, and if I want to grasp any of the insight to the other side I'm seeking, I'm going to have to keep it real with him. Already feeling exposed and in such a short amount of time, owing to his keen perception and invasive gaze, I decide to go in with a personal truth.

"There's a famous picture," I rasp out, "called "The Vulture and the Little Girl." It was taken by a photojournalist named Kevin Carter,"

I glance back at Easton, who's now standing beside me. I see his gaze gliding along my profile, his own dimly lit by the spotlight on the sculpture. "Do you know of it?"

He gently shakes his head as I flit my focus back to the installation.

"In this picture, a Sudanese girl is starving to death." The image I stared at for endless days appears in my mind with little prompt. "The way she's postured, on her knees, hunched over, it's as if she's in the midst of desperate prayer." I draw upon the memory of the image, and the details become clearer. "She's got nothing but a necklace on, her outline skin and bones, clearly on the verge of death. She looks so small, so tiny, so helpless, and it's easy to conclude her time is running out. And, Jesus," I say, unable to help the tremble in my voice as Easton inches toward me. "Just behind her sits a vulture who's close to the size of her. His presence is menacing because you know it's just waiting for the chance to pick her apart." I swallow, trying desperately to reel my emotion in.

"Anyway, the photo appeared in the New York Times, and Carter won a Pulitzer for it. But the only question I had after seeing it was what action he took to protect her after he snapped that photo." Anger surfaces at my initial reaction and the mixed reports I read on the web just after. "And I wasn't the only one. Soon after, the paper and Kevin were put under fire regarding the fate of the girl and what Kevin did personally for her after he snapped the photo. You see, by industry standards, Kevin did his job. He reported the truth of the situation with a powerful image bringing awareness about the famine. Still, the fact that his actions after were put into question is another thing entirely."

The image again flits through my mind, forever burned in my brain. "In my eyes, there should never have been a muddled story behind what happened *after* he took that photo. One report stated he was standing near a waiting plane and used a long lens to take the shot and had no way of helping." I shake my head. "An excuse I found inexcusable. How could *any* human being walk away from a dying child who was about to be picked apart by a bird?" I close my eyes in disgust. "Not only that, it was a separate team of people altogether who investigated what happened to that starving girl—who turned out to be a *boy*—after the photo was taken. Initially, there were so many conflicting reports, facts seemed impossible to come by."

Silence stretches for a few seconds before Easton speaks up. "What happened to him?"

"He didn't die that day, and according to Kevin's recount, he chased the bird away, and the "girl" managed to make it to camp where they were unloading food. What still infuriated me is that Kevin received the greatest of honors for the shot but never once investigated her fate for himself. It was the concern of others and the criticism he received for not knowing after taking that shot that became a defining moment for me. Then and there, I decided exactly what type of truth-seeker and journalist I wanted to be and that I would never aspire to be Kevin Carter."

I look over to Easton. "And I won't be the vulture, either." His eyes bore into mine. "Nor will I be the one to feed them. If you don't understand or care to know anything else, please know that about me."

I look back at the sculpture. "But that's the thing about perception. I initially hated Kevin for his lack of action and the vague reports about the after and fed into the negative beliefs about his judgment and character...until I found out he committed suicide months later due to depression. Clearly, his work was affecting him on a massive scale. His empathy for having witnessed far too much in his career had taken a significant toll on his mental health.

"In his suicide note, he stated he couldn't handle the amount of pain in the world. I assume the backlash he took from having shot that picture added to that. Even though it was taken almost two decades before I was born, I was just as guilty, so quick to condemn him like everyone else. Maybe he did lie to save face, or perhaps he'd already become so ill from what he'd witnessed that he wasn't in the right frame of mind to step in because he was too busy trying to find reasons to continue his own life. Maybe he saw himself in that little girl, and in turn, those who judged him became the vultures. That's when I became obsessed with getting the *whole* story, gathering *all the facts* before I put out any human-interest piece. Sadly, his suicide isn't even mentioned in some of the articles, and I have no doubt it's because people are so quick to villainize someone and keep negative perceptions prominent in the world we live in. The day I read about Kevin's suicide was the day I realized the true power of the media and what damage an incomplete or biased story is capable of causing. Even now,

I don't think we'll ever know the facts or complete truth of that story." I shrug, "Maybe *my theory* is wrong."

With the slight tilt of his head, Easton weighs my words.

"Easton, tell me why you're so hesitant to give an interview for something you're signing up for."

He focuses back on the installation as bated silence ensues but surprises me when he finally speaks up. "The most I have to give to anyone is my music. That's personal enough."

"But it discredits you as a human being."

"I don't want to be human, not for them, because I'll be crucified no matter what, and you can't convince me otherwise. I want to—strike that—I *have to* keep a piece of myself for me and those close to me."

"But what if your music inspires people so much they can relate and want to know more about you?"

"Then it's the *music* they relate to, my feelings, my experiences, maybe my politics or beliefs *at the time* I was feeling them when I wrote it. I don't want to be held to some inhuman standard. I want to be able to make mistakes and evolve, just like everyone else. So, no, I'm not signing up for anything. I'm sharing my music. That's it. I don't want anything else from it."

He looks over to me, his voice grave.

"I wasn't made for this, Natalie. Creating and playing may be the only thing that comes naturally to me—and might be construed as talent—but the fame aspect is not something I've ever wanted, and I was born into it. It makes me feel *less* than human. I feel trapped, imprisoned by it, and for that, yeah, I'm just fucking unappreciative. As selfish as it may seem, I don't want to be responsible for people that way. If I play, it will be for entertainment. I'm no one's messiah and don't strive to be. Kind of like your Kevin Carter. I know exactly what I want and what I don't. I want my music heard. I want to play it for those who enjoy it. That's it. I don't want you to print any of this to paint a picture of another fucking ungrateful rock star's kid, who already feels trapped by fame before he even releases. It's my worst nightmare. Pick a different angle, any fucking angle."

"It's the truth."

"It's part of the truth," he insists, not giving me anything else.

"We don't have to be friends, Easton, and I may grill you for the truth, but I can promise you that I won't sacrifice any part of *you* for *them*."

He remains silent, his jade gaze magnetic as we stare off.

"I know I haven't given you a single reason to trust me, and I may seem a little out of..." *my fucking mind*, "sorts, but I assure you I am capable of writing an honest story full of whatever your truth may be. If you decide to grant me an interview."

He nods, unrelenting in his observation of me as more silence ensues.

"Will you at least tell me what you're thinking right now?"

"I think you're beautiful," he rasps out, "and I feel sorry for you."

I can't help the bark of a laugh that bursts from me as my pride takes another solid hit. "*Screw you, Crowne.*"

His lips lift slightly in another almost smile before he extends an open hand toward me. "Come on."

Frowning, I stare at his outstretched hand as he extends it further, urging me to take it. Hesitantly I grasp it, and he encases it in his warm palm before leading me into the next room.

We don't exchange a single word as we go through the rest of the property. Still, he remains close, our arms brushing as he glances over at me every couple of minutes—strangely in silent support and apparently ready to listen.

He probably thinks I'm a little crazy or cracking up.

Currently, I fear he might not be wrong.

Once we leave the garden, he drives around the outskirts of the city. The music blaring as the whipping wind circulates through the ancient Chevy, and the heater blows at our feet. Every so often, I glance over at him as he drives, seemingly lost in his own thoughts. I have no doubt those thoughts are keeping him in better company because, for the umpteenth time since I got to Seattle, I'm questioning why I'm here. All I do know is right now, I feel incapable of taking the lead. The self-assured, confident, steadfast, focused woman I was before I opened those emails is nowhere in the vicinity.

Sadly, but truthfully, I'm thankful for the distance between myself and the people that know me best—especially my father. But even that tiny relief brings its own type of guilt.

After endless miles of relaxed silence with music continually flowing, Easton finally asks me where I'm staying. Not long after, he pulls up to the circular entrance of The Edgewater Hotel. The sliding doors are to our right, and a fire roars in the large stone column on the left. The heavy repeat of the engine amplifies to an obnoxious level when he puts the truck in park and turns to me.

"As odd as the day was, thank you," I say, too exhausted to be embarrassed.

He dips his chin, his gaze dancing along my windblown hair before his eyes snap back to mine.

"Um...look, I fly home on Sunday, so if you are still willing to do an interview, I guess...well, you have my number."

Another subtle dip of his chin gives me no inclination either way as I drink in his features. Knowing what the odds are, I'll probably never see him again. In all honesty, I wouldn't have blamed him if he dumped me roadside hours ago.

"It's been...," a laugh bursts from me, and his lips lift slightly in response. Something inside me mourns the fact I'll never see Easton Crowne smile.

"Bye," I whisper, shutting his truck door before walking through the lobby doors, fighting not to look back. I don't hear his truck engine rev until I'm well past the reception desk.

SEVEN

Devils Haircut
Beck

Easton

Entering the front door, I hear music drifting throughout as I start the trek across our expansive sunken living room before stepping up into the kitchen. I find Mom dressed in her usual at ease attire—one of Dad's tour T-shirts, baggy sweats, and a messy bun. Studying her while she dutifully stirs a pot, I can't help but notice she seems smaller in frame than she used to.

"What are you cooking?"

Mom jumps a foot off the floor before turning to me, eyes wide, one palm flattened to her chest, a partially coated wooden spoon gripped in the other. "What the fucking scary stalker type of an approach was that?" She widens her eyes as I chuckle. "Seriously, son, why didn't you announce yourself?"

"Because you're blaring Beck while cooking…" I eye the pot and the clock on the stove behind it, "…spaghetti at midnight. Seriously, Mom?" Chest heaving, she snatches a remote from the counter and taps a button furiously, lowering the volume.

"I couldn't sleep. You didn't text."

"This again," I sigh, ripping off my hat and running a hand through my hair. "I'm moving out."

"Not yet. I have to mentally prepare."

"You said that six months ago. It's about *four* years past time, two at the very least, don't you think?"

"Says who?"

"Every other self-respecting twenty-two-year-old human with a set of testicles."

"You're *safe* here, and you'll be on tour soon anyway, so it's pointless to get a place now that will essentially be a storage unit. Save your money."

"A tour?" I scoff. "That's a bit premature."

"Mark my words, you'll be on the road by summer," she says with surety.

"That's a big *if*," I remind her, knowing there may be some truth to her statement. While music distribution has changed substantially in the last fifteen years, making it far easier to release with the mere push of a button, the road aspect to perk ears to new sound remains the same. Especially if I don't get the airplay or streaming results I hope for within the first few months. My hopes will most likely be dashed anyway, due to my hesitance to sell myself and my music by placating the media. Much like in my dad's day—and the days before—if I want my music heard, I'll have to pay dues by playing clubs and smaller stadiums to get the word out. Playing live still has the potential to have as much impact as it's always had. It's also a way to sharpen sound, bring bands closer on a personal level, and is considered by many musicians as a rite of passage.

Her prediction is still farfetched, considering I don't exactly have a band—*yet*.

"Either way, you live *here* until we know. Deal?"

For my mother, it's all about security, and I can't say it hasn't been needed over the years. A few months after I was born, a crazed fan broke into the infamous A-frame house my parents reunited at while we were home. Dad managed to get the disturbed woman outside until the police arrived. In an effort to protect me, they moved us into the security guarded, gated community where I've grown up. It was a wise decision on their part. My mother still remains bitter about the fact we had to move out of a house that meant so much to them both. I've heard the story dozens of times over the years of how their chance meeting at that open house solidified them together for good. To this day, each time my mother tells it, her eyes cloud with sentiment.

"Elliot Easton Crowne," my mother prompts, breaking up my inner musings. "You will stay here until your tour is over, right?"

"This is not full name serious," I taunt.

"To you," she digs in, ready for this fight.

"Fine," I concede, running my hands through my hair in frustration, but wanting no part of the oncoming rant if she doesn't get her way on this. Mom tends to get emotional more often than not, forever wearing her heart on her sleeve. She's always felt things on a deeper level than most people do.

It's one of the character traits I love most about her and identify with, which is why I'm well equipped to handle her because I have them myself at times.

A smile threatens at the memory of Natalie having her own moment hovering above me in the bar parking lot. Her long, strawberry hair whipping around her face, sticking to her lips. Even in the midst of her wardrobe crisis, she looked like a beautifully wrapped disaster, emotions warring, cheeks pinkening with embarrassment as her eyes battered mine with a plea to keep my company. She won that battle far too easily, and I let her because I would have been hard-pressed to leave her there looking as lost as she seemed. She reminded me of Mom a little then—and myself, too, her emotions prickling just beneath her skin. The exchange only sparked my interest.

Upon first meeting her, I assumed the conclusions I'd drawn about her since her threatening call were right. That she was privileged and ruthlessly abusive because of it. Turns out, she's the opposite of what I expected, showing clear remorse for that call by apologizing more than once. Mom speaks up while stirring her sauce again, and I shoot up a silent prayer that she's planning on dining alone. "What did you do today?"

"I cruised around and went to the Chihuly Garden."

She tosses an inquisitive glance over her shoulder. "Alone?"

I nod, refusing to add words to my lie, but for now, respecting Natalie's request that our parents remain out of it. I could easily relay anything to either one of them. As furious as they would be about how she cornered me, they wouldn't interfere if I asked them to stay out of it, but I allow the white lie anyway.

Mom opens a box of pasta and dumps it into boiling water as Natalie's confession about our parents' dating comes to mind. Her back-pedaling today and request to forget she mentioned it has me curious.

"Hey, Mom? Did you ever seriously date anyone other than Dad?"

She turns to me, her brows furrowing. "What?"

"You heard me. Did you?"

"Yeah, I did. We didn't get back together and marry until I was on the downside of my twenties, so of course I did," she replies easily enough, her eyes going a little distant before focusing back on me. "Why?"

"Just curious..."

She narrows her eyes suspiciously. "Oh, shit."

She does the sign of the cross, and I snort. "Mom, you're not religious."

"I am religious, more so now if you met a girl. *Did* you meet a girl? Please lie if it's serious, especially since you're about to hit stardust." She sighs dramatically, placing her palms on the island between us as if to draw strength. "Look, no matter which way *JR*," she dips her chin to insinuate I call my junk JR, "is directing you right now, *walk away* from the light."

When I give no reply to the utter ridiculousness of her statement, she mutters a curse before pulling the fridge open to check the egg carton for a count. Realizing what she's up to, I quickly speak up.

"Mom, chill. No open eggs under my bed, or white sage, or whatever superstitious voodoo shit you're conjuring up in that crazy brain. You don't even really believe it."

"Eggs are for bad dreams anyway. I think I'm supposed to clean your bedroom door and then bury the rag or something. I'll check with your grandmother." Mom is half Latina and practices the superstitious rituals her aunts in Mexico instilled in her—which Dad finds hilarious. I did too, until middle school when she chaperoned a field trip near Cedar Lake for a picnic. The second I set foot in the river, she placed her hand on my head and screamed my name three times, explaining if she hadn't, the river spirits would take me away. The kids around us immediately fled the water, some crying. It embarrassed the shit out of me, and I still haven't forgiven her. Even as I inwardly roll my eyes at her rituals, she pinches and disperses oregano into the bubbling saucepan in a cross formation.

"Do you really believe in that shit?"

"You know I do. Your father and I have had some really insane crap happen over the years, mostly in a good way. I believe in fate, karma, and things that work together for the greater good. If a little practiced superstition helps negate the bad, what's the harm?"

"Well, don't call Grandma or bust out the Hocus Pocus handbook just yet. I'm not getting married."

"Ever?" She deflates. "Look, I know your generation doesn't really believe in marriage anymore, but there are perks."

"Not saying never."

"Oh, thank God. I want grandkids."

"Those I can deliver in spades," I wink. "Married or not."

She points her weapon of choice—a wooden spoon she used to threaten me with—at me, "That's not even remotely fucking funny."

"I disagree," Dad says, walking in half-asleep in nothing but sweats. "What in the hell are you up to, Grenade?" He circles her with his arms and presses a kiss to her temple. "Or should I say burning?"

"Sorry, did I wake you with the music?"

"No, you woke me up by not being in bed," he eyes the pots behind her. "But it seems I woke to a living nightmare."

"You both want on my shit list today?" Mom snaps, wriggling free of him and looking between us. "Seriously? What have I ever done but love and adore the two of you?"

"I can think of a few hundred headaches," he chides. Her eyes narrow, and he lifts his palms in surrender. "Easy, baby," Dad says, pressing a quick kiss to her temple before grabbing a water from the fridge and eyeing the clock on the stove. "Why are you attempting to cook for the first time in a decade at midnight?"

"I'm hungry, and I cook," she defends weakly.

Dad and I collectively bite our lips.

"I *do* cook. Sometimes. Occasionally. Okay, *never*," she turns back to the sauce and stirs. "I'm just a little restless," she adds with a shrug.

Dad's lips quirk as he studies Mom carefully. I see it the second he pegs the reason for her unease.

"Babe, we talked about this. You have to be patient."

He runs a reassuring hand down her back, her shoulders slumping forward as she softly dips her chin in response. Dad looks over at me, and I frown, unsure of what's happening. "What?"

He gives me the pointed look that reads, 'see what you're doing to her?' just as it dawns on me.

"Mom—" I start as she speaks up.

"It's fine," she lifts her tone in an attempt to try and hide her disappointment, her back to me to keep me from seeing it. "I understand. I didn't let anyone read my articles early on." She glances back at me, hurt clearly visible though she's trying her best to hide it.

"It's not that I don't want you to hear it—"

"I'm a critic."

"No, Mom, you're *The* critic," I add, *and the one that matters most to me.* But I don't voice that, opting for a different part of the truth.

"I don't want you to feel torn between your bias for me and the truth of how you really feel about it."

"So, you want to release it to the rest of the world *first*?"

I give the firm dip of my chin as she studies me. "I know that hurts you, but I promise all I'm trying to do is protect us both."

She's never going to write about my music. We agreed on that when I decided to entertain releasing it. Even though she wrote about the Sergeants early on, that was a different lifetime ago before they became synonymous with the greats like The Rolling Stones, U2, and other classic rock bands that have a place in the Rock & Roll Hall of Fame. The Dead Sergeants were inducted a year and a half ago, and it was a surreal experience seeing my father and his band honored and revered that way, though they've been bestowed so much already.

Natalie is right, I have a legacy to live up to, and I fucking hate that aspect of it. When I sat down to record years ago, I didn't take that into account. I just wanted to make music. So I did, with no real intent to release it. Now that I'm about to expose myself in this way, all of the bullshit I kept out of it is coming into play. My mind drifts again to the beauty who rode in my truck, seeming as confused as I was today. The longer we rode together in comfortable silence, the longer I drove, nowhere near as anxious to leave her as I was back at the bar.

Though she cornered me in the worst imaginable fucking way, nothing about her confession at the garden seemed contrived. She was far too vulnerable to have made any of that up. Though I swore to myself I would never give a single interview—no matter how well my music did—I find myself wanting to trust her with the insight as to why I won't.

"Mom, if there's anyone in the world I want to hear it, it's you."

"I understand, I do. I'll deal," Mom assures me as the water boils over and the tell-tale fizzling sound goes off behind her. Oblivious and intent on our conversation, she ignores it. Dad snaps into motion, turning off the heat fueling both burners before smoothly sliding the saucepan to safety, his chuckle rumbling through the kitchen.

"Babe, you're not going to turn into Gordon Ramsay tonight. Let's spare your pride."

She keeps her gaze fixed on me. "No matter what, I'm proud of you. I know how unbelievably talented you are, no matter what, okay?"

I can't help my grin. "Thanks, Mom*my*."

Dad gives me his signature scowl, but Mom smiles, her watery eyes gleaming with pride. "That natural shift to smartass is *all me*," she declares proudly to Dad.

"Let's not exaggerate by taking all the credit," Dad quips back, opening a drawer full of take-out menus and tossing them on the counter. "I'm sure something's still open."

"It's spaghetti," Mom defends, scowling at Dad's profile. "Jarred tomatoes, meat, spice, and noodles, not rocket science."

"Tell that to your finished product," Dad grumbles, the smell of burnt sauce starting to permeate the air. Mom gets a whiff of it, and her expression falls. "You were distracting me."

"Babe, face it, you'll never be a cook."

"Only if you face the fact that you'll never be a mechanic and get that piece of shit out of our garage."

"It's coming along," he defends.

"It's been eight months," she chides. "You still haven't turned the engine over, and I'll make sure it never does. You're not riding a fucking motorcycle. That phase of your life is over. Window closed."

Dad remains mute, his version of 'we'll see' covering his expression, and I can't help but observe the two of them as my thoughts again drift back to Natalie.

Something shifted between us today from our hostile meeting to the time I dropped her off. Despite us being complete strangers, I felt just as exposed and raw watching her. Even as she tried to defend her integrity to me, I sensed some sort of break inside her beneath the surface and glimpsed it in bits and pieces. Oddly, I found myself wanting to show her the beauty in them and help her try and make sense of it, whatever it may be. One thing I'm growing more suspicious and sure of, is that she's not here for an article, even if she's refusing to admit it. The second thing is that she wasn't expecting to be attracted to me, at all.

That surprise was mutual.

It unexpectedly took me hostage in much the same way it seemed to grab her. I got swept up in it, and it was fucking intense. Every second that ticked by after her confession felt like an invitation I didn't take.

The weight of my cell phone increases where it rests in my jeans pocket as I debate whether or not to use it. Does the reason she's here have more to do with our parents' involvement? If so, why? What could the draw of that possibly be after all this time? It's definitely not newsworthy at this point.

For the first time in a long time, I examine my parents closely, their body language, their knowing glances and effortless exchange as Dad jerks back in fear while Mom raises a spoon of burnt sauce to his lips.

"Not a fucking chance, baby," Dad says, his grin fading when he turns to me. Before I know it, they're both looking at me quizzically, studying me back just as carefully.

Opting out of the inquiry sure to come, I turn abruptly. "I'm going to bed."

"You okay?" Mom asks, a fair level of concern in her tone as I stride across the living room.

"Yeah, I'm just wiped. Night."

Before she can pry any further, I take the winding staircase up to my room. An hour later, I lay in my briefs, buds anchored in my ears, cell in hand, staring at the Pulitzer Prize-winning picture of "The Vulture and the Little Girl." At first sight, I felt the same sting anyone with a conscience who's viewed it must have felt, terrified this is still a reality for some, fighting daily simply to exist.

Studying it, I recall Natalie's admission of how the picture changed her and how her researching the story behind it shifted her perception more drastically. Part of her confession had the hairs on my neck standing on end. If she only knew how close she'd gotten to verbalizing my fears, which were fucking eerily similar to her own, the difference being *me* on the opposite side of the pen.

It's as if she knew exactly what to say to me. If I still believed her capable, I would have considered her story a ploy to get what she wanted. But no matter how closely I watched her for any sign of manipulation, I couldn't find it. Instead, I felt the vulnerability rattling from her, which put me at ease. There's no way she would have that type of insight into me anyway, especially when my own confession came *after* hers. My music is the most personal thing I have and ever will have, and my parents understand that about me. For some reason—though I shouldn't have any—I find myself wanting to make her understand it. Or maybe I just want to be in her space again to figure out why she seems so fucking…lost.

Clearing the screen of the picture I can no longer stomach. I pull up my messages and shoot off a text.

Hey, you still up?

I can't help my grin as dots immediately begin to roll along the screen.

I was just about to text you and let you know I'll leave your jacket at the reception desk.

Keep it for now. It's clear you didn't pack nearly enough clothes.

I program her in, waiting on her response.

Natalie: Hilarious. Eye-roll emoji.

Want to go somewhere with me tomorrow?

More bubbles appear, her response time drawing out in ridiculous length before she gives me a one-word reply.

This woman.

Natalie: Where?

Not telling. Be ready at 6.

Natalie: Okay.

AM.

Natalie: Wtf, that's like five hours from now!

And this is strictly off the record.

Natalie: Seriously?

Yeah. What's your room number?

The bubbles start and stop for a full five minutes before the room number appears.

EIGHT

Firestarter
The Prodigy

Natalie

I jerk awake as sharp knocks sound against my hotel door. It's only when I open my eyes that I realize I'm not at home, and I fell asleep with my laptop open after failing to set an alarm.

"Shit!"

Scrambling, I pull on the Seahawks sweatshirt I bought from the hotel gift shop and crack the door. On the other side stands a handsome, well-dressed man who looks to be somewhere in his early forties, grinning at me with a phone lifted to his ear.

"Good morning, *Natalie*?"

"Yes," I say, partially shielding behind the door to hide my slightly revealing pajama bottoms.

"Yeah," he says with a low chuckle. "She most definitely overslept."

"I'm sorry," I blurt loudly, knowing Easton is on the other end of the line. "I can be ready in ten minutes."

The man shakes his head, his grin widening. "He says too late."

My chest deflates.

"Yeah, she looks like you just kicked her."

I narrow my eyes at him as he pulls away from the phone and covers the speaker.

"Hey, I'm Joel," he whispers.

I frown in confusion. "Hi."

He elevates his voice for Easton. "He says ten minutes, fifteen if you bring coffees from the lobby and have an apology ready." He pulls his phone away again and whispers conspiratorially, making him an instant ally. "He'll wait twenty."

I project my voice again. "I already apologized and tell his entitled ass, it'll be *twenty.*"

Joel grins as Easton speaks on the other end of the line. I find myself leaning in and can't make out a word. "Uh huh, got it," Joel says before hanging up and giving me a wink of reassurance. "See you in twenty, Natalie."

With that, he turns and begins to make his way toward the elevator.

"Wait," I call out to his retreating back. "How do you take *your* coffee?"

"Black."

"Got it," I say, slamming my hotel door and bracing myself against it for a few seconds before I burst into motion. I use the first four of my twenty minutes in the shower and accidentally wet my hair when I drop my rag.

"SHIT!"

Bringing my soapy hands up to see how much of it got wet, a splatter of soap lands directly in my eyes. Eyes burning, I curse as I jump around in pain before finally immersing my whole head under the spray.

Once I'm out, I manage a quick towel off before I frantically dig through my amenities bag, praying I have enough product to tame the inevitable curls I inherited from my mother. While Dad gave me the color, my mom graced me with the just electrocuted ringlets sure to appear as soon as the air starts to dry it. I spent the rest of my ticking time blow drying and crunching it as my unused flat irons stared back at me in judgment.

Without a single second to spare, I slide on clean panties, jeans, and my Van high-tops before pulling back on my Seahawks hoodie. With less than five minutes to spare, I haul ass to the coffee shop in the lobby and stand in line, shooting off a text to Easton.

How do you like your coffee?

EC: On time.

Then stop wasting mine. What will you have?

EC: I'll take a triple shot espresso with lots of sugar and cream and a dash of cinnamon and nutmeg.

What the hell are we doing that constitutes that kind of caffeine buzz? Or are you in need of a substitute for testosterone due to that need for a cinnamon and nutmeg dash?

EC: I know you're adjusting to the time change, Austin, but your Seattle time ran out two minutes ago.

Ten agonizing minutes later, I walk out of the hotel without a single trace of makeup, looking like a freshly laundered poodle with pink eye. Balancing the beverage tray with Joel's man coffee and Easton's girly drink, I tighten my small backpack on my shoulder as I spot the celebrity-typical idling SUV with blacked-out windows.

Joel pops out as I near and opens the back door for me as I pluck out and extend his coffee his way. He thanks me as I slide in, keeping my gaze averted, embarrassment already coating my neck. Aware we're all our own harshest critics, I still need a few confidence-boosting steps to feel comfortable, especially when attempting to go all-natural. I had no time for any of those.

"You really expect me to take you seriously as a reporter?" Easton chides as I thrust his apology espresso towards him.

"We're off record today, remember?"

He refuses the piping hot offering in my hand, and I look over to him to see his gaze fixed on my hair just as he reaches up and rubs one of my curls between his fingers. "I like it like this."

"Clean?"

"Natural," he says, taking his coffee as a tinge of exhilaration shoots up my spine.

"You can't be serious."

"I am."

"Well, thanks, but that makes *one* of us. I guess I'm glad you're not embarrassed to be seen with a human poodle since all-natural seems to be the running theme of this trip because I can't seem to get acclimated to a simple two-hour fucking time difference."

He smirks before sipping his liquid crack as I take a tug on my own.

"I'm sorry, Easton. I forgot to set my alarm after you texted and fell asleep reading."

"Is that why your eyes are so red?"

"No, they're red because I've been crying over your mistreatment of me," I quip.

A loud chuckle escapes Joel from where he sits in the driver's seat.

I catch his eyes in the rearview, flashing him a smile before turning back to Easton, who's not quite as amused. "Okay, so what's with the butt crack of dawn wakeup call?"

"How we doing on time, Joel?" Easton asks, ignoring my question.

"You'll only have about an hour once we get there," Joel replies.

Easton scowls in response at me. "Thanks to Goldilocks here."

"I'm sorry, man. Geesh. How many apologies do you need? And where is the fire so early?"

It's then I scan his dress. He's in snug jeans and a mesh, black, long sleeve shirt with black boots. His raven hair tucked behind his ears catching a ray of sunlight, thanks to the morning sky.

Great, sun rays follow him wherever he goes, amplifying his hotness tenfold, and I don't even have my eyebrows shaded on. It's a good thing this isn't a date because he's far too damned good-looking for me to handle in this state of disarray. The upside is, graced with the three hours of sleep I managed and my escalating coffee buzz, I don't feel nearly as terrified as I was yesterday. Easton's somehow put me at ease even while giving me shit. I again study his all-black dress and decide to grill him about our destination.

"Are we going to rob someone? If so, am I an accomplice? Because I'm not properly dressed, nor armed."

"You wouldn't hurt a fly," Easton says as if it's a fact.

I narrow my eyes. "Assumptions make most people assholes, but you already have that market cornered, don't you?" I widen my red eyes as Joel audibly snorts.

"I said wouldn't, not *couldn't*," Easton mutters dryly, giving Joel a warning look in the rearview. Joel doesn't so much as flinch. They're close, from the looks of it—*really close*, and Joel seems to be on Team Natalie today.

Take *that*, gorgeous man with visible eyebrows.

"Once again, I must insist on asking. Where are we headed to, Mr. Crowne?"

"Patience," he says, kicking back in his seat and crossing a booted foot over his knee before speaking up to Joel. "Hey man, give me something." Seconds later, loud bass fills the car, a song I've never heard thrumming throughout as Easton stares out the window.

As I ease further into consciousness, I glance over to see he seems to have checked out—as in transported elsewhere—his fingers tapping along to the music.

I lean forward to Joel behind the driver's seat.

"Hey, what's this song?"

""Firestarter" by The Prodigy," Joel answers.

"Thanks," I say, sliding back into place and making a mental note. If I was writing a story, I'd be taking a lot of notes, both mentally and physically. If I want my ruse to seem convincing, I need to keep up with my norm. Pulling up my phone, I start a new playlist and add the song before flipping through to see the sad list I started and forgot about years ago. Pulling up my texts, I quickly add some of the songs Easton played yesterday on our drive that I'd texted myself to remember, the only true notes I made.

Meh, if anything, maybe my eleven-hundred-dollar plane ticket will have me back in Austin with a better music library.

Not long after I add the music, we arrive at what looks like a small arena. Pumped I might get to hear Easton sing or play, my hopes get dashed when I read the marquee on the front of the building. "Are we here to watch motocross?"

Easton ignores my inquisition and grips the headrest of the passenger seat, his question for Joel. "Where are we meeting them?"

"Here they come now." Joel nods toward two men who appear at the front of the building before making their way toward the SUV.

Easton's eyes light as he turns to me, pulling a packed duffle I hadn't noticed from between his booted feet.

"Wait," I grip Easton's arm, slightly stunned by the zing that accompanies touching him as he pinches his brows, his eyes dropping to my tightening fingers. "Easton," I glance toward the men now waiting outside of the SUV, "you can't be serious."

Another almost smile upturns his lips as he slowly lifts his hazels to mine, and I see just how serious he is. "Let go."

I pull my arm away quickly as he leans in on a soft whisper, his woodsy scent invading my nostrils, sweet coffee breath hitting my ear and neck, "I said, *let's go*, Natalie."

"Oh," I whisper back as he plants a foot out of the SUV and turns, extending a hand toward me. The second I place my palm in his, his eyes snap to mine and flare slightly before he turns and ushers me toward the building.

NINE

Safety Dance
Men Without Hats

Natalie

Anxiety slithers through me as I gape at the track behind Easton, who is currently conversing with Jedidiah, one of the two guys who met us at the SUV. On the floor of the arena, I've patiently stood at his side, being completely forgotten for the last ten minutes. Feeling oddly put off by his blatant brush-off, I entertain calling an Uber and giving him the one-finger salute. As I entertain the thought, Easton finally looks over and smirks as if he can sense my aggravation. Just as I narrow my eyes, he reaches back and pulls off his shirt. Olive skin stretches over perfectly muscled pecs, down to a crystal-cut eight pack. His upper body is every bit as impressive as that of a top-tier athlete, and my appreciation for his efforts threatens to escape as I fight to keep my jaw clamped closed. As he busies himself back into the conversation, I drink in his long, muscular torso, my eyes bulging as he starts to unbuckle his belt, the sheer sight of it doing something to my insides. Belt dangling, he pulls another shirt from his duffle as I step back to where Joel stands idly by.

"He's not actually planning on—" my question is cut short as Easton pushes his jeans off his hips, and I'm struck sideways by the sight of him in nothing but black boxer briefs.

Jesus by the river.

Toned, muscular calves, thick thighs, a prominent LELO-HEX-XL bulge hanging between them. He's most definitely been graced with the body to match the face. His tinted skin helps to showcase the shadow of the ridiculously deep V-cut that peeks out of his boxers. A dark trail of hair lining what I can see of the top of his navel. His eyes flit to mine briefly, and the faint curve of his lush, red-tinged lips follow before he plucks some pants from his duffle. A deep chuckle sounds from next to me, and I turn to see Joel eyeing my reaction with amusement.

"Is it customary for men to strip—" I'm cut short again as Jedidiah manages to get into his own underwear within a blink. His body is just as insanely toned, muscles rippling with his every movement as he jokes with Easton like they're old friends—and maybe they are.

Easton again glances over at me as I narrow my eyes.

I'm onto you.

I fight my tongue from escaping my lips as the two of them banter as if standing beachside, golden skin, muscles taut and taunting for everyone without a swinging dick to admire—which makes me a lone party of *one*. Ripping my eyes away, I shrug.

"Well, big shit, so he's pretty." I cross my arms, "They make 'em just as pretty in Texas," I spout to Joel, which has him belting out another loud laugh. Easton turns at Joel's outburst, his eyes darting curiously between Joel and me as we share a smile. In the next second, both Easton and Jedidiah are dressed in riding gear.

It's when I see the bikes being rolled up that the fear kicks in, and I step up to Easton in an attempt to be some sort of voice of reason. He gazes down at me with glittering eyes full of mischief, seemingly ready for my protest. It's then I notice they're far greener in color than a mix of both. The light honey-brown color surrounding his pupils threading out like tiny sun rays before disappearing in a sea of emerald green.

Pretty man on motorbike, destination—death. Focus, Natalie!

"Look, I know it's not my place, and we just met, but are you fucking crazy?!" My voice of reason sounds more like the screech of a grandmother with a fanny pack full of Bactine and Band-Aids. Supplies that won't help Easton one damn bit if he loses control on the massive track behind him.

"I wouldn't argue with that assessment," Easton retorts. "Seems I'm in good company."

"Har, har," I whisper-hiss, leaning in, "just so you know, you don't opt to ride a death trap on Mt. Suicide before you drop your first album and break every bone in your body!" I mentally search the endless articles I read last night about Easton—or any mention of him—and not one of them cited motocross or anything else helpful for that matter. Fear escalating, I eye the monstrous track behind him. Intimidating mounds of dirt are piled high, expertly architected for the Evel Knievel-type motherfuckers surrounding him in encouragement.

"You've done this before, right?" I ask, further invading his space. "Right, Easton?" I press when he doesn't answer, the early morning wind whipping around my face, my wayward curls sticking to my lip gloss.

Wordlessly, Easton slides on his gloves as an amused Jedidiah nudges him before handing him a helmet and goggles. "Little lady is worried about you."

"I'm not his little lady," I snap. "I'm just the journalist who will not get her story if her subject ends up in a damned coma!"

"Ah, now don't go hurting my feelings," Easton chides, "you're acting a lot like my little lady…and I kind of dig the concern. If you feign indifference now, it will only hurt my confidence."

"Oh, you'll survive," I snark with an eyeroll before I straighten and sober considerably. "You *will* survive, right?"

Easton weighs my expression before he slides on his helmet. He's doing this.

"You know if you break your neck, you'll never know if your album goes platinum! Does your mother know you're doing this?"

"Why, you going to call her?" I can only see the tips of his smile, but I can tell it's full by the devilish glint in his eyes. My heart begins to pound erratically inside my chest as I dart my attention between Easton and the track.

I know fuck all about motocross, but I've seen it in passing on TV, and from what I can tell, you have to be close to a professional level to take on a track like the one looming behind him.

"Easton," I plea. "You've done this before, right?"

He gestures for me to step back, and I lay my hand on one of his gloved hands where it rests on the handle of the bike and shake my head. It's then he lifts a gloved hand and takes the hair I'm close to eating away from my lips, the gesture intimate but short-lived. Instead of replying to any one of my protests, he lowers his goggles and kicks the bike to life, forcing me back.

Jedidiah looks back over to me, a smirk firmly in place to match my horror-filled expression. His shout barely registers over the hornet-sounding engine ringing in my ears. "Trust him. He's got this."

I nod as Joel grips me by the shoulders and ushers me back toward the stands.

The next few minutes are a battle to keep my coffee down as Easton keeps to one area of the course, opening the bike up, his wheels catching once or twice in a way that has my stomach roiling.

"He's in the rut," Joel says.

"I'll say. Is this some sort of cry for help?"

Joel belts out a hearty laugh. "No, the *rut* is the most technical part of the track and hard to get through. He's just warming up."

"Oh, greeeeaaat," I reply dryly. "Some bodyguard you are."

All I get is an answering smile as his eyes trace Easton on the track. There's definitely a friendship there, a brotherly type of love. It's easy to see by Joel's expression. He doesn't want him hurt, which eases my nerves by a fraction.

"This isn't his first time," Joel finally relays, "or second."

"I've gathered that," I harrumph as Jedidiah fires up his own bike and makes his way toward Easton. Jedidiah's a little older, and I know just by the look of the way he's riding that he's a pro. To his credit, Easton seems to have his own way with the bike, his posture just as natural and impressive. After a few minutes of racing around each other in the rut, they both seem to appear out of thin air at the top of the starting line, wheels edging on a pile of dirt at least a few stories high. Prompted by fear alone, I do the sign of the cross just as Easton's helmet tips down in my direction. He seems to pause when he sees me praying as if the gesture stunned him.

Anxiety partying in my gut, I twist my hands in my lap and shake my head in denial. Why the hell did he want me here? To witness his senseless end? Does *he* believe in God? Does he want a funeral? Cremation or burial? Am I responsible for reporting his last words to the world? If so, he should have at least given me something worthwhile. My memory is shit in times of extreme stress, so I doubt I'd do him justice.

Before I can contemplate any more questions, Easton takes off, and Jedidiah remains at the top of the hill. I barely have time to gulp back air before he speeds over a series of short hills, and in the next second, he's airborne, a thousand feet high—well, maybe not a thousand—but enough to make me scream out in panic as he begins his descent. Covering my eyes with my palms, I space my fingers just enough to witness his demise.

When he manages a smooth landing, I'm only able to relax for a few seconds, and then he's airborne again, his hangtime surreal, while he manipulates his body and the bike sideways.

"Oh my God!" I exclaim, and this time my body reacts on its own, an encouraging fist-pump winning. Unable to help it, I stand, my arms above my head as I scream my praises, as do the floor of spectators—all of them staff. This time his landing is better than the first, and a strange sense of pride fills me for him. I glance back at Joel to see he's recording my reaction with his iPhone, and I flip him twin middle fingers, knowing Easton will see this footage at some point. Even so, I keep my grin firmly in place before Joel again trains his camera on Easton, who's owning the track.

When Jedidiah takes off, I spend the next few minutes in a mixed state of anxiety, awe, and slow budding arousal as I watch the two of them navigate the complex path with expertise. Jedidiah does a lot more tricks, but Easton runs through it just as remarkably—and more importantly—in one piece. By the time Easton makes his way back to where I left him, the waiting staff are cheering as he pulls up and huddle around him while he takes off his helmet. His sweat-matted hair falls in a heap across his forehead, his eyes lit with adrenaline. Jedidiah races up next to him as the small crowd parts, and they fist-bump gloved hands before killing their bikes.

Easton and Jedidiah talk animatedly as I take my time descending the few steps, shaking in relief while invigorated by the rush of just seeing him this way. Easton isn't an all-around grump, he's just... private, and it seems he saves his smiles for his people.

Just as I think it, his eyes find mine, his lips lift, and he beams at me with the most beautiful of full smiles, and the thunder roaring through my chest increases exponentially. I approach him with a similar grin and ready scold.

"That was reckless, stupid, irresponsible, and fucking amazing," I say, evident awe in my delivery.

"You're the only person in my life right now who could appreciate it," he says with sincerity, pulling off his gloves and again separating some wayward hair from my lips. The gesture seems natural, a little intimate—but not overly—and still, my heart skips briefly as it sputters out rapid beats, and I'm forced to catch myself.

Back, Natalie, back!

Clearing my throat, I will the adrenaline and threatening butterflies to kick rocks. "How long have you been riding?"

"Since I was four. Dad encouraged me, and Mom kicked him in the balls for it, *literally*. Now when I hit the track, I hide it from her. There's some ammunition for you."

"Well, if this singing thing doesn't work out for you," I shrug and am rewarded with a half-smile. "So, are you done for the day? Or are we going to base jump off a skyscraper?"

"I'm good for now." He glances over my shoulder at Joel. "All set?"

Joel nods and hands Easton a fob, which I assume is for the SUV. "Good to go."

"You're leaving us?" I ask, frowning.

"Taking a day off," he answers with a grin. "It was nice meeting you, Natalie."

"You too, Joel," I say as he lifts his chin to Jedidiah and disappears into a small tunnel between rows of stadium seats. I turn back to Easton, narrowing my eyes. "So, we *aren't* done for the day?"

"File the questions away, would you?" He says, rummaging through his duffle.

"This is me, being *me*."

He rolls his gaze up and puckers his lips sourly. "Well, that's *annoying*."

"Kiss my ass," I sass back. In a sudden move, he stands, grips my shoulders, and tilts my body before his gaze dips.

"What the hell are you doing?" I ask, craning my neck over my shoulder.

He playfully rakes his lower lip, his brows lifting. "Seeing if you have enough ass to kiss."

"My ass is perfectly up to par, sir," I fire confidently, shaking my shoulders free of his hold as he lets out a low chuckle. "I ride *real* horses, not manufactured death traps." I deadpan, determined not to let his proximity get the best of me as I scan his face, zeroing in on the sweat trickling down his forehead. Sweat that is quickly wiped away by the shirt, which he rips off his body. I turn slightly and avert my eyes. "Okay, well, modesty is definitely not an issue for you," I let out a nervous laugh.

"Nope," he replies dryly, all traces of humor gone as I look back at him with furrowed brows. He shrugs. "Why the hell would I care anymore when I've been considered *public domain* for the last twenty-two years?"

"I'm sorry," I say softly.

"Not your fault," he says, pulling out his jeans.

"Well, I apologize on behalf of everyone," I whisper. Kneeling at his bag, head snapping up, hazel eyes bore into mine, searching for the sincerity of my words—which he finds. He slowly stands and wipes his chest dry, and my own eyes dip briefly before he leans in on a whisper. "Want to know a secret?"

"Sure," I say as he continues to wipe his body before tossing the towel. Without warning, he fingers his pants and shoves them down midthigh. "I've raced a few times."

"Professionally?" I swallow.

He pulls on his jeans as I admire the bulge of his bicep, the clink of his unbuckled belt again doing more unwelcome things to me.

"Yeah," he confirms, "I did okay."

"How did they not know?" I ask, my eyes roaming over his rippling torso as he retrieves a can of body spray, steps back, and unloads it like a deodorant, shooting a few squirts over his muscular chest before pulling on a fresh, long sleeve T-shirt. Even while standing in a stadium full of dirt, the exchange feels intimate. It's as if we are sharing a bathroom, like a couple chattering as he dresses for a workday.

"Covered from head to foot."

"Huh?" I ask, completely immersed in my wandering thoughts as he zips his bag and hoists it from the ground.

"That's how I got away with it," he says, his eyes catching mine, a whisper of a smile on his lips. "Covered from head to foot."

"Oh. That's awesome."

Easton lifts his chin in goodbye to Jedidiah and the rest of the crew, and I follow his lead and wave my farewell before he gently tugs my arm, ushering me out of the stadium.

"Are you going to tell me your alias?"

"No," he says simply.

"Of course not," I grumble, working a little harder to match his long strides.

"Well, I figured since you think I'm ungrateful to be born into privilege, I would highlight some of the perks. And there are a lot of them, Natalie," he says softly. "I don't hate it all the time."

"Just when you want to eat a cheeseburger publicly?"

I'm graced with a featherlight smile. "Yeah. I can still get away with that sometimes, for now."

"But that might change soon."

Mixed emotions flit across his features as he shrugs because he doesn't know his fate—neither do I. Either way, media attention is about to shift in his direction again in a highly invasive way, and that's the tradeoff. It's clear to me that he considers it the price he'll have to pay to share his music. As we make our way toward the SUV, I glance over at him.

"I think I'm starting to understand."

He meets my watchful gaze briefly. "I think I thought you might."

TEN

Lovesong
The Cure

Natalie

Easton adjusts himself in the driver's side, fixing the rearview before turning to me.

"What?" I ask as he starts the SUV and raises an expectant brow.

"Seriously, I've got a high IQ, but I'm no mind reader—"

I'm cut off by the sheer force of restraint when I come face-to-face with Easton Crowne as he covers my body with his in an effort to buckle me in. Despite being slightly sweaty, his raven hair smells incredible—as does the rest of him—as I'm struck senseless by just how accessible he is at the moment. I drink in what I can—the ridiculous length of his lashes, the dark freckle imprinted near the corner of his jaw, and the texture of his lips, which are at the moment dangerously close to mine.

Don't inhale. Don't inhale. Don't inhale.

In the next second, he's gone, and I'm left in near heart attack status as he resumes his position behind the wheel as if he didn't just assault me.

"You could have just told me," I chide lightly as he puts the SUV into gear, amusement twisting his lips. In less than twenty-four hours, I've become dangerously attracted to this man. It wasn't instant, but it's now evident, and it's a no-fly zone. I decide to nip it in the bud by putting him on the offense.

"We're on record now," I declare, setting the boundaries.

"Don't want to ease into this at all, huh?" He shakes his head, reaching behind my seat into his duffle—again invading my space—his eyes rolling down my profile before he produces his cellphone. Unlocking it, he taps it a few times and hands it to me. I grab it to see he's opened his music app, and not only that, a compiled list of songs. Curious, I scroll through to see it's never-ending. There are hundreds, if not thousands, on the playlist.

"Are you trying to distract me by letting me play DJ, Crowne?"

He remains silent as he pulls out of the parking lot.

"That's a lot of pressure considering..."

"You can't choose wrong," he assures, pulling to a stop at the main road and looking in each direction in indecision.

"Don't know where you're going?"

"Nope."

I close out of his playlist and pull up a GPS app.

"Do you have the address?"

"Yeah."

"O*kay*?" I drawl out.

"Lost."

"We're going to get lost?"

"Why not?" He says, taking a right turn. "You said yourself you don't want to do the tourist thing."

"How can you get lost when you've lived here all your life?"

"I spent a good amount of my childhood touring with my parents and the band. Trust me, I can get lost *anywhere*."

"Okay. But you will answer some questions," I state with emphasis.

"The ones I want to."

"That's not really fair."

His expression hardens. "Pretty sure we should keep fair and *ethical* out of our conversations due to *hypocrisy*."

"Touché, and I already apologized for that."

"Hurry up and choose," he nods toward the phone in my hand.

"Not a fan of silence?"

"Not when I have an alternative," he quips.

"Should I be insulted, considering you're in my company?"

"It's me being *me*," he muses.

"Fair enough."

Tapping back into his music app and list, I scroll through and press a random song. Unfamiliar music fills the cabin of the SUV as I note the title, "Lovesong" by The Cure. Easton immediately starts tapping his fingers on the wheel and turns it up. Reaching for the volume on the console, I turn it down, giving him a pointed look.

"Just relax," he sighs, "we'll get to it."

He drives a few miles when his phone rings, and we both zero in on the ID on the dash.

Mom.

Our stares linger on the screen as he turns into a nearby gas station. When he answers the call my eyes bulge.

"Mom, hold up a second, okay?"

Stella's easy reply comes over the line. "Okay."

The need to flee engulfs me and must be evident on my face as Easton disconnects the Bluetooth and leans over. "Want to grab us something?"

I nod as he goes to pull out his wallet.

"I've got it," I whisper, "what do you want?"

"Coffee, sugar and cream. And water."

I nod, exiting the SUV like my ass is on fire, bypassing an elderly man sitting on the side of the gas station next to the door. Deep creases mar his face, and he looks badly battered in his current state, a cup gripped in his hand like a lifeline. He glances up at me as I open the door, muttering something I'm unable to decipher.

Going along the aisles, unsure if Easton's eaten, I decide to grab an armful of snacks for our road trip to nowhere. I can't help but be thankful he invited me out today. If not, I have zero doubts I'd be wandering around Seattle aimlessly. At least my fake motive for being here gives me a distraction. Nerves fraying in the wake of Stella's call, I try to focus on the man just outside the door and opt to pay with what little cash I have.

This is already too close for comfort, Natalie.

Rattling with tension, I exit the store and bend down, putting the entirety of my change—including a few bills—into the man's cup.

"What the hell, lady?! That was my coffee!" The man screeches, standing abruptly and taking a threatening step forward.

"Oh, I'm s-s-sorry, I thought, I apologize," I manage weakly, taken aback by his aggression while walking backward with my bag of snacks, Easton's piping hot coffee, and my purse clutched to me. Eyes fixed on the man cursing me while fishing the sopping bills out of his cup, I open the passenger door of the SUV and jump into the seat, seeking refuge as the outraged loiterer's eyes pin me with a withering glare. It's the clearing of a throat that brings me to the realization I'm in unfamiliar surroundings. A whole new wave of terror runs through me as I turn to see a stranger in the driver's seat. A stranger who's gawking back at me in confusion.

"Uh, can I help you with something?"

Horrified, I study the older man whose passenger seat I just highjacked when Easton's face appears through the glass *an SUV over*, a 'what the fuck' reading clear on his lips. Shifting my gaze, I glance back at the man sitting on the driver's side as he stares on at me expectantly.

"Oh my God, I'm so sorry. I—*sorry!*" Exiting the wrong SUV, I round the rear and race back to Easton's passenger door before opening it and diving in, securing his coffee in his cupholder while giving orders. "Go, go, go! Drive!" I demand, embarrassment racing through me as I bury my face in my hands.

"Seatbelt," he orders evenly, not budging an inch.

"You can't be serious, Easton, go!" I say frantically, reaching blindly for my seatbelt.

"Afraid so. It's apparent if anyone needs a safety net right now, it's you." I turn to glare at him as laughter bursts out of him, and I manage to click myself in.

"Please just go." My neck heats as he puts the SUV in gear and pulls away while I fumble through an explanation.

"The m-man outside, I put money in his cup, I thought he w-was, you know, in n-need of help, and he started screaming that it was his coffee," I stutter out as Easton's laughter amplifies.

"This is a black SUV. It's a *common car*!" I defend. His laughter only increases as I shrink in my seat, and for the next mile, short bursts of laughter sound from him. Unable to help myself, I glance over at him with a sheepish smile on my face as he turns, his eyes flickering over me with head-shaking amusement.

"Whatever, *asshole*, it was an honest mistake. It could have happened to anyone," I spout weakly, only mildly annoyed.

"I'm not entirely sure that's accurate."

Exhaling harshly, I train my smile out of the window until his chuckle finally slows.

"All right, Crowne, I've given you eight songs to start speaking," I summon, turning the music down and staring over at him.

He sighs heavily and nods in resignation but speaks up. "What you want to know is trivial and doesn't matter."

"Says you."

"If it's about me, *personally*, then it has nothing to do with the bigger picture. You haven't even heard my music, so there's nothing to discuss."

"And what's the big picture?"

"The body of work I've created. For the most part, I have it all mapped out."

"How mapped out?"

"Sixty-three songs," he says simply as my jaw drops.

"There are sixty-three songs on one album?"

"No, I've recorded sixty-three so far."

"You're fucking joking, right? That's like the equivalent of what… five albums?"

"Yeah," he says, glancing over at me for a few lingering seconds.

"How long have you been recording music?"

"Since I was fifteen."

"So, your band—"

"I don't have a band," he mumbles as if he's embarrassed by it.

"Wait…you play all the instruments yourself?"

He drops his eyes, his voice low. "I grew up playing with professional musicians, so it's not that big of a deal."

I give him a hard stare. "Oh, bullshit. Don't try to humble your way out of this, Easton. You lied to me when you said you weren't a prodigy."

"You haven't even heard it," he defends.

"I'm suspecting you know exactly how good it is. You do realize that amount of music is considered a lifetime's worth of work for some musicians, *right?*"

He scoffs. "Because, if this does well, I can kick back and take it easy, *right*?" Anxious energy rolls off him as his posture tightens.

"So, when you say you have no choice—"

"I mean it," he says, glancing over at me. "I can't sit still for long without playing, listening, writing, being a part of it. I'd be empty without it. I've felt that since I was very young. But instead of expecting open doors, I worked my ass off, doing everything I could to pave my own way."

"How so?"

He remains silent for a stretch before finally speaking.

"When I was nine, we were on vacation in Lake Tahoe at one of my parents' very wealthy, very affluent friends, and Dad found me washing one of said friend's boats for cash."

"Why?"

"Mom had just taken me on a trip to Mexico to visit family, and it was there I recognized the different types of social barriers between people and the mindset it must take to get from one place to the next. It wasn't the first time I was exposed to the way other people live, but it was there it resonated with me most. That's when I realized the bars behind the gated community I grew up in were exactly that, *bars*, no matter how shiny they were. That's also when I started to resent the separation from the rest of the world. Even feeling that, I also recognized how hard my parents broke their backs to get us behind them, to keep all they had worked for and built together, *safe*."

With one hand hung on the wheel, he runs the other down his jeans. "Dad got it. He's all about work ethic and allowed me to earn cash when I found the opportunity. Sometimes I carried lighter equipment for the crew or cleaned toilets at the studios. I did everything I could to save money for my own studio time. When I was fifteen, he put me on the payroll, making the same wages as everyone else because I was determined to earn my way, like he did."

"And you don't think this would endear you to your future fans?"

"Sadly, it would probably be thought of as a ploy, so I don't ever want them to know."

Expelling a breath, I shake my head as he glances over at me long and hard.

"I once saw a documentary where John Lennon was speaking to a fan outside his house. It was clear the guy had mental health issues to the point a simple conversation wasn't going to convince him that John wasn't his answer. He invited that guy into his home, fed him, and had the best conversation he could while trying to relay that he wasn't the solution. That's a scary scenario for people in the limelight. Like how the fuck do you handle that responsibly?"

He shakes his head. "I don't want to be responsible for the way people behave, think, or live, or the decisions they make. If anything, the message in my work begs them to think for themselves." He gives me a sideways glance. "I don't think you can live a genuine life being inspired by others—everyday lives anyway—but you can be inspired by their *creations*. There's a big fucking difference. If some guy wants to propose because of a love song I wrote, great, that's where it should end. I'm not saying famous people don't have a responsibility, or if they're reckless with it and do horrible things, they shouldn't be called out. They should. But for those who just want to quietly contribute at this point, it's next to impossible to keep their private lives out of it. Not only that..."

"Don't you dare stop now," I warn.

"Seeing my father in a state of utter disarray for months regarding one of his fans changed my perception completely about what I want out of this."

"Are you referring to Adrian Town's suicide?" Adrian was a Sergeants' fan who committed suicide at one of their last concerts. It was in the headlines for weeks. Easton's expression darkens.

"I don't think a lot of people realize they live around echoes of defining moments in their lives."

"He was mentally ill. It wasn't anyone's fault."

"Tell that to my dad. He was a fucking wreck for almost a year. We still feel the echoes of that night to this day. But everyone seems to take great pleasure in pointing fingers in claiming crazy on those they don't understand." He rakes his lower lip, and his chest bounces as irony covers his expression. "Everyone loves *The Starry Night* by Vincent van Gogh, but I wonder how many know..."

"Know what?"

"That's the point. I don't want to spoil it for anyone or change their perception of an artist or take away any merit of his art for any reason."

"How so?"

"You really want to know?"

"I have to now."

"All right. He painted *The Starry Night* because that's what he saw during one of his most manic states while staring out of his asylum window."

He glances over at me to weigh my reaction as I picture the painting. "You're right. I didn't know that."

He nods. "Most people don't unless they look into the artist or listen attentively to the Don McLean song. While some people will appreciate the art, those curious will want to know more about where it stemmed from. When they dig, they'll get the dirt under their fingernails and hate how it feels."

"It's a natural curiosity."

"I get that, really, but from what I've seen and learned, expressing yourself creatively and becoming successful at it always comes at a cost."

His voice is solemn as he exits the highway and glances over at me as he parks in a recreational area, a picnic bench and charcoal grill a few feet away. Light droplets of rain coat the windshield as we remain idle.

"The truth is, ordinary humans are capable of doing extraordinary things every single day without living extraordinary, *extra* lives. It's the art, the creativity that sets them apart, not what they fucking eat for breakfast or who they're fucking. Let them have their eggs in peace." His jade eyes find mine, and I briefly get lost in them as the intimacy in the air becomes tangible. "But then I look at you and see you have a natural inclination to seek out what makes humans tick. Of how they came to be who they are, and I can't fault you for that, no more than you can fault me for not wanting to be under your microscope. I don't hate the press. I just hate the microscope and what it's done to the people I love."

Soaking all his admissions in, it dawns on me. "This is why you haven't set a release date. You're not sure you're going to release at all."

He turns to stare out of the window, his jaw tensing. "I've thought about doing it anonymously, but *fuck that*, if I go in, I'm going all the way in. I'm not missing the experience of performing, or else what's the point. It's a bonding experience I've seen and felt—so much love. It's surreal, and that's when I'll be with them. That's when they'll have all of me." He turns to me. "I'm not missing that for any reason."

"Easton, you can't let—"

"Can't I?" He interjects, dread in his tone. "I've waded through the scary parts with my parents, watched people I love implode under pressure, buried family friends too soon, and observed people close to me tear their personal relationships apart year after year due to insecurity."

I try to place who he's talking about as he turns back to me, his expression full of anxiety.

"Fame is my biggest fear, Natalie."

Unable to help myself, I reach over and grip his hand as he shifts his focus back out of the windshield. After a few minutes of silence, he turns to me.

"I want you to remember this moment. Right here, right now, just you and me in a fucking SUV, taking a drive to nowhere." He looks at me pointedly. "Promise me you'll remember this."

It's kind of hard to forget, but I voice his request anyway. "I promise."

He turns my hand over and slides his finger along my palm as my spine prickles with awareness.

"Now I wonder how you'll view *The Starry Night* when you see it again." He pins me with his inquisitive gaze. "Will you see the masterpiece or the mental illness?"

"I honestly don't know, probably both."

He closes my hand and releases it. "Sometimes I feel so fucking simple. It's painful."

"You're not simple," I counter without pause. "I've known you for less than a day, and you're *anything* but simple."

"And you're *exhausting*. We done?"

"No, how do you like your eggs?" I jab in an attempt to lighten the mood.

He's silent for a long moment, so long I'm unsure if he heard me or is even listening.

"Sorry, that was in poor taste. Forgive me," I say as he speaks up.

"Joel's been with me since he was twenty-two," he mutters absently, speaking his thoughts aloud. "My whole life."

"It's apparent you two are close."

"Thank fuck for that," he says. "I love him." His admission comes so easily that my heart warms, and inwardly, I sigh.

He senses my cogs turning. "What?"

I shake my head as he prods. "Tell me."

"You're a lot freer than you think, Easton."

"How so?"

"Because you seem to live and speak with *intent*."

"What's living according to Natalie Butler?"

I nod toward our surroundings. "I guess, right now, what we're doing today is my current definition. Coasting along to see where a day leads." I smooth down my frizzy hair. "You know, in *real* life, I'm not really the mess you've been subjected to."

"That's a fucking shame," he says, his eyes trailing down my profile.

"Sorry to disappoint, but my life is…highly structured, and while I wouldn't change a lot about it most days, something happened recently that made my clear path…fuzzy." I glance around. "Where are we anyway?"

His lips lift in a triumphant smile. "Lost."

I return his grin. "I can't say I hate it."

He traces the steering wheel with his fingers. "I have this theory that if you don't have enough days like this, then you're pretty much living out someone else's expectations, which is my definition of prison."

I pause. "I know exactly what you mean by that."

He nods, gripping the wheel. "I thought you might."

ELEVEN

Cult of Personality
Living Colour

Natalie

Once the rain stopped, we ate the small haul I bought at the gas station sitting on a weathered and slightly warped wooden picnic bench. We laid off the heavier talk, though with Easton, he refused to make it small. After a few minutes, he steered the questioning to my side of the table. He was probing me for more about myself and seemed to absorb the answers rather than just hear them with the intense look forever in his eyes. When the sun finally made an appearance, we raised our collective faces to it, soaking it in.

As Easton chauffeurs me back to my hotel, we sit in comfortable, amicable silence, wind whipping through the cabin, both occupied by our thoughts. In lieu of me playing DJ, Easton tuned into an oldies station. The music is at his usual level—a few obnoxious decibels over loud. As each mile passes, I find myself staring over at him, processing all he'd divulged today, my empathy for him increasing tenfold.

He's seemingly in the midst of a crisis of his own—a battle about his future, and his predicament is far more daunting than mine. In order to venture into his career dream, he has to overcome his fear of the spotlight. The fact that he relayed why he hates the medium of the press and that he trusted me with that information says a lot. With every mile we travel, it's on the tip of my tongue to thank him and ease his worries about what I'll do with what he revealed. Just as I go to speak, he beats me to it.

"What do you listen to?"

He gestures toward the radio for me to take over.

"Nuh-uh, I'll only disappoint you."

"Go on," he says, a barely-there lift of his lips.

"Okay, but you asked for it."

I look at the time and calculate the difference at home before switching the dial to AM and Hearst's national news radio. The puckered look of distaste on Easton's face has me cackling. He listens for a few minutes and shakes his head.

"Two tornadoes killing sixteen people, left and right fighting, as usual. Tell me how this is uplifting?"

"It's my life."

"No, it's other people's lives."

I raise a brow. "Careful, you're getting offensive."

"And you're getting defensive," he quips back. "Why is that?"

"I'm not a music fanatic." I shrug. "We just march to the beat of different drums, pun fully intended."

"No, no, Natalie, *no*," he shakes his head profusely. "Not with music, *never* with music. It's where we discover *common ground*."

He stares at me for a few long seconds, turns off the news, reconnects to Bluetooth, and flips through the playlist on his cell.

"Eyes on the road, Crowne. I don't feel like playing airbag roulette today."

He ignores me and shifts his attention between the road and his phone. "Don't you jam when you're out with your girlfriends?"

"*One* girlfriend and one boyfriend, they're my best friends. Damon's my dad's best friend, Marcus's son. We're like brother and sister."

Shut the hell up, Natalie!

"And then there's Holly. She's the daughter of one of my mother's closest friends. She's a year younger than me, but we all grew up together. Anyway, I guess we jam out occasionally, but I never fight for control of the radio."

"What do you listen to when you work out?"

"News radio mostly…stop looking at me like I'm an alien," I mutter, only to get another slight lift of his lips.

"Got it," he says confidently, referring to a choice from his playlist. "We'll start here."

"What?" I laugh at his animated expression as he cranks the volume up and kicks back in his seat. A second later, what seems like the middle of an old news bulletin sounds through the speakers—*'and during the few moments that we have left, we want to talk right down to earth in a language that everybody here can easily understand.'*

Easton lifts a mocking brow at me, and I roll my eyes in response just before a jarring guitar riff blares through the speakers making me jump.

Easton immediately dips his chin, his head bobbing perfectly to the heavy beat that follows. It's fucking sexy as hell, so natural. He holds me captive for a few minutes as I listen attentively. When his eyes dart my way, I avert them to the title—"Cult of Personality" by Living Colour. Adding it to the list of songs Easton's played during our time together, I allow myself to sink into it. In minutes, I'm immersed in the powerful lyrics, the attitude of the song ringing in unison with Easton's thoughts about the power of media and his personal beliefs.

I glance over to find he's full-on smirking and know he was waiting for me to grasp the point of it.

Touché, Crowne.

As Easton continues to rock out at an ear-bleeding level, I can't help but glance around self-consciously as we pull to a busy stoplight. Easton ignores the odd looks coming in our direction from the idling cars beside us and turns it up louder in response, which has me bursting out in nervous laughter. Grinning, I start to mimic his movements, which earns me another half-smile.

It's when he pulls up through the drive-through of the hotel—the song still blaring out of our open windows—that my face flushes.

"Easton!" I exclaim with wide eyes as the music echoes through the wind tunnel of the entrance and into the hotel lobby. He continues to tap on the steering wheel, his fingers ticking off in perfect time with the drums, no fucks at all to give. Reddening by the second, I glance out the window to see an older couple exiting the hotel. Instantly, I reach for the volume, and Easton bats my hand away. Hand stinging and tempted to flee, I look back to the couple just as the older man animates and starts bobbing his head, giving Easton a thumbs up.

More hysterical laughter bursts out of me as I track the couple in the passenger's side view mirror as the man continues to jam-walk until they disappear from sight. Shaking my head ironically but still smiling from ear to ear, I turn back to see Easton carefully scanning my profile.

"Well played," I clap my hands sarcastically as the song comes to an end. "I got your point, but did you have to bang me over the head with it with such a heavy hammer?" I exaggerate my eyeroll upward. "But that's you…isn't it?"

My smile begins to slip as his gaze burns me from face to boot and back up. Swept up in his sudden intensity, I unbuckle my seatbelt as I try to compose appropriate parting words. He beats me to it with a rough whisper. "You just fucking fell out of the sky, didn't you?"

The cabin of the SUV clouds with energy as a surreal gravity threatens to draw us closer.

"In a way," I swallow, "I guess I did." My mouth dries as he refuses to free me from the power of his perusal. As I opt for honesty, my heart begins to thrum harder with each passing second. "Thank you for giving me a soft place to land, Easton." Fumbling, I find and tug on the handle of the truck before slamming it closed. Gripping the top of the open window with my fingers—unsure if I'll see him again—I peer over at him and try to convince myself that if this is the last time, I'll be fine with it.

"I'll…" a nervous laugh escapes me, "thanks again, and good night." Turning abruptly, I stalk toward the lobby, my pounding heartbeat and footsteps in sync. I don't have to look back to know. I can feel his eyes on me.

TWELVE

White Noise
Exitmusic

Easton

Adding more weight to my press bar, I glance down as my phone lights up with an incoming text.

Natalie: I just want you to know that you don't have to regret or worry about what you confided in me today.

Downing my water, I take the bench seat and text back.

Still not claiming to be villain or vulture?

Natalie: Exactly.

So, if my secrets are safe with you, what will you write?

Natalie: Let me worry about that.

The bubbles start and stop for almost a full minute before stopping altogether.

"East!" Mom calls from atop the stairs of our basement, which Dad converted into a state-of-the-art home gym and theatre years ago. "I left a plate of dinner on the counter if you're hungry!"

"Okay, thanks," I call up to her, distracted by the image of Natalie's panic-stricken face when Mom called earlier today. It was obvious by her reaction that the answer to some of her mystery lies there, but I surprised myself by letting her off the hook without explanation.

What are you so afraid to tell me?

The bubbles start and stop again for over a minute, and I can't help my grin. I've got her cornered, and she's flailing.

Are you really that afraid of me?

Her answer is immediate and defiant, just like her.

Natalie: No.

It's clear she's got a surface confidence, some of it ingrained, a lot of it natural. I have no doubt what she told me today is true, that her life is structured, and she probably prefers it that way. But I've been loving every second of watching her guard slip willingly and unwillingly in the short time I've known her. The more we spend time together, the more I find myself increasingly captivated by her own disbelief during those times, as if she's surprised herself. If she only knew how fucking beautiful she is when she allows herself to unravel naturally. My fingers dart over the screen in easy invitation.

Want to get lost again tomorrow?

Natalie: Don't feel obligated.

I don't.

I bark out a laugh at the hangtime of more bubbles without reply. This woman.

Natalie: Okay.

I'll text you.

Natalie: Night.

My fingers linger over the screen as renewed energy courses through me. I can't pinpoint what possessed me to reveal so much to her without ample reason to, especially when it's obvious she's still hiding a lot from me. My own confessions poured from me as if I've been saving them specifically for her. For some reason, I want her to understand my logic, *me*. Oddly, I didn't battle with myself over it after I dropped her off and am more unsettled by how I felt when she walked into her hotel, away from me.

The adrenaline I feel now lingers, thanks to the odd connection I feel to her. The attraction is heavy and growing stronger, but more so by her mystery and what she wants from me. I saw her hesitate—more than once—as she looked over at me on the drive back. I have little doubt she wants to confess whatever is weighing on her, but I'm not about to demand it because odds are, I won't get it all.

Laying back, I resume my reps as I replay the day, the light in her eyes as she looked at me with the same curiosity, like maybe she's searching for similar answers from me.

She's shying away from our attraction, and I'm not the man to press it, but today I fucking wanted to. She's become one hell of a distraction from the unease I've been feeling for weeks about releasing.

Maybe that's why I'm becoming so attuned to her, because if I've been in need of anything lately, it's a diversion.

"Are you going to come up sometime tonight?" Dad's voice sounds from the bottom of the stairs as he lowers the volume on "White Noise" by Exitmusic, a song I find fitting for my career predicament.

I push up on the bar and lower it on the rack.

"What the hell are you doing pressing without a spot?" He says as I sit and wipe my face with a towel.

"You're turning into a soft old lady," I jab.

"It's fucking dangerous," he grumbles, and I lift both brows in response.

His eyes flare in the realization that he's being a helicopter parent, and he flashes me a sheepish grin. "I blame your overprotective mother," he sighs and cups the back of his neck. "Shit, I really am that dad, aren't I?"

Dad didn't have ideal parents. Both were drunks and died within a four-year period after I was born. According to Mom, Dad had to support them when he didn't have two dimes to rub together, and sadly, it almost kept him from realizing his career dreams. I don't have a single memory of them. However, I'm well aware that though they weren't deserving, Dad took care of them financially up until they died. Knowing that, I don't give him too much shit about being overprotective of me. But together, they have a tendency to be a bit much. Neither of them can go long without checking on me. I sometimes wish I had a sibling to take some of the pressure off.

"It's fine. I'll make you spot me next time. You can scrutinize your cuticles while that gut of yours keeps expanding."

He gives me his signature glare as I chuckle. In truth, Dad is still in pretty good shape and often hits the gym, though not nearly as hard as he used to.

"It's one of the perks of retiring," he defends.

I can't find any good in that statement and say as much. "Are you really done for good?"

He shrugs as if he's unsure, but more and more, Dad and the rest of the band are turning down gigs, even if they're just isolated events.

He gives me a pointed look, and I tense, knowing what's coming. "I'm more interested in what's about to happen for you."

I sigh, and he reads the 'I don't want to talk about it' in my expression but doesn't ease off the gas.

"Just tell me where you're at."

Dad is the only one who's heard *my* music. Mom has heard me sing and play plenty of times, but hasn't been made privy to a single song I've recorded.

"You're biased," I say.

"You know how gifted you are. And it's not just talent, Easton. It's an *astounding* talent. And I think you know that too." He shakes his head in irritation. "Do you think for one fucking second, I would encourage you in any way if I thought your music didn't deserve an audience? What you've done is mind-blowing, and I'm proud."

He stuns me with the easy admission, though I've seen the way he looks at me after I let him hear a new track. I've only allowed him to help me sharpen the sound. So in truth, he has helped produce to a small extent, but most of my work is untouched by anyone. He's got a lot to do with strengthening my backbone and sharpening my skills as a musician and lyricist, but he's given me, and continues to give me ample creative space when it comes to my music, knowing I want to do this all on my own.

"It's all I can do daily to keep from telling your mother we're finally going to have to share our son—*indefinitely*."

He draws the conclusions for my hesitance easily because he's been absorbed in the meaning behind my lyrics time and again.

"You're in control of this, son. You made it that way, and I wish to fucking God we'd had it that way when we started out."

I nod, knowing it's the truth. Though the Dead Sergeants got signed with one of the biggest labels in music, they were pressured to carry out the will of the label and the other powers that be for years before they were able to negotiate themselves into calling their own shots. I have no intention of following suit in that respect at all.

"It's just...You've worked so fucking hard for this. Now that you're seriously thinking about doing it, it's literally all I can do to keep from tearing into you to go for it because you know goddamn well the minute you do..."

He reads my aggravation and lets out a heavy sigh.

"All right, I'll drop it for now. But if you don't come upstairs, you know she's going to—"

"To what?" Mom snaps halfway down the stairs. Dad visibly flinches, a slight fear in his eyes when she reaches the landing, crossing her arms. "What's *she* going to do?"

"Jesus, Grenade," he turns to her, a sparkle in his eye as he pats himself down. I bite my lip to hide my smile because I know what's coming.

"What are you looking for?" Mom asks, frowning.

"Your muzzle," Dad deadpans, and I can't help my chuckle.

"I think I saw it next to my *How to Surgically Remove Your Husband's Testicles While He Sleeps for Dummies* handbook."

He doesn't miss a beat. "Have I told you lately what a pain in the ass you are?"

"Daily," she lifts a brow, letting Dad know she's not changing anytime soon—or *ever*. Their tit-for-tat has me thinking again about the blue-eyed beauty I dropped off only hours ago. We've been going back and forth similarly the last two days, and I can't help the widening of my grin because of it.

"What's that?" Mom asks.

I frown. "What's *what*?"

She gives me a keen stare. "You haven't smiled like that since you got a digital valentine from Aurora Long in the fourth grade."

"That's bullshit, and how would you know?"

"I know things...and I know that smile."

"Stella," Dad sighs. "Lay off. He's finally sleeping at home again."

"Seriously, Mom," I chime in, taking Dad's out. "I'm going to go grab that plate."

"Evading," she pipes, turning to tail me as I take the stairs two at a time.

"I'm moving out," I threaten again, knowing it's low but will be enough to throw her off my scent for now. Truth is, I'm not sure what's happening with the woman who's invading my life—and now my head.

I hear Mom's yelp from the foot of the stairs as Dad hollers from below, mirth in his voice. "Run for your life, son! I'll take this one for the team."

"You jackass—" Mom's protest is cut short, and I don't have to look back to know Dad is shutting her up in a way I don't want to witness. Grinning, I click off the light at the top of the stairs and hear their collective protests muddled as I shut them in. Swiping my dinner off the counter, I jog up the stairs to my bedroom for some privacy. I've rarely slept at home in the last few years, my obsession taking precedence and consuming me to the point I almost lost sight of any sort of outside life.

Standing under the steaming shower spray a short time later, I catch myself immersed in thoughts of deep blue eyes, glossy lips, and strawberry-kissed curly hair. Thick suds gathered in my idle hands, my body reacts to the images stirring me up, and I go with it, releasing some of the tension before I towel off and toss on some sweats.

It's when I hit the sheets that I find myself becoming more thankful for the invasion and more determined to seek solace in her for the time we have left.

I might only have a few days remaining to find some reprieve in the distraction who crash-landed on my doorstep, but it's enough for now.

I wake hours later in the exact position I fell asleep in, having slept better than I have in weeks.

THIRTEEN

Bad Day
Fuel

Natalie

I didn't sleep.

As much as I tried to blame it on the jet lag, I found myself warring with Easton's admissions and the fact that he seems to know exactly who he is, the questions he posed to me a lot harder for me to answer than I let on.

Last night, as I stared at the low-lit flames burning in the fireplace tucked in the corner of my hotel room, I listened to the music from his playlist and physically *felt* the weight of the lyrics wrapped inside the expertly created rhythm, amplifying their meaning.

For the first time, I became fully aware of their capabilities as Easton's prodding questions circled in my head.

As I mulled those questions over for deeper, more meaningful responses, I replayed every song on the rapidly growing soundtrack I've compiled in our short time together. I examined the lyrics, wondering which parts of them he personally identifies with before questioning which parts I, myself, could relate to.

The irony that though none of the lyrics were lost on me, I hadn't really experienced much to coincide with what they entail—which began to eat at me the more I listened.

Words have always been what light me on fire. The stories they create fuel me, and the more I tuned into each song, I realized the art of fusing a story, message, or layered emotions in fewer words to paint a picture is fascinating. Composing lyrics with the right notes is an art form widely recognized and celebrated by billions of people. Though aware of it, I'd spent most of my life idolizing the noteless side of composition.

Which led to an even deeper question—why hadn't I ever taken notice before?

Music had always been more background noise for me than anything else, and I couldn't remember a time in my life when it played a central role.

I also couldn't remember the last time Holly and I did something between our busy schedules, other than lunch, or a recent time where I laughed as hard with her as I did with Easton.

As more sleepless hours ticked by, I calculated how long it'd been since I had sex—or even dated—which only pulled me deeper into my own head.

The conclusion I drew after hours of contemplation—I've considered working '*living*' for so long that the lines have completely blurred. I gave my parents the excuse that I hadn't taken a break since I graduated last year, but am *living* the totality and consequences of that truth at present.

Which led to another forgone conclusion—I'm quickly becoming the living definition of burnt the hell out.

Those realizations—combined with the fact that I found myself going further into Dad and Stella's emails again—kept me tossing and turning until the early morning hours. The insurmountable guilt continued to pile up to the point that I felt I was suffocating. Thankfully, my mind shut down, granting me a few short hours of reprieve. Seeing the email thread the second I regained consciousness this morning inevitably led to my current, ongoing battle with my conscience.

Nate Butler
Subject: Look at me.
March 31, 2009, 4:22 p.m.

Right girl,

I may be the pompous ass who feels he's rarely wrong, but if I'm right, then I take it back. I can't fucking stand the hurt in your eyes or the fact that this day is dragging out, as is your silence.

I'm so sorry I hurt you. I was being honest, but even if I felt I was right, it wasn't worth it. I love you too much to allow this to drag on. Please, baby, look at me, or I'm not going to make it through the rest of the day.
Nate Butler
Editor in Chief, Austin Speak

Stella Emerson
Subject: Look at yourself, asshole.
March 31, 2009, 4:53 p.m.

Nate,

I'll break my silence, but only to tell you that you are, in fact, the pompous asshole who can claim he's right as much as he desires, but it doesn't make it so. Case in point, you're partially colorblind, and you refuse to believe it. Therefore, your green tie doesn't match your blue suit today. But because you're such a smug son of a bitch, no one in this newsroom will likely tell you to add to your disillusion. You can critique me all you want. That's your job inside of this building. Outside, your position doesn't play a part. You just smiled smugly at me, and now you're walking toward my desk. Yeah, that infuriating smirk is growing as you approach. You really should have heeded the warning I just gave you with the jerk of my chin. I'm about to embarrass you. By the time you read this email, it will be too late.

In the doghouse, you'll remain.

Stella Emerson
Entertainment Columnist, Austin Speak

Stella Emerson
Subject: RE: Look at yourself, asshole.
March 31, 2009, 5:14 p.m.

What you just did was sketchy and absolutely unfair. I will never look at you again...until you stoop to that level again...and again. And again.

I have work to do. Stop looking at me like that.
Stella Emerson
Entertainment Columnist, Austin Speak

Nate Butler
Subject: RE: Look at yourself, asshole.
March 31, 2009, 5:22 p.m.

I love you so much it hurts.

Nate Butler
Editor in Chief, Austin Speak

Stella Emerson
Subject: RE: Look at yourself, asshole.
March 31, 2009, 5:23 p.m.

Good.

Stella Emerson
Entertainment Columnist, Austin Speak

Nate Butler
Subject: You
October 5, 2009, 3:00 p.m.

What's wrong? And don't lie to me and tell me it's nothing. I know we're okay because I know when we're not okay, and this doesn't have anything to do with us. Talk to me.

Nate Butler
Editor in Chief, Austin Speak

Stella Emerson
Subject: RE: You
October 5, 2009, 3:04 p.m.

I'm just tired. Really, please don't read too much into it. But can we skip our dinner plans with your mother tonight? I don't want her to think I don't want to be there because I won't. Please don't be mad I'm asking. While I love you for encouraging me to earn my masters, school is kicking my ass, and I really need to buckle down on my studies.

Stella Emerson
Entertainment Columnist, Austin Speak

Nate Butler
Subject: Re: You
October 5, 2009, 3:09 p.m.

I've got you, baby. I just texted her and cancelled. Sometimes I forget I'm in love with a college student. Forgive me. We'll cram in a study session tonight while we stuff our faces. I'll make you come before I tuck you in.

Nate Butler
Editor in Chief, Austin Speak

Stella Emerson
Subject: RE: You
October 5, 2009, 3:11 p.m.

Sounds like a dream. I love you so fucking much Nate Butler.

Stella Emerson
Entertainment Columnist, Austin Speak

Nate Butler
Subject: Re: You
October 5, 2009, 3:12 p.m.

Feeling is mutual, Right Girl. Now, get to work. I'm not paying you to ogle me.

Nate Butler
Editor in Chief, Austin Speak

Nate Butler
Subject: The When and the Where
January 12, 2010, 8:03 a.m.

Just got off the phone with your sister. Please don't let Paige bully you into a venue choice. This is about us. Her crazy makes yours seem sane, which is no easy feat. Regardless, I'm siding with my Right Girl and always will. By the way, I can't fucking wait to marry you.

I love you, Stella.

Nate Butler
Editor in Chief, Austin Speak
Sent via Blackberry

They were *engaged*.

The revelation shook me to my core when I read it last night and is no less debilitating now as I ready myself for another stolen day with my father's ex-fiancée's son.

Feeling all kinds of fucked up, the reason in black and white feet away, I slam my laptop closed as I plaster on concealer. As I apply my makeup, I contemplate sending Easton a message to cancel our day, just as he texts he's on his way to collect me.

The thought of getting lost again with Easton currently outweighs my need to flee, which is only further proof of just how far I've taken this moral hiatus. My fear now is how much I will continue to play into this lie, especially now that I feel my attraction building for Easton the more time we spend together. Even worse, I'm catching myself becoming more drawn to him in every way that matters—and I'm thinking I'm not the only one.

This pull can't be one-sided, not with the type of energy passing between us.

Or maybe Easton's just this intense with all the people in his life. He doesn't seem to have an off switch for it, though he clearly knows how to relax and enjoy himself. Something, until recently, I had no idea was a serious issue for me.

Maybe sleep deprivation has me reading too much into everything.

I've never had insomnia and it appears to be a slow thief, robbing me daily—by chipping away at my confidence, my sense of purpose, my moral compass, and everything that's made me feel like a respectable human being—until this week.

"It's just a bad week," I snap, closing my compact, and palming off the bed when a heavy knock sounds from the other side of my hotel door.

Music blaring from my cellphone, I snatch it up and immediately turn it down, embarrassment threatening that Easton might hear it until a light and unintrusive "housekeeping" announcement is bellowed. In my haze last night, I'd forgotten to put the digital Do Not Disturb on the lock.

"I'm fine, thank you," I call out as I dart into the bathroom to stare at my reflection. Even after layering thick paste beneath my eyes, it's aided poorly in concealing the darkening circles. Opting not to wash my hair, I spray it with some dry shampoo, and luck is on my side when my curls bounce back with a kick. Taking the small victory, I wrangle them up with a hair tie. Somewhat appeased by my appearance—though thrown together—I war with going through another day of deceit.

Part of my solution is clear. At some point, I need to come clean with Easton, if only to ease his worries about what I will do with his confessions. He's taken special care of me in my time here, and because of that, it's my biggest hurdle. My fear is, once I confess, he'll tuck and run. If I'm holding off the truth, it's one hundred percent because I want his company and am now starting to crave his warmth.

Humming along with "Honest" by Kyndal Inskeep—a fitting song for my mood and one of my favorites on my rapidly accumulating playlist—I lightly mist my thickest sweater with my favorite Black Orchid perfume. Upon exiting the bathroom, my eyes catch on Easton's jacket, which is draped over the side of my bed. Selfishly, I decide not to pull it on in an effort to keep it just a bit longer. Unable to help myself, I sniff the collar, his scent enveloping me as my phone buzzes in my hand with an incoming text.

EC: Be there in five.

The butterflies I'm trying to deny wake me up far more effectively than the cold coffee I toss back before setting the cup next to my uneaten breakfast. Grabbing my tiny travel purse, I take in my appearance one last time and discard the tray of food outside my door. In the elevator, I give myself a good sound lashing.

"You will be the professional journalist you were trained to be today, Natalie Butler," I command as the doors open. Determined to take charge of the situation—despite my consistent deterioration in simple, everyday functioning—I find myself rattling in anticipation for the roar of Easton's truck motor just before it sounds and he appears.

Sliding onto the seat, I slam the door and turn to greet him with a low "Hi," before I'm hit by the sight of him. His clean scent circulates through the cabin as I drink him in.

His presentation today—fucking edible. He's got a solid black hat on, the bill of it turned backward, covering his damp onyx hair, its ends curling naturally around his ears. He's dressed from head to toe in black—a thermal layered with a V-neck jersey, jeans, and high-top Vans. His lips lift in greeting, a low "Hey," in reply to mine as he puts the truck into gear, a frown pulling at his features as he weighs my expression. "You okay?"

It's then I feel the surge of threatening emotion as guilt consumes me.

"I don't have a favorite song, and I work too fucking much," I admit, blowing all redeeming expectations I demanded of myself within seconds.

He laughs, full-on *laughs* at me, as I avert my gaze and buckle in. I feel his eyes on me as I battle to keep my guilty tears in, my confessions threatening to roll off my tongue.

Easton puts the truck back into park, and grips my chin gently, turning my head, his eyes lingering on the circles beneath.

"Is that what kept you up all night?"

"It's part of it," I admit. "I don't know if I'll be very good company today."

"That's assuming you're capable of improving it?"

I narrow my eyes as he lets out another infuriating chuckle. Releasing his grip on me, he leans forward and peers through his windshield at the clear blue sky. "Pretty sure it isn't going to fall today, so you're okay." He glances over at me. "Trust me?"

I nod because I'm too close to letting my emotions overrule me, and the only thing I'm sure of is that I don't want to cut our time short, so I rein it in.

"I've got you, Natalie," he assures softly before gassing the truck. A minute later, a light melody drifts through the speakers, the lyrics wrapping around my heart in solace. Even as he keeps his eyes on the road, I feel his gentle, soothing caress from feet away.

FOURTEEN

Feel Like Making Love
Bad Company

Natalie

"Oh my Glod, Easthon," I mumble around a mouthful of succulent white crab, butter dripping down my chin as my eyes roll up in pleasure.

His lips tilt up in amusement. "Yeah? We loving it so much we're calling out to a higher power?"

"Hell yes, thank you, and you," I chime happily to our waitress when she delivers another half-pound of snow crab tableside. She and Easton exchange a conspiratorial grin, both entertained by my enthusiasm as I use my butter-coated hands to lift my dark beer, greedily gulping back the cold suds before blotting my face briefly without much care.

Clearly, I'm at the no-fucks-given stage of my almost quarter-life crisis.

But as the beer eases the sting and the crab goes down, I find myself gradually lifting out of my weeklong funk, thankful for the reprieve—even if it turns out to be short-lived.

The mouthwatering company chuckling across from me—delighting in the utter ass I'm making of myself—hasn't hurt either.

After a long, long drive filled with music, Easton decided to draw an end to my pity party by luring me into conversation. Not long after, he insisted we eat at The Crab Pot, which sits on Miner's Pier perched on the edge of Puget Sound.

Due to the lunch rush being over, we managed to secure a table on the enclosed porch, spaced away from others with a waterside view. With Easton's back facing away from prying eyes, he's hardly recognizable to most.

So far, we've managed to escape the paparazzi, but I can't help feeling that our luck may run out the longer we linger in public. Even though he's been out of the public eye for some time because of the Sergeants' gradual withdrawal from the spotlight, he's still newsworthy—especially if sighted with a female who happens to be stuffing her face with shellfish.

Right now, I can't bring myself to care as I inhale the bounty before me.

"Do they feed you in Texas?" Easton taunts.

"I feed myself," I quip back emphatically, using my mallet to smash into a claw.

"But no seafood?"

"Shrimp," I shrug, "my mom has an aversion to seafood, especially shellfish, so we never really have it, even when we travel. Trust me, if I had eaten this, I'd remember it."

"Oh, I believe you," he pokes through another chuckle.

Ignoring him, I pull apart the cracked claw to draw out a chunk of meat before popping it into my mouth.

"Easton," I whisper breathlessly, grabbing my fork and shoving the outer tong into the softer side of the leg before ripping into it the way he taught me. He leans forward, bracing his forearms on the table as I toss my prized meat into one of four drawn butters. "I'm dead serious when I say this…you may have to cut me off."

"I don't think I'll be able to. This is too entertaining. In fact, I can guarantee I'll be enabling you. Psst," he whispers, giving me the come-hither finger and drawing me closer to him. Eyes locked, he gives me a sexy flash of teeth as he retrieves a piece of crab from my cheek and discards it amongst the mountain of shells I've accumulated.

Temporarily distracted by him, I try unsuccessfully to push out all wayward thoughts—including his full lips—before returning to my mission.

"God, I really needed this." I lift my beer with the clean sides of my palms and take a sip, nearly dropping the heavy glass mug onto the table. Exhaling happily, I lift my finger when the background music cuts off and the first few notes of a new song chime in.

Ready for the challenge, Easton kicks back, sipping his beer, listening attentively before he confidently speaks up. "'Every Little Thing She Does Is Magic' by The Police.".

Grabbing my phone, I pull down my screen and tap my Shazam app as the title comes up, along with the band name.

"Unreal," I say. "You haven't been wrong once today."

"Maybe, but true connoisseurs know the *B-side*."

"B-side?"

"The flip side of the vinyl record, on a forty-five, the B-side is on the opposite side of the hit song, which is typically on A."

"Oh, so are you a true connoisseur? Do you know the B-side songs too?"

"A lot of them. Some of them I like a lot more than the A-side."

"How many of the songs on your infinite playlist can you actually play?" When he goes silent, I lift my gaze to where he runs his finger along the rim of his frosted glass.

"Easton?"

"Most of them," he admits softly.

"Jesus…that's incredible!"

"Maybe it's remarkable to you, but I've been doing it my whole life, so it's kind of an unconscious thing."

"It's a gift," I say pointedly. "*Own* it."

"Fine," he negotiates, putting both his forearms on the table, "but I bet you could just as easily name the date on a lot of key headlines."

"Well, they coincide with US history, which I love, so maybe a few."

"But you took the time to study it, probably just as avidly as I have music."

"Okay, let's put it to the test." I wiggle butter-covered 'hit me' fingers.

He presses in. "Reagan assassination attempt?"

I surprise myself when the answer comes easily. "March 30 nineteen eighty-one."

"End of the Cold War?"

"Third of December…" I squint, "'89." My smile widens. "Hit me again."

His half grin briefly dazzles me. "Roosevelt's death?"

"Twelfth of April, 1945, eighteen days before Hitler, which I hated for Roosevelt, he deserved to know the fate of his nemesis."

"See," Easton reclines, seeming satisfied as I blow a wayward lock of curly hair out of my face. Hair Easton set loose a mile marker into our drive before tossing the tie out the window. Sensing my distress to keep from feasting on my hair, he leans in and tucks the cascading lock behind my ear.

Thanking him, I push my plate away and rip open another lemon-scented packet to clean my hands.

"You sure you're good?" He glances down at my sparsely covered plate, "Or should I order another beer and reload the trough?"

"I can't fit anything else into this mouth," I declare in surrender, and when my word choice strikes me I roll my eyes, my couth unreachable. Ripping my bib off, I take a sip of beer.

"Feel Like Makin' Love," Easton delivers, and I reject a little of my beer on a cough.

"Pardon?"

"The song," he muses, not missing a second of my discomfort. "Feel Like Makin' Love."

"I walked right into that one, didn't I? Who's it by?"

"Bad Company." He smirks, pun fully intended.

"Another zinger, impressive. You know, as much as you hate media, you'd be an amazing radio host. Your dry sarcasm is undetectable on delivery sometimes, so you could insult half your guests at will."

"Hard fucking pass," his features twist in clear disdain and I decide to dig a little further. His musical knowledge was expected, considering his upbringing and the company he's grown up with, but not at such an astonishing level.

"How far back does your mental library go?"

"Roaring twenties, but mostly thirties and up."

"Wow," I say, pulling out my wallet and lifting my card.

"Hell no," he argues upon the sight of it, and I glance over to see his nostrils flaring in irritation.

"This isn't a date…and anyway, I think I ate the equivalent of someone's salary in crab," I declare through a laugh.

"You maxed out your AmEx to be here," he reminds me.

"Wait…I said that out loud?" I ask in horror.

"Yeah, I think you might not be aware of just *how much* you've said out loud."

"Easton," I sigh. "Why are you being so nice to me?"

"Fuck if I know," he fires back, his candor making me laugh. "But I'd pay an annual salary just to witness you do that again," he gestures toward my destroyed side of the table.

"You know, you're really a nice guy on the *B-side* of that mastered A impression of a total asshole."

"Well, as far as I can tell, you're still a terrible journalist," he declares as he places his card on the table, tossing mine back toward me like it's useless. "You haven't asked more than a few questions today, most of them trivial."

He's calling me out, and I don't know how much longer my bullshit pretense is going to hold up.

"Oh, they're coming." I sass with a bitter edge.

"Uh huh," his smirk deepens as my eyes narrow, though I'm feeling the opposite effect.

"Laid," he speaks up, "by James."

"Now you're just showing off. You win, Easton."

"Yeah?" He cocks a sculpted black brow. "What's my prize?"

"A queasy passenger." I palm my stomach as it roils. "Look, if we're going to continue to hang, I probably need a shower and wardrobe change. That bib proved worthless, and to be frank, my breasts are covered in butter."

He barks out a laugh and I smile back at him while our waitress picks up his card.

"Full, sweetheart?" she asks with a smile, looking between us. She's a little older, I gauge early-forties, and has kind, warm eyes and a sweet disposition.

"Yes, ma'am, and please know we're tipping a hundred percent," I smirk over at Easton, costing him double, "sorry about the mess I made."

"Oh, honey, don't worry about it." Gathered plates in hand, she hesitates briefly. "But if I may say," she looks between Easton and me. "It's been my pleasure. My daughter is around your age," she flicks her gaze at Easton, "and I pray every day she meets a man who can make her smile the way that you are her."

I speak up at the same time Easton snakes the compliment. "He's not—"

"Yeah? Thanks. It's our anniversary."

And you thought you were a deceitful shit.

"Oh?" She says, her grin broadening. "I can get the chef to whip up something—"

"I'm so stuffed," I interject, tossing Easton a warning look, "but thank you, that's not necessary."

"I'll be right back," she says, taking Easton's card.

"Thanks for lunch, honey," I spout sarcastically when the waitress glances back, seemingly smitten by the two of us.

In the next instant, Easton's out of his chair, his fingers curling around my neck as he pulls me in. "My pleasure. Come here, baby."

"Easton," I hiss, just before he presses his full lips against mine. He holds the kiss a second longer than hoax-appropriate before gliding his tongue in a smooth sweep along my lower lip. I gasp against his mouth before he abruptly releases me.

"Don't want to shatter the illusion for her," he whispers thickly, easing back into his seat as a heavy, potent pulse starts between my thighs.

"You can't do that," I scold, rather unconvincingly.

"That's a word I refuse to acknowledge."

"ButIhavecrabbutterbeer breath," I mumble incoherently.

"And a perfect fucking mouth," he whispers in reply, an admission that comes far too easily as his gaze lingers on said mouth. Retrieving his glass, he casually tosses back the rest of his beer, like he didn't just assault me.

"Smooth," he whispers as our waitress nears the table. "Rob Thomas and Santana."

Easton breaks our stare off and thanks her, his long lashes flitting over his cheeks as he tips her and scribbles his signature. The sight of it has my stomach churning for an entirely different reason.

He kissed me.

He *licked* me.

I want a repeat, or at the very least, a *do-over.*

"Ready?" he asks as he stands and tucks his wallet back in his jeans. Feeling seduced for a plethora of rapidly accumulating reasons, I simply nod.

Instead of bringing me back to the hotel to change, Easton and I end up standing outside the entrance of the Museum of Pop Culture. I glance up at the structure of the connecting buildings, which look like nuclear plants smothered in colorful, ghost-edged blankets.

"You're intent on making me a tourist," I harrumph.

"Well, technically, you are, and this is an epicenter of a lot that interests you," he shrugs as he pulls my hand into his warm grip. "Come on."

Minutes later, we're walking past a theatre-sized screen with an abstract reel playing as he guides me along highly polished floors. As we bypass a story-tall, inverted tornado sculpture made up of musical instruments, I release his hand and lift my phone to take a snapshot. Easton turns back and catches me, an amused glint in his eyes.

"What?" I shrug, "might as well go *all in* and finish with a T-shirt from the gift shop."

Simpering, he jerks his chin in silent command. We soon enter a section of closed-off rooms with glass displays full of worn instruments and other paraphernalia, many solely dedicated to one music artist or band. A few minutes later, the two of us stand side by side, staring at Kurt Cobain's green sweater.

"April 5, 1994," I say, "one of the few entertainment headlines I can easily recall because it made national news for weeks."

"One of the innovators behind what's known as grunge, a title some bands tossed into that genre resent. Though, it was Mother Love Bone who really kick-started it all. When their lead singer, Andrew Wood, died of an overdose, the remaining members found Eddie Vedder, and Pearl Jam was born. Two months after Pearl Jam released *Ten*, Nirvana released *Nevermind*. What seems fated was Andrew's roommate at the time of his death was Chris Cornell, the lead singer of Soundgarden, his eventual fate the same as Kurt's," Easton adds in a subdued tone, studying the Nirvana front man's sweater. "They're truly the ones responsible for putting Seattle on the map." Easton's eyes glide over the display thoughtfully. "Mick Jagger from The Rolling Stones called Nirvana's music morose, but ironically, Cobain and the rest of the band were influenced heavily by The Beatles. If you listen to *Nevermind*, you can easily pick up some of the upbeat, catchy similarities in rhythm relative to The Beatles' earlier works."

We collectively gaze at the late singer's sweater, knowing the tragic end of Kurt's life was suicide. The circumstances of his death are still speculated by many, even forty-one years later.

Easton speaks up again. "Kurt's one of many in the infamous 27 Club."

"27 Club?"

"The age several prominent creatives died, many of them musicians, for some shitty reason or another. A lot of those reasons being drugs."

"I think I read about it somewhere. Who else is in the club?"

"Shit, too damned many. Jimi Hendrix, Janis Joplin, Jim Morrison, Brian Jones, Amy Winehouse." He lifts his chin, "Some of them are in a few of the rooms here."

I harrumph. "For someone so intent on keeping his own details so close to the chest, you sure seem to know a lot of the details of others."

"I study musical *evolutions*, mostly by listening to their *music*. I don't pay attention to the useless details so many seem to obsess over."

"Yeah, well, as a human-interest writer," I look back to the sweater, "I would love to know what was going on in his mind."

"*Pain*," he surmises easily. "Kurt and Eddie both notoriously hated fame and media, so if nothing else, we have *that* in common." He flashes me a condescending, full-toothed grin, and I lift my free hand giving him the bird. He squeezes my other in jest before leading me to the next room. It's when we reach the entrance that I see the reason he brought me here.

"This is…wow," I shoot him a grin as we walk into the circular room full of glass cases dedicated solely to the Dead Sergeants.

Slightly starstruck, I turn to Easton. "How does it feel to know your dad aided in keeping Seattle known for the talent it houses?"

"Dad came from *your* neighborhood. The whole band originated in Austin."

"True, but they're synonymous with Seattle now, and you didn't answer my question."

"All the things I'm supposed to feel, I guess," he relays easily. "Mostly proud and…inspired."

I walk to the first prompt, reading about the various memorabilia on display—all donated by the band members. The first section is dedicated to Ben First, the Dead Sergeants' lead singer. A life-size picture of him on stage in the back of the case. The photo speaks volumes as Ben sings, clearly in his element, hand wrapped around a mic. His wardrobe consisting of nothing but a Home Depot apron, tapered jeans tucked into calf-length black boots, his toned, muscular build alluring. It's obvious why the photo was chosen because it captures his stage presence perfectly—curly blond hair untamed, eyes beseeching, expression unguarded.

I read the eye-level explanation of the display, which states Ben wore the apron during their first tour as part joke and nod to where he started. I grin. "One day, his most useful tool is a box cutter, the next, it's a mic, and he's singing for a crowd of *thousands.*"

"Took a whole lot longer than a day," Easton relays absently, seemingly lost in a memory as I study Ben closely.

I can see the appeal he had then and find myself empathizing with Lexi, his on-again-off-again ex-girlfriend who eventually mothered his only child. In the movie, Ben and Lexi's relationship was hot, volatile, and ended when Lexi cheated on Ben after the Sergeants were signed. Her insecure actions forced Ben to walk away. From the way she was portrayed—much like Stella—Lexi was a pistol, and it saddens me that even the most confident of women must feel helpless at times, thanks to the constant threat of those who want to take their place.

"I can't imagine dating a man so sought after, so *wanted*," I find myself saying aloud. "It would drive me insane."

Easton scoffs. "Ben's just like *you* and *me*, and *them*," he lifts his chin toward a few people wandering into the room opposite ours. "Temptation can be both avoided and ignored. I've seen it for myself. Granted, most of the band were settled down by the time I was born. When we toured, *no one* got backstage. We had security on every floor of every hotel. It was mostly all business until the show."

"I hear you, but those who can't put together a group of meaningful words and pair them with an emotion-evoking melody are heavily intrigued by those who can. Not to mention the stage presence. It's sexy as hell, Easton. I might not be a music fanatic, but even *I* understand the allure and am not immune to it." I nudge him, "But for all I know, you sound like a gorilla on the mic, so you're no threat to me."

The biggest lie you've told thus far, Natalie. Going for the gold, are we?

I drink in his profile outlined in clear view in the reflection of the glass case, wondering if he's mirroring his own future as he looks into Ben's past. When he catches my gaze, instead of shying away, I smile, and he returns it, his fingers brushing mine as we walk down to the next display. Just inside is a picture of Rye Wheelan, the Sergeants' lead guitarist, playing the Fender he donated, which sits propped in a battered case covered in old bumper stickers. I laugh at a few of them.

A step over, homemade T-shirts from Adam Shaw's raunchy collection are displayed along with a bass in two pieces, only held together by the strings.

"I take it these two are the goofballs?"

"Most definitely," Easton says with a grin. "I've had to parent them on more than one occasion."

"This is your *family*," I hear the slight awe in my voice, "in a glass case."

"I have to admit, it's a little fucking weird."

"Do you remember a lot about being on the road?"

"Plenty. It took up most of my childhood summers. But only for three or four months out of the year. My parents were determined to give me some semblance of normalcy, so I missed a lot of the European dates. Yet by the time I was old enough to crave it, I was foaming at the mouth along with my dad to hit the road. I loved it," he admits freely, "I really, really fucking loved it."

I nudge him. "So, you have that to look forward to."

He dips his chin noncommittally before sauntering over to the last case. Like Ben's display, at the back sits a life-size black and white picture of Reid, fingers firmly gripping his sticks, arms raised and poised to rain hell on his drums. Shirt tucked in his back pocket, Reid's expression is much like Easton's when he gets lost in the music.

Though I've attributed Easton's skin and hair color to Stella, in this photo Reid and Easton's likeness is striking.

Inside the case, situated in front of the life-size picture, sits a Drummer's Workshop kit. A battered set of Reid's drumsticks—one with the tip broken off—rests against the large, tattered bass drum. Reading the prompt, I recognize I was right in assuming it's the set of drums Stella won by chance and sent to Reid after they broke up.

Her gesture was a plea to encourage him to keep going, even *after* he broke her heart and left Austin. A slight bitterness seeps into me, but at the same time, I know the gesture was probably what kept him from quitting.

"They saved him," Easton confirms, staring at the kit. "It cut him deep to donate them, but he didn't want them rotting away in storage. He figured at least they'll be preserved here. Mom saw in him what he couldn't see for himself," he utters, unmistakable pride in his eyes for what his parents have.

I nod, ashamed my confidence is shaky in the same respect, and I allowed—*am allowing* it to happen. Easton trails me into a nearby room as I stare blankly at the next display. His warmth surrounds me before he rests his chin on my shoulder, my body reacting in kind as it begins to thrum with awareness.

"I'm right here," he whispers, the words resonating a second before bringing me to a scene in *Drive*. Reid typed out those exact words for Stella on her laptop minutes before they collided in their first kiss. Just as I question the implication of Easton's whispered words, his warmth vanishes and he steps away, his expression imperceptible. He scans the room briefly, seeming to get lost in thought before turning back to me and extending his palm. "Come on, buttery breasts," one side of his mouth lifts. "I'll take you back to your hotel."

I do the only thing that's felt right since I landed in Seattle and place my hand in his.

FIFTEEN

Only You Know

Dion

Natalie

For the first few minutes of the drive back to the hotel, I fight the urge to try and extend our time together. Somehow, Easton's managed to turn *another* shitty morning into an extraordinary day. An unforgettable day. As hard as I try to muster the courage, I can't manage to get the words out thanks to the lie I'm continuing to feed into. His effort to give a little background by taking me to the museum to help me with my fictional article hasn't gone unnoticed.

It's when the surroundings start to become familiar that the overwhelming urge overtakes me. Just as I go to speak, Easton lifts a finger, asking me to wait. The now recognizable, faraway look in his eye is present as he becomes absorbed in the music. Ears perked, he turns the song up and I quickly pull up my Shazam app to identify it when it doesn't appear on the ancient truck's radio display. Seconds later, the title pops up on screen—"Only You Know" by Dion. I look up the year it was released, 1975, and make a mental note of it as we reach the hotel.

Limbs growing heavy with disappointment, I ready my goodbye, but instead of pulling up at the entrance to drop me off, Easton parks and wordlessly exits his truck. In seconds, his warm hand surrounds mine as he pulls me from the cab before turning and stalking toward the hotel, ostensibly on a mission. Instead of questioning what he's doing, I speed up to keep up with his determined strides. Ambling into the lobby with me in tow, he stops and scans it. Seeming unsatisfied, he continues his search to the adjacent lounge. I nearly collide with him as he pauses briefly when we reach it before making a beeline to the back of the large room. Glancing around, I soak in the atmosphere for the first time since I arrived in Seattle.

I'd picked The Edgewater on a whim after seeing that several known celebrities and musicians have stayed here. Ironically, it was a picture of The Beatles fishing in the Puget Sound from one of the room windows that sold me. One of a few growing coincidences I purposely haven't pointed out to Easton.

As Easton speed walks through the room with me in tow, I note that the large, clustered seating area is adorned with posh, comfortable-looking furniture. Branches extend from tree trunk-shaped support columns through the space, and much like my room, cemented river rocks make up the massive fireplace to our right. The fireplace currently hosts a low burning flame, making the atmosphere romantic in feel. A large, amber-lit antler chandelier rests low in front of a row of floor-to-ceiling windows. Just beyond one of the windows, a cluster of seagulls dip along the water, leaving it rippling in their wake.

It's when I peek over Easton's shoulder that I spot a baby grand that faces away from an amazing view of Puget Sound.

Unclasping my hand, Easton leaves me standing beside the polished instrument, discarding his hat on top before taking the bench seat. It's then I notice the moisture coating the hand he just released.

He's nervous.

I barely have time to register what's happening when Easton closes his eyes. Time seems to stand still as his fingers search for and easily find the keys as he runs down a few chords.

Just after, he begins to play as I stare at him, stunned. Within a few notes of the intro, I pick up the melody, which mimics, note for note, the song we just heard on the oldies station. It's when Easton opens his mouth and begins to sing that I feel the full gravity of what's happening.

Easton Crowne is singing, *for me*, in my hotel lobby. Not only that, but the man's voice is staggeringly perfect.

As if on cue, the water begins to glitter dramatically with the sun's descent, the warm hue drenching him in a surreal, golden glow. Rays filter across his dark locks which start to unravel as he plays, the sun casting his features in perfect light as his velvet voice wraps around each lyric with expertise. Within seconds, I'm intoxicated—completely drunk on the sound and sight before me.

Easton moves naturally behind the piano, the scope of his talent no longer a mystery as he breathes new life and soul into a song over a half-century old. His fingers instinctively move along the ivory keys, and his raspy, melodic tone guides it the rest of the way as the song hits its crescendo.

Disbelief clouds me, and my eyes sting in response to the emotion he so easily evokes. Though borrowed, Easton owns every second of the song, the lyrics, and the very essence of the music. Unable to do anything but gawk, I fly over the edge of his mystery into infatuation.

It's not just the way he plays. It's the way he deconstructed the song, implementing every instrument while only using the piano. It's as if he calculated an exact compilation for this very purpose.

But how?

My full being lights up with understanding as he continues to play, entirely in his element as a level of certainty overtakes me.

Easton Crowne is not some budding star. He's a *supernova.*

He's undoubtedly a prodigy—a genius disguised in a beautiful, but highly breakable—human package. At any time in the future, if he so desires, he will become a world-renowned star.

If I take advantage of this knowledge—and my current position—and write this story, an exclusive with him could very well kickstart my career and get my name out of the grey and into a bolder black. Even so, no part of me wants to share this moment with anyone in *any capacity*. More than anything, I want to cling to his star as it burns the brightest—if only to be with him for a little longer. If what Easton said is true, and we live in echoes of defining moments, I want to remain in this one for as long as I possibly can.

When Easton finishes the song, he glances up, his eyes focusing on me as if he's coming out of a trance. A blooming smile slowly spreads across his gorgeous face as though he's surprised himself. Unable to help it, I take another dangerous step with the edge of gravity continually urging me toward him. Thunderous applause explodes from adjacent rooms, along with those he drew into the lounge. The sound of their cheers snaps me from my dreamlike state into the present as Easton gives them a brief dip of his chin in a silent thank you. His eyes remain fixed on me and my reaction to him.

I interrupt my own applause by wiping an errant tear, feeling a pride I have no business feeling.

"I was close to begging," I whisper hoarsely, "and Jesus, Easton, I should have. That was…fucking *incredible*." I shake my head, completely bewildered. "You memorized that song after hearing it *once*, didn't you?"

He slowly nods, his hazel eyes sweeping my face, soaking in my response as if he wants to remember it. Undeniable warmth bounces between us as I laugh at my continually watering eyes, my voice hoarse as I step up to him. When he clears the piano and peers down at me, his jade eyes gleam with what can only be perceived as happiness.

"Easton?"

"Yeah," he rasps out, his gaze penetrating mine in a way I could never look away.

"Can your *first fan* buy you dinner?"

Shortly after, I run up to my hotel room to shower and change while Easton has a beer at the bar. We end up dining at the hotel restaurant, Six Seven, tucked away at a comfortable corner table—both of us severely underdressed. With the sun absent, soft amber light filters throughout the restaurant, making it feel unavoidably intimate.

We've been drinking dark beer and taking bites from each other's plates since we sat down, and I felt another shift between us.

A soft glow from the candle licks along Easton's profile as he bites on rare steak and shiitake mushrooms, his eyes scanning the eatery occasionally for prying eyes. Surprisingly, I'm at ease. We've been out and about for days without encountering paparazzi, but I'm no stranger to the game. I know the rules, as does he. "Paps aren't allowed inside."

"Like that will stop them," he huffs in disgust.

I can't help but feel the threat of that truth and glance around briefly. If anyone should be nervous about getting caught on the opposite side of a lens with Easton Crowne, it's *me*. Even so, I ask a question that's come to mind more than once, as casually as I can muster. "Do you have a girlfriend?"

He pulls on his Smoked Porter, shaking his head. "No."

"Is it purposeful? Do you fuck for sport?"

He pauses his fork halfway to his mouth, his eyes flaring at the invasion.

"Off-record, of course," I add.

"Women aren't a sport for me," he says, bracing his forearms on the table and leans in, his whisper loaded, "so I *fuck* because it feels good."

Heat covers me at the suggestive implication in his voice as I press my lips together before replying. "Well, that's just as good of a reason as any, I guess," I hold up my dwindling beer to our waitress, signaling for another before eyeing him, "and practice makes perfect."

Stop flirting with the supernova, you idiot!

"You haven't mentioned one either," he says, wiping his perfect mouth with his perfect hands as his perfect eyes continue to poke gaping holes in my rapidly disintegrating resolve. According to my third dark beer, the truth is that I'm already missing the feel of his hand as I try to push down thoughts of what his skilled fingers are capable of.

If I'm reading him right, he's been mentally undressing me since we took our seats at the table. The buzz that's been brewing between us since we met is now palpable and moving rapidly in a dangerous direction.

Shut it down now, Natalie.

"I have no man to speak of at the moment."

Idiot!

"Dated a guy—Carson—in college for a year and a half until we graduated. He took a job in New York, which ended us. That's about the extent of my serious dating history. I'm at that 'career comes first stage' anyway."

He lays his knife and fork on his plate and tips back, his posture screaming 'bullshit' before he calls me on it.

"So, that's what you're telling yourself."

"Damn, and here I thought you were going to make it a whole day without going A-side asshole." I flash him a sarcastic grin.

"Okay," his shoulders go rigid as he tosses his napkin. "If we're blowing smoke up each other's asses, I guess I can give you the, 'I'm a guy who has to be careful because I have famous parents and am about to start a music career, so it's not an optimal time to have anything serious going on' spiel."

"Makes sense," I concede easily.

His eyes flare in warning, and I harden my stare in return.

"No, it fucking doesn't. You don't deny yourself *anything* you want in life because of *timing*. That's a coward's excuse."

"I disagree. But you might want to watch yourself pointing out bravery as a barrier."

My remark cuts both ways as his eyes fill with fury. Regret saturates me, and I instantly backpedal. "Easton, I didn't mean—"

"So, I hit a nerve, a *big one*, apparently," he delivers smugly, pinning me with his hardening gaze, searing me. "What was it exactly?"

"This is nice," I sip my beer. "I'm having a good time. Let's not fuck it up with brutal honesty."

"It's the only way I function," he delivers with a harsh bite before turning and glaring out of a nearby window for several seconds. Seconds that don't tamp down any part of his anger before he flicks his furious gaze back to mine. "You're really going to check out on me *now*?"

"What do you want from me, Easton? I've been a train wreck since I got here."

"And so…what? You don't have to go into hiding now."

I glance around because his bark isn't light. Seeing the warning consume his posture, I lean in.

"Look, I'm just trying to keep things profess—"

"Oh, hell no," he says, pulling his wallet from his back pocket and tossing his card on the table. "Fuck this."

"Easton," I fumble for the right thing to say to start damage control. "I told you I'm paying for dinner." Definitely *not* the right thing to say. "It's the least I can do."

Way to go, Natalie. You might as well have punched him in the dick.

He silently glares at me as he tugs at his beer. Panic starts to set in as I realize he's probably weighing his decision to stay or go.

"I'm sorry, I'm so sorry. You're right, and I had no right to turn what you told me in confidence against you. It's unforgivable, but please try, if you can, to forgive me. I'm projecting. *I'm* the asshole, okay? But like I told you, you're freer than you think."

"And that trap is in *your mind*," he hisses, "you're doing it right now."

"I envy you, truly, the way you—"

He snaps to his feet, decision made, patience evaporating as I grip his arm to stop him. "Easton, I have my reasons. Please don't be upset."

"Fuck that, Natalie. I'm not going to watch you build a wall between us after I—" b*ared myself to you.*

Even though he doesn't say it, it's heavily implied truth. He has bared himself, and I've done nothing but play into my lie, giving him nothing concrete. He fists his hands at his sides, his patience long gone as my window to come clean nears an inch from slamming shut.

"Easton, as much as a hypocrite as you think I may be right now, you have a public persona too."

"I didn't create it, and I sure as fuck don't feed into it," he spits, animosity radiating from him, putting purposeful space between us. It's surprisingly painful, and while I hate it, I understand his anger.

"No, you don't feed into it, which makes you braver than most—than *me*. I'm not denying that, but we all can't walk around running rampant with our feelings. It's exhausting."

"Have you ever once stopped to think that's maybe *why* you're exhausted?"

"Jesus, it really is all or *nothing* with you, isn't it?"

He gives me a dead stare because the question is redundant. I knew within five minutes of meeting him that he despises a disguise or even a thin coat of armor.

"I'm sorry," I repeat, knowing I made the wrong call as he stares down at the hand still clutching his arm, nostrils flaring. He's holding back wrath I deserve, and for that, I'm thankful.

"Just so you fucking know, that was my first time playing in public," he delivers to my heart which explodes into a chaotic rhythm.

"Ever?" I ask, gaping up at him. His silence has me sputtering as I realize just how much of himself he's bared to me. "Easton, oh my God, Easton, I'm so sorry. I'm honored and...f-flattered and completely unworthy. Jesus," my eyes water with guilt as I make my decision. "You're right. You deserve better. So much fucking better."

The side of his jaw ticks as he flicks his gaze back to mine, trying to get a read on me.

"Will you take a walk with me? *Please.* Before you leave pissed and decide you hate me, at least let me give you a better reason to."

He remains silent, his jaw like granite as I stand.

"Take a walk with me, Easton, please."

He gives me a cautious, slow nod as our waitress walks over and grabs his credit card. Eyes on Easton, I raise a hand to stop her. "Please charge it to my room, 212. Natalie Butler."

Pocketing his card, Easton pulls out a large bill and hands it to her for a tip. She takes it with thanks, failing miserably at concealing a flirtatious grin. "You two have a great night."

SIXTEEN

Come Undone
Carina Round

Natalie

It's close to midnight as a silent, brooding Easton walks next to me along a short pier a few blocks from my hotel. Dots of brightly lit houses surround the water in the distance as I figuratively walk the plank toward whatever disaster lies ahead. As sleep deprived as I am and have been this past week, I'm surprisingly alert. As we reach the end of the pier, I palm the railing, wondering if I jumped in now, how far I would make it.

Sensing my hesitance, Easton steps closer to me, his quiet electricity surrounding me as I try to think of a way to explain my actions.

"Are you tired?" He asks softly, surprising me by speaking first, and with concern for *me* before darting his gaze to the dark water.

"Not really. I was just thinking that. You?"

"No."

"Either way, I'll see myself back to my hotel. I'm sure you have more important things to do than babysit me."

"Kind of necessary since I'm parked there."

A burst of tense laughter escapes me, and I shake my head at my idiocy. "Maybe not tired, but it's clear I'm in dire need of sleep."

Turning, I step up on the wooden base hitching my arms on the railing. The breeze whips around my face, a few strands inevitably sticking to my freshly glossed lips. Just as I lift my hand to free it, Easton grips my arm, moving to stand in front of me. Stunned and immobile, he cups my jaw before running a sure thumb over my lips, completely wiping all traces of the gloss away. A stuttered breath leaves me as he leans in, palming my stomach before sliding his hand into the pocket of my jeans. Glancing down, I watch him retrieve my gloss before tossing it into a nearby trash bin. I gape at him in disbelief. "What the hell?"

He shrugs. "Seemed like the easiest fucking solution."

"Yeah, but you see," I manage to get out as he inches closer, "you just erased all the allure."

"Not fucking possible," he whispers heatedly, eyes probing as my libido lights fire, his every word stoking it. He dips dangerously close, and I palm his chest, determined to get my confession out. He steps back, his posture rigid.

I glance back at the water briefly to stop myself from tossing caution to the wind and giving in to my desire before looking back up at him. "You want honesty? I've never been so attracted to a man in my life."

He stares down at me, expression unwavering as if that's not news.

Tough room.

"*But* if I entertain it, it will be the second-worst thing I've ever done."

His jaw ticks as I start to defend that statement.

"However, not for the reasons you might think. I asked you to walk with me because I'm going to try to explain myself. I've just been stalling because I know when I do, you might turn around, walk away, and never speak to me again—and you'll be well within your rights to." I wince. "You probably should."

His brows lift. "That bad?"

"For me, in my heart," I press my hand where it lays, "it feels like the worst thing I've ever done, especially now, because I like you a lot, and I don't want to deceive you another minute."

"You're not here for an interview," he delivers with a relaxed tone.

I nod.

"I gathered that much," he utters simply. "So, this *is* about our parents?"

I nod again. "Partially, but not for the reasons you might think. How mad are you?"

"You're pretty transparent, Natalie. So, I'm more fucking relieved than anything."

"Well, don't be," I blow out a harsh breath. "Our gossip columnist is still going to run a story Monday speculating you're coming out with a debut album. That's out of my hands...and it's out of my hands because I can't...no, I *won't* protect you."

He rakes his lip with his teeth, eyes cooling considerably.

"Reason being, if I try to stop her from running it, questions will be raised by both her and my father, who will demand an explanation as to *why* I'm protecting you." I swallow. "Reasons I can't give because I'm not allowed to and was never supposed to know you, Easton." I test the waters. "How angry are you now?"

"I'm still standing here," he clips out.

"Well, you are partially right in your assessment," I admit in a whisper. "I didn't come here to meet you as a reporter...but as the child of the other half of a broken love story between our parents."

"Guess you've got a story now," he grits out with a venomous bite.

"Despite the fact that you shouldn't trust me at all at this point, I won't use a single word of what you told me, even if it could boost circulation and my career. I've already decided that."

He remains in front of me, his profile backlit by a nearby dock light.

"The truth is, it was never *my story* to begin with. I got the information from my columnist and used it as an excuse to meet you." I palm my face briefly. "Jesus, yeah, it sounds really, *really*, bad out loud."

He remains mute, demanding the rest of my explanation.

"I told you that something happened recently that threw me off."

A slow nod.

"The thing that happened is...fuck it," I shake my head, deciding not to attempt to arrange the words and just let them fly. "I was digging through Austin Speak's archives for excerpts of stories for our thirtieth-anniversary edition of the paper and, in doing so, stumbled upon emails between my father and your mother. Some of them were very *personal* emails, and it did something to me...I can't really explain it, which is pathetic because I'm supposed to excel at describing through words."

Easton's expression remains unreadable. Unsure if he's about to turn away in disgust, I rush through the rest of my explanation.

"At first, I only read a few. The beginning of their relationship and the end. I was stunned to discover they'd dated at all. As close as my father and I are, he's never once mentioned it. Anyway, I guess you could say that once I read them, they created an alternate universe. Like," I swallow, "like everything I knew about my parents, their history, and the fact that they even exist is more thanks to a decision on *someone else's* part rather than the soulmates, kismet type of thing I've always believed. The truth is, if our parents had stayed together, they would be living entirely different lives." I cringe. "Jesus, I know I sound like a lunatic. Especially since, in that alternate universe, you and I don't exist." My chest flutters with awareness and ache. "They loved each other, Easton, your mother, my father, they were really, *really*, fucking in love, and not for just a few months, for *years*. It was serious, and what I read rocked me to my core. It shook my beliefs. It made me question a lot. And for the life of me, I cannot figure out why I'm taking it so personally or why it *hurts* me so much. I mean… everyone has exes, right?"

I brave a look at him to see that he's staring at me intently.

"I don't know why I flew *here* and sought you out. I swear I'm not asking for anything, nor would I ask…or do I want to meet Stella or Re-y-your parents. That's not what this is. I guess it's just a morbid type of curiosity that brought me here to meet you." After a harsh exhale, I relay the rest of the truth. "It's just…that revelation kind of cracked my sky. Those emails…the love exchanged. It's altered how I view things and my parents' relationship as a whole, and I can't change it back. So, I just had to get away, and I came here. That's it, that's the whole truth."

I shake my head and let out a low, strangled laugh. "You probably think I'm crazy now."

Silence stretches for long seconds as I avoid his eyes.

"Crazy people don't question their sanity," he utters assuringly.

"Well, I *feel* fucking crazy. I just couldn't look at my father anymore with a thousand unanswered questions I have no right to ask swirling in my head. I had to get the hell out of there. Not only because of that, but because I violated his privacy in an unforgivable way. Some of those emails were so intimate."

Tears threaten, and my voice shakes. "Nate Butler is the person I love and respect most in the *world*. My father is my *everything*. Maybe *that's* why I took it so personally. So, I came here, I guess, wanting to meet you, doubtful I would get any more of a story you probably had no idea existed, either. And now…though the why is killing me, I don't think I want to know the rest. Knowing the full truth will probably sting worse than not knowing, but I'm sorry," I whisper. "I'm sorry for the way I did this, the way I roped you into my bullshit. It was just a lot easier to do it in a professional capacity than to admit that..." I palm my face briefly and smile, "is twenty-two too early to have a midlife crisis?"

Fear swallows me as his eyes remain intent, and I turn back to the water. "I'm sorry, Easton, if you want to walk away, God, go. I won't blame you, but everything you've confided in me is safe, I swear to you."

I feel the brush of his hand against mine, and an involuntary shiver runs up my spine. My lips part as I glance back at him, his face impassive as he grips my arm and turns me back to him.

"Stop fucking ducking away from me," he commands, his order warming me, even as I shiver in the cold.

"Do you hate me?"

He slowly shakes his head before he speaks. "Are they happy?"

"My parents?" I ask.

He nods.

"That's the thing, they seem to be totally content...I have no right to ask you...but are—"

Easton nods quickly, confirming what I already knew.

"So, it's all for the best, and I should be able to put it to rest, except that..."

"What?"

"They were engaged, Easton."

Easton's eyes widen slightly in surprise.

"Yeah, I discovered that last night, which is why I didn't sleep. Like I said, it was serious, and I felt it. I *felt* the love between them down to my marrow."

He sorts through my confessions for several beats before his expression changes, and I don't miss its implication.

"Great," I roll my eyes. "I know *that* look and what you're thinking."

"Enlighten me."

"You're thinking that maybe if I had a love life of my own to concentrate on, I wouldn't currently be obsessing over my father's ancient history."

"No—"

"Oh, shut up. You're thinking it." I call bullshit. All pretenses are gone as I bare myself in return because he deserves it, no matter how humiliating it is.

"I'm not thinking that. Not outright."

"Okay then, what do you think? Don't hold back," I snort. "Not like you would to spare me."

The space between us crackles as I blow out a nervous breath. He waits for my gaze to lift, his silence deafening before he finally speaks.

"I think reading those emails affected you this way because you might be envious. Maybe you crave a connection, a love like my parents have, like our parents had together, maybe something more than the relationship you've idolized your whole life." He leans in, his every word striking like a blow.

"Jesus. Is this who I am? The girl inventing drama?" He blocks my attempt to cover my face before pinning my wrists to the dock and stealing my breath.

"I'm also thinking you've never been properly *kissed, fucked, or loved* and that you caught a glimpse of something you want for *yourself*."

My foot slips, and in an instant I'm in his arms as his whisper caresses my temple. "Okay?"

"Yes," I snap. "No, hell no," I admit, stepping out of his reach.

"Natalie—" he murmurs at my back.

"Fuck—this is humiliating." I feel my eyes burning as the truth of his words resonate with me. "I've been so wrapped up in it, I couldn't see the forest for the trees," I scoff. "But you're right, you're absolutely right. Hell, maybe this was inevitable…I've been reading and writing human interest stories my entire life. Incredible moments," I sniff. "*Other people's* defining moments and echoes. So, what do I go and do?" My eyes spill over. "The worst fucking thing imaginable to a man who means everything to me. Just being here, meeting you, is a betrayal in itself, Easton—of the worst kind." Fear rolls through me at the idea my father might already know where I am. "If he found out I was here, with you, I don't know if he could or would ever forgive me."

"There's nothing wrong wit—"

"There's everything wrong with this," I snap. "She broke his heart in a way that probably changed him. So maybe there is a lot of truth to what you've gathered, but it's not just envy…"

He turns my chin with gentle fingers, forcing my watering eyes to his. "Say it."

I gaze up at him, feeling as lost as I was when I got here. "What if…my father *settled* for my mother? What if she's felt it over the years?

Or worse, what if she fucking knows it and has lived with it all this time?"

"That's *your* fear, which might not be the truth."

I nod.

"And not just fear for your mother, but for yourself."

I nod again, tasting the salty evidence of that truth pooling on my lips.

"But it's not your life, Natalie," he gently reminds me. "You don't even know if it's true, and if it is, that's on them."

"I hate not knowing."

"Then you have to ask."

"Never." I sniff. "God, I would never. I just have to let it go, and I'm going to, here. Here and now. This is completely destructive and serves no purpose." I glance up at the most beautiful man I've ever laid eyes on. "And being with you—"

"You aren't doing anything wrong."

"Yes, I am. Even you, Mr. Brutal Honesty, can't truly deny that."

He remains quiet because he can't. I let out a self-deprecating laugh. "Easton, why aren't you hauling ass in the other direction? Seriously, why are you being so nice to me? Especially after what I just told you?"

"Not sure," he says as I lift my palm to his chest, and he covers it with his own. "You're cold."

"I'll live," I say, ripping my eyes away from him so he can't see the desire begin to blind me. I focus on a seagull who drunkenly lands a few feet away. Where before it was easier to distance myself, it's now a constant struggle not to touch him more intimately, especially feeling as raw as I do. "So, there's my sad little tale, which isn't even mine. Pathetic."

"You're bored. You've realized it. You followed a trail that piqued your interest, and it led to a little self-discovery. It's not a fucking crime to realize that you feel you're lacking in some ways. What would make it a crime is if you didn't do shit about it. You're an intelligent woman, and now you know what you want and what you don't. Figuring it out is all part of it, right?"

"God," I grin while wiping away the few errant tears gliding down my cheeks. "That pep talk must have been so painful for your A-side."

"I got close to jumping in," he jests in a velvet tone that has me inhaling an extra breath.

"Yeah, well, I guess thank you for not throwing me over. You're a pretty decent guy, Easton Crowne."

Gripping my hand, he surrounds it with his own and pulls me to his side, "Come on, let's walk some more until you get tired."

"I'm sorry, Easton," I repeat because it bears repeating.

As we walk away from the pier, he laces our fingers together in response. Relief trickles in as I glance over at him just as we pass the dock light, and I see no trace of judgment but an accepting warmth in his eyes. It's then I feel the totality of the warm embrace Stella described when she first arrived in Seattle. That and the knowledge I'm exactly where I'm supposed to be and with the right person—even if I don't understand or have the crystal clarity of why. He pulls me into his side as we stroll along the edge of the water, my head resting on his chest before we get lost in our footfalls.

Easton stops short of the sliding doors outside of the hotel and wordlessly lifts our clutched hands before pressing his lush lips to the back of mine. Heat sparks through me as the buzz between us amps up, crackling and intensifying with every passing second.

"So, you don't hate me?"

"No," he answers, quickly crowding me on the sidewalk. His potent, desire-filled gaze destroying my will to keep him at arm's length by the second.

"Not even a little?"

"No, but do you want a little more clarity?"

"Think I can handle it?"

His lips lift in a barely-there grin. "You're a little more villain than you think."

"Yeah," I sigh. "I have to agree with that."

"We all have one in us," he imparts.

"You're completely different than I thought you would be," I admit, "but in the best way." My limbs thrum with recognition that the gorgeous distraction towering over me is taking up every inch of my headspace.

"Easton, maybe I've been presumptuous in thinking...but if I wasn't," I whisper as his body cradles mine without contact, the invisible thread between us strengthening, "if I wasn't—"

Using our clasped hands, he jerks me flush to him, his breath hitting my ear a second before his heated declaration. "If you weren't so determined to keep me out of your bed, I'd be fucking the breath out of you right now, Natalie."

I let out a shaky exhale as his erection brushes against me. "In my mind, I've already sunk inside you a thousand times."

A whimper leaves my throat as he pulls back, undeniable heat burning in his darkening emerald gaze.

"This is crazy," I swallow.

"No, it's not," he says, brushing his thumb seductively over the back of my hand. Allowing it briefly, I lose myself in the sweep of his touch as I imagine the type of lover he would be. He seems to read my thoughts easily, as he has since the day we met, all the while naturally disarming me.

Exhaling heavily, he pulls back slightly, reaching into his jean pocket where he retrieves a pack of breath mints. His dark lashes flit over his cheeks as he unwraps the candy. Lifting a piece of it, he gently pushes it between my parted lips. Embarrassment threatening, I draw my brows just as he pops a piece into his own mouth before flicking the mint skillfully along his tongue. "I'm so tempted to ignore your words and listen to everything else you're not saying."

"Please don't," I whisper, knowing if he moves in, I won't stop him. It's when he inches closer that I realize I'm fisting his jersey for support.

He cups my face, running his thumb along my creased brow before lowering it to slide it across my bottom lip. "At least now I don't have to wonder what your mouth tastes like."

My entire body trembles with need as his earthy scent engulfs me while he presses a slow kiss to my temple. "Sleep in. I'll pick you up tomorrow at three." Releasing me, he turns just as abruptly and stalks toward the parking lot as if forcing himself to walk away.

SEVENTEEN

Damn I Wish I Was Your Lover
Sophie B Hawkins

Natalie

Exiting the hotel, I catch sight of Easton leaning next to the passenger door of his truck. As I draw near, I'm struck stupid by the sight of him—dark brown leather boots crossed at his ankles, whitewashed fitted jeans, and a form-fitting, buttoned flannel accentuating his lean, muscular build. His thick, chin-length raven locks are partially tucked behind one ear. The rest cradles his jawline pulling attention to his naturally stained, crimson lips.

Dear God, please make it stop.

His current look battering my libido, I can't help but be happy about the extra effort I put into my own appearance today. After waking refreshed from a coma-worthy twelve hours of sleep, I ate a breakfast fit for a queen. Finding myself with a few hours to spare, I ordered a car and took a little trip to Pike Place Market. I explored the tourist destination before dipping into a boutique and treating myself to a sexy, low-cut halter sweater that accentuates my cleavage and bares a few inches of my midriff. I've paired it with skintight dark pleather pants and black suede ankle boots. After a long, steamy, life-altering shower, I left my hair curly, despite my temptation to straighten it, and managed to tame it in large ringlets. Keeping my makeup clean—knowing my expensive gloss was en route to a nearby dump—I settled on a matte nude. It's not at all lost on me that every effort I made on my look coincides with his preferences. The appreciation for said effort shines clear in his eyes as I stalk toward him. At the last minute,

I slipped on his oversized jacket, and that finishing touch is where his gaze lingers longest.

Hastening toward him, I can't help the gradual lift of my lips with every step as his eyes again sweep me, holding on the bare skin of my stomach before trailing back up.

"Hi," I beam at him as he opens the passenger door for me.

"You slept," is his reply as I slip into the truck, inhaling his heavenly sage and woods scent.

"Like a rock, *finally*, and I feel amazing," I glance over at him as I settle in.

"It shows," he replies low, closing me into the cab. My eyes follow him in the sideview, his natural swagger in full effect as he rounds his truck bed. As he eases into his seat, nervous energy engulfs me. Though it can't be, this feels everything like a date.

Easton unlocks and hands me his cellphone to play DJ, in time with the routine we've established in just a few days of knowing each other. Though I'm still a bit surprised he picked me up today as promised, considering he's had time to absorb the full extent of my deception.

"So, you still don't hate me?" I ask, taking his extended phone.

"No," he starts his truck, "I think you're punishing yourself enough." He glances over at me, a smile flirting along his lips. "But since we both know you're currently a danger to yourself and others if you're alone with your thoughts, you're going to run an errand with me today."

"That's a dramatic assessment."

He raises his brows.

"Okay, so there may be a small amount of truth to that." I laugh lightly, and he gives me another whisper of a smile as he puts the truck into gear. Aside from humiliating myself unintentionally, and publicly for his amusement, I wonder what it takes to get Easton Crowne fully animated.

"What errands are we talking about? We know you're all stocked up on condoms," I jab, flicking his playlist exaggeratedly with my pointer as the tracks tick down the screen by the dozen before pressing play on a random song. It's when I roll my window down halfway that I feel him pause on the other side of the truck and glance over. "What?"

He eyes my hand on the knob of the window, which mirrors the current position of his own hand, and shakes his head in reply. As he pulls out of the parking lot, I fill him in on my morning activities.

"You'll be happy to know I'm a full-fledged tourist now, Mr. Crowne. I watched the tossing of the fish at Pike's Market and even visited the saliva-infested bubble gum wall, and before you ask—no, I didn't add to it. I was a little grossed out by it."

Though Easton remains quiet while I fill him in, his expression reeks of amusement from my ramblings before we fall into a comfortable, but music-filled silence. Not long after, we pull up in front of a glass storefront, and I draw my brows. "A tattoo is an errand?"

Easton wordlessly exits his truck and gathers me from my side with an offered hand before pulling me to the entrance. On his heels when he steps inside, he releases my hand before lifting his chin to a man running a tattoo gun. His subject is a twenty-something woman propped on a leather table that sits a few feet behind a small reception desk.

"Hey man, almost done here." The tattoo artist's eyes drift to mine. "And who is this pretty kitty you dragged in?"

"A friend," Easton replies simply. This time, I'm the one who lifts a brow his way.

He gives me a dead stare. "Shut up."

"So, we're going A-side Easton today?"

Ignoring me, he sits in one of the nearby lobby chairs as I scan the parlor. In short summary, it's clean and modern and looks more like a posh gentlemen's club rather than a tattoo parlor. A sleek counter-height bar sits in the far-left corner, craft beer nozzles ready to pour and pint glasses stacked next to them. Next to it sits a glass refrigerator full of everything imaginable to wet a dry tongue. The furniture at the stations throughout consists of rich, expensive looking leather with chrome touches.

The lobby houses several matching chairs, the walls lined with digital displays that blink in and out with professional photos of completed projects. The finished product work atypical of what one might expect. I note as well there are no drawings on display to choose from for basic, uninspired tattoos. It's obvious this isn't the place to come without a clear idea of what you want. This parlor appears to be the crème de la crème of spots to get inked. From the digital signatures on the bottom of those displayed, it seems only three artists work here.

Behind the guy currently running his gun, neither of the other chairs are occupied.

Glancing back at the gallery, I question if I would ever permanently mark my skin or want to endure the pain in doing so. Sensing Easton's eyes on me, I turn to see him scanning the fit of his jacket on my frame. I swear I see slight satisfaction in his eyes before he pulls his cell from his pocket and begins to tap the screen.

Looking beyond the reception desk when the gun stops buzzing, I eye the artist as he starts to tick off aftercare instructions to the highly attentive twenty-something staring up at him as he dresses her fresh ink in plastic wrap. From the look she's giving him, she'd like a little more aftercare than what he's offering—and I can't blame her at all. Upon closer inspection, I note he's gorgeous and…mammoth in size. His height is similar to Easton's, at around six-foot-two, and his curly dirty blond hair is cropped short, a lock of it loosely swept over midnight blue eyes. His build is immaculate. Not only that, but he's also dressed to kill in a dark red collared shirt and designer jeans.

With sleeves rolled up a few inches on his forearms, it's easy to surmise both arms are covered in ink. What appears to be bold black feather tips peak along the side of his neck. He's the gasp-worthy blond in contrast to Easton's breath-stealing tall, dark, and strikingly handsome.

They sure do seem to make them pretty in Washington.

Smiling at the thought, I glance over at Easton to see his nostrils flaring in my direction before he darts his eyes back to his phone.

Guilt I shouldn't feel for ogling another man threatens as I walk over and take a seat next to him. Easton's posture remains rigid, which has me scrambling to get some semblance back of the comfortable dynamic that we've managed to easily find since we met. Unable to help it, I glance over as he types out a fast text. I only catch a part of it to see it's an apology.

"If I'm interrupting your plans—"

"Fucking shameless," he scolds, clicking his phone closed before pocketing it.

"Sorry, I'm sitting right here. I *am* press."

"How could I forget?" He mutters dryly.

Feeling stung, I slide back farther into the seat. Apparently, there is some grudge here because there's no way he's jealous.

"Ready for you, man," the artist says as the girl gathers her purse to exit, her eyes scouring Easton greedily when she catches sight of him. Standing, Easton smirks at her just as she pushes out of the door. A jealous heat blooms in my chest at the interaction. Still hovering above me, Easton glances down at me as the artist speaks up. "Got a chair for her back here."

Sensing my budding contempt, Easton grips my hand and pulls me to stand, locking eyes with me as if daring me to protest, and I feel every bit of the jolt it evokes. Turning, he guides me behind the counter as the artist gestures toward an empty chair beside the table.

"How's it going, G?" Easton greets.

"Good," he replies with an easy grin and the lift of his chin before the two embrace in a brief hug and exchange back claps. As they do, G's dark blue eyes focus on me.

"So, who do we have here?" A perfect white smile dazzles me as I beat Easton to the punch.

"Natalie. I was just admiring your work. It's *incredible.*"

His receptive smile reaches his eyes. "Thanks, Natalie. My friends, and friends of my friends, call me G."

"Okay, will do." I say in reply. "Nice place you have here."

"Thanks. Is that a hint of a Southern accent I detect?"

"You caught that, huh?"

He gives me an inch between tatted fingers. "Li'l bit, and it's adorable."

"Well, I'll take it," I grin at him. "I'm a proud southerner, but not to an obnoxious extent, I promise."

"Tell me, Natalie, what is a sweet Southern belle like yourself doing with *this* asshole?"

"Trust me, I'm no belle."

"She's lying," Easton mutters as we begin to talk over the other.

"She's drowning in propriety—"

"Those are called manners, Mr. Blunt and Moody."

"Pure as the driven fucking snow." Easton quips.

"What am I doing with this *asshole*?" I narrow my eyes at Easton. "Right now, I'm wondering the same thing."

Easton turns and snaps at G. "Are we doing this or what?"

Amused by our back and forth, G grins my way. "Someone's in a mood today."

"Right?" I agree, widening my eyes as Easton's nostrils flare in response, and G fails to hold in his chuckle.

"He's got a nasty temper," G reveals. "He can get downright street dog fight dirty at times."

"Does he now? Interesting," I muse as we both comically turn back to Easton, staring at him like parents expecting an explanation.

"Fuck off with that," Easton snaps. Unphased, G palms Easton's shoulder.

"Yes, darling, we're doing this. Did you get what you needed?"

"Yeah, but I want it altered now, and it's going to take a little sketching." Easton retrieves his cell and presents a picture of the sculpture we conversed at the day we met.

"Ah, so there *was* a reason we were there," I say, "and I didn't see you take that."

"Yeah? Well, did you see him take this?" G asks, thrusting the phone in my direction. Squinting to peer at the screen, I barely make out a black and white image of what looks like my silhouette. He must've snapped it while I was lost in thought, staring at the installation. Not a second later, Easton rips the phone from G's hand.

"What was it?" I ask, feigning ignorance of what I saw as Easton glares at G, who's chuckling at his discomfort. G somehow placates him with quick words I can't decipher. Shortly after, the two begin conversing about the tattoo as I take my designated seat, grappling with the fact Easton took a photo of me within an hour of us meeting. Feeling Easton's gaze dart my way, I avert mine and glance around the parlor as the flutter in my stomach intensifies.

As I contemplate the reasoning behind it, Easton and G stand at the sketch table at the station as G gets to work. In a matter of minutes, G produces a surreal-looking 3D likeness of a section of Chihuly's sculpture. Several lone stalks of the red glass resembling lightning rods make up the whole of it. The difference is one prominently hovers over the top of the others, sweeping into a full loop before it breaches a few inches above the rest and shoots jaggedly upward.

It's beautiful and…different.

G glances over at me as I study it. "This is just phase one," he explains, "he's got a lot planned for his virgin skin."

"I don't doubt it," I reply. Eyes on the sketch, it saddens me that I'll only be able to see the finished product in mixed media, and that's only if Easton decides to release. Further contact with him after I take off tomorrow isn't an option.

Eyes back on the sketch, I contemplate its meaning until I see Easton start to unbutton his shirt in my periphery. Instantly my attention shifts to his impeccable build and the memory of his heated eyes, his words, and the rest of our unspoken exchange last night. We'd come so close to crossing an uncrossable line. Panties soaked and breathless, I retreated straight to my room, tortured with *what-if* thoughts every second of the ride up the elevator and through a long soak in the tub. I woke this morning surprised but thankful sleep claimed me before my imagination got a chance to steal more much-needed rest.

Toeing the line again, I stare at his defined hard lines and feel the throb of want pulse through me as the need to flee threatens. Easton's fingers slowly release each button, revealing more of what I'm in want of as G readies his supply cart. This is the second time in as many days I've had to endure the sight of this perfect man and his sculpted body, and the ask at this point is a bit much.

Mouth watering, I eye his belt briefly, picturing my fingers releasing the heavy buckle and the clank that would follow. The mere thought of the sound has my clit pulsating with terror as this unrelenting attraction rips through me. Panicking, I spring from my seat, my question coming out louder than intended.

"Bathroom?"

G grins at me, the twinkle in his eyes and the smug twist of lips letting me know he caught me as Easton discards his shirt and lifts his eyes to mine point-blank.

Bang.

Clearly, my prayers are going unanswered today, possibly because I'm committing heavily to one of the deadliest sins. Said sin coats me in a flooding shade of fresh red, and my damned neck flushes as G speaks up.

"In the back on the right. Extra TP under the cabinet if the roll is empty, and it usually is, so sorry in advance."

"No problem, thank you."

I march toward the bathroom as I berate myself.

WhatthefuckareyoudoingNatalieButler?

"Jesus help me," I mutter behind the closed door of the bathroom, attempting to catch my breath. I realize I'm clutching my pint-sized travel purse to my chest like a human shield.

As if it would help.

My thoughts race for a solution to help me sidestep my increasing attraction for Easton Crowne as the answer boomerangs the second the question is released, hurtling back and bitch slapping me with truth.

Nothing.

Easton Crowne is a human masterpiece. He's cruelly alluring looks-wise, and he's got intelligence and depth to boot. He's also insightful and warm, despite his frank way of speaking and his broody nature. Even after all he's revealed, there still remains an air of mystery that's only drawing this moth further into the flame. A flame I didn't fully see until now, which is growing hotter by the second.

In short, Easton Crowne is the biggest threat to my well-being ever created.

"In my mind, I've already sunk inside you a thousand times."

He wants to act on it, I want him to act on it, and there's no way in hell that's a possibility.

No way.

The upside to my current battle? In less than twenty-four hours, I'll already be in the air, halfway to Austin, and he'll no longer be a danger to me. Meeting him today—especially after my confession and our near-catastrophic flirtation last night—was a mistake. We should have parted there.

Instead, I dressed up for him, and now I'm obsessing in a fucking bathroom.

Who are you?

I blame the situation. I do not bow or blush for men, nor do I cower from attraction and hide from it in bathrooms. The man's out of his damned mind comparing me to *snow*. I've roped and ridden my fair share. Not that the draw is comparable.

Simply put, it's not.

Attraction aside, I can't help the fact that I want to soak in every single second with him until I leave, even if we can't act on it. He's been one hell of a friend to me, and he's being respectful of the line I've drawn, which makes me feel safe with him—to an extent. Images of him at the piano snake their way into my psyche as I repeatedly smack my head against the back of the door while Easton's words filter through again.

"I'm also thinking you've never been properly kissed, fucked, or loved and that you caught a glimpse of something you want for yourself."

Exhaling harshly, I make my way toward the vanity sink and give my reflection a pep talk. "Less than a day, woman. Get your shit in check. Right. Now. Butlers don't back down. Seriously, he's just a man. You can scratch the itch back in Austin." I roll my eyes at my reflection, but even as I think it, and though Easton's respecting the boundaries, his withdrawal from me when we got to the parlor has me sorting through the reason for it.

I haven't said or done anything out of sorts. Nothing near as bad as what I confessed last night. Has his resentment grown? Is he masking some underlying contempt for me? Does he plan on toying with me? He's more than capable, especially knowing I'm attracted to him.

If he's planning on acting out, maybe getting even somehow, he'll probably enjoy every second of watching me squirm. He's probably enjoying the panic he no doubt saw back there. Determined to keep some of my self-respect, I flush the toilet to complete my ruse, wash my hands, and toss my shoulders back. It's when I grip the bathroom handle of the door that realization dawns about the company we're currently keeping.

My friends call me G.

Gi.

As in Benji First.

As in *Ben*—the son of the lead singer of the Dead Sergeants—and *Lexi*—Stella's lifelong best friend and confidante's—*lovechild.*

Oh fuck! Oh fuck! Oh fuck!

Racing from the bathroom back into the parlor to beg Easton not to disclose a single detail about me or my reasons for being here, I'm stopped short by the sight of Easton laying on the table, the purple outline of the sketch running from his hip bone to the top of his ribs. Buzzing gun in hand, Benji lifts his head when he spots me. "So, Easton tells me you're from Texas, and your dad used to date my tía Stella."

Fuck.

EIGHTEEN

Lost in You
Phillip LaRue

Natalie

Slumping back into my seat next to the table, Benji frowns as he reads my dread-filled expression. "I'm sensing you didn't want me to know that?"

Technically, Stella's not his aunt by blood, but I have zero doubt that she has been present in his life in a way blood isn't at all relevant.

Easton's eyes catch mine before I flit them away, jaw tightening.

"If it helps," Benji says, "I can tick off at least a dozen things we haven't made our parents privy to."

Easton remains silent as I begin to fume, face burning in response, unsure of how much has already been revealed. All it took was a trip to the bathroom for him to break my confidence. Benji continues, a smile growing on his face as he pauses his gun. "So, you blackmailed my boy into a story to get dirt, huh?"

"Jesus, really, G?" Easton snaps as Benji's eyes challenge me for an answer.

"I…I," I falter as I try to decide whether to flee or attempt damage control.

"It's okay," Benji assures, placing two black latex-covered fingers across the outline before running the needle along the pattern on Easton's side. I can't even look at him for fear I'll take Benji's gun and start working on a different sort of art. "It's cool, Natalie. East explained it, and believe it or not, I get it. My own parents are a shitshow."

"Well, apparently, it was poorly explained because mine aren't," I snap, standing and glaring down at Easton. He stares back at me, remorse shining in his eyes. "Is this fucking funny to you?" I shake my head, not believing that he sold me out so easily. "I guess I deserve it," I shoulder my purse, "but I assure you, your secrets are still *safe with me*. Have a nice fucking life."

"Fuck, man, sorry," Benji whispers as I stomp toward the door.

"Natalie, stop," Easton calls as I push out of the parlor and glance around, having no idea where I am or which direction to go. Choosing right, I lift my phone and start to order a car when it's ripped from my hands. Keeping my eyes down, I refuse to look at Easton as I go to retrieve it from his hand, his bare, heaving chest in my line of sight as he easily holds it out of reach. "Hey, hey, it's not like that."

"It's exactly like that," I snap. "You told him everything!"

"I'm sorry, okay, he's a dumpster fire at subtlety."

"Well, now it's obvious where you get it." I'm so pissed, I still can't look at him, but I hear the shake in my voice. "If you're intent on humiliating me as payback, you've done an amazing job already, and maybe I do deserve it, but game over, okay? This can't get back to my dad, Easton, or your mom, not ever."

"That type of shit is not in my makeup," he snaps. "I'm not capable of manipulating a situation that way."

"You mean not like I have? Do you even realize you just insulted me, *again*?"

"That's your guilt twisting the words into something other than I intended." He grips my shoulders. "Look at me."

I flick up my gaze as Easton stares down at me in earnest, a glint of the panic I felt last night reflecting back at me.

"Benji is as real as they come, and he gets shit like this—people like us—who live a little emotionally further above the surface than most."

"That's not me."

"No? Maybe it wasn't, but it seems to be now."

I exhale as he squeezes my shoulders in prompt.

"He's a brother to me in every sense but blood. I trust him with my *life*, just like I'm trusting you, fucking blindly, I might add. All I'm asking you for is the same." He exhales harshly as I trail the goosebumps erupting across his exposed skin. Gripping the sleeve of his jacket, I go to return it, and he stops me, his voice sharp. "Don't."

"It's freezing."

"I don't give a fuck about the jacket," he snaps. I look up at him and see the same soft expression he's given me glimpses of in our time together. "I'm the one you chose," he rasps out softly. "Like it or not, for some reason, I'm the one you *chose* to come to, to work this out with. Benji's a little older than me, not by much, but he might have some insight that I don't. That's why I told him. I'm sorry I didn't give you the heads-up."

"Fine. I'll try, but do you mind telling me why you're so moody today?"

"Do we need to hash everything out right now while I'm standing half-dressed in the fucking street?"

"No...sorry," I say, screwing up my lips. "It just seems like you're out to hurt me today."

"Then you aren't reading the situation correctly. Come on," he says, his jade eyes imploring. When I remain where I am, posture tense with indecision, he cups my cheek with a gentle palm, bending so we're eye level. "This time, I'm the asshole for blindsiding you. I'm owning it."

"It's not just that, but Easton," I damn near close my eyes at the feel of his thumb whispering along my cheek, "maybe I should just go. I mean, I'm leaving tomorrow anyway."

"You don't want to go," he fires back with conviction, gripping my hand and jingling it within his. "And I don't want you to go, either."

His admission stuns me briefly as he looks down at me the way he did last night when we nearly combusted outside the hotel. Judgment clouding and damned near seduced, I don't argue as he turns abruptly and leads me back to the shop. We glance at each other as he opens the door, the slight lift of his lips fueling my steps inside.

"Cool," Benji says, seeming unfazed by my outburst. Easton releases my hand and takes his place back on the table, his watchful eyes pinned on me as I sink back into the seat.

"You look like you could use a drink," Benji says, readying his gun. "Pour yourself a beer. There's wine in the cooler, too."

"You're right. You two want one?"

Benji shakes his head. "He can't drink as he's getting inked, and I won't while I'm inking him. The bar is more for those waiting. We'll take waters."

"Got it," I say, deciding it's not the worst idea. Tipping the glass into the nozzle, I pour myself a Smoked Porter overhearing a little of their heated exchange, grinning at the "stupid motherfucker," curse coming from Easton as the music changes. Beer in hand, I grab two bottles of water from the fridge before walking back over and passing them out. Benji thanks me as I place his on the counter of the station next to where he works, and hand Easton his. His eyes probe me as if to ask, 'we okay?' and I nod easily. His shoulders visibly relax, and the sight of it warms me further. We hold our connection as I resume my seat and tip my beer. Gun buzzing in short bursts, Benji speaks up after grabbing more ink.

"The reason I admitted my parents' relationship is a shitshow," Benji says without looking up, intent on his task, "is because if their history is screwing with your head, I can relate." Stopping his gun, he scoffs and shakes his head before pressing the needles back into Easton's skin. "Their relationship has been a thirty-year saga."

"How so?"

He looks at me pointedly.

"Anything you say is off the record. You have my word."

He weighs my promise, and I speak up again.

"I have a paper to inherit, and I'm not gambling it or my integrity away for *any* story, no matter how in demand it is."

Benji dips his chin. "It's not like it's a secret anyway. They've been on and off my whole life. To this day, they live separately but are crazy, and I mean fucking craaazzzyyy in love, which, for them, has never really been a good thing."

"If they're so in love…why aren't they together? Is it because of her infidelity?"

"Yeah, after Mom purposefully sabotaged their relationship because of her insecurity, Dad was never able to forgive her, but neither have ever really let each other go."

"So, they haven't been together since?"

"Yeah, they have, but not long term and never exclusively. I guess that's Dad's fucked up way of punishing her over the years, and Mom's so stubborn that she's never fully admitted to him *that* punishment has worked all too well. Dad went as far as to get engaged, even though he was still clearly in love with her. This is also the reason neither have ever married. I would love to say I came out of their drama unscathed, but it's not the case. In fact, it's no secret to those who know me well that I would rather shoot off my cock than get serious with anyone. That's what I was trying to convey—"

"Fucking horribly," Easton scolds over the buzzing gun and music.

"Fucking horribly," Benji concedes, tossing an apologetic expression my way. "So, all due respect to tía Stella and both of *your* relationship examples," he looks between Easton and me, "I have other ideas on how to live without the weight of commitment. And I can guarantee I'm going to be the groomsman ready with the getaway car."

Drawing on my beer, I nod.

"So, tell me what really brought you here, Natalie Butler," Benji demands.

The sound of my last name has me tipping my beer back further, hoping it will loosen me up enough to speak as candidly. I'm not at all at ease with Benji the way I am with Easton, and it's becoming more evident by the second.

"She likes to be the one to ask questions," Easton interjects. Translation—*it's hard for her*.

He's dead on. I'm not all that much a 'share my feels' type of girl. At least I wasn't until Easton challenged what I thought was a truth about me.

When I've been hurt in the past, I usually use it as fuel to better myself somehow. Incorporating the ache in a new workout routine or using it to push myself harder in my studies or work. Using my pain to better myself has always been my method to come out stronger. Only when I'm truly at my lowest do I confide my hurts to Holly or my mom. When I do that, that's when they know I'm down for the count—at least temporarily.

From what I've gathered, these two seem completely comfortable sharing things that seem highly personal. Easton managed to draw my truths from me like no one ever has, peeling me back easily, layer by layer, in just a few days.

"I think I'm going to need another beer first," I admit. "I don't have that swinging dick honesty you two seemed to have pegged."

Easton and Benji glance over at me with raised brows.

"Or maybe it's already working, damn," I grin, holding up my pint. "What is in dark beer?"

Benji chuckles. "It's the man's version of red wine. Women don't talk about the difference in the buzz between a chardonnay or merlot, but it's legit. Two glasses of red will get your blood pumping like no other and can make a hard day a little more bearable."

"In that case," I down the rest of the beer, and they both chuckle. I strain to see Easton's accompanying smile and miss it because of the way he's laying. I stand to get another beer. "Sure you don't mind, Benji?"

"Not at all. It's what it's there for."

Benji projects his voice as I draw another beer. "So, I'm guessing you figured out who I was before you came out of the bathroom?"

"Yeah," I say, walking back toward my chair, trying really hard not to notice the bulge of Easton's bicep as his hand cradles his head.

"I guess I'm just surprised the place isn't crowded with groupies, but I guess that's partly a result of your parents keeping you all out of the spotlight?"

Benji nods. "Our whole lives. When the Sergeants stopped releasing and then touring, the paparazzi started to lose interest in all of us, making it easy for me to open up shop. To most who walk in here, I'm just the hot-as-fuck blond who inks excellent tatts."

Easton rolls his eyes, and I grin.

"Well, to credit your parents, they did their job. The only reason I pieced it together is because I crammed in as much research as possible before I got here and watched the movie."

The bitter edge in my tone rings clear as they both glance my way.

"The movie was more about the evolution of the band and Stella's career," Benji explains simply.

"Yeah," I agree curtly, and Easton doesn't miss it, doing the prodding voodoo thing.

"Hollywood," Benji says, dipping for more ink. "Only they could make my parents' story seem romantic when it's anything but."

"But the whole of their start and their relationship took place before you were born, right?"

"True," he agrees, seemingly unconvinced. "Which places tía and your dad's relationship before the movie, too, right?"

I shake my head.

Understanding flits over his features. "Ah, so *that's* why you're curious."

"It's a little more complicated than that," I admit. "So, you've never heard about my father or his role in Stella's life?"

He squints as if in thought and shakes his head. "Sorry, can't say that I have."

"It's okay." I wave the apology away. "I thought as much. It just threw me for a few days, that's all."

Easton's expression calls bullshit as I harden my gaze on him. "I guess it's just the journalist in me. I'm not really a bits-and-pieces type of girl."

"But you won't ask your dad?"

"No, I don't want to bring up anything from his past that might hurt him."

"But it's hurting you," Benji fires back point-blank.

"It's my own fault for prying. But it's more the mystery of what happened that is bothering me. It's like watching a movie halfway. Even though you know the end, you still want to see how they all got there. I blame a lot of it on the journalist in me."

"I get it. I do." Benji stops his gun and cracks his neck. "All right, you're doing good, but let's take a little break, man."

Easton shakes his head. "I'm good."

Benji snaps off his gloves and trashes them. "Well, I need a piss and a smoke, so sit tight."

Easton lifts to sit as Benji looks between us. "You two hungry?"

"We'll probably grab something after this," Easton states, though it's news to me. I watch as Benji makes a beeline for the back door of the shop, pulling cigarettes out as he goes. The door closes as I stare into the foamy head of my beer feeling Easton's watchful gaze on my profile, knowing what's coming.

"Downplaying your need for answers won't help you get them."

"He doesn't know anything anyway. I told you I was going to drop it, and I will as soon as my plane wheels go up tomorrow. I was never here," I say. "I have to let it go for my own sanity."

"If you say so," Easton mutters, clearly disbelieving.

"Has *your* mother ever mentioned my dad?"

"I thought about it last night. Growing up, the stories I paid attention to, no, but I wouldn't expect her to talk about him if they were as serious as you say they were—"

"They were *engaged*, Easton," I clarify for both our sakes, beating it into my psyche as I try to keep my gaze averted from the living, breathing temptation feet away from me. "It doesn't get much more serious than that."

Easton nods as he shifts on the table, clasping his hands between his knees.

"So, yeah, I don't think Mom would mention him much. If she has, it's probably been in the context of her old editor."

I nod. "You could have invited Benji to dinner," I attempt to change the subject.

"I didn't want to," he admits readily, and I lift my gaze to his.

"What pissed you off about the movie?"

"You really don't miss anything, do you?" I sip my beer.

"You're really not that great at hiding what irks you. What is it about the movie that bothers you?"

"From what I read in their emails, he helped shape her into the writer she became," I shake my head. "She didn't even acknowledge him in the movie. Or maybe I'm wrong. Maybe it was intentional because she didn't want to hurt him. I wonder if she reached out or just decided to leave him out altogether." I brave a look at him. "Are you even remotely curious about this?"

"I'm confident in what my parents have and know they're in a good, solid place, but yeah, I'm growing more curious because it struck you hard enough to get you here."

"I don't want to project what I'm feeling on you."

"That's a needless worry. I don't let others' perceptions change my mind about *anything* unless I agree with it."

"It's that simple for you, huh?"

Silence. That's my cue to look at him. Right now, I can't because the beer is not only loosening my tongue, it's making me more aware of his effect on me.

"Look at me, Natalie."

Jesus, the way he rasps out my name. It can't sound so good, but it does.

"Natalie," he repeats, "look at me."

I don't. "It's not just that he helped shape her as a writer...they seemed solid, and I think—"

"What?"

"I think Reid...I think your dad—"

"Broke them up?"

"Maybe he had something to do with it. To be fair though, it's pretty clear from the emails that your mom made a choice because she and my dad broke up months before she moved to Seattle and stumbled upon your dad at that house. I'm just unsure of what broke them up in the first place. After reading in their own words how much they loved each other, it was hard to imagine that anything or anyone could come between them."

The back door of the parlor slams shut just before Benji closes the bathroom door behind him.

"Keep talking," Easton prompts.

"The last email between them was an apology from your mom about the headlines regarding your parents' engagement," I relay, blinking up at him. "As I was reading, it was like experiencing the heartbreak myself...after they broke up, it hurt like hell. It was so strange. It was like, as my dad's heart was breaking, mine was too. How can two people who claimed to love each other so much just walk away from each other?"

"Natalie. The only way to know is to *ask him*."

"I can't. Trust me, I wanted to at first, but I can't help feeling like he hid this because it's too painful for him to talk about and he buried it so he wouldn't have to."

"But your parents' marriage—"

"A rough month here and there, but...good," I grip my beer and sigh, "this is ridiculous." I toss the rest of it back as Easton eyes the glass in my hand, knowing I'm purposefully numbing. "It's a stupid, unhealthy fixation on a past that doesn't even belong to me. I need to shake it off and let it go—"

"But if you don't..."

"I have to. My entire future—every dream I have envisioned for myself, is based around my relationship with my father, and that's *by my choice*. He didn't raise me to follow in his footsteps. My love for storytelling came naturally, and my admiration for him is what led me on this path in the first place. Now that I'm a year or two away from inheriting his legacy, losing his trust would be detrimental—not only to the future I have waiting but, most importantly, to our relationship. I want that paper, Easton, and I want my father to trust me with it. It's my career dream."

Easton hums his understanding, and Benji joins us as we stare off, reading the room. "You guys need another minute?"

"Yes," Easton says.

As I answer with a firm "No."

I widen my stare at Easton in a plea to stop as Benji snaps on new gloves before resuming the needling along Easton's side. As Benji resumes working on him, I search his face for any sign of discomfort. "Does it hurt?"

"Not really, no. It's like being pinched."

"Wait until I get to your ribs, motherfucker," Benji grins, keeping his eyes on his task.

Even as he taunts him, brotherly love is stamped in both their expressions. Loving the look of it, I soak it in until dark jade eyes flit to mine with a sadness of reality seeping in. I won't ever see Easton again after tomorrow. My heart grows heavy at the thought of it. Somehow, in the short time I've known him, I've grown attached to our budding friendship and easy connection, and it's becoming painstakingly evident.

It seems reciprocal—*has to be*, because he stopped me from leaving. He forgave me for a deception he shouldn't have. He could have let me go last night, but he didn't. Instead, he's been adamant I stay with him—and in his jacket. Not only that, it seemed to pain him when I tried to take it off earlier. The woman in me shamelessly rejoices in that slight show of possession on his part. But that's what I feel now as I stare at him, possessed by this inescapable attraction and the need to get closer to him in every imaginable way.

But this isn't a game, and I no longer have a lack of sufficient sleep to blame for my behavior. I showed up a shell of myself, questioning everything, and he's been nothing but a beautiful sanctuary—a comfort to me. A comfort I'm becoming dangerously needy for. Yesterday, we bared our souls to one another. More than that, we revealed our hopes for our futures while exposing our biggest fears.

Easton pinpointed the sum of mine to me last night, one of which opposes his own. Though I don't exactly want to become a headline, I want to live a headline-worthy life. My other fear coincides with my first—I'm afraid I'll settle for less down the line, in life, in my career, and more importantly, in love. Gazing back at him, I find myself grateful for his presence in my life—even if temporary—while mourning the fact I don't get to know him after today.

"Neither of you has said a word in five minutes," Benji speaks up, embarrassing us both. Easton and I have been staring at each other the entire time, even knowing that—we don't break our gaze. The ache churning in my chest intensifies as I imagine he's feeling what I am, what his eyes are conveying.

It's insanity. The last few days have been a whirlwind of confusion and revelation. I couldn't imagine a better human soul to be with, and I find myself grateful. His expression softens as I pray that he can read as much from mine.

Not long after, the buzzing of the gun stops. Benji begins aftercare and instructions, wiping the tattoo down before covering it with salve. Easton inspects it in the mirror, his flawless olive skin only enhanced by the tattoo. Appreciation for it runs clear in Easton's features as Benji wraps his muscular torso in plastic.

"Fucking sick choice, man," Benji prompts as I study the finished project, my fingers itching to trace and soothe the lines of the angry, red skin. Easton turns back to me.

"It's beautiful...and wicked."

"I agree," Easton says, buttoning his shirt and turning to Benji. "Thanks, man." Easton plucks his wallet out, and Benji holds up a hand, his eyes filled with a hard edge.

"Don't fucking insult me."

"I'm going to get you paid one way or another."

"Someday, I'll call in a favor," Benji assures him.

"Bet," Easton says as they clap each other's backs.

Benji grins at me over Easton's shoulder as they separate. "How about you, Texas Belle? Up for a little ink tonight?"

Smiling, I shake my head. "Not for me."

"You sure? It's on the house," Benji offers as Easton glances over to me, brows raised.

"Some other time."

Benji chuckles. "You mean the next time you have a meltdown and fly to Seattle on a whim?"

I can't help my return smile, the beer buzz prominent as I reply. "Exactly."

"Bet," Benji grins as the parlor door opens. A good-looking and beautifully inked man—who looks to be in his late twenties—saunters in, his eyes zeroed on Benji before he glances between the three of us.

"You need me to come back?"

"You're good. We're just finishing up," Benji replies to the new arrival while giving him a look that's anything but friendly. It's more a look that says he's about to devour him.

Oh.

Oh.

"We were just leaving," Easton assures him as a searing sexual tension fills the room, and my blood starts to heat from the loaded looks being exchanged.

"I'll text you tomorrow," Easton says to Benji as he turns to me, a rapid storm brewing in his dark ocean eyes.

"Nice meeting you, Tex, and don't worry, I've got your back."

"Same," I say with a smile. "Promise."

I stand, discarding my empty pint glass as Easton grips my hand and guides me toward the door while Benji walks us out.

"Stay safe, love you, bro," Benji adds, clicking off the parlor lights and locking the door just after we both step out of the shop, the only light coming from a nearby streetlamp.

Sliding into Easton's truck, unable to help myself, I peer into the parlor as two shadows collide in a heated kiss just behind the reception desk. I manage to make out just enough so that my eyes bulge before I turn to Easton, whose gaze is trained on me. I let out a nervous laugh and a "Wow," my face rapidly heating. "I've never seen two men kiss. I mean, I have, but not like *that*."

"Yeah?" One side of Easton's mouth lifts. "And what do you think?"

"Honestly, it's hot as hell."

"Into voyeurism?"

"I just may be if it's *that hot*. Others though, not my own."

"Poor bastard," Easton glances up briefly as he turns the engine over.

"Is Benji really that bad?"

He sighs as he puts the truck into gear. "He warns every single one of them, but they fall anyway. He was being one hundred with you when he admitted he has no plans of falling for anyone. But what he *omitted* is that he already fell, a long time ago."

"Who is he in love with?"

"A girl we grew up with."

"Girl?"

"Yeah. He has no preference other than what he's attracted to. He's got nearly two years on me, so I've laid witness to his bed being a revolving door since he was fifteen. Shit," he glances over at me. "He would fucking kill me if he knew I told you that."

"You'll learn in time that his secrets are safe. I can only promise you in the here and now, they are."

Nodding, Easton pulls out as I let my inner perve go a little wild, imagining what's happening back in the parlor.

"And you?"

"Me what?" He draws out with a knowing smirk. "You can't even say it."

"Do you like a little cock on occasion?" He brakes in the midst of pulling out and floats a dead stare my way. I can't help my dark beer-induced giggle. "I'll take that as a *no*."

"I have a very specific preference," he admits readily. "I'm not hating on him in the least, just the way he goes about it. He's unapologetically reckless."

I lean back in my seat, rolling my window partially in unison with Easton. As he presses the gas, I unabashedly drink him in. "Easton?" I don't wait for his reply as I grip the hand he has resting on the seat and squeeze. "Thank you for today."

His eyes flit to mine. "It's not over yet."

NINETEEN

Dive Deep (Hushed)
Andrew Belle

Easton

Natalie gazes up at the towering Space Needle as I park, no expected sarcastic quip or trace of amusement in her expression, despite being lured to the most well-known Seattle tourist destination.

Instead, she turns and peers back at me with indigo-colored trust, which only further widens the crack in my chest as she pries her way in deeper.

She's sobered considerably since dinner, which consisted of tacos. Our conversation at the table drew out my frustration, and the lingering stares added up as she skillfully skirted around our attraction. Without prompt, she recalled what it was like growing up in Texas, shared stories about her favorite horse, Percy, and gave some background on her closest friends, Holly and Damon.

In return, I revealed more of what life was like touring in the early years—getting educated by a tutor before clutching Mom's hand side stage, and watching the Dead Sergeants' reign before I was tucked in by both my parents. Parents who opted on most nights to nurture me rather than pass me off to my nanny to party.

Even though they did at times.

In some ways, we couldn't be more different. Yet, I feel myself as drawn to her as I have been since she bulldozed her way into my space days ago. Somehow, at present, it seems a lot longer than that.

She's not so much a mystery to me anymore as she is a fixation becoming fucking impossible to ignore. The longer we linger, the physical curiosity becomes a beating, breathing presence between us.

Every part of me wants to grip her in my hands, dominate her with a kiss, unwrap her, taste her, and fuck her so thoroughly that words become unnecessary. But, I know she can feel it and stated as much last night.

Wordlessly, I round the truck and take her hand in mine, which she gives freely, loving the feel of the small fit of hers in my own. We lace our fingers together, the energy between us buzzing as we silently walk toward the entrance. Within minutes, despite her protest, I'm pushing my wallet back into my jeans, collecting our tickets as she scans the gift shop for onlookers while keeping her hand firmly in mine.

She's leaving tomorrow.

It's that fact alone that has my pulse amping up, while the urge I've been suppressing for the last few days threatens to overtake me. I do my best to bat the idea away because of her hesitance and plea last night.

If she doesn't want to give in to this attraction, I'm sure as hell not going to force her. I've never had to coerce a woman into my bed, and I'm damn sure not going to start now. Ironically, the physical isn't the most significant part of my draw to her. This…feels different, and it's different because I've allowed her to get close to me. I've shared enough truths and insight about myself that she could burn me with little effort if she so desires. Power I've never granted to any woman, not even when I considered myself smitten with women I've dated in the past.

We walk to the elevator and wait for the next car to the top of the Needle as I pull out my cellphone and flip through the music. Pausing on a song, I mentally hear it start to play, the melody, the lyrics, every aspect of it as I observe her.

When her eyes dart my way, I decide to swing the bat in the opposite direction, intent on some sort of satisfaction for what we're denying ourselves before I let her go. Digging my earbuds out of my pocket, she grins when she sees me produce them.

"Can't go long at all, can you?" she taunts in a whisper, her attention fixed on my lips, which hover close to hers. "You truly are an addict."

"It's my only vice," I admit, pushing back her silky curls and securing the wireless buds into her ears. "Don't you write to music?"

"No, not really. I mean, it's not a habit I have."

"You should. It enhances *everything*."

She lifts a skeptical brow. "I love a good song as much as the next gal, but *everything*?"

"Everything," I insist. If I hadn't seen her tear-stained cheeks after I played for her yesterday—a reaction I burned into memory—I'd believe she was more left-brain oriented than she's letting on. Though it's true that a certain amount of the population isn't as affected by music as others, it's most definitely not the case for her. She's just not aware of how necessary it is for her as she should be. "It could be as much of a tool for you as your keyboard. It has the power to draw everything out of you that you can't fully grasp on your own. For you, it's fuel, trust me," I tell her.

"Well, when you put it like that, I will."

She's looking up at me with the same expression she has had for the past twenty-four hours—*touch me*. I inhale a breath of patience, fighting once again to keep from capturing her perfect lips and owning them as the seconds continue to tick toward goodbye. She's determined to snuff us out before we can become another mistake and leave our time together as nothing but a memory when she boards that plane. While I understand it because of how she's explained it, and how it's clearly affecting her, I can't help but want to make her departure as hard for her as she's continually making it for me.

Neither of us notice the arrival of the elevator, just as lost in each other as we have been for endless minutes today until the attendant speaks up, holding the door to usher the few of us now gathered inside.

As instructed, we all do an about-face and turn in the direction of the glass wall at the back of the car. As the attendant begins spouting off facts about the top floor and the car starts to move, I press play on "Dive Deep (Hushed)" by Andrew Belle. Natalie's reaction is instantaneous as the music begins to play. I feel the shift in her, the vibration and exhilaration rushing to the surface as the Seattle skyline appears while we gradually ascend. Unknowingly, Natalie tightens her hold on my hand, and I turn the music up, drowning out the attendant and the rest of the world around us to emphasize my point.

As we continue to rise, I can feel myself falling further into infatuation with her. In a matter of days, she's managed to captivate and draw confessions from me that I never saw myself making to anyone, let alone a practical stranger.

When the door opens, I guide her out and onto the slowly revolving floor, away from probing eyes as the soft beat and lyrics work their way into her. Her chest begins to rise and fall as her breathing picks up. A minute later, we're collectively standing in front of the wall of glass which overlooks the brightly lit cityscape. Opting out of the view, I study her and see her expression soften when the lyrics start to resonate with her. Ignoring the view along with me, she turns to face me, her eyes boring into mine as she falls under the spell, listening intently. Lips parting, she keeps her gaze locked with mine as my heart thrashes in my chest.

Fuck.

I've never felt so exposed, so raw with another human being in my entire fucking life. She's leaving in *hours* with absolutely no intention of looking back, and I've never been so unsatisfied.

Adding to her confusion with my own won't help her, but it's not confusion I'm feeling when I stare back at her right now. Everything she's drawing from me feels imprisoned. If I'm unable to act on any of it, I at least want to relay to her what she's making me feel, and it's through borrowed words I'm doing it, which keeps us both relatively safe. That is until she makes safe impossible when she whispers my name, shattering my patience as I will time to slow—to fucking stop, altogether.

Unable to keep from touching her a second longer, I glance around to make sure we're alone for the moment, then glide my knuckles appreciatively down her cheek. In the next breath, I'm exhaling a groan into her parted lips as she grips the back of my neck, clutching my hair, clutching *me* to bring me closer.

Because we're kissing.

Body tensing with the realization, I grip her face and take control. I lose that control just as quickly as I gain it when she presses against me, seeming starved as we furiously explore each other's mouths. Chest detonating at the feel of her lush, hungry mouth, I grip her chin and thrust my tongue against hers, invading, consuming, taking every second we're allowed as she kisses me back without an ounce of restraint.

The craving is instant, the hunger unmanageable.

Tilting her head, I feed. She opens further, our mouths fusing naturally. The crack in my chest becomes a gaping wound as I free-fall into what I'm feeling, pouring myself into her, which ignites a crazed need to possess her.

Seconds away from unleashing, but hyperaware we aren't alone, I crack my eyes as an older couple comes into view at the edge of my periphery. Her moan vibrates in unison with mine as I allow myself a second longer, her hands fisting my hair as she sucks my tongue. My cock twitches in response, forcing me to break our kiss. Pressing my forehead to hers, she slowly opens her eyes, whispering my name with hunger while gazing up at me in confusion as to why I stopped our kiss. I lift my chin toward the couple as she pulls her hands away, eyes dimming considerably while she walks closer to the glass, crossing her arms.

Furious with the knowledge that I got a taste of something I know I'll be craving for the foreseeable future, I turn and stalk toward the small bar coming into view on the revolving floor and order us two beers. Uncomfortably hard and pissed about the fact that taste was my first and last, I glance back to see Natalie blankly staring into the skyline.

Beers in hand, I approach to see her eyes trained on my reflection and notice she's watching *me* intently. Keeping the connection, I walk back to stand next to her, offering the beer to her reflection. She takes it, thanking the man in the glass softly.

"This, here," she says, nodding toward our clear outlines. "This is where we can..." She doesn't finish. She doesn't have to. I gaze back at her in the glass as we both lift our beers to drink, remaining in the only place we're allowed to be more than figments of our imagination. At least in her mind.

I've been wrapped up in her mystery since she went apeshit on me in the parking lot of the bar on day one. Something about this woman is driving me to the brink of insanity, and I've loved every minute of it. I can't pinpoint exactly when it happened, but all that matters to me right now is how strong this pull is; though foreign, it feels fucking amazing.

If I could bottle or needle it, I would inject myself regularly, even as its danger presents itself, and despite her warning, it's lethal.

I want more.

I want her.

Even if I have some idea of how fucked up the situation could get and know this can't go further than tomorrow, I can't bring myself to stop imagining something with her on this side of the glass. In this reality. Feeling bitten and battling the venom of her kiss, I only grow more aggravated as the threat of the clock eats away at me.

Kissing her was heaven, but fucking her before she flees from her self-confessed biggest mistake would be a hell I don't want to sign up for.

I don't even have to know what it's like getting that level of personal with her to understand it would draw me further under and maybe alter me more than her sudden presence in my life is starting to. This is no longer just about what *she's* missing. She's starting to make me believe *I'm* missing something vital too.

Knowing we ended with that kiss, I pull out my cellphone and kill the rock now blazing through her speakers and turn her to face me, forcing her to deal with the reality on *this side* of the glass, back into the universe we exist in.

Just before we step off the revolving platform, I pull out my cell, open my camera, and focus on our shoes which fit perfectly inside opposing edges of the frame, an inch of the sidewalk far below between our feet, before pressing the shutter. Satisfied with the snap, I adjust the exposure a little before sending it to her via text.

When her phone rattles in her pocket, she pulls it out and opens it, a sad smile lifting her swollen lips. Gently, I push her hair back and retrieve both earbuds before sticking them into their case and tucking them away in her jacket pocket. Her eyes dim as I down the rest of my beer, hoping it will douse some of the racing in my veins.

"I'm so glad I met you, Easton," she relays softly.

I can't say the same now, so I guide her off the platform. "Come on, I'll take you home."

On the way down, I don't hold her hand and refuse to so much as brush against her as we walk soundlessly to my truck.

When I turn the engine over, she murmurs my name and I ignore it, knowing whatever words she's devised will come out as some sort of effort to placate me, which is bullshit because she's battling the same war. The difference is, she's winning hers.

"I get it," I say gruffly, unsure if I do, my anger boiling over at this fucking predicament. I've never been so hard for a woman in my life, and I've been cut off before even getting a chance to explore all aspects of the attraction. Resigned to let it go, I remained silent the entire ride back to her hotel.

When I pull up through the circular pass-through, I glance over, granting myself one last look at her. I allow my eyes to linger just long enough to see the regret in her features before I tear them away to focus on the flames burning in the large fireplace on the other side of my window. "What time does your plane leave?"

"Four tomorrow afternoon."

"Will you text me and let me know you got home okay?"

"No," she answers apologetically. "I'm sorry, but I can't."

Without looking her way, I know she's staring out of her own window.

"I don't regret coming," she says softly, "but something tells me I will." She turns to me, and I keep my eyes averted as I white-knuckle my wheel.

"Don't fucking thank me," I warn with the firm shake of my head. "Don't."

She doesn't because she knows it would be insulting. We got way too personal for any sort of bullshit or formal goodbye. We got way too close too soon to be anything but fucking miserable right now, and that's all I feel.

Words are futile at this point, so I don't bother with them. Touching her isn't an option either, so I remain caged.

I know what this is and what it isn't, and there's not a lot on the *isn't* side. If I say another word, I won't be able to give her anything but my truth, which will only make shit worse. Thankfully, she frees me of the burden.

"You deserve every amazing thing coming your way, Easton Crowne, and when it happens for you, I'll get to kick back and say I knew him when." Her hesitance is palpable as she pushes open the door. "Take care of yourself. I-I'll…bye."

The burn in my chest intensifies as she slams the door closed. I immediately hit the gas, refusing myself the chance to stop her.

No matter how we parted or what words were spoken, it was going to sting like a bitch. What I didn't expect was the full-fledged, continuous punch in the gut the whole ride home.

TWENTY

No One is to Blame
Howard Jones

Easton

I drive for miles avoiding home as the last three days repeat on a loop. Music blaring, melodies filter in and out of me, not a single one of them soothing as I continue to play track after track, unable to pinpoint a song that encapsulates the mix of shit I'm mentally sorting through.

Another first that infuriates me.

I reason with myself that she's just some woman who's lost her way and needed a weekend to get her head straight, but the memory of the way her smile *felt* shoots that down. I've already memorized her expressions, the size of her hands, the lilt in her voice, and now, the feel of her lips.

Every rational explanation I feed myself as to why she's had such an effect on me continues to be shot down as another memory surfaces. Especially the one where she moaned my name.

Knowing I've already lost the battle, I pull up to my childhood home drowning in defeat and sit in the driveway, wanting to be anywhere but here. Tempted to be the late-night knock on her hotel door, the mistake that fucks her until the sun lights the horizon, I regrip the wheel.

When the front door opens, no doubt owing to the repeat of the loud-as-fuck motor in my dad's old classic, he comes into view as I curse my fucking fate and the night in equal measure.

I want to be pissed off and alone, not parented, and as long as I allow this dynamic, things will remain the same. Dad stands outside the truck I commandeered from him on my last birthday as I sigh and exit.

"Something happen?" He asks.

"No."

"You been drinking?"

My father is militant about drinking and driving because of an accident he had decades ago in my truck. He hates the fact that I drive the ancient relic, but I've used it more with Natalie than I have in the last year, opting for it instead of utilizing Joel so we could have the time alone.

"I had one beer at the Needle," I sigh out in reply. "*One.* Can I brush my teeth and go to bed now, *Daddy*?"

"Fuck," he grins sheepishly. "Point taken. Sorry."

"Yeah, well, don't take this the wrong way, but I'm moving the fuck out as soon as I find a place. It's way past time, Dad. You two can't protect me forever."

He blows out a breath and nods. "Your mom's going to lose her shit, but I get it."

"Thanks. I won't let her know until I'm halfway packed. Deal?"

"Yeah."

We start the walk to the front door, and he mulls over my mood.

"Is this about the release?"

"No."

"Are you really going to leave me wondering?"

"This time, yeah, I am."

"All right," he says as we take the stairs to the front door. Hand on the knob, he turns to me. "Even when you move out, you know I'll always—"

"I know, Dad," I clip out in a biting tone that he doesn't deserve.

He glances over at me, reading the tension in my posture. "Come on, you aren't sleeping anytime soon." He turns abruptly away from the door, down the staircase, walks around the house, and I follow him down the cobblestone path. What he's offering me comes a shitty second to what I would rather be doing right now.

At this point, I'd settle for watching her watch the world around us or watching her watch me.

Dad unlocks the detached studio with the pushbutton code and turns on the lights before we both step in. Every inch of his dream studio is state-of-the-art, a musician's multimillion-dollar dream. Within minutes of entering, Dad and I keep a steady beat on our drum kits along with the accompanying guitar and bass. It's a ritual we started when I was old enough to start playing and remains an impromptu appointment we keep every time I get restless, or my anger starts to get the best of me.

Frustrated silence is a state I inherited from him, and so he's always known just how to handle me when I get this way. Taking my aggression out on the skins of my drums, I build up a sweat, which glides down my back as unrest continues to surge through me, no matter how hard I play.

Nothing is fucking working tonight.

Fighting the urge to get back into my truck, I glance over at Dad as questions begin to flit through my mind. Did my mother really love another man to the point she almost married him? Does Dad even know how close he was to losing her? Or is he the reason things went the other way?

Did he fight another man for her? The man in question being the father of the woman I'm currently fixating on.

Even if I have no issue posing these questions to Dad, he wouldn't keep them to himself. Not something this serious in nature, or maybe he would. God knows Dad and I have purposefully told our fair share of white lies to keep Mom's nerves from fraying to a dangerous point. Dad and I have a firm understanding to keep Mom out of harm's way due to a condition she's battled most of her life, but I can't risk it.

It's Natalie's desperation to keep her discovery between us and only us that keeps me silent. Beating the instrument into my submission, I try to pinpoint the attraction and rid myself of the incessant need crawling inside of me to go back.

The fucked-up part?

Everything about her seems to be what draws me closer, even the denial she seems comfortable swimming in, which irritates the shit out of me. She might feel safe there, but she felt safe with me outside of that, too—her raw vulnerability clear evidence. But only with me, and she admitted as much today at the parlor. It's as if she saved it for me, bared herself completely, and fuck if I don't want every part she's offered up.

Fatigue sets in, my body covered in a sheen of sweat as I recall the minutes and hours before. Her pale red locks dancing along with the breeze in the truck just before her indigo eyes meet mine. The curve along her top lip, her fucking perfect mouth, and how it wraps around my name, especially when she's breathless.

I could live a hundred more years of life and will never forget the way she looked at me while I sang for her in the hotel. That will go untouched in memory, as will our kiss tonight.

I'm still unsure who initiated it, but what I do know is that I've never had to question who struck first before.

I've never lost myself in my senses like I did then.

As ridiculous as it may be, in a matter of days, I've become utterly and completely fucking bewitched by Natalie Butler.

Raw ache continues to build as I mentally tick through a small list of dialable, no-strings distractions that could come close to satiating me. A warm body to lose myself in that may help this gnawing that won't let up.

Within seconds the answer is clear, and she's in room 212 at The Edgewater Hotel. "Fuck!"

Dad's head snaps up at my outburst, his brows drawing tight as he stills his hands. It's then I realize I've stopped playing and failed to lose myself in the music, something I've rarely if ever, fucking done.

When Dad moves to click the track off, I jerk my head to stop him. Knowing I'm worrying him but unable to help myself, I lay my sticks to rest on the snare and walk out of his studio without explanation.

TWENTY-ONE

Crazy for You
Madonna

Natalie

Zipping my suitcase shut, I roll it to the edge of the bed before stepping out onto the balcony of my hotel, which overlooks the water. The sun hovers brightly above as a cluster of seagulls flock together and swoop in my direction, flying eye level with me a few feet from where I stand.

Nervous laughter escapes at the way they're stalking me, no doubt trained by previous guests to wait for breakfast leftovers. As I take in the view, I realize Seattle has truly taken a back seat, playing more of a backdrop to Easton during my time here. Only now, as I prepare to leave, do I find myself appreciating the view I've had access to the entirety of my trip, yet, I have no regrets about why. I also can't bring myself to regret coming, but hate the way we parted last night. The second I closed the door to his truck and entered the lobby, I felt the loss of him strike. The idea of missing him is insane, but it still rings just as true now as it did last night. Just as I switch my camera to capture a panoramic view against the invading glare of the sun, a knock sounds on my door. Ears perking up, I step inside, unsure if housekeeping announced themselves.

"I'm still here!" I call out. "I asked for late check-out," I explain, nearing the door.

"I was hoping you were," rings out in reply as I open the door to find a grinning Joel on the other side. The instant burn in my chest leaves my hopes of seeing Easton before I left dashed.

I manage to muster a smile. “Hey, you. What brings you here?”

“Thought you might want a lift to the airport.”

“Thank you, but my flight doesn’t leave for another four hours.”

“I’ve got time to kill,” he brushes past me to grab my waiting suitcase. “We’ll take the scenic route.”

“Joel, that’s really not necessary. I don’t want to take up your day.”

“You aren’t. It’s either chill with you or be bored in a parking lot,” he says, glancing around the room.

A dozen questions surface, mainly consisting of which parking lot it would be. If Easton occupies the building he’d been waiting outside of and where it’s located.

“Joel, seriously, thank him for me, but—”

“I’m not taking no for an answer, so give it up. Besides, I can think of a lot worse ways to spend a day.” His warm smile puts me at ease.

“Okay,” I agree.

He looks around again. “Got everything?”

“Let me do one last walk through, and I’ll meet you at the elevator.”

“Sounds good.”

Unable to help myself, I grab the remaining two pieces of toast from my breakfast tray and toss them onto my balcony before quickly sealing my door shut, narrowly avoiding the explosion of fluttering wings that follows.

After checking the drawers and bathrooms, I place a bill on the desk to tip housekeeping and glance around the room, knowing my time is up, but the source of my melancholy rests somewhere outside this hotel room. Even so, I find myself grabbing the forty-dollar teddy bear dressed in a red sweater brandishing the hotel logo before I exit, a souvenir of my time here, of the memories I’ll be hard-pressed to forget anytime soon. Especially the minutes in which Easton sang for me, and for the first time publicly.

Joining Joel, who’s already inside a waiting elevator, he ushers me in, eyeing the bear and flashing me a grin. I lift a shoulder in reply.

Once outside, I follow him to the SUV parked at the pass-through. Taking Easton’s jacket draped on the top of my suitcase, I slide it on, unwilling to part with it just yet. Joel barely conceals his smirk as he opens the back door for me, and I give him a “pshh” before circling him and hopping into the front passenger seat. He chuckles as I close the door, and once in the driver’s seat, he turns to me.

"I know of a place that serves the absolute best seafood in the Pacific Northwest. You up for it?"

"Sounds perfect," I lie.

"It's a little bit of a drive."

"Well, we have time," I remind him.

"All right then, it's a plan."

I use the drive to get acquainted with the person who's probably closest to the man I haven't been able to chase from my thoughts since the day we met. Long minutes into our drive, our polite chatter turns more personal in nature. So far, I've discovered Joel's ex-Army and served four years before getting hired as Easton's private driver and bodyguard.

"No wife or kids?"

"Not by choice. I'm ready for it, but I'm being patient. I haven't found her yet. It will happen when it happens."

"Do you think it's the job?"

"No, I've had a few long-term relationships," he shrugs, "they just didn't work out. Mostly because the women I'm typically attracted to turn out to be bat shit."

"Well, that's dangerous."

"Yeah, more so than this job."

I run my fingers along the fabric of Easton's jacket. "How will you know when you've found the right one?"

"When I miss her too much to go from one day to the next without her, only then will I consider putting the job last."

"Not a bad way to gauge it," I agree, glancing out the window at the trees blurring past us on either side of the road. Briefly, I wonder how good the fare is for what seems like a drive to nowhere. It's when Joel begins to slow as we approach a deserted, small, dilapidated-looking, one-story building that I turn to him with drawn brows.

"What's this?"

"A pit stop."

Confused, I scan for clues until I catch a glimpse of the tailgate of Easton's truck parked at the side of the isolated building. My heart leaps into a fast rhythm when Joel parks just in front of the entrance.

"You tricked me," I scold.

"Yeah, you look *really* unhappy about it," he replies with a grin I know mirrors my own. "Go on, I'll be here waiting for you," he urges as I look back toward the building when Easton appears at the door, knocking the wind out of me.

His eyes sweep me as I exit the SUV in his jacket and prance toward him with a grin. "Hey," I say, nearing him.

Easton replies with a soft "Hey," before shifting his gaze to the SUV and lifting his chin to Joel in thanks. I duck under Easton's arm as he holds the door open and come to a dead stop.

"Where exactly are we?" I ask as the door slams closed behind us, shrouding us in darkness. The only light comes from a dimly lit hallway several feet in front of us. Eyes adjusting to the lack of light, I make out a seating area full of worn leather couches on our left and a small kitchenette to the right.

Easton stands just behind me, his chest brushing my back. I sense some slight tension rolling through him as he speaks. "I wanted to show you something before you go."

"Okay," I acquiesce as he takes my hand, a balm to last night's rushed goodbye.

Even though I know he withdrew for both our sakes, I can't deny it was painful in a way I wasn't prepared for. Butterflies swarm me as he gently nudges me forward to give him space before he takes the lead, guiding me down a short hallway. A single door is closed to our left before he stops at another closed door on the right. Opening it, he ushers me in, and I glance around.

"Oh," I say, taking in our surroundings. Straight ahead is a large soundboard with two comfortable-looking chairs edging it.

A long, newer-looking leather couch takes up a good amount of the wall immediately to my right. Next to it is a glass door leading into a sound booth which sits opposite the board. The booth is so small, it's got barely enough space to fit the instruments it currently houses. Though it seems equipped, it's severely outdated. Even with all the necessities, the room looks to be something straight out of the '70s era, the surrounding walls made up of paneled wood. I turn to Easton, confused.

"*This* is your studio?"

He chuckles at my obvious surprise. "Not impressed?"

"It looks like a '70s porno set and smells like mothballs. Seriously, Easton, why *here*?"

"I'm here mostly because of this soundboard, and I told you, I earned every single dime to record myself. This is the only place I could afford."

"Don't get me wrong, it's um, nice enough—"

"Liar," he grins and scolds simultaneously. "It's a total shithole. But it's been my home on and off for years. I've slept on that couch more than I have in my own bed."

"Did you sanitize it first?" I jab.

"I bought it new, asshole," he growls, nudging my shoulder.

"So, do you own this palace?"

He shakes his head. "I fucking should with as much time as I've spent here, but no. I lease it long term because no one else wants it."

I open my mouth to talk, and he covers it with his palm, his eyes lit with humor.

I peel his hand away. "I was only going to say a coat of paint, or…a wrecking ball, and this place could really be…something."

Wrinkling his nose, he pinches my sides, and I jump as our smiles collide. My heart flutters in my chest as we get caught up in the other for a few seconds while his palms rest on either side of my waist. Sucking in my lip as my body begins to thrum, I glance around and try to imagine him holed up in this relic he labels his studio. "And you're by yourself when you're here?"

"Most of the time. You say that like it's a bad thing."

"Don't you get lonely?"

"Not with all the music in my head," he says, tapping his temple.

"You're beautiful…" His eyes snap to mine. "…and I feel sorry for you."

I'm graced with a full grin before he leads me deeper into the room.

"Come on, it won't bite, and I got rid of the rats years ago."

"That's reassuring."

He smirks as I take one of two seats behind the soundboard. Putting on my most serious expression, I straighten my shoulders. "So, you going to teach me how to drive this spaceship or what?"

"Only if it lands us in an alternate universe," he rasps out, taking the seat next to me. His eyes bore into mine, the sentiment hitting hard.

"Then what are you waiting for? Let's go."

"I'll do you one better."

I feign busy, pushing up a lever I know he can easily adjust back. "I don't quite see how that's possible, Mr. Crowne."

He ducks under the board and retrieves a set of headphones, and I gape at him. "You're going to let me hear it?"

"How are you going to write your article without hearing it?"

"We both know I'm—"

The 'play along with me' look in his eyes cuts me off.

"Exactly," I snark, tossing my shoulders back and exaggeratedly clearing my throat. "I can't perform miracles. I don't know how you expect me to sway people otherwise."

"Let's remedy that," he says, a nervous underlay in his tone.

"How many people have heard it?"

"My dad—so that makes you—number two."

An audible gasp leaves me. "Easton."

"Yeah, not even my mother," he says softly. "I didn't want her feeling pressured."

I gape at him. "You trust me this much?"

"Guess so."

The urge to launch myself at him intensifies and I do my best to sidebar the plethora of emotions threatening. "Sure hope it doesn't suck, or this could backfire badly."

"Clock's ticking, Butler, and you have a plane to catch and seventy-seven minutes of music to listen to."

"Seventy-seven minutes. Is there a significance to that?"

"You tell me." He gently pulls the tie securing the pile of curls on top of my head, teasingly ruffling them loose before placing the headphones on my ears.

"Why the headphones?"

"Because I've heard it far too many times, and I don't want to concentrate on the music."

"Perfectionist?" I ask.

"You have no idea," he says, his expression tightening.

"I have some idea."

"You going to shut up anytime soon?"

"Sorry, I'm excited," I clap giddily. "You don't really intend on watching me, do you?"

"Since I've been waiting seven long years, yeah, I absolutely fucking do."

"Geesh, no pressure," I spout nervously. "If I'm this nervous, I can't imagine what you're feeling."

"Comfortable?" He asks, dodging my question.

"Yeah," I say, bobbing my head with emphasis.

"Close your eyes," he whispers. Immediately, I flutter them closed, thankful for the reprieve of being so close to him and unable to touch. It's a special kind of hell.

All words fall away as the intro—an atmospheric sort of melody—surrounds me before notes begin pouring through the headphones.

I can feel Easton's gaze as he keeps the seat opposite me, our knees touching, his earthy scent surrounding me as his velvet voice sounds with the first lyrics. In seconds, I'm transported from the dimly lit room we're sitting in into his universe. Heavy drums kick as he sings between searing guitar riffs, my lips parting at the heaviness of the song's message.

The introduction song comes to a close, the last of the lyrics lingering as I melt further into the chair, mind blown, keeping my eyes closed. When the next song begins to play, my eyes bulge open in response, and I see Easton's expectant smile in place due to the drastic difference in sound from the first song to the second. Both are different in feel, yet just as phenomenal.

My eyes flutter closed as he sings of mistrust. When it ends, I open my eyes briefly, and his lips part as he conveys something unintelligible, but I purposefully refuse to lift my headphones in fear of missing a single note. By the third song, I'm completely in orbit, unable to give him a second of my attention as I'm swept further and further into the journey he's so effortlessly taking me on. There's a theme mixed in the brilliance, but even as I try to mentally take notes, I'm unable to formulate a single coherent thought.

I feel it all, goosebumps erupting over my skin over and over as I'm continually seduced, brought up to immeasurable highs only to be swept into sorrow. I lose time, fully absorbed, emotions warring as the music continues to play with only a few short seconds of reprieve between songs—which isn't nearly enough time to recover.

The journalist inside desperately wants her poker face back, but even as I try, I fail to formulate a single cohesive sentence for what I'm experiencing. Ultimately, I bat her away because the journalist that resides inside me is not who he's playing his music for.

So, I sit, failing to hide the totality of the feelings he's evoking as my throat constricts and his voice pulls at the last of my restraint, my eyes burning with tears as they escape and trickle down my cheeks. I don't stop them, nor do I wipe them away. He deserves every one of them.

Easton Crowne makes beautiful music, his sound unlike any I've ever heard. Faint echoes of musicians—past and present—thread through his soul-searing lyrics and complicated melodies, but in a distinctive way I know will be trademarked as his own.

The truth becomes evident as I continue to listen and realize he's probably not at all ashamed his father helped him produce it. He's proud of it. I conclude he doesn't want it publicly known he got the help because the sound he created is uniquely his own.

I know if I open my eyes, it may well ruin me, so I rest my head back against the leather seat—my senses heightened exponentially as he continues to wage war on my every emotion. His brilliant, beautiful lyrics and carefully laid out melodies drown me for endless minutes as I'm swarmed in the sensation of his mindboggling creation. I embrace every second of the feeling.

Just as I reach immeasurable heights by the beauty of new lyrics, Easton removes the headphones and unplugs them, the gorgeous ballad surrounding us both as I open my eyes. The ready praises on my tongue are silenced when Easton's lips capture mine.

TWENTY-TWO

Wicked Game
Johnnyswim

Natalie

I gasp into Easton's mouth as he thrusts an eager tongue between my lips with a hunger I could only dream of.

Instantly I cling to him, my kiss just as greedy, my thrust just as desperate as our tongues intermingle at a frenzied pace. It's as if he has waited the entirety of the time I was listening to unleash on me. I feel every bit of that truth and see it on his face when Easton pulls away just long enough to gauge my reaction. In his search, he seeks and finds permission before his lips again capture mine in another soul-searing kiss. This one deeper than the last, as his hands cup my face and he surrounds me.

In the next breath, I'm wrapped around him, licking along his neck, inhaling his scent until our mouths again collide. My entire being lights on fire as our lips and tongues desperately move against the other as wetness floods my core.

His kiss gives me new life as I'm tossed further into orbit, feeling the vibration of his groans which coax me as I open myself for him.

"Easton," I rasp out between kisses as his eyes burn through me with a searing heat. Seeing his reaction to us, I free myself completely, letting the need I've been suppressing take over entirely. Just this once, I'll allow myself to have him. Just this once, I'll give him all of me, without restraint or thoughts of another living soul.

In this universe, only we exist.

The music continues to pierce the deepest parts of me as I grip his face and still him. It's then I realize we are in the middle of the room, and I'm wound around him. For several seconds we simply stare at each other. One beat passes, and then another before our mouths collide again. Body vibrating with a need for more—to get closer—he walks us over to the couch and lays me down gently, nestling between my legs. The thrust of his tongue into my mouth matches the drive of his hips as I gasp at the feel of his hard length against my core. Crazed with lust, I grip his thick hair in my fingers as he trails his kiss down my neck, laving every inch of bare skin with his lips and tongue.

He trails his carnal kisses between my mouth and neck before sinking his teeth into my shoulder and thrusting against me with more pressure. I cry out, gripping his shoulders as he does it again and again, bringing me close to the brink.

"Easton—" I plea, body coiling as sensation threatens to overtake me. He stops, reading my ask. I don't want to go anywhere without him.

"Fuck," he breathes as he stares down at me with a hooded gaze. The sight of Easton Crowne aroused is by far the sexiest fucking thing I've ever seen in my life.

"More," I demand as he braces his muscular arms above me and rears back. The next drive of his hips has me seeing stars as he hits me perfectly. And with the next, my entire body shudders.

"Tell me what you want ..." he urges. I reply by ripping at his buckle, the clank of it damn near bringing me to orgasm by sound alone as I dip into his navy boxer briefs and grip his cock in my hand. Cursing, he keeps himself hovering above me with his arms locked as my gaze dips, and I stare down at the glossy drop of arousal seeping from the fat head of his perfect, thick dick before sweeping my thumb over it.

"Goddamn," he swears as I look up to see him react to the feel of me, *us*.

"Now, please, now," I order, unable to take another second. He fists off his shirt before helping to free me of my own. Gazing down at me, he thrusts again, keeping me primed and wanton. I spread my legs further just before he backs away, pulling off my UGGs and tossing them over his shoulder. Staring down at me with nothing but fire in his eyes, he unbuttons my jeans and peels them away along with my panties.

Lifting my upper half, he unclasps my bra and dives for the spoils, pulling the whole of my breast into his mouth as he lowers his jeans and boxers to mid-thigh before driving against me, his bare cock gliding against my soaked center. We both call out as the lust overtakes us, and he grips the back of the couch before driving into me in one claiming thrust.

Our blue flame turns blinding white as his hooded eyes lock on mine, and I gasp at the stretch and invasion. I gaze up at him, my mouth parted, my vision blurring. Nothing has ever felt so good.

"Fuck, Natalie," he hisses, his voice full of restraint. "Are you okay?"

"Please, please move," I whimper as he stares down at me with lust and wonder.

"Condom," he blows out a harsh breath. I lock my legs around him.

"I'm covered, please, Easton, please just fucking move," I grit out on the verge of orgasm as my thrumming clit pulses against the edge of his buried cock. In the next breath, he rears back and thrusts in harder, burrowing further into me.

That's all it takes for me to detonate, and I tighten around him, my body pulsating from head to toe as my orgasm rips through me.

"Fuck…Christ," Easton rasps, eyes closing before he begins furiously pumping in and out of me. Expression coated with desire, he grips my hips and grinds me onto his cock with each deep thrust sending me over the edge a second time. He captures my cries with his mouth, seeming to feed off them before stopping suddenly.

"Hold on, baby," he murmurs, gently pulling out of me and standing abruptly, toeing his shoes off before shoving his jeans down and kicking them away.

I gaze up at him, fully bared, lips and legs parted, chest heaving as he stares down at me in a way that makes me feel perfect. The sight of him naked, cock hard and glistening with my orgasm, has me reaching for him, wanting every part of him touching every part of me. Planting his knees on the couch, he lifts my right leg, kissing his way from my ankle to my calf before trailing his tongue up my thigh and capturing the whole of my clit between his lips, sucking with fervor. Back arching from the sinful workings of his mouth, he kisses his way along my stomach, flicking my nipple with his tongue, briefly surrounding it with his lips before trailing his kiss up my throat and thrusting his tongue into my parted mouth. We moan in sync as he nestles himself between my thighs and slowly, so slowly, presses back into me. His shoulders tense beneath my palms as he pauses and stares down at me. "You're so fucking perfect," he whispers hoarsely, "so incredibly beautiful," he murmurs as he rolls his hips gently, thrusting harder and deeper as he continues to keep his pace.

Endless waves of pleasure roll through me as he draws it out, watching me come undone for him. He presses his forehead to mine. With every sure thrust, I lose myself further to him as we pant against each other's mouths.

"Look at me," he implores, cradling my face in his hands. Our eyes collide as he gazes down at me, mouth parted as he picks up his pace. I murmur praises until all words fall away, heart lurching toward his. With the next drive and skilled shift of his hips, I tip and fall, tightening around him and gasping into his mouth. My orgasm sets him off, and he unleashes, frantically fucking me as I lose my voice with the cry of his name. Gathering my hair in his fist, he pulls it back so I'm focused on his face as his expression twists in an exquisite mix of pleasure and relief. He releases a long, breath-stunted groan, as he slows his hips and pulses inside me. Visibly spent, he dips and captures my mouth, kissing me for lengthy seconds as our bodies quake in the aftermath.

He murmurs my name with reverence as he pulls away, his biceps shaking as he hovers, placing worshipful kisses along my face before drawing me back into another life-altering kiss. His tongue glides against mine as I run my hands along the perfection of his slick, muscular back in exploration, careful not to touch the healing ink along his side. Still between my parted thighs, Easton eases more weight on top of me as I stroke his skin, gathering as much as I can of him to me.

We lay there for wordless seconds as the music stops and silence fills the room. The only sound left is our mingling breaths. I live in the moment, knowing the instant we separate, all thoughts of existing in the place we've just created will be over, and so will we.

Sometime, in the immediate future, I'm going to have to fight hard to rip myself away. But I do the opposite now in this precious time we have left, which is rapidly ticking out.

Clutching him tightly to me, I bask in the feel of him, of how perfect we fit, of how beautiful he made me feel.

"Natalie," he scratches out, withdrawing slightly from my touch and staring down at me.

"Not yet," I whisper hoarsely. "Please. *Not yet.*"

He nods, his features shadowing with the same knowledge—that we both just stole something we were never supposed to have. We both made the decision to exist in this moment, and we both have to live with it. He pushes himself further into me as if to refute it as we allow ourselves to briefly rest in our connection, chasing the last of the sand together.

The thought occurs to me that if I leave now, I may be able to outlive this.

His lips begin to caress my skin as his cock starts to harden inside me, and I softly say his name. Lifting to hover, muscular arms braced above me, he sees my decision as I gently push at his chest. He curses softly as he slowly pulls out of me.

Flushed and covered in a sheen of sweat, I start to dress, increasing my speed and frantically pulling on my clothes in an attempt to start the long, seemingly impossible trek back to reality. Guilt swarms me as my reckless decision to give into my attraction for him begins to catch up with me. "I'll take the morning after pill, just in case."

"Natalie," he rasps softly as I pull up my jeans and fasten them.

"You have nothing to worry about, okay? I've been very careful. I haven't had sex in a long time. I'm clean, I swear to you. Jesus, I'm so sorry I did that."

"I'm not," he snaps, this time with a bite. He's already refuting my attempt to play off what just happened between us as nothing more than sex, seemingly ready on the other side of the battle line I'm drawing.

"Natalie. Look at me." I hear his zipper and the clank of his belt buckle, and instantly, I want more. I'd give literally anything to replay the minutes before this one and escape the cold reality I'm thrusting myself back into.

I hate so much that Easton Crowne is the most beautiful secret I'll ever have and will forever be the one I'm forced to keep.

"Natalie—"

"I can't look at you, okay?" I admit honestly. "I have to go home, *right now*. I have to go." I fasten my bra and yank on my shirt in haste as the weight of his jacket hits my shoulders when he covers me with it. I sink where I stand, ache taking over. "That's yours."

"Not anymore," he forces my arm into one sleeve before I hesitantly take the other. Once I'm cloaked in the soft fabric, he snakes his arms around my waist and pulls me back firmly against him, my back to his chest.

"Please, let me go," I whisper.

"I don't think I can," though quietly delivered, his reply is a direct hit.

He turns me to face him, and I inevitably lift my eyes as the searing pain of loss starts to unfurl in my chest. Trapped in his depths, it's all I can do to get my breathing under control. As I pull myself fully back to earth, it strikes me. If this is the last time I'll see him, the last time we speak, what just happened between us—though earth-shattering—can't be the sum of our time together and everything we've trusted the other with. He's given me so much in such a short time. It's only fair I reciprocate with honesty. Brutal honesty, which is no less than he deserves. "Easton, please listen to me, just for a second."

He dips his chin before cradling the back of my neck with his hands, his thumbs resting on my jaw, eyes searching.

How am I going to move on from the way this feels?

Eyes stinging, I press on, because I'm desperate for him to hear me.

"It's not going to matter," I utter, my voice shaking. "It's not going to matter if Reid had a hand in helping to produce it. That's not the Sergeants' sound. It's yours. What it is…is undeniably…I-I-I. I felt *everything*, Easton. You have every reason to be protective of it, but I swear to God, that's some of the most amazing music I've ever heard in my life."

My lips tremble as I grip the hands cradling my face, peeling them away and kissing the tips of his fingers before I release them. "Please, please, don't allow your fear to win and deny the world your gift. You have absolutely nothing to worry about. You are about to exceed every imaginable expectation, and I'll be cheering you on from the sidelines."

Reeling, I turn and open the door before glancing back to see him fisting his hands at his sides. His expression darkens as I close my eyes and force myself out of the door, the burn in my throat and chest intensifying unbearably.

I reach the door to the studio and open it, a ray of sunlight beaming into the room and disappearing as Easton slaps it closed with a palm.

"Don't go. Don't fucking leave like this."

"Easton, this has to stay here and remain here between the two of us."

"Fuck that, I—"

"In the history of all bad ideas," I warn in a grave tone, "this would top *both* our lists. You have to trust me on this. If our parents ever found out, this could be detrimental to *all of us*. It will do so much fucking damage."

He presses his forehead against my back as an unparalleled crack of awareness runs through me. I turn to look up at him, able to make out his profile in the dark as the look in his eyes begins to shred me. He seems just as bewildered as I am. It's as if we're being pulled by a tractor beam toward the other. It's undeniable. Stupidly, I try to deny it anyway.

"It's attraction. Probably because of the situation. It will pass."

"Don't fucking lie to us both," he bites out, batting my words away.

"Easton, even if we could act on this, we live worlds apart."

"Not anymore," he declares vehemently.

The truth of his statement hits hard. He believes what he's saying, and I can't, at all, afford to.

Get the fuck out of here, Natalie!

"We have to be sensible—"

"Being sensible isn't what got you here," he murmurs.

"I wasn't expecting—"

"Me neither," he fires back, "but I refuse to fucking deny whatever is happening here. You know I won't."

Closing my eyes, I let his words set me on fire because I deserve it. It rages inside me as I draw every bit of strength I have remaining to douse the flames.

"*I can't,*" I say in clear resignation.

"Fuck," he slaps the door behind me, making me jump. "Stay, one more day. I'll fly you home."

"Let me go," I order sharply. "Right *now.*"

He releases me immediately and steps back. Turning, I open the door and slip out, flinching when it smacks closed behind me in finality. Easton's curse rings out behind it as Joel leaps from his driver's seat, his smile fading as he takes in my expression and concern morphs his features. Without hesitation, he opens the back door for me, and I crack, managing to slip inside just as the first tear falls.

Joel closes my passenger door just as I lift Easton's jacket to shield my face when another tear joins the first. The second Joel presses the gas, the burn becomes too much, and it's all I can do to muffle my sobs.

In an act of mercy, Joel turns on the radio, and I keep myself shielded in the jacket, drowning in unexpected grief. Easton's scent surrounds me as I replay every second of our time together.

It's only when I hear my name being softly repeated that I come to. Eyes puffy, vision cloudy, I lower Easton's jacket to see Joel standing at the back door of the SUV, the entrance of the airport, and the bustling traffic of people behind him.

"I'm sorry, sweetheart. I drove around as long as I could, but if you don't check in now, you'll miss your flight."

Wiping my face and knowing it's useless to try and sort myself out, I step out into the sunlight, realizing he must have driven me around for well over an hour. "Joel, I'm so—"

"Please don't apologize," he assures, his features twisted with the same concern. With my suitcase already in one hand, he ushers me out gently with his other.

"Thank you." I go to take my bag, and he jerks his chin before handing it off to the skycap approaching us. "Ticket?"

I pull out my phone and present my barcode. He scans it as I stand in a fog, all activity around me a blur. The skycap and Joel exchange words and Joel tips him before turning back to me.

"Jesus, I'm embarrassed," I wipe my face.

"You have no reason to be," he assures me.

"Well, you better get used to it," I sniff, "because you have so many jilted women in your future." I suck in much-needed air and miraculously manage a smile. "Joel, he's going to be..." I curse the fresh tears threatening, "I mean, you know how incredible he is, but brace yourself."

Joel nods, his eyes softening further as the skycap calls out to the two of us. "All set. Best get to your gate. You board in ten."

"Okay," I nod and turn to Joel. "Thank you." He steps up to me and pulls me into him, hugging me tightly. I manage to keep it together long enough to hug him back and pull away, my hands resting on his shoulders. "Take care of him, and please don't tell him I was in this state when I left, okay?"

"Natalie—"

"Please, Joel, it won't do a bit of good," I swallow. "He's got so much to look forward to. The next few months are going to be the best of his life. Trust me on this. Keep this *one thing* between us. *Please*."

I release him when he nods reluctantly.

"You're too fucking cool. He's so lucky to have you, and I'm so happy to have met you. Take care of yourself for me, too." Lifting, I kiss his cheek before turning and hauling ass into the airport.

Standing in line to board, I hear Easton's plea as clearly as if he's still standing behind me, whispering in my ear. Shielding my mouth, I do my best to avoid the mix of odd looks I feel scanning my profile as I choke back a sob. Once free of the line, I charge down the jetway and onto the plane, eagerly searching for and finding my seat to take refuge. Curling myself toward the window, I will the plane to move as I sit in a haze of the aftermath. As the plane slowly taxis down the runway, I burrow into Easton's jacket.

He's everywhere—my skin drenched in his scent; my panties soaked with remnants of the most intense lovemaking of my life while my lips still faintly tingle from his kiss.

Plastered to the window, I slip my hand inside his pocket and run my fingers over the lighter, the condoms, and the earbuds he tucked into the jacket last night. Pulling them out, I quickly plug my ears and connect them to my Bluetooth, frantically opening my music app and searching for the song he played for me as we kissed. The opening of "Dive Deep (Hushed)" unleashes a fresh round of hurt.

The lyrics envelop me as the land begins to blur beside me, and I cover my mouth as more hot tears wet my fingers. As the wheels go up, I set the song to repeat and pull up a blank document on my phone to compose.

Heart raw, music fueling me as Easton assured me it would, I begin furiously typing while grieving what might have been as the miles between us increase, and our worlds start to separate. Even as I try to reason with myself that it's impossible to feel so much for anyone so quickly, my heart defies that logic as it roars in protest. As the space increases between us, I frantically type in vain to close it, the music pulling me further into my every emotion as the blurry truth I type becomes bolder with every mile. By the time I land in Austin, the truth I laid out in black and white is crystal clear. In Easton Crowne, I got a glimpse of exactly what I was searching for when I left Texas, and now I have to live with it.

*"Utterly brilliant, a sound impossible to box in any genre, and we dare you to try!"—**Mojo***

*"Easton Crowne has managed to do what no other artist has ever done—outlive a legacy only to become a legend in twelve songs."—**Rolling Stone***

*"False Image is everything we've been missing. Easton Crowne is blue printing the future of rock, and we're here for it."—**Pitchfork***

*"I think it's safe to say not one musician worth their salt has slept soundly since Crowne released False Image."—**Spin***

TWENTY-THREE

Dead in the Water
James Gillespie

Easton
One Month Later...

Just past the bridge of Metallica's "One", I hear the distortion and lift my hand, halting the momentum we've been building. In response, I get a frustrated lick of a guitar followed by the bash of a crash cymbal. Annoyance flaring, I glance back at Tack, who sits behind his kit, wary eyes focused on LL before he lifts his soaked T-shirt to clear the sweat off his brow. LL mutters a curse from next to me, the tips of his taped fingers bright red from endless hours of nonstop practice.

From beside me, Syd dumps his bass in his stand as if he doesn't have a care in the world before twisting off the top to another beer. Taking a long pull, his eyes lift in dare for an objection from me. Surprisingly, he hasn't once lost rhythm, so I don't bother with one. He's not the problem.

"Let's take five," I snap, harsher than I intend, glancing back at LL. He stares back at me with muted contempt. He must know full well it's his continuous fuckups holding us all back from mastering the song.

"*Five*, seriously?" LL prods, eyeing the clock perched above the glass partition in Dad's studio, his British lilt punctuating his disdain. "We've been at this shite for nine fucking hours, mate."

Walking over, I hop onto an old amp and rip the clock off the wall before tossing it on the floor and driving my boot through it. "It takes as long as it fucking takes." Dad pops out of his chair as I stalk toward the door. Hot on my heels, I take a few steps onto the cobblestone pathway before reeling on him. "You don't have to say it. I already know."

"So, he's off today. *One day*, East. Just give him time to regroup."

Dad reaches me in a single stride before lifting my bandaged fingers. "You're fucking bleeding on your own Strat. It's time to take a breather. You're wringing them and *yourself* dry."

"He can do this. He's better than he's playing."

"He knows it, and it's only pissing him off. Just let him even himself out."

I fist my hair and let out a harsh exhale, and Dad smirks. "You're placing too much importance on the wrong shit. Your collective sound is tight, East, damn near seamless, so give them a little fucking grace."

"Dad, you can't intervene."

Cigarette dangling between his lips, lighter ready, he pins me with his stare. "Don't go there. I haven't said a single word inside that room without you instigating my involvement."

"You ever stop to think *you're* the one making them nervous?"

He scoffs as he lights his cigarette, exhaling as he speaks. "Professionals they may be, not one of them can exchange instruments on a whim and play with expertise the way you can. Thank fuck they don't know it yet, either. It'll only humiliate them, but the more you point out, the more they're catching on."

"All right," I snap, feeling the adrenaline coursing through me start to wane. I'm drained. We're all drained. We've been busting our asses for a solid month to get our sound together. We've only got a few days before we hit the road, and we aren't where I want us to be. The fact that we've only had weeks to play together is my fault because of my indecision on releasing. To their credit, they've been practicing their parts solo while on standby in case I decided to pull the trigger.

Now that there's gunpowder on my hands, I feel the pressure mounting daily.

"You have time," Dad reads my thoughts, offering assurance. "We weren't nearly as strong the entirety of our first tour."

"I hear you," I reiterate, as he takes a long drag from his cigarette and shakes his head incredulously.

"No, you don't, and the fact that you think it's me they're intimidated by is laughable." He blows out a steady stream of smoke. "Truth of the matter is, they weren't at all prepared for *you*. Think about your ask, son. You're demanding they master a song with different time signatures that starts in four-four, shifts to three-four, and then occasionally measures down. Then there's the change in the chorus. A song they were only vaguely familiar with before today. That's the equivalent of handing a fucking four-year-old their first violin and the sheet music for Mozart on day one."

Reading my expression, a prideful grin lifts his lips. "I don't know whether to love or hate it that you still don't believe me, but that," he jabs a thumb over his shoulder, "what's happening in there has got *nothing* to do with *me*."

He tosses his cigarette and stomps it out before stepping up to me. "You can't let frustration and anger take over, or you might as well hang it up now. Whether you like it or not—and for the first time in your life—you have a band, and you'll have to learn how to play well with others. Stop being so selfish with your demands and recognize your own talent is one in a *billion*. You know all too well how to bounce off other musicians because you've played with some of the best."

"We can do better," I mutter.

"Perfection is an illusion. Half the fun of being in a band is fine-tuning sound together and letting their creativity blend with yours. You have got to relinquish some of that ingrained control."

Sweat begins to dry on my back as I consider his words. I need a shower and a day of sleep. A lot of my frustration has nothing to do with the hired musicians we recruited months ago and everything to do with the woman who left me trapped between infatuation and unsatisfied curiosity. I predicted before she left that time and space wouldn't do a damn thing to curb either, and I was dead on. Instead of dwelling on what I can't control, I've thrown myself into perfecting what I can. "All right."

Seeming satisfied, Dad turns and heads back into his studio. When I step in behind him, I see three sets of eyes lift past Dad's shoulders, and land anxiously on me, driving his point home. I am meticulous and often a perfectionist. When recording, I consider it a good thing to be able to get the melodies and notes cemented exactly like I composed them. But if I want to make this work, I'm going to have to leave a part of that perfectionist in the studio.

Making a fast decision, I look over to LL, who I've been dueling lead with for the better part of two hours due to the difficulty of the song.

"One more time," I prompt, keeping the demand out of my tone, "this time, follow me to the split."

LL's technically our main lead on guitar, so I expect a little opposition. Instead, he cracks his neck before securing his guitar strap just as Tack lifts his drumsticks. Looking bored—which seems to be my bassist's MO—Syd tosses his empty beer bottle into the trash before strapping himself up too.

Though they are professionals, all of them are experienced bandmembers who have never managed to attain the industry's definition of success, and I've put them through their paces. They've taken it, mostly, in stride. Today, I pushed them past their capabilities and was rewarded when I saw the shock on Tack's face. He surprised himself, which I considered a small victory, but that was hours ago. Even his adrenaline is starting to dry up.

"We're too fucking close to fold." I look at each of them pointedly, strumming a few chords, relaxing my posture. "So, just give me everything you have for seven more minutes. Seven minutes." I search their faces for relief that this is our last attempt and find none. They want to nail it too, and it's in that I find my own respite.

I close my eyes and take a calming breath as Tack clicks his sticks together to start the count. Within the first minute, it starts to *feel* different. My breathing becomes labored between playing and singing, and I avert my gaze to LL, who's paling rapidly but keeps rhythm with me like we've been at it for years, not weeks.

My lips lift in a slight grin when we surpass the first hurdle. It's then I see the determined flare return in LL's eyes, some of his confidence restored.

Because of our grueling practices, these men are still strangers to me in the personal sense. Our only common ground at this point is tightening our sound for the few gigs we've managed to line up since I released. I've pinpointed their flaws as meticulously as I have my own. The fact that they're aware of them, and that Dad stepped in with sound advice when asked has made all the difference.

Going hard, I duel with LL to thicken up the lead to one of the most notorious metal guitar solos while raging through the lyrics. When Tack nails the break, and LL and I fall effortlessly in sync with our solos, victory begins to roll through my veins. When the last of the notes pierce the air, we mutely glance over to Dad, whose megawatt grin confirms what we all know just before he belts out. "Fuck yeah, you just did that."

The four of us howl in victory as Syd pops another beer in celebration before doling out cold bottles to the rest of us. Turning it up, I soak in the moment, glancing at the three men I'm about to embark on a journey I've imagined a thousand times or more since I began recording. Walking over to a nearby table, I lift the sketch I've spent hours drafting. "What do you think about REVERB?"

They scrutinize the drawing as I explain the motive behind the name. "R3V3RB short for reverberation. Since we're planning on paying tribute to music of every genre during the tour while introducing our own sound, I think it suits. The three's in replace of the e's are a nod to the old school LP's."

Surprisingly, I'm met with no resistance as they individually and enthusiastically agree to the name. My chest lights up as we toast to the decision while *what if* drifts through my psyche and the road ahead expands beyond the mental barrier I set.

Clinking bottlenecks with my band, I process the fact that I finally have the backup I've been holding out and hoping for since I started. Even if we didn't find each other in some sort of kismet way like I've read about in countless other stories, there's a reason we chose every single one of them. There's a place for them and for me. Though the shift from me to us is uncomfortable, the payoff of relinquishing control marks our true beginning.

In this moment, I realize there's only one person I want to call and share my elation with. It's the unanswered phone calls in the last month that keep me from attempting to do so.

She's barricaded us on opposite sides of a dead end.

Victory diminishing by the second due to her blatant rejection, I finally understand the crushing weight of defeat in the word I most despise—can't.

I decide to hate her a little for it because her refusal has made the word part of my vocabulary. The attempt to get back to that euphoric place we created has proved futile. The more she sticks to her stance, the more frustrated I become. This only leads to me concluding she's far more villain than she believes herself to be.

Daily, she's stealing my peace of mind with her cruel indifference and purposeful absence. Try as she might, I'm positive I wasn't the only one who felt a sort of revelation, an undeniable shift during the time we spent together, especially the last few hours. She can feign ignorance and apathy all she wants, but I felt it too substantially—and from her as well—to believe otherwise.

What she's made abundantly clear is that I'm no competition when it comes to her love and loyalty for Nate Butler. Over that, I have absolutely no control.

She may be a vulture too, for picking me to the bone and consuming my waking thoughts. Draining my beer, anger simmering for the list of can-nots when it comes to Natalie Butler, I do the only thing I *can* and numb the imprinted details of her face to a blur with my new band.

TWENTY-FOUR

Here with Me
Susie Suh, Robot Koch

Natalie
One Month Later...

"Earth to Natalie." Holly impatiently snaps her fingers in front of my face and I find myself ripped from another daydream. The budding summer sun burns hot on my shoulders as I lower the fork raised halfway to my mouth.

Mere seconds ago, I was in Easton's truck, hair whipping around my face just as he glanced over and our eyes locked, resulting in the inevitable jolt. Crashing back into my current reality, I dart my gaze over to Holly, ready with a quick apology. "I'm so sorry. What were you saying?"

"That's the third time you've spaced out on me in fifteen minutes. I'm not rehashing *all of that* again," she utters dryly, glowering at me. "What is with you lately?"

Easton called, again, and I didn't answer, again.

"It's like every time I talk to you, you space out when I get to the goods."

"I'm sorry," I offer weakly. "I told you I've been working my ass off. I'm just tired."

"Yeah, well, you aren't the only one, or did you forget I just graduated?"

"I know. I was there," I grin, "and I'm so proud of you."

Seeming satisfied for the moment, she runs a manicured finger through her glossy dark brown ponytail, her matching eyes imploring.

"We need to have some fun. I don't start my internship for a few weeks. Want to take off this weekend?"

"I've got a lot of work to do. It's not the best time."

"You always have a lot of work to do," she whines. "Come on, if I get Damon in on it, we can hit Nola and get a stupid expensive suite on his dime."

"Maybe," I avoid looking at my phone that rests face down on the table. Easton's called me twice a week for the last two months. Every time I don't answer, he lets it ring to voicemail. Every time I check it, the message is full of dead air and background noise as if he wants to speak but stops himself.

No texts, just two weekly calls without a message which I consider just punishment since I'm vying to hear any word from him but can't bring myself to answer.

By the time I touched down in Austin, Easton had released his first single. I'll never be able to wrap my head around the shock of hearing the news on the ride home before frantically scanning the radio to listen to it playing. It wasn't just any song, either, but the one we'd made crazy, life-altering love to a few hours before. It felt like he was calling me back to him.

As soon as Easton's single hit the airwaves, it went viral on every forum and media outlet. Even ESPN made a comment about it during a sportscast.

In the end, no marketing ended up being the best imaginable marketing, gaining him consistent airplay and respectable nods from other artists. Both his music and the news of his sudden and unexpected release spread like wildfire through the media. Rosie was furious she'd been scooped by none other than the man himself. A fact that still brings a secretive smile to my face—*daily.*

Less than a week later, he published the entirety of his album along with the would-be article I'd typed on the plane and sent via text. He'd rearranged parts of it and managed to turn it into more of a blanket statement-type press release while protecting my anonymity.

The second I saw it, I ran to the bathroom and tossed up my breakfast, tears streaming down my face, phone in hand, wanting nothing more than to call him. That, combined with the fact that I could barely look at my father, had me going home early that day. It was the lone day I allowed myself to wallow in my misery like a lust-crazed teenager and let the ache rule me wholly.

"Okay," Holly says, her fingers flying over her phone screen. "I just shot a text to our boy to see if he can manage an impromptu trip."

"He might be our boy, but he's *your man*, remember? So, when do you plan on telling him?"

She pauses, pulling sculpted brows together. "How about never. I'm getting over that crush."

"You think eight years is a crush?"

"It is if I deem it so," she sasses.

"Do you even know how beautiful you are?" I prop my hand under my chin, eyes gliding over the fit of the slinky halter dress she's pulling off so effortlessly. She pauses, a fork full of chicken salad halfway to her mouth, her expression bemused.

"He's a fool, Holly," I emphasize. "Because I'm not just talking about your appearance. You have the heart he needs."

"He's not looking. He's too busy hustling for his career and fucking for sport."

The familiar words jolt me back into that hotel restaurant.

"Do you fuck for sport?"

"Women aren't a game to me, so I fuck because it feels good."

God, did it ever feel good.

So damned good I've had actual wet dreams—which I swore were a myth—good. An image of Easton flitters in, above me, inside me, hazel eyes intent, jaw slack. An image I've replayed an embarrassing number of times. Slamming my fork down in irritation, I let out a long exhale, and Holly jerks back.

"What the hell?"

"It's just..." *I'm losing my focus over the gorgeous, budding rock star I slept with two months ago, and I would like my sanity back.* "I'm... just...tell the man you love him already."

"He's not ready to couple up, and I don't want the "I'll text you" version of Damon. I'm better than that. I'm *worth* more than that. Sure, we flirt a lot and have come close to crossing that line, but I'm not willing to risk his judgment when it comes to us. It would ruin twenty-one years of friendship—so, yeah, I'll pass. If this ship sails before he's ready to board, then it sails." She flips through her phone, though

I know she's completely tuned into this conversation. "Why are you so worried about this all of a sudden?"

"Because. I'm…," *wishing on a shooting star every night, every time I ride Percy toward a sunset, and every time I close my damned eyes.* "I just want you to have who you want." *Because I can't.* "I'm sorry I'm being pushy, it's your decision. I just know you both would fit so perfectly, and the fact that you *can* be together and are both being idiots about it, irks me sometimes."

She lowers her fork, eyes cast down. "I'm sorry if I've talked about him too much over the years," she withdraws slightly.

Cloudy head clearing immediately in response to her rapidly dimming expression, I grip both her hands tightly, including the one still holding her fork, and her eyes bulge at the crazy I'm showing. "Never, don't you ever think that. You can talk about my other best friend all you want; do you hear me? Tell me you hear me."

She grins at me as I release her.

"What?"

"You love me," she declares, "like a crazy person."

"Hell yeah, I do, and I love Damon just as much. I just wish you two would finally get together, that's all."

"Maybe someday," she sighs, "but you're forgetting one important thing."

"What's that?"

"He never talks to you about *me*."

"He does." I pull on my iced tea.

"Not the way I do, and I know it, so let's drop it, 'K?" She picks her phone back up and begins scrolling and typing, her embarrassment clear. I hate that I did it. What I hate more is that the next time she wants to talk to me about Damon, she might hesitate, or worse, not tell me at all. The whole thing is ironic because all I want to do is confide to her at the top of my lungs…finally confess the secret that's been bleeding out of my pores for eight straight weeks. Instead, I need her drama—or any drama for that matter—to distract me.

While it may be true that Damon doesn't talk about her in that context, he's been looking at her differently more and more over the years, and I want to box his ears for not paying attention to his growing feelings. I don't relay that to Holly because Damon truly is a wild card. He's also one of the most lusted after men I've ever known, coming a close second to my last lover, who's currently being worshiped by an increasing number of women on the daily. As I suspected, Easton's refusal to engage with the media has only made him more alluring to the masses, women especially.

And he's calling *me.*

The facts are, I haven't gone more than a full hour without thinking of him since I left him in that studio.

No matter how much I want to shelve those days we spent together in their respective place, I can't. Even if I could, he's *everywhere.* Videos of his first few concerts on the tour he kicked off weeks ago are not only being spread like wildfire on social media, but his performances are making headlines. So far, the world has done nothing short of worship him since he dropped *False Image.* A title I find perfectly fitting with the album's message—defaming fame.

The critics have done nothing but give massive props to the prodigy, who's broken up the monotony and splashed onto the music scene like a 'modern-day Elvis,' *Wall Street Journal's* words, not mine.

He's calling *me*, and I'm not answering.

The idea that one day he'll stop is a heavy weight in my gut, but the idea of being anything significant to him while fighting said masses for his attention is beyond comprehension to me.

"Thank God I don't have to deal with that," I say aloud.

"Well, aren't you an asshole."

I recover quickly. "I mean dating. Does he like me? Does he *not* like me? Does he have more than one sexual position in his arsenal? Is he worth the price of admission?"

Holly laughs as I roll my eyes exaggeratedly.

"If anyone needs to get back on a horse other than *Percy*, missionary or not, it's you. It's been, what, over a year since you broke up with Carson?"

"Who?" I taunt.

She glowers at me. "Exactly, but still."

"I'm in no hurry. I'm not saying this shop is closed, but I'm definitely not going to spread myself thin trying to find a decent date."

"As if you would have to. Girl, do you know how pretty *you* are? Your summer body is on point this year, bae. Look at you, all ripped and tan."

True to my nature, I've been using the ache in the weeks that have followed Seattle to fuel me and have been hitting the gym harder than ever.

"Forget men," I declare, gripping her hand and squeezing. "Forget sex, and let's just date each other."

"That's called friendship," she says. "Sorry, but I need the sex. Are you going to eat this garlic toast?"

"Nope."

"No bread till September?"

"Yep," I confirm with a chin dip.

She confiscates my toast, eyeing the clock on her phone. "Shit. Damon says raincheck. Between you two workaholics, I'll never get a weekend away. I need new friends."

"Good luck finding better," I taunt.

"True. I have to run." She stands before bending to kiss my cheek, smacking her lips exaggeratedly. Feigning disgust, I wipe it with my napkin as she exits the patio and power walks towards her Audi, giving me her signature diva farewell wave. "Don't make any plans for tomorrow. I'll dig around and see if I can find something for us to get into."

"'K. Love you."

"You too."

Sipping the last of my tea, I watch her pull away. Holly is by far one of the biggest blessings in my life. We've been through it all, from diapers to every part of puberty-driven awkward adolescence and so forth. Even though she's the perfect ride or die—and I know I can trust her with anything—I've kept my time with Easton completely to myself. Because of that, I've painstakingly fought through the ache and lingering desire alone.

I did not, at all, make it out of Seattle unscathed.

It was apparent when I got behind the wheel after my flight and saw my tear-splotched reflection in the rearview.

For the first week, it felt like I was hiding a breakup from everyone—especially my parents, which was the hardest task. Even though said task seemed impossible, I went to their house nearly every night and rode Percy until my legs went numb. Sadly, after having the most romantic interlude of my life, I was left talking to my four-legged best friend, who couldn't produce a word of advice. But riding Percy calmed me, as it so often does. After the first few guilt-riddled days and avoiding non-work-related conversations with my father, I decided I could ride out the guilt until it subsided as long as I kept my secret.

It was when the first call came from **EC** after week one that I regressed. It took everything in me to keep from answering.

The thing is, I will his calls to continue and can't bring myself to text him to stop. Even though, deep down, I know it's only prolonging the inevitable.

Sadly, the workaholic repetition I sought escape from when I went to Seattle—and identified as one of my issues—I resumed with ferocity. Easton told me point blank if I did nothing about it, that I would be responsible from then on.

I know he would be disappointed to find I let myself down.

My temporary cure?

After a grueling day at the paper, I spend my nights recalling the spontaneity in Seattle. It's been blissful getting lost in those memories, even if I have to walk through hellfire while fighting my pillow after.

Dad was pleasantly surprised when I went into overdrive and says the time away had done wonders for me.

But it wasn't time. It was a who and a culmination of things about him that inspired me—his honesty, his observations, our jam sessions, and getting lost together. In getting lost with Easton, I discovered new parts of myself—parts that are grossly unsatisfied with the way I'm currently living.

I spent the first few days with his earbuds in, immersed in sensory overload. I finally had to tuck them away in my desk, having decided anyone who listens to music while emotionally compromised is a masochist. It's utter agony knowing my mind now associates certain songs with a man forever trapped in a place and time I don't want to outlive.

It's hard for me to rationalize my feelings or even romanticize any part of them. Every time I play a song from his playlist, I feel every emotion I felt during that time and still manage to summon images of us during certain lyrics.

It's in the after that I fully realized the truth about the power of music Easton spoke so emphatically about.

Last night, at the feed store getting food for Percy, I heard an old '80s ballad and nearly lost my shit mid-aisle.

Crazily enough, no matter what I try, I've been grieving the loss of Easton like I am going through a full-fledged breakup. Which. Is. Insane.

I didn't even mourn Carson this long, and we damned near lived together for a year. But the fact that I'm having such a hard time letting go makes my embarrassing reaction as I left Seattle a bit more bearable.

It might have been a flash of days, hours, and minutes, but they remain with me. Easton remains with me, and it's bittersweet.

Easton properly kissed me, fucked me, and I'm certain—if we gave each other a chance—he might have been the one to properly love me.

Pulling up my phone, I see another missed call notification and blink in surprise. *Two* calls today. He's about to give up. It's only a matter of time before he does. Appetite gone, I toss my fork and pull down my sunglasses, the elation of his call cut short when his name evaporates from my screen.

Inside my car, AC blasting, tapping my thumbs on the wheel, I eye my phone where it rests just outside the lip of my purse as it re-lights with the missed call notification from **EC**. Just after, a text from Dad comes through with praise for my latest article.

Daddy: Great job. I've got a few notes. We'll go over them when you get back from lunch.

Guilt wins again.

Tucking my phone back into my purse with a sigh, I shift my focus—the paper, my father, my goals, our joint plans—I press the gas, and the truth painfully settles in. There's no place for Easton Crowne anywhere amongst them.

TWENTY-FIVE

Pets
Porno for Pyros

Easton

My cell vibrates in my hand, and I brace myself for the inevitable as I slide it to answer. "Hey, Mo—"

"And I quote, 'Easton Crowne—'"

"Mom, stop," I can't help my growing smile as I exit the coffee shop while she talks over me.

"'Easton Crowne and his band, REVERB, are leaving their fans stunned and mystified with every performance, and for good reason. Young Crowne seems to be making a statement by way of a nod to his predecessors. His nightly encore is a purposefully intended tribute to a diverse list of influences. Last night, he finished his set with Porno for Pyros' "Pets," the context clear—we're all missing the unattainable point of a pointless world.'"

"Mom—"

"Do you know who fucking said that about *my* son?"

"Don't tell me. I told you I don't read the reviews."

"Then don't. I'll read them all to you."

"Don't you have an interview with Chris today?"

"He's here, on speaker."

"Hey, man," he chimes in, "I'm so happy you finally did it, though I kind of hate you right now. But everyone else does too, so take it as a compliment."

I can't help the zing that runs through me. "Take some credit. You're the one who taught me to play the piano."

"I wish I fucking could," he says, "but sadly, I won't. We both know this is all you."

"Thanks, man. Means a lot. Don't let Mom talk your ear off."

"Too late," Mom chimes in. "Chris is going to sneak into one of your shows."

"No shit?" Anxiety spikes as I shake my head, imagining one of my heroes watching me perform. Though a family friend he may be, he's one of my favorite songwriters.

"I would love to catch up, but I have to jump off."

"The hell you do," Mom protests, "I want my five minutes."

"Can't. We have sound check in twenty, and I'm driving today."

"Fine. But I'm saving all of these, and we will be reading them together when you get back."

"Maybe."

"Oh, by the way, your father is still sick, so I don't know when he'll be able to join you."

"Bad?"

"No, just a really nasty head cold and ear infection, so he shouldn't fly."

I bite my lip. "Mom, can I ask a favor?"

I hear it the second she takes me off speaker and tells Chris she'll be right back before she speaks up. "You know you can ask me anything."

"Can you hold him back for the next few shows? I do want him here, but I want a little time alone with the band. If it comes from me, he might think—"

"Say no more." She convincingly fakes a cough. "I'm sick."

"Really?"

"My sweet boy, I'm a fucking scholar on the subject of Reid Crowne. I've so got this."

I can't help my chuckle. "Thanks."

Stopping at the crosswalk with the rest of the pedestrian traffic, I glance over to see a blue-eyed baby girl staring up at me from her stroller as Mom ticks off her regular list of orders. "Remember, no drugs, girls, or bar fights."

"Gee, thanks. But you do realize you're about a decade late with this lecture?"

"What!?"

"Kidding." *Partially.*

"Easton, you better damn well be wearing your—"

"Gotta run. I'll call you later. Love you, Mom."

Mom barks my name, and I hang up, feeling a pride from the call I wasn't expecting. Especially with a huge nod from two of the people I respect most in the industry.

Tack texts me for my location. Just as I go to pin it, I glance up at the street sign as those around me begin to walk forward. The walk sign blinks in haste for me to obey just under the glaring street name—BUTLER.

Unable to dismiss the irony, I take a page from my mother's book and dial her number, knowing she's probably watching her phone ring. Not once in the two months since she left has she declined a call, but she hasn't answered a single one, either.

Knowing it's a lost cause as her voicemail prompts me to leave a message, I consider telling her why I continue to call, but at the last second decide to hang up because she must know.

She knows, and she's willing to let go of it, so it's past time I give up.

Tack texts me back, and I shake my head in exasperation as I glance at the time. A time stamp I've been encouraged to wish upon my entire existence thanks to my mother's superstitious rituals and the part she believes it's played in her life.

11:11 AM.

TWENTY-SIX

Come Find Me
Emile Haynie, Lykke Li, Romy

Natalie

"Hey, love," Elena sounds through my console. "I'm going to head home. Do yourself a favor and get some rest this weekend."

"Is that your way of saying I look like shit, Elena?" Silence ensues on the other end. I know it's because she hates it when I use profanity. My father can cuss like a jilted, drunken sailor, but God forbid I swear around her. Sadly for her, I'm just the asshole to keep doing it. "Tough room," I joke. "I'm right behind you. I'll lock up."

"'K. Have a good weekend, sweetheart."

"You too."

The pit lights dim as Elena makes her exit. I revel in being the last in the office some nights, especially when the sun sets late because of the time change. Behind my desk, I light a tiny candle for a slight shift in atmosphere before ambling down the hall to claim a dark beer. A taste I acquired in Seattle and refuse to part with, allowing it to be a small consolation.

Twisting the top off, I wander back toward my office as I scroll through the latest hourly headlines and stop altogether when my phone rings. **EC** fills the screen as it rumbles in my hand, feeling like a five-alarm bell though I keep it on silent. With the slide of my thumb, I could hear his voice and possibly stifle the ache that's been nagging at me for endless weeks. At the very least, I can congratulate him.

"Maybe you should fucking answer it this time, 'cause from where I'm standing, it looks like you want to."

The bottle damn near slips out of my hand as I look up to see Easton standing just short of entering the pit at the edge of the lobby. His phone rests in his palm, his eyes damning, his beautiful features twisted in a mix of irritation and hurt, chest heaving like he just ran here.

I stand stunned, tempted to fly to him and rain his gorgeous face with kisses. He's nothing short of breathtaking in a simple T-shirt, board shorts, and high tops, his black cap flipped backward, giving me a clear view of his face and rapidly darkening expression. His hostile eyes dip and rake me over in a slow, appreciative sweep. Today I wore a plaid tennis skirt and matching collared shirt, which bares an inch of my midriff. I left my hair down and tamed my curls before painting my lips a hot pink to match my pumps.

"Easton," comes out more like a moan, and his eyes hood slightly in response as he takes a step forward, and I jerk my head. Coming to my senses, the exhilaration kicks in, and I rush toward him, then past him, yanking his arm to follow. He chuckles as I nearly rip his arm off, his laugh amplifying as I shove him against the exposed brick wall of the lobby near the door, praying we're out of view of the cameras.

"You been working out, Beauty? Because I'm feeling a little manhandled." His clean, woodsy scent envelops me as I palm his chest before looking up to him, and the awareness hits me like a freight train. My mouth refuses to do anything other than lift in a full smile.

Damnit!

We drink each other in for a few thirsty seconds before he speaks up.

"I should've just walked out of here, but Jesus Christ," he rasps hoarsely, "you look so fucking beautiful." His pained, faraway gaze shifts to focus fury on me as I try to register the fact that he's standing in front of me.

"Easton," I croak out, equal parts terrified and enthralled, before glancing toward my father's empty office. "You can't be here."

"The fuck I can't," he snaps, his eyes roaming my profile again as if he's fighting himself.

Panic takes over as some vampire-like motor functions kick in.

"Just…wait here," I demand, and he nods quickly in reply. "I'm serious. Stand *right here*. Not an inch to the left or right, *okay*?"

He nods slowly as if *I'm* the dummy as I rush to gather my purse, blow out my candle and flip off my office lights before hauling ass back into the lobby.

"Don't move!" I bark as I set the alarm.

"If you're this bossy at the office, I'm not sure we'd make it as co-workers," he jests.

A nervous laugh escapes me, and as soon as the alarm begins to beep, I rush him out and remotely lock the door. Turning, I start at a dead sprint around the side of the building and past *Speak's* designated parking area. Glancing toward the street in a panic, I feel his eyes on my profile as I weigh whether or not we're far enough away from the security cameras. Dad should already be on the golf course with his best friend, Marcus. I know this because I spoke to him half an hour ago. Mom is at the spa with her girlfriends from the station. Even knowing they'll have no reason to scan the cameras, my anxiety spikes significantly at the idea they might. Easton's minty exhale hits the side of my neck, causing my lashes to flutter briefly as his arms encase me. When his fingers curl around my waist I look up at him and feel nothing but the same debilitating attraction that's been haunting me for eight straight weeks.

"Are you fucking crazy?! What were you thinking?"

"That there was only one car in this parking lot, and I doubt your dad drives a hybrid with a bumper sticker that reads 'World Dominance' with a stiletto heel running through it."

"This isn't funny," my scold contradicts my smile. The friction of his fingers against my bare skin has goosebumps erupting on my flesh, despite the heat, as I grapple with the fact Easton's in Austin. "Seriously, what are you doing *here*? You're supposed to be on tour."

"I am. I was in the neighborhood…on Butler Street."

I frown.

"In Oklahoma, where I have a show in," he pulls out his cell and checks the screen, "six and a half hours and another tomorrow night in Dallas, so we need to get you packed."

"Yeah, right," I scoff, loving the feel of his hands on my hips, putting my entire focus on him and instantly wishing I hadn't. I can't bring myself to remove his hands as he continuously sweeps lazy thumbs along the bare skin above my skirt.

He gives me the barely-there lift of his lips. "Tell me you aren't happy to see me."

"I am…really. I am. It's just…I can't come with you to Oklahoma, you know that." I glance around nervously. Dad's probably three beers in with Marcus already. Damon's supposed to join them both. I could text Damon to confirm they're occupied. When I look back at Easton, everything starts to dull, the world around him blurring into nothing but a backdrop.

"There you are," he whispers.

"I'm just…I'm freaking out. You can't ever do that again, okay?"

His grip on me eases as his nostrils flare. "Right, bad idea. Got it."

"I'm serious."

He ignores my blatant reprimand. "You have weekends off, right?"

"Yeah, but—"

"Come with me then," he says, his eyes sweeping me intimately.

"You're making this so hard for me."

He smirks. "I could say the same."

"Not funny," I snap, my heart picking up rhythm.

"Then why are you smiling?"

I push against his chest so he's forced to loosen his grip on my hips, his touch too seductive. "I'm so happy for you. Seriously, I've been watching the progress. Are *you* happy?"

"Yeah," he gives me the half-smile I love so much. "I am."

"So, where is everyone?"

He lifts his chin in the direction of the back of a coffee shop less than a block away. "They're waiting in a van out front."

"You're really doing it."

"Yeah, I really am," he lifts a hooked finger to trace the side of my face, "and it's been a mix of awesome and fucking terrible. I brought them with me so you can get to know them on the way back to Oklahoma."

"You seriously drove from Oklahoma to pick me up, thinking that I would come after not answering your phone calls for two months?"

"Fuck yeah, I did. I'm pissed at you, but I can't bring myself to act on it yet because I want to give you a proper tongue lashing."

"Easton," I admonish with a sigh.

"Beauty," he fires back, unphased, continually running his fingers down my cheek. "I'm not letting this go, *yet*, so if you're going to let me down, you'll have to do it gently over the weekend." His eyes trail his fingers as he caresses me, "Because we really don't have time to argue."

"I'm supposed to be having dinner with my parents later."

"Well, you'll be dining on peanut butter and jelly in a van that smells like blue cheese instead."

I can't help smiling. "You really know how to sweep a girl off her feet."

He leans in. "I'm planning on doing my fucking best."

"Easton," I smack his chest playfully. "You're putting me in the worst imaginable position."

"Seriously, you're killing me with the easy puns. Clock's ticking," he taunts, running his fingertips up and down the bare skin of my arms. "It's hot as fuck here," he glances around curiously as if just now seeing my corner of the world.

"This is so unfair. This is entrapment."

"Come on," he urges gently, "just this weekend. I'll have you tucked in by Sunday at midnight."

"If I go, there will be no tucking in."

"Uh huh."

"And this is a really, really bad idea."

"Senseless and reckless," he murmurs heatedly, bringing it all back so effortlessly, "so *come*."

"If I do come, I *will* be turning you down gently."

He replies on exhale. "I have a feeling you'll try."

"I'll *succeed*, but I'm dying to see you play."

Victory flits through his eyes. "I'll give you the best seat in the house, baby."

"Uh huh, after I travel for hours in a van full of sweaty men."

"Five hours, six tops, depending on traffic, and I'm so fucking pissed at you right now," he repeats, his eyes flaring, "so expect a fight."

Before I can speak up, a horn blares obnoxiously a street over, and Easton chuckles, glancing in that direction before turning back to me. He looks so beautiful. His hair is longer, his skin darker, seeming drenched from the summer sun, which beams down on him as it lowers in the skyline.

"Natalie," he murmurs, pulling my chin by his fingers back toward him. "I really just want to talk to you, so please don't force me to play dirty because I have time to kill between gigs, and if you don't get," he bites his lip, "your perfect ass in my van, I'm going to bend you over Monday morning and bite it right in front of your daddy. *Bet.*"

I gape at him. "You did not just threaten me."

"Yeah, I did, and don't look at me like that. It's par for the course, but don't mistake me. I'm just A-sided enough to make good on mine."

"This is serious," I snap.

"You've made me painfully aware, Beauty," he runs his hands down my back and presses his forehead to mine.

"Jesus," I sigh, sinking into his hold.

"Easton," he corrects, pointing to himself.

My grin wins again. "Stop being so..."

"Irresistible?"

He grips my face and licks his lips, and I follow the trail of his tongue.

"Easton, please," I say breathlessly as he flashes a devil's grin. He closes his eyes briefly before reopening them, the intensity of the man I met still there. Inside them I see nothing but a reflection of my own desire. It's as if a second hasn't passed at all, but so much has changed. So much, at least for him.

"You know, Mr. Crowne, months from now—probably a lot less, you'll be selling out stadiums."

"We've already sold out the Staples Center at the end of August."

"Oh my God! That's incredible! I truly am so...so very happy for you." Sentiment waters my eyes as he stares at me, seeming satisfied by my reaction. "I mean, I knew it was going to happen...and I'm happy to say I told you so, and Easton, the things the critics are saying...it's..."

His eyes glint as though he's justified a thought or a notion.

"What?" I prompt. "What are you thinking about?"

"I'll tell you later."

"Well, you seem happy," I say. The creased line I thought was permanent between his eyes appears to have all but disappeared. He seems more approachable and, altogether...lighter.

"I'll be a lot happier when you get the hell in the van."

I shake my head, and he pinches his dark brows. "What?"

"Nothing. I just can't believe you're here and that you came all this way for me."

"Would have come a lot sooner had you answered the fucking phone."

"East—"

"Like I said, we'll fight later. Let's get you packed, okay?"

I bite my lip and find myself nodding. "Okay. But I have conditions."

"Of course, you do," his smile stretches his lips as his hands ghost over my skin. He can't seem to stop touching me. I can't seem to stop wanting him to any more than I can turn down his invitation.

"Follow me home, and I'll pack a quick bag."

"I'll help," his gaze dips to my navel.

"I'll be packing *alone*."

His eyes flick up before he grips my neck and crushes our mouths together, his kiss promising and demanding. He ends it just as abruptly.

"You can't—"

"I just fucking did," he replies smugly before releasing me. Running a hand through his hair, his eyes shine suspiciously as he rakes his lower lip with his teeth, dangerous plans seeming to formulate as he does. "Lead the way," he orders, his expression flashing with smug surety before a satisfied smile blooms on his face.

He turns and saunters toward the coffee shop, natural swagger on full display. Studying his silhouette, I bite my own lip, loving the snug fit of his board shorts and the spectacular outline of his muscular frame beneath his T-shirt.

"I'm *not* sleeping with you," I call after him. With his back to me, he shakes his head in obvious annoyance before jogging in the direction of his van.

I can't help but watch him go, my heartbeat ramping up as I walk toward my car. Once behind the wheel, I catch my beaming smile in my rearview as I buckle in and take a few sobering breaths.

"Just the weekend, Natalie," I tell myself. Just the weekend. Two more days.

Just to see him play.

And then I'll let us *both* down gently.

TWENTY-SEVEN

Space Age Love Song
A Flock of Seagulls

Natalie

After battling Easton for minutes—minutes he argues we don't have to spare—I relent and let him into my apartment. The thought of being intimate with him again and suffering a similar aftermath is too much to bear. Even if we can't become anything resembling what we left in Seattle, I decide to live in the moment, if only to witness him realizing his dreams.

He's mostly quiet as he prowls around my apartment, pausing at my built-in bookshelf before focusing on the digital photo frame that fades in and out with years of pictures.

"Is the brunette Holly?"

"Yeah," I reply from beside my bed in front of my open suitcase, flattered he remembered her name. A second later, his posture stiffens.

"What?"

He lifts the frame that hosts a picture of Damon and me the night we graduated, arms thrown around each other, smiles beaming. "Please tell me this isn't fucking Damon."

I can't help my answering laugh. "Yeah, and sadly, he's even prettier in real life."

"Seriously?" he mutters under his breath as I press my lips together, trying desperately not to read into the hint of jealousy. As pretty as Damon may be, not once have I ever felt a tenth of what I do when I look at Easton.

At my closet, I glance over to see him pulling my Cactus yearbook from the shelf.

"What's this?"

"It's the oldest publication at the University of Texas. It's kind of like a yearbook for each graduating class."

"Did you like college?"

"Yeah...well, in hindsight, it's kind of a blur to me."

His chest bounces as he puts the book back. "In other words, you didn't cut loose much."

"Didn't have time. I spent a lot of it working at *Speak* when I wasn't helping at *The Daily Texan*."

He lifts his chin in prompt.

"The UT paper," I clarify.

"Overachiever," he mutters, closing the book before shelving it and gazing at me with an intense stare. "Good thing you now know you're capable of more, at least with me."

"Think so?"

"I know so," he says with a level of certainty that has anticipation rolling through me.

"Well, that's not possible," I mumble, grabbing a skirt from a hanger and tucking it into my suitcase.

"What's that?" He asks, temporarily distracted by the mini maracas I got as a souvenir on a family vacation.

"I'll only be a few more minutes," I amplify my voice and make a mental note the man has bat hearing. "Those are from a beach trip to Mexico," I say as he rolls the tiny instruments between his skilled fingers.

"Yeah? I've never been to the coast."

"It's a must. Dad used to take us annually to this spot he loves. It's less touristy, and—" I turn and falter when I see Easton standing in my bedroom doorway, his hands braced on the frame above him, biceps bulging. He's so fucking perfect that I pause my packing to admire him.

"Your place is nice. Comfortable."

"Thanks," I can't help my smile, "I'm sensing a but..."

"It's a little small. I guess I just expected bigger."

"Wow, Easton Crowne skirting around a question?" I pull some panties from my delicates drawer and toss them into my case. "What you really want to ask is why I'm living in seven hundred square feet when my parents are well off?"

"Pretty much," he says.

"Because…we have more in common than you think." I tuck some bras into the zipper bag. "I maxed out my AmEx to go to Seattle, remember?"

He nods.

"Well, that's because wet-behind-the-ears college graduates don't get high spending limits. I, too, intend to fully earn my way. I live on the salary I make at the paper, not off some trust fund. I will admit, like you, my parents still attempt to and often spoil me pretty damned rotten."

His probing stare trails me as I grab my amenities bag from my bathroom and start to load it into my suitcase.

"You didn't say anything," he whispers softly.

"No, I didn't." I pause with a T-shirt in hand, "I was having a hard enough time with," I gesture between us, "you know."

"Who's skirting now?" He dives in—relentless in his pursuit of the truth—as I roll up the T-shirt for the second time and shove it into my suitcase.

"I didn't think it was that important."

"No, don't backtrack. You didn't want to highlight how much we had in common."

"Easton," I sigh, "make no mistake. I am happy to see you. I do want to hang out with you and watch you play, but we can't go further than that. After this weekend—"

"You won't even answer my fucking phone calls," he quips coldly. "So, it's pretty safe to assume I'm wasting my time with that."

I nod solemnly.

"Like I said," he sighs, "we can argue about this later."

I cross my arms. "All that means is that you're not hearing me."

"What makes you so fucking sure I'm here for *that* anyway? We only hooked up once." He shrugs. "You're being mighty presumptuous."

"I…oh," my neck heats as I drop my gaze to my overpacked suitcase. A low chuckle rumbles from where he stands, and I glare at him while he runs his teeth along his upper lip.

"You're a real asshole, you know that?"

"Yep, but don't worry. I'm not in the business of forcing my will on women who won't even bother to pick up the phone for me."

"I wanted to answer," I say. "I really did."

"I saw, but you didn't."

I wrangle more clothes into my suitcase as he pipes up, mirth in his tone. "We're only going for two days. You do know that, right?"

"I like options. So, how do you like the band?"

He grins, seeming thoroughly amused by my abrupt change of subject, but he allows it.

"All of them have some years on me, but I don't consider it a bad thing. Every one of them is crazy talented."

"That's awesome."

"Yeah. So far, the gamble's paid off. They play my originals just like I laid it out, but if it all works out and we decide to move forward, we're going to collaborate on the next album, and I'm really hoping it works out. It's definitely an eclectic mix."

"Uh oh, you want to give me the rundown so I know what I'm in for?"

"Nah, you can handle them and get their stories when you meet them."

"Do *you* like them?"

"So far. We were practically fucking strangers when we hit the road a month ago, but that's the whole point of doing the van thing, to remedy that and see if we vibe. We're basically living in the fucking thing, stuck together for endless hours on the road. It's been…" he widens his eyes with a chuckle, "something."

"Already collecting war stories, huh?"

"You could say that."

"I'm sure." Even I hear the hint of jealousy in my tone and berate myself for it.

Ewww, Natalie.

Still, it's hard to imagine he's immune to the staggering amount of female attention he's getting. He probably has hourly opportunities to get his needs met, and damn if that doesn't sting. The memory of the feel of him inside me that day at his studio hits me like a tidal wave as I look over at him.

I swear I catch a hint of a smile on his face before he turns and stalks back over to the digital photo frame just as an old picture of my dad and me appears. I'm in my softball uniform, holding my glove awkwardly. Dad's kneeling behind me, surrounding me in his large build as we flash twin smiles for the camera.

"I'd just made catch of the year," I tell Easton as he holds his finger on the photo to keep it from changing.

"You were that good?"

"Just the opposite, I was terrible," I laugh as I pull out a drawer. "Outside of riding horses, I don't have an athletic bone in my body. See how big that glove is?"

"Yeah, it's huge."

"I'd forgotten mine that day and had to use my coach's. I think that's the only reason I made that catch. Dad was in the stands as the ball was popped right to me. I just stuck my glove out to shield myself and miraculously caught it. Stunned, I just stared at it in my hand as Dad screamed at me from the stands to throw it to second. When I did, it earned us a double play, and we won the game." I giggle at the memory. "That was my first and *last* season. I quit when I was on top. Played soccer for a few seasons though, Dad coached. Turns out I was just good at running, and he liked it because I had a lot of energy and would pass out on the way home. So, basically, he wanted to be seen as a doting father but was just a bad parent."

Easton chuckles, releasing the picture as more snapshots of my life unfold on screen. Scanning the suitcase, I opt to pull on some white shorts beneath my skirt before discarding it.

"Keep the heels," Easton orders thickly, glancing over at me as I turn my head, and our eyes collide.

The air charges between us as I lift a brow.

"Please," he adds dryly as if he's reached his limit for the day and the word is now leaving a bad taste in his mouth.

"Thought you weren't here for *that*," I snark.

"I'm here for *you*. But we're not going anywhere if you don't hurry the hell up."

I slip on my worn checkered Vans and opt to toss my favorite heels in the suitcase before zipping it up.

Without prompt, he walks over and lifts the case from my bed, running his fingers over my patched quilt comforter as if he couldn't resist feeling it on his fingertips before extending his hand toward me. The familiarity of the act brings forth everything lingering between us, and so I do what feels natural. I take it.

TWENTY-EIGHT

Steal Away
Robbie Dupree

Natalie

Gaping at the footage on the cell phone, I glance back at Jason Garett, aka Tack, Easton's hired drummer, as he grins back at me from the first row of the van. Stunned, I flit my gaze to Easton, who opted to drive while I ride shotgun.

"You outran a fucking tornado?" I scold in my Bactine and Band-Aid maternal tone.

"We were at a safe enough distance," Easton defends weakly, a grin brewing on his lips.

"That's a bit of a stretch. Look at this," Tack admits, thrusting a picture of golf ball-sized hail cradled in his heavily tattooed hand toward me.

"Jesus, Easton," I chide, which only makes his smile bloom.

"Crazy, right?" Tack shakes his head before pulling a beer from the cooler on the floorboard and thrusting it toward me. "Want one, Nat?"

"No thanks, I'm kind of a lightweight," I admit. "I'll wait for the show."

A question strikes me then. "Easton?"

"Yeah?"

"We aren't *sleeping* in the van, right?"

He chuckles. "I wouldn't subject you to that."

"We tried a few nights the first week," Tack says with clear annoyance, lifting his chin in Easton's direction. "This fucker insisted on it, but it was a nightmare."

"Too fucking right," Syd pipes from next to him.

"So sorry you missed your morning tea, darling," Easton says unapologetically.

"As you should be." Syd snarks back in his British accent.

Easton shrugs. "I tried. But the vote was three to one, against me."

"Not that our win did much good. Now, after endless hours in this filthy fucking van, we're stuck staying in the cheapest hotels," Syd adds, his prominent accent making his snobbery sound a bit more comical. "I draw the line sleeping with these smelly bastards, and bologna is not proper food."

"Ah!" I say, turning to Easton, "that's what's lingering in here. I couldn't place it!"

Easton chuckles and glances over at me. Much to my dismay, upon entering the van, I had to control my gag reflex. Easton's blue cheese assessment far kinder than reality. I would go so far as to say the van smells like a blue cheese-covered, heavily used gym sock that's been freshly baked in the sun.

Easton had laughed hysterically at my reaction as I immediately rolled down the window, trying to mask my gags.

It took the better part of the first hour of our trip for me to be able to handle it. Still, I wouldn't want to be anywhere else. The band has been nothing but welcoming in a way I wasn't expecting, and I got the eclectic part of Easton's warning right away.

Tack was raised in the Midwest. His monstrous meat and potatoes build bred deep in a slice of Americana. He definitely sports the rocker look with dark brown hair and darker brown eyes. His mismatched clothes somehow work, and he's got more ink than visible skin. So far, he's been the most talkative of the three.

"Now this was a good fucking night," Tack says fondly, lifting a picture to LL, aka Leif Garrison, Easton's lead guitar player, who sits with his back to the window, his arm stretched out on the second-row seat. Though Scandinavian born, with white-blond locks and sparkling blue eyes, his Sussex-raised accent is unmistakable. LL's looks are striking in contrast to the other three's dark and broody.

Syd Patel, the oldest at twenty-nine, is Easton's UK-born bassist. His skin is the most beautiful hue of dark brown, thanks to his Indian heritage. The quietest of the three, mainly because he hasn't stopped vaping and drinking since I got into the van, he's been forthcoming enough to make me feel at home amongst them.

"This crew," Easton muses between us, "it's almost like a setup for a joke."

As I take them all in, LL returns my curious gaze the longest, a Guinness can clutched in his hand.

"Maybe," I say, turning back toward Easton, "but this is really happening. You're doing it. You're on your way to play another show right now."

"Yeah, it's amazing. But something wasn't right." He glances over to me. "It hit me in Oklahoma that I needed to pick up my favorite instrument." Jumping on Easton's bold and slightly infuriating declaration—knowing he didn't really mean the misogynistic insinuation—I unbuckle my seatbelt and turn on my knees, gripping the headrest. Easton objects immediately by slapping my ass, *hard.*

"Just for a second," I say, waving him away.

"Put that buckle back on, *now*," he barks.

"Chill," I dismiss. "So…" I give each of them a pointed stare. "Tell me about the ladies," I waggle my brows, "how's the action?"

LL is the first to smile, and I point at him. "Ah ha!"

Glancing over at Easton in time to see his nostrils flare, Tack speaks up as Syd smirks out of the window.

"What do you want to know?" Tack asks.

"Well, do any of you have a lady in waiting back home?"

"Fuck no," Tack replies, "and it's a good thing because—"

"Don't you fucking finish that," Easton warns, all too aware of what I'm getting at. Right now, it's my only line of defense, so I press in.

"Oh, but Tack, I think you should," I draw out.

"I'm divorced," Syd offers, tapping his bare ring finger, "no birds to speak of at the moment, which I also consider a good thing."

"And you, sir," I ask LL, whose looks could vaporize panties worldwide. The man is stunningly gorgeous, though no Easton Crowne.

LL's lips curve in a devious smile. "I'm a gentleman."

Even Easton protests with a loud sigh of "Bullshit" as various debris retrieved from the floorboard flies toward LL's head. As the chaos erupts, Easton's fingers discreetly skim up my thigh, and I immediately turn toward him and catch the opposite of what I was expecting. He's glaring at me in warning, a take no prisoners look marring his features. "Seat belt, *now,* or I'm fucking pulling over."

"Geesh," I turn back and buckle in. Seconds later, Dion's "Only You Know" comes on through Easton's playlist, a rare repeat. Easton turns it up, keeping his gaze on the highway as more anarchy erupts from the back of the van.

"What the fuck is this, golden oldies?" Tack wrinkles his nose.

"Exactly, it's a classic. Listen up, and maybe you'll learn something. Also, if you're not *driving*, you don't get a say," Easton barks in his no fucks given tone.

Apparently, it's a van rule.

Not long after, I get lost in the melody, in the memory of those minutes he played for me in that hotel. For several seconds, I mentally trace his profile. Though he doesn't look over at me, I know he's right there with me. When the song ends, his gaze finally slides over to mine.

"Your first time," I whisper between us. "I wish I would have recorded it."

"It's better you didn't," he says in a way I know would tarnish some of the intimacy of that memory, and I slowly nod in agreement.

I'm tempted to fling myself at him, even with the burn of the groupie talk chattering in the back of my mind. I can't help but ogle him freely, and I do, for miles. That is until Tack grips both our headrests with his heavily inked hands, his head popping up between us.

"So, what's the deal with you two?" Tack cants his head toward Easton, his question directed toward me. "This fucker was tightlipped the entire way to Austin and only admitted we were picking up his girl five minutes before we pulled up."

Easton shoots a quick look my way, forcing me to answer on our behalf, his expression muted.

"We're friends," I say, with a lead tongue, the words feeling like a betrayal. "*Close* friends," I emphasize, glancing over to see Easton checking his blind spot as he shifts lanes, his reflection revealing he's not at all happy about my answer, jaw ticking in response.

It's not like I'm happy about it either, but we can't be anything else, and somehow, I have to figure out a way to make him understand it while continuing to convince myself of the same thing. I wonder how many times you can lie to yourself before it becomes habitual. That's what I feel like right now, a liar, because how in the hell am I going to resist this man? But I must. I have to make those words true. My father always taught me the right thing and the hard thing are often the same thing. In the case of Easton Crowne, my resistance to him will be my biggest test.

Unsatisfied, Tack presses in. "How did you *close friends* meet?"

That's the crux of it, and I say it out loud to remind us *both*. "In the most impossible of situations. Trust me, you wouldn't believe me if I told you."

"Try me," Tack challenges.

"Hey, man, sit back," Easton bites out lightly, "I can't see out of the rearview."

Tack rolls his eyes at Easton's blatant attempt to end our conversation. It's effective enough. Soon after, the guys start to chat amongst themselves, beers popping at random.

Briefly, I worry that they'll be drunk by the time they have to play, but Easton looks unconcerned as he stares out at the rapidly darkening road.

After too many miles of uncomfortable silence, a rarity for us, I finally state my piece.

"I'm sorry…I didn't know what else to say."

He gives me the subtle dip of his chin, but I know that's not the answer he wanted. In the next two days, I'm determined to make him understand it's the only answer I can give.

The minute we pull up to the small auditorium, the guys exit like their asses are on fire, having only half an hour to spare before the show starts. Easton had refused to pull over for a third piss break, and the guys threatened to unload in the sea of Gatorade bottles on the floorboard. Needless to say, there was no going back after they'd broken the seal. We ended up stopping four times before we made it to the venue. They all seem in good spirits now, even Easton, who I had refused to let go radio silent on me the rest of the way to Oklahoma. Surprisingly, he seemed just as eager to get us back to the cheerful place we were in when he picked me up. As we caught up, I could see such a change in his posture from the time we met. His smiles are granted far easier. The more I observed the differences in him, the more I realized some of his ill demeanor was due to the fact he was at his own crossroads when ours merged.

We'd been there for each other when we both needed someone to help us put things in perspective. It's no doubt one of the reasons why we bonded so quickly, and it seems so—unforgettably. One thing I know for certain is that he gifted me the perception I need. Unfortunately, he's done it in a way that's brought on a whole new set of challenges. Challenges like trying to keep my legs from wrapping around his naked waist for the next forty-eight hours.

It's clear now we're both on the other side of the road we merged on, having chosen our respective directions. Unsurprisingly, I've stayed the same course—a course I've chosen my entire life, as has he. My path isn't as full of solutions as his is, though—something I'll be hard-pressed to admit to him.

As much as I love the intense Easton I met who was weighing a major life decision, this Easton is just as alluring, if not more enigmatic, which will make the next couple of days much harder.

Mulling over the task at hand, I catch sight of a familiar face as an identical second van, which was absent during our road trip, pulls up beside us.

"Oh my God!" I exclaim, and Easton flashes me a grin before I haul ass toward the driver's door of the second van. Joel steps out looking gorgeous in a simple white T-shirt and jeans, a ready smile for me as he opens his arms and I fly into them. "Hey, you!" I greet, feeling the warmth in his embrace as we hug tightly and pull back slightly with matching grins. "Is it weird to say that I missed you?"

"Not at all. We bonded fast, and we weren't the only ones." He lifts his chin, gesturing behind me, and I follow his line of sight to catch Easton's gaze darting warmly between us before Joel leans in on a whisper. "And in case it's not evident, you've been missed, too." Before I can get a read on Easton, the back door of the arena bursts open. Easton's eyes slip from the two of us as he's greeted by a man who eagerly pumps his hand with both of his own. Joel and I chuckle as Easton widens his eyes at us helplessly. The man talks a mile a minute, clasping his palm on Easton's shoulder before ushering him toward the door.

"You told him, didn't you?" I turn back to Joel as Easton disappears inside. "That I was crying when I left, you told him."

Joel shakes his head, not a trace of guilt to be found in his expression.

"I didn't have to."

TWENTY-NINE

Worldstop
Roy English

Natalie

Blindsided.

That's how I felt during the first half-hour of the show. The online experience of watching Easton perform doesn't do him or the band nearly enough justice. Just a few minutes in, I decided it would have been a tragedy if I missed this opportunity. Though Easton said they were jelling well as a band and making good progress in tightening their sound, I can't imagine them sounding better. Easton's stage presence is an experience within itself. Combined with his astounding vocal range and his music, it's utterly mesmerizing.

He came out guns blazing, the most natural showman alive, and I was instantly hot for him. Though dressed the same as when he collected me, the look somehow turned more rock and roll as he performed, his hat backward, the visible tips of his hair dripping sweat within the first few songs, his T-shirt plastered to his muscular chest.

Hidden between the first and second curtain, side stage, I really do have the best seat in the house, away from the audience's view. From my vantage point, I witnessed every damned facial expression and close of his eyes. I felt every change in pitch, every emotion he's feeling, relaying and evoking as he plays and sings seamlessly, like a veteran—God help me. Now well into the set, it's astounding they all have the same energy as when they started playing, as if they're just warming up.

Drinking in the scene before me, I briefly shift my focus to the rest of the band. Tack remains a powerhouse on the drums as LL edges the stage on lead, his retro and badly faded Hawaiian shirt hanging open as he draws out every note with perfect clarity. Syd remains on the other side of the stage, far less animated, his bass lines steady yet expertly provoking.

But it's the man center stage that is wrecking us all past repairable. He's spent most of *this* song, "Tumble Dry," cupping the mic—his current weapon of mass destruction—with both hands, sweeping us away with the haunting melody and cut-throat lyrics.

I sway where I stand, maybe ten feet away, singing along, giving the starstruck fangirl dwelling inside me her fair share of indulgence.

They've surpassed my expectations. I'm already dreading when the second show ends, but still thankful I'll be gifted one more.

One more will be enough, Natalie.

Chucking the heels I put on before the show, I lift my arms in praise above my head as sweat trickles down my back, and I allow myself to get swept away.

Easton's voice flows like lava throughout the small auditorium of six thousand, the place packed to capacity. Peeking out through the curtain at the beginning of the show, I saw that many of the fans taking up the first row are women, their expressions nothing short of worship, as if they reach out to him, he'll cure them all. For them, in these few minutes, he's worthy of those starved and reverent looks. He would also be the cure for me if I acknowledged the continually growing ache and pounced on the opportunity to temporarily pacify it with him.

But I'm no idiot.

I've had a long drink, and I know of the addictive thirst that's sure to follow. Easton now belongs to the world—and for him, for me—I have to live in this moment because I know it's fleeting. He's space-bound, and my roots are firmly planted. Refusing to let my mood be altered by those thoughts, I cheer along with the crowd and take endless minutes of footage before putting my phone away. The last few songs of the show I decide will be for memory alone.

As a journalist, it's sometimes hard for me to distinguish which moments to live in and which to capture with total mental clarity for my own creative outlet down the line. But this moment is definitively mine, and he wanted *me* here. Natalie *Butler*, not Natalie Hearst. Even if we are one and the same.

Closing my eyes, I get lost in the lyrics, mouthing them in tandem. It's when I open them and see Easton angled toward me, watching me intently from where he sings, that all the breath whooshes out of me.

Bastard.

I'm so close to the fire now. I know exactly what parts would remain intact if I so much as take a single step toward what I'm feeling, the truth of it continuously plaguing me.

A tale as old as time as far as human nature is concerned.

I want what I can't have.

Even as I think it, his quiet electricity runs rampant throughout my body, engulfing me as the hairs on my arms and neck stand on end. I inhale the charged air between us as memory floods in, of the desire in his eyes, of how we bared ourselves, pulled each other apart, and examined our pieces before fusing ourselves back together so effortlessly. I feel those seconds with every fiber of my being as he engages me fully, his guitar strapped on his back, guttural lyrics of longing pouring from his lips. The tidal wave of his gaze ebbs away, slowly receding as they drift closed, unmistakable ache in his voice just as he sings the last line before the stage goes dark.

When the lights come back up, I'm utterly seduced, drenched in him from feet away, my desire for him at an immeasurable high. Forcing my selfish needs down, I smile and extend my hands in a clap as the crowd roars to a deafening level. Even without seeing them, I can physically feel the bond between Easton and his audience, of the love he spoke so fondly of. Not only that, as Easton scans the throng of fans, taking it all in, I can see the elation on his features as he engages them. "Thanks so much for coming out, Oklahoma City," he places a hand on his chest before his eyes flick to mine. "I'm so glad you came."

"Me too," I mouth, still cradled inside the curtains asking myself the question again.

How the fuck am I supposed to resist this man?

How could *anyone* resist this man?

It's then I decide the pain will be worth it. Just to know him, to witness him start his life path, his career path, because of who he is. Briefly, I entertain the idea we could have some sort of friendship eventually, but that notion is shot to hell the second the image of him hovering above me at the studio shutters in. His hand gripping the end of the couch, the other cradling my jaw, his beautiful features twisted in pleasure when he pulsed inside me.

Here and now, Nat. Here and now.

These precious moments with him, witnessing the start of his journey, will be my consolation when I'm forced to tear myself away from him a second time.

This, right here, is the sweet spot, somewhere between easily recognizable and the full blow stardom sure to come. It's taken only months to build an audience this size, and he's already sold a stadium out for the end of his first *van* tour. A year from now, I won't be able to get near him so easily or possibly at all. This knowledge instills some fear for him. Because by the time he's done touring, he'll probably be swept into a level of fame he doesn't want. Ironically, on stage now, he seems completely at ease. I know he's at peace because, despite the fears he confided in me, his connection with them is his consolation.

"Give it up for REVERB! Baseline by Syd Patel, ripping on lead LL Garrison, and on drums Tack fucking Garrett!" Easton shouts, nodding toward the band before addressing them. "How about one more?" he asks, bouncing his gaze between LL, Tack, and Syd, who ready themselves in agreement, their faces lit due to recognition from the crowd. I love the fact that he spared the audience the ego-driven walk off stage and silent demand they cheer for an encore because that's not who he is.

A devilish grin lifts his lush lips, and I get buzzed by the sight of it as he easily shifts his shiny black guitar in front of him, making the transition look effortless.

I hold my breath—along with the rest of the audience—in anticipation of what cover they'll play. So far, he's covered several eras and genres and made more headlines due to one of his latest encores in which he nailed a rap song to the point it seemed like he's been rapping his whole life. I must have replayed that footage a hundred times and felt the same pride for him every time. It seems no matter what he tackles, he nails it.

Easton leans into the mic as they continue to cheer for him, his answering smile amping them up before they finally quiet down as he readies his guitar pick.

The lights go out a second time as Easton's drawl echoes.

"And during the few moments that we have left, we want to talk right down to earth in a language that everybody here can easily understand."

"Oh my God!" I spring like a Jack in the Box as the lights come up and Easton rips through the first chords of "Cult of Personality" with expertise. Eyes fixed on him, I geek out, bobbing my head and rocking on my heels, hair flying around my face wildly as the stadium explodes in chaos.

Easton rips on his guitar like it's an extension of him through the solo, running his head back and forth as he plucks the strings, expertly pulling it off alongside LL while I lose all sense of self. The band doesn't miss a single layer of the song as the four of them blow the roof off the fucking place.

Like me, I suspect most of the post-millennium-born audience has never heard the song. Then again, some of them probably have because if Easton's taught me anything in our time together, it's that though music is dated with a time stamp and divided by genre, it's timeless.

I understand that now more than ever because Easton has proved it so and made certain music eternal for me, this song included.

This revelation isn't news because not only is Easton outselling every mainstream artist out there, but he's also breaking demographic barriers, selling to multiple generations, a feat very few artists have managed to do. As he explained to me in the truck that day, he's creating common ground between us all. Knowing him—and his aversion to media—I'm not even sure he's aware of it.

Before I can take a full breath, the song is over, and the auditorium is roaring and organically begging for an encore Easton doesn't grant as the curtains close. The go-to-hell lights come up as I bounce on the balls of my feet, filled to the brim with adrenaline. Feeling euphoric, a sheen of sweat glistening on my skin, I laugh hysterically when I realize I'm becoming trapped between the first and second curtain as they close.

"Oh, bollocks!" I exclaim in mock Brit. "I would applaud you gents, but I can't seem to find me way out of these!" A whiff of Easton's scent hits me along with the smooth rumble of his chuckle just before I'm swallowed by the sight of him, the curtains billowing around him as he stalks toward me. In the next second, he's plastered to me.

Our chests collide before he grips the back of my neck and crushes my mouth with his.

His eager kiss elicits a moan from somewhere deep within, representing two excruciating months of longing. Easton uses it, pressing his tongue past my lips before invading me. I'm climbing him in seconds as he molds us together while playing *me* effortlessly. Ripping at his hair, I feel the vibration on his tongue and suck it feverishly as his hat thuds somewhere below us. Wet and aching, I moan into his mouth as he continues to draw me deeper into the kiss, utterly destroying my every defense until I'm clinging to him, unable to support my own weight. Our tongues furiously duel until he eventually pulls away, staring down at me intently before letting out a low, "Fuck, Beauty."

Panting, I gape at him, my clit demanding attention between my legs. "Damnit to hell, Crowne," I mutter in an attempt to catch myself, "you're *already* playing *dirty.*"

"No," he licks along my lower lip and pulls it briefly between his teeth. "Not yet." His nose brushes mine, "Not even close, but don't put it past me."

"This isn't a game," I whisper hoarsely.

He sobers, pulling back slightly so I can clearly see the look in his eyes. "No, it's not. You punched a hole in my goddamned chest in Seattle, only to leave me in the dark to try and figure out how to fill it."

His admission has me gravitating toward him just as he releases me and retrieves his hat.

"You keep interrupting my praises," I tell him in an attempt to sidestep the paralyzing effect of his words. His grin doesn't reach his eyes as he opts to place his retrieved hat on my head, pulling it down over my hot mess of curls. "It's like you don't even care about my opinion."

Something sparks in his eye as he dips in a whisper. "That's the thing, Beauty. With me, you rarely have to say a word."

"You keep calling me that."

"Yeah, well, it's a large part of the reason I drove to Austin to collect the girl I met. Because that's all I see when she reveals herself to me." He runs a gentle thumb across my lower lip. "Raw. Fucking. Beauty."

"Ohhhh," I draw out in my best Texas twang and another useless attempt at self-preservation, "you're really good at that. You should be a songwriter or somethin'. Women will fawn all over you for pretty words like those—"

"—while other parts of her remain purposely oblivious," he retorts dryly, rolling his eyes before knocking the brim of his hat down, temporarily blinding me. Gripping my hand, he starts to navigate us from within the confines of the curtains. Once we're free, I notice that LL and Syd are closing their cases, and Tack's made good progress dismantling his drum kit. The noise from the audience on the other side of the curtains is now noticeably absent.

How long were we kissing?

"That was amazing!" I belt out in an attempt to draw their attention, extending my clapping hands toward them. "Bet you fellas good money you make all the OK headlines tomorrow." Syd and LL flash me grins. LL's cerulean gaze flicks between Easton and me, letting me know he's onto us. Dodging his prodding assessment, I turn to Easton, his expression drawn up in amusement. Gripping his arm, I lift on my toes, commanding his attention and pulling him closer for his ear. He snakes his arm around me, his warm skin sending a shiver up my spine. "What I was going to say before you interrupted me with your *tongue* is that performance was every imaginable adjective for incredible, Easton. Thank you for sharing this with me," I pull back as he wets his lips and shakes his head.

"What?" I draw out, frowning. "Not enough praise for your highness? Still think I'm a shitty writer?"

"You really have no idea, do you?" He asks as I look helplessly over to Joel, standing guard just a few feet away.

"What am I missing?"

"The whole point," Easton taunts, running his knuckles down my cheek.

"Enlighten me, then," I say in a stupor, as all nearby hands-on-deck blur while I get distracted by the intimacy still bouncing between us.

Easton's chest pumps with his silent chuckle.

"Well?" I prompt.

"I'm working on it," he murmurs as a stagehand approaches with a water bottle. Easton takes it and thanks him before downing the whole thing in a few swallows. "I need to help break down and load up," he relays apologetically through a hasty inhale.

"How can I help?"

"You can't. Joel is going to get you checked into the hotel. Are you tired?"

"Hell no. I could run a marathon." I turn his hat backward and pretend to push up my sleeves as his easy grin returns.

"Let's have a late dinner with the guys at the hotel. Two hours?"

I curl my lip, renewed energy coursing through me. "Sure I can't help?" I point to myself. "I've got all this pent up..."

Easton lifts a brow as Tack speaks up from behind him. "Do you know how to break down a drum kit?"

"I'm a quick study!" I shout, sidestepping Easton and heading in Tack's direction just as Easton grips my arm.

"Deal with your own kit, asshole," Easton snaps as Tack gives him the bird without glancing up.

It's then, over Easton's shoulder, that I spot a handful of women waiting side stage, not a single swinging dick to be seen. Their view of us is obstructed by Joel as he moves toward them, arms outstretched before he ushers them further back. Easton leans in, forcing my eyes back to his. "I'm not trying to get rid of you, Natalie."

I muster a shrug as if I haven't a care in the world. "It's not my business."

His nostrils flare in clear irritation, and he gives me a dead stare.

"I'm golden, and it's not my place, so let's drop it." Turning, I start a search for my heels just inside the curtain and fish them out one by one. Without prompt, Easton grips my hip for support as I push into them, his fingers brushing my skin when he releases me. Swallowing, I brave a look up at him to see the same intensity I've seen several times before.

He leans down, so we're eye level. "Your lips are swollen from my kiss, and I'm willing to bet *good money* that your panties are fucking useless. Should we find a place backstage where I can make my point clearer?"

"You don't have to...say things like that." I feel my neck reddening as he presses in.

"I don't say anything I don't want to, and you fucking *know* that. See you in two hours." He leaves me then, panties drenched, head in a fog, body screaming, demanding satisfaction, my heart an inch from orbit.

"Ready, sweetheart?" Joel asks, suddenly standing next to me, jarring me out of my stupor. Narrowing my eyes, I look over at him as he presses his lips together in an attempt to hide his smile.

"You really didn't tell him?"

"I really didn't *have to*," he replies without further explanation before ushering me toward the exit. Glancing back, my gaze finds its way to Easton as he secures his guitar in his case before flicking to the eager group of women standing in wait. Easton's assurances whisper through my mind as I run my fingers over my tingling lips.

I am so fucked.

"Hey, Daddy," I say, tossing my overpacked suitcase on the hotel's king bed. He starts in immediately.

"What's with the vague text and skipping out on us?"

"I got caught up with a story. You know how it is."

"I do, but your mom's pissed. She cooked."

"Apologize for me."

"You're on speaker, brat," Mom chimes in as I unzip and begin to load the dresser.

"Sorry, sorry," I plea as the guilt sets in that I'm again lying to them both, and with far too much ease.

"Raincheck," Dad chimes in. "How about Sunday dinner?"

"No can do. You two will have to entertain yourselves this weekend. I've got plans."

"With whom?" Mom asks unabashedly.

"Addie," Dad scolds. "It's her weekend and her business. If she wants us to know, she'll tell us."

"Fine," Mom concedes easily. "I'll push dinner to Monday."

"I'll be there. I love you both…so much."

"Love you too," they say in unison.

"Oh, Daddy, if you want to look over the specs for this week's edition, I uploaded the layout before I left the office. I don't know if it's exactly what you want, but it's there."

"I trust you," he murmurs with pride as my heart drops. "I'm sure it's fine."

"Okay, well…Night."

They both echo goodnights as I end the call and fling myself across the bed, feeling like an altogether shitty human. I know I have their complete trust, but with the acts I've committed, I no longer feel worthy of it. With Easton's kiss still fresh on my lying lips, I tell myself for the umpteenth time that this weekend is all I can give him because my entire future resides on this secret being precisely that, a secret.

Even though remaining close-knit with my family is sewn into my future, I try to remind myself that I'm also very much a grown woman. A grown woman who shouldn't have to answer to her parents for every move she makes, especially when it comes to her personal life.

Guilt refusing to dissipate, I take a quick shower in an attempt to wash off the shame as I try to figure out how I'm going to hide for the next few days.

With the paparazzi earning high dollars for personal shots of Easton, the stakes are much higher now than in Seattle. The chances of us getting caught on the other side of the lens are far greater, so I can't be seen with him—in any capacity—in public. Standing side stage tonight—even between the curtains—was reckless and dangerous. Not only that, but Easton's eyes also strayed in my direction enough that anyone watching closely, especially with a keen, trained eye to pay attention to those particulars, could catch on.

Did they? Surely no one was able to get a good shot. I was too far back, practically buried between those curtains. Yet, anxiety begins to run through me as I shoot off a quick text.

I don't know if dinner is a good idea.

EC: It's taken care of.

What do you mean? I haven't told you why.

EC: You don't have to. I've got it handled. Trust me and get down here.

So demanding.

The bubbles start and stop before a text comes through.

EC: I miss you. That's what I called to say the first time.

Heart pounding erratically, I manage to type a reply.

And the second time?

EC: Maybe I'll tell you when you get to the table.

THIRTY

Through the Glass

Stone Sour

Easton

Spotting Natalie at the entrance of the hotel bar, I lift my chin as she searches and finds me, Tack continuing to prattle on beside me. He's still playing off the remaining energy from the stage, as am I. The high of playing is better than I could have ever anticipated. The woman standing side stage sweetened the feel of it exponentially tonight. Her reaction was everything I hoped for, as was she. She's everything I remembered but somehow even more beautiful, more alluring. Simply put, she's just fucking more.

So much more. I'm sure she's intent on ruining me dressed in tight jeans that hug her long, muscular legs, a plain white T-shirt, and a thin as fuck bra. Tack and I stand as she nears the table. It's when I'm able to read her expression and sense the hesitation in her posture that all of my hopes for the rest of the night slip into murky territory.

Somewhere between the kiss we shared backstage—that left me hard and uncomfortable as we packed up—to now, something has shifted, and she's back in the no-fly headspace she's been forcing herself into since I picked her up in Austin. Knowing I'm up against reinforced mental barriers, I allow her to choose her seat just as Tack pulls the chair next to me back in offering.

I dip my chin at him in silent thanks. Tack and I have managed an easy friendship since we started touring, and it's got a lot to do with the fact that he's basically a better person than most of the musicians I've met. He's got no bitter chip on his shoulder thanks to years of falling short of his dreams with his other bands. Like me, he plays purely for his love of music, and that fact alone earns him a lot of my respect.

Natalie takes a seat, freshly showered, her face only slightly made up, her curls still drying as a whiff of her clean, floral scent hits me. A scent she drenched me in and left me pining for after she opened herself to me. She gives me the opposite now, posture closed, avoiding eye contact before relinquishing a soft "Hi."

"Hey," I answer back, draping my arm along the back of her chair.

"My room is nice, comfortable, thank you," she says, glancing around the restaurant. "Where are LL and Syd?"

"Preoccupied," Tack offers up easily.

Hating the fact that she's deducing exactly what my bandmates are up to, she glances over at me, and I feel her unease before she addresses Tack.

"And you didn't want to be preoccupied?"

"I'm good here," he says. "I need a breather, and we have that thing tomorrow night."

She looks to me. "What thing?"

"An after-party in Dallas," Tack speaks up.

"Oh?"

"Yeah, we probably won't be going," I inform her.

"The fuck?" Tack asks as I stare back at him in warning.

"What am I missing now?" Natalie asks me directly, and I don't reply because the answer is different for each question, and I don't want to go there tonight since she seems to be on edge.

"Nothing. What are you hungry for?" I lean in, brushing her arm with mine, doing my best to put her at ease. "I don't think they serve crab legs here."

Her lips gradually start to lift as the waitress arrives, dropping us dark beers and water. "I'll give you guys a minute."

Natalie thanks her and turns to me. "You ordered for me?"

"Yeah, it's cool if you don't want it. It's last call soon."

"No, thank you, I do," she says, glancing around, "I was wondering why we were the only ones in here."

"No one else is here because your *very close friend* closed the fucking place down for you," Tack interrupts as I full-on glare at him. He stands and jabs a tattooed thumb over his shoulder. "I'm going to get us some shots before they close up. Order me a French dip?"

I nod as Natalie turns to me. "You closed the restaurant down?"

"A bit of an exaggeration. There wasn't many dining. I've got this," I reiterate, "so stop worrying."

She studies me as I scan the menu. More than anything, I want her at ease, like we were. The fucked-up part is that the clock is ticking just like the last time. A clock I decided to kickstart the second she closed the door in my face in Seattle. Sadly, it is her unearthed fears for herself that've aided in my decision. I don't want to die with regrets at *any* fucking age, and I sure as hell don't plan on letting this crazy chemistry and undeniable connection go to waste if I have any say in it. I've never been so drawn to another human being, and I'll be damned if I give up without a fight. Even if she plans on spending the weekend letting me down gently, by the time she leaves, she'll know exactly how much those days meant to me.

If my efforts prove futile and this goes nowhere—which seems inevitable—I can't fucking seem to stop wanting to explore it, explore more of her.

As crazy as the last two months have been for me professionally, I've spent a large part of all the combined moments quiet and otherwise absorbed by thoughts of her.

"What's up?" I ask as she traces her coaster with her finger.

"Nothing, I'm good."

"You spoke to your dad," I conclude, her resistance too familiar, too easy to read.

"Yeah," she floats her eyes around the table before lifting them to me. The purple around her irises hits like a fucking lightning bolt to the chest as memories of us without a trace of Nate Butler come to the forefront. I grip her hand beneath the table, and she gently pulls it out of reach.

"Already?"

"No, not already, always have been. Facts are facts." She lifts her voice as Tack approaches, fully armed. "And the fact is, tonight, you all ruled that stage, and I want to celebrate that." She taps the neck of her beer against mine.

"I'll drink to that," Tack adds, tabling a fistful of shots. We each take one and tap glasses before tossing them back.

As if out of thin air, Syd appears with a tumbler full of liquor and vape smoke clouding around him. The man is a tank and seemingly unflappable. Although we've become acquainted enough, he's still a bit of an enigma to me. His preference for the finer things is the only real *defining thing* about him so far. That and the fact that he's a beast on the bass.

"Another?" Tack asks the table.

I shake my head as Natalie nods and Tack ushers Syd away from the table to accompany him.

"...feeling like a third wheel," Tack says while they're still within earshot, and I clamp my eyes shut briefly to summon more patience. I had no plan other than to capture Natalie and demand a conversation. But the discomfort—thanks to the need for explanation of what we are and aren't—makes that simple tactic far more difficult to execute.

"He thinks we're together," Natalie utters.

"They all signed the strictest of non-disclosures. If they so much as utter a word about anything personal regarding me, or anything else to do with the band, other than regular interview bullshit, they'll pay, *dearly*."

"I'm sorry," she whispers, "I don't want to make things weird. I just...you know."

"I'm good, *for now*, being your dirty little secret, even if you're refusing to be mine."

She pinches my thigh hard beneath the table, and I chuckle. Seconds later, she flips the script. "You're a real rock star." Her hoarse declaration has me turning my head, and it's when I see the look in her eyes that I'm struck by the same intensity I've come to crave from her. "You *are*, Easton. You were incredible tonight."

We face off as the moment time stamps itself across my chest.

"You're all just so insanely talented." She lifts her voice, indicating our time alone is over. "That was the best concert I've ever been to."

"Yeah?" Tack asks, dropping more shots at the table as Syd remains at the bar, no doubt clearing them out of the top shelf.

"Really?" I grin over at Natalie and nudge her. "The best, huh? Compared to what others?"

She bites her lip.

Busted.

"Who else have you seen live?" I prompt as Tack takes his seat, his eyes volleying between us in earnest.

"I'm not saying," Natalie says, tossing her hair back as she pretends to study the menu.

"Come on, Nat. Now I have to know," Tack prods playfully.

"Wait for it," I mouth to Tack, lifting my arm and pointing over the top of her head.

"Fine…Dance Disney," she spouts, palming her forehead as Tack and I burst into hysterical laughter.

"Oh, fuck right off," she says between us. "Both of you."

"It's cool, baby," Tack chuckles. "I'm flattered to be the front runner over Dance Disney."

"Football," Natalie interjects, neck reddening. "That's my thing. My dad and I have season tickets and regularly attend UT games. It's Butler tradition. I might not know much about music, but I know *football.*"

"*That* we can get into," Tack says as he looks over to me and dips his chin. His stamp of approval, not that I needed it. Even so, it doesn't hurt he'll watch out for her.

"You," she snaps as I give her my attention. "Take a damned compliment from me already," she grits out as Syd sidles up to the table with a goddamn tray full of shots.

"I would much rather shut you up while you attempt to," I whisper back.

"I'm sorry I mentioned my dad," she utters low for me.

"I've got nothing against your dad, Natalie."

She narrows her eyes. "Speaking of, where is your room?"

"Okay, now maybe I have something against your dad," I jest.

"Not funny," she smiles.

"Same floor as yours," I grin back. "Think you can handle it, or should I bolt my door?"

"Are you…planning on being preoccupied?"

I grip the edge of the table because I know I wasn't fucking alone between those curtains. She's already shrugging that kiss off—if it can be called that. It was more like a make-out session while hiding in plain sight. Though I loved every minute of it, she seems to have completely blanked it out, as if it didn't happen. She reads my irritation and bristles in her seat next to me. "All I'm asking is, please don't play me for a fool. I know what this atmosphere truly is about, and shielding me from it isn't going to change my perception."

My chest pumps with my scoff. "Is that what you think I'm doing?"

"Yes," she says without hesitation. "Don't protect me. If some crazy fan wants to run in here, titties blazing with a sharpie in hand, I'm here for it." She gives me the most sincere smile she can muster as more laughter bursts from me. I push a partially damp curl from the side of her face, hating the fact that I can forgive her so easily. Unfortunately for her, I won't forget.

"What?" she grins.

"You're beautiful."

"But you feel sorry for me?"

"No, it's clear you're sleeping better now."

"Yeah, I am."

"Then I guess I feel sorry for myself," I scan the menu again and make a quick decision.

"Not that well," she admits as I turn to see her lips parting slightly. It's physically painful to stop myself from claiming them if only to shut her up. Seeming to read my mind, Natalie pulls a shot from the tray, deciding to numb away the red elephant, denying us both. After the few prompts this morning from my mother's cosmos—not that I really needed them—I made a split decision to pick her up, knowing the attempt might have me making a damn fool of myself. The sight of her in the office instantly made the drive worth it before I dialed her.

Watching her let my call go unanswered felt like a glass bottle to the temple, while seeing her expression because of said call felt like a simultaneous jolt to the chest.

Minutes later, I watch Natalie pick at her food before she opts for more numbing. A few shots later, I give up the struggle. Whatever conversation she had with Nate ruined everything we were building up to during the drive and after the concert. Even with the clock ticking and a well-formed bone to pick, I decide to leave it untouched, at least for the night.

THIRTY-ONE

Not Enough Time
INXS

Easton

Not long after the last of the drinks are consumed, Natalie's eyes begin to droop. After paying the tab, Tack and Syd opted to leave us and hit one of the downtown bars for a night ender, while LL remained unaccounted for. At first, I thought Syd would be the one to watch, but as it turned out, when we hit the road, LL became the front runner for the possibility of becoming the most problematic. Since we started, he's opted to partake more often than not and shows up for band engagements a clammy, shaking mess. So far, he hasn't missed a sound check or showtime, nor has anyone been forced to summon him, so I'm not touching it for now.

Once alone, Natalie and I head up to our floor in the elevator as easy, liquor-induced chatter and mixed laughter erupt from her—her buzz far outweighing the few bites of pasta in her stomach.

"And when you started playing *Cult*, I totally lost my shit," she recalls enthusiastically. Safely behind the closed doors, she turns to me and diminishes the foot of space she's been putting between us since the restaurant. "How do you feel, Easton?"

"Good."

"No, really," she grips my T-shirt, stretching it until I give in, and pulls me down so we're nose to nose, imploring me. I can't help my grin.

"In comparison to you right now, I think you've got me beat."

"Shut up." She widens her eyes. "It's happened, it's happening! You kicked your fear's ass, and now," she gestures a hand grenade toss and makes an explosion sound.

"Not quite kicked, but it feels good," I admit honestly.

"You're downplaying it. Tell me all the good parts. Did Stella freak?"

I can't help my growing smile when I think of Mom's reaction. "That's been the best part. She's pretty emotional. She pukes when she gets excited or upset, and that day was no exception. It was hilarious. Every time she started to talk, she'd gag." I clear my throat and spout my best impression, "'Easton, I'm so proud-bleck,' 'Easton, I can't believe—bleck,' and then she'd run away. I thought we were going to have to sedate her."

Natalie throws her head back in laughter, and I join her as the elevator doors open once we reach our floor. She stumbles a little with her exit, and I reach out to steady her. "Good?"

She looks at me with 'touch me' eyes before blanking them out. "T-those shots are catching up with me," she laughs. "Sorry, I can usually hold my liquor a little better."

I don't bother to call bullshit, but in truth, they caught up with her a few minutes after she took the first shot. I can't say she isn't an entertaining drunk because she is. Back at the table, she bombed us with stories that had Tack and me laughing hysterically, which only endeared her to me further while, in turn, frustrated the fuck out of me. I couldn't get a word in edgewise or pull her chair closer to mine. Things I could have easily gotten away with in Seattle—but didn't attempt—seem off the table now.

She and Tack went back and forth for most of dinner, acting more like old friends than new acquaintances. I know some of her eager interest in him was an attempt to skirt around *us*. But I found myself becoming increasingly disgruntled as she allowed Tack to monopolize her time just to avoid me.

"I knew all the words," she speaks up as we head down the corridor full of rooms. "The critics can't stop raving, Easton. You're going to be a household name," she shoots me a fearful look. "Sorry, I don't mean to spike your anxiety."

"Well, that's a hell of an exaggeration, so I'm good."

"You need a reality check," she makes another emphatic hand gesture, "because it's not at all an exaggeration. I've read everything, every single review on the web. Even the toughest critics are testifying to your talent."

"Thanks, but I wouldn't know."

"I knew you weren't reading them!" She shakes her head, "You really have no idea what's going on out there, but you need to trust what I'm saying and trust the screams in that audience tonight. You're only going up from here," she points skyward with her finger.

"You're so drunk," I muse.

"I'm a li'l tipsy," she spouts, producing her keycard from a pint-sized purse. "I can't invite you in…so," she unlocks her door and opens it a few inches.

"I wouldn't accept," I say as she draws her brows adorably.

Crossing my arms, I lean against the jamb. "You look disappointed, Natalie. Tell me, why is that?"

"No, it's not—"

I turn her toward her door and smack her ass. "Go on, enjoy your denial."

She does an abrupt about-face and damn near clocks me with her forehead as she postures up to tell me off. Fuck if I don't want this to turn into a push and pull, ending in me pushing into her as I pull on her wild, light strawberry curls.

"I'm not the *bad guy*," she announces. "So, stop making me out to be one. I'm trying to protect us *both*."

"Go to sleep, Natalie," I push her door open to usher her in, her exotic floral scent wafting into my nose as the moral battle ensues.

We have a fight coming, an important one, but I'm not about to reason with liquor.

"I kissed you back," she blurts, as if I need a reminder. "You know I did."

"Is that what I know?"

"Fine…okay, all right, I guess…you must be so tired," she stalls, her eyes begging me to act on what we both want. A victory I refuse to give her when she's gone out of her way to avoid this very thing. More underlying anger flares as I imagine pinning her down and punishing her for it. Spreading her wide and fucking the truth into her mind only to have it pouring like a confession out of her mouth.

Right now, I don't trust myself even though she seems cognizant enough for me to trap her denying lips with mine before gagging her quiet with my tongue. But she's mistaken if she thinks I'll allow her to use booze as an excuse to relapse on me. She's playing dirty to avoid culpability. If anything happens this weekend, she's going to have to fucking own it. She's going to be stone-cold sober when we have this out for good.

"Yeah, I am tired. I'm driving tomorrow, so I'm going to turn in. Night, sleep well, Beauty," I say, dipping to kiss her cheek and lingering, feeling her tense as I pull away. She grips the side of her door as I stifle my chuckle and move to head toward my room. "Hey, uh, Easton?"

"Yeah?"

"What's the second…you know, the reason you…called the second time?"

"Nuh-uh. You closed that window when you flew away with Grey Goose."

"I'm not the bad guy," she repeats defensively.

"Okay."

"I care about you, *a lot*."

I dip my chin in response.

"Why won't you talk to me? I'm being honest!"

"Well, don't hurt yourself."

She glares at me. "I missed you too, when I left."

Despite her state, her neck reddens a little with her admission, and it's all I can do to keep from snatching her to me.

"We can talk about it tomorrow."

"Why?"

"Because I'm not doing this with you right now." I take two strides away as she speaks up.

"You really missed me? Even with all you have going on?"

I pause and glance over my shoulder. "No, I've only called you twice a fucking week—every week—since you left because I haven't thought about you at all."

"What do you think about?"

"Don't go there," I warn, fishing my keycard out of my jeans.

"Tell me."

"We'll talk in the morning," I snap, the fight to keep the space she needs me to keep diminishing by the second.

"Fine," she slams her door behind her as I tap my keycard against my lock before trapping myself inside the room adjacent to hers.

Aggravation for our situation begins to eat at me as I smack my head against the door, fists clenching at my side. She's fucking infuriating, but no matter how hard I try, I can't stop wanting her.

"I thought about your hands," I hear in muffled confession from the other side of the adjoining suite's door. "Your beautiful hands."

In three strides, I'm pressed against it like a stalker, eager for her alcohol-induced revelations because it's the only way I'll get any real truth from her right now. What pisses me off the most is she's got a warped sense that there's some chase going on between us, but her feelings are so fucking obvious that it makes the notion ludicrous.

"...the way you looked at the hotel the day you sang for me... it was like the damned clouds parted just for you, and because you're *you*, they probably did." A long, exhausted exhale follows before shuffling ensues. I can only assume she's struggling to get those tight-ass jeans down her legs.

"I think about the day I left," I hear this admission clearly, seriously questioning the quality of our hotel as I catch the faint sounds on the other side of the door—the clank of her bracelets hitting the dresser, the unzipping of a bag. "Best sex...ever," she proclaims.

"Couldn't agree more," I mutter, rolling my forehead along the inches-thick wood that separates us.

"I think about your dick. *God*, just wait until some groupie discloses the size of *that* particular gift," she bites out. "You'll have to load up on tasers."

I bite my fist to stifle my chuckle as another bang echoes with an "Oww, oww, oww, shit!"

Grinning at the sound of the small crash that follows, I resign myself to another sleepless night. I don't do the hard-up, beat-around-the-bush bullshit, but somehow, she has me participating in her fictional chase. The truth is, this battle was over for both of us the day she let me in. While I've already accepted defeat, she seems to want to die on this hill.

"Seeing you is going to screw me up all over again," she whisper-yells, confirming it, as if she knows I'm within earshot. I manage to draw some inhuman strength and stay still to keep myself from going to her, from being in the same space with her, even if I can't be with her the way I want to.

"I didn't tell a soul, not a soul, and it's because I wanted to keep you...all to myself."

"Feeling's mutual," I sigh.

"Well, I told Percy, but our secret is safe with him. I feel...protective of you. I sent you what I wrote because I want to protect you so much."

"You did," I whisper, feeling the bite of my fingernails in my palms while managing to keep my groan inward. "Please, Beauty, go to sleep."

"You don't even realize you're too good for all of us, for me."

"Jesus," I grip the frame, knuckles turning white. I bat all notions of giving up as the girl I sought out speaks to me from the other side of the door.

"I cried," her mournful voice becomes clearer, as if she's only a foot away, "the whole way to the airport."

"I know, baby," I whisper.

I'd opened the studio door after she slammed it on us to see her crack just before Joel shut her inside the SUV. I had to fight myself for ten minutes in my truck not to call and have him stop so I could drive to her, but I knew it would be pointless.

"Who does that? I felt like a lunatic."

"You're still not crazy," I murmur, stepping back and ripping off my shirt before unbuckling my jeans. "Because if you are, so am I."

I slip into the cool sheets and grip myself in my hand. Frustration and lust battle as I hasten my strokes at the memory of her spread out before me, post-orgasm, skin flushed as she reached for me. She murmurs my name a few minutes later, the need in her voice sending me over as I tense and shatter, holding in my groan as cum glides down my fist.

"I can't fall for you, Easton," she whispers hoarsely. "I'll lose everything I've worked for...my whole life is in Austin, my future."

"You're already mine," I declare, knowing that's the truth for us both.

THIRTY-TWO

I Want You

Concrete Blonde

Natalie

A knock on my hotel door jars me awake, and I snap to on the mattress. Wiping the drool from my face, I look down to see I'm in a cami, my panties discarded nearby on the floor, yet I somehow manage to have kept one pant leg clinging to my ankle.

Dafuq?

How is that even possible?

"Uh, just a second."

After pulling my jeans on and straightening my cami, I search and fail to find a mirror as the knocking resumes. Wincing at the thrum starting in my head, I embrace defeat and open the door.

Easton stands on the other side looking mouthwatering, hair darker probably due to a recent shower, two coffees in hand. His lips stretch into a smile as he extends one toward me in offering.

"Thanks, and don't bother saying it. I'm sure I look like a freshly drowned rat."

"Actually, I was wondering if you plan on sitting on your tuffet today, Miss Muffet."

"Huh?" I wince, his words not registering as he scans my room, his eyes landing on my discarded panties before pinning me.

"While eating your curds and whey." He lifts his chin, and it's then I realize I may have mismanaged undressing, but I did manage to put my silk bonnet on.

Oh, fuck you, Grey Goose.

"Har, har," I say before darting into the bathroom and seeing I also managed to take exactly half my makeup off with a remover wipe. Desperately trying to pull myself together, I scrub my teeth and start to clear the debris off the other half of my face while briefly going over the events of last night, heavily regretting the excessive vodka intake.

"Sorry I got a little buzzed last night," I call out through the cracked door. "I haven't let loose in a while."

"You were a real animal. In bed by one fifteen," he says, his tone indecipherable.

I eye the time on my cell phone where it sits on the counter. "Is everyone waiting on me?"

"No. We pull out in thirty. I was sure you would oversleep."

My alarm goes off at that exact moment, and I hold it out of the bathroom for his view along with a middle finger and hear his chuckle in response.

"So, what's with the action cap?" He asks from behind the door.

"If you must know—"

"I must."

"It's to keep my curls in decent shape."

"Thought you hated them," he jabs.

"I've recently reembraced them."

Fresh-faced and feeling slightly better about my appearance, I open the door to find him sitting on the edge of my slightly rumpled bed. A smart quip dies on my tongue as I fully take him in. A black titanium cross dangles from his neck and peeks above the collar of his dark blue T-shirt which clings to his build in all the right places. Light denim jeans accentuate his muscular thighs tapering down to well-worn, dark leather boots. As if that wasn't enough, inch-thick leather cuffs are secured by large silver snaps around his wrists, along with the titanium thumb ring and tiger's eye pinkie ring he wore the day we met, making him look every bit the rock star he is. I feel his perusal as I pluck my tablet from the bed and begin to scroll.

"Well, do you want the good news or the bad news?"

"No news," he clips, sipping his coffee.

"Tough shit, and it looks like all good news anyway." I clear my throat. "And I quote, 'REVERB blew fans away last night at the Civic Center during an eighty-three-minute set, cementing themselves as the act to see this summer and securing their place amongst this year's top performers. I'm here to tell you to believe the hype because Crowne's stage presence and delivery alone is worth the price of admission.' I agree," I declare, continuing my search and peeking over my tablet to see he's completely unaffected.

"Ah, here's another. 'REVERB, specifically Easton Crowne are single-handedly giving mouth-to-mouth to a genre that seems to have been long forgotten, reviving Rock 'n' Roll one show at a time.'"

"Please stop," he says before I again lower my tablet.

"Why?"

"Because in about an hour, my mother will call and attempt to read me the same reviews."

"Really?" I grin. "Stella does that? I love it!"

"Yeah, and I hate it when she does it too, so don't take it personally."

I take a sip of my coffee and gag, and he chuckles at my reaction to it.

"What the hell is in this, *nitro*?"

"Drink it and say thank you."

"Geesh, thank you." I take a seat next to him on the edge of the bed and nudge him. "Why are you so grumpy this morning? I'm the one with cymbal crashes going on between my ears."

"Oh, yeah," he stands, and I take immediate advantage of the view, my eyes focusing on the natural bulge at his crotch and drifting up to the dark hair partially covering his face as he dips into his pocket before producing a pack of Advil. "Got these for you downstairs, too."

"Oh, you rock, literally," I can't help my laugh at the roll of his eyes as he starts to fight the package. "You truly don't care about the reviews?"

"It's not that."

"Tell me."

"It's just…personal to me."

"Okay, I get that." I shake my head. "Maybe I don't. You do realize this is *praise*."

"It only truly matters when it comes from the people that matter most to me," his eyes sweep me, and a shiver runs up my spine, "and from those I respect."

"It's just the things they're saying," I read his unwavering expression and toss the tablet on the bed. "Fine. You're no fun."

"Sorry."

"No, you're not," I grin as he opens the package and hands me the pills.

"Thank you," I say, tossing the pills back and sipping my coffee. "For last night, for putting me up. For all of it. I honestly can't wait for the show tonight."

"I read your article," he completely throws me off guard, "about that couple from Houston who got lost on vacation in Australia."

I gape at him as he leans against the dresser opposite the bed.

"You read my article?"

He nods. "Yeah, and honestly, I'm relieved. You write so much fucking better than you speak."

I glower at him. "Many writers do, jerk, and I don't know whether to slap you or..."

He lifts a brow at option two, which I decide not to verbalize.

"I could feel their desperation," he adds thoughtfully, "because of how you wrote it. It's pretty miraculous how after two days of panicking and arguing, they said 'fuck it' and adapted to their surroundings to survive until they were rescued."

"And they were on the verge of divorce," I grin. "It's crazy how it didn't push them over but brought them back together."

"That's my favorite part," Easton relays softly.

"Maybe there's a song in there?"

He nods.

"Well, I'm flattered, Mr. Rock Star."

"Stop with that shit. I'll let you shower." He walks over to the door, and I call out.

"Hey, you're kind of hard to gauge this morning. Are *we* okay?"

"Sure," he opens the door.

"Easton," I draw out his name. "Are you angry with me? You seem...frustrated."

He glances at me, a small smile on his lips. "It seems to be a constant state with you."

"I said or did...something, didn't I? What was it?"

Closing the door, he steps toward me and hovers, his gaze gliding over my bared skin as my treacherous nipples draw tight in my cami. Ignoring the ever-present pull, I bat it away briefly and press in. "What? What are you thinking?"

He shakes his head. "Nothing. What do you say when we get to Dallas, we get lost for a while? Just the two of us?"

"I say that sounds perfect." I inwardly sigh, fighting the urge to get closer. He smells so fucking good, a mix of bergamot…and smoky wood.

"Good," he leans in and stops suddenly, pulling back, a secretive smirk playing on his lips.

"Okay, that's it. Subtlety is not even remotely your thing. What the hell is going on up here?" I tap his temple, and he gently grips my fingers, lowering them before releasing them.

"Nothing you want to hear." His smirk spreads to a full-on grin.

"You're so sure."

He chuckles as he opens the door. "Positive."

Without another word, he slips out. Irritated, I swipe my tablet from the bed and open the door calling out to his retreating back.

"'A legend in the making'- That's a direct quote from the *Oklahoman*. You're a star, Mr. Crowne, own—" the words die on my tongue as he reaches his hotel door, the door to the room adjacent to mine. His grin turns into a megawatt smile as he sees me mentally start to question my life choices last night before slipping inside.

Twenty minutes later, I exit the hotel to find the guys lingering in and around the two vans. The first van is filled skillfully to the brim with equipment, and Joel is already behind the wheel, waiting to rollout. Grinning, I wave to him and get one in reply as Syd spots me just outside the open door to the second van and lifts his chin in greeting, a plume of vape smoke pouring from his lips. Easton spots me next, his eyes doing a shameless sweep as he opens the passenger door for me in greeting.

"Thank you, kind sir," I say as he lingers at my side between my passenger seat and the van door. "Nothing happened last night. I wasn't *that* drunk," I utter confidently, "so, the jig's up."

"Good to know." A smirk.

"What, Easton, *what*? I remember our conversation, too."

He gives me a dead stare before I finally catch on.

"Oh, for crying out loud," I say, yanking my seatbelt and buckling in. "I'm a grown woman, you know."

He shuts the door on me as I roll my eyes and spot LL already sitting in the second row, focus fixed out of the window. Though seemingly unapproachable, I greet him anyway.

"Morning, LL."

"Morning," LL replies absently. I look to Easton with pinched brows as he takes the driver's side before glancing quizzically in the rearview and shrugging.

Tack ends a call at the back of the van before stepping in and giving me a warm grin. "Morning, beautiful. How you feeling?"

"Not bad, considering I drank my weight in potatoes."

"You had four shots, lightweight."

"And two beers," I remind him.

"Right," he winks.

"Did you read the reviews?"

His smile widens. "A few."

Tack and I engage in easy conversation as Easton pulls out, following Joel's lead. Our conversation fizzes out the first hour of the short drive to Dallas as we wait for our caffeine buzzes to kick in. Most of the guys screw around on their cellphones as LL continues to stare out his window.

I lean over in a whisper to Easton. "Is everything okay with LL?"

"Have no idea," he replies. "He's not really an open book."

I chew on my lip and avert my gaze just as Easton's eyes drift over to me. Last night, he seemed in fantastic spirits and talkative. Today, he seems more the thoughtful introvert I met.

Before my obsessive thoughts can take over as to why he's acting so out of sorts, Stella's promised call comes through.

Anxiety already spiking as Easton answers, Tack demands Easton put the phone on speaker. My fears put to rest slightly as she spends the first five minutes of the call spouting off reviews for Easton and the band. Her personality on full display, I find myself stifling my laughs a few times, especially due to her and Easton's easy banter, which reminds me a lot of my father and me.

As she shamelessly reads his praises, I carefully watch his expression for any sign of satisfaction but only find it when the feedback comes directly from her. This only confirms he was being one hundred with me when he said the only opinions that matter to him are those of the people closest to him. Something more to admire about him, as if I didn't have enough already.

Tack joins in on the conversation talking to Stella like they are the best of friends, clearly already well acquainted. Even Syd speaks up with a greeting and makes a little conversation while LL remains mute, his gaze trained on the rapidly passing surroundings.

I focus on LL and his concave posture as Tack's words register.

"...picked up our friend in Austin last night before the show."

Easton rips the phone from Tack's hands and takes him off speaker as I shake my head wildly at Tack, pressing a finger to my lips. Mortified, I glance over at Easton as he skillfully clears the speed-bump with Stella before ending the call and turning to me, his expression apologetic. Not a second later, Tack's inevitable question comes.

"What's up with that, Nat? You don't want Stella to know you're with us?"

"Well, I guess you could say it's out of respect for our mutual profession. We're both journalists, and since we haven't met, I don't want her to think I'm trying to exploit my friendship with Easton for a story, you know? That's what I would think."

Lies, and I'm getting too good at telling them. Easton spares me further by speaking up. "Or how about this? My mother doesn't need to know who the fuck climbs in and out of this van or my hotel room or anything else of a private fucking nature regarding me, period," Easton bites out in nasty warning.

"Shit, I get that," Tack cups his neck. "Sorry, man. Guess it's already a bit of a family affair with Dad, right?"

Easton dips his chin in confirmation as the hotel room part of his blanket statement gnaws at me.

Not yours. He's not yours.

"So, when's Reid coming back, anyway?" Tack asks in a quick change of subject.

"Not until next week," Easton clips out, ending the conversation.

For the rest of the short drive, I feel a low-lying tension brewing between Easton and me and know that—true to Easton's nature—it's only a matter of time before he confronts it, us, all of it.

Despite his confrontational nature, he's been oddly evasive this morning, which has me pondering why. At first, I thought he was doing it just to rile me up. But after replaying his stunted actions this morning, I decide he's definitely holding onto something. Knowing he'll inevitably come clean when he's ready, I make the most of the rest of my time with the band and use it to dig into their individual histories.

I discovered Syd's father was a musician—as is most of his family—and Syd started to play at the very early age of five, tackling piano before finding his love of the baseline. He played in his last band for five years before two of his bandmates became romantically involved and, in his words, "fucked it all to shite."

Tack was a member of a high school garage band for years and reported they came close to getting signed before they broke up. He then jumped to another band that broke up when the lead singer quit by not showing up for a stage call and took a full-time job at the urging of his wife. Tack packed his sticks away and went to work full time for UPS eighteen months before he got Easton and Reid's call, further driving home Easton's point that no success happens overnight.

Due to LL's blatant tune-out, I don't press him for his own details, but it seems they've all traveled very different roads to get to this point. Between Tack's recollection and Syd's contributions to the conversation, it seems their goal is the same—to play music for a living. The underlying desperation is indicative that they feel this may be their last chance to do it. I find myself hopeful for them all as I listen attentively.

The minute we pull up to the auditorium, the band immediately disperses. Upon exiting, I find myself stopping LL before he can reach the back of the second van where Easton converses with Joel as they open the back doors.

"Leif?" I call softly to his back.

He turns to face me, his expression indiscernible.

"I-I know it's not my place, but I just wanted to ask you if you're okay?"

Hovering a foot above me, his pale blue eyes lower before focusing on me. It's then I notice the thin sheen of sweat on his forehead, his skin practically translucent in the early morning light. He remains mute as I stand in front of him, feeling like an idiot. "Sorry, it's not my business." I move to step around him, and he stops me with a gentle grasp on my arm.

"Sorry, love, you took me by surprise. Truth is…it's been a very long time since anyone asked me that."

"I hate hearing that, I really do. So...are you feeling well?"

"To be honest, I'm a bit knackered this morning, but I'll be fine."

"Well, if there's anything you need, don't be afraid to ask, okay?"

He tilts his head at me curiously, and my chest tightens with ache. Does the man really have no one looking out for him? Feeling that may be the truth of it, I muster a smile. "I hope you have a great show tonight."

"Thank you." His lips lift in an appreciative smile before he turns to grab his equipment from the van. I catch Easton's gaze—which lingers on me briefly—before he turns back to help unload the wall of instruments. The second I step up to offer a helping hand, he speaks up. "Joel's going to get you checked into the hotel. I'll pick you up in an hour."

"Sure you don't want me to help?"

"We're good," he quickly replies before turning and striding toward the building, guitar case in hand. Turning back to Joel, he gives me an easy smile. "Want to catch up over breakfast?"

"I would love that," I say, glancing back in the direction Easton left. Within minutes, Joel secured both Easton's and my luggage in his hands and is rolling it toward a waiting SUV in the parking lot with me in tow.

"I see we're traveling in style today."

"Thank fuck for that," Joel says.

"Do you get lonely driving the second van?"

"Hell no. I prefer it."

"Are you having a good time at least?"

"For the most part, yeah." He nods as he starts the SUV, a fond sparkle in his eyes. "I'm so fucking proud of him, Natalie. I didn't think he was going to do it." He turns to me.

"Nuh-uh, oh no, don't credit me for that. He did it all on his own."

Joel puts the truck into gear and shakes his head. "You know as well as I do, that's bullshit."

"Ha! And you know all too well that man doesn't do a damn thing he doesn't want to."

"Well, some*thing* or some*one* shined a light in the right direction," he adds as I shake off his compliment, ignoring the bat shit flutter threatening in my chest.

THIRTY-THREE

Stuck in the Middle with You
Stealers Wheel

Natalie

"What the fuck?!" Easton barks as we fly past another sign on the interstate, and I try to decipher it, equally as confused as I was when we passed the last one. In the next second, Easton taps the brakes hard, lurching me forward before screaming out of his driver-side window. "Fucking idiot!"

Unsurprisingly, it's the same sentiment he's spouted toward every driver who's come before the last. He braves a glance over at me, another car whizzing past us, coming dangerously close before darting into the next lane. "Did you see what the speed limit is?"

I scan the side of the highway for another sign and try to make sense of it. "I think there are four speed limits. It depends on the type of vehicle you're driving and whether it's day or night."

"Are you fucking serious?"

I shrug. "I say go with the flow of traffic?"

Just as I say it, multiple cars blur around us as if we're in a Formula One race.

"With the flow?!" Easton shrieks, his expression bewildered as I press my lips together to stifle my laughter.

"So, I'm guessing *this* is the downside of having a driver most of your life?"

"Don't give me that shit. I've driven nearly every fucking highway since we left Washington. This isn't fucking normal or in any way acceptable!" He declares, his posture ramrod straight. His eyes frantically dart across the six-lane highway as he white-knuckles the wheel before glancing over to see my amusement. "Think this is fucking funny? This isn't fucking funny!"

"S-s-sorry, I've just never seen you so wound up."

"Is your seatbelt on?!" He doesn't bother looking this time, his panicked eyes focusing on the road.

"Yes, Easton."

"Double check! I'm not kidding, Natalie!" He screeches as another car darts in front of us, narrowly missing our front bumper. A long, colorful, and I'm almost certain not entirely English string of curses follows, which has my levee breaking as repressed laughter bursts out of me. After a full thirty seconds, I manage to get it to a rolling cackle.

"Natalie, this isn't funny," he whines. "Get us the fuck out of here!"

Pulling up my GPS app, I make a fast decision to lead us out of the city, knowing it doesn't really get any better.

"Natalie!"

"I'm on it! Pfft, JEZUZ, Crowne. It's clear *we* wouldn't make it back united if we got lost in the Australian Outback if you act like *this* during times of extreme stress," I jest. Another bout of laughter flows out of me before his desperate plea cuts through it.

"Please, baby, *please*," he whimpers, "get us the fuck off this highway."

"I'm on it," I reply instantly, stunned by his term of endearment as the directions populate. He darts his gaze between the rearview, side view, and the road while my heart rate continues to spike, beat after beat. He's said it before, when we were intimate, in the moment. I know why this one hit so differently. It's because of how he said it—so naturally, as if we already exist as an us, as if I already belong to him in the most intimate sense. It's also because I know I want so much for it to be a possibility, to be the truth. The hope circulating through me brings about the same damning conclusion I've been avoiding, curbing, side-stepping, ignoring, and mourning since I left Seattle.

I *want* to belong to Easton.

I want *us* to exist.

Again, I want what I can't have.

After our very short and terrifying ride outside downtown Dallas, we ended up in Fort Worth, ironically landing at a local tourist attraction. This one of my choosing is The Herd, a longhorn cattle drive that takes place twice a day downtown in the Stockyards National Historic District.

After a brief shopping trip—my suggestion for anonymity's sake—Easton managed to secure us the entirety of a tiny patio of a Mexican restaurant facing the street with just enough greenery to keep us out of view of prying eyes. Nestled away from the public while managing to be a part of it all, we've spent the afternoon alternating sipping frosted schooners of light beer and water while stuffing our faces with tortilla chips and salsa.

Even with the crowds gathering on the street for the cattle drive, I feel relatively safe we'll be undiscovered. No one would ever suspect Easton Crowne to be wearing a ten-gallon cowboy hat with the wide brim pulled down just above his Ray-Bans. Not only that, he covered his T-shirt with a western embroidered shirt and finished his look off with black, metal-tipped cowboy boots.

"Your disguise is ridiculous," I taunt, sipping from my schooner. Easton gives me a pointed look as the fringe hanging from my Dallas Cowboys cheerleader vest dances across the top of the salsa. The traditional long-sleeved colt blue shirt tied just beneath my breasts bares every inch of my midriff down to my low riding jeans, and I find myself thankful for the thousand Easton-induced crunches that fueled my recent workouts.

Adjusting my solid white Stetson, I stretch out my legs to admire my new boots. Boots that cost a pretty penny and won't go to waste.

The feeling in the air between Easton and me has been breezy since we managed to make it out of Dallas in one piece. With sound check and set up out of the way, we find ourselves with a day's worth of hours to just be together without the threat of any other outside worries. It's here we find our groove, with no pressure to define our relationship. My guard is comfortably lowered, even though every passing minute with Easton continues to threaten said guard's existence.

"Aren't you going to tell me I look ridiculous?" I ask, gripping the top of the solid white hat currently covering my frizzy ringlets and dipping the brim toward him in proper cowgirl etiquette.

"No," his grin disappears into his beer as he sips it.

"Why?"

"Because you don't."

"Seriously?" I push back my chair and stand, waving a hand over myself with exaggeration. "There's being nice, and then there's charity. I spent a fortune on this shit, and I'll never wear it again. Well, aside from the boots."

"I would have paid for them, Natalie."

"But we settled that argument…quick," I draw imaginary six-shooters from my hips and blow them out, "fast…" I flip and holster my fake guns back at my hips, "and in a hurry, didn't we there, partner?"

His nostrils flare in response, and I'm pretty sure if he lowered his glasses, I would be on the receiving end of a dead hazel stare. I must admit, it's so fucking sexy to see him riled up, despite his overall look being completely foreign in nature. Unsurprisingly, it works on him. Then again, the man could decide to wear nothing but a banana leaf to hide his junk and would still look mouthwatering.

"Natalie?" Easton prompts.

"Yup?" I check out briefly, the summoned image of naked Easton and his banana leaf disappearing as I focus on him.

"Worth it?" He asks, his tone full of smug assumption. I blame the heat. Heat makes people crazy. Case in point, I'm parading around like an idiot in downtown Fort Worth playing cowgirl, waiting to see a parade of cows.

"Worth it?" Easton repeats.

"I already decided it was." I take another sip of my beer. "Oh, I know. I could wear this again role-playing with my future husband, who *will be* a Dallas Cowboys' fan."

He chuckles. "Good luck finding one of those."

"You better have meant a Cowboys' fan, not a husband, and blasphemy, sir. That's America's team you're talking about."

"Only claimed by Cowboys' fans."

"I'll bet you they win the Super Bowl this year."

"I'll take you up on that bet."

"So, you *do* know football?"

"I've observed enough to know that most people love or loathe the Cowboys, more the latter."

"Whatever. Cowboys aside, not being a Longhorns' fan, that would be the true nonstarter. Wha, wha, whaaaa," I mock in my best game show buzzer impersonation.

"That's a real tall order, Butler," he mutters dryly. "Don't sell yourself short or anything."

"Hey, grumpy, take a drink. The heat is making you irritable."

"Or maybe it's the annoying-as-hell, buzzing, blue bee that can't seem to sit still."

"Fine," I sigh, "The show's over, but just know you missed the grand finale," I tease, reclaiming my seat and discarding my hat. "Today is a good day." I take another sip of my beer, the light buzz filtering through me as I soak in an authentic Texas experience with my favorite rock star. "Though, I don't get the appeal of this lifestyle." I glance through the iron bars, which sit just below lined planters full of thick green ivy, and spot two cowboys mounting thoroughbreds across the street dressed in full riding gear, chaps included.

"Why?" Easton prompts. "Why don't you get the appeal?"

"For one, it looks…uncomfortable. Covered in dirt all the time, working in extreme heat only to stare at cows' asses. Struggling through half the day to get a whiff of fresh air instead of inhaling the stench of their shit, bleh. No thanks."

Laughter bursts from Easton as I look over and smile at him sitting next to me, his own boots propped and crossed at the ankles on top of the dark blue and red-tiled table.

"Where's the reward? Starry nights of solitude playing "Home on the Range," next to a campfire with a harmonica?" I shrug. "Seems like a lonely life."

"Only if you base a cowboy's life on the few Western movies you've seen."

"First of all, if I've ever seen a Western, it was completely by accident—I promise you that. And I mean, hey, I know there's a lot more to it. Just seems like a lot of work for little-to-no payoff. Some of the folklore surrounding it has got to be true, or it wouldn't be the standard. Bet you'd dig it, ya *loner*."

His smile fades when I reach for my schooner, and he grabs it and sets it next to him on the table, just out of reach. "How about you hold off on that for a second."

"I've only had one," I defend. "You made me drink four waters between that and this one."

"For good reason. Just for a minute," he adds. "Okay?"

"Okay." I bite my lip as he bends and pulls my chair closer to his, the stifling summer air instantly charging as I run my sweaty palms down my jeans, more sweat trickling down the nape of my neck. "Are you about to start a fight?"

"Is the road anything like you thought it would be?" He asks, dodging my question.

"In a way, but I know there's a lot more to it." I saw the warning looks he gave to Tack last night when he relayed a few road stories. Honestly, I'm too terrified to know if Easton has his own to tell yet.

"Okay," he accepts easily, too easily, as I follow the drop of sweat gliding down his Adam's apple before it disperses over the top of his cross.

"Tell me why you wrote that article."

The question stuns me as he lifts my chin with gentle fingers, demanding my focus.

"It was just a what-if type of thing. I never expected anyone to see it."

"But you wanted *me* to see it."

"I wanted you to know I understood your stance, and if I had the chance to plead your case for keeping your private life *private*, that's how I would have written it."

"So that's why?"

I dip my chin. "Yes, of course. I wanted you to know that I understood." In my periphery, I see the first longhorns gather behind the fence across the street. "Oh, look! It's happening."

I jump to my feet, and Easton slowly joins me before we walk over to the iron partition separating us from the rapidly crowding street. Crouching low enough where we won't be seen, Easton opts to stand just behind me, my shoulder resting against his chest, his scent surrounding me as heat drips down my back. He whisks one away with his thumb at the top of my jeans, and my lips part at the gentleness of his touch. Hyper-focused on what parts of him are touching me, I try to concentrate on the commotion behind the gate as Easton begins the slow sweep of his thumb along my spine.

Thoroughly seduced and his lips just inches away, my pulse quickens as he pulls the damp hair away from my neck and blows. Closing my eyes, I try to inhale some restraint, refusing to look his way.

"It's starting," I rasp out, nodding toward the street, Captain Obvious diarrhea spewing freely.

Easton continues to sweep his thumb along my back as the cowboys make a small show of lassoing ropes overhead and begin to usher the massive steers onto the street. The parade lasts only a few minutes, and I frown before turning to Easton to see his face equally drawn up in confusion. A second later, we burst into incredulous laughter.

"That was so fucking anticlimactic!" I huff as we head back to the table. "Glad we didn't come out of pocket for that."

Easton shrugs. "I think it was just about the experience of seeing something so Old World in the new one."

"I get that, but," I look around and wipe my brow, "maybe not worth sitting in Texas hellfire for two hours to wait for it." I lift my hair and wave a hand to cool my neck off.

"But you had fun, didn't you?"

Our eyes meet and hold. "I always have fun with you."

"Good," he murmurs before reaching out and scooping me into his lap to straddle him. Shocked by the public display, I quickly glance around and am stopped by his gentle palm when he cups my face. "I can fucking do anything with you as long as you're looking at me the way you are right now." His expression arrests me, keeping me immobile as his voice and words reverberate through me.

"Easton," I manage to breathe out as the world around us inevitably fades away in contrast to him.

"I called you the second time because I remembered how this felt, and I wanted to feel this way again. It's that simple."

"It's so not simple," I argue breathlessly as I move to get up, and he pins me gently with his palms covering my thighs.

"Then it's time for a fight," he declares roughly.

"We don't have to fight, we agreed—"

"No. You decided. I allowed it because you could have turned me down flat yesterday, but you didn't. You didn't turn me down knowing full well that I would want to—and try to—kiss you…touch you…fuck you." He grips my chin tightly before lifting it to brush his finger along my neck. "I don't have the urge to call my friends and share my highs and lows. I don't miss them with an ache so deeply etched inside that it keeps me awake at night, and I sure as fuck don't drive for hours in hopes they'll spend a few days with me. And I definitely don't jerk off to the image of them coming on my cock. I don't feel this way for my friends, Natalie—close or otherwise—so I dare you to call me your *close friend* again," he warns. "I fucking dare you."

"It's all we can be, okay?" I whisper with a clear shake in my voice.

"Well, if friendship is all you're offering, you're a shitty friend to start with because those I claim as friends would have at least answered the goddamned phone."

"I explained this before I left Seattle. You didn't read the emails—"

"You mean the emails that are nearly three decades old and might not even hold any relevance to any of us here and now?"

I shake my head. "You don't know what you're saying. It still haunts me. Every day. Maybe if you read them—"

"It's history, Natalie."

"It's our parents who almost *married* each other's history, Easton." I fire back. "If you would just read them—"

"I look at you, and honestly, I just don't give a fuck. It physically fucking hurt me when you slammed that door on me."

"It hurt me, too. But please understand, I still can't do this with you."

"You *can* do this with me, but you *won't*. There's a difference, and I would drop it, but I know how you feel about me. You don't want this limited to friendship any more than I do."

"Don't presume to tell me how I feel," I snap.

His nostrils flare as he lifts us both, his eyes wreaking havoc even as he gently sets me on my feet. "I don't have to fucking presume shit. You already told me, and even if you hadn't, I'd still know."

"What do you mean?"

He takes a step away before pulling out his wallet and tossing a few bills on the table. Eyes cast down, he lingers where he stands for a long beat, seeming to focus on the pattern of the tiles on the table before he slowly lifts his gaze back to me. It's strikingly hollow. The distance between now and seconds ago has my stomach dropping. There's not a trace of warmth to be found. He's checking out. "Fuck it, let's go."

"What do you mean fuck it? Or are you really saying fuck *me*?"

He swipes the keys to the SUV from the table and turns abruptly, his biting words stinging repeatedly as I softly call his name. Ignoring me, he rips open the chipped blue fenced door to the patio and stalks through, striding away in the direction we parked the car. Feeling condemned, I follow him to the parking lot, juggling our bags until he relieves me of them before shutting me into the truck.

The ride home is painfully silent, aside from the blaring music. We're now in this horrible place—at such painful odds, which has me panicking because our time is once again running out. The panic increases with every mile we get closer to reality and my window alone with him is cut short. Because tomorrow, I'll be stuck in the same place I was two months ago—replaying our time together, obsessing over him, his touch, the way he looks at me, his whispered words, mourning what could have been. A cycle that I can't bear to think about repeating but can't do a thing about.

I'm certain I've been lying to myself in thinking I was trying to get on with my life after returning from Seattle. While my head tried to convince me that was the truth of it, my heart was still holding out hope for the chance to see him again. He's here, now, and still within reach. He's validated every feeling I had about us that I chastised and ridiculed myself for. He's telling me he missed me. Telling me he wants more, that he wants us to be real, and I'm once again forcing the door closed on us.

Shadows that weren't present yesterday darken his features as I remember the light in his eyes when he picked me up, the ease in his posture, and the easy smiles he so freely gave.

God, was that just yesterday?

With no traces of that Easton to be seen, I mourn that loss more than anything and turn down the radio. "I've spent so much time thinking about you," I deliver my admission that feels much too late as his face remains like granite, his eyes fixed on the road. "The days I've spent with you are some of the most unforgettable days of my life, Easton, but my stance hasn't changed, and it's only because I can't hurt my father this way. I know that's not a good enough reason for you, and I wish, so much, that I could make you understand."

He bites his lip, his features tensing as his phone rings and Joel's name flashes on the screen from where it buzzes in the console. I lift it within reach for Easton to answer, and he takes it from my hands and tosses it on my floorboard. It's then I know the fight is over for him, and my words are useless. I've lost him. Dread settles in my chest as I speak up one last time. "I'll see myself home after the show."

THIRTY-FOUR

STAY(Faraway, So Close!)

U2

Natalie

The auditorium grows mostly silent with palpable anticipation as sweat glides down my back. The distance between us when we parted today at the hotel making the concert a bittersweet experience, knowing goodbye is just on the other side. If I'm granted that. Easton didn't so much as utter a word to me, other than he'd see me later, exiting the SUV before quietly closing the door. His indifference as he walked into the hotel without a glance back stung worse than his anger. I'd briefly entertained leaving early, but Joel had once again shown up on his white horse to summon and chaperone me to the show uplifting my spirits enough to get me here.

Under Joel's watchful eye—who stands like a sentry to the left of me—I stand partially cloaked on our side of the cleared stage. The rest of the security are lined at the foot of it to keep the screaming fans at bay. This arena hosts thousands more than the last, and it seems not a single seat went unclaimed tonight. Every so often, I feel Joel inching closer in silent support but also on guard as if Easton ordered him to protect *me*, while my focus remains glued to the man where he performs feet away. A man currently strapping his guitar around his body as he walks back toward the mic and away from the piano he's occupied the last four songs. Songs where he continually bruised my battered heart and stole valuable breaths without apology. Even if this is goodbye, the experience of seeing him perform one last time has been worth it.

At least, that's what I'm trying to tell myself.

I've been standing in the same place the whole show waiting for any recognition from Easton—which he hasn't granted, his grudge clear. Since the concert began, he hasn't so much as glanced in this direction, and despite my resolve, it stings like a bitch. Even as he played what I now consider *our* song, I got absolutely nothing.

As thousands of his newly acquired fans start to scream for him again as he approaches the mic, I feel just as desperate for an ounce of his attention. He's hurting me purposely, giving me a taste of what it's like to be nothing more than a spectator in his life, and he's driving his point home with a sledgehammer.

For the whole of our time together, he's been subtly and not so subtly reminding me what we started in Seattle is worth the risk, but it seems he's done trying and I can't blame him. I should be relieved. Instead, Easton's cold shoulder feels like a thousand needles digging into my chest all at once.

Even with him a few feet away, it's the broken connection that has me stalking his every move for any sign that I'm not already a part of his past. Determined not to cower away from the fact he's acting like an ass—and his A-side is most definitely running the show tonight—I decide to try and reason with him once more before heading home, or at the very least to attempt to part from him on speaking terms.

The spotlight illuminates his sweat-soaked hair as he runs his fingers through it, his thin cotton T-shirt drenched and clarifying every muscle that makes up his build. Electrified, insides warring, and breathless in anticipation of what cover he will play tonight, I glance over at Joel offering up a smile.

"Let's go back a little," Easton speaks into the mic as the stadium roars in approval. Grinning at the reception, Easton glances back at Tack before he and LL pluck the first chords. The intro to the song has a funky, upbeat vibe, and I find myself bouncing a little on my heels along with the easy beat. Though I don't recognize the song—as I haven't ninety percent of his library—the crowd seems to and screams in approval. Or maybe it's just Easton because he's got that effect.

When he begins to sing, I pay close attention to the lyrics knowing that's half the appeal for him—a habit I've kept since our time together. It's when the lyrics start to register and resonate with me that I feel the implication.

Only a few lines in, Easton turns his head, smug eyes connecting with mine, his expression cool, as he delivers each line like a blow.

He sings of a lost woman, resembling a car crash, who's stuck in denial, incapable of paying attention to the world around her due to indecision. Of a woman who sees and hears nothing but what she's programmed herself to see and hear. A woman who looks *through* him and talks *at* him, blind to her needs and therefore incapable of discovering something real with anyone.

My chest caves as the insults are hurled with ease due to his delivery. His posture relays his satisfaction as he holds my gaze while I stand stalk still, under attack.

Fury begins to roll through me as he continues ripping me to pieces using the vulnerabilities I hand-fed him. He breaks contact as he delivers the last part of the song to the audience, the lyrics a hauntingly clear warning that if I don't wake up, I'll become another casualty destined to implode due to my own ignorance.

Bastard.

Tears spring to my eyes as he bellows the last line, his plea to an angel going a thousand miles an hour without purpose. I can feel Joel's eyes on me as I turn to flee when the last line is repeated, and the angel Easton sings of inevitably meets her demise.

Joel calls after me, but I'm already gone, racing down the long hall backstage toward the exit. Applause erupts, and pandemonium ensues just as I burst through the back door. Humidity instantly covers me in a sheen of sweat as I reenter reality before I'm pulled under by the crushing weight of what just happened.

Feeling betrayed in a way I could never have anticipated from him, my vision blurs as I bypass a few lingering fans smoking outside, dodging their stares in seek of refuge. Bolting away from the auditorium, I make the quick decision to order a car and pin my location several blocks away, giving myself a little time to physically try and burn through some of the hurt. Ten minutes later, a Honda pulls up to where I'm waiting before the passenger side window lowers.

"Natalie Butler?"

"That's me," I say, the driver's inquiry of my full name a reminder of exactly why I've gone to the lengths I have to ensure I don't in any way forsake a name I take pride in.

I *am* my father's daughter.

I'm his legacy, and his legacy is my future.

Nate Butler has been my rock, my hero, and the man in my life my whole existence, and I can't forgo him or our relationship so easily. Our relationship is precious and sacred to me, and I'm done explaining that to Easton because it's falling on deaf ears.

Safely inside the car—feeling like I just ran an emotional marathon—I let the anger take over.

Smug, self-righteous, son of a bitch!

As if he's got me so easily pegged—along with my flaws—like *he's* some sort of solution. For a man who claims he wants no part of ego, he damned sure seems to have procured a massive one when it comes to *me*, what he thinks of me, and my actions.

"Just come from the concert?"

Glancing up, I meet the eyes of the driver, who my app told me is Tom and looks to be close to my age, if not a little older.

"Yes," I clip out.

"I wish like hell I'd gotten tickets. How was it? Is he any good live?"

My verbal lashing dies on my tongue, and I deny myself the petty satisfaction in place of the truth.

"He's incredible. He's better than you could ever imagine."

"I fucking knew it," he replies as I wonder if that was Easton's version of a sendoff, the notion of us parting ways like adults now laughable.

So be it.

Having a reason to despise him will make things a hell of a lot easier because right now, I can't reconcile the mess between what my heart is screaming and what my head is trying to explain. But one thing is for sure, both are roaring mad and jointly jaded by his shitty behavior. He once told me vindictive behavior doesn't come naturally to him.

Tonight, he made himself a liar.

"I'm going to the next one," Tom vows as I dodge his watchful gaze in the rearview, the Dallas skyline lighting in the reflection of my passenger window.

"You should, Tom, because he's unforgettable," I sigh out the painful truth.

Tom's attempt at conversation becomes background noise as a blanket of regret cloaks me. Regret now underlined by anger. A large part of me wishes I'd never flown to Seattle, never laid eyes on Easton, never raced after him out of that bar, and got into his truck. That I didn't know the feel of his hands, the pull of his scent, the warmth that emanates from him. That I'd never got lost in his blazing kisses, or discovered the intensity of our chemistry, or felt the weight of his body on top of mine. I wish I'd never become privy to the intensity of his lovemaking, the mind-blowing feel of his thrusts and the rippling of ecstasy that follows.

That I didn't know what it feels like to be the sole focus of a man so brilliant, so beautiful, so insightful, and so intoxicating. I hate that he tuned into me so expertly and managed to get truths about me in such a personal way that his words and behaviors with me reflect those points home so thoroughly. I hate that he's taken so much from me already without me truly realizing it—until now—and I resent the fact that I'm the one who gave them to him.

As I pull up to the hotel feeling defeated, I decide it's for the best. Easton did me a favor by dismissing me so cruelly. Otherwise, I might have always wondered what might have been. A small part of me wonders if alienating me was his intent, to spare me some of the heartache. Because, despite his disgusting behavior over the last six hours, he is just that type of selfless man.

I hate that I'll never know that for sure.

All I do know is that it's time to go home.

THIRTY-FIVE

Poison
Taylor Grey

Natalie

Freshly showered, I glance around my hotel room and decide to bide my time by packing. With the late hour, I've missed every available flight home and can't manage to secure a rental car. With nothing but time to kill, I take care folding my clothes before spotting my discarded Stetson on the table. Tears I refuse to shed threaten as I think past the hurt to the raw honesty he fed me just hours ago—of how I again refused him and rejected us.

I told him I wouldn't change my mind. He didn't think I could or would hold my ground.

I hate that I have, while at the same time, am glad I did because screw him for being so cavalier with my feelings because his were hurt.

Stuck in the hotel but determined to make my exit as quickly as possible, I decide to do one last search in hopes of finding a twenty-four-hour rental car company and see a missed ping from Easton to a nearby hotel.

EC: Penthouse.

He must have sent it while I was showering. I note the time stamp.

He sent the message twenty-three minutes ago. A *go to hell* ready on my fingertips, they hover over the screen as I continue to stare at the text. My stomach twists as the thought occurs to me that maybe the invitation is just a formality on his part. Maybe he feels obligated to host me. Either way, he can take his half-assed invitation that reads more like an order and shove it up his over-privileged ass.

I told him I would see myself home, and I will. Maybe he'll assume I'm already bound for Austin by not replying. No part of me believes entertaining said invitation is a good idea, especially with how furious I am with him. The longer I linger in his universe, the more susceptible and vulnerable I become.

Fuck my feelings. They don't take a back seat to my self-respect.

Annoyed with myself for letting him be the victor while painting me the villain for trying to spare our parents—us—nothing but grief and heartache, I set the phone down and continue packing. I stare at the back of the phone like the ticking time bomb it is. I have got to get the hell out of here. Even if it means switching hotels for the night, I can't give him any more access to me.

I'm not in the wrong for doing the right thing, and he's got no right to make me feel as though I am. He's not thinking about anyone but himself—his wants, his desires, even if they do heavily mirror my own. Once packed, I zip up my bag as my phone rattles again with an incoming text.

EC: Joel is on his way up.

Just as I read it, a knock sounds on the door. "Son of a bitch!" I roar, jumping out of my skin as Joel's chuckle and amused voice drift in from the other side.

"Sorry, sweetheart, did I offend?"

"Tell him I already left!" I call out.

"Well, considering he heard you—along with half the hotel floor—he's not going to believe me."

Glaring, I roll my suitcase with me toward the door and open it. "I'm leaving," I lie. "So, tell him I got his message loud and clear."

Joel's infuriating grin greets me as he lowers his eyes to the bag in my hand. "Yeah, she's packed."

I narrow my eyes at him. Apparently, he's on Team Easton tonight.

"Will do," Joel says.

"If he's got anything to say to me, he can say it himself."

A second later, Joel holds out the phone, and I barely manage to conceal my flinch.

Okay, *that backfired.*

Joel chuckles at my reaction as I take the phone and open my mouth to speak, but Easton beats me to the punch.

"Don't make me come after you, Beauty. If I do, you won't like it. Neither will your *editor*."

"You can't be serious."

"Turnabout is fair play."

"That's so—"

"Fucked up? I agree, but I'm taking a page from your handbook tonight, and right now, I swear to Christ, I'm just the motherfucker to make good on the threat. See you soon."

My jaw drops as he hangs up, and I glare at Joel, who has the good sense to look remorseful as he palms the back of his neck. "Shit, he kind of makes it hard sometimes for people not to hate the messenger."

"He's an infuriating—" I tick off on my finger.

"Daily—" Joel counters.

"Entitled—" I go on.

"At times—" Joel agrees.

"Relentless—" I fume.

"Only when he really wants something—" he tosses in.

"Selfish prick!" I finish.

"Oof," he winces, "I *felt* that. So, I guess, here's your chance to tell him?"

When Joel's phone rings in my hand, I go to answer it just as he snatches it out of my grasp. "I'll be waiting downstairs." He turns and strides toward the elevator as I glare at his retreating back the whole way, a 'traitor' on the tip of my tongue. But he's not a traitor. He's Easton's people, not mine, no matter how much I want to claim him.

When the doors slide open, Joel turns to see me fuming in the hall and mouths a quick "I'm sorry."

I shake my head emphatically, refusing to let him off the hook.

"Properly," he mutters into the phone, "I would say somewhere along the lines of a bull in a china shop," he reports of my temperament, scratching his temple in obvious discomfort just before the doors slide closed.

I slam my room door shut and fume while pulling my phone up to call and read Easton the riot act. Unable to compose a text to convey the thousand and one insults I want to hurl his way, I drop my phone and fist my hands.

"All right, you son of a bitch," I snap, "you want a fight. You've got one coming." Opening my suitcase, I pluck the navy dress bag I packed last minute and unzip it. Though already showered, I take my time getting ready, hoping to tick both Joel and Easton off by making them wait.

Furious, even though I've given myself ample time to cool off, I paint my lips a glossy nude and slide into a form-fitting, shimmering white V-neck dress. The cut bares inches of my midriff, connected only by tiny gold loops on each side. The deep cut also gives ample glimpses of side-boob while remaining classy in fit, hanging a few inches above mid-thigh. It's my 'dressed to kill' dress, and right now, there's a real possibility of that turn of phrase becoming a reality.

Satisfied with my makeup, I grab a thin gold chain from my jewelry bag as an afterthought. I decide it pairs perfectly with the dress after I clasp it around my waist, flicking the two small chains at the end that dangle over my exposed navel.

After taming my curls into larger ones with my iron, I slide on my blue suede Louboutin's. Satisfied with the look I plan to neuter Easton Crowne in, I grab the small clutch which matches the red soles of my heels before tucking in my phone and travel wallet. After walking through a few shots of orchid perfume, I march out of my hotel room, mind set on making Easton pay.

Once downstairs, I find Joel parked opposite the circular drive. As I approach, he reads my ready-for-war expression, his eyes dancing down my armor as he holds open the wrong door. Shaking his head with a grin, he closes the back passenger door and opens the front before I slide into the car. He lingers there as I buckle in, knowing I'm none too happy with him, which he clearly finds amusing.

"Don't be angry with me."

"I'm not."

His smile broadens. "You're a stunning liar, and to be frank, he's going to shit himself when he sees you in that dress. It's the perfect choice."

Unable to help it, my eyes soften. "Thank you."

"Natalie," he sighs, gripping the top of the door. "He may seem entitled at times—and maybe he even acts like it, but he's tried since he's become aware not to be."

"I hear you, and I know that about him, but let him defend himself, okay?"

Joel nods and lingers a bit longer. I can tell he wants to speak up again on Easton's behalf, but he shuts the door instead.

Deciding to keep Joel out of our newly declared war, I ride in silence to the hotel feeling the restless energy bouncing off his frame. He's nervous for Easton, or for me—probably both. Either way, this is our battle, and he's respecting the boundaries. When we reach the hotel, the valet beats Joel to the door. I grab his hand and thank him as Joel joins me and walks me toward the entrance while I mentally go over my battle plan, which is straightforward—to enjoy myself.

It's the best revenge.

Walking around like a forlorn and lust-sick puppy isn't going to do me any favors. Reacting to his tantrum and giving him the attention he wants won't either. If he's intent on forcing me to a party, that's precisely what I intend to do, *party*. Joel stops just outside the door of the hotel. "Just give your name at the door. I'll let them know you're on your way up."

Swallowing, I look up at the towering skyscraper. "You're not coming?"

"I'll be around if you need me," he assures with a wink before heading back toward the idling SUV.

So, the asshole's not even going to allow me my only ally? It's clear he wants me vulnerable. He's probably enjoying every second of this.

Game on, rock star.

THIRTY-SIX

Get Down, Make Love

Nine Inch Nails

Natalie

The thump of bass vibrates heavily at my feet as I step out of the elevator. Slightly shaky on my stilettos, I amble down a long but highly decorated hall full of expensive art. At the end of it—just outside a set of massive double doors—stand two equally massive security guards.

"Natalie Butler," I announce to both the intimidating gatekeepers, the first of which is standing next to a clothing rack full of small plastic bags. He holds out his hand for my clutch, extending the other while proffering a red ticket.

"It's just my wallet and phone," I open my clutch for him to view.

"You can keep the wallet, but no phones or cameras tonight."

It's then I realize the rack is full of confiscated cellphones.

"Um…I'm with…" I feel the heat creep up my neck, "Easton. I'm a guest of his."

"As is *everyone else* inside. No exceptions."

Bile climbs up my throat as he gives me a brief sweep, full of judgment. I mentally hear the smack of his gavel and read the 'she thinks she's special' look in his eyes as he glances over at the second guard.

Just like that, offense fills me as the hypocrite in me takes a huge bite of humble pie. I vow to never again mentally berate another woman for vying for the attention of my beautiful, talented rock star or any other in his company. Reason being, that every minute before now, I've been heavily adrift in a similar boat with no intention of looking for land.

Even if I do know Easton personally, I can easily relate to the appeal from a distance and know I would be filled with an equal desire to get closer.

Slapping my phone unnecessarily hard into his hand, he cocks a brow. "I don't have enough time to talk sense into *stupid*, but you can take that judgmental look and shove it up your ass, pal." I snap. "I have a degree and a penchant for writing from which I make my living. Which means I can pay my own fucking bills. I can also cook a five-course meal and change a flat tire. I even have my own set of power tools. And while I can do all of that, I can *also* embrace my femininity, rock this dress, these heels, and enjoy the feel of both while I feast on the dick of any worthy man of *my choosing*." I step up to the asshole who put me on the offensive with a mere look, "But I assure you, any man *I kneel for* will be intelligent enough to understand why I'm doing it."

Guard two chuckles behind him. "Fuck, man, she just burned you to ashes."

Keeping the asshole's stare, I know I've already gone too far. A lot of my venom is meant for Easton. "In the future, you might want to rethink looking at women with such clear judgment and consider them past their appearances, and maybe, one day, you'll be worthy of any woman who kneels for you."

"I do just fine, sweetheart," he dismisses me as the elevator pings and the doors open behind me, but I step up and am forced to look up after deciding I'm not quite finished.

"I'm sure you do just fine…off of another man's *merit, talent, and allure* because they're worthy of the fantasy. Damn, how that must chip away at your ego."

The man's scathing eyes turn murderous as the guard behind him opens the penthouse door for me. "After you, *beautiful*."

"Thank you," I say, sidestepping guard one, satisfied with his reddening complexion as guard two dips to address me.

"If you don't find what you're looking for inside, I'll be here all night."

We share a smile as he ushers me inside, his eyes sweeping me appreciatively just before he closes the door. The second I take a step into the party, the change of atmosphere hits me, and I'm instantly transported.

Holy. Fucking. Shit.

The massive penthouse has an open floorplan, and the partygoers are bathed in blue light and shadows from spotlights lighting up the walls. To the right, a full kitchen seemingly fit for a Michelin chef. A floating spiral staircase sits just to the left of an expansive marble island—the only barrier between the kitchen and massive living space. A living space where several women dance between an array of plush, oversized circular couches. An audience of men and women alike lounge on and around the furniture, watching them in clear appreciation. Many of those dancing look like models of the *super* kind—long legs, curvy, and dressed the part. Amongst them, I feel sexy in my own skin as a few stares drift in my direction. Feeling the tingle of awareness and the music pulsing throughout the room, there's a clear implication of sex in the air which amps up the forbidden feel in the ambiance.

A massive wall of floor-to-ceiling windows sits just beyond the living room, giving way to a majestic view of part of the city skyline. The long, u-shaped balcony is filled to the brim with guests, billows of smoke erupting from various corners of the vast space. Instinctually, I find myself scanning the first floor for Easton, who is nowhere to be seen. The idea he might be *preoccupied* gives me a sinking feeling, which I bat away, allowing my anger to lead me further into the party.

Stick to the plan, Natalie.

Plastering on a smile, I navigate my way around the crowded space satisfying my curiosity for a gathering of this magnitude. It's always been a hope of mine to see how the one percent parties. Continuing my search, I spot Syd in a corner of the room talking to a group of twenty-something women who seem to be hanging on his every word. He's a respectable foot away from them, but the expressions on their faces are priceless. This is most definitely a night they will remember. As if sensing my stare, Syd spots me standing unmoving in the middle of the room, surrounded by dancing bodies. He gives me a onceover before the hint of a smile lifts his lips. I give him a small wave, and he gives me a quick nod in return before averting his attention back to his captive audience.

Drawing closer to the patio, I make out fire red cherries burning at the end of cigarettes as countless silhouettes take up the space. It's dark, but not to the point I can't make out some of the faces of those clustered around the sporadic stone firepits, blue flames dancing along various profiles. It's ominous enough to make those who want to keep their presence here lowkey feel secure.

Averting my gaze to discourage a few prying eyes away from me, I pause when I spot a familiar face in the corner of the balcony.

Is that the star of the latest Marvel movie?

Seconds later, the object of my focus turns his head, flames lighting up his face confirming it.

Lucas Walker.

Holy shit!

Taming the fangirl threatening to burst out of me and denying the urge to call my mother over our mutual crush, I rip my eyes away, knowing he's probably one of the reasons no phones are allowed. Lucas walked away from Hollywood years ago and came back kicking ass in a Robert Downey Jr. way and set new box office records with his first movie in over a decade. He's the definition of a silver fox, and due to the iconic teen movies Mom turned me onto, he remains one of my earliest crushes. Lucas also co-starred in *Drive*, which makes his presence here relevant, but has my anxiety spiking. Surely Stella and Reid aren't here?

I quickly dismiss that thought. Easton wouldn't do that to me, no matter how angry he is. Intrigued by whomever else might be here, I sweep the bottom floor one last time before heading toward the floating staircase.

The music changes as I take it all in, the entirety of the penthouse vibrating with introductory bass before a woman's breathy moans sound through the speakers accompanying industrial-sounding rock. Realization slams into me, the tone of the music reeking of a lack of inhibition.

Scalp prickling with awareness, the music slithers its way through me in a seductive caress down the back of my neck before giving me the come-hither finger. I follow it, sauntering through a sea of writhing bodies. The further I step in, the more my intuition spikes. The music seducing me along with everyone else, a tangible change in an already voyeuristic type of vibe.

Arousal pulses in the air, and anticipation flutters through my chest as I make my way up the spiraling staircase. I take the last few steps up, a sway in my hips, the ambiance causing my own inhibitions to inch down slightly. It's when I reach the landing that I see the first floor was a fluke, a ruse in comparison to the *real* party happening upstairs. I draw the only conclusion I can to the theme of tonight's party—sin.

And Satan is most definitely cleaning house tonight.

Keeping my "holy fuck" inward, I damn near laugh as I take in the full-blown ominous circus taking place before my eyes. Everywhere I look, there's something more brazen than the last sight to behold.

A crowded, wall-long bar sits to the left of the gigantic room. Half a dozen or so large couches are filled to the brim with celebrities, socialites, and the likes. Scantily clad women, many topless, writhe in every part of the room, their bodies twisting to the music in salacious offering.

To my right, a few of said women kiss on a loveseat opposite an executive-looking type in a suit. He's got his back to them, conversing with the man next to him as if they're in a breakfast meeting. No doubt a music exec.

Just to the right at the end of the bar sits a DJ booth, mixed-colored strobe lights dancing around him. He bobs his head to the trance-inducing beat, the illicit lyrics projecting while sung on the wall behind him.

The more I observe, the more it feels like walking into a dark fantasy. While this may not be my world, right now, I'm a part of it, and I plan on enjoying every second. My plan becomes a lot easier to follow as the music continues to hypnotize me, the deep bass and mechanics drawing me into the thick of the theme.

Everyone in attendance is of varying ages, from early twenties up to their fifties, and very few seem to be acting age-appropriate, which has my smile lifting substantially.

At the bar counter closest to me, credit cards are being utilized to separate a variety of spices, only to be snorted a second later. On the other side, scantily dressed bartenders—men and women—distribute liquor in mass quantities, dueling bottles in each of their hands as they pour freely. Just as quickly, their concoctions are tossed back like water by those on the other side, empty glasses being slammed down, summoning for more.

Scattered throughout the rest of the room, I spot a few more half-naked women grinding on the laps of several men in various chairs and footstools. If I had to guess, I would say an orgy may be in the works, and it won't be long before it elevates to a level that might be too uncomfortable to feed my curiosity. I've never been a prude, but I've never been confronted so brutally with sexual barriers before. The thought of just how far away I am from my norm has a nervous laugh escaping me as I take one gigantic step straight into the thick of it.

If this is Easton's kind of party—Easton's world—I conclude I've nailed my assessment of what he's been trying to shield me from. Even so, I can't help the exhilaration I feel knowing this kind of thing truly does exist.

It's everything I thought a rocker party would be—complete fucking mayhem. Feeling attention start to drift toward me, I slink away from the center of the room and inch toward the bar as I scan the cluttered space once more for Easton and come up empty. Upon doing so, I temporarily become distracted watching a woman lower her top for a man who looks like he's about to devour her. I damn near jump out of my skin when a voice sounds from my right just behind me. "And who are you?"

A quick assessment has me noting a paper-thin V-neck sweater and dark jeans before I turn to address him. His eyes are a sparkly kind of grey, or at least they look that way in contrast with the amount of light in the room. He has a slim but muscular build, and thick dark hair. In seconds I assess he's hot—substitute teacher hot—and a little older. My best guess is somewhere in his early thirties. His watch isn't too expensive or flashy, so he probably wears it for practical reasons.

Responsible.

"I'm Natalie, and you are?"

"Chad."

"Hi, Chad."

"Nothing in your hand?"

"Just got here," I scan the room again for any sign of the band and come up empty. It seems since the last time I blinked, a dozen or so more people have sprouted up in every direction. Ignoring the stomach drop that follows my fruitless search, Chad speaks up.

"Allow me?"

"Please," I say when Chad holds out his elbow, and I wrap my hand loosely around his bicep as he escorts me toward the bar.

Whatever he's doing is none of your business. Whomever *he's* doing *is none of your business.*

Even as I think it, I feel a possessive stab start running rampant through me. Why drag me here if he had no intention of being here with me? I'm positive Joel alerted Easton I was here, which only fuels my irritation. The thought that Easton might be trying to toy with me rears its ugly head. Repulsed and becoming more certain that's the case, I decide I want no part in whatever sick game he's planning on playing with me.

Plan, Natalie. Party.

After a few fruitless attempts to flag the few tending bar, Chad takes matters into his own hands and hoists himself up and over the bar counter. He ducks out of sight before retrieving two bottles, one vodka, and one rum. I point to the unopened vodka bottle, and he winks. "Smart!"

"Not my first rodeo!" I yell back, my thoughts drifting to the makeshift cowboy I hung out with today.

He's not this callous, Natalie.

Shaking off the threatening urgency to find him, I command myself back into the moment and watch Chad pour a healthy shot of vodka over ice.

"Can you please mix it with something? Club soda, if you can find it!"

He grins. "Got you!"

"I'm a good tipper!" I yell.

"What?!"

We collectively laugh because the notion of conversation is ridiculous. Chad busies himself looking for a mixer as I step aside to make way for another in need of the bartender and stumble into a warm body. Righting myself, I go to apologize and come face to face with LL. Feeling slightly relieved to see a familiar face, I open my mouth to greet him noticing his eyes are hooded. My jaw unhinges when I discover he's *heavily* preoccupied.

"Natalie," he greets me casually as my eyes drift down to where his hand is fisting a brunette's hair. A brunette who's on her knees, sucking him off with wild abandon as he guides her bobbing head with his firm grip.

"Apologies, love," he relays, "the Molly hit her pretty hard."

Doing my best to conceal the shock—while a bit jealous his day has gone in a spectacularly better direction than mine—I take a small step back and can't help my wandering eyes from lowering again as his impressive length glides in and out of her lips. Unable to stop the train wreck, I watch him caress her face with his free hand like she's a good pet. My eyes fly back to LL's for a few seconds, his mouth parting slightly as his arousal spikes, his surreal crystal blue eyes piercing.

Slight apprehension threatens for the degradation taking place before me, and I ignore it, knowing the power is ultimately *hers*. With that notion, I find myself turned on, chest heaving with my increased intake of breaths. LL seems to read my expression as I allow my eyes to again dip in time to see his companion swirl her tongue skillfully around the tip of his cock.

"Fuck, you're going to have to stop staring at my cock like that, love," he exhales gruffly as his hungry eyes sweep me, and I avert mine to check the room in search of Easton. My nipples draw painfully tight, an intensifying ache growing between my legs just as a cup appears in my line of sight.

Chad.

My Drink.

Embarrassment covers me, heat blanching my neck as my eyes fly to Chad, whose own lower to discover the scene playing out before slowly lifting back to mine, the effect on him clear.

"I…um…," I shake my head, knowing my skin is betraying me as I take his offered drink, "thank you."

Chad's eyes bounce between LL, his current situation, and back to me before he leans in on a whisper, his voice charged as his breath hits my neck. "I would give anything to know what you're thinking right now."

I can't blame him for his own response, I feel exposed in a way I've never been before.

"What am I thinking?" I laugh. "I'm neither a prude nor saint, but I wasn't expecting to get so close to the fire during the length of a single song. Obviously, I'm embarrassed and..."

"And..." Chad draws out, a knowing grin on his lips.

"Turned on," I shrug. "Wasn't expecting to become a full-on voyeur before sipping my first cocktail."

Chad dips his chin in understanding, a spark of mischief in his eyes before we step away from the show and glance around the party, purposely avoiding LL's grand finale. Just as we move away from the first sexual landmine, we spot another, almost landing on a couple fucking mere feet from the two of us. I damn near jump back in shock, and Chad seems to grow uncomfortable too. I can feel his eyes on my profile as he leans in again. "Do you want to go someplace..."

I laugh. "Way too presumptuous, Chad."

His white smile beams brighter due to the reflective lights as he moves to stand in front of me. Though he maintains a comfortable distance from me, he braces his palms on the bar on either side of me before leaning in. "Not at all," he shouts, "just somewhere where I can actually hear you talk?"

It's when he pulls back to wait for my response that unease hits me, and I glance over his shoulder. I almost flinch at the sight that greets me. Sitting deathly still amongst the chaos in the middle of one of the couches, with cutting hazel eyes unmistakably zeroed in on me, sits Easton Crowne.

THIRTY-SEVEN

Skin

Zola Jesus

Natalie

My throat dries instantly, the intensity in Easton's gaze stifling my reply to Chad. My chest rises and falls rapidly from sensory overload as I drink him in. He's dressed like he was this morning, short black boots with a metal ring clasp, dark cuffed jeans, and a black T-shirt. His hair damp from a recent shower, one side of it tucked behind his ear. The leather cuffs he wore today clasped around both wrists.

My cheeks heat from the desire spike due to the amber jade flames being thrown my way. It's a heady mix, those eyes…and an expression I've never seen on him—accusation, possessiveness, lust, jealousy… judgment? We stare off for several seconds as Chad suggests he secure us another drink before we head downstairs. All I can do is nod as Easton and I stare off and remain planted, waiting at the bar. Despite my conflicted state, I can only hope my return gaze reads something like, *I'm here, asshole.* Now *what?*

Because he forced me here. He wanted to see my reaction to this. I'm sure of it.

I lift challenging brows to him, praying my skin doesn't betray me as my ache for him escalates. He's so fucking beautiful, especially sitting stock-still, a statue surrounded by a thousand-mile-an-hour world, expression filled with lividity. The joke's on those surrounding him, though, because *he's* the supernova, the one passing them at lightning speed.

Sadness laces the thought, and I briefly wonder if this atmosphere will eventually end up curbing his momentum or worse, deter him, as it has countless others. He's made me aware of just how unappealing that fate is for him, but as it seems right now, it's not the case.

Do I even truly know him?

That thought pains me more, that I might not—at least not after his actions today.

Chad's subtle cologne wafts from where he stands next to me, and though it's all wrong, the innate need to rub up against someone, anyone, to relieve the pulse between my legs and numb the growing ache in my chest starts to overpower me.

All I can feel now is the masculine presence surrounding me, but it's the lone, extreme look of the man staring that's weakening me with each passing second. Still, I'm determined to finish this fight with my dignity intact.

Doing my best to gauge Easton's expression, a woman disrupts my view as she moves to stand in front of him, hovering between his spread knees. A spear of ice smashes into my chest, driving in deeper as I study her. Gorgeous—dark skin, dark hair, dark eyes, curvy figure—absolutely beautiful. It's the appearance of his fingers resting casually on her hips as she bends to talk to him that sets my insides ablaze.

"Natalie?"

Chad rejoins me, a vodka bottle secured in his hand and a mixer in the other as she walks away, giving me a full view of Easton without interruption—he slowly lifts his chin to me in summons. My chest visibly bounces once with my laugh and refusal.

My answering expression? *Go fuck yourself.*

"Oh shit, that's Easton Crowne, isn't it?" Chad shouts, following my gaze and tuning into our stare-off. Hands full, he bristles next to me, his lingering question breaking me out of my stupor.

Focus on Chad, who's attainable, present, and who wouldn't be a life-altering mistake.

A safe choice, albeit temporary, but one I desperately need to make to save myself from the heart demanding a quick exit from Chad to flee to Easton.

Don't you dare abandon me now, you worthless muscle!

"He's staring at you like—"

"We're friends." Even as I draw my own battle lines, the words still feel like a filthy betrayal coming from my lips.

"It's clear he thinks differently by the way he's looking at you." My attention flits briefly back to Easton as static fires between us before his gaze drifts to Chad, who turns back to me with a quizzical look. "How do you know him?"

"Work, w-we were working, we worked together, temporarily—I'm in media," I answer, unable to rip my eyes away from Easton when the dark-haired goddess rejoins him, offering him a water. From the way she situates herself against him on the couch, it's clear they have history. Maybe they're going to make more tonight. The thought has my stomach turning as I toss back the remnants of my first and last drink, snapping my eyes away and giving Easton his victory.

I don't want to play adult games with a childish heart. I'm unsure which one of us is acting more like the child at this point. I just want to take what's left of me, go home, and nurse it back to health.

I'm fucking out.

Done.

Imagining him in this life will make it so much easier for me to let go. If this is truly his world, there's no way I can be any part of it. I'd make myself fucking sick obsessing over this very scenario nightly. Even if our parents' history weren't a barrier, there's no way this could ever work.

"Natalie, are you okay?"

"No, I'm not, Chad," I speak up, refusing to look back in Easton's direction as I feel the sting start in the back of my eyes and will it away. "Can you please walk me out?"

Chad nods, discarding his haul on the bar before gently gripping my arm above my elbow and guiding me through the sea of warm bodies. As the music switches, my anger morphs to hurt.

Did he mean a single fucking word he said to me in the past few days?

Is this some sort of payback for leaving him in Seattle and not answering his calls?

Chad ushers me toward the stairs, his hand on the small of my back as I walk away with purpose, thankful I came and saw what I needed to in order to let the fantasy go. I exhale heavily and let resignation sink in. The second Chad and I make it to the landing at the top of the stairs, I feel the shift in the air before warm, calloused fingers grip my shoulder. My scalp prickles as I glance back to find Easton glaring between us both.

"Where the fuck are you going?" Easton hisses, his eyes raking me in a possessive sweep.

"Pretty rude, man," Chad interjects, winning points with me.

Easton's gaze darts to him. "And you are?"

"Chad, this is Easton Crowne. Easton, Chad. Chad was just escorting me out." Catcalls sound from feet away as I motion over Easton's shoulder. "Thanks for the invite. Great show tonight, I mean that. It was exceptional. I wish you every success and…enjoy your orgy." Hating the jealous edge to my voice, I stand firm and turn again as Easton grips my wrist, his gaze locked with mine.

"Nice to fucking meet you, Chad," Easton clips. "Read the fucking situation and take the hint." Chad eyes Easton's hand on my wrist. "I'm asking nicely."

"Natalie," Chad reasons, shaking his head. "I've obviously stumbled into something."

"No," I speak up clearly. "No, you really haven't," I place a placating hand on Easton's chest just as he tightens his hold on my wrist. I may as well have tossed jet fuel on the fire. "You go on. I'll find you downstairs before I leave."

Chad frowns. "Sure?"

"No, she fucking won't," Easton snaps, "so make peace with it now and move the fuck on. I'm done asking nicely."

Chad looks at Easton with a 'you're a dick' expression before he leans in.

"Nice to meet you, Natalie." Chad concedes, pulling out of the ring because he's no idiot, and the air around Easton has turned deadly.

"You too," I sigh as Chad glances between us once more before starting down the stairs. Easton's eyes rake down my dress as I spot the stunner who was catering to him standing at the edge of a nearby couch, her eyes darting curiously between the two of us.

"Uh, I think that woman needs you…or something."

"I'm not with her," he says bluntly.

"Okay. Well, she's got a different impression."

"No, she doesn't," he pulls me a step back into the room.

"Easton, stop this shit, *now*, and let me go."

Ignoring me, he pulls me into him. Panicking, I glance around. "You're making a scene. People are staring."

"That's your hang-up, not mine," he growls. "We need to talk. We're talking. Right fucking now."

"No, we're good. I came, I saw. I got the T-shirt, thank you for a lovely—fuck!" I shriek as Easton moves like a freight train through the room, bypassing hordes of people toward a heavily guarded hall. He stops and addresses a security guard, and the guard nods, letting Easton pull me past him.

In the next second, I'm being tugged down the corridor before being yanked into and released inside a hotel suite fit for royalty. Glaring at me, Easton slams the door behind him and closes his eyes, fists clenched at his sides.

Averting my gaze from the tall, dark, gorgeous temptation blocking my exit, I sweep the room. Floor-to-ceiling windows on one side, a sunken tub, and an opulent master bath on the other. In the middle of the room, beneath a sea of white-washed glass, sits a massive four-poster bed. It's posh, pristine, and wildly romantic, but I'm far too pissed off to appreciate it.

"What in the hell is wrong with you?!" I shout as Easton remains standing at the door, seeming to gather himself. He's angry in a way I'm not familiar with, though I've been warned of his temper. He seems to be trying to rein it in now as he stands motionless for several seconds. But when his eyes finally open, it's all I can do to keep from taking a step back. He's positively furious.

"Admit it," he commands in a lethal tone.

"Admit what? That you're acting like a fucking child? That's your admission to make."

"Admit you didn't want to leave what happened in Seattle any more than I did, and you still don't."

THIRTY-EIGHT

Torch Song
Shady Bard

Natalie

Our chests rise and fall as he shakes his head in irritation. "Jesus, you really are intent on seeing this through."

"Easton—"

"Fine," he interrupts, pointing to his chest, "I'll go first, *again*. I've thought about you every damn day since you left, but I've made that pretty fucking obvious. Your turn."

"What is this? A tantrum for not getting the reaction you hoped for?"

"Oh, I got it," he scoffs, "I saw it, I can still see it, feel it, all of it from *you*. You just fucking refuse to admit it to *me*." He blows out a harsh exhale and rolls his head up on the door, his tone biting. "I want to hear you say it."

I stalk toward him, more so, toward the door. "I don't know what you're trying to do to me, but you win, Easton, okay? You win." I stop a foot away and can physically feel the contempt rolling off his frame.

"You think I can't see what hurts you? Fucking admit it, Natalie."

"What do you want to hear?"

"Admit you were just fucking jealous! Admit that it hurt you when I didn't look at you on stage tonight. Admit that you want this to happen just as badly as I do."

"It can't happen."

"It already has, and you know it."

I drop my gaze as the sting again starts behind my eyes. "Easton, I've explained this over and over again, okay? I should go. I need to go."

Several heartbeats later, he speaks up.

"Then go… Run." My eyes flick to his as he averts his and takes several steps away from the door, giving me a wide berth. "Run. I promise you won't ever hear from me again."

I grip the knob as he keeps his back to me.

"That's not what I want."

"It's what it is, Natalie."

"I'm not running."

"Sure, you aren't. But just know, the second you step out of that door, we'll both be settling for whatever's out there after. At least I know I fucking will."

The burn in my throat worsens as I remain where I stand. "Easton, I'll admit I have feelings for—"

"Right," he cuts me off, shoving his hands in his jeans.

"I don't want to leave like this."

"You don't want to leave at all," he utters.

"You're so sure."

"Yeah, I fucking am because you're still here."

"Because I hate this animosity between us. Can't we just try to—"

"No." He shakes his head adamantly. "No. Fuck no. You know why. We started out heart to heart, and we can't go backward from that."

"I don't fit in your world."

He darts cutting eyes back to me. "What's wrong? Didn't like the party?"

"Sure," I retort dryly. "It was grand."

"That's what you expected, right?" His chest bounces. "This is how you see me living?"

"Whatever, Crowne. It's your life."

He reels on me. "That's the opposite of how I live my fucking life, Natalie. I've been there, done it all. That's so far from how I'm living—it's comical."

"Seemed pretty comfortable to me," I snap.

"Easier for you to believe because it makes leaving easier on you. But it's just another lie you'll tell yourself."

I cross my arms. "So, what, are you telling me that party was just for show?"

Within a heartbeat, he's lifting his phone to his ear and barking a command. "Get them downstairs and cut it in half."

"What are you doing?" I ask. "What is this?"

The music stops abruptly, the pulse of bass now absent from the walls as mixed protests sound from the partygoers down the hall. Easton takes a step toward me.

"You've been making backward comments for the last two days, Natalie. Apparently, *this* is how you see me living, even though you spent four days witnessing the opposite back in Seattle. I could tell you all day, every fucking day, that this is not what my life is on the road, but...*actions* speak louder, and though *words* are supposed to be your kryptonite, mine don't seem to do *shit*."

I gape at him as he draws closer.

"I've been bashing myself against you painfully for the last forty-eight hours, fighting like hell to get past your barricade—back to *you*." He slaps his chest. "I've given you more than I have most after a lifetime of fucking knowing them. What the hell do I have to fucking do?"

"I don't understand what you want!"

"Oh, the fuck you don't, Jesus," he cups the back of his head in exasperation before pointing toward the door. "*That* is not my fucking life. That's not my future, either. The truth is really fucking boring. I'm up by 7 a.m. running, and I eat my fucking vegetables. I listen to podcasts or music if I'm not driving. I write, rehearse, play, work out again to exacerbate the energy I never seem to run out of after a show, and it's lights out after a shower." He takes another step toward me. "I've already lived my rock fantasy bullshit out and had my fill—in my early *teens*. I want no part of it. That's not my life, Natalie, and it won't ever fucking be."

He takes another step forward, forcing me to look up at him.

"You can say it's our parents' history keeping this from happening—"

"It is," I interrupt.

"That's not *all* it is," he fires back vehemently. "I heard you in Seattle. Every word you said, and I took them to heart. So, what is *this*? This is my way of getting rid of what doubts I can control because this thing, this thing between us, to me, is worth the fucking effort." Another step. "Intelligent men don't let life-changing women pass them by without trying to grasp onto them with both hands. I don't need endless months to figure out you're that woman for me. I'm not most men, Natalie. I know exactly what I don't want, and it's everything outside of that door. What I do want is standing in front of me, and the idea of letting her walk away from me a second time is fucking eating me alive."

Unable to swallow, I try and fail to control my breathing as he palms the door on either side of my head. "I haven't touched another woman or even had the desire to since I was inside you."

My lips part in shock, while somewhere deep inside, I get confirmation I already knew that to be the truth.

"Try as I may—because you're fucking infuriating—I can't get you out of my goddamned head." His eyes dip to my lips and then back up. "I can't even get off anymore without thinking about you. I don't bother trying."

"It's the c-chase," I stutter out.

"Oh, yeah, the chase," he chides. "You mean the one and only thing about this situation that makes me want to *run* in the *opposite* fucking direction?"

His eyes roam down my body in a lustful sweep, and it's all I can do to hide my involuntary shiver.

"Okay," he grits out, jaw ticking. "I'll go again. I didn't realize I was a jealous man…until tonight. I have you to thank for that."

He crowds me against the door as I battle the instinct to pull him closer, his scent invading as my arousal spikes immeasurably while his words crash through me.

"Have you let anyone touch you, Beauty?" He lowers a hand before tracing his fingertips along the fabric at my stomach. Panting, I sink against the feel of his touch as his eyes light in satisfaction. "Thought so."

Keeping my eyes, he releases the sterling silver buckle I picked out for him hours earlier, the clank ringing in my ears as my panties flood. "Did you like watching LL get his cock sucked?"

His question has my eyes bulging as his own gaze begins to rapidly heat.

Briefly, I lower mine to see the buckle release is as far as he went. Disappointment seeps into me, my need for him gripping me by the throat.

"You think I didn't see you scanning that party for *me* every time you got turned on?"

The path of his finger trails down my neck before he sweeps it lightly along the cut of my dress, tracing the swell of my breasts. My chest heaves as he lowers it to circle my hardened nipple through the thin material before his molten gaze flicks back to mine. I manage a swallow as he presses in, dipping his finger to trace the thin, delicate chain running along my waist. "Easton—"

"Did you like watching, Beauty?" He abruptly pulls his finger away, and I flinch at his sudden withdrawal. "Answer me, Natalie."

"Yes and no," I say, my eyes again dropping to his dangling buckle.

"Look at me," he snaps. "Why?"

"Because…I don't want him."

"Who do you want?"

"Easton, if we do this—"

"I know, baby, I know," he says, pressing his forehead against mine as if he's trying to both mentally and physically rid me of my position against us. "Jesus Christ, I heard you, I hear you, but I won't let this go. I fucking won't as long as you're with me, and I know you don't want me to, either." Unbuttoning his jeans, he takes one of my hands and guides it into his boxers. Instinctively, I grip his impressive length. A moan escapes me as his thick cock twitches in my palm.

Blinding need surges through me, attempting a takeover as I note the set in his jaw and the desire pooling in his eyes. Before I realize it, I'm lowering to my knees and gripping his boxers to feast. Because he's worthy. Because he's my fantasy turned beautiful reality. Because I want him so fucking much, the ache is unbearable.

Gathering my hair in his fist, he tightens his grip and tugs so I'm forced to look up at him. "Is this what you wanted when you were looking for me?"

Leaning forward, I lick along the fat head jutting out of the top of his boxers, my fingers hooking on the hem to lower them. His grip on me tightens as he pulls me away, refusing access.

"We can have tonight," I offer softly, gazing up at him.

"Admit it," he grits out, jerking himself further out of reach as I attempt to take him into my mouth again. "Admit it. Goddamnit," he grits out in heady demand. When I refuse, he yanks me up by my arms.

"Admit it, Beauty," he cups my cheek, his eyes searching, imploring. "Please just fucking admit it."

"I can't," I whisper, the apology in it unmistakable.

Eyes flaring with renewed anger, he lowers to his own knees while slowly pushing my dress up to my hips to reveal my silky white thong. Palming my thighs apart, he presses his forehead to my navel in obvious frustration as his fingers ghost up between my thighs. He skims the fabric at the apex before moving the material to the side and running his index finger through my center.

"Jesus." He grazes my clit with the pad of his finger, and my legs start to give as he anchors me between himself and the door.

Nostrils flaring, he gazes up, adding another finger and crooking them in beckoning. A cry escapes me as muted satisfaction flares in his eyes. He's declaring war, and I've allowed him to corner me, knowing this can't go in any other direction than the way we both want it to—but on *his* terms. I've already waved my white flag for tonight, but he won't be satisfied until I've voiced it aloud, and in a more permanent way that may damn well ruin me.

"God, I want to fucking punish you," he rasps out, hastening his fingers as another moan escapes me. His eyes snap up. "Don't moan like that, baby. That's my one and only fucking warning," his threat carries a dark edge, which only fuels me. In the next second, he fists the crotch of my panties and yanks, ripping them down mid-thigh until they give and fall. The ruined remains slide easily down my legs before they pool at my stilettos. Another moan escapes me as a wicked smile curves his lush lips.

"Too bad," he sits back on his heels and spreads my slick flesh with his fingers before leaning in and flattening his tongue in a thorough swipe up my drenched center. My responding cry comes out more of a scream just as he takes it away before darting the tip of his tongue out in targeted strokes against my clit. Grappling and already on the brink, I brace against the door, my orgasm starting to unfurl when he pulls away.

"Easton," I croak out, chest furiously pumping as I claw his head in an attempt to grind against him, chasing my denied orgasm. Smirking, Easton teases with one finger, slowly pumping it in and out of me. Dragging it lightly along my walls, keeping me there, but only enough to have me chasing the friction with the desperate grind of my hips.

"Want to come, Beauty?"

"Please," I beg hoarsely. "D-don't—"

"Don't what? Dangle what you want in front of you, only to tell you that you can't have it? That would be cruel."

My thighs shake uncontrollably as he hooks a leg over his shoulder, lifting my lower half and further wedging me between himself and the door. Finger plunging noisily due to my arousal, he looks up at me, and pulls my clit into his mouth, sucking lightly to keep my cries coming. Furious, I fist the material of his T-shirt as he stares up at me.

"Tell me."

"Please make me come."

"I can't," he mimics as he spreads me wider so I have a clear view of the illicit act. "I can't," he taunts before darting his tongue along my clit again. I feast on the look of it, his hot breath and raspy voice lighting me on fire. "This taste," his lashes flutter as he closes his lips around my clit and gently sucks, edging me to insanity. The vibration of his moan has my back bowing as his light stubble rubs against my thighs. In seconds, I'm whimpering his name.

"Please, please, Easton," I beg.

Ignoring my plea, he drops my leg and shakes his head.

"Sorry," he inches a tongue-filled kiss up my stomach while gathering the material of my dress beneath my breasts. Massaging one with his thumb, he stands to his full height, eyes full of condemnation as I fall completely and helplessly under his spell.

Gripping the back of his head, I run my fingers through his thick hair as he brushes his erection against my stomach, smearing the pre-cum onto my skin. He again guides my hand into his jeans, his velvet cock rock hard as we get lost in each other's gaze. The desire between us rages, our stare-off lasting a painful eternity due to our stalemate. His own stance doesn't waver a bit despite the desperate need bouncing between us. Even with the permission I'm so clearly giving him, he's dead set on winning this war.

"Easton, please, you don't know what you're asking of me."

"You want to talk about I *can't*? How about I *can't* fuck you again and watch you walk away from me, *again*. Once was plenty."

He stops the hand I'm using to stroke him and flattens my palm against his stomach before sliding it up to rest over where his pounding heart lays. "I want more for myself, and I want to give you so much fucking more. So, think of what you're asking me because I know exactly what I'm asking of you," his voice cracks with emotion. "This is me fighting dirty for us *both*, so please just admit it so I can give you the best parts of me, because I want every fucking part of you."

A fast tear falls as the first confession tumbles from my lips. "I cried the whole way back to the airport because I knew it would never feel the same with anyone else, so I haven't bothered to look. I couldn't." Another tear falls. "I wrote that article because I wanted you to know I saw you, and I love what I saw *inside you.* Because I was frantic on that plane to keep a piece of you—of us—as close to me as possible. And because I felt the dire need to try to protect you, and that was the only way I could think of doing it." I swallow. "I've thought about nothing but you since I left Seattle." My voice shakes with my next admission. "I didn't want to leave you that day, and I sure as hell don't want to leave you tomorrow. I didn't want to leave us there. All I truly want—and have wanted since the day we met—is *you*."

A cry escapes me before he swallows it with his kiss. Mouths fusing, we collide past the barricade he just blew to ashes. Plastered to him, I pour every feeling I have for him into our kiss as I'm flooded with the warmth I've been continually denying myself. My eyes burn with a prick of fresh tears as he consumes me with his kiss. Tongues dueling, our fire burns brighter and hotter than any other I've felt with him, confirming my worst fear while at the same time filling me with the most profound sense of freedom.

Ravenous, Easton breaks the kiss to take the whole of my breast into his mouth. His head bobs as he suckles, lashes fluttering along his sculpted cheeks as he eagerly feeds while gathering my dress in his hand. He only pauses to lift it from me and toss it away like a nuisance. Hands pinning my wrists to the door, he kisses and kisses me as I feed him more truth with my own—allowing my emotions to take over, allowing him to see.

Frenzied, we take and take until he breaks away. With one inhale, his dark expression seizes me as I stand in nothing but desire-filled anticipation and heels. Lust and intent in his hazel eyes, he abruptly turns us, his hand on my throat, calloused fingers pressing gently into the sides of it as he walks me backward to the edge of the bed. Lifting my leg over his hip, he hastily lowers his jeans and boxers. The instant my back hits the mattress, Easton buries himself inside me in one unforgiving thrust. The second he rears back and presses in again, I start to come apart. My entire body ripples in ecstasy as he stares down at me, mouth parted while hastening his thrusts.

"Jesus...fuck," he curses as I tighten around him, my body quaking as pleasure unfurls through every fiber of my being. Grappling as I come down, I barely manage to grip the sheets in my fists before he drags me to the very edge of the bed. Unleashed, he frantically begins fucking me as I cry out to him, for him, over and over—the full feel of him is ecstasy in its purest form.

Within seconds, I begin to meet him thrust for thrust, following his gaze to where we're connected to see my stretch around him—the sight of it driving me straight back to the brink.

"Look at us, baby," he growls, the edge in his voice the sexiest thing I've ever heard. Eyes closing, Easton dips, swallowing my cries with the thorough sweep of his tongue before he methodically begins rolling his hips. His stuttered exhale hits my neck as I begin to spasm around him, "There it is, baby. Let go."

I obey, and he lifts my hips, grinding himself into me—running the ridge of his cock along my clit and prolonging it, satisfaction gleaming in his hooded gaze.

Panting, chests collectively heaving, he dips and kisses me thoroughly before pulling out of me to fully undress. His shirt is the first to go, and the sight of it bare is nothing short of glorious. I devour him, my eyes trailing his defined chest, sculpted torso, and further down, drinking in his deeply defined V.

"Let me see you," he commands, ripping off his boots.

Heels still on, I spread my legs as he sheds his jeans and boxers together, his gorgeous cock bobbing as he grips it and strokes it from root to tip while biting his lip.

"So. Much. Fucking. Beauty," he whispers roughly before releasing himself and kneeling on the mattress. Gliding his palms simultaneously up my thighs and further up my sides, he grips my hands and threads our fingers before pinning them next to my head. Eyes roaming, he aligns his body with mine, the cross dangling from his neck gliding through the valley between my breasts before he lines the head of himself up with my entrance. Arching my back, I lift my hips in invitation, greedy for more as he hovers above me.

Unwilling to damn myself with more words, I lock my legs around him as he watches me intently, waiting. I soak in the details of his face as my heart goes completely raw for him, and his eyes search mine.

"Say it," he whispers.

"I'm scared."

"Good."

"God, you're a real bastard," I murmur, writhing beneath him, squeezing our clasped hands as he keeps them pinned.

"On this, we agree," he murmurs in reply.

"Good," I fire back, "because we don't seem to agree on much lately."

"And we won't when you fight me on what feels like mine."

"I want *that* part to be true. It feels true."

"It is, Beauty," his possessive lilt hits before he slowly, so slowly, pushes back into me. "I'm making fucking sure of it." He presses into me the rest of the way, staking his claim.

Fully connected, we call out to the other skin to skin, heart to heart, as he pulls back and buries himself again and again, watching me intently. Body flooding with sensation, heart soaring, I free myself to believe his words. To believe in what I feel. That this is real. That *we* will work.

Heart rocketing to a marathon pace, I stare up at him, mouth parting as he palms my thighs further apart and watches himself disappear inside me. Keeping his thrusts slow and deliberate, forcing me to acknowledge this is so much more than attraction and sex. A truth I've known all along but have been too terrified to admit to both of us. The more I allow myself to feel, the more frantically we begin to move as if we've been apart for far longer than eight weeks.

My entire body trembles as he takes us both to the brink repeatedly and past, while staring back at me with soul-stealing intensity.

Lost in his rapture, I find myself feeling whole, and then I lose the pieces I've been grasping onto so tightly right back to him.

We exhaust ourselves to the point my throat dries, my voice going hoarse with my whispers and cries as he ravages me, body, heart, and mind.

At the sight of something he sees in my eyes, he dips and gives me the longest, most intoxicating kiss of my life. Inside of that kiss, I collide with my supernova going a million miles an hour, all space between us diminishing in its entirety.

Easton's groan rumbles against my lips as he stills on a deep thrust, spilling into me again. Exhausted and spent, he rolls us and situates me on his lap, still inside me, refusing withdrawal. Feeling like I'm floating, I rest on his chest as he cradles me in his warmth. It's only when I notice sunlight flooding the hotel room that I realize we've been so immersed in each other that I'd lost all sense of time.

"Easton," I whisper, my cheek to his chest while mentally recalling I got to the party shortly past one. "We've been—"

"Yeah," he runs a gentle palm down my spine, "we have."

"I didn't even realize."

"I know."

Still straddling him, I lift, glancing around in a daze before staring back down at him and palming his chest. Sweat glides down his temple, and my skin erupts in chills as I realize the sheets are soaked through. Bewildered, I shake my head. "What in the hell just happened?"

He grips my hip with one hand and strokes my face with the other, his eyes injecting me with the truth. "What's been happening since the day we met," he lifts to sit before pressing a long, slow kiss to my lips. "Welcome to this side of the glass, Beauty."

THIRTY-NINE

Heaven Sent
Mr. Little Jeans

Natalie

"You owe me one hell of an apology," I scold as Easton's lips roam over my stomach.

"I believe," he licks a slow, seductive path along my gold chain, which is surprisingly still intact after endless hours of intense lovemaking, "I've been apologizing profusely for *hours.* But I'm sorry," he offers, pausing to look up at me. I expect to see a smirk, or at the very least, a sly smile, but instead am met with sincerity.

"Do you know what you're apologizing for?"

He frowns. "Have you been dating nothing but toddlers? I'm sorry for being a dick yesterday," kiss, "and last night," kiss, "and for the song. I'm not proud of myself."

"That song…you believe that's who I really am?"

"No, I believe that's who you portray yourself to be when you're uncomfortable dealing with real shit." This time he does smirk, "*Sleeping Beauty*."

"Ah, so there's the double entendre to my nickname. Thanks for ruining it."

"It will only feel condescending when you play immune."

"I told you when we met that I'm aware of my behavior at all times, even if I'm not acting in a certain way or saying things *other people* want or expect me to." I run my fingers through his thick, damp hair. "And those are two distinct definitions. Playing *immune*—not affected or influenced by and *acknowledging*—to accept or admit the truth of.

I've never been immune to you, Easton, I just refused to acknowledge it, and you know why."

He runs a lazy finger around my navel. "Desperate times, drastic measures. You were leaving, *again*. You weren't going to answer my calls, *again*."

"So, you threw a party to try and convince me?"

"No," he clips out, lowering his gaze.

"Oh, way too abrupt of an answer. What are you omitting?" I pull his hair—hard—so he's forced to look up at me.

"Damn, woman," he grits out as I continue to pull on his thick tresses. "Jesus, okay. Fuck, okay."

I soothe his scalp with a caress as he blows out a harsh exhale. "The party was already planned because I was going to attempt to hook up to try and get my mind off you."

Truth stinging, I nod as he covers my torso with a warm palm. "But I made a better, wiser decision by picking you up in Austin."

"I can't hold that against you, and I won't. I gave you no reason—"

He shakes his head. "Let's not go back there."

"Okay, and technically, Tack told me about the party anyway."

"Because I decided we weren't going the minute I got you into my van. So, was the party planned for you? No." He rakes his bottom lip to cover a smile. "Did I decide to lure you to it after I ramped it up to prove a point? *Maybe*."

"You sure you're not a toddler?"

"I know it was bad. It was meant to be, but only because I wanted to confront your suspicions." He groans in frustration. "It took you fucking *forever* to get here."

"*That* was purposeful," I grin.

"Trust me, I know."

"Well, you threatened me."

"I'm sorrier for that than anything else. That was the biggest dick move of them all." His expression turns earnest. "I wouldn't have carried through with that threat."

"I know that…*now*."

"I was so fucking miserable thinking you weren't coming."

"Poor baby, it must have been sooo agonizing with all those *titties* and *bare-naked asses* bouncing around you." Batting my lashes, I dole out my best Southern drawl. "However did you cope until I arrived? Bless your little heart."

He digs his chin into my stomach, and I giggle and squirm, palming his jaw to stop his assault. "Sorry, but it's just a little hard for me to imagine that you were waiting so impatiently for me with designer drugs at your disposal and a literal clitoral circus running rampant around you."

"I told you it's not my thing anymore. Drugs aren't either. I prefer to acquire my adrenaline and endorphins naturally."

"By riding motocross and chasing F3 tornadoes, I'm aware."

"It was an F4," he corrects with a grin.

I roll my eyes. "So, no parties, *ever*?"

"I mean, yeah," he lifts a shoulder, "sure, occasionally. Why the hell not? I'm in this life for the ride like everyone else, and I want to make the most of it—but everything in moderation. And a party like *that*? Only with you next to me."

"That was some show," I widen my eyes.

"Truth?" He lifts to hover over me, sporting a devilish grin. "That was tame compared to some of the crap I've been exposed to."

"That's..." I shake my head, "I can't even imagine what that would look like."

He turns on his side and props his head on his hand, eyes glittering down on me. "My parents tried their best to shield me, but I've snuck into far worse." He sobers with his next admission. "I'm no saint and won't ever claim to be. I've done my fair share of questionable shit over the years. But since I've been on the road, I've created a new norm. After we play, I write, work out, order some good food—*real* food—shower, and crash." He holds my chin with gentle fingers commanding my full attention. "And now, when I can work it in, I'll add my new favorite pastime," his accompanying smile lights my chest, "making my beautiful girlfriend come so hard I put her to sleep."

"Girlfriend?"

"Moving too fast?" He groans before collapsing back against his pillow. I catch his gaze on me in the mirrored ceiling above us as he addresses my reflection. "Are you really going to keep denying this didn't get serious back in Seattle? I did patiently wait eight fucking weeks in between dates."

Sliding my leg over his torso, I lift to straddle him. Soaking in his every detail, I trace his beautifully healed tattoo with my fingers. So much is clear to me now since I've allowed my rejection cloud to disperse. Part of that clarity is the fact I've never in my life wanted anything more than to keep the connection I feel with the naked man beneath me.

"No. I'm not denying it. My reality is on *this side* of the glass now, remember?" I admonish with ease, utterly done with that aspect of it, no matter how much the potential consequences scare me.

Easton's eyes flit with relief. "*Finally,* Jesus."

"Oh, shut up."

He runs his fingers gently through my damp hair before pushing it behind my naked shoulder. After an explorative and thorough shower, we changed the sheets with a spare set we found in a closet. After a handful of hours of sleep, we woke up hungry, only to soil them all over again. We've spent most of the day exhausting each other before collapsing, naked and entangled while grabbing cat naps.

Rinse and repeat.

When day turned into late afternoon, we dragged ourselves into the shower to wash off one last time with the intent to dress and get me in the direction of home. Joel had picked up my suitcase for me and checked me out of my hotel before delivering it to this room. Even with my luggage waiting nearby—and a long workday looming tomorrow—we only managed to make it as far as the bed, wearing nothing but our jewelry. Admiring his now, I run my finger along the smooth black cross resting against his chest. "Speaking of messiahs. When did you become religious?"

"I'm not."

"So then, not a believer?"

He tilts his head. "I believe in the soul," his response thoughtful. "I've heard too many bleed and crack through my speakers not to, so it's only natural I believe that a higher power created them. But if there's a religion I subscribe to—"

"It's music," I finish for him, and he dips his chin as he pinches the cross between his fingers.

"This is a talisman of defense to ward off evil gifted by an overprotective mother. I guess you could say 'it's a Stella thing.'"

When I tighten my grip on his hips with my thighs, he frowns. "What? Is that more of a deal-breaker than me not liking the Cowboys?"

"It's the Longhorns, Crowne. Get it straight. And no, it's not that at all. I feel exactly the same. I don't buy into all the condemnation in organized religion, but I do believe in God and love. So, I guess if *I* have religion, it's human-interest stories because that's what feeds my soul and makes me a believer in the miraculous."

"Okay, so we agree there, which is a good thing."

"Right."

He palms my thighs. "So why are you bruising my hips?"

"It's just…what you said afterward. It took me by surprise."

"What did I say?"

"Don't get weird, but 'it's a Stella thing' reminded me of our parents."

"Don't get weird?" He rolls his eyes upward. "We're fucking naked, in bed, and you're thinking of our parents."

"Unfortunately…yeah."

"Do I want to know why?"

"It's just that my dad used to say that exact thing to your mom verbatim when he was wooing her. 'It's a Stella thing' was *their* thing, an inside joke between them I read in some of the emails."

He grimaces. "Their history really fucks with you, doesn't it?"

"No, I've only been ignoring your phone calls twice a week for two months because it doesn't affect me at all." I deadpan.

"Point taken," he chuckles before resuming his intoxicating touch.

"Will you at least read the emails?"

"Because you're having such an awesome time dealing? No fucking thank you."

"Easton, this is serious." I sigh, and he grips my hand, threading our fingers.

"Okay, then let's talk about it."

"Seriously?"

"Yeah, baby," he murmurs, studying our clasped fingers. "Seriously."

Eager for the conversation, I go to slide off him, and he grips my hips to stop me.

"No way," he rakes his lower lip, "if we're going to finally have this talk, I'm keeping my view."

I can't help my smile even as I roll my eyes. "Okay."

He brushes his thumb along the crease between my brows in an attempt to erase it. "I don't want this, *us*, to hurt you or your career. I also don't want you to have to sacrifice anything, especially your relationship with your father."

"I don't see any way around that," I shake my head. "I mean, how can we avoid it?"

"As much as I don't want to have to—and as juvenile as it may seem—we're going to have to hide this relationship from *everyone*." He presses his lips to my knuckles before resting my palm on his chest. "For now, we're in this to see what's between us, so we'll keep it solely *between us*."

"Okay," I agree readily, too readily, according to his rapidly darkening expression.

"But not for long, okay? I don't lie to my parents." He grimaces. "I've never really had to."

"Same, and I hate it."

Fear starts to slither its way in while my mind sifts through worst-case scenarios.

"Stop it," Easton commands sharply. "We'll figure us out first and feel them out later before we come clean. We're only touring through the end of summer, and if we keep adding shows, possibly through fall. We can do it this way until I'm off the road. For now, I just want to concentrate on us, and I want you to know you're safe…" He brushes my chest where my heart lay, "that *this* is safe with me."

"Agreed…then, can I ask who that girl was?"

He bites his lip to hold his grin. "I was wondering when that was coming."

I narrow my eyes. "Stop stalling."

"I'm not. She's the daughter of one of my dad's friends who owns a studio here in Dallas." He eyes me warily. "Do you want the whole truth?"

"Yes."

"We fucked when I was nineteen, and she was my potential hookup for the party, but I shut that shit down for good the second she showed up last night."

I swallow, hating the fact I was right about them having history.

"I didn't want to disinvite her after I already called, but I didn't give her any inclination we'd be hooking up when I did. I was just fucking…frustrated. But before you got here, I made it clear I was waiting for someone."

"Such a gentleman," I sass.

He traces the faint tan line on my neck, his hands seducing and soothing, as his words bite. "I'm sorry if that bothers you."

"It would bother me more if you weren't honest about it."

"Sure about that?" He lifts his hips, jostling me. "You look pretty bothered."

"Shut up."

"I'll never lie to *you*, Natalie."

"I know you won't, and I love that about you."

"I told you last night, nothing outside that door has ever compared to what I feel on this side of the door with you, and I mean it." He grips my hips to command my attention. "I've never in my life been jealous in a way that could incite violence, so, touché, Beauty, because Chad *bothered* the fuck out of me."

"Well, he caught on quickly to what was going on between us. That should tell you everything you need to know, but can we have a 'no exes within ten miles' rule?"

"Let's make it a fucking hundred."

"Suits me. But in my case, you don't have an ex to worry about."

"Same."

"So," I grin. "What's an *amped-up* party like that cost anyway?"

"Don't worry about it."

"Oh," I giggle and pinch his sides. "You going to get *funny* about money again?"

"No, but you're already a flight risk, so I'm not telling you shit."

"Thirty grand?"

He schools his expression in refusal of answering.

"Forty?"

"It doesn't matter. It was worth every fucking penny. Couldn't you tell how miserable I was?"

"I wasn't really paying attention because I was too busy trying not to leap over a couch of naked women to claw your eyes out."

Said eyes roaming, he shifts his hips, his cock hardening beneath me. "I saw your curiosity the minute you hit the landing, how intrigued you were," he lifts to take my nipple into his mouth, sucking noisily before releasing it, "how turned on you were getting." He grinds his hips beneath me, eliciting a low moan from my parted lips. "I was going fucking blind with the need to touch you," he murmurs before laying back against his pillow and jostling me again, this time with his thick dick. "I wanted to pluck every filthy thought, every fantasy from your beautiful head and play it out with you."

"How do you know they were filthy?"

"Are you kidding? I can read you so easily it's ridiculous."

"Well," I hear the arousal in my voice as I plant my hands on his chest before running my center teasingly along the ridge of his cock. "You punished me instead."

"It was a *just* punishment. But I've got so much more in store for you—for us—for that curiosity that was written all over your face." He rakes his lower lip. "I'm going to be the man to satisfy every filthy fantasy you come up with. *Bet.*"

"Mmm, so what am I thinking right now?"

"That you want to be kissed, fucked, and loved properly, and you want me to be the one to do it." His words stun me briefly as he grasps my hips, controlling my movement while rolling his own, pulling me straight back to the brink of orgasm. He's already mapped my body to the point he can get me *there* before I'm even aware I'm capable.

The part that has my heart fluttering faster is that he's right. I do want him to be the one to kiss me, fuck me, and love me properly, but instead of admitting it, I grip his impressive length in my hand and lift to take him inside of me.

Seeing my intent, he jerks his chin in command, challenging me as he rubs me back and forth, inching lower to cover more of him with every teasing thrust. "You're going to come first," he declares, determination in his heated tone, "just like this." He quickens his pace for emphasis.

My thighs begin to shake from the delicious friction he's creating as his expression smolders.

"Fuck," he whispers hoarsely, "you're so goddamn perfect."

His praise sends me into orbit as I rock against him, fueling the fire. Just as I start to come apart, he lifts me and thrusts in slightly. I tighten around him as the orgasm takes hold, the wave crashing into me so abruptly that I score his chest with my nails.

"Easy, Beauty," he grits out as the shudder subsides. Sweat beads at my temple as pain and pleasure mingle in the most delicious mix. "I know you're sore."

"I don't care. I want you, please, Easton, now," I grind my hips in demand while trying to accommodate his size. As wet as I am, and even after the orgasm, I struggle to take him in.

"Damn." Easton stills my hips, keeping my gaze before gently easing into me with prodding thrusts. I call his name as he slowly feeds me every delicious inch until I'm fully seated. Impaled on his perfect dick, he releases my hips, and I take over, palming the back of his thighs for leverage while slowly starting to circle my hips.

Jaw slack, eyes hooding, Easton gazes up at me like no one else on earth exists. And I feel that truth because when we're connected like this, for me, no one else does.

"Everything," he groans, gently pumping up and into me as I swivel my hips. "Every fucking thing about you," he rasps out.

Together, we sync into perfect rhythm as I stare down at him, drunk on his expression, on the feelings he's drawing out of me. Using the pad of his finger, Easton begins to lazily trail the chain around my waist, gliding his finger back and forth in a hypnotizing sweep in time with my hips. We maintain our silent tempo as I widen my thighs to take him deeper. His eyes go molten at the richer connection, his expression one of bewilderment.

I murmur his name, hearing the emotion in my tone, and his finger stops as he searches my gaze. Unable to voice what I'm feeling, I pray he can read my thoughts now as he seems to do so easily because what I feel for him in this moment is indescribable. In an instant, he lifts to sit, cradling the sides of my face. It's there he holds me captive, as I vibrate inside my skin, on the precipice of handing myself over while giving him a clear view of the emotional overload—withholding nothing.

"Let go, baby," he urges softly, "I'm coming with you." My heart rockets as his words surround me. Knowing he's with me in every way that matters, *physically*, *spiritually*, *emotionally*, I leap.

FORTY

Woman
Mumford & Sons

Easton

"Wake up, Sleeping Beauty," I murmur against her temple resting on my chest as Joel pulls the SUV to a stop.

She rouses, her hand sliding up my chest as she lifts and glances out of the window. "Where are we?"

"A private airstrip at Love Field." Covering her hand with mine, I raise my chin to Joel in the rearview. "Give us a minute, would you, man?"

"Sure," Joel replies, winking at Natalie before making a quick exit.

"What the hell?" she turns to me, voice still coated in sleep. "Easton, please tell me you did not charter a plane to get me home."

"I did not charter a plane to get you home," I repeat robotically before she playfully slaps my chest.

"Seriously? I could have flown commercial. It's like fifteen minutes in the air from Dallas to Austin."

"I promised to get you home and tuck you in by midnight. This is the only way to keep half of that promise because if I tuck you in, I'm not going to make it to my next show."

"I understand," she smiles. "I really do. I don't want to leave you either. Especially now." She leans in and presses a kiss to my throat.

Briefly, I flashback to a memory of the way she looked hovering above me as I stroked the chain secured around her waist. The feel of her wet heat clenching around me as she stared back at me was the hottest fucking thing I've ever witnessed. But it was the feeling bouncing between us that burned that moment into memory as one I'll never forget.

My attraction for her hums through me now—a beastly threat that I, in no way, want to cage. Even if the depth of what I already feel for her intimidates me, I won't do a single thing to stop it. It's the ferocity in which I want her—in my need to possess her—that has me leaping over hurdles I've never dared attempt before. This is why it's important we finish this conversation before she takes off. She presses another kiss to my throat before pulling back to trace my jaw.

"Baby, hold up," I groan and put a little distance between us.

"Why?" She pulls back and glances around in alarm. "Can they see into the windows?"

"No, but I'm already hard, and if you do that again, I will fuck the hell out of you in this SUV with Joel standing feet away."

"You act like I don't have a say in that."

"Want to test me?" I taunt.

"No," she replies with a smirk as I force myself back to the point.

"We haven't managed to get a full conversation in all day."

She arches a brow.

"That wasn't a complaint."

Her lips curve into a sultry, reflective smile, and I shoot a quick prayer up to the creator of souls that this feeling never leaves me.

"I can't believe you chartered a plane for me."

"There will be a car waiting when you land to take you home."

"Easton, it's too much."

"No, it's not," I defend, running my fingers through the curls resting on her shoulder.

"I hate that you spent the money."

"Worth it for me, especially since I now know what death traps Texas highways are. I don't want you driving on them, fucking *ever*, but that's not something I can remedy tonight." I lift my chin toward the window. "This is the fastest, safest way to get you home, and something tells me it won't be your first time flying private."

She nods, her neck reddening slightly. "Hearst Media owns a jet. So yeah, I can't say it's my first time on a private plane." She glances at the waiting plane just outside the window. "But it's a bit much."

"You know that matters fuck all to me, right?"

"I just don't want you to think I expect these things."

"Expect a lot from me," I urge her. "A lot."

"Easton," she murmurs back, our hands gathering momentum as we stroke each other, "you don't have to cater to me."

"I want to, so let me."

"Okay," she sighs, "as long as you allow me the same freedom."

"We'll see."

She rolls her eyes. "You're an unbearable ass. So, are you going to keep me in suspense?"

"I want this to work," I declare, putting her on guard, causing her smile to dim.

"Me too."

"So, this is going to seem hard to navigate for a while, but there are some things we can agree on now to make it easier. Going caveman jealous last night…I hated the feeling."

She laughs and shakes her head before ducking a little under my glare.

"Sorry, but it is a bit ridiculous. You are aware that by now, there are thousands of women just dying for you to bed them."

"You could have just as easily had any man at that party by simply looking at them last night. We're on an even playing field, and don't think for one second that we aren't."

"I hate to disagree, but men don't exactly toss their boxers on my desk while I'm working."

"I'm pretty sure it wouldn't take much to make that happen."

She smiles, and as much as the sight of it lights me up, I have no choice but to dampen the mood. "We really need to have this conversation."

"I'm listening."

"Name all the people you trust."

"Easy, my parents and my best friends Holly and Damon. I trust them all implicitly. Then there's my dad's sister, my Aunt Nikki, and his cousin, Sierra, but she lives in California now. Why?"

"From this moment forward, you can't trust any of them."

"What?" She squints like the notion is ridiculous.

"Not when it comes to us. Hear me out," I plea. "If you really want to keep us under wraps, we have to go completely off the fucking radar. No confidants. Just for the time being. Percy excluded."

"My *horse*? Seriously?"

"Has to be this way."

"But last night—" she starts, and I lift my hand.

"Last night, a few people noticed me leaving the party with a stunning but unrecognizable woman. With a party like that, it's par for the course. That's why I wasn't worried."

"Geesh," she widens her eyes, "groupie point taken."

"That won't be the case the first time the media gets a clear shot of us together."

"Why do you think I've been so paranoid?"

"We really had nothing to hide but our association before last night."

"Now we do." Her smile reappears.

"Yeah, baby, we do," I grin back. "As much as I hate this next part, and I think you're going to too, I don't think you should attend any more shows for a while. Especially since my dad will be at a lot of them and lodging where the band is after."

"You're right. I hate it. Watching you play is my new addiction."

"I want you there. I love singing to you, but seriously, Natalie, if you want this to remain a secret, we can't let anyone see us together. And until we come clean with our folks, I'll be doling out nondisclosures like candy. Even then, we really aren't safe."

"I am the media, Easton, so I understand, *obviously*, but not even *Holly*?"

"It's a good thing you didn't tell her already and hear me out on why."

She gestures for me to continue.

"So, you tell Holly but leave out the details of *who*. Guess who she's going to tell?"

"No one. I told you she—"

"Until she accidentally slips up around Damon or during dinner with your parents. From any point—and I mean *any point* at all—that you cave and confess, no matter who it's to, it could snowball. Take it from me. The people you trust the most have people *they trust* most. Your life-or-death secret becomes a secret they have coffee over in hushed whispers."

"Holly would never—"

I lift a brow.

"Damn, okay, I've got it." She nods. "I see the logic."

"Joel is the only human alive I truly trust to keep us safe, and we're going to need him, a lot if we're going to pull this off."

"Okay, I believe you, and I adore Joel."

"I know you do, Beauty. He feels the same."

I unhook her seatbelt and pull her to straddle me.

"I'll have to be all of it, your boyfriend, your best friend, and confidant. I'm fine with that, just until we come clean with our parents. Okay?"

She nods firmly. "Okay. Percy it is."

"Or me," I try to assure her. "You can bitch about me to *me*."

"That's not the way it works," she grins.

"I know. Doesn't matter anyway. I'll know when you're pissed. You're almost as bad as my mom at hiding your emotions."

"First of all, I'm not an emotional—"

"Just with me," I finish, every speeding heartbeat due to her proximity confirming what I already know—this woman is very close to *owning me*.

"And while the 'no ex within a hundred miles rule' is very fucking much in effect," I add, "insecurity and jealousy will end us faster than our discovery might—at least when it comes to your line of thinking."

"It would be yours too if you knew what I do. Easton, please just read the emails."

"No," I say firmly before swiftly changing the subject. "So, we have to keep our heads at all times. Any photo or anything you read in print gets *discussed* before it's argued about."

"Tell that to yourself and my battered vagina. You really are a jealous idiot, which is ironic because I'm the one who has to deal with hordes of women trying to weasel their way into your hotel room."

I shake my head in frustration. "You don't have to deal with that. You won't ever have to deal with that. I've—"

"Been there, yes, I know. That's *all* I need to know, thank you very much." Her eyes dim. "Atlanta next, right?"

I can't help my grin. "You know my show schedule?"

Her neck reddens, and I grin. "She blushes."

"You're making me a weak woman."

"You're kidding, right?" I chuckle and brush my thumb beneath her lower lip. "You fought like a four-star fucking general last night."

"Before I lost," she adds.

"No, baby. Coming clean with me, that took strength, and thank fuck you did."

"I've never been happier about losing," she murmurs as Joel taps once on the hood, signaling our time is up. I fight the urge to fly with her and spend a week in Austin, getting lost in her world, inside her. Although, I doubt that will stifle enough of the rapidly increasing ache. "The next few stops are going to be brutal schedule-wise, but can you fly out in two weeks? Lake Tahoe?"

"Yes," she nods, "I'll make sure I can."

"I'll get us the perfect spot."

Joel knocks on the top of the hood again.

"Shit, you have to board now, or it will fuck up their flight plan."

"Okay," She presses a quick kiss to my lips, and I grip her and bruise her lips in return. "See you in two weeks," she inhales, sliding off my lap and latching onto the door handle, her expression going bleak.

"Natalie—"

She turns back to me, her stare filled with trepidation. "I just hate feeling like we're being robbed straight out of the gate, you know?"

"Tell me how to fix it."

"There's no fixing it…but at the same time, you gave me…" she shakes her head, her electric blue eyes stunning me along with her broadening smile that lights up my whole fucking world.

Damn this woman.

"Easton, last night was the *best night* of my *life*."

"Mine too," I caress her cheek. "We'll have so many more, so don't let errant thoughts take this away from us, okay? Don't let your guilt ruin this. Text me. Talk to me about it. Make that your first promise to me."

She nods as I press my forehead to hers. "Say it."

"I promise, Easton."

"Good. And I promise to do everything in my power to keep this between us until you're ready to talk to your dad."

"Thank you," she murmurs against my lips.

"Go, before I do something *really* stupid."

Anxiety overtakes me with the thousand ways this could go wrong, and she quiets my erratic thoughts with the tenderness in her kiss, soothing me as we desperately draw upon each other's mouths. I sink into her affection, into her need for me, into the promises we have yet to make, and the declaration dancing on our tongues as our time ticks out. She breaks the kiss with Joel's last knock and exits the SUV, stalking toward the plane and boarding without a glance back. Though it stings like a bitch, I know why. For the same reason I can't fly with her and tuck her in.

I revel in what this ache means, in what my heart is relaying.

My chest tightens unbearably as I watch the plane taxi down the runway, flashes of the last forty-eight hours flitting through my mind as our connection continues to buzz through me with the strength of a tsunami. As her plane floats into the late summer sunset, the ache in my chest begins to rage, only confirming the deep-seated truth that began to take shape inside me months ago.

The truth that our souls clicked seamlessly together before our bodies ever aligned, and it can no longer be denied or undone.

FORTY-ONE

Girl, You'll Be a Woman Soon
Rafferty

Easton

"It's a good one, man," Tack claps my shoulder as he and Syd exit the stage searching for sustenance. Our sound check lasted longer than normal—thanks to my insistence we start working on a new cover I decided we would master after leaving Dallas.

"I agree. See you tonight."

Syd jerks his chin to LL and me in silent goodbye, vape smoke billowing in his wake. Aside from his base line, I've deduced grunts and gestures are Syd's chosen love language. Syd's private, and in that, we have common ground.

For the most part, I've got my bandmates figured out—quirks and all—except for one. I glance over at LL, who's taken residence on my piano bench to jot notes down on the margin of his sheet music. When he senses my gaze on his profile, he stops his pencil and stares back at me.

I've been borderline hostile with him since Dallas, and he must know why. In response, he's been playing ignorant. The apology he should have already made feels pointless now, but I can feel the indecisive energy emanating from him when he finally speaks up. "Look, mate, I didn't know—"

"The fuck you didn't," I interrupt. "Let me make myself clear. I don't care that you're talented and will be hard to replace. If you ever so much as look at—or pursue—any woman who's with me like that again, you're fucking gone."

"That's a bit fucking petty," he fires back. "I was already midgame before she caught us in the act."

"Then maybe don't make it a point to have your cock sucked in public."

"It was *your party*, and it wasn't exactly rated PG. If I recall correctly, it was quite the contrary."

"And that makes me responsible for your behavior?" I roll my eyes and take a step toward him. "I was already skeptical about you personally when we hired you, so any chance of my opinion changing was shot to shit with the way you reacted."

"She was watching *me*," he defends.

"She saw something that piqued...shocked her. In turn, you saw an opportunity," I snap. "That's the behavior of a fucking predator. I know it when I see it, so don't play innocent."

"Far from that, mate."

"I'm not your fucking *mate*," I snap, turning to retreat off stage before my anger bests me.

"No, you're not my mate. You're a fucking spoiled cunt. I'd almost be relieved if you carry through with the threat to fire me," he snaps at my back. "At least I'd get half my salary and be free of your Type A fucking arse. I don't see the issue. She's just another fucking bird."

Red streams through my vision as I turn, and in two strides, land a right squarely on his mouth—knocking him backward, along with the piano bench. Tempted to pounce, I take a few steadying breaths as he sneers up at me, his lip bleeding freely.

Sighing, I grab the towel from atop the piano and squat so we're eye level as he continues to glare at me. Indecision appears to flit over his features, like he's deciding whether or not to strike back. I give him ample opportunity to do so before thrusting the towel toward him. "You deserved that, and now I know where we stand, but let's cut the bullshit. I'm just as observant as you are, Leif, and you know damn well she's not just *another fucking bird.* Regardless of what she is or isn't, it's not your business to try and figure that out. Your business is to show up and play guitar."

"Whatever you say, *boss*," he snaps in clear condescension before snatching the towel and wiping his mouth. "I don't give a fuck what you think about me because you know fuck all."

"Well, by all means, LL, if I'm wrong about you, feel free to fucking surprise me."

He spits blood into the towel and tosses it back at me before standing. "Whatever, like I give a damn who you stick your prick into."

"Just keep your shady shit away from me and—"

"The fuck's going on here?" Dad yells, striding on stage, and I flash LL a warning look.

"Just a misunderstanding," LL offers quickly, eyes fixed on mine. "Apparently, I mis stepped with Easton's *special* bird," he declares with blood-laced teeth, sealing his fate with me.

Fuck.

I can practically predict the future issues he's prone to cause, and not just for me personally. At this point, I'm hopeful the band only remembers Natalie's first name. I wasn't thinking long-term, or at all, about the future when I picked Natalie up because honestly, she had me convinced we weren't happening. Long term is what kept me awake the second she passed out in my arms in that hotel room in Dallas.

"What special bird?" Dad asks.

"Just a girl I met on the road," I lie. "It ended in Dallas."

LL's lingering stare and budding smirk tells me he knows I'm lying, and he just gained leverage. Thank God he's got no real idea of who Natalie is or the damage it could cause. I'd parked a block away from *Austin Speak*—in front of the coffee shop—but I have no doubt Leif was privy to every word she spoke on the road and caught her mention she was media. It's too much. The web is already spinning in a direction I don't want, and we're not even a week in.

I hate lying—especially to my dad—but I will for her, her future, her happiness, and our relationship. For now.

"If it ended, then what's the problem?"

"Seriously, Dad?"

Dad, of all people, should understand my need to protect any woman from walking STDs like LL. Just the memory of how turned on she got watching LL get head has my hackles rising. It's not so much jealousy—though it's a large part of it—but his reaction to her natural curiosity. I practically saw him licking his wolfish chops as he weighed her reception. I've never wanted to physically end another human life like I did when I saw LL's intent to try and lure her into participating. Even from ten feet away, I could *feel* his intent.

Shaking those thoughts away, I kick what's important to the forefront. My priority right now is that Natalie's identity remains safe. I'm her secret, and sadly, she has to be mine. For the next three months, four tops, it's doable, but it will be fucking tough with all the media attention starting to focus our way.

LL's lips curve as he obviously reads my panic—despite my attempt to hide it—hammering another nail into his coffin.

"See you backstage," he says to Dad before smugly sauntering off. Dad watches him go before turning to me, silently demanding an explanation.

"He made a pass at her in a very lewd way, knowing she was with me."

"So, you punched him *now*? After the fact?"

"He deserved it. That's why he didn't retaliate."

I move to organize the sheet music scattered along my piano, but Dad yanks my hand, my reddening knuckles in clear view. "Going to sting like a bitch playing with this tonight." He shakes my swelling fist. "This fucking thing is a lot more valuable than fighting over some meaningless road fling."

I rip my hand from his grip. "Well, maybe you treated women like dish detergent in *your day*, but that's not my style."

"The fuck?" He explodes. "You say this shit to me? I've been faithful to your mother well before and during your whole *existence*."

"Have you?" I ask, having no idea where I'm going with this line of questioning. I exhale heavily when I see fury flare in his eyes. "Sorry, Dad. Shit, sorry."

When his anger dissipates as a result of my apology, I deem his ability to let it go so easily a superpower I wish I possessed. But it's her. I know it's her, and meaningless is not a word I would associate with her. She's under my skin, fueling my days, lightning in my veins. I'm already gone.

"What the fuck is going on with you? And don't lie to me."

"I'm stressed out," I say honestly. "I have a lot on my mind."

"So, take a day. Take two. You don't have to be writing on your days off. Find something else to get into."

"I can handle this, the road, on my own," I snap.

"You gunning for me now?"

"No, Jesus." I run my smarting hand through my hair. "I just fucking clocked a guy. Sorry if I haven't leveled out yet."

"I'm aware you can handle this on your own, East, and I'm not doubting you." His watchful eyes trail me before I turn my back to sort the music.

"What aren't you telling me?"

Briefly, I entertain broaching the subject with him. Natalie and I did agree to feel our parents out at some point. I open my mouth to speak, but the words die on my lips as he pulls the piano bench LL took down with him upright.

"Your fucking temper," he barks, eyeing me in a way that makes me feel an inch tall. "You need to get a hold on that, son, and fast, or it's going to fuck things up for you in the long run. Big things, important things. I have the same temper, but I've never let it get to me like it's starting to eat at you."

"It's a matter of respect," I tell him. "He doesn't have any for himself, let alone anyone else. I told you I had a feeling about him, and I'm usually right."

"He's a musician in need of a paycheck who backs you on stage every night without fail," Dad scolds. "Is it really worth the hassle to go at him over a random road hookup?" He shakes his head. "And just so we're *clear*, all the money in the fucking world can't repair the damage of a bad temper."

"He deserved it," I explain. "He was getting sucked off at a party and was trying to lure her into the mix, knowing she was with me. She's not the type. She's innocent. That's why he didn't fight back."

Dad doesn't miss a beat. "Then he deserved it."

"Fucking thank you." I straighten the sheets in my hands. "I can't stand him. We're replacing him after the tour," I lift my chin in the direction LL left.

"Fine. I'll take your word on this." Long minutes pass while I pack my messenger bag. Dad lets out a heavy exhale before he breaks the silence. "I love him, son. I love that boy with everything in me, but his acid may be leaking a little too much into you."

Confusion blinds me briefly until it hits me. "Benji?"

"He's like a son to me, but he's jaded as hell, and sadly his perception is a bit fucking skewed because of what he's been through with Ben and Lexi. He's smart. I'll give him that, probably more intelligent than all of us. Buried somewhere inside him is a good heart, but make no mistake, he's got more acid than blood running through him at this point."

"He has a strong aversion to our government and commitment issues, but that's *Benji's* prerogative. Credit me for having a mind of my own."

"I do. I just don't like the path he's on. He's starting to worry me, and I don't want you mistaking his word for gospel, especially right now."

"Stop. This whole conversation is unnecessary. We may be as close as brothers, but I don't share all his beliefs."

"Fine." Dad gestures toward my hand. "You need to ice that."

"Yeah, I'd better."

"Come on then, I need a smoke and I'm starving," he prompts, already digging in his pocket for his cigarettes.

Shouldering my bag, my phone buzzes in my pocket with an incoming call. Figuring it's probably Natalie, I resist the urge to make an excuse to answer to pursue the conversation with Dad instead. "What exactly happened with them?"

Dad shrugs. "Lexi cheated, and Ben couldn't forgive her. I couldn't blame him at the time. They were heavy, and it was pretty brutal. When she tried to move on, he couldn't forgive her for that, either. Neither of them could truly let go, so they went back and forth for years. He got her pregnant the night I married your mother."

"I didn't know that."

"Yeah. He was good to her when she was pregnant, too. You could see the potential there for reconciliation, but it never happened. I never really understood why they could never manage to get it together until a few years back. I decided the reason was and still is what it's always been, the band."

"Lexi couldn't handle being a rock star's wife," I add, recalling the same conversation with Natalie in Seattle.

"Exactly." He glances up thoughtfully. "As close as Ben and I are, I realized her cheating changed something inside him for the worse. It's like their relationship going south slowly poisoned them both."

"What about you and Mom?"

He draws his brows as we walk the hall backstage. "What about Mom and me?"

"Where was your head when you were together?"

"We got together when I was at my lowest point, so it was scattered. You know that."

"Yeah, but did you two ever get dicey like Ben and Lexi?"

"We were dicey from the start because of my circumstances. I had absolutely nothing to offer her. Your aunt Paige was fucking furious and didn't want me near her baby sister. That was a nightmare in itself. Sad part was, I agreed with Paige back then, but thank fuck your mom didn't."

"Did Mom cheat?"

Dad pauses as we exit the building, cigarette dangling from his lips. "What? No. You can't cheat if you're not with the person. We broke up, I got signed and hit the road, and she had to finish school. We were in entirely different places."

"So, did she sleep around?"

"You're seriously asking me about your mother's sexual history?"

"I'm just curious." I shrug as he pushes open the door and instantly lights his cigarette before exhaling.

"We weren't apart for days, son. We went years without each other before we got back together. I can't speak for her, but it was hell on earth for me for the first two and only got worse as time went by because I knew if we stayed apart much longer, I would lose her for good."

"What aren't you telling me?" I turn his question back on him, knowing he'll come clean.

"Nothing to tell. Your mother wrote our story," he grins, "and it's available for rent on Amazon."

A foreboding feeling sets in as I realize even my dad is reluctant to talk about Nate.

"So, how did you get her back?"

"The way she wrote it. We found each other at the house on Lake View. It happened just like that."

"Would you have forgiven her if she had cheated?"

He stomps out his cigarette with a black booted heel. "Back then, I would have forgiven her for anything," he says. "Absolutely anything. Probably still would. But I wasn't always capable of that. She's the reason I became capable."

Joel hops out of the driver's side of the SUV as we approach and opens the back door for Dad, who shakes his head in irritation.

"Twenty years of telling you to stop opening the door for me. You think you would get it by now."

Joel grins. "After twenty-two years of paying my salary, you would think you know I don't do anything half-assed."

Dad splits his attention between Joel and me. "I'm not paying it anymore, so cut that shit out. You up for a burger?"

"Hell yes, I'm starving," Joel replies as we all get in. Dad shoots me a look from the front seat as he buckles in, prompting me to do the same. "The truth of the matter is some people work together, some people don't, time will tell, and trust me, it always fucking does."

Shit. The summary.

Otherwise known as Dad's way of ending a discussion.

Joel eyes me in the rearview as he starts the SUV while Dad checks his phone. I jerk my chin to Joel to let him know all is well, but in truth, it's anything but. In the last twenty minutes, I lied to my father. The worst part?

He lied to me, too.

FORTY-TWO

Baby I Love You
Aretha Franklin

Natalie

My phone rumbles in my pocket as I pull to a stop and retrieve my cell to see EC requesting Facetime. Wiping the sweat from my brow, knowing there's not much I can do about my appearance, I slide to answer with a ready smile. "Howdy, handsome. Just in time, I want you to meet someone." Unable to see Easton clearly due to the glare of the sun, I lower my phone. "Percy," I introduce enthusiastically, practically lying atop him to lower the phone, "this is my boyfriend, Easton. Easton, this is the other man in my life, Percy."

"Hey, man, nice to finally meet you," Easton greets, the smooth rumble of his velvet voice spiking my heart rate. "Heard a lot about you, but why the long face?"

I lift the camera, giving him a dead stare. "Har, har."

"Fuck, you look beautiful."

"You need your eyes checked, buddy. I'm a hot, sweaty mess."

"You were the last time I saw you, too, and you looked just as beautiful."

I can't help my smile as I swat a fly away from my flushed face. "It's hotter than Satan's anus out here," I say, and he chuckles in reply. "You're lucky you're up north, where summer doesn't feel like a three-month sentence."

"I'd much rather be where you're at. So you're *home, home*?"

"Yeah," I turn the camera around and scan the house and surrounding grounds for him to view. "My parents flew to Chicago last night for a few days on Hearst Media business, so I'm housesitting for the pool privilege and to bitch to Percy about you."

"Oh yeah? Any complaints I should know about, Percy?" Easton muses.

Cupping the phone from the glare of the sun, his gorgeous face fills the screen. "You're too far away," I say mournfully before whispering a more intimate. "Hi."

"Hi," he repeats, black hat on backward, buds in his ears.

"So, you're on the road?"

He turns the camera on Joel. "Riding with my man here today so I could call you. Say hi to Natalie."

Joel turns and waves. "See the way he abuses me, Nat?"

"I see it," I tease. "It's just wrong."

"He can't hear you," Easton points to his buds.

"Well, tell him I'd ride with him any time."

"You're *my* date tonight. He can find his own."

"Are we on a date?"

"Yeah," he grins, tilting his head back against the rest. "That okay?"

"I'm all yours."

"Yeah, you fucking are," he declares with a possessive edge. "So, show me around."

"And this is my one and only riding ribbon," I say, holding the camera up to the corkboard still mounted in my childhood bedroom closet.

"My little equestrian nerd," Easton muses as I turn the camera back on me.

"Do you ride? Well, I mean, *would you*?"

"Yeah, sure. For you I'll try it," he says softly, the view of him doing a number on my insides.

"Don't expect to see me on a motorbike, but you can teach me to play an instrument."

"That's a decent compromise. Which one do you want to learn?"

"Maybe the drums?"

"Done. I'll give you your first lesson in Tahoe."

"Seriously?"

"Of course."

"I'm so excited."

He chuckles. "Easy to please."

"Well, I hope you're patient. I have no rhythm."

"I disagree," he fires back. "You sure give one hell of a lap dance."

I bite my lip and shake my head. Every day I read headlines that praise Easton's genius—declaring him a revolutionary—and every night since Dallas, I talk to the man I met in Seattle. The man who took my hand and helped me make sense of the state I was in.

Sometimes it's hard to believe he's one and the same. As a journalist, I finally understand the distinction between the fantasy life most believe celebrities dwell in and the reality of their every day. Insight that not many people can truly understand, unless they live behind the scenes.

Not that the jet setting, yacht life isn't possible, because it is. It's just not practical for everyday living. Easton's daily routine is exactly as he described, far from that luxurious life, but he's anything but boring as he claimed to be. He's insightful and brilliant, and I love hearing him talk about anything and everything.

We bicker—sometimes outright disagree—but at the end of every conversation, we just stare at each other with longing in our eyes and voices when we're forced off the phone. He's texted or called me every day without fail since Dallas. We've spent a few late nights on the phone, which has only made me more of a believer that I'm a priority for him.

"I never saw a picture of your mom," he remarks as I exit the closet filled to the brim with years full of juvenile junk I left behind. Crap that my sentimental parents never threw out, despite turning my old room into a guest suite.

"Really? Well, I can remedy that." I exit my bedroom and walk down a long hall. Framed photos line the wall between guest bedrooms, and I search them to find a recent picture before flipping the camera.

"This is my mom, Addison Warner Hearst Butler," I laugh.

"That's a lot of last names."

"She mostly goes by Butler. This was taken two years ago, at Thanksgiving." Dad grins behind Mom in the kitchen, his arm wrapped possessively around her chest as she grips it, smiling more at him than posing for the photo. "It's one of my favorites."

"She's beautiful," Easton says, "but you look so much more like your dad."

"Which she unfairly holds against him."

"They look happy," he observes.

I sigh. "Yeah, they do. They are," I agree, turning the camera back on me. "Is this weird?"

"Not for me. Not at all. I hate that it is for you."

"It's just guilt."

"We aren't doing anything wrong," he insists.

"Says you."

"Baby, can we not do this today?"

"Okay, sure. Sorry," I turn the camera back to the wall of photos and accidentally scan one I'm not crazy about, just as protests come flying out of my cell speaker and my ears redden. "You weren't meant to see that."

"Fuck that, turn it back," he commands.

I shake my head.

"Right now."

Sighing, I flip the camera back to a picture of me in a bikini top and tiny shorts, standing in front of Percy and holding his reins at the pasture fence.

"A little to the left," he commands again.

"Geesh, bossy."

"Got it."

"What?!" I turn the camera to see the notification that EC took a screenshot.

"You perv, I was barely seventeen."

A satisfied grin covers his beautiful face. "I'm going to lose some skin, servicing myself to that one."

"Shameless," I grin. We've been on the phone for hours. Most of the time, he was on the road but refused to let me go as he checked into his hotel. As he unpacked, I cooked dinner. As he ordered room service and called his business manager from the hotel phone, I showered. I've loved every minute of it, and the fact that he refused to end the call no matter what was happening lit me up from the inside out because it's as close to *together* as we can be. Easton's exceptional knack for making ordinary days extraordinary and menial tasks seem substantial, unchanged. Even on FaceTime.

"Your parents live in a palace, and you live in a shoebox," he chuckles.

"Yeah, and how many square feet is that house you described as a prison?"

"I didn't mean it like that. I'm moving out when the tour ends. I tried to find a place after you left Seattle, and my dad ratted me out, so Mom went postal. Trust me, I'm aware I'm too fucking old to live at home—and have been for years—but in my defense, I slept at that studio. It wasn't embarrassing until now."

"Don't be embarrassed, and don't think for one minute I don't know you're frugal."

"Did you just call me cheap?"

"Maybe a little," I grin, entering my room.

"I know how to manage my money," he states, "there's a difference."

"I'll take your word on that, and you did spring for a private plane," I lay back against my pillows, and his gaze dips.

"About that, I actually called in a favor," he admits sheepishly.

"You shit, you let me believe you paid for that. That's some favor."

"It doesn't hurt to have friends."

He averts his gaze briefly, and I realize he's checking the time on his hotel nightstand. "It's getting late. You tired, baby?"

"A little, but I don't want to get off."

He lifts a brow.

"The phone," I grin. "I mean, I'm not saying I want to get off, either, you know what I mean."

"There's that gift by way of words. Thank God I speak fluent Butler gibberish."

He full-on laughs at my answering expression. "Kiss my ass, Crowne."

"God, what I wouldn't give to do just that and more."

My cheeks hurt with the width of my smile. "And just like that, you're forgiven."

"Good. Put on your pajamas," he orders softly. "I'll tuck you in."

"Uh…" I eye my duffle bag. "I'm good."

His chuckle fills the room. "What's with the hesitation?"

"No hesitation."

"Your neck is turning tomato, baby. No sense in ever lying to me… Ah, I know what this is about." A smug smirk graces his face. "Grab your sexy cap, Miss Muffet."

"I don't know what you're talking about."

"I know it's there," he taunts. "Come on, let's see it."

"Fine." Sighing, I walk over to my duffle and put the phone down next to it, giving Easton a view of the ceiling. "But I'm not sure you can handle this three-alarm fire I'm about to start."

"Oh, I can handle it."

"Yeah? Think so, big boy?" I tease, tucking the last of my hair in before I rapidly start to undress and redress.

"Hit me, Beauty."

Once dressed, I whip myself into view, my hat and quilted snap button robe aging me about thirty years as unguarded laughter bursts out of Easton.

"Seriously? Babe, what the fuck?"

"The house is drafty at times," I assert.

"So, you decided to make your grandmother's robe a staple?"

"It's comfortable," I contend.

"God," he muses. "I fucking miss you."

"That's a mutual feeling, Mr. Rock God."

Mid eye-roll, he lifts from his bed. "So, what's next, a gooey green face mask?"

"It's gold, and it's not gooey, but I'm not subjecting myself to any more of your shit. Self-care for women is already a pain in the ass without adding your testosterone into the mix. Besides, it's your turn. Let's see *your* pajamas."

He disappears from the camera, making me dizzy with the rapid change of hotel scenery before I'm knocked stupid by the sight of him walking into the bathroom, his reflection showing nothing but tan, rippling muscles, and perfectly filled black boxer briefs.

Well, that backfired.

"Oh, screw you, Crowne," I shake my head, soaking in every inch of his mouthwatering physique.

"No? Don't like 'em?" Teasingly, he lowers his phone.

"I did not say that I don't like your choice of sleepwear, but I'll need another peek to make a well-informed decision."

Grinning, he props his phone against the bathroom sink before lining his toothbrush with paste as I prop my own phone. We wordlessly brush our teeth, the buzz of a brush motor sounding on his end. It's when our foaming mouths overflow—showcasing our twin smiles—that I decide to take a quick screenshot.

He rolls his eyes when he sees the notification on his end and rinses while I speak up. "You have your idea of screenshot worthy. I have mine," I defend. Exiting the bathroom, I prop my phone on the nightstand and grip the first snap button on my robe as he slips into his hotel bed and holds his phone up, so his face fills the screen. Seeing me hesitate, fingers paused on the top button at my neck, he quirks a dark brow. "You got something going on under there?"

"Nothing special," I squeak.

"I'll be the judge."

"Okay, but no screenshots."

"Everything under that robe is for my fucking eyes only," he proclaims adamantly before grinning. "I'm also the only one who gets to know how truly filthy you really are."

"I am not," I feign offense.

"'*Harder, Easton. Harder!*' Who the hell do you think you're fooling? Well…my dirty girl, on with it."

"You realize you've been ordering me around a lot today, right?"

"Sorry, I would just really love to see if there's a girdle under there."

"Just for that, show's over."

"Baby, please," he murmurs before giving me Puss in Boots eyes. "I'll play nice."

"Jesus, you can be a manipulative shit at times."

"But it's about to pay off, right?" His lips twist in an infuriating smirk. "Come on, Beauty, it's been too long." His voice heats. "I need to see what's mine."

Careful to keep my ridiculous cap out of view, I slowly unsnap my robe to reveal myself wearing nothing but a black cami and hip-hugging black panties.

"Fuck me," he groans, "had to go there, didn't you?"

"It's not exactly lingerie."

"Tell that to my cock because he's weeping."

My neck heats as I quickly slip into bed.

"Hell no, you can't do that. Tease."

Plucking my phone from the nightstand, I bring it to eye level, ensuring my cap is still out of view as Easton lifts his chin in prompt. "A little more? For my cock's sake?"

Lowering the sheets, I reveal the cleavage poking above the top of my cami.

"Better, but not nearly enough."

Anxious, but too entranced by the heat in his voice, I manage to wiggle out of my panties while holding the phone. I lift them into view for him to see before tossing them next to me on the bed.

His eyes instantly heat as he speaks up in a throaty whisper. "More."

"Easton," I protest, skin flushing.

"Show me," he demands, shifting to rest his back against his headboard.

"You first," I tease.

In the next second, I'm graced with the sight of his ripped torso, and the small line of dark hair sprinkled along his navel before he lowers his boxers an inch, revealing the glistening head of his cock.

"More," I urge, my mouth watering as he slides his briefs down slowly to reveal his long, thick dick that is currently standing at rapt attention. Filling his hand, he pumps himself once before turning the camera away and jerking his chin.

"Your turn."

Eyes roaming his face, I lower my cami giving him a brief peek-a-boo of my hardening nipples.

"Jesus," he murmurs. "A little more."

"Are we really about to do this?" I giggle nervously.

"Have you ever?" He asks, his voice strained.

"I've tried, but honestly, it was so lame I didn't finish," I confess. "So yes and no."

"I love that I'll be the first to make you come."

"I do, too. You are a first for so many things already, Easton," I admit, lifting the phone to my face, heart pounding.

His tone softens in response. "Like what?"

I shake my head. "I'll tell you when we're together."

"Really? You going to hold out on me?"

"Yeah."

"All right, I'm going to get it out of you, *bet*. Now, let me help you come."

"Okay," I say, raking my lip as we stare at each other for several seconds, the ever-present pull palpable as I lose myself in the look in his eyes. Certain he can see the arousal building on my face, he bites his lip and slowly releases it.

"I'm so fucking hard for you already."

"What are you thinking about?" I ask.

"All of it," he pants, pumping his cock again.

"Easton—" I breathe as he lowers the camera giving me the most amazing view. "I'm aching so bad right now," I whisper, hearing the need in my voice.

"Will you let me see more of you?"

"Okay, but promise me, no screenshots."

"Not fucking ever," he says with a dangerous edge. "Are you wet?"

"Very."

"Spread your legs," he commands with little restraint, "show me."

I do and am instantly rewarded with an answering groan. On fire and anxious to earn more of them, I lower the camera further, spreading myself with my free hand before drawing my wetness up to my clit.

"Jesus. Fuck, Beauty," he pants. "Now suck those fingers," he orders gruffly, "like you would suck me."

I lift the camera and swirl my tongue over the pads of my fingers, tasting myself before sucking them down to the knuckle.

"Put them inside you, nice and slow." I groan his name as I do. "That's where I want to be right fucking now," he grits out, tension in his voice. "Your face," he whispers. "I can't look at what I can't eat anymore. All I need to see is your face." Lifting my phone, I'm met by the fire burning in his mesmerizing depths, his lust-covered expression bringing me closer.

"Massage your clit."

Soaked and panting, I stroke my sweet spot and find myself on the brink within quick seconds. "Easton," I gasp. "I'm already..."

He starts to stroke himself furiously as I press my head back into the pillow and close my eyes.

"Look at me while you come."

My orgasm unfurls through me in soft waves as I exhale his name. His eyes close briefly at the sound of it before he covers his stomach with his own release.

"How was that?" He asks, heavy breathing subsiding.

"Definitely not lame, but not nearly enough. Thanks a lot. You've ruined me."

"That's just the start," he assures as he heads back into the bathroom and wets a rag to clean himself off. The act of watching him do it is so intimate that I somehow feel closer to him in those seconds.

"It's been the perfect night, the perfect date. How in the hell did people do long-distance before FaceTime?"

"Phone calls, letters," he says.

"And emails," I add, which earns me a warning look. "It had to be so much harder back then."

"I'm glad we don't have to fucking deal." He slips back into bed, palm cradling his head, bicep bulging next to him, eyes glittering with warmth and affection. I burn the sight of it into memory.

"Get some sleep, Beauty. You've got an article to write for me tomorrow."

"You're reading my columns?"

"Every day, like religion. Why wouldn't I read them? It's your passion, and you should know," he gives me a warm half-smile, "even though I rag on you, I love the way you tell stories."

Momentarily speechless, I battle threatening tears. "That means a lot to me, Easton, really."

"You mean a lot to me. But I really do love the way you write. That one about the two brothers who got separated for twenty years got me emotional. I wrote some lyrics after I read it."

"Really?" I ask, my chest exploding. "Will you let me read them?"

"Of course," he whispers.

"Eight days," I remind him. "If you're wondering."

"I'm counting them. I'm fucking *counting*," he exhales harshly.

"Me too," I admit freely, heart swelling.

"Go to sleep," he orders. "I'll hang up when you're dreaming."

"Okay," I say as he clicks off his lights and the shadows from the TV begin to dance over his profile. He flicks through the channels as I settle in. Not a minute later, his eyes focus back on mine.

"Night, Beauty," he murmurs.

"Night, Beast," I jest, keeping my eyes trained on him until they give out.

The next morning, I wake up to see he never hung up and am granted the perfect view of his face from where he sleeps on his side. His long, black lashes rest over his sculpted cheekbones, his crimson lips slightly parted. The rise and fall of his chest is barely perceptible due to his comatose state. Ache intensifying as I rouse, I watch him far past the point of acceptable, but I can't help myself one bit.

I'm in love with him.

FORTY-THREE

Somewhere Only We Know
Lily Allen

Natalie
2 months later…

"He's Connecticut-bred, so we come from different planets," Rosie relays, crossing her long, toned legs in the chair opposite my desk. The reason for her impromptu visit the second I flipped on my office light? To report on Dad's most recent hire, Jonathan, a financial advice columnist who recently claimed the vacant office next to mine. "I conjured one too many daydreams before my gaydar went off. I confirmed it this morning with a social media search. I had to dip way back into his archives for proof. He's not closeted but doesn't advertise his sexual orientation, which is cruelly misleading. Needless to say," she whines, "I'm going back to California broken-hearted."

I can't help my laugh. "Rosie, he's only worked here for *two* days."

"Exactly, my gaydar betrayed me," she sighs.

"He's handsome," I say, catching sight of Rosie's current crush as he saunters out of Dad's office, coffee in hand, "but seems pretty aloof,"

"I *love* aloof. Oh well, plenty of fish, right?" She waves a dismissive hand, her heartbreak lasting as long as it takes her to retrieve a nail file from her tiny Fendi purse. She slowly runs the file along her immaculate manicure while fixing her interrogational stare on me. "In *other* news. You need to spill on the reason for your current daydreams because, girl, you are *glowing*."

Panic sets in as I school my expression and shrug. "I've been working out a lot." *Truth.*

I now have *four* abs.

"That smile you're sporting is not a result of exercise but rather *who* you're working out *for*."

"Nothing to report," I lie through my teeth as she narrows her eyes, calling bullshit. "I've been spending a lot of time outdoors, catching a lot of rays. It's been good for me."

"Sure, it's the *sun* that has you floating around this office like you're living out the best parts of a Jane Austen novel. No," she dismisses, packing away her file, "there's a Mr. Darcy hidden somewhere in this, and you know I'll sniff him out if you don't come clean. So, out with it. Who is he?"

Her sudden attention on my personal life has my throat closing, but I manage to speak through it in an attempt to thwart her efforts.

"I'm actually *relaxing* on the weekends now, so yeah, I'm spending a lot of time with the sun."

Reid and Stella Crowne's *son.*

I credit myself for the partial truth while trying to figure out a way to leap off her radar.

"Natalie, line four," Elena sounds through the intercom interrupting Rosie's interrogation. It's all I can do to hide my relief. Rosie stands when I roll my chair closer to the console in a hint for her to make an exit.

"Lunch next week before I fly home?" She asks.

"It's a date," I say, with zero intention of keeping it. Feeling the walls closing in—especially as she lingers, suspicious, in my doorway—I give her my attention, finger inching toward the speaker button.

"I'm going to get the truth out of you before I head home," she warns, giving me a shifty side-eye before sashaying into the pit.

The hold line blinking, I click my mouse to run a spell check on my latest article before pressing speaker. "This is Natalie Hearst."

"Beauty," Easton's sexy, sleep-coated voice fills my office, "you broke my cock."

Snatching the phone from the cradle, it escapes my grasp before I can get a good grip on it and lands with a thwack on my keyboard. Taking the phone off speaker, I eagerly search the bustling newsroom for anyone within earshot.

"What in the actual fuck, East—" I stop myself in the nick of time and duck behind my monitor. "You're supposed to call me on *my cell phone*." I whisper-yell.

"I tried. You didn't pick up."

"That's because I have a job," I scold, glancing at the console screen, relieved to see the name and number on the caller ID are blank. "Thank God you're unlisted."

"Always unlisted," he sighs, "but this is an emergency."

I straighten in my chair and respond in my professional tone. "I've heard *Eastern medicine* can be helpful in that particular area. Maybe you should soak that issue out." I cup my mouthpiece to continue my quiet rant. "I'm going to kick your ass. I had you on speaker. Thank God I was alone."

"Sorry," he says, clearly amused.

I roll my eyes. "Yeah, you sound *really* apologetic."

"Because you're smiling."

"How can you tell?" I catch my grin in my monitor's reflection.

"Because I've memorized you, Beauty."

"Fine," I sigh in mock irritation as my chest flutters. "So, you called to discuss the state of your—"

"My cock, yes," he replies, mocking my tone as if discussing the weather.

"I'm sorry to hear that."

"No, you clearly aren't."

"Because now *you're* smiling," I click my mouse to make myself look busy while briefly lowering my guard.

"Not denying that," he rasps out softly, "I've been doing a lot of that lately."

"According to the gossip columnist, who *just left my office* seconds before your issue announcement, I'm suffering from the same condition."

"Shit…be careful with her."

"Well, you aren't helping with that. She was sniffing me out before you called, and trust me, I'll be doing everything I can to avoid her. I'm thankful she's going back to California next week."

"Sorry," he whispers sincerely. "It's just…I'm driving today and wanted to talk to you before we hit the road."

"I see."

"And then there's my issue."

"Yes, your emergency. Mmm. Any symptoms?"

"It's like it's turned on me and doesn't even wake me up anymore."

"Do you know when this issue started?"

"It could've started when my girlfriend gave me incredible head on a balcony in Lake Tahoe."

An instant image of me on my knees, mouth wrapped around him as he fisted my hair, fire in his eyes, praise pouring from his lips, has me squeezing my thighs together.

Lake Tahoe cemented our relationship. The second Joel deposited me in the three-story palace Easton rented us for the weekend, I went to work and lit every candle in the place before I waited for him in bed—wearing *nothing*. The second he breached the door, we didn't separate until Joel whisked me back to the airport. Though we've only managed to steal a handful of days together over the last two months, what we have is rapidly turning into the most intimate and committed relationship I've ever been in. My living reality is far better than any Jane Austen scenario I can recall.

"Or maybe it was this past weekend," he continues, "in that chalet in Idaho."

"Sounds serious," I murmur as a vision shutters in of a naked Easton, arms splayed on the sides of the rustic outdoor tub, expression smoldering as I undid my robe, wearing nothing but a smile before stepping in. During both rendezvous we spent our days getting lost in our surroundings and our nights and mornings getting lost in each other.

"If I'm being one hundred," Easton continues, "my cock really hasn't been the same since I met her."

"Hmmm. Sounds like a real pickle." I glance at my father's office, seeing him fully occupied, which relaxes my guard a little. "Who did you tell my receptionist you were?"

"A man who really needs more one-on-one with his girl."

Ache seeps in further as I start to dread the upcoming weekend without him. "Any idea when that will be?"

"Working on that now. I kind of hate that we added more dates to the tour."

"We talked about this. I'm nothing but happy for you. To be honest, I expected it."

"But it means we have to keep this charade going on longer."

"It's not a charade," I defend sharply, a little too sharply.

"No, it's not," he exhales audibly. "That was a poor choice of words."

"Well, if you're in need of words, I'm your girl." I muse. "So, is your dad still with you?"

"Yeah, but after the Salt Lake show, we're off the rest of the weekend. Maybe after the show, I'll come to you?"

"You would do that?"

"Seriously? Right now, I would fly into the fucking sun to get back to where we were last weekend. I felt sick when I had to leave you in that chalet."

"So, if I'm hearing you correctly, what you're really saying is that you're completely and utterly whipped?"

"You don't want to start this spar, Beauty," he warns. "You'll lose."

"Have I won a single argument with you yet?"

His chuckle rumbles over the line. "No, but you keep starting them. You're such a little asshole."

"Well, I am a ginger," I boast. "Rumor is, I have no soul."

"Only because I stole it."

"That may be true," I sigh, allowing him to hear the smitten in my voice because that's what this is—smitten, and every accompanying synonym—taken, enamored, infatuated. Though it's been a struggle to keep us under wraps since Dallas, when doubts threaten to take over, all I have to do is replay the beautiful words he spoke to me to convince me to bet on him, to believe in us. In the two months we've officially been a couple, he's delivered on every promise, mainly in the way of giving more pieces of himself to me without reservation. In return, I've done the same. He's made and kept me a priority without putting me through my paces or questioning his intentions. His only motive seems to be to keep us together and me happy. In short, he's perfect.

Every day, I find myself fighting to withhold the words I so desperately want to admit. The struggle to hold them in becoming unbearable, as is my need to tell the people in my everyday life that I'm in love with the most incredible man I've ever met—my dad excluded.

"Thank you," I whisper.

"For stealing your soul?"

"No, for…making it…like this."

"Like what?"

"Easy," I say, "and...happy."

"You sure you're a words girl?"

"Shut up, *dick*," I laugh at his predictable jab.

"Ah, back to the subject currently in my hand," he coos.

"Forget toddler. You're an infant," I giggle before looking up to see my father filling my office doorway.

My heart skips several beats as he stares back at me with a quizzical expression, hands stuffed in his slacks just before mouthing, "Who is that?"

I roll my eyes in an attempt to play off the surge of panic racing through me.

"Dad just walked into my office," I report to Easton, praying I managed to keep the shake out of my voice.

Dead silence greets me on the other side of the line before Easton whispers a faint, "I'm sorry," and hangs up.

"Sounds good." Line already dead in my hand, I hang up just as Dad steps forward to eye the caller ID on my console.

"Who's making things easy...happy and is a dick, toddler, and infant?"

"I think the better question is, why are you at my office door spying on my phone conversations?"

A dozen lies form, scatter, and retreat on my tongue as his brows draw in confusion as to why I didn't simply answer him. Because normally I would, and without hesitation.

This is how it starts, Natalie. Kill it now.

"Who else would it be? Holly. She was on a call with me during a consult for a *lady stuff* appointment and cracked an inappropriate joke." Lady stuff is code in our family for anything having to do with my vagina and menstrual cycle—a subject my father will happily sidestep at all costs. I shake my head. "Never mind, what's up?"

Dad grimaces, a reply ready on his lips as Elena buzzes in again. "Natalie, line one, Holly."

Thank you, merciful God, for this circumstantial miracle. I'll do better.

I snatch up the phone like the lifeline it is. "You are an infant," I recite the same way as I did to Easton a minute earlier in hopes of making my lie more believable.

"Well, that's no way to greet your best bitch," Holly claps back as

I keep my eyes trained on my dad. Thinking on my toes and in an attempt to thoroughly cover my tracks, I put her on speaker. "Say hi to Dad. He's lingering at my office door because he's all up in my business this morning."

"Hey, Uncle Nate," Holly bellows out. Though they aren't blood related, Dad watched Holly grow up alongside me, and they're as thick as thieves, hence his honorary title. Easton's warnings in Dallas ring as clear as a bell as this situation becomes increasingly similar to the scenario he described and far too close for comfort.

"Hey, sweetheart," Dad greets her fondly, "Addie and I have been missing you. Come by the house soon for dinner."

"I will. If your daughter wasn't so damned b—"

"Shut it," I interject playfully, taking her off speaker before she can incriminate me. Certain a heart attack is in the works, perspiration glides down my back as a full-on panic attack threatens, and I do my best to mask it.

"Call Addie and set it up," Dad belts out for Holly to hear despite my attempt to separate them, his grin growing at my obvious agitation. "I'll tell her to expect your call today."

"Dad!" I draw out, my blood pressure spiking to an unsustainable level. Dad knocks on my doorframe, satisfied he's thoroughly ruffled my feathers. "I'll let you two get back to your talk about *lady stuff*."

Holly catches his parting words and squawks in my ear. "What lady stuff?"

"You're a pain in the ass," I call after his retreating back, testing the waters.

Dad turns back to me, his expression a mix of amusement and adoration. "And you're the light of my life." He retreats then, walking through the pit towards his office as a tidal wave of guilt washes over me.

Jesus Christ.

Heart pounding, back soaking wet, I shift my focus on Holly while mentally replaying the last few seconds of lies as she prompts me for a reply.

"Natalie, what lady stuff?"

"Oh, I made that appointment with your waxing lady." *Truth.*

"So, that makes me an infant?"

"I said, bare as an infant."

Oh. My. God.

I'm met with what can only be described as a horrified silence before banging my earpiece against my forehead. "Can you hear me?" I ask, "My desk phone has been acting up this morning. What's up?"

"I hope like hell I misheard you. Why are you being weird about a lady wax and honestly…fucking disturbing?"

"It's been the longest first hour of a workday in the history of ever, Holly. I haven't even had my first cup of coffee, and Dad's already driving me crazy."

Lie.

My secrets are driving me crazy.

Being in a secret relationship with my father's ex-fiancée's son is driving me crazy.

Being in love with a man I haven't admitted it to is driving me crazy.

Reporting every exciting aspect of my new relationship to my *horse* is driving me bat shit.

The fact that I'm lying to everyone close to me—and doing it so horribly—is making things much, much worse.

"I'm j-just frazzled…and busy. Can I call you back?"

"What the hell? Can I not get five minutes? You canceled Chuy's on us. You never miss Chuy's, and that's why we chose the damn restaurant because you were *guaranteed* to show. Even Damon is starting to feel jilted by you. He thinks we're being replaced."

"He said that?"

"Yeah, he did, right before he picked up our waitress," she utters dryly.

"The one with the beauty mark?"

"That's the one."

"Well, she's ugly."

"You're a terrible liar," she sighs.

"Trust me, I'm aware. I'm sorry, babe."

"Whatever. It's just Damon being Damon. You think I would be used to it by now, right?"

"He's an idiot."

"An idiot who's now shitting where we eat. Not cool."

"Damn right it's not," I agree. "So if he ends up with a tainted burrito on his plate due to his whoring, that's on *him*."

"Thanks for reminding me why I keep forgiving you. Miss you."

Her reply has me coming to a quick conclusion.

I'm now that girl.

The one who's neglecting her friends and family due to a new relationship. A nasty habit I swore I would never participate in after my last breakup. Though I have managed to keep most of my dinner dates with my parents. Maybe it's paranoia, but I swear I've felt their lingering gazes on me more than once when I do show. Every time I pull out of their driveway, the guilt becomes a little bit harder to shoulder. With Rosie's observation this morning, it's clear the people I'm so purposely deceiving are starting to catch on.

Even though I chastised Easton for saying so a few minutes ago, this is starting to feel like a charade.

"This coming Wednesday, I'll be there," I declare in a promise I refuse to break. "I'll buy all the margaritas you can consume. Deal?"

"Deal."

"Then we'll ditch Damon and make it a girls' night. No distractions, just us."

A headache begins to build as blood furiously pumps at my temples. Despite wanting to comfort Holly, all my racing thoughts begin to collide as I make a quick excuse. "Hey, babe, Dad is flagging me down. Can I call you back after lunch?"

"Sure," she utters. The blatant disbelief in her tone only aids in my conclusion that along with being an unworthy daughter, I'm becoming a shitty friend.

"I will call you back. Love you."

"Love you, too."

For the next few minutes, I palm my desk and practice breathing techniques while gathering my wits and what's left of my sanity. Flipping my cell phone face up on my desk, I prepare to properly bitch Easton out for being so careless. But as I read his texts, my anger quickly disperses.

EC: Answer the phone. I need to hear your voice.

EC: Fuck. Answer the phone, Beauty.

EC: I can feel your anger from Wyoming. That was reckless and fucking stupid. I won't call your office again. Please don't be mad. I'm sorry.

Kicking back in my seat, I read his texts again as my heart swells. He's just being a boyfriend, or trying to. We've fallen into a surprisingly easy rhythm—even in hiding—and despite our hectic schedules. This week has been an exception with his back-to-back shows. While he's missing me, I'm aching everywhere for him.

Though I wouldn't trade the last two months with Easton for anything, the juggling act is starting to wear on me. Glancing over into my father's office, I feel the sting due to the purposeful distance I've been putting between us. I miss being candid with him about every aspect of my life, including my relationships. I miss having beers with him after work, an invitation I've been turning down more frequently as of late. I briefly wonder if Easton could be right—if I am making too much of a deal about our parents' history. I've never been afraid of my father, no matter how badly I screwed up. Maybe the solution is just a matter of walking into his office, confessing, apologizing, and explaining myself.

Being with Easton no longer feels like a decision to hurt him but a choice that makes me happy. Deliriously happy. The past eight weeks have undoubtedly been the best granted to me personally, and Dad has made it clear throughout my life that my every happiness is his. Intent on coming clean sooner than later, I begin to type out a text to Easton, knowing I've gone too long without a reply. Especially since he thinks I'm angry with him.

I compose a quick response, the same text I've typed a dozen times in the past week.

I love you.

I backspace those three words because delivering them via text is not how I want to admit my feelings for him, but right now, it's the only reply I genuinely want to give. Instead, I dole out the raw honesty he's made so easy for me to relay back to him in our time together.

I miss you, too. So much. I needed to hear your voice, too.

I hit send and immediately start typing again.

I don't want to hide anymore. If that means being reckless and stupid, then I'll be reckless and stupid with you. Being with you makes me happy. Everyone close to me can see a difference in me, and I want to tell them why. I want to tell them who you are and what you mean to me. Who I belong to and with. I'm

not mad, I swear, and I'll relay that to your cock myself, which by the way, isn't broken, but only answers to its new owner. 😊 **Drive Safe. XX**

I shoot out the second text without an ounce of hesitation before I start to spell-check my article. Ten minutes pass without a response, and I deflate, knowing he's driving.

Making good on my promise to Holly, I call her back during lunch at the three-hour mark, chatting as if I don't have a boulder growing in the pit of my stomach with every minute my text goes unanswered.

Pissed I only have my fucking horse to vent to over my emotional vomit-induced texts, I read them repeatedly, worrying I might have revealed too much. When five hours pass by without a reply, and I am certain he's already parked the van in Salt Lake, panic sets in. I didn't say anything out of the ordinary for us. He's expressed far more about his growing feelings for me than I have thus far, and never once has he led me to believe this relationship isn't serious. If anything, he's catapulted us in this direction, and I've flown fearlessly with the ease in which he lavishes me his affection.

My fear only increases as I check my phone throughout the duration of my workday until the office slowly starts to empty because, for the rest of the day, my texts are unanswered.

FORTY-FOUR

Wild Horses
The Sundays

Natalie

Feeling glum on the drive home, I do my best to bury my growing insecurity away. Did he turn off his phone to avoid a fight? I reconsider that train of thought because that's not Easton.

I teased him about being whipped, but he must know it was said in jest, and I'm equally as enamored. He said I wouldn't win in that standoff, but would he purposely not reply to prove that point?

"Stop it," I scold myself as my seatbelt alarm dings, a ding I now associate with my boyfriend's constant harping. Buckling up, I slow at a stoplight behind a row of cars and glance out of my window, pausing when I see Emo's, an Austin venue the Dead Sergeants often played when they started out. This detail I remember well because, in the movie, it's where Stella caught Reid singing in memory of her. I conjure the scene clearly—the actress who played Stella crying hysterically at the foot of the stage as Ben pointed out she was there. Reid had leaped from behind his drums and collided with her. For me, it's the most memorable scene of the film. A substantial part of Reid and Stella's history lines these streets, especially Sixth, the one I'm currently on. Briefly, I imagine a younger Stella roaming downtown Austin, daydreaming of making a name for herself in journalism while tirelessly working toward her future. An image of Reid behind his drums, fighting similarly for his own dream, skitters in as a horn blares behind me.

Jarred back into the present, I press the gas, my eyes lingering briefly on the well-known club.

Thoughts drifting back to Easton, stomach continually churning, Lexi and her past with Ben pushes into the forefront of my mind. This same type of insecurity caused Lexi to sabotage her relationship with Ben. Something else Easton warned me about. It's then a decision quickly forms.

I can't behave in the same way. I won't. If I'm going to be the girlfriend of a rock star, I will have to suck it up.

I'm not the only one going through the mounting pressure of lying to everyone while keeping this relationship under wraps. I'm not the only one battling the pressure of my job. Easton's enduring the same battles, if not more, due to the rapidly increasing spotlight. Maybe balancing our relationship while touring is becoming too much for him, and we need to talk this out.

At the same time, Easton's a private man. Even if we weren't hiding from our parents and went public, he would still be concealing our details—ferociously.

Facts.

I reason with myself that I'm feeling especially vulnerable because I spilled some of my heart into a text.

Unlocking my apartment door, I stand on the other side, letting my purse drop from my shoulder to the floor while I glance around the empty space. Deciding to grow the hell up, I shoot out another text for my sanity's sake.

Have a good show tonight. X

I hit send and am surprised when I see reply bubbles instantly start dancing.

EC: It will be.

Unsure what to make of his cryptic reply, I text back as though I haven't run through a gauntlet of conflicting emotions the entire day.

Feeling a bit cocky, are we?

EC: Maybe...Knock. Knock.

Who's there?

EC: Joel.

A knock sounds on the other side of my apartment door, and

I scream in surprise. Joel's laughter echoes just outside before he speaks up. "We've got to stop meeting like this, Natalie."

Opening the door, I can't help my smile before I leap into his arms, relief coursing through me. "That's Easton's freaky timing, or yours," I scold. "You two have these surprise attacks coordinated down to a science."

"Come on," he says as I pull away and beam up at him. "You have to get packed."

"Packed?" I ask, my spirits lifting insurmountably as my phone rumbles in my hand.

EC: Do as you're told, Beauty.

"Case in point," I say, lifting the message for Joel to read. "It's witchcraft."

Joel chuckles, "We're a well-oiled machine, don't even try to figure us out."

I narrow my eyes. "Do I want to know exactly how many women you two have practiced this act on?"

"You're the first. How are we faring?"

"Meh." I shrug.

"No more time for chit-chat, the plane is waiting, and we're going to have to fight traffic to get to it."

"It's kind of presumptuous of him to assume he can summon me on a whim." Even I can hear the bullshit in my statement. "What if I had plans?"

"Then I would have had to kidnap you because I was ordered to, in no certain terms, 'collect his soulless ginger and get her side stage.'"

"Reid isn't there?" I ask, excitement clear in my voice.

"Nope, he left this afternoon." Joel claps his hands together. "No more time to explain. Easton wants you at the concert. We can get there in time for the second half if we hurry."

"Hell yes! Twenty minutes?" I ask.

"Better shoot for ten." He jabs a thumb toward the elevator. "I'll wait downsta—"

"The hell you will! Get in here." I yank him inside my studio, and he chuckles as I race to the fridge and pluck a Coke and a beer from the shelf before holding each up to him. "Thirsty?"

"I'll take the Coke, sweetheart. I'm driving, and your boyfriend will have my balls if I take a sip of alcohol before I do."

"He's overprotective," I say, another surge of relief coursing through me.

"Of you, yeah, he most definitely fucking is." I hand Joel the Coke and lift a brow.

"Are you being cryptic right now?"

"Little bit," he glances around. "Cute place," he muses silently at the size of it before he pops the top of his Coke.

"Thanks," I grab the remote from my ottoman and thrust it toward him. "Make yourself at home. I have every sports channel imaginable. I'm going to," I jerk my head toward my bedroom.

"I'm good, *go*," he waves me away as I race to pack.

FORTY-FIVE

Here Comes My Girl
Tom Petty

Natalie

Though Joel drives like a bat out of hell to get us to the interstate, we end up stuck in over an hour of traffic, which has me fuming and Joel panicking. The second we board the plane and are buckled in, we're cruising toward the runway.

"Whose plane is this?" I ask, checking out the large cabin, this private jet far more luxurious than the first plane Easton chartered for me.

"Not sure," Joel averts his gaze.

"Bullshit. Please tell me this plane isn't on loan from a big-breasted pop star or anyone of a similar nature."

Joel chuckles. "I'll let him explain himself."

I search for any clue and come up empty. "Oh, I'll make sure he does."

"Of that, I have no doubt," Joel says from the oversized, plush seat opposite me, opening our window shade as we turn onto the runway.

Vibrating with excitement, I reroll the sleeve of Easton's jacket to my forearms and secretly marvel at the quick outfit I made out of it. Keeping the top open enough to show a little side boob, I belted the rest around tiny black shorts. I finished the look with black stilettos that are already killing my feet but will hopefully be worth the pain. "I can't wait to see him play. It feels like it's been forever rather than two months."

"He had the whole stadium on their knees last night. It was fucking epic."

"I know I texted you, but I just want to thank you again so much for sending me the videos. I've seen some of the footage online, but it's entirely different because you take them side stage, so it's almost like I'm there." I press my hand to my chest. "Means a lot, Joel."

"It's my pleasure, sweetheart."

"Does Easton know you take them?"

"He's caught me recording a few times, but I don't think he suspects I send them to you. I think he believes it's a proud papa-type thing."

"Is it?"

"Oh, hell yeah, it is," he grins. "But I know he hates it that you aren't there."

"I wish I could be. I would go to every single show."

"He knows." Joel unbuttons his suit jacket, looking every bit the bodyguard he is. "You know, I can tell, even from the few concerts you attended, that his energy is different when you're there. Don't get me wrong, he's still incredible and brings it every night, but it's just different."

Within seconds of speeding down the runway, we're airborne.

"You don't have to tell me these things, Joel." I grin, "but you can keep telling me if you want to."

"I'm paid to protect him, nothing more. I wouldn't lie to you, Natalie. Not about stuff like this."

"So, you'll lie to me about other stuff?"

He responds partly through a chuckle. "You forget I've seen you in 'hell hath no fury' wrath mode, so maybe?"

We share a laugh as I glance out the window while we ascend through a cloud. Once on the other side, amber light fills the window and the cabin as we chase the sunset. Replaying the emotional hours I suffered prior to this moment, I find myself speaking up. "Has Easton explained why we're being so secretive about our relationship?"

Joel nods. "He told me when you left Seattle."

"Damn, so back *then*?"

Joel nods.

"Wow. Hard to believe that was only four months ago. So much has happened since then. Especially for Easton."

"For you both," he prompts, "and that's some story."

I harrumph. "Easton doesn't even know the half of it, the stubborn ass. But which part are you referring to?"

"Theirs, yours, how you ended up in Seattle. All of it is pretty remarkable."

"Do you know Easton and I were born only *six days* apart?"

Joel nods. "That's crazy coincidental too."

"Did you decide *I* was crazy when he told you why I came to Seattle?"

"No. I knew you were good people minute one. We all go through things, Natalie. It's nothing to be embarrassed about."

"Have you seen the movie?"

"Yeah, back when it first released. I loved it."

I nod, deciding to let it rest until Joel speaks up. "Easton says you don't know why Stella and your father broke up. That the reason wasn't in the emails."

"I've searched them relentlessly and came up empty. It's the only thing that still haunts me about their story. I can't make sense of the *why*. One day they were happy, planning a wedding, engaged. The next, the emails ceased for months. The movie doesn't have a hint my father even existed, so I can't make heads or tails of what went down or when. My dad and Stella broke up *months* before Stella and Reid reunited. You wouldn't happen to know, would you?"

"Wish I could help you. Reid and I are close, but he doesn't talk about the past that much. At least not that in-depth about his history with Stella."

"Men," I roll my eyes. "Why can't you guys overshare like girls do, and know every sordid detail?"

"Sometimes we do," he winks, and my neck reddens as I recall Easton's musing about his now infamous Tahoe blowjob. Joel reads my expression and holds up his palms. "Oh shit, Natalie, no, not like *that*. He's not spilling intimate details. He's keeping you all to himself in that respect."

"Oh, thank God. I thought I was going to need a parachute."

"You dive. I have to follow," he chuckles.

We sit in comfortable silence as I run my hand down the rich leather of the seat.

"It's been hard on me, you know," I admit after a few minutes, looking over at him. "Only having my fucking horse to confide in." We share a lengthy stare-off before bursting into laughter. "I know, right? It's ridiculous, but he's a faithful horse and a good listener."

"Hang in there, sweetheart. Things will work out."

"God, I hope you're right." I swallow as I reflect on this morning's close call. "Joel, c-can I ask your opinion?"

"You know you can."

"Do you think we're doing the right thing by keeping our relationship from our parents?"

"Honestly, I think it's a tough situation for you both to have to navigate. In a way, it seems really deceptive, but at the same time, I completely understand why you both decided to go about it this way for now."

"I came really close to walking into my father's office this morning and confessing all."

"What stopped you?"

"What's stopped me from the start. The emails. That combined with the fact that I'm happy. I chickened out." I swallow. "Do you think our parents will understand...I mean, eventually?"

Joel grimaces, and I already know his answer before he voices it. "I don't know their history, so it's hard for me to say one way or another. I wish I could ease your mind, and I really hope for both your sakes they do."

I nod. "I'm sorry, and I'm sorry I put you in the position to answer that."

"Hey," he prompts sharply, drawing my eyes from the landscape below. "I care *a lot* about Easton and *you*. This isn't just a job for me."

"I know. He loves you."

He seems to stare through the passing clouds. "I would lose my damned mind if anything happened to him."

"So, is it really like a proud papa thing for you?"

"It's weird," he says, easing back in his seat slightly. "It's like I remember every part of his childhood, and I've had to stop myself a lot over the years from overstepping when Reid and Stella aren't around... but now? I truly recognize him as the man he's become, who's got to make his own choices and mistakes. I wouldn't say it's a father's love, but definitely an uncle's. A very close uncle."

"I get that. I love that."

"It's a balancing act sometimes for me, more back then than now," he admits. "But when it comes down to it, this really hasn't been a job for me for a long time. Blood or not, we are family. Even when the job ends, I know for certain our relationship won't. I don't even question that." His chest bounces. "Hell, I have a designated bedroom at the Crowne house and put it to good use during the holidays."

"That's awesome."

Melancholy sneaks in at the thought I might not ever be welcome or accepted in the Crowne house—in any capacity. That Easton's parents may never embrace me and vice versa. Even worse, I can't picture my father accepting Easton, at all.

What future can we have?

"You have to live your life, Natalie," Joel speaks up, sensing my budding apprehension. "You can't base important life decisions on the feelings of others. That's one thing I can say for certain. What you two found with each other and have now is rare, really fucking rare, and I can attest to that because I've watched it happen. So, embrace it for what it is and let the worries for what might be go for now, because those are out of your control."

"Thank you," I say. "I really, *really*, needed to hear that." I look around the cabin of the plane. "I'm sure you've witnessed a lot over the years."

"Yeah, I really have." He chuckles, his eyes going glassy. "Stella and Reid were pretty mild, though they had their moments. Stella was a pistol as is, and when her Latina came out, everyone took cover." He full-on laughs. "Reid has a temper, and most of the time, he kept it subdued. But put those two together on a bad night, the turbulence took place *inside* the plane."

"I can't imagine."

"They've provided a fair share of drama over the years, but were always quick to make up and often did before the wheels hit the ground. Ben and Lexi—whole different animal. Lexi wouldn't let Ben take Benji on tour without her, so those were *good times*." Joel widens his eyes and tips his head back. "Picture an entire rock band, their spouses and kids, and mix that with some of the company the band kept," he harrumphs. "It was a circus."

I wince. "That bad?"

"Mostly when they toured with another band who gave zero fucks around toddlers and infants." He shakes his head. "Put it this way, certain people with egos and unlimited money shouldn't be granted the freedom that comes with it—no matter how talented they are—because they're fucking terrifying to be around. I've had to deal with that in abundance, some of it on this fucking plane."

"This is the Sergeants' plane, isn't it?"

Joel shrugs. "Well, it doesn't belong to a big-breasted pop princess."

"So why not tell me—" I widen my eyes. "Shit, Joel, did Easton steal the Sergeants' plane so you could pick me up?"

"Wouldn't be the first time," he chuckles. "Or the second."

"Jesus," I can't help my smile. "And I thought sneaking my dad's Audi out for a joyride made me a rebel."

"Easton has an *amazing* track record of busting Reid's balls."

"Apparently. So, speaking of band dynamics, how are the guys getting along?"

"They're killing every show without fail."

"Yeah, but backstage? Easton said he and LL don't vibe well. Easton thinks he's on something."

"Something is going on with him. I'm not sure it's drugs, but he's definitely wrestling some demon. As long as he keeps his shit away from you and East and does his job, I really don't give a damn."

"I think LL's misunderstood," I say honestly.

"Natalie." The warning in his voice jars me. "Do us both a favor and don't look into it."

"It's escalating that badly?"

"For now, Reid's keeping them both in check, but Easton's been a lot less tolerant of LL since Dallas."

"Really?" Anxiety spikes. "I'm partially to blame for that. I'll talk to him."

Joel goes to object, and I lift my hand.

"I won't say a word about this discussion or rat you out, I swear. I'll figure out a way to work it into a conversation."

"Thanks. See, this is a prime example of when it gets dicey," he relays.

"I totally understand, but you can trust me," I promise.

"Why don't you just enjoy tonight and let them work their testosterone issues out for themselves."

"I think I will. I can't believe he sent you for me."

The pilot announces our flight time to Salt Lake City as our attendant approaches us with champagne and orange juice. Taking both glasses of champagne, I extend one to Joel, bristling with renewed excitement.

"I'm not the only one who needs to enjoy themselves." Joel eyes the champagne, and I press in. "Come on, Joel, just one. Celebrate with me."

"Just one," he says, taking the glass before clinking it with mine.

FORTY-SIX

Hypnotised
Coldplay

Natalie

The minute we touch down in Salt Lake, I am thankful for the slight champagne buzz as Joel's mission to get me to the concert becomes an instant flurry of activity. As it turns out, Joel has a driver waiting on both of us. The second my luggage is transferred into the blacked-out SUV, we are speeding toward the venue. I spend most of our drive primping as Joel begins a series of phone calls, barking orders to security to ensure our passage to the stage with strict instructions to keep us under the radar. Easton wasn't at all exaggerating when he said we'd need Joel. He's been a white knight for us the last two months, being our lone driver, getting us to and from our hideaways safely and undetected.

Joel champions himself now as he synchronizes our arrival and immediate escort to the stage. I spend what minutes I have left touching up my half-assed makeup job, having spent three of the ten minutes I had to pack in the shower. Thankful my curls are in decent shape, I spruce them up with a bit of dry shampoo, and they bounce back due to the lifesaving miracle in a bottle.

Stilettos nervously tapping the floor of the SUV, I finish myself off with a spritz of perfume while glancing over at Joel, who grins as he composes a text. "Don't be nervous. You look beautiful."

"I don't know why I am. He's seen me at my absolute worst."

"As you have him," he adds, "don't forget that."

Nodding, I grip his hand and squeeze as he glances over at me. "Thanks, Joel, seriously, for everything. I don't know what we would do without you. I hope Easton makes you feel appreciated because I know I do."

"He does, and so do you, and you're welcome, sweetheart."

Unable to help myself, I pull out my compact again and run my fingers around the edges of my lips, catching a little excess of the deep rose matte lipstick I decided on. I barely packed, and in my excitement, I have no idea what's in my suitcase, but I don't care. Clothes have seemed optional during our previous times together, and I send a quick thanks to the cosmos that my period came and went last week. All I can imagine right now is the feel of his lips, the emotion inside his kisses, the weight of him, and the sound of his groans. The ecstasy that comes every time we connect, the pillow talks that can last for hours, the way he gazes down at me, and the way I can predict what he'll say. All of it.

My stomach begins to flutter uncontrollably as Easton-induced butterflies dance around my insides while we race toward my supernova. After what seems like an eternity, we finally pull up into the garage of the auditorium, right next to an elevator.

"Ready?" Joel asks as I eye the five monstrous security guards who swarm the SUV.

Jesus, Crowne.

"Let's do this," I take Joel's hand and step out, keeping my eye-roll inward as security engulfs us on all sides. In seconds, we're out of the service elevator and being led by the guards down a series of halls. The noise level heightens the closer we get, in turn amplifying my need to get to Easton. If I knew which direction we were headed, I would already be running.

"How long have they been on?" Joel asks one of the mute guards.

"A little over an hour," the guard answers before barking at a few girls loitering outside a dressing room door. "Get back!"

"Damnit to hell," I grumble in disappointment. Easton's sets normally run an hour and twenty minutes. When we take a hard right down another hall—this one abandoned—I curse that I missed the show as the click of my heels echoes with my hurried steps. When LL's guitar rings out in introduction—the last song of one of two sets Easton rotates—the roar of the audience explodes.

"Hurry, please," I beg, unable to help myself, speeding up, spirits dipping with the knowledge I'm close to missing the entirety of the concert. Joel grips my hand and squeezes. I manage to muster a smile when he grants me a reassuring wink.

Even a song away from his encore, I find myself thankful we made it in time to catch at least some of it as security stops and parts for us at the foot of the stairs. Joel leads me up by the hand, and in the next second, my anxiety-ridden reality morphs into something more on a fantasy level when Easton appears in my line of sight.

Already midway through "Brimstone," one of my favorite songs, which just claimed number one on the Billboard charts, I inhale my first full breath since we landed. Soaking him in, Easton reigns hell on the mic, wringing out chords while wailing on his guitar, T-shirt predictably soaked and clinging to his chest, his hair dripping sweat. Closer to him but unable to find my chill, I feel the innate need to fly to him. Immersed in seconds, the rest of the world blurs as I zero in on Easton and see the slight change in his posture the minute he senses me standing there. I don't miss the faint smile that upturns his lips just before he flits his gaze to mine. My entire body heats as he sweeps me in one long drink, his eyes lingering on his jacket. Even from where I stand, I don't miss the satisfaction in his expression as I beam at him.

Keeping out of view of the first row, I find myself inching toward him when he breaks eye contact, bowing his head while ripping through his guitar solo. Tack pounds the drums into submission as LL and Syd rock alongside Easton, the song roaring through the packed auditorium. His audience has grown staggeringly in size in the two months since Dallas, which isn't surprising. Being present to witness it brings the truth of it next level. The second the song ends, the lights go out, and the auditorium filled with thousands upon thousands of fans scream out their praises. Refusing to remain disheartened, I missed the show—save Easton's encore—I clap enthusiastically along with them as the lights come back up.

I'm here, Easton's here, and somewhere in the very near future,

I'll be surrounded by him, *privately*. That knowledge has my smile growing substantially as Easton steals another glance my way, and I mouth, "I'm sorry."

He gently shakes his head, his answering smile breathtaking as I drink him in. He's dressed in all black, including his jeans and boots, along with the leather cuffs I bit into, leaving an indentation on them the last time he took me roughly. The sight of them has me reliving it briefly as I squeeze my thighs together.

Easton grabs a water bottle from nearby, gulping it back as pandemonium ensues in the auditorium. He glances back at the band, his expression slightly bewildered as Tack, LL, and Syd all give him a nod as if they can't believe this is their reality as well.

It's clear he's having the time of his life, and they're feeling the same. Whatever differences he's having with LL seems to have been cast aside to enjoy this. Easton saunters over to the mic, his natural swagger in effect as he grips it. "Thank you so fucking much, Salt Lake," he gestures toward the band. "Give it up for REVERB."

The reply sends a wave of pride through me. I shake my head, amazed at the path they've traveled thus far, along with the change in the conflicted man I met versus the heart-seizing performer oozing confidence feet away from me. My admiration for him grows as he speaks up again.

"I know you guys have busy lives to get back to, but we were wondering if you've got time for one more?"

Easton grins at the response, eyeing the crowd humbly. The budding emotion clear in his face, only magnified by the view of him on the large screen which sits on stage behind the band. The perspective then shifts to Easton's as the cameraman scans the stadium, and I gape as I get a glimpse of his view.

"How about we set the mood first?" In an instant, the auditorium is cloaked in darkness. Anticipation thickens the air, and it takes a few minutes for the noise to die down before Easton's velvet voice circulates throughout. "Pretty dark in here. Can I get some help from you, Salt Lake?"

The darkened stadium roars in response, the screen no longer giving access to the audience view. Unable to help myself, I edge the stage and peek out into the crowd. The sight of thousands of floating lights steals my breath as they continue to pop up, hundreds at a time.

"Perfect. Thank you," Easton says, just before a lone spotlight shines down on him, where he now sits at his piano, facing me. I light up at the fact he's far closer now than when he sang on the mic. From where I'm standing, I can see him clearly—the set of his jaw, even the light in his eyes. Easton adjusts himself behind the piano while the rest of us wait with bated breath for whatever cover he has planned. Try as I might, Easton consistently refuses to reveal which cover song he'll perform at his next show, no matter how I bribe him. Even when I've gotten sexually creative, I've gotten no dice.

Settling in, Easton leans in and addresses us while trickling his fingers along the keys of the piano.

"I'm going to attempt something tonight, so bear with me."

Another worshipful rumble reverberates in reply, which gains them one of his signature half-smiles. A flirtation, though he's already got everyone in the palm of his hand. Adjusting himself one last time, he sweeps his soaked hair away from his forehead, giving me a clear view of his flawless face. He's never looked more beautiful to me, my supernova, shining so brightly in his element. He's happy, and it's so apparent. "I borrowed this one from a family friend." he says, "He taught me to play piano, so I don't think he'll mind."

He postures himself to play as the audience grows more subdued, the lone spotlight on him dimming slightly. Easton dips his chin, and somewhere from the stage, a synthesized yet beautiful melody begins to play. Easton joins in shortly after and falters, muttering, "Shit, well, he might mind *that*, sorry, Chris." His embarrassed chuckle elicits a round of helpful and encouraging cheers, and I can't help my smile.

He's nervous.

The raw vulnerability he's displaying for the world, a world he fears, has me tearing up as he begins again. During that magical moment, as all I feel for him threatens to burst from me, he sweeps us all away in the most beautiful of melodies.

Soon after, Easton begins to sing the first of the lyrics about being lost, of an inner struggle, just before he lifts his eyes to mine. Within a matter of a few stunted breaths, I replay the first time our eyes met at the bar and the second he held out his hand to me in offering at the garden. Tears already shimmering in my eyes, I gaze back at him as the rest of our story unfolds through his chosen cover song. Through the lyrics, Easton sings of the state of the world, our differences, the belonging we all hope for…and of finding it in another's eyes.

It's then I realize he's serenading me, singing to me, and the song represents us. I relive it all as my chest goes raw. Within a few more bars and heart-stopping lyrics, the band starts to play along, scattered around him in the pitch dark.

Easton raises his voice, tipping it up and beyond a surreal level as every lyric strikes me to my core, and I allow my tears to spill over. Heartbeat escalating, chest pumping, his words from Seattle come back to me.

"I want you to remember this moment, right now, right here, just you and me in a fucking SUV, taking a drive to nowhere. Promise me you'll remember this."

"It's just us," I whisper, entranced, gazing back at him as he captivates me wholly. Steadily pulling me closer and closer to him, despite the distance between us. I don't feel an inch now, and I've never in my life felt anything like it—this intimacy, this feeling of belonging to someone so completely.

This can't be bought or bottled.

It can't be replicated, duplicated, or imitated.

Being with Easton in any capacity is like trying to cling to a shooting star, and somewhere inside, I know that if I don't relish this time with him, I'll miss it as he burns his brightest. Even if it seems impossible that he'll burn out at all, I know for certain that I want to burn with him for as long as humanly possible.

No…there's nothing to compare this feeling to, and that's why it's the meaning of life. Love is purpose, belonging, and the very definition of living.

He continues to sing of my effect on him as his voice caresses my entire being, covering me head to heel in goosebumps while searing itself permanently into my heart. With every fluid stroke of his tongue—his weapon far too lethal for any sort of armor—the needle drives in deep, infusing me with a euphoric, indescribable high.

Surrounded by thousands, he holds me captive as I become helplessly attuned to the fact I'm utterly, hopelessly, and desperately fucking in love with Elliot Easton Crowne.

A rock star he may now be, but for me, he was first a man who reached in with a gentle soul and discovered some of my veiled truths before forcing me to acknowledge parts of who I am—and what I want. A man who made me feel important at a time when I questioned my direction and everything else I thought I knew. A man who has since freed me to be that woman, all the while addicting me to new needs. Needs he himself sparked and created before gifting me with the type of love I dreamed of. The love I hoped to experience for myself.

In becoming her, we both fell—unguarded, raw, and vulnerable—the only way *to* fall. The most potent aspect of all is that he helped blueprint our love, just as my heart conjured it.

It has nothing to do with anyone else, despite how it happened.

This love story is ours and ours alone.

All of these truths hit me within seconds as he expertly plays an intoxicating, romantic melody—a symphony seeming to consist of only the most beautiful notes. Easton's gaze remains focused on me as he hits every single one with ease while his fingers glide over the keys.

As the song builds, spotlights begin to pop up on clustered musicians gathered on stage, the last a group of violinists who begin to play.

He planned this. Every second of this, for *me*.

Standing in a living dream, while floating on the love I feel for him, our eyes lock, our affection clear during the most beautiful minutes of my life.

The song hits its crescendo, shooting a tingling through me before he dips closer to the mic, stare intensifying, his admission clear when he speaks.

"I love you."

The chaos of the crowd drowns out my gasp as I clutch my chest, my eyes flooding. Refusing to miss a second, I furiously wipe at my tears as my heart thrashes wildly in my chest. Whoever I was before this moment exists no more. Inside, I'm aware I'll never be her again, the woman who doesn't know what this kind of love feels like. Whatever I presumed my loves expectations to be feel insignificant for the moment, because his declaration makes me feel immortal.

My decision comes easily.

I'm done hiding. From everyone. I'm done hiding my love for this man, period. Endless daydreams of a repressed future start to unfurl as he continues to pour himself, his love, into me with the most beautiful of love songs.

He loves me.

He. Loves. Me.

As if reading my thoughts, a shy smile graces Easton's lips as a screen full of swaying lights from the audience become his background.

The power of our connection flows over every inch of the stadium, or at least it feels that way, as it blankets me while he sings the last of the lyrics. Piano notes linger in the air as the violins rush out on high and the stadium goes black.

An explosion of praise fills the air as I manage to make out the slide of Easton's piano bench due to a small backlight shining brightly just beneath it.

Face covered in the aftermath, I brace myself, my eyes still spilling, scalp tingling as he rushes toward me.

Six feet…five…four…three before he comes into view. I leap for him, and he catches me easily, his mouth capturing a sob as he kisses me like there isn't a stadium of people screaming for him. But it's me he soothes with his gentle hands, my tears he wipes away as our kiss intensifies. There's so much conviction in it on both our parts, yet he fuses more in with every sure swipe of his tongue.

For those precious and monumental seconds, it's just us.

Natalie and Easton.

He breaks our kiss as the lights go up and immediately starts ushering me out of view and toward safety.

"N-no," I say, pulling my hand away, "No. N-no more h-hiding."

He stares down at me, weighing my words.

"You're sure?"

"Positive," I sniff. "I l-love you, Easton. With e-everything in me. No more hiding—from anyone."

Elation brightens his face as he sweeps me back into him and kisses me, this kiss even more intense than the last. I grip him to keep from buckling as he deepens it further, our hands caressing in worship. A blur of bodies starts to move around us as we continue to bind ourselves to the other, our tongues tangling as silent promises flow between us. We seal ourselves together this way until forced apart. Smiling at each other, noses brushing, I speak up. "And to think I was f-freaking out because you hadn't texted me back," I murmur.

"I wasn't going another fucking day without telling you," he pushes the words against my mouth.

"Jesus, I can't believe you did this…like this."

"Easy…and happy?" He teases, repeating my words from this morning.

God, was that just this morning?

"It's y-you, only you, that gets me t-tongue-tied and flustered like this. I'll have you know I'm an a-authoritative woman in every other aspect of my d-damned l-life," I stutter out horribly. "I h-hope you're happy," I sniffle as I try and fail to gather myself. "I-I-I'm ruined. You've r-ruined me!"

"Only fair." I read his lips more than I'm able to hear him due to the increasing commotion surrounding us.

"W-w-wh-hat the hell am I s-s-s-upposed to do now?" I sniff and shake my head as he clears the mascara beneath my eyes.

He grips the sides of my face, his gaze prodding. "Marry me."

FORTY-SEVEN

Space Song
Beach House

Natalie

"W-w-what?" I stutter out as Easton speaks up, but not to me.

"I'm done tonight, man," he barks to an approaching stagehand, his intense gaze still trained on me. "Please walk away," he orders more aggressively. There's no sign of a bluff anywhere in his expression as he watches me while weighing my reaction to his proposal. The stagehand scurries away as I gape up at him before he calls for Joel. I faintly make out Joel's approach in my periphery, eyes bolted to Easton's. "Please grab us a car. We're right behind you."

"On it," Joel replies as Easton continues to hold me captive, eyes searching.

"Marry me," he repeats, "let's do it, let's make a life together." He slowly lifts my left hand and presses a soft, full-lipped kiss to my empty ring finger. "Marry me because we're the rare, lucky ones who managed to find something together so many others don't have—it would feel criminal not to. For both our sakes, marry me, Beauty, right now, marry me *tonight*."

"Yes," I whisper in answer. The *only* answer that rings clear in both head and heart. "Yes."

Easton cuts off my third "yes," with another soul-altering kiss that he ends far too abruptly before gripping my hand and leading me off stage and down the stairs. And then we're running down the halls, purposefully ignoring *everyone* and *everything* that could interfere with our hasty getaway. Easton's euphoric smile is all I can see as we race toward the garage. I return it, knowing my skin is splotchy, and I look an utter wreck. Plastered to his side, I keep my eyes on him as we silently ride down the elevator, the guards caging us before we're ushered into the back of an SUV. The second the door closes, Easton curses and addresses Joel, who's already in the driver's seat.

"Joel, we need privacy, *now*. Can you please make that happen?"

He glances back and effortlessly reads the situation. "I've got you."

Joel exits the car, and in minutes we're exchanging the back seat of the SUV for a limo. As the privacy glass rises, Easton speaks up with another request. "Play us something, *anything*."

"You got it," Joel muses just before the window seals shut.

Soft melodic music begins to fill the limo as I turn to him.

"What are you doi—" Easton cuts me off, kissing me with wild abandon before his calloused fingers dip into my jacket, and he palms my bare breast.

"Jesus, are you trying to kill me?" He cuts off any reply by again sealing our mouths together and thrusting his explorative tongue against mine. Hands roaming, mouths fused, we get lost in each other before he breaks away, pressing our foreheads together.

"Fuck, baby," he murmurs. "I can't get close enough." He pulls me to straddle him before elongating the seatbelt and buckling us in together as I giggle against his lips. Not long after, all traces of humor disappear as he pushes the shoulders of his jacket down. My hardened nipples brush his T-shirt as I moan my request for more into his mouth. Overcome with the need to feel him, I manage to ease back enough into the restraint to unbuckle his jeans. Dipping into his boxers, I grip his velvet, hard length before brushing a bead of moisture over the fat head of his cock.

"See, not broken, just mine." I pump him firmly to reiterate my point while he trails kisses down my neck.

"No question about that. Fuck, I missed you," he hums as he tugs his jacket cinched around my waist. "I fucking love this."

"I hoped you would."

"I love *you*," he breathes. "Feels good to say it."

"I love you too, Easton, so damned much. I've been stopping myself from saying it for weeks," I admit before playfully scolding him. "You freaked me out a little today when you didn't text back."

"I had work to do," he pauses between kisses. "I wanted it to be perfect."

"It was, but you screwed yourself and set a high bar."

"Oh yeah?" he grins, pulling my hand from his pants to slide his own hand into my shorts, running teasing fingers through my soaked center. "Give me ten minutes with this perfect pussy, and I'll set it higher. *Bet*."

"Shameless," I croak out, my voice coated in lust, my desire spiking as he latches onto my nipple. Gasping, I watch him feed, riding his fingers while running my own through his sweat-soaked hair. "Please, Easton, please, I need to feel you." I grind onto him as he pulls away, shaking his head.

"I can't love you the way I need to in this fucking limo," he groans in frustration, withdrawing his hand. "I want to lay you down somewhere soft and…white," he insists, looking at me with a love-soaked expression, one I immediately burn into memory.

"Please," I whimper as he gently shakes his head again, his eyes glittering over me as he threads my wandering fingers between his.

"No, baby, no. The next time I cum inside you, you're going to be my wife."

He takes my lips again, so lovingly that my emotions get the best of me, and an elated tear escapes me as he continually feeds my euphoria. We kiss, hands tenderly exploring until the light of the cabin flashes in warning.

Easton pulls his lips from mine and stares down at my breasts. "As much as I hate to do this," he gently suckles each of my nipples before lifting the jacket.

His gaze prodding, I relent and push my arms into the sleeves as he secures it back into place so I'm covered.

"That was just mean," I protest, unfastening the seatbelt and sliding off his lap. Securing his jacket in place, I pull my belt tighter as he tries to wrestle his raging hard-on into his jeans. I can't help my smile as he struggles to conceal his massive erection and notices my smirk.

"You think this is funny?"

"I think it's fair. I mean it. You've ruined me completely with that grand gesture, and not just tonight—*forever*." I blow out a harsh breath. "I hope you're happy."

His smile broadens as he wins the battle with his jeans before he grips my hand and begins kissing my fingertips.

"Stop smiling, you ass. There's no undoing this."

"Good."

I snag his hair and pull gently. "You better mean that."

"I'm about to pledge my life to you—proof enough?"

"We're really doing this?"

Determination takes residence in his tone. "Fuck yeah, we are. Reckless and stupid maybe, but stupid *happy*."

"Couldn't agree more." Unable to help myself, I climb back onto his lap and start to shower him with kisses. "You," kiss, "told," kiss, "*everyone*," kiss, "that you love me," kiss. "The *world*."

"Hold up, baby," he says, jostling me on his lap.

"Nope, we're decent enough," I fire back while continuing my kisses as he chuckles.

"Hold still, Beauty. Just for a second," he muses, trying to juggle me as I turn to see that he's plucked his favorite black star pinky ring between his fingers. I stare at it before he grips my left hand and pushes the ring on—the fit perfect—my eyes misting before looking back at him.

"Just until we pick up something else."

"I don't care," I exclaim. Giddy, I screech out my bliss before continuing my assault, drawing another laugh out of him. "I love you," I murmur, working my way along his jaw, his neck, the hollow of his throat. He snakes his arms around me and lures me back into a slow, exploratory kiss which quickly sets us both ablaze. I pant into his mouth, grinding against him before belting out my demand.

"Fuck me," I murmur. "Fuck me right now, and make love to me *later*."

"I'll do both later. Jesus, Beauty, we have to stop. We're about to pull up to the hotel." I groan as he gently lifts me by the hips and deposits me back into my seat. He rakes his lip, eyeing my heaving chest and the flush in my skin. "I promise I'll make the wait worth it."

"Jesus, Easton, as if I need *anything* other than what you've already given me."

"It's only going to get better," he assures me as we straighten ourselves while we approach the hotel. The second we're stopped, the back door to the limo opens, and a valet greets us warmly. Behind the valet,

I get a glimpse of sliding glass doors just as Easton grips the door handle. "Not yet, man, thanks." Easton turns to me, his finger on the partition button. "Tonight?"

"Yes," I nod repeatedly. "Yes."

Joel comes into view and glances back in the rearview at the two of us. My neck heats as Easton speaks up.

"Hey man, change of plans. Just grab our bags and check us out. We're going back to the jet."

"Yeah?" Joel turns back, grinning between the two of us. "Where are we off to?"

"You tell me, *best man*," Easton declares, brushing his thumb along my newly occupied ring finger while holding it up for his perusal.

Joel's eyes widen, his smile amping. "Vegas it is."

Frowning at our destination, Easton glances over at me, a plan clearly forming behind his eyes. "You know what, man? I have a much better idea."

I exchanged vows with my supernova while the rest of the hovering stars lay witness, enviously blinking before fading into dawn. Easton pushed the matching black titanium wedding band onto my finger just as the sun peeked over the horizon. Though our ceremony was simple, and our traditional vows have been recited countless times by others before us—it was still uniquely ours.

While Joel checked them both out and gathered their luggage, Easton conducted a brief internet search, keeping me out of arm's reach, and his private loop by shielding his phone from me. By the time we got to the idling plane, he solidified the plans, only sharing them with Joel. We touched down at a private airstrip in Arizona just after one in the morning. The next few dizzying hours were an array of unanswered questions, *my questions,* as Joel and Easton gathered what and *who* we needed to elope. The patience I kept during those clueless hours paid off the second Easton led me from the back of another SUV.

Easton's idea had been to unify us beneath a glittering sky, rather than neon lights, in a far more private part of the desert.

Our guest list short—Joel, a local officiant, and a pastor Easton managed to bribe out of bed by paying off a good portion of their mortgages. Between the look in Easton's eyes, the sincerity in his voice, and our starlight to sunrise wedding, his vision easily superseded anything I could have ever dreamt up.

It fit.

It was us.

It was perfect.

The point was driven home further within the length of a song. A song I requested Joel play as he whisked us toward our resort. The song Easton serenaded me with before proposing. A song now embedded into my heart's playlist alongside the others that mark the milestones between us.

Too overcome with excitement to sleep but every bit in a dreamlike state, Easton carried me over the threshold of what could only be described as a honeymooner's paradise. Nested into a ridiculous four thousand square feet, our private, two-story, adobe-style villa at the resort felt constructed from a dream. It was clear Joel came through again in a major way—plush furniture, the best linens, a fireplace, a jacuzzi, an outdoor hot tub, and windows that gave way to spectacular views.

Not that it mattered where we were the second we were alone.

Within a minute, maybe two, of closing the door, Easton laid me down on a soft white bed and proceeded to kiss every inch of my skin before we consummated our marriage in the most incredible way. Wedding rings clinked together next to my head on the mattress, and my husband's love-filled eyes bored into mine. We quickly lost all sense of time as he brought me to completion over and over again before he succumbed himself. Early morning light fully invaded our piece of desert paradise before Easton and I finally spent ourselves to the point that exhaustion took over. After a shower, I barely remember being ushered back into bed before Easton blacked out the sunlight, and I sank into a blissful coma.

Staring at the black titanium band on my finger, I'm warmed by the memory of rousing to his kiss as he pressed worshipful lips to my occupied ring finger before pressing into *me*, whispering, "Good afternoon, Mrs. Crowne."

Glancing over at Easton now, I soak in the gravity of what my ring means, unable to summon any regret. Thick hair whipping around his face, Ray-Bans shielding his eyes from the desert sun, Easton navigates the winding road, both hands on the wheel. My eyes pause on the thicker black band on his left hand as I mentally pinch myself. Though I wanted to stay in bed for more consummation, Easton insisted on driving me through the backdrop he'd chosen for our honeymoon. Forcing my gaze away from my husband, I marvel at the terracotta-smeared mountains and clustered boulders of a similar shade that make up the Sedona landscape.

Breathing in the reality that today, I woke up Easton's bride, I can't help the joyful tears that fill my eyes as I slide my thumb along my newly christened ring finger.

"It's so beautiful, Easton."

And hot.

But a different kind of heat than Texas hellfire. The AC on full blast in the cabin making it bearable. It's the feeling of serenity here that has me melting into the seat, relaxed, the atmosphere unlike any I've ever known. Being in this part of the desert is like existing underwater, tranquil and slow-moving. Like the outside world exists, but it's muffled and seems unimportant. As if all of the rest of the world's chaos doesn't apply here.

"This is a dream," I declare over the music. Easton doesn't reply but lifts my left hand as he has a dozen or more times since we woke, pressing another gentle kiss to my ring finger. The pleasure he takes in the act is clear in his features when he does it. Easton turns the radio dial to settle on another song. We'd turned off our phones last night before we boarded the jet and have taken every precaution since to keep ourselves concealed and under the radar.

We only let the top down when we are miles into the drive on the two-lane road. Our surreal surroundings only add to the fuzzy haze of the hours preceding this. Less than twenty-four hours ago, I was slumped against my apartment door, questioning my fit into Easton's life.

Thumbing my ring now, I decide the fit is fucking perfect.

Feeling utterly at peace in my surroundings and my position and place with the man by my side, I appreciate him more due to the fact he didn't want me to miss this, even when we have the divine right to be naked hermits. Still, I fight to keep my eyes on the spectacular terrain instead of the view next to me.

"Space Song" croons through the cabin as Easton drives quietly at my side. Turning to him, I realize he hasn't replied to me because he's lost somewhere in his music subspace, far beyond my reach. Silently, I wait for him to come back to me, knowing whatever magic going on inside his head deserves the attention he's giving it. A few minutes later, he speaks up.

"Sorry, did you say something, Beauty?"

I grip his hand and kiss along his knuckles. "Nothing important."

"What was it?"

"I said this is a dream, and I love it here, but then I noticed you were doing your thing."

"What *thing*?"

"You know, when you blast off into a musical coma at random."

He chuckles. "Sorry."

"Don't be. I'm not getting in the way of that for *anything*."

"That so?" I'm graced with a half-smile.

"Honestly? I'm dying to know what's happening in there. Where did you go?"

"Playing around with a melody that sounds a lot like you."

"Will you play it *for me* sometime?"

"Of course," he quips as if it's a given. "And I'll try to be more conscious about my space travels, especially now."

"No!" I shout, and he flinches, gripping the wheel tighter.

"Beauty. I love you, I do, but please fucking refrain from screaming out when we're on narrow, winding roads in the middle of the mountains."

I wince. "Sorry. Didn't mean to scare you. It's just…if you get lost, stay there. I'll come for you when it's important."

"It's not exactly a habit I want to maintain when we're together."

"Fuck that noise. It's your process, Easton. I won't disturb your momentum for *anything*." I tilt my head back and get the perfect panoramic view of red mountain and turquoise sky. "God, Easton, you make the most beautiful music. I cannot wait to hear what you come up with next. Neither can the world and," I spout with pride, admiring my band, "the next show I attend, I'll be stage side as your *wife*."

Easton slides his glasses onto his head and slows on the straightaway, his eyes trailing over my profile before he flicks his gaze back to the road.

"What?" I ask as he slows to a stop and parks on a designated shoulder next to some giant evergreens. "Why are we stopping?" I glance around, looking for a landmark of some sort. "Are we taking pictures?"

Without a word, he closes the top, and locks us in, turning down the music as the air cools our skin. Glancing over, I lift a brow.

"Good sir, we cannot *do*...whatever it is you're thinking of *doing*, and I'm pretty sure what you're thinking will include an *arrest*. This is a state park."

Eyes intent, he reaches over and caresses my face, his features relaxed, his eyes softening.

"What?" I grin. "What is it?"

"You know what my father calls my mother?"

"Grenade."

"Yeah. That's his pet name for her. Because that's the way he saw her when they met. A ball of destruction."

"Are you saying—"

"Oh, hell yes, you are. That's what you are for me. Charging into my life wearing a dozen mismatched sweaters, pissed off about the fact that you hadn't been properly loved, kissed, or fucked."

"I said no such thing."

"You didn't have to," he murmurs.

"You pulled me over to tell me I'm a nightmare?"

"Yes, but there's more, so shut up, Beauty." He positions his thumb over my lips, and I give him a dead stare which makes him chuckle.

"I always wondered why I never gave too much of myself away to *anyone* in a personal capacity and felt more comfortable in isolation. Sometimes it would worry me. Like maybe I was lacking some basic human need...until I met you." His confession lingers between us as my eyes begin to water. "I've also never shared a comfortable silence with *anyone* but my parents—until you. I've never felt as seen, known, or understood as I have with you." He swallows before his lips twist ironically. "Who would have thought I would find so much comfort in who I am with—a Texas fireball full of opposition who disguised herself as a journalist."

"Damn it, man," I scold, tears spilling over.

"Thinking back now," he continues, "I think I knew you existed and was waiting." He kisses me soundly and pulls away. "My *wife*," his tone full of wonder. "You found me."

"Easton," I sigh, as my heart swells unbearably, "you have *seriously* got to stop this. I was okay with you being gorgeous, brilliant, talented, selfless, and really, *really*, good in bed, but adding hopeless romantic is going way too far."

He chuckles before brushing his lips across mine. "Baby, you have no idea how good it feels to know that you love me the same way I love you."

"And how do we love each other?"

"Wholly, unconditionally, and *definitively*."

"Jesus," I sniff, climbing over the console. "You just *had* to play hardball, huh? *Fine*." I situate myself around him in the tiny space, deciding to risk jail time.

He's worth it.

FORTY-EIGHT

Nothing's Gonna Hurt You Baby
Cigarettes After Sex

Natalie

At the peak of some of the mountainous terrain we just traveled through, we park and stretch our legs before taking a short walk to the overlook that sits past a waist-high brick partition.

"Oh, wow, Easton. Wow," I say, glancing around. "Sucks we don't have a camera."

"I have my phone," he offers, pulling it out of his pocket.

"No phones," I say.

We stare at the other in trepidation briefly before he whispers, "Fuck it," and powers it on. Not long after, a grin lights up his face as he turns it to me. "No service."

"Thank God," I exhale a breath of relief we were spared the roulette bullet as he keeps it powered up long enough to take a selfie of us. Twin smiles the main focus, he also manages to capture the blanket of tree tops in the valley below along with a little of the surrounding cliffs. He takes a few more shots of the panoramic view before powering his phone back off and taking my hand. On our way back to the car, I stop at the group of clustered craft tables that we bypassed on our walk and cautiously pause at the first, eyeing the woman sitting behind it for any hint of recognition for the rock star lingering close by. She greets me warmly, nothing telling in her answering expression as I lift a solid white dream catcher from where it hangs on the side of her table.

"This is beautiful," I tell her before holding it up to Easton, who's shopping a table over. "Babe, mine?"

Easton instantly nods in reply as he lifts a plate-sized, hand-crafted drum, dark wooden sticks dangling atop it. "Also yours, for your next lesson."

"Yes, please."

Seeming pleased, he pulls out his wallet, doling out the cash for each vendor, both older women of Native American descent.

I walk over to where he stands and snake my arms around his waist, pressing a kiss onto the soft cotton of his T-shirt-covered shoulder, inhaling his scent. "I'll pay you back. I thought we were just going for a drive, so I left my purse at the villa," I whisper as the vendor speaks up.

"Are you two on your honeymoon?"

"Yes," we say in unison, our proud need to share that information with *anyone* obvious with our enthusiastic reply. Once our purchases are bagged, we browse along the other tables picking out new treasures, each of us procuring silver spoon rings with turquoise stones. The next table over, I find a hand-carved wooden Christmas ornament with a tiny dream catcher hanging inside of it and decide I have to have it. By the time we make our exit, Easton's hands are full of bags of locally crafted, one-of-a-kind gems, each bought from a different table. As we retreat back to the parking lot, we're waved away with warm goodbyes and congratulations. The feeling continues as we reach the convertible. I breathe in the day, and Easton secures our haul into the trunk. Smiling, I glance over at him, and it's not reciprocated.

"What?"

"You'll pay me back?" Easton stares over at me across the convertible. I'm thankful his Ray-Bans are on, so I'm unable to see his complete mean mug.

"I don't know how we're going to do money yet, and I can buy my own shit." I shrug as his jaw ticks. "Fine, I'll consider it my wedding present," I concede, getting into the passenger seat and buckling in before he orders me to. "Now we have to figure out your wedding present, and it has to be *good*. Something special and one of a kind," I demand as he takes the driver's seat.

Famous last words.

Easton's wedding present turned out to be a gift a little harder for me to bear, *literally.* "Easy, baby," Easton grits out, the strain in his voice evident as he tries to ease into me, and I whimper at the discomfort. In the last few hours, we've gone from emotion-filled love-making to downright filthy and experimental fucking. I've given my body over to him as I have my trust, my heart, and my future, which is why I'm on all fours now on a plush towel he laid out on a large ottoman in our heavily mirrored bathroom. Easton towers behind me, gloriously naked, our eyes connected in our reflection, his mouthwatering cock in view as he pushes another inch inside me. Seeing me wince, he eases back out.

"Don't stop," I protest.

"I don't think I could if I wanted to," he murmurs as he massages my backside. With that, he grips my hips pulling me toward him before dipping to ready my exposed flesh with an explorative tongue. My last orgasm still dripping between my thighs, Easton laps at me from behind, gathering my wetness onto his fingers before pushing one of them back inside a formerly untouched place. The second I admitted I hadn't explored that particular sexual boundary, I could see the fireworks go off in his eyes and knew exactly what my wedding gift would include. Before he could voice it, I fled his arms, running around our villa, and he gave chase while I screamed like a banshee.

He caught and punished me by running his tongue between my legs for endless minutes. In return, I surrendered, my white flag inching higher with every orgasm. Not once since we got back to the resort has his stamina wavered, nor has he gone more than a few minutes without growing hard—and I've loved every literal fucking second of it. He stands behind me now, the man I've fallen hopelessly obsessed with, sun-tinted dark olive skin covered in a sheen of sweat, his eyes hooding as he gently probes me.

"Better?" he murmurs after adding another finger and pumping them in and out of me until he's able to do so more easily. My eyes go half-mast, mouth parting as the foreign sensation becomes oddly pleasurable. The carnal lust in his own hooded eyes spurs me on as I gaze at his reflection, just as lust drunk. Jade-amber fire licks flames down my reflection as he positions himself back where we started on our second attempt. In the last several hours, he's made diligent work of claiming as many sexual firsts as I've listed, this one his final frontier.

"Push out, baby," he orders gruffly, and I do as he thrusts in. My legs nearly give out as a wave of pain courses through me.

"Look at me, Beauty," he orders, "watch me take your ass." I do, soaking in the pleasure in his expression, not wanting to deny him this or anything else for that matter. Abs glistening, eyes darkening by the second, he keeps me engaged as he grips my hips and pushes in further, *claiming*. I can practically see the 'mine' in his eyes even as he whispers encouragement. "Almost there," he grits out. "Fuck, you're so goddamned tight."

"Easton," I whimper, the shake in my voice a dead giveaway. "Do it, now, please," I beg, the discomfort becoming close to unbearable.

He thrusts all the way in as I arch my back, the pain briefly blinding me as he mutters, "Jesus Christ." His eyes frantically search my face. "Okay?"

"Hell no," I croak, "but don't stop."

"Sure?"

"Easton," I whimper, the pain overtaking any pleasurable sensation.

He guides my hand between my legs before gripping a lone finger and running it along the side of my clit, the result surprising as pleasure comes instantly. "This, right here, is your sweet spot."

Apparently.

"Don't stop," he orders, and I nod, bracing myself with one arm while massaging myself with the other. The pain subsides slightly as he dips and darts his tongue along my back. "So fucking sweet. Ready?"

"No," I pant.

"You have to relax."

I narrow my eyes. "Want to switch positions real quick, husband, so I can give the same lecture? Pretty sure this wasn't anywhere in the brochure."

He barks out a laugh. "Baby, we can stop," he pants. The pleasure due to his subtle movement quickly draining all humor away. "Let's stop," he murmurs, palming my back as I object.

"Don't you dare! We're doing this. Just...make it better."

Expression tense, nostrils flaring, I know he's restraining himself as he slowly pulls back and thrusts in. When he manages a few more without an answering whimper, I start to relax a little. The second I do, his strokes become easier as he starts a rhythm, lust oozing from him as he watches me massage myself.

"Better?" He grits out, running a palm over my ass cheeks.

"Yessss," I hiss as I relax a little more, the foreign sensation overtaking me in a slightly more pleasurable way. He picks up his pace watching my every movement, his jaw going slack.

"F-f-feel g-good?" I ask as I begin to sync into the slow-building rhythm with him, the worst of the discomfort behind me.

"So fucking good, baby, I love you so much," he rasps out, his voice velvet. "You're so goddamned beautiful. I can't get enough."

"Then take more," I order as I push back, meeting his thrusts. The act spiking my arousal further as his hunger increases, his eyes flaring unmistakably.

"Fuck, Natalie…don't, I'm going to fucking explode."

But I do, and in return, I elicit a groan I've never heard from him that spurs me on as I massage myself faster and begin backing onto him with every thrust. He slows our pace enough to press thick fingers inside me before running them along my walls. Sensation instantly overwhelms me as he simultaneously seems to push every button I have. Within a few more targeted strokes, my entire body succumbs before seizing. Pleasure rips through me like a tsunami as I toss my head back and scream out his name. A string of curses leaves him as he bites his lip, grips my hips, and begins pounding into me, prolonging my orgasm before he himself capitulates, belting out a harsh "Fuck! Fuck!"

I continue to shudder with release as a flood pours between my legs, coating my thighs as Easton collapses forward with me.

The pleasure subsides, and the discomfort again sets in as he carefully pulls out of me, rimming my ass gently with his fingers before collapsing on his back on the ottoman. Staring over at me, chest pumping, he pulls my upper half to rest atop him and kisses me like I'm the air he needs. Pulling away, he gives me a devilish grin. "That was fucking insane, baby."

Nodding, I subtly run a hand down my thigh and feel it's soaked before wiping it on the towel discreetly beneath me.

"Will you start a shower?" I ask, and Easton nods, kissing my lips before turning to give me a grand view of his naked backside.

The last thirty hours or so have been the happiest of my existence. The last few especially. Feeling filthy while at the same time blissed out on the never-ending high that seems to endlessly fuel us both, I discreetly wipe between my legs as he sets the water temperature. Unable to stop thinking about what just transpired, I speak up.

"How do you know about all those places on me?"

He tosses a grin over his shoulder as steam rises from the shower, his dark hair cresting over his forehead. I take a mental snapshot. "I made it my business to know, and now it's my *job*."

"Sadly, I didn't even know some of those places," I bite into his shoulder. We've been adventurous before, but our honeymoon has turned into our dirtiest adventure to date.

As it should be.

Like Easton, I refuse to let anything, anyone, or any thought take the happiness from our first day of marriage. Since we agreed to turn our phones off before we got here, we haven't bothered acknowledging the disaster that awaits us outside the door. But, the longer we keep from discussing our cocoon has an expiration date—which sadly is tomorrow—the more anxious I start to become. I need a plan of some sort in order to feel secure. Even so, I don't want to broach it just yet. In fact, I want to prolong every second of the high we deserve as newlyweds.

"How do you feel?" He asks as he steps in and pulls me under the spray with him. Limbs feeling like Jell-O, it's all I can do to nod, fatigue taking over. A few seconds under the water has me replaying our most recent interlude, and I turn my face away as he murmurs his compliments to his "filthy little wife."

It's when he sees the blush shading some of my afterglow that he tips my chin in concern. "Was that too much?"

"Yes, Easton, far too much. You don't have a cock. You have an Amazonian water snake in your pants."

"Seriously?" He asks, holding in his smile briefly before it breaks through.

I dispense some jasmine-smelling soap onto one of the luxury sponges that feel like angel's wings on my skin before giving him an eye roll. "It was painful but glorious, and you damn well know it, so stop smiling like that." I hesitate before I run the sponge across his chest and glance over at the towel uneasily. Too late with my recovery, he pinches his brows and follows my line of sight before sensing my hesitance. This man wasn't lying when he said he's memorized me. He's far too perceptive, making it hard for me to hide anything. Both a blessing and curse.

"What? Are you hurting more than you're letting on?"

"No…it's not that."

"Well then," he ducks under the spray before spouting a stream of water onto my chest. "Spit it out."

"Cute."

"Natalie," he warns, "what is it?"

"I've had sex before you," I start. "Some good sex."

"Fucking really?" he groans. "That's what you're going to start with?"

"Hear me out. I've had a handful of partners."

Nostrils flaring, his jaw ticks.

"There's nothing to be jealous about."

"I'll be the judge."

I roll my eyes. "I can't talk to you when you go all paleolithic man."

"Then maybe you need to skip the sexual history and get to the point."

"Forget it," I say dismissively, turning and ducking under the spray. He instantly turns me back to face him and positions me to the shower wall. Palming the tiles next to my head, he runs his nose along mine.

"Sorry, I'll put the jealous asshole on a leash. Tell me what you were going to say, Beauty."

"Well, in my experience, I've never…" I dip my eyes to my nether region before widening them. "You know…"

He frowns in confusion before a slow smile begins to build on his lips.

"You mean—"

"Don't you dare say it!" I clamp my hand over his mouth as he completely ignores me, his reply muffled against my hand.

"Femaw ej lation."

"I said don't say it!" as he chuckles and removes my palm.

"Porn word—squirting." He barks out more laughter as I shake my head in irritation.

"That's absolutely disgusting."

"Didn't seem that way at the time," he muses at my discomfort.

"Just forget it. This conversation isn't happening." Thoroughly embarrassed, I do my best to free myself under his scrutinous confines as he presses in, holding me in place. "This is highly unfair," I say, unable to move, "you've got a lot of muscle and inches on me."

His lips quirk higher. "You walked right into that one, and I must admit, my ego is thankful for the boost."

"You're an idiot."

"Ouch," he chuckles, "is this our first marital spat?"

"You're being disgusting, and I'm...never mind."

When he sees my disappointment, his smile dims.

"I'm sorry, baby. Don't let it freak you out. It's natural for some women when they have an intense orgasm and is nothing to be embarrassed about. Honestly? I think it's hot as fuck and can't wait to make it happen again." He crowds me as I look anywhere but at him.

"I don't share your enthusiasm," I retort dryly.

"But you did," he chides, "you were *very enthusiastic* about it. You sang opera." Face flaming, he presses in further, forcing me to look up at him. "No way, don't hide from me." The sight of him in the massive shower, seeming fully relaxed and *mine*, takes my breath away.

"You can talk to me about anything, Beauty, absolutely *anything*. Don't be embarrassed to talk to me, ever. We're one now. Okay?"

I dip my chin. "Okay."

"Not good enough. Look at me and really hear me," he murmurs as his velvety voice surrounds me, as does he, keeping my chin up with gentle fingers. "Don't ever hide from me. We're as close as two people could ever be."

Studying his expression, I see nothing but conviction in his eyes as his words feed my soul.

"Do you get that?"

I clasp my fingers around his neck and pull him closer. "We're one," I repeat. Loving the sound of it. "You know I've been *one* my whole life too, much in the same way—an only child and a *party* of one most of my adult life. This meaning is so much different and so much better."

"Yeah?" He graces me with a beautiful half-smile as he palms my stomach. "Maybe one day we'll be two, or three?"

I nod. "One day. Yes. I want that, too."

His entire demeanor shifts as we conjure a glimpse of a future, our future, his eyes lighting with it as he gazes back at me with reverence.

"Now is the best time for us, just the two of us, and we get to have these kinds of days for as long as we decide to." He lifts our banded hands, palm to palm, before tethering them together and kissing my wedding band. "I want so many more of these days with you."

"Me too."

He nods. With at least a thousand days worth of decisions made, he begins to bathe me with gentle care, using a silky sponge to wash every inch of my body. His eyes trail the workings of his hands, and as much as I want to reciprocate, I'm too exhausted for the moment. At my feet, he glances up at me while gently running the sponge between my legs. I wince, and his eyes soften.

"We're going to have to give it a rest," he says in a mournful tone. Even as I go to protest, he shakes his head and nuzzles my neck before whispering. "I do, means the rest of our lives. We've got time."

Even as he says it, I feel the desperation building for us both to keep that reality mixed with his fierce need to protect us. I cling to him as he continues to wash me before working on himself. It's when he glances over that his expression falls. "Don't, baby. Please don't. The minute you start thinking that way..." he shakes his head. "We have to be and *stay* united on this, okay? We can't apologize for loving each other, or we'll give others the power to condemn us."

"Right," I nod. "You're right."

I'm graced with another breathtaking smile as his long, wet lashes mat together under the steady spray. "Concentrate on us tonight, and don't let fear or doubt destroy a second of it."

"Okay, I'm sorry."

"You're safe with me..." He traps my hand, squeezing my fingertips together before pressing them to my temple. "Here," he rasps out before flattening my hand over his heart, "here..." He glides it down his muscular chest and navel before cupping his cock. "And most definitely here."

I can't help my grin as I wrap my hand around his hardening length and pump him.

"Don't start," he scorns, "you need to rest."

"I need you."

"You have me, Beauty."

"Is this real?" I rasp out, love drunk, spent, blissed-out, but already yearning for more.

"Real in every fucking way," he declares vehemently.

"When did you know you loved me," I ask.

"I knew something was happening between us hour one."

"Me too."

"The girl that met me at the bar was a far cry from the cocky bitch previewed on the phone."

I lift a brow. "That was *also* me."

"Yeah, but she no-showed." He palms my cheek. "And this version showed up in her place, searching for something I also wanted for myself."

"What?"

"The type of love that defies rationality, that trumps all reasoning, that's uncontrollable."

"We have that."

"We do. The best part is, I didn't have to want to be the guy for you. I already was."

"So, you're saying it's fate?"

"Maybe a little," he admits, pushing soaked hair away from my face, "and every other thing that pulls two people together."

I can't help my smile. "Careful. You're starting to sound a lot like your superstitious mother."

"I might not buy into it all, but I love that about her and inherited a few traits from her."

"Like?"

"Sometimes, I can get irrational due to my emotions. My mom's the same way and has been her whole life. Instead of trying to change it, she found someone who accepts and loves her more for it and has thrived because of it." He exhales and grabs the shampoo, pouring it into his hand. He runs it through his hair before I take over, digging my nails into his scalp.

"What traits did you inherit from your dad?"

"My temper," he admits, "and that's where it gets tricky."

"Are you afraid of it?"

"On the day-to-day, no, but my dad is. He's afraid I'll do something I can't take back." He lifts his gaze to mine. "Honestly? I'm a little afraid of it when it comes to you."

He stills my hands.

"I would never hurt—"

"Jesus, Easton, don't even finish that." I press in, ensuring he hears me as he rinses his hair. "*Unconditionally*," I remind him. "I love all of you," I whisper on a shaky breath, "I really, really fucking love you and will continue to, come what may. I can handle your bad moods," I laugh, "I met you in a bad mood."

"Good," he murmurs, "because you promised me you would."

I rake my lip. "So, don't let what I'm about to say put you into one, okay?"

He sighs. "Out with it."

"I'm a plan girl, you know that. So, when we walk out of that door tomorrow—and after we face whatever consequences that we have waiting—what then? Like, where will we go?"

"Depends," he replies easily.

"On what?"

"On what you want," tilting his head back, he rinses his hair of conditioner while keeping my stare.

"You do realize when we leave here, reality kicks in."

"This is fucking reality," he snaps defensively. "We just got married."

"I know," I snap back. "But you're a fucking rock star, and I'm a reporter, and we don't live in the same *state*."

He turns off the water, his back to me, and I clasp his shoulders as he lets out a harsh exhale. "I was going to talk to you about all this tomorrow morning."

"Don't get upset. I just want to figure this out."

"I know, I'm not," he concedes easily while grabbing a towel and glancing over at me. "Tell me what you want, and we'll go from there."

"The paper is a legacy I want to uphold. I can't just abandon that."

"Is that truly what you want?"

"Yes. Dad's always given me the option to go my own way, but I love every aspect of it."

"Then that's what you'll have. I don't expect you to follow me around the globe, Natalie. It will be hard on us to be apart at times, but I've grown up in this world and knew what not to do from the get-go. That's why I made damn sure not to sign a record contract and to *own* and *distribute* my own music. I'll never be any label's fucking dog, which grants me luxuries off the leash that a lot of others don't have. Because I made it that way, I tour when *I want to*, and break when I want to. Which means I'm not chained to anything but the tour dates I set myself."

"Okay."

Securing a towel around his waist, he takes the towel from my hands and begins gently running the soft fabric over my skin. I revel in his attentiveness as he bends, and I grip his shoulders as he looks up at me.

"Your dreams don't and won't come second to mine. I want to be the man that stands beside you or behind you when you need me to. I can and will be there for you when it matters most to you."

"You've thought about this, haven't you?"

"I have, a lot, and honestly don't give a damn where I live, as long as my wife is there when I get home."

"You would move to Texas?"

He turns sharply. "You. Are. My. Wife."

"I know that, but—"

"No, you don't. *Nothing* comes before you now, not even my career. All I have to do is make music. I lived as a rock star's son. I don't have to live that lifestyle to fulfill my dreams. I just have to make music. In fact, I would prefer the opposite. I don't want to be homesick on the road. I don't want to spend endless months apart from you. Not even weeks. Not even *a* fucking week. That's what I don't want."

"You're serious?"

"Yes," he says. "And I won't be sacrificing anything to change zip codes, Natalie."

"Okay," I say softly.

"Okay," he brushes his knuckles down my cheek and presses a slow kiss to my lips. "I'll fulfill the rest of my obligation to this tour, and we'll figure out what to do from there." He swats my ass with a towel. "And I know you think I'm funny about money, but owning my masters and writing my own songs means that every time I sell a song or get airplay, I collect the majority of the money. Because I made it that way, and as the album did what it did, we can have more than one home."

I wrap my hair turban-style in the towel. "That would be… incredible."

"We could have a spot in Seattle close to my parents and build a home in Texas, close to yours. Fucking anywhere."

"Anywhere," I repeat.

"As long as we're together."

"Agreed. But I make my own salary and will be contributing. I'm no squatter."

"Fine," he says with a shrug, "see, not so impossible."

"You're making it seem easy." I cup his shoulder as he turns to me. "Just promise me, if there's any part of this you can't live with, you'll speak up."

He lifts a brow. "Have we fucking met? You're such a pain in the ass. I know we'll have plenty to fight about."

"And you're a real Sunday picnic."

"This is going to be epic," he grins.

"I can't believe you're looking forward to fighting. What a weirdo."

"Only the good fights, the ones where you end up coming. I didn't ask for the rest of your life thinking short-term. Now we have a plan." He kisses the tip of my nose. "Feel better?"

"Currently, you're the reason for the literal pain in *my ass*."

A wicked gleam shines in his eyes. "But you liked it. You got so into it and went *freaky*!" He morphs his voice as I slap his chest.

"It will be an *anniversary* type of occurrence."

He flashes me a brilliant grin. "We'll see about that."

Images of our imminent future, of the backlash we're about to endure threaten to creep in, and despite wanting to keep inside our bliss bubble, I can't help my next question. "Are we being young, reckless, and *naïve*?"

He bites his lip briefly. "Maybe a little, but we *are* young, *in love*, and fucking *happy*, so it's worth it, right?"

"So worth it."

"Good, now we can drop the adulting because it's time to get ready for dinner."

I glance at the clock as he walks over to my suitcase, pulls out the lone purple negligee I packed and tosses it to me.

"What restaurant is open at midnight and serves its patrons wearing lingerie?"

I slide it on as he tugs on a pair of boxers before giving me the come-hither finger. I trail him to the door before he opens it. On the other side sits a waiting cart, several chilled champagne bottles submerged in a large ice bucket. Two large covered platters rest in the center. Assorted chocolates and sweets are arranged around a tiny vase full of baby pink roses. Six unlit tapered candles sit in crystal holders next to it.

"This is incredible. I've been with you every second. How did you do this?" I can't help my giddiness. Easton grins and retrieves the rolling cart, parking it next to the twelve-seater dining table in our villa. We quickly unload the haul, and I light the candles and lower the lights as he takes a seat at the head of the table, holding out his hand to me. I take it, and he pulls me into his lap before lifting both cloche covers to unveil several steaming crab legs and melted butter.

"You're so damn predictable, Easton," I utter, as my genuine appreciation rings clear in my voice.

Grinning, he moves my wet hair from the nape of my neck and presses a kiss to it. "No more talk of tomorrow. This is a time of celebration, so no more adulting tonight, deal?"

"Deal," I concede easily as candlelight flickers over his profile while he untwists the wire cap on a champagne bottle before popping it. The overspray oozes down the side of the bottle, and he flicks it off like a pro before generously pouring two glasses. "Good, because tonight, we're dining like Crownes."

FORTY-NINE

Natalie

I wake up in a stupor as Easton eases out of my grip. Moaning due to the arrival of a rapidly progressive champagne hangover, I blindly reach for the bottle next to the bed.

Gulping down the lukewarm water, I pray it does the trick as memorable pieces of our private party last night come back to me. As promised, we dined like kings on succulent crab and chocolates before having a private jam session. After washing myself clean of crab debris, I joined Easton in front of the adobe-styled fireplace just as he lit the match. Cushions and pillows surrounding him for support, he pulled me to sit between his spread legs while situating my newly purchased drum in my lap. Using his skilled hands, he guided mine, which held the sticks in an effort to help me grasp the basics.

Easton kept the champagne flowing, which in turn prematurely ended my lesson when I lost all semblance of rhythm. By the time we polished off the second bottle, an overly animated version of Easton made his first appearance—a version I quickly decided was a favorite. By the time we uncorked the third, we were exchanging sloppy words and kisses, consuming the last drop on the roof of our villa. Feeling no pain, tangled together in a large chaise lounge, we stargazed while conjuring up more immediate plans for our future.

Easton's demand for a longer honeymoon in a more exotic place had us chattering in excitement, the sky above us feeling like our only limit as we discussed the possibilities of where and when.

Sometime after, I passed out only to wake up dangling in my husband's arms as he carried me to bed. During the night, we'd stirred at the same time and reached for each other in the dark. It was as if our bodies were aware of our need for the other before our senses kicked in. When they did, we collided into motion, hands exploring, tongues dueling as we made love until dawn crept into our room. A mental snapshot of Easton hovering above me, bathed in the blue morning light flits in just as he calls for me to wake up from somewhere in the villa. I groan in reply and move to sit, head screaming.

It's the muffled sound of Joel's voice that has me coming to, just before a door slams. Easton's curses precede him before he stalks back into our bedroom.

"What's going on?" I groan as the thumping reminder of the amount of champagne we ingested continues to batter me.

"Baby, get dressed," Easton orders, the alarm in his tone putting me on guard.

"What is it? What did Joel say?" Tightening the knot on my resort-provided terry cloth robe, I walk over to my suitcase and fish out my last clean pair of panties. I slide them on and turn to see Easton pulling on a pair of jeans as the reality of today's dreaded task sets in.

We're set to jet out of Sedona later this afternoon on separate planes with the intent to explain ourselves to our parents. The night we got married—with both of us knowing full well marriage licenses become a matter of public record as soon as they're filed—we begged the officiant to wait until the very last minute in an attempt to buy us some time.

Knowing the threat the outside world poses to us, and along with turning off our phones, Easton instructed Joel not to update us if the news broke. We both banked on the slight chance we would be able to reach our parents before we made headlines. "Easton, tell me. How bad is it? What did Joel say?"

He hastily pulls on a T-shirt, expression full of dread, just as yelling ensues outside the door. "He's *here*."

The question of *who* is answered when my father's voice booms in reply to Joel's. All the blood drains from my face as our honeymoon bubble bursts in the same instant.

"Oh my God," I cup my mouth in horror, the impact of what's happening jerking me into full consciousness.

"Fuck," Easton mutters. "How in the hell did he find us?"

"He's a seasoned journalist and very resourceful, but if he knows, that means we made headlines and—"

"—my parents know too," Easton finishes, his venom meant for his suspect. "That motherfucker, I knew he wouldn't sit on our certificate."

"We could have been outed at the concert," I say, fairly certain someone might have seen or captured our overindulgent lip-lock on the side of the stage. Anyone with footage like that would be granted a substantial payday for it.

Panicked tears threaten as I imagine my father laying witness to his worst nightmare while I scan our destroyed room, knowing the rest of the villa is in similar shape. We'd opted out of maid service to remain in our cocoon, and because we did, the state of our temporary home is damning. Forgoing a useless attempt to clean up, I rush to a nearby floor-to-ceiling mirror. Frantically running my fingers through my sex-tousled hair, I spot several unmistakable love bites on my neck and chest. Pulling my robe tighter, Joel's voice comes in more clearly on the other side of the front door. "Sir, please, calm down."

"Open the fucking door! Natalie!" My father's reply elevates my panic into a full-on attack.

Don't shut down.

Even as I imagined the wrath we were both sure to face at some point today, I never once thought it would be in *this* setting. Easton's return gaze tells me he didn't either. I'd hoped to deal with my father privately, at home, without Easton present. Panic rears its ugly head, paralyzing me as Joel and my father argue outside—their voices becoming more aggressive. Turning back to the mirror, I continue to try and wrestle my appearance.

"Beauty, look at me," Easton commands in a level tone from where he stands a few feet away, and I lift my eyes to focus on his reflection. "No, *look at me*."

Glancing over to where he stands, I find no trace of fear before giving him a firm nod. We silently exchange assurances in our decision to live permanently on *this* side of the glass. This is our reality now. We made it this way.

Unified, position clear, Easton heads for the door, and I trail him a few feet behind. When Easton opens it, I instantly catch my father's eyes as they blaze down Easton's frame over Joel's shoulder, his features twisted in undeniable fury.

Joel stands as a human shield in the doorway, a wall between

Easton and Dad as they stare off for the first time. That is until Dad's eyes catch mine.

"Daddy," I croak, feeling the crippling impact of the hurt and rage in his stare as Joel's shoulders go rigid in preparation.

"Joel, let him through," Easton says, opening the door further in invitation for my father.

"Easton," Joel objects as Easton shakes his head and cuts through it.

"Let him through," Easton says more firmly.

Joel glances back at him warily but relents. "I'll be right outside."

Easton nods, and Joel steps aside as my father's scowl returns to Easton before he strides into the room and stops, his arctic gaze zeroing in on the bed behind my shoulder before he surveys the villa. I take in the view as he does—empty champagne bottles everywhere, clothes that were discarded in haste to get naked exactly where we left them. A slew of used room service trays cover the table and kitchen island. Dad stops between the living and dining room, chest heaving, seeming to try and collect himself while casting his gaze out the sliding glass doors that lead to the patio. His gritted first words are meant for me. "Please, put some fucking clothes on."

His scathing order covers every inch of my exposed skin as he keeps his back to me. I make a mad dash to our room and pull on some shorts and a T-shirt before racing back to the living room. As I do, I glance over at Easton, who stands a few feet away, his expression like granite, posture guarded, which means he's already on the defensive. Even so, I know he's determined to keep his temper in check to try and reason with my dad—which gives me a ray of hope.

The longest minute of my life passes before Dad finally turns and shoots daggers directly at Easton. "Who the fuck does this? What respectable man does this?"

"Daddy, I'm just as much to blame," I start as Easton speaks up.

"Your approval was never coming," Easton relays in an even tone. "There was no way around that. But I do have respect for you, sir, and it comes from how you raised her, her core beliefs, and the incredible woman she is. Respect aside, the truth of the matter is, we both know you don't want to know me."

"You knew," he clips out accusingly. "You *both knew,* and you did this, *knowing.*"

"Daddy," I speak up in an attempt to gain his attention, and he swivels his head in my direction, his expression filled with something I never thought I'd see directed at me in my lifetime—*revulsion.*

"How long?" he rasps out. "How fucking long has this been going on?"

"Four months," I admit with a shaky voice.

"How?"

"The archives," I confess, "I was looking up old articles for the thirtieth edition and found emails between you and Stella, and so I—"

He takes a step toward me, cocking his head. "You *what?*"

"I know it was wrong, but I got…immersed in your love story with her, and I…" How can I possibly explain this to him *now*? No part of his current disposition indicates he's capable of an ounce of understanding, but I press on as my worst nightmare unfolds. "I didn't want to ask you about it because I know when it ended…y-you got hurt." I catch his flinch as though every word of my confession is a physical blow. "You never told me about your relationship with her…I-I contacted Easton—"

"And started a goddamn *fling* with the one human being on earth I would forbid you to see?"

"Far from a fucking fling," Easton defends in a clipped tone, "never was. That was the problem."

Dad's features distort in indignation as he turns to address Easton. "You're walking a very fucking thin line, considering," my father warns, his tone deadly.

"I understand you're pissed, but please don't come at me that way," Easton grits out. "I'm trying here."

"Daddy, I'm just as much to blame, *more so even* than him."

Tension rolls throughout the room, and I can physically feel Easton begin to battle his temper as he speaks up. "At least give us a chance to explain ourselves. I don't expect your understanding."

"You better not expect my goddamned acceptance either!" Dad roars, upturning a nearby tray which crash lands on the floor. Broken dishes shatter while water runs in rivulets away from my newly-scattered, glass-embedded pink roses.

Never in my life have I seen my father lash out physically in anger, not like *this*. Trepidation fills me as he pins me with his glare. "I won't fucking accept this, Natalie!" His eyes dart to Easton and back to me. "Is that why you married him?"

"No," I speak up, finding strength in the truth. "Just the opposite. The night I married him was the first and only time since he and I met that I allowed myself to be with him without a single thought of you. I married him because he understands me. Because being with him makes me happy. Because I love him with every fiber of my being. Every minute we were together before this weekend, it was thoughts of you, of how you would feel, that kept—"

"But they didn't stop you," Dad rages. "Do you have any idea what you're asking?"

"Daddy, I tried. I tried so hard, but Easton and I, we," I shake my head as hot tears fill my eyes and my vision blurs. "I know you know what this feels like—"

"Don't you dare!" Dad roars, and I jump back.

"Please stop screaming at my wife," Easton bristles, nostrils flaring, voice dangerously low, "you're scaring her."

"*Your* wife," Dad snarls, before immediately stalking toward him, posture threatening. "*Your* wife!"

"Daddy!" I cry out in fear as Easton lifts his chin, eyes darkening, posture tensing. In that moment, I don't even recognize my father until he stops a few feet away, hands fisted just as a lethal warning slices through the commotion.

"Take another threatening step toward my son, Butler, and I'll fucking end you." The entirety of the room fills with a dangerous air as the three of us collectively turn toward the front door of the villa, and all eyes land on Reid Crowne.

FIFTY

Easton

Storming into the villa, Dad steps around me to go head-to-head with Nate, and I palm his chest, his outrage tangible.

"Dad, don't," I press in and can physically feel the anger in Dad's shaking frame as he barks around me while I try to step between them. "What the fuck, Nate? Were you seriously going to strike my son?!"

Nate scoffs, "I'm not the man to take the underhanded route, Reid. That's more *your* fucking specialty, isn't it?"

"Didn't look that way to me," Dad grits out, frame still coiling beneath my hand. As they weigh each other, I glimpse a view of the history between them before Nate claps back.

"Well, we both know things aren't always what they seem, don't we, Reid? I prefer to use my intelligence over my fist to make a point, which may be a foreign concept for you."

"Sure seems like your fucking IQ is lacking today," Dad grits out, rare anger in his voice.

"Because you're an authority on controlling your temper, right?" Nate shakes his head with a scoff. "Don't insult me by acting like you're okay with this."

"I won't, but this is news to me, just as much as it is to you."

Joel, who's already standing behind Dad, speaks up. "Reid, do you want me to call security?"

"We all need to take a breath," I say as calmly as I can muster, pushing at Dad's chest again, this time with more force. Dad steps back, eyeing Nate with a disdain that borders on hate.

Joel speaks up again. "Reid?"

"No," Dad barks in reply. "We're good."

Natalie involuntarily shudders from where she stands, her tears coming faster as I try and fail to catch her eyes.

"What the fuck did you do?" Dad barks, and I look over to see his venom is meant for me.

"I fell in love," I admit unapologetically as Nate speaks up, eyes still on Dad, his order for Natalie.

"Natalie. We're leaving. Right fucking now."

"What?" She croaks, her eyes meeting mine as I whip my attention to Nate.

"That's not happening," I say, slicing my hand across my throat.

"They're getting it annulled," Nate fires at Dad.

"Couldn't fucking agree more," Dad concedes with just as much aggression as they attempt to take the fight away from Natalie and me.

"The hell we are," I bark between them. "We aren't a bunch of lovesick teenagers, and this isn't some rebellion against you. You both need to check yourselves and your personal issues. Your story is *history*. She and I, our marriage, are in the here and fucking *now*."

"Is that so?" Dad turns to me. "Well, in the *here and now*, son, your mom almost had a fucking episode."

All the wind gets knocked out of me, and Nate's hostile posture collapses in the same breath, his attention instantly on Dad as he speaks up. "Jesus Christ, Reid, did she?"

"Easton," Natalie rasps out, briefly stealing my attention as the weight of Dad's words settle in my stomach. "What does that mean? An episode?"

Dad speaks up, his reply for me, and surprisingly, for Nate as well. "She's okay, but they've had to sedate her for nearly two days as a precaution." He fixes his glare back on me, "Because she's *inconsolable*."

Two days. We never had a chance.

"As is *your mother*," Nate relays to Natalie, who looks helplessly between the three of us.

"What episode, *Easton*?" she presses frantically, "What does that—"

"She's got a rare condition," I speak up before Dad can, "when she gets too upset, is under a tremendous amount of stress, or goes from one extreme temperature to another—or a combination of both—it can cause her to stroke."

"*Stroke?*" Her eyes widen as they continually spill over.

"She's only had three episodes in her life," I admonish quickly, "twice before I was born, once when I was young. It was the mildest. She's on medications now—"

Dad speaks up, condemning us. "That number got pushed too fucking close to four with headlines her only son married the daughter of her ex-fucking fiancé!"

Nate steps back and cups his neck, staring up at the ceiling as Dad's words reverberate throughout the room. Feeling my resolve start to slip thanks to the outrage of our fathers and the intense emotions flowing from all sides, I run a hand through my hair at an utter loss for what words to say. Right now, no matter how we plead our case, our actions feel indefensible, and there's no way to curb that. Not at present.

"How the fuck did this happen?" Dad demands between Natalie and me.

Nate crosses his arms and drops his gaze as if bracing himself to hear Natalie's confession a second time.

"It was me…I-I s-started this," she sniffles.

"Natalie, don't," I object, but she ignores me by walking herself directly in front of the firing squad.

"I found years' worth of personal emails between my father and Stella while searching our paper's archives. I contacted Easton under false pretenses," she twists her hands nervously in front of her, the sight of my ring on her finger bringing a surge of brief relief before I again attempt to stop her.

"Beauty, don't," I jerk my chin, knowing that she's not going to let me take any of the brunt of this.

"It's the truth," Natalie says softly. "We owe—"

"What, son? You don't think we deserve the fucking truth, especially *now*?" Dad scoffs as Nate shakes his head in clear contempt.

"It was me," she confesses. "I found the emails, read them, and then used a tip-off from our paper's gossip columnist, Rosie. She got word from a credible source that Easton may be releasing a debut album without so much as a press release, so I used it…" Natalie rushes out the rest of her confession as Nate's head snaps to her, his arms going slack in disbelief. "…I used it to catfish Easton into a false interview."

"You fucking *what!?*" Nate growls. "Jesus Christ, Natalie!"

"I know it was wrong," Natalie utters as Dad's expression zeroes and hardens on her.

"Dad," I grit out, my patience running thin as he shifts his gaze to mine. "Don't."

"You know it was *wrong*?" Nate repeats, fisting his hands at his sides. "Is that the word you're choosing?"

"She came clean to me in Seattle," I speak up as Dad's expression morphs into one of livid accusation.

"You flew to Seattle?" Nate prompts her, his tone bone-chilling.

Natalie's face falls. "Daddy, I was—"

"You had no right! No goddamned right!" His snarl has Natalie flinching as I struggle not to go to her, knowing it will only escalate things. My only solace is knowing that no man in this room will lay a hand on her, but it's doing fuck all now as she's battered by condemning glares from *both* our fathers.

"I'm so sorry." Face crumbling, she cups a hand over her mouth to muffle her cries, and all at once, I feel helpless, my dad's behavior turning up the heat on my simmering anger.

"And then what?" Nate presses as Dad remains silent, seeming just as intent on more explanation.

Natalie's neck splotches red as I fist my own hands to remain idle. "I was…I wanted to see if Easton knew—"

"She told you, Easton. You knew?"

"Yes," I nod. "She did."

"So, you knew she was off-limits and still fucking pursued a relationship with her?" Dad shakes his head, his question rhetorical, as Nate gapes at Natalie, equally as mortified.

"How long has this been going on?" Dad asks between us.

This time, I answer for us both. "Four months."

Searching for the right words to explain the truth of us and how we came to be, I fail us both. What the hell can we say right now? We didn't mean to hurt them?

Too cliché and more insult to injury as I grasp for anything I can think of to temper them both—because I knew this fight was coming. I just didn't know it would be coming so ferociously. It's when Dad eyes Natalie suspiciously that I start to boil over.

"Stop looking at her like *that*," I explode at them both as Natalie continues to shudder with her cries. "Need I remind you both that you're happily married?" Two sets of hostile eyes fix on me, and I'm thankful for it. I shoot Natalie a reassuring look as her chest heaves, and sob-induced hiccups escape her lips.

"Yeah, you're a real fucking wealth of knowledge, it seems," Nate quips dryly. "You could write the book."

"My mom *did* write the fucking book, and you weren't *in it*," I snarl over his blatant insults.

"Only the version *you* know of." To my surprise, that reply doesn't come from Nate but from my own father, as my anger starts to best me.

"You know what? Both of you need to ease up, or we're done here. We might owe you an explan—"

"Easton, it's ok-kay," Natalie says in assurance. It's the involuntary jerk of her chest that makes my patience run dry.

Dad chooses that moment to turn and lay into me. "An explanation," he scoffs, "you two are fucking with a history you have no business becoming a part of."

"That's probably the attraction," Nate adds sarcastically.

"No doubt," Dad agrees.

"Fuck this," I yell, fury taking over. "You two don't get to assume shit about us. We might be privy to some of your history, but you sure as hell don't know ours, and this situation right here is why we've been seeing each other behind your backs for months. As it is now, you are the ones acting like children."

"Don't try to turn this around, Easton. We aren't at fault here," Dad fires back.

"The fuck, Dad?!" I shout.

As it seems, on this, he's siding with Nate, which is the worst imaginable fucking twist of fate. I expected his anger. What I did not expect was for him to *take sides* with my wife's father. The two of them seem hell-bent on their own agenda—which is to end us, *swiftly*. Fed up, I make my stance clear.

"Don't belittle what we have to justify your attempt to control what you don't want happening. It happened. It's *still* happening. We're married. We're staying married."

"Because you're too fucking selfish to realize just how over the line you leapt!" Dad belts as Natalie's soft sobs start to echo throughout the room. Unrelenting, Dad looks her over, "But *you know* how far over the line you went, don't you, Natalie?"

"Dad, that's enough!" I shout before I move to console Natalie as Nate speaks up, his tone barely above a whisper.

"Please, Easton, please don't touch my daughter." His eyes redden as he chokes on his next words and turns to Natalie. "I asked myself a thousand times on the plane how I could have fucked up with you so horribly that you could find it in yourself to deceive me this way. To hurt your mother this way." Natalie crumbles where she stands, her eyes overflowing as Nate turns to my dad, devastation coating his voice. "Is this my fucking life, Reid? Is a Crowne man destined to swoop in and take everything that's precious to me?"

Dad blows out a harsh breath as his eyes drop.

Nate speaks up again, his voice a plea. "Please..." He cups his jaw, "I'm asking you *both*, just give me and my daughter the room."

Dad glances over to me and then to Nate before nodding, giving in way too easily. "Come on," he says, pulling at my shoulder in an attempt to usher me out with him.

"I'm not going anywhere. We aren't children," I snap at Dad before looking to Natalie, whose face is buried in her hands. "Natalie," I implore with as much tenderness as I can muster. "Baby, look at me. Please look at me."

Natalie lifts her red-rimmed blue eyes to mine, her expression defeated as Dad continues to usher me toward the door.

"We aren't wrong," I tell her. "Baby, we aren't a mistake."

"Goddamnit, Easton, *now*!" Dad barks out as he shoves me out the door.

FIFTY-ONE

Easton

Dad slams the villa door before blocking me from it. Fury rolls through me like a tidal wave as I slam my fist into the back of it, because for the first and only time in my life, I'm close to striking my own father.

"What the fuck are you even doing here!?" I roar.

"I've *been here* since last night!"

I look over to Joel. "You fucking told him?"

"You hijacked my fucking plane!" Dad barks in Joel's defense. "But you have him to thank for keeping me from this door until he calmed me down."

"Sorry, man. I was forced to make a judgment call when Nate pulled up to the hotel," Joel confesses.

"Yeah, well. It was the fucking wrong one," I rip at my hair and shift my animosity to my dad. "As much good as it did to have you here."

"What did you expect?"

"For you to have my back!"

He gapes at me in disbelief. "Like you had your mother's and mine?"

"You would never allow this to fucking happen if it was you and Mom!"

"That's where you're wrong," he grits out. He pulls out his cigarettes and lights up. "That's the problem with not knowing the full fucking story."

"What in the hell are you talking about?"

"I did let it happen. I made it happen. That situation in there started because of me. Your mother never would've been with him if I hadn't left her, but I couldn't get myself together enough to be the man she needed, so I walked away for both our sakes. That's when she fell for *him*."

"Well, that's your fucking cross to bear. I'm not backing down, and I'm not walking away from her."

"And it's starting to tear her apart already!" He tosses his hands up. "I let your mother choose, and it was the hardest fucking thing I've ever done."

"We aren't you. We chose each other. She's my wife!"

"And his *daughter*," he emphasizes, "and as your father, I'm in my own hell right now."

"Yeah, and what's so fucking hard for you? You got Mom."

"Yeah, but I lost pieces of her and *years* to him in the fucking process, years I'll never get back. And you're right, that's my cross to bear, but yours is going to be too much for you to handle!" He runs a hand through his hair. "Easton, FUCK!" I notice the dark half-moons beneath his eyes as his jaw works back and forth. "I can't believe you did this knowing full well the shitstorm it would cause."

"Not to hurt you. It was never about you, Mom, or Nate. I married her because she's the only woman who will ever fit me and because it's too fucking painful to be away from her. Sorry, but that alone negated my need to know your whole history. Because it's history, Dad. Those are *your* mistakes, and I'm not going to let them cost me my wif—"

"Say you have babies," Dad interjects, argument ready, "and your mom comes face-to-face with the man she nearly married twenty-six years ago. Do you think we can honestly be comfortable or cordial enough to manage some sort of harmonious fucking relationship?" Dad's chest bounces with incredulity. "Maybe for your sakes, we should. Maybe it's the right thing to do, but it's too much to ask of *all* of us. I've resented that man half my life because of the faraway look I sometimes catch in your mother's eyes. And the worst part is, I don't even fucking know if it's him she's thinking about, or it's just my paranoia. Either way, I don't ask. I can't, and I won't blame her if she is because it's my fault for walking away."

I stand, stunned by his confession. "Then why—"

"Because she loves me *more*, Easton, and always has. And thank God for that." He shakes his head. "For a lot of other reasons too, but this isn't so simple or cut and dried. You say it's history, son, and it is, it *was*, but what you've both done is drag it all right back, front and center." He takes a long drag, hotboxing his cigarette, his exhale clouding the air. "Here's a history lesson," he grits out. "Other than in passing and only vaguely aware of each other before everything went down, we've never crossed paths."

Cigarette pinched between his fingers, he points toward the door. "That's the first goddamned time Nate Butler and I have ever *truly* come face-to-face," he seethes. "You're responsible for that, and if you stay married to her, you'll be forcing us all to the sidelines to avoid each other. Do you want that?"

"That will be your decision."

"No, it was yours. Even your *wife* is aware of it."

Panic seeps in for what's happening behind the villa door. "Dad, I need back in there."

"No. He deserves his time with her."

"He's ripping her apart!"

"He has a right to be furious."

"Do you want me to fucking resent *you*? Because I will if you continue to try to tarnish the thing that matters most to me."

"Yeah, *fuck* your family, right? I just held your mother's hand and watched her check out, but that doesn't matter." Dad's eyes redden as he stares at me like we're strangers. "The whole time I watched her disappear inside herself, I told myself I can get past this with you, because you are what matters most in the fucking world to us both. But if you keep looking at me with zero remorse, I don't know if I'll ever be able to forgive you."

Every word strikes like a blow to the chest as reality sets in deep. No matter how much Natalie warned me of the blowback this would cause, she was all I could see. My willpower wavers slightly as I gaze at my father, who looks like he's aging by the second.

"I fucking love her," I rasp out, "with all that I am. She's everything to me. You want me to give that up?"

"Love isn't selfish," he says evenly. "If there's one thing I learned from waiting on your mother, it's that."

I heard those same words in my vows two nights ago as he speaks up again, his tone a mix of anger and hurt.

"You need to give this thing some space, step back, and let the dust settle. If you don't, you'll implode it from the inside out."

"You don't know anything about us."

"Whose fault is that? And maybe not," he exhales a plume of smoke, "but I've observed enough to know that woman in there, who's wearing your ring, who just took *our* last name, loves and respects her father. And she is crumbling fast because she's being put in a situation to choose between Crowne and Butler. Sound fucking familiar?" He crushes his cigarette beneath his boot. "She wants to keep him in her life, and that's not going to change, Easton. That's never going to change. You may no longer give a fuck about your mother and me—"

"You know that's not true—"

In a flash, I'm nailed to the door, exasperation in his eyes as he searches mine. "Then act like it! Where in the hell is the son *I raised?!* Because from where I'm standing, I see no signs of him!"

"That son is trying to be a husband!" I defend before he releases me and steps back as a long silence lingers between us.

"How could you..." his voice breaks as he lifts tormented eyes to mine.

Chest tightening unbearably, I run my hands through my hair, feeling more helpless than I ever have in my entire life. He's never shown so much emotion in front of me, and the knowledge that I'm the cause of his devastation starts to undo me. "Dad, is Mom," I rasp out. "is she—"

"She's home, but still heavily sedated. Lexi is with her." He chokes before he speaks. "I'm hanging by a thread right now, Easton." An unchecked tear drops to his jaw, and I die a little at the sight of it. "I need you to come home. She's not talking."

"All right, Dad," I say, gripping his shoulder, knowing it's pointless to tell him I'd planned on coming clean the second I got to Seattle. The state of him is enough to pacify me. I'm all too aware this fight between us is far from over. Once his hurt subsides, his anger will come back with a vengeance. That's how we're made because aside from me, when it comes to Reid Crowne, there's only one other thing in his life you can't fuck with, and that's his wife. To him, I committed the only thing he considers a cardinal sin.

"Let's go," I force the words out though they pain me, even if it was our original plan. "Let's go home."

"I'll be on the plane." He nods toward Joel, silent communication passing between them before stalking down the stone-covered path toward the parking lot.

Joel steps toward me. "Easton, I tried, man—"

"It's…fuck it," my shoulders slump, "we'll talk later."

Joel nods, appearing condemned, my emotions running far too rampant to do anything other than shift my focus.

Today, I made my father cry, and it's going to be hard to live past that.

Taking a breath, I knock on the door before entering. Natalie meets me on the other side of it, fully dressed, expression bleak, face thoroughly tear-streaked. I stride into the room to see her purse sitting atop her packed suitcase. The sight of it cracks my chest. Nate stands stock still against a floor-to-ceiling window, scanning our view, hands stuffed in his slacks. Natalie blocks my view of him and reaches for my face, the metal of her wedding ring against my jaw has emotion lodging in my throat as her eyes fill. "I have to go home now, Easton, and so do you."

I nod my head into her palms as the crack in my chest widens.

Natalie turns back to Nate. "Daddy, can you please give us a minute?"

Nate drags a hand down his face as if contemplating giving us that much, and it's all I can do to keep silent before he turns abruptly and I step in his path. He pauses, his body averted along with his gaze as if it's too fucking much to look at me.

"I'm truly sorry for what you're feeling right now, but I do love her, Nate, and I have no intention of letting her go. Can we not do this? For her?" Burning blue eyes the exact color of my wife's meet mine. I recognize so much of Natalie in this man. It's uncanny. Do the parts of my mother that loved Nate Butler exist in me, as well?

I conclude they do, and every other part along with them. It strikes me hard in that moment—even with as many times as Natalie's pointed it out—my mother was going to marry this man. She was going to build a life with him, and maybe he loved her just as fiercely then as I do his daughter now. From my father's confession, my mother still harbors love for him and always will. I try to reason with that man even though he's almost impossible to see. "Please don't make her choose—"

"You have no right to ask me for anything," Nate clips out. With a slight tilt of his head, I see the resolution in his eyes along with his declaration of war. A war he has no fucking intention of losing. We hold eyes a beat longer before he brushes past me.

Biting my tongue, I fist my hands at my sides as Nate slams the door closed with his exit. Nothing I can say to him will make a difference. He wants me gone, and he's hell-bent on making it happen.

I feel the first pang of genuine fear as Natalie stares back at me, looking utterly lost.

"I'm so sorry, baby," I murmur.

"I'm okay," she sniffles. "I mean, I'll be okay. I knew this was going to be bad."

"Not this fucking bad," I murmur, gathering her to me tightly before she pulls away with her question.

"Is Stella—"

"She's home with Lexi. I'm going straight to her."

She nods.

"Dad got in last night. I'm willing to bet he and Joel had it out in a way they never have before to keep him at bay. They're overreacting."

"*Are they*?" She croaks. "Jesus, Easton," she glances toward the closed front door, "I've never seen him like this. Ever."

"He's never going to accept us," I relay, knowing it's the truth of it.

"He's my first love and sadly the only man you'll ever have to compete with for my affection…and it may not seem like it right now, but he's a good and typically more reasonable man. He's just unimaginably hurt." She shakes her head. "It's not just who you are. It's the culmination of everything. The extent of my deception. I did this in an unforgivable way."

"*We* did this. Which he will also hold against me."

Are you going to choose him?

Irony of the worst kind strikes me as I realize Dad's right. History is repeating itself to an extent. Her love and loyalty for Nate is our biggest threat. It's been our only real issue from the start. What's worse is that I can't ask or force her to choose.

"I'll get through to him," she declares, despite a shaky conviction.

But will she feel the same conviction she did two days ago when the dust settles? In a week, a month from now?

Even as my heart demands an answer, I have to believe the ring on my finger is all the assurance I need. I keep the question brimming beneath the surface because if I do ask it right now, it may sharpen the point of a wedge capable of separating us.

"Let me go home. Let me try and figure out a way to get through to him."

I shake my head, unable to let it go yet. "He's not going to let you find one—"

"I love you," she burrows further into me. "I love you. I belong to you. I meant every word I said."

"Then remain my wife," I plea, unable to help myself. "Keep your promises, your vows to me."

"Don't do that," she whispers.

"Okay." I relent easily and pull her to me, and we cling to each other, her tears coming freely as she cries into my shoulder. Even with her close, there's not an ounce of solace to be found. There's no solution, and it irks me that I can't find one. I can't see one, either—at least, not in the near future. The overwhelming feeling hits that in her mind, she might no longer see a future for us on the other side of that door. The thought starts to eat at my resolve to give her the decision to fight alone as we break in each other's arms. Preparing myself for war, I pull back and firmly cradle her face. "It's up to us. It's our fucking choice."

"I know."

"Please don't let go."

"Stop! Easton, please," she cries, "I'm paralyzed!"

My throat burns as my head begins to pound. Every tear gliding down her beautiful face eating me alive. In our shared silence, we fruitlessly search for a potential solution and find none. She's right. For the moment, we're completely gridlocked. If we continue like this—the way things are—we'll destroy our relationships with our parents, eventually destroying us. We can't allow it. Dad's warning and our vows reverberate through me.

Love isn't selfish.

The crux is that I have to share her with a man determined to make that feat impossible. Despite needing her, despite wanting her, despite the pact we made to remain unified, we were just divided by an atom bomb. I have to be the man she needs me to be right now, even as it rips me apart.

With a lump lodged in my throat, I'm reluctant to let her go. Heart splintering in my chest, I tip her chin with gentle fingers. “Okay, baby. Go. We will work this out.”

She looks up at me, a glimmer of hope reflecting back. Cupping her face, I dip and kiss her, our tongues tangling in desperation as I infuse it with all I feel for her. I shake my head when her sobs interrupt it and manage a smile, wiping her tears with my thumbs.

“I love you, my beautiful wife.” Even as I say the words, the ominous premonition threatens again. This time, I can’t shake it, even as the fight continues to build inside me.

Jagged, cutting bitterness takes hold for everything that just went down in the same place we made some of our most significant memories. We tear ourselves apart before she grips her suitcase and shoulders her purse. Our red eyes hold when she glances back at me from the open door of our villa. I fist my hands, forcing myself to remain idle while trying not to let her see what’s raging beneath the surface. She does anyway.

“I love you, Easton,” she declares vehemently. “And despite what just happened, I don’t regret it, and I won’t, no matter what,” she regrips the handle of her suitcase while gliding her thumb over her ring, a new habit that strengthens my pulse just before she turns and walks out of the door.

FIFTY-TWO

We Belong
Pat Benatar

Natalie

Dad slams the garage door behind him as I stalk toward the patio, anxious to escape him, if only for a bit of reprieve. I'm halfway to the sliding back door when he sounds up behind me from the kitchen. "You're suspended from *Speak* until further notice."

My gasp is audible as I turn back to see him bracing himself on our island.

"Daddy," I choke out, "please don't take the—"

"You invaded an employee's privacy," he cuts in, his tone laced with finality. "Not only that, but you completely fucking discarded your ethics to lure a subject into an interview under false pretenses for personal gain." With that, he lifts damning eyes to mine as he lists off the crimes he deems fit for his punishment. "You used the guise of my paper to do it," he exhales as if he doesn't believe the words he's saying, "and annihilated my trust… Do you really believe you deserve a desk chair right now, let alone still be considered the best candidate to take over my life's work?"

I bite my lip as my eyes water and shake my head.

"You can work for your mother until I can trust you to help run my paper again."

"Yes, sir," I choke out before I flee, unable to take another second until I can handle it. I'd suspected it would come to this, but the reality of it is too much to bear. Dad didn't talk to me during the short plane ride home as I stared out the window, stifling tears while replaying the devastation in that villa. Since he arrived in Sedona, I try to shield my occupied ring finger from him while refusing to take it off. The act seems impossible and feels more like a betrayal as my heart continues to mourn for the husband I left behind.

Though he tried, Easton failed to hide his fear, which only made me love him more. As much as I wanted to stay, to convince him we were in this together, he was just as much at a loss as I was. The difference is, Reid was right. I had a clear idea of what we were going to face. It's the aftermath that I could never have prepared for.

As if his silence isn't enough punishment, Dad drove me straight to our family home to face my mother without a single word of warning of what I am in for. Ironically, when I was young, Dad refused to spank me, even at my mother's insistence. He would get me behind a closed door and tell me I better start crying and make it sound convincing. That protection is painfully absent now as dread courses through me. Tears brewing, throat raw, I slide the back door open and jump as my father slams a door nearby before I draw it closed. Glancing around the grounds for my mother, I come up empty and begin the trek to the stable, every step draining more than the last.

Entering the barn, I find her brushing Percy's coat. Like me, Mom always seeks refuge with our horses when she's too stressed or distraught to *people*, so it was a given I would find her here.

The second I near her, I feel the charge shift in the air. Standing beside her outside the stall, I nuzzle a greeting to Percy, waiting for her to speak. Silent, agonizing seconds tick past before she finally does, her eyes trained on Percy.

"Parents live separate existences outside of their children," she admits, her voice coated in irony and edged in bitterness. "We play ignorant to a hell of a lot, for your sake, so you can experience life and learn your own hard lessons. It's one of the hardest parts of being a parent." She swallows. "Your father and I gave you a ton of leeway, because you never—not once—disappointed us, even when you made mistakes." Her eyes sweep over me in obvious devastation. "You have utterly and completely destroyed that faith and trust."

My face heats as fresh tears fill my eyes. "Mom, I—"

"I was in love with another man before I met and married your father. He was fucking beautiful…and good in bed." Shocked by her candor, I'm stunned speechless. "He was everything I thought I wanted, but nothing at all that I needed. Eventually, he took advantage of my love for him and turned me into someone unrecognizable. He used me up before he let me go, and because I loved him so much, I let him."

A tear glides down her face, her voice surprisingly strong when she starts again. "If you're lucky enough, you get a few chances at love in your life, but you don't really get to decide which loves get the best and worst of you…at least at *first.* In hindsight, that's the conclusion I came to. A naïve heart always gets hit the hardest, but a mature heart makes better choices. Some of that comes with age, but a lot of it has to do with the amount of break it can withstand before it wises up. I knew about Stella. I've always known." She resumes running the brush along Percy's thick mane. "He told me their story not long after we met."

The damning curiosity that cost me, keeps me mute.

"I was just as forthcoming with my own story. It was our first bonding point and common ground. We couldn't keep our hands off each other *physically*, but because we were so raw—so straightforward—with each other, we came together as the most honest versions of ourselves. Truth is, neither of us gave a damn if we turned the other off with the bluntest version of our personalities. But that thing we had when we met was so hard to ignore, though it was heavily lust-induced and comforting. Until it wasn't, and when the dynamic changed, it terrified us both—more so him. I don't think he expected to love me. I don't know if I even wanted to love him. We both held out as long as we could. I knew your father was getting nervous that he was starting to fall, and he'd been burned just as badly as I had." She shakes her head as memories surface clearly in her eyes, a soft smile lifting her lips. "Eventually, I acknowledged that I was crazy in love with him, but the truth is, he fell for me *first*. And when we gave in and clicked together, *hearts* and *bodies*, the same way we met, it was the most beautiful thing I've ever experienced." She swallows, and I can feel the anger vibrating from her frame. "I walked down that aisle toward your father without any hesitation in my step. With a mature heart still capable of being set on fire, and I've never once resented Stella or her place in his." She turns to me then, eyes brimming. "At least, not until last night."

"Mom, I wanted to tell you—"

"No, you didn't," she snaps crossly. "It took me a hot second to figure out why you were asking me so many questions about how your father and I got together, about the timeline…until it clicked." I see the utter devastation in her expression as her voice begins to shake. "It clicked that my own daughter questioned the authenticity of my twenty-three-year marriage and believed it to be such a farce that she sought answers from someone other than *me*."

"M-mom, I'm so sorry. I know Daddy loves you. I was just—"

"You had your chance," she interrupts as she aggressively wipes her face with her T-shirt sleeve. "I had to know," she continues. "So I went to your desk, and I found the file and the emails between them," she bites her lip as tears roll freely down her cheeks and she draws her brows. "I can only imagine how inspired you were by them and how boring we must have seemed to you over the years. I felt *everything* between them, right along with you." Her lower lip trembles. "I felt how much he wanted her, loved her. I felt his pain, too," she shakes her head as tears collect and pool at her chin. "It did something to me I can't really explain…but I guess that's why you couldn't either. Why you wouldn't come to me." She turns and faces me fully, the desolation in her expression ripping me apart.

"So now, sweetheart, I guess the question you couldn't bring yourself to ask me is, if I ever feel like your father settled for me? Never. But if the one person who has lain witness to our marriage day-to-day isn't convinced, why should I be?"

"Addie, Jesus Christ, *no*," my father rasps out as we both turn to see him standing at the door of the barn. The thud of the brush on the stable floor clatters as my mother's face collapses in an expression of grief, and she buries her head in her hands. Dad reaches her in a few strides, pulling her into his arms. My mother cries briefly into his chest, and he strokes her hair while whispering into her ear. "No, baby, no. Fuck no. Why didn't you tell me?"

She rips herself from his arms abruptly. "Just…give me a goddamned minute, Nate." Mom's cry echoes into the barn, and she steps out of it.

"Fuck!" Dad shouts, making me jump before raking his hands through his hair. He stares after her for several heart-shattering seconds, looking utterly lost as I clutch my chest.

This isn't happening. This can't be fucking happening.

"I'm…D—"

"Go," he says in a lifeless tone, watching the direction my mother disappeared in. "Go home, Natalie."

FIFTY-THREE

Meet Me Half Way
Kenny Loggins

Easton

Just past the front door, I follow Dad through the living room and down the hall toward the master bedroom. Dad walks in first and motions for me to follow, opening the door. I trail him inside the large room as he pads over to the oversized chair tucked next to a bay window. Mom lays on her side, her head resting against the edge as she blinks vacantly into a view of the thick trees edging our backyard.

Dad kneels in front of her, brushing his lips on the top of her head. "Hey, baby," he murmurs, pulling back. She continues to look through him in the absence of a reply. "He's home," Dad says, my mother's cloudy eyes finally floating in my direction. Dad sighs and stands, walking over to Mom's vanity and pulling a pill bottle from it. He taps one into his hand, but she shakes her head in refusal. "Baby, please. For me," he implores. My gut churns, and his anger toward me becomes incredibly justified—it's like a punch in the gut.

"I don't need it," she says, lifting to sit. "I'm okay."

Dad sighs again, looking down at her helplessly, overflowing me with guilt. He stalks over to me, where I'm standing next to the chair, stopping when we're shoulder to shoulder.

"You come fucking get me as soon as you're done talking. You hear me, son?"

"Dad—"

He jerks his chin. "Do you fucking hear me?"

I nod, feeling every ounce of his resentment. The hurt turned to anger before the wheels touched down in Seattle. The worst part? He was done arguing with me at the hotel. No matter how hard I tried to engage him, he successfully ignored me. For the first time in my life, my father doesn't have my back. I feel that implication everywhere.

Dad pulls the door closed as I look over to my mother, whose eyes are scanning me from head to foot as if I'm not the son she raised, but some mystery to her.

"Mom," I greet softly, walking over and mimicking Dad, kneeling at her chair. "How are you feeling?"

She stares at me, probing. "You really married her?" She asks, barely above a whisper. "You married *Nate's daughter*?"

I nod.

"Easton," she croaks. "You *married* her."

"I love her."

"Why? Why did you marry her?"

"It's the way it happened and has nothing to do with you, Nate, or anyone else."

She moves to stand, a completely different woman than the one I saw mere weeks ago on tour, and begins to pace.

"Please don't get worked up, Mom. Do you need anything?"

"Do I *need anything*?" She parrots incredulously, a little life coming back into her eyes as a storm begins to brew inside them. "I need to wake up from this fucking nightmare." The look in her eyes cuts me to the bone. "How?"

"I don't want to upset you anymore. It's dangerous. Can we table this until you're okay?"

"Absolutely fucking not," she delivers with a targeted bite before reclaiming her seat in the chair. "Start from the beginning."

Three hours later, exhausted and distraught, I walk out of the bedroom in search of my dad. I find him in his studio watching a tape from one of his early concerts. The second I step in, he stands and brushes past me.

"Dad—"

"No."

"She's okay, she's not happy, but she's talking."

He stops a few feet from the door and launches a livid expression at me.

"I practically begged you to come clean with me when I knew you were lying. You could have handled this situation a dozen different ways—better ways—but you didn't fucking respect me, your mother, or our marriage enough to take any one of them, if only to keep her fucking *safe*. I *trusted* you to help me with that."

"Dad, I'm sorry—"

His reply is the slam of his door at his back, which says it all.

FIFTY-FOUR

Ever the Same
Rob Thomas

Natalie

The heart-stopping melody of "Hypnotised" gets cut abruptly from where it plays on my nightstand, adding to the tally that now totals four missed calls. It doesn't include the dozens of others from Holly, Damon, and Rosie, who've also sent me a slew of furious texts that I've left unanswered for now. The overwhelming domino effect that started in Sedona is still scattering around me, even a thousand miles away. Seconds later, a text message pops up on display, and I grab my phone and strain to read it, my eyes swollen.

EC: Damnit, Beauty, answer me.

I haven't heard a word from either parent since I got home yesterday, not that I expected to. With Dad's ban from *Speak*, and the knowledge I'd be working for my mother at Hearst Media, it's up to me to be a responsible adult and figure out the when, where and *who* to report to, but I haven't been able to leave my bed since I got back to my apartment. Easton flew out of Seattle this morning, meeting the band on the road due to his rapidly filling concert schedule. While he has some semblance of normalcy to immerse himself back into, I feel as paralyzed as I was in Arizona.

Opening my laptop had proven to be a mistake. The headlines and social media kickback is a mix of support and condemnation, the latter from women who seem to have banded together and deemed me unworthy of Easton. My initial search led me toward a rabbit hole I quickly opted out of and refuse to feed into. Because I've seen so much internet evil over the years, I've developed a healthy immunity to it. Regardless of the tolerance I've built, it still stings being scrutinized and judged. What confidence I have for the moment has nothing to do with the headlines, but it's being stripped away by the complete lack of communication with my parents—the current state of *their* marriage unknown. The isolation I feel in their silence is both uncomfortable and foreign. It's as if I've cracked vital pieces of a foundation I thought impenetrable. Every step I take moving forward in either direction feels damning, like it could be the misstep that costs me everything.

Even if Easton and I wait for the initial shock to wear off, it seems we've alienated our parents in a way that feels irreparable. Because of that, we may never get an invitation, let alone an open door for conversation.

Reid's scathing glare yesterday continues to haunt me. Upon first sight, it was undeniable just how much of Easton's looks are inherited from his father. Reid's eyes, like my husband's, are both capable of the same type of injury without a spoken word. Like my own father's.

In many respects, so much of our lives mirror the others. Despite the toll, it still seems like kismet.

Not once had I added 'wreaking havoc on my own parents' marriage' into the number of scenarios I'd come up with when picturing this fallout.

What baffles me the most is how the incredible, colorful world Easton and I created together has been muted to a lifeless shade of unknown grey.

Love is meant to be celebrated, not mourned, and it seems mourning has been all I've done—to some degree or another—since I found it with Easton. My cowardice in answering my husband's call is because he wants me to fight. It's a fight I agreed to. A fight I intend on seeing through. But a fight I feel was ripped from me the second I witnessed the detrimental difference between what I imagined the battle with our consequences would be, to the war I fear it will become. It was made abundantly clear to us both in that villa.

Our fathers hate each other.

Maybe to the point our love for the other won't ever matter.

Whatever lies ahead, Easton's worth it. We're worth it, but I don't want him to know just how shaken I am or that he unknowingly broke promises he had no grounds to make.

Loving him, marrying him, cost me everything he assured me it wouldn't—my relationship with my father *and mother*. As well as my desk at the paper and the possibility of losing my future at *Speak* altogether. The question now is the permanence of the damage. Damage I refuse to guilt him for.

My phone vibrates again with an incoming call from **EC**, the song taking me right back to that beautiful place and time I first heard it, stirring some strength from within me. Other than changing my ringtone, I have yet to program his name to something more, to clarify his significance in my life and the happiness it brought me before it was ripped away. Holding the phone in my hand, I take a calming breath before sliding it to answer.

"Beauty?" he gasps, before I get a chance to get a word in.

"I'm here," I murmur.

"Jesus. I'm so fucking pissed at you. How could you not answer my calls?"

"I texted you," I mumble. "It's, it's been a day. I'm sorry," I wipe at my stinging cheek.

"Okay. It's okay," he exhales harshly. "What's happening?"

"How is your mother?" I fire back.

"She's fine," he replies quickly, too quickly.

"Don't lie."

"I'm not, but fine is a stretch. She was still somewhere between furious and devastated when I left this morning, which was an improvement from when I got there. Dad isn't speaking to me."

"Same," I say. "But her health?"

"She's fine, baby. I'm not stretching that truth at all. She didn't stroke and was only sedated as a precaution."

"Jesus, Easton. You never told me about that."

"Because it's been over a decade since her last episode. I didn't think…Jesus, I didn't think…"

"*We* chose not to think. Young, reckless, and naïve," I remind him.

"Please don't try and validate their behavior yesterday. That was not fucking okay. Tell me what's happening."

"I messaged our receptionist, and she told me *Speak* is surrounded by paparazzi, which is expected, so I'm working from home for now."

"Okay, that's not so bad, right?"

"No," I lie. I hate that I am lying, but if I reveal the whole truth and the consequences I'm facing, I have a feeling he'll come straight to me—and so will his temper, which could be even more destructive. His next words only confirm it.

"Come to me, Beauty. Come on tour for a few days. You can work anywhere remotely. I'll fly you here."

"Easton, we have to face this, face *them*. Our parents are integrated closely into both our lives."

"Yeah, well, now I'm beginning to think that's not such a good thing."

"It's a large part of who we are. We can't change that. I don't want to."

"Dad's not touring with us anymore, so it's changing regardless."

"I'm so sorry."

"I'm not. That cord needed cutting a long fucking time ago."

"That's not true. He's your touchstone."

"You're my fucking world."

"You're angry," I know the hurt will soon follow as he speaks up.

"Joel helped me clear out most of my shit this morning. I'm not going back home anytime soon. I wasn't going to anyway, right? Fuck, I can't stand this."

"We just tore our families apart. My mom," I whisper, "she figured out what I was hiding and where to find it. While Dad was on the plane, she went to the paper, searched my desktop, and found the emails. She read them all, and when we got home…it was bad."

Silence lingers before a low, "Fuck."

"I was so wrong, Easton," I manage to keep the shake out of my voice. "She knew about our parents, about Stella, and never once resented her until I dragged her into their past. This could harm my parents' marriage. Maybe it already has."

"I get they have a right to be upset, but they're just as in the wrong as we are, with the way they're reacting. What the hell are we supposed to do?"

"Find someone else to fall in love, marry, and have children with."

"That's your solution?" His tone is biting.

"I have your ring on my finger." I lift the black band into my line of sight, loving the weight of it, its significance—and the memory of his expression when he slipped it onto my finger fills me with warmth. "It means more now than it did when you put it there. I can't stop staring at it. It was the happiest moment of my life."

"We'll have more."

"I know," I do my best to control my involuntary hiccup and fail. A second later, he requests FaceTime.

"Easton—"

"Answer," he snaps. "Answer right *now*. I need to see you."

I accept the request, and Easton appears, the sight of him like a lightning strike to the chest. Was it only a little over twenty-four hours ago we left each other? It feels like an eternity already. Looking as distraught as I feel, hair in utter disarray, he runs his bloodshot gaze along my face. His expression pained, his eyes linger on my raw cheeks before they close. "Fuck this, fuck all of this, I'm coming to you."

"No," I shake my head. "Easton, you know you can't."

"Don't say that to me," he warns.

I slide my finger down the outline of his profile, his eyes boring into mine through the screen.

"We need to give them some time. I haven't had a moment of peace or a chance to breathe since we touched down. Holly, Damon, and the rest of my circle are impatiently lining up to take a crack at me. I've got a lot of damage control to start."

"I'm sorry."

"I'm not," I manage a small smile. "I married an up-and-coming rock legend. I hope you know it will only get crazier from here."

"Beauty," he rasps softly as I heartily drink in every detail of his face.

"We can do this, Easton, for them. With the way we deceived them, especially me, we owe it to them to give them some time to accept us. In the meantime, you have an entire globe to entertain, and I have obligations here. Our plans don't have to change."

"I can come to you between gigs. They don't have to know."

"Sneaking around is what got us into this mess. If we're going to try and repair this, we have to stop deceiving everyone we love. It's the only way it will work."

"So, we don't see each other? No. Fuck no."

"My future at the paper depends on mending my relationship

with him. Running off and doing the same thing that damaged it won't help. You're going to have to trust me, too."

He searches my eyes and seems somewhat satisfied. "Fine. But this can't last long. *We* aren't their decision, baby. Do you hear me? The state of our marriage is not a decision they get to weigh in on. We can't let that happen."

"I know that," I agree, "and we made our decision. They just need time to learn to live with it. We have to be patient."

He opens his mouth to speak, but pauses, instead running a hand over his jaw. "Are we being that selfish, Beauty? Or are they?"

"I think we all are, but they're reeling because we blindsided them. First with the fact *we* exist at all, and then by eloping."

"Doesn't give them the right to…God damnit!" He roars and begins to pace.

"You have to keep your head, Easton. We both do."

"I know," he nods, his exhale ragged. "I'm just…I'm fucking…" He stops pacing and looks pointedly at me. "Don't say goodbye to me, Natalie."

"I think the whole point of this conundrum is that I can't, husband." I lift my finger, and it earns me the slight lift of his lips before he drops his jade gaze and runs his hand through his thick hair again. A knock sounds on the other end of the line before a male voice breaks through, words muffled.

"Everything okay?"

"Yeah, I have to get on stage."

"Shit. Please try to have a good show and not worry so much. The bomb went off, and even through the smoke, I can still see you, Easton. I can still feel you."

"Fuck, I love you." His tone drops heatedly with his next words. "All I want right now is to be back in that bed, pushing inside my filthy little wife, and making her come."

I close my eyes and physically feel the fullness of him inside of me just before it's replaced with ache. "I want that too, so much."

"I'll deliver on that, but Beauty," he eyes me warily, dread setting in with his abrupt change in tone. "They want to add a few more dates to the end of the tour. That will have us booked through most of fall."

"I'm not surprised in the least," I say truthfully. "I'm so proud of you."

"I don't know what to do."

"What do you want to do?"

"I want to play."

"Then get to work, *rock star*."

"I want my wife more."

"You can have both. The plan stays the same," I reiterate. "I'm not going anywhere, and I'm behind you all the way. I'm *with you* on this."

Soft eyes caress me as relief covers the rest of his features. "I needed this before I could go out there. I needed you. Answer my fucking calls, especially when it's important like this, okay? I get that you can't sometimes, but don't pull that shit again, Natalie, or I *will* come to you."

"*Bet*?" I manage another smile.

"This is serious."

"I'm aware, and I won't. I'm sorry."

"I love you, Natalie Crowne," he rasps softly as I close my eyes before he ends the call.

FIFTY-FIVE

No One
Alicia Keys

Natalie

Sitting on the other side of the booth from two pairs of affronted eyes after long hours of confession, I suck down the rest of my third margarita as Damon and Holly process.

"So..." Damon draws out as he reclines in the booth. I briefly admire him as he gets lost in his train of thought and seems at a loss for words. Hair trimmed perfectly to his signature quarter-inch, skin a beautiful shade of light mocha, honey-colored, sweetheart eyes cloaked with thick, dark lashes which naturally curl up. The eyes mixed with the cut cheekbones and jawline makes him the most lethal of combinations. He truly is the most gorgeous man. His build is no less than perfect, as he sits across from me wearing a perfectly cut, tailored suit that only accentuates the hours he spends working on his body. His father and mine have been best friends for decades, and though I see him as more of a brother, there's no denying his masculine beauty. No one can. Holly turns to him in question and gets equally as distracted as he scratches his jaw before finally speaking again. "That's just...," he shakes his head. "Can you repeat all that?"

"Which part?" I scoff.

Holly leans forward, resting her elbows on our table—a table the three of us claimed years ago when we decided to make this one of our rituals. "And you didn't think you could trust *us*?"

"I explained that part to you. Easton—"

"I get it," Damon says.

"Well, I fucking don't," Holly quips back. "We tell each other everything. At least we used to. I don't even know what's going on in either of your day-to-day lives anymore, and frankly, I feel like I'm the only one who even cares."

"I'm sorry," I say for the tenth time. "We didn't even know what it would become until we did, and from there, it went *whirlwind*."

"A whirlwind that included a wedding we both missed," she hisses.

"Please," I say hoarsely.

Damon sharply scolds her in name alone. He's been surprisingly calm, considering he hated my ex and had no issue speaking his mind about him.

"I need you two to do the impossible and forgive me quickly. Please. I'm…"

Damon leans forward and takes my hand over the table. "We're here, Nat." He turns to Holly, brow cocked.

"I'm irrationally angry," she sighs, "but I'll let it go for now. But just for now. But you're going to catch hell later. Probably some side jabs for years."

"I'll take it," I say. "I'll take them all. I think you two are the only people in my life who are on speaking terms with me."

"So what now?" Damon asks.

"I don't know. Easton and I have our plans, but as far as my parents go, I'm too much of a coward right now to call or message either of them. I'm just going to show up at the Hearst Media's satellite office tomorrow and hope I'm expected by upper management. I know I'm being a coward, but I just need a little time to get my strength back."

"I can't believe Uncle Nate was engaged to Stella Crowne. Wow."

"You and me both," Damon says thoughtfully. "I can't see them meshing." Damon grins, "But it's not like I can imagine you meshing with Easton, either."

"Well, they did, and we sure as hell did," I say, holding up my ring finger. "And it was perfect until we got pulled into the undertow."

"But you and Easton are okay?" Damon prompts.

I nod, for the most part believing it to be true.

"You're not going to tell him what Uncle Nate's doing?" Holly asks.

"Not now. I think that will infuriate him to the point he comes here for another confrontation with Dad. I don't want to risk it."

"Do you think your parents are okay?" Holly asks as the idea of them still being at odds rips into current wounds.

Damon says, "They'll be fine."

Just as I say, "I don't know."

Damon drains his beer and pushes his plate out of the way, leaning forward, commanding my attention. "Listen to me. We're here for you, and we're not going anywhere. You can trust us, and you should've. Respect to your husband—and I get what he was saying—but this is us, and we've been around long before he fucking got here. So, from now on, we're all going to do better, no matter how busy our lives get," Damon turns pointedly to me. "Or who we decide to fucking marry in secret, which warrants a phone call at the very least." He pulls the sleeve from the cuff of his jacket. "We're all going to be better."

I nod, and so does Holly.

"Good, that's settled," he pulls his wallet from his back pocket.

"Tonight's on me."

He rolls his eyes. "You don't know if you even have a job."

"And we both know you're not taking a dime from your husband," Holly fact checks right after. Which is the absolute truth.

My heart lights with hope as I look between them. "So, do you forgive me?"

"For lying to us for four months and eloping with the world's hottest rock star?" Holly condemns before she and Damon look at each other, their stare off resulting in a shared grin. Ironically, while *I'm* being lectured on transparency, these two idiots are clearly in love and doing a shit job of hiding it. Pushing away my margarita, I deny myself another sip to keep from blurting it out as Damon turns back to me.

"We do, but if you ever fucking ice us out again when shit such as this is going down," he warns as he tilts his head toward Holly. "I'm going to let her kick your ass."

"I've been working out, too," Holly adds as Damon grins over at her in adoration.

"I'm sorry," I swallow over the lump in my throat, "I love you guys."

"We love you," Damon softly reassures.

"You too," Holly reciprocates. "Now, tell me about Dallas again."

"Holly," Damon cuts through. "Once was plenty."

"Not for me," she props her hand under her chin, looking glorious in a black sheath dress, makeup flawless, and sporting a sleek, high ponytail. "I love it when a man has enough balls to lay himself on the line for a woman."

Damon lifts his beer to our waitress as Holly steals a glance at him.

It's clear by her expression she thinks he's playing immune. My guess is he's heard every word.

Three days later, my mother rides alongside me on her temperamental Haflinger, Daisy Buchanan. She named her after the heroine in *The Great Gatsby*, one of her favorite books, despite my father poking fun at her for her depressing preference for romance classics. Unsurprisingly, *Wuthering Heights* takes the number one spot. She trots next to me along the fence after having greeted me at the front door to ease my concern with a quick, "I sent your father for beers with Marcus. It's just you and me tonight."

She'd texted me to come home for a ride after another day at my new but temporary office. Despite wanting to avoid my father—something I never thought I'd do—I immediately accepted the invitation, hope lighting my chest. I'd even gone so far as to call Easton to hear Stella had called him once too. Though their conversation was short, it is a start we both celebrated with quiet smiles.

"Mom," I speak up, "I'm so sorry I hurt you this way. My actions were selfish, but I wasn't thinking…and I know I owe Dad his own apology, as well—if he'll ever be receptive to it. But I want you to know, I do respect you immensely. I respect your marriage to Dad and what you've built together, now more than ever."

She rides for a few seconds before turning to me. "I'm still ridiculously angry and disappointed with how you handled it all, and I will have to work hard to forgive you, but I'll get there. Your father will come around eventually…but Natalie," she shakes her head.

"I know, Mom. Trust me, I know."

"He finally told me everything that happened in Sedona."

"Is that why you texted?"

"Again, I'm still pissed at you to the point I might get hostile." She gives me a stern side-eye, her curly dark hair whipping around her face. "But I love you too much to let you sit at home alone a day longer thinking the things you were."

"Thank you, I've been," I shake my head, refusing tears. "Are you two…" my question lingers in the air briefly.

"We're still fighting, but for different reasons than you may think." She turns to me, her voice unapologetic, "But just to be clear, it's *our* fight, and you have no place in it."

"Okay."

She averts her gaze to the large line of oak trees that edge the back of our property. "We'll be fine. Hell, we already are." A loaded smile lifts her lips. "Sometimes fighting can be really good for a marriage."

I can't help my smile. "*Really*?"

"You'll learn soon enough." With that, she taps Daisy with her heels in command and shoots forward, and I laugh before prompting Percy to catch up.

We ride hard for a short while before trotting along the fence to cool our horses down.

"How are you liking it at Hearst?" I glance over at her, and she beats me to the punch in reply. "Yeah, I thought as much."

"It's not that."

"I think we've had enough lies between us."

I nod. "You know you shocked the shit out of me the other day. You've never been so brutally honest when we talked in the past—but I loved it."

"Can't say that I hated it either, just the way it came about. The good part is we get to share a little more in that way. For the most part, you're all grown up, now."

We share a smile. "In the spirit of full disclosure then, I wouldn't say I hate it. But yes, I'd rather be at the paper."

Seeming satisfied, she nods as I take in her profile, my perception of her different now while I study her with new eyes.

"You know, I made peace with it when you were just a tiny thing that the two of you would be closer than we would. It's just the way it is." She glances at me. "But I know you far better than you think I do, just by the way you are with him and from the conversations your father and I have."

Tears threaten again as I battle them back.

"I know which parts of you I can take credit for and which I can't.

I raised you right along next to him. Hearst women are *strong*, Natalie, and you might feel a little weak right now in finding your footing, but you inherited a hell of a lot of the fight in you from me, so don't go thinking otherwise." She lightly pulls on her reins to slow Daisy to a stop and dismounts. I do the same as we begin to guide Percy and Daisy toward the barn. "The stubborn streak inside you, I'll grant that as *his gift to you*. It's infuriating, but we'll figure it out. Now that you're fully aware your own parents aren't always capable of acting age-appropriate and make rash decisions, let's skip the bad parts for now." She turns to me, her expression surprisingly receptive, an inquisitive look on her face. "So let's go uncork a bottle so you can tell me the good."

Unable to help myself, I pull her to me, tears of relief escaping me as she holds me tightly to her. "Thank you, Mom."

FIFTY-SIX

Mayonaise
The Smashing Pumpkins

Easton

Strapping my Stratus around me, I adjust it as the cheers ring out in encouragement. I muster a smile I don't feel in response, because tonight, I feel a disconnect, not from the music but from those I'm playing for. Far too into my own head, I've tried for the entirety of the show to get there with them and failed. Stepping up to the mic now, frustrated, I even myself out, scanning the packed three-story bar before I speak.

"Thank you," I say, feeling my typical 'time for one more' spiel disingenuous, so I don't bother with it. "This is for my wife."

A roar filters through the space as ache-filled electricity hums through my veins. LL starts the repetition of the fill chords of "Mayonaise" just before I start to pluck in the whisper of my own, milking the notes while feeling them festering inside me. Using every bit of my reserves, I tap into my frustration while coated in my exertion. At the peak of momentum and in perfect time, Tack drops the beat, and Syd nods to me, joining in on cue. The heavy guitar-filled melody fuels my contempt as I start to recite lyrics about someone who believes themselves cursed by the people closest to them, attempting to strip away all hope and happiness. At least that's the way I'm interpreting it for myself—because for me, and where I'm at mentally—it's all too fucking fitting.

Glancing over to the side of the stage, I envision my wife in place of a shadow currently taking up residence where she belongs. My slow leaking destruction bleeds through my voice to those witnessing my slow implosion. My plea into the mic for something to give, for things to be different, for a change in the stagnant water I've been treading. Screeching into the mic, I plea to be heard and understood by those who know me best, by those refusing me everything I'm begging for.

Unleashing my anger fully, I run the guitar up and down the solo and turn to address my mother just after, every lyric following the electric riff meant for her. Her lips part on an audible gasp I can't hear before I turn back to address the swaying crowd, confessing the hell I've been forced to dwell in since Sedona. Fusing myself with the music, I allow those few minutes to break apart, for her, for myself, and for the man intent on keeping us both in purgatory.

My resentment now borders on hate for Nate Butler, because I haven't seen my wife in forty-three fucking days.

So on stage, I rage against him.

Rage against the circumstances in which we found each other.

Rage against the way I feel daily about her continued absence.

Rage against her inability to wage a war she won't allow me to fight.

Rage against the promises we're breaking every day we remain divided.

I rage against it all until the lights go dark. Exhausted as the applause explodes throughout the club, I exit the stage without a single ounce of relief. Joel meets me at the side of the stage, reading my mood in silent support as we walk toward the back of the club. In the next second, a tropical scent wafts into my nose as I'm gripped by the neck, and lips that don't belong to my wife smash into mine. Pushing the woman who accosted me away by the shoulders, I assess her and jerk my chin. "Not fucking cool."

Clearly drunk, she stares back at me with wide blue eyes, on the verge of speaking before Joel gently takes her by the arm and away from me, handing her over to security.

Joel joins me again as I stalk toward the dressing room, bypassing everyone, including my mother. Slamming myself inside, I fume at the fact that my wife is no longer the last woman to kiss me and that security was stolen from me. In the next breath, I begin to wonder if she'd even fucking care.

You can always find me,
in your own story
Lost and found
Our whispered confessions
A thousand hours apart
For a few seconds longer

Found then lost,
Remember our story,
Our screaming secret
Every memory pushed inside you
A thousand hours apart
For a few seconds longer

Replay our past
To destroy seconds of theirs
Erase their memories
To consider our future
A thousand hours passed
To earn a few seconds longer

You could have found me
In those thousand hours
Waiting
for just a few seconds longer
choose me

I write out the last of the lyrics in my notebook as the band bustles around me. Feeling the burn of the last two words, I take a numbing swig of beer before staring at my phone screen in indecision. In the same time zone, a state away, I note it's 1 a.m. in Austin, and all I want to do is talk to my wife, who is, no doubt, fast asleep. I pull up her last text.

Wife: I hope you have a good show. I love you.

Even though the message is sincere, it rings hollow for me. The chaos in the room quiets briefly, the sudden stillness in the air credited to my mother, who's standing in the doorway. Throats clear as she makes a beeline for me. One of our roadies lifts his chin in question, and I nod. In fast response, he starts evacuating the room, as if her sudden appearance wasn't enough to do so. In seconds, the noise outside the door is the only sound in the room as her presence batters me with hurt.

"Really fucking subtle, son," she says, her voice shaking.

"Wasn't meant to be," I mutter, unsure of how to react to this new dynamic and exhausted from the struggle of trying to figure it out.

"I can't believe you just walked past me," she takes a seat next to me on a long, black leather couch. Turning toward her, I feel the same animosity that's been brewing between us, which never existed before. "Hey, Mom, good to see you. What are you doing in New Orleans?" she snarks before continuing. "Good question. Well, the truth is I came to see my kid play," she spouts sarcastically, "since he hasn't answered a single call from me in a week." She tilts her head in taunt. "Where's your father, you ask? Well, he's currently at the hotel because he packed a fucking bag and flew halfway across the country only to take a stand by not showing up, even though he's dying to see you play. So, on principle alone, he's refused to accompany me because you two fumbling idiots are determined to be the death of me. Enough of this shit," she barks, "Easton, I'm serious."

"What bothers you more now, Mom? That you can no longer order me around or that you can't control my emotions?" I keep focused on the beer cap I'm flipping between my fingers.

"That's completely unfair. We both realize and accept you're your own man. Before, you were apologetic, and now this icy shoulder? What point are you trying to make? Tell me, Easton, I need to know."

"I'm not changing my mind. I'm not divorcing her. You can't just snap my happiness away like it's a toy I'm no longer allowed to play with."

"We reacted and overreacted the way we did because it was warranted.

We never asked you to end your marriage. And where is *she*, son? This woman you chose to give yourself to, knowing the damage it would do to your family and hers?"

I lift my eyes to hers.

"My *wife* is currently trying to salvage her relationship with her father, trying to earn back his trust. Meanwhile, we're both trying to work around all of your fucking collective tantrums and mood shifts. So, where is my wife? In hell, that's where she is. Blaming herself, punishing herself, because she doesn't feel like she deserves happiness with me, because *your fucking husband* made her feel like she didn't—along with her own fucking father, who still doesn't!"

The first three weeks, we threw ourselves into work, her getting ready for the thirtieth edition of the paper while planning the party to honor him. Instead of rewarding her, Nate's made it nearly impossible for us to connect. Filling her schedule, he's sent her as a liaison for Hearst Media to every party, every convention, and every *thing* imaginable on the East Coast to keep her from joining me on tour. What's worse? She's allowed it. His ploy to keep her away from me, a calculated chess move as he forces her to pay penance for loving me. As of a week ago, she's home. But, he's kept her scrambling to keep up with his demands, all the while keeping her locked out personally. I have no doubt that right now, she's only placating her father to try and get back to me while he does everything he can to hasten her future without me—continually driving an axe between us. Something is going on that I can't place. At this point, I think we're being polite to protect the other from what's truly happening in each of our lives. Her more so than me since my accumulating resentment is the only thing I'm withholding.

She's hiding, and there's not a fucking thing I can do about it—or I might lose her. Even as we make time to keep connected—every chance we get—I feel the drift, and because she's allowing it, I'm losing wind.

I can't fight alone. We've fought twice since we got married, and both times ended with her tears and my murmured apologies—even if I felt justified in my anger. She hasn't so much as tried to come to see me because she believes she can still get through to him.

Every day I ache for her, and every single day she assures me of her returned affection. Though I believe her, I need something more because I feel like I'm swinging in the dark. Thirty years ago, Nate rivaled my father for the affection of the woman he held most dear. History is repeating itself now, and he's doing it again, but this time he's *winning.*

"She's coming," I inform my mother. "And when she does, it will be *your* choice to make."

"This is supposed to be the happiest time of your life," Mom says, shaking her head, her expression bleak. "I want that for you so much."

"Yeah, I believe it's called the honeymoon phase." I finally look over to her. "Do you know my wife didn't recognize my body on FaceTime the other night because Benji's been to two shows and inked me, and I forgot to mention it. Does that sound like a good honeymoon to you?"

"I'm talking career-wise."

"Having a blast," I say dryly, tugging on my beer. "Can't you tell?"

The silence that follows cuts us both as her expression falters and her eyes fill with tears.

"Mom, please don't get upset."

"What the hell am I supposed to do? I have no idea what to do here."

"My fight is with Dad and with my wife's father. I'm not in a good place." I roll my head against the back of the couch. "Go back to your hotel, okay? Get some sleep, and we can have breakfast before we roll out tomorrow."

"You're pissed at me, too, and taking it out on your father because you're scared of putting my health at risk. You've made a bad habit of doing that over the years. He's not your enemy."

"You always hurt the ones you love, right?" My chuckle lacks all humor.

"Easton, you have to understand that what you did was..." she shakes her head.

"What? What was it, Mom? Because you never fell in love and made a single impulsive decision?"

"Jesus, Easton. Do you think I ever anticipated *this*? There's no fucking handbook for this. I'm sorry. The very last thing I ever wanted was for you to marry the daughter of my ex-fiancé."

"And why is that?" I vent. "It's not like I ever had the full story. I asked you months ago, and you skirted it. You couldn't even say his name. I asked Dad the same. He did the same shit. Turns out, it wasn't just me. You lied to the world, letting them think you and Dad lived out some romantic rock and roll fairytale. You totally omitted Nate. No wonder he hates you both."

She clamps her hand over her mouth and speaks through it. "I can't believe you just said that to me."

"He shaped you as a writer, did he not?"

"Absolutely," she says. "So, you're blaming me for his reaction, but not your own actions?"

I grip the leather of the couch, my gaze dropping. "I blame myself for thinking our parents give enough of a fuck about our happiness to act like mature adults."

"That's not fair."

"Maybe not," I swallow back my drink. "But I don't see what's so damned impossible that the four of you can't get over it, so my wife and I can move on with our lives."

She drops her head and sighs before opening her purse, pulling out a large bound script, and tossing it on my lap.

"I omitted Nate because my agent reached out, and he wanted no part of it."

I lift it to see the title. *Drive.*

My mom did write the fucking book, and you weren't in it.

Only the version you know of.

"You really wrote a book about them both? It wasn't just you and Dad?"

She nods.

"And Dad read this?" I hold it up.

"Yes, he did. He wanted to."

"Jesus."

"Son, I love you more than any soul on earth. I carried you in my body for nine grueling months. Your father and I gave you everything we could as parents. I'll freely admit that you're wise well beyond your years, and while you can write and sing a thousand songs about your *perception* of things, that's all it is right now—your *perception.* Until you've actually lived through it, that's all it will ever be. All I'm hearing right now is a rant about your *perception* of a person's life to the *person* who actually fucking *lived it.* Experience is what truly shapes the soul, your *own* experience, and you haven't gained enough or lived enough yet to fully form yours. So don't tell me what I lived through and what you think you fucking know. I don't give a damn about *your perception* of one of the hardest trials of *my life.* But if you want insight into what can *never* be fully experienced through words alone, that's the full story. You want the truth. It's all there. There's your option to know exactly why the three of us—Nate included—have reacted the way we have and why we don't mention the other in passing. It's not because we hate each other, and it's not because of *one thing* that happened. It's a culmination of things that fucking hurt." She lifts her chin in defiance. "So before you preach another word to me, know what the hell you're talking about. Now you can invade my privacy the way Natalie did and no longer blame me for keeping my fucking personal life my own."

She furiously wipes a tear from her face as I sit stunned, and shame sets in.

"Do you think I'm not sorry for hurting you and Dad? Because I am, but this," I pick up the book, "is your past."

"My past turned into your future. Jesus, you told me your own wife tried desperately to warn you, but you're still dismissive. You aren't this selfish, Easton. You're just too wrapped inside your pain to realize what a shit you're becoming. Look at me, son," she orders, and I lift my eyes to hers.

"Twenty or thirty years from now, let's say Natalie isn't a part of your life anymore. Do you think, for one second, your experiences and love for her, your recollection of the way you're feeling right now, the bitterness, the ache, won't be bittersweet? Especially if you're forced away from each other *permanently* with as much as you love her *right now*? You're *living* the love story that will help shape your soul, Easton."

"So why choose Dad?" I seethe. "If you harbor so much lingering love for another man?"

"Stop," she says. "That's enough. You want an explanation?" She gestures toward the manuscript. "There it is. That book is a product of the peace I made letting Nate go, along with an affirmation of all our decisions. Which were the right ones. I have never, not once, regretted it."

"Might want to let Dad know. He thinks you still think about Nate."

Mom pauses. "Well, I did. It's natural. But I hadn't in a very, very long time—until you married his daughter."

She stands and shoulders her purse. "You're everything I hoped for. You're all of it. You're the best mix of your father and me, and I couldn't be more proud of the man you're becoming. But as cocksure as you're acting, you have plenty of growing up left to do. We, as your parents, deserve better, and your *wife* does too. You want to be a married grown-up, fine, *grow the fuck up*. Your father and I aren't at fault here, and I'm done trying to bridge this. This is a conscious decision you made, knowing the hurt it would cause. Try and simplify love all you want, Easton, but you're still just a punk-ass twenty-two-year-old kid. Try living with the intensity of the love you feel for *years,* only to lose it to another you feel just as much for, and then come to me and tell me how fucking simple it is. You made a decision, son. Now you have to live with it."

Tossing my bottle, it shatters against the wall as I stand and face off with my furious mother. "Okay, Mom. I'll stop loving her. I'll start fucking groupies and live an empty existence like the little rock star you raised me to be. Maybe I'll come home addicted to something fun for Christmas."

The slap across my jaw echoes throughout the room as her eyes spill over. She's at the door when I catch her.

"Mom." I circle her waist and pull her body to me as it shakes with her cries. "Please, Mom. I'm sorry. Fuck, I'm so sorry. I'm sorry."

Sniffing, she turns and hugs my waist, holding onto me just as tightly. "I see and feel how much you're hurting," she cries, "but I can't control how everyone else feels. No matter how much I want to ease your pain, I can't make this go away."

Terrified I've pushed her too far, I run a soothing hand down her back.

"I'm sorry, I am," I say. "I didn't mean it."

"Some of it you did, and that's okay. Jesus, I feel so helpless right now. My baby's hurting, my husband is hurting, I don't know how to fix this."

"We'll figure it out, Mom, we will. I just…" I swallow. "I love her." My eyes burn. "I can't stop it, no matter who it hurts."

She nods and pulls away, cupping my burning jaw. "Crownes don't know how to love halfway, do they?" I shake my head. "God, baby. What if she breaks your heart?"

"She already is," I say. "She doesn't realize she's choosing him."

"And you're sure giving her the choice is the right thing?"

"She has to be the one to make it, or else she'll blame me."

She nods. "Please, please, beautiful boy. Please don't shut me out anymore. Easton, I miss us."

"Me too," I confess honestly. "I'll come by the hotel tomorrow morning and talk to Dad, okay?"

"Really?"

"Yeah," My voice cracks as my eyes continue to burn. "I promise."

The truth is I'm lost. I need him more now than I have in some time.

"Okay," she sniffs. "Well, I'm sorry I broke up the party."

"I'm not," I say. "I'm glad you came to the show."

"You're incredible, Easton," she laughs. "Even when you're bitching your mother out on stage."

We share a smile.

"You sure you don't want to talk some more? Are you hungry?" She asks, reading my expression as I duck away.

"No, I'm going to head back to the hotel, get a run in, and some sleep."

"Okay," she kisses my jaw before stepping away. "I love you."

"Love you, too."

She gives me a hint of a smile. "It was an incredible show tonight."

"Did you feel my disconnect?" I ask as she opens the door. She pauses and turns back to me.

"Only because I know you. But they had no idea, I promise."

"I don't want to act out there," I say.

"That's something for your dad to help you with."

"Point taken. I promise I'll be there tomorrow."

"I'm so proud of you, baby."

The sentiment rings in my chest. "I feel it," I say honestly.

Freshly showered and back at the hotel, I flip open the manuscript I tucked in my messenger bag and only get a few pages in before closing it. Even now, I don't want to know Nate Butler's fucking love story with my mother.

I don't want to know the reasoning behind the man currently dividing and conquering my wife and me. I don't want to fucking empathize with *him* or understand his side in any way.

Furious with thoughts of this going on much longer, I push send and lift the phone to my ear before it goes to voicemail.

"This is Natalie Butler. Leave a message."

The line beeps.

"It's Crowne. Your name is Natalie Crowne," I snap as the accumulating acid starts to pour out of me, "or did you fucking forget?"

FIFTY-SEVEN

Unsteady
X Ambassadors

Natalie

"Your name is Natalie Crowne…or did you fucking forget?" I replay the message Easton left last night, hearing his anger and frustration over the distance I've allowed between us. The last six weeks have been hell on earth for me, personally and professionally. On the rare occasions we've seen each other since Sedona, I clung to the hope that my father would finally look at me instead of *through me,* and I am always disappointed. Whenever our paths do cross, it's primarily thanks to my mother's attempt to bridge the gap. Even so, he remains unreceptive. Dad still hasn't called me back to my desk at the paper but instead has kept me scrambling to keep up with his demands. Demands I've met to keep him pacified while trying to reestablish some of the lost trust. A confrontation is coming and soon, because after the anniversary party wraps, I'm going to try and mend my rapidly deteriorating relationship with my husband.

Exiting the stretch limousine I commissioned for the night, I stand waiting in my parents' driveway in a glittering, deep jade gown my mother had her stylist choose for me. The neckline runs snugly against my collarbone, while the back rests at the curve just below the small of it. It had to be taken in a little last week due to the grief-stricken pounds I've lost and kept off. It's both elegant and sexy—her style—and it's only now, as it glitters in the setting sun, that I start to appreciate it.

After the glam squad left my apartment, I couldn't muster a single reaction other than feeling like a glossed-up lie—a living, breathing *expectation* of my father. That seems to be the sum of my value now, at least when it comes to Nate Butler. Though I argued the same point with Easton recently, it isn't the case. I've made the choices I have in recent weeks to be at my father's side in an effort to fight for my future and his legacy. It feels like the aspect of choice got lost somewhere in my neck-breaking efforts to appease him. I can't keep allowing him to dangle the paper over my head while keeping me at arm's length—in exile.

In truth, I'm absolutely devastated and utterly shocked by my father's behavior.

Dad's done nothing to guard me from his anger. He's not only furious about my part in the deception with Easton, but for hurting my mother and indirectly causing a small rift between them that could have cost him dearly. Even though they seemed to have bounced back, he refuses to truly look at me. More deplorably, I've allowed it. Allowed him to continue to order me around like I'm a grounded teenager instead of a nearly twenty-three-year-old woman capable of making her own life choices. But the truth is, I knew this is what loving the man I chose—marrying the man I chose—would cost me.

At this point, I feel I've paid enough.

Even if I'm justified in a lot of ways for my feelings, I also damned myself because I miss my father. His absence continues to rob me of security and peace of mind. I miss our easy camaraderie and our stress-releasing walks to the bar we used to frequent near *Speak* after meeting excruciating deadlines. What I miss most are the moments that followed as we shared beers chattering bluntly, more like friends than father and daughter.

All traces of that dynamic are painfully absent, as my need to please him and get back into his good graces overshadows my relationship with Easton. I've been put in the impossible position to try and please the two men I love the most—and like I predicted—I feel like I'm losing no matter what steps I take and in what direction. The only assurances that we have a chance at moving past this come from my mother. She has tried her best to play referee between us, despite the utter disruption in our lives that my marriage has caused.

It's only when I speak to Easton—when I soak in his face on the screen, evident with the love I reflect—that the cost feels like less of a burden. But in the last week, I can feel Easton's resentment starting to overflow. It's apparent my neglected marriage needs nurturing, and I know the only way to try to keep it together is to fly to Easton's side or allow him to come to mine.

As luck would have it, tonight is all about the other man in my life. A celebration of Dad's contribution to media, his accomplishments, and the empire he built in our corner of the universe. A universe he's silently and painstakingly pointed out exists without a place for Easton Crowne.

With every day that ticks by, it's become clear Easton is right. My father is at war with my husband, and it's tearing us apart.

My bitterness toward Dad continues to build as I continue to wait next to the limo, too timid to walk through the front door of my own family home due to his ill-treatment.

Ironically, Dad insisted we arrive at the gala as a family, which for the moment, also feels like a lie. As I try to temper myself and hold it together, Dad exits the house looking gorgeous in a perfectly fitted tux with my mother in tow. Mom approaches, looking stunning in a glittering black gown that hugs her tiny frame. Her freshly colored, curly, dark hair is pulled up and pinned, her makeup flawless. "*Baby*, it's chilly out here. Why didn't you come inside?"

Because it's even colder inside.

"Mom, you look…incredible," I dodge her question. She reciprocates by side-stepping my compliment.

"And you look absolutely gorgeous, my sweetheart. The dress is perfect on you. Do you like it?"

"Love it, thank you," I reply, grateful she went to the trouble to dress me. Most days, I feel like I'm on autopilot, simply going through the motions. Mom has tried her best to help me through it, taking long rides with me and simply listening. She's been amazing in the boss department as well. Though my schedule has been grueling, if I wasn't being constantly tasked, I'm not sure I would know my own direction. Inside I'm still fighting for the woman I dreamt I'd be—the one with her head straight and ever-changing goals within reach. Every day, I'm fighting for the bride I became, blooming rapidly under my husband's loving gaze.

I glance over to Dad as he locks their front door, and Mom's gaze trails mine. It's then I feel the shift in energy. Seeing the light in her eyes start to dim, I muster a smile. "It's going to be an incredible night."

"No more bullshit," she reminds me, warily eyeing Dad as he approaches.

"It will be," I assure. In reply, she dips her chin noncommittally. Dad reaches us at the end of the walk before wordlessly and gently ushering Mom into the car. Hoping to create a small window of truce for tonight, for both their sakes, I speak up.

"Hey, Daddy?"

Dad tenses before dismissing the driver, who's patiently holding the open door of the limo. When the driver's out of earshot and Dad finally lifts his violet-blue eyes to mine, I find myself on the receiving end of a tattered stare. Inside it, it's all there—the anger, the hurt, the betrayal, and the toll it's taking.

"I just wanted to say congratulations," I continue, "in case I didn't get a chance to later." He gives me a brief dip of his chin and stands in expectation, refusing to see all I've done to resume the role of the responsible adult he raised. Even as he stands impatiently waiting for me to join my mother in the car, I soak in his expression, knowing that no matter how much he's accomplished or how well pleased he is by the occasion, I might have ruined this milestone for him.

"Daddy, I-I'm sorry I hurt you," I stutter out sincerely. His expression falters slightly before his eyes glaze over.

Now is not the time, Natalie.

"Okay. That's all I wanted to say." Unable to handle any more of his disappointment, I slide into the long leather bench seat opposite Mom. Averting my eyes from hers, I opt to stare out of the window as Dad slides in beside her. Within a minute of the car speeding toward the downtown hotel, a motor whirs, and I glance over to see my mother closing the privacy partition before addressing both of us.

"Okay, enough is fucking enough. I don't care what occasion this is, Nate. Your daughter is hurting, you're hurting, and you're hurting *her*, and if you continue to ignore her pain, you won't forgive yourself, and I won't forgive you either. Look at her, damnit!"

"Mom—" I say, as Dad bites out at the same time.

"Addie, now is not the time."

Clearing his throat, he unbuttons his jacket as Mom turns to him, digging her heels in.

"It's the perfect time," she snaps. "How in the hell are we supposed to celebrate anything as a *family* when we have this much space between us? A space you continue to add to every time you ignore her pain for yours."

Dad bites his lower lip as Mom turns and commands my attention. "Look at me, Natalie."

Eyes stinging, I look over to my mother. "Your father and I are okay, and we will continue to be okay. We've been through a lot. That's marriage, but this..." she gestures between us, "this is unacceptable."

Dad stares out the window, his frame vibrating with emotion before she speaks again. "Have I ever told you what your father said the minute I placed you in his arms?"

She doesn't wait for me to answer as Dad rasps out a low, "*Addie.*"

"He said, 'I've found the perfect love.'"

A strangled noise escapes Dad as his eyes redden, and I cup a hand over my mouth. She turns back to Dad, addressing him as if they're alone.

"What in the hell are you doing, Nate?" Her voice shakes with emotion. "I did my part, but you've been molding our little girl since the first minute you held her, shaping her into a tiny replica of you. She's just as willful and intelligent and loves just as fiercely as you do." Dad grips his knees, his knuckles whitening. "But the more you punish her," my mother urges, "the harder you make it for her to believe that *I* come in *second.*"

Dad whips his head toward her as she grips his hand and runs her finger over his wedding ring, "But only to *your daughter.*"

Raw ache seeps through his gaze as he looks over at her, and she speaks up in a plea for both of us. "Look at her, Nate."

Dad's watery eyes drift to mine. "That baby needs you right now." His expression falters as a fast tear forms and falls, trailing slowly down his cheek. My own tears begin to blind me. "She needs you more than ever, and you're hurting her. So, I'm asking you, again, what the hell are you doing, Nate?"

Dad's expression crumbles as I bury my head in my hands and let out a guttural cry. In the next second, I'm whisked into his arms as he encases me fully. His love surrounds me as I shake with grief, completely overwhelmed while he holds me to his chest.

"Daddy," I croak, just as he does.

"I'm sorry, too. I'm so sorry, Natalie," he rasps out. "You're my life, and there's nothing, *nothing*, on this earth you could do that could erase an ounce of my love for you."

Doing my best to catch my sobs, I fail when I feel my mother's palm run down my back as Dad continues to whisper to me. "I'm sorry I've been such a bastard. It ends now." I feel him shift his focus to Mom. "I'm sorry, baby."

I continue to cry in his arms as he speaks to me in broken whispers. "I just…I thought we were closer than that."

"We were, we are," I croak.

"Why didn't you come to me? Why couldn't you just ask me?"

"I wanted to, so much. I should have. I know that."

In my father's arms, and with his words, I feel some semblance of the peace I've been so desperate for. When we pull away, I see a reflected glimmer of hope in my dad's eyes as he gazes back at me with unrestrained love.

"We'll talk tomorrow, okay?"

I nod in quick agreement, my heart beating steadily in my chest, an incredible amount of weight starting to lift from my shoulders. It might take some more time, but the knowledge we both want to figure it out is all I need. Our gazes linger with that knowledge as hope starts to bloom in my chest. The idea that the universes I've been praying to merge together may become my future reality further stokes that hope.

Inhaling Dad's scent, wrapped in the warmth of his budding forgiveness, for the first time since we went wheels up in Arizona, I take my first full breath.

FIFTY-EIGHT

Outside
Stained

Natalie

My parents exit the limo, eyes slightly splotched but sporting matching smiles. Mom and I did our best to repair the damage done to our makeup with the emergency kit the glam squad gifted us for our clutches. I watch them ascend the carpeted stairs surrounded by waiting paparazzi and give myself a little extra time to gather my emotions.

Glancing out of the window now while they pose at the top of the entrance of the hotel for a few pictures, I prepare myself for the long hours ahead. Even with the relief of knowing my relationship with my father is reparable, for the next few hours I'll still have to play my part in the life I used to comfortably exist in—a life before I fell in love with Easton Crowne.

Urgency continues to build for me to shift my focus on the consistently aching part beating inside me—every one of the beats filled with longing to get back to its owner. Unclasping my clutch, I check my phone to see he hasn't replied to my earlier text, and my heart cracks a little. He's purposefully not answering me. More punishment. Briefly, I try to imagine where he is right now in his universe and what he's thinking.

A soft knock on the limo window has me snapping to attention to see Jonathan—looking handsome in a fitted tux—standing just on the other side of the door. Opening it, he bends down and scans the cabin of the limo before sweeping me with his gaze.

"You plan on depriving the public of this view all night?"

"No, I was just..."

"Stalling," he finishes for me, eyes roaming my face before confirming my upset. Before I was shunned from the paper, Jonathan and I became acquainted enough for me to be aware Rosie's crush assessment of him was close. Jonathan is private, but shy would be a more accurate word to describe him rather than *aloof*. In our short time as work colleagues—close to bordering friendship—he gathered enough about me to be aware of where my head is at. If anything, the headlines I'm positive he's read that speculate my marriage is a nonexistent farce have undoubtedly added to the sympathy in his gaze.

"Quite the dramatic entrance you planned," he quips, rubbing beneath my eye with his thumb and then showing me a smudge of mascara I missed before offering his hand. Scattered chatter of the photographers engulfs us when I take his offered hand, exiting the limo, plastering a smile in place.

Jonathan eyes me as we turn toward the waiting chaos. "For God's sake, Debbie Downer, straighten your shoulders because you're rocking that fucking dress."

Following orders, I toss them back as he shifts to guide me toward the stairs, placing his hand on the small of my back. I glance over at him just as he leans in, sporting a devilish grin. "I was hoping for a more masculine, mascara-smeared Cinderella to save me from looking stag and pathetic. But you'll have to do."

Releasing a strangled laugh, I shake my head at his candor as the flashes continue to fire off while he escorts me up the stairs.

An hour into the gala, pride sneaks into me as I, along with several others, watch my parents dance. Dad smiles down at Mom as they sway on the floor, his eyes filled with intimate amusement at whatever she said. The look he's gracing her with is a telltale sign of a man who knows the details of the woman he's holding because of the time he's spent memorizing her. I know this because my husband looks at me much the same way. Immersed in the other in those few seconds, they seem completely unaware they're being admired by those surrounding them.

How could I have been so fucking blind?

Maybe their story and beginning wasn't as much of a fairytale as what I perceived in those emails—or perhaps it was. Just because I'm not privy to the details of their beginning doesn't make it any less substantial.

No matter how they started, they've solidified their lives together for nearly a quarter of a century, and blind to it, I didn't have enough faith in them to keep my curiosity from harming something they hold sacred. A marriage I'm sure they fought for over the years to keep together.

Remorse consumes me as they continue to dance surrounded by friends, colleagues, and *Speak* employees. As I watch, I wonder if I would have been satisfied if I had witnessed them in this capacity, just after discovering the emails.

Can I even regret what I did now?

Yes, but only for the hurt it caused.

Regret Easton? Never.

My phone buzzes repeatedly in my purse, and I ignore it, knowing Easton has to be prepping for his show. Everyone else can wait. Grabbing a glass of passing champagne, I toss it back, determined to get some enjoyment out of the night I'd planned down to the last detail for months. When Jonathan's eyes catch mine from across the dance floor, his expression bleak as he lifts his cell phone up, I realize he's the one texting.

Frowning, I set the glass down on a linen-covered high top and pull my phone out to see the link Jonathan sent. Clicking on it, I sway in shock and fear when a damning picture of Jonathan and me out front of the gala pops up. Bracing myself on the high top, I take note of every incriminating detail—his hand on the small of my back, face inches from mine, not to mention the smile we're sharing. Every point of focus condemning even before I scan the scathing headline.

Is the newly *Crowne*d media heiress already stepping out? An inside source reveals why being the wife of a rock star isn't a fit for Hearst Media's princess."

Oh, fuck. Oh, fuck. Oh, fuck. Oh, fuck.

Rushing toward the balcony doors adjacent to the ballroom, I feel the weight of the implication of the picture hit me as I continually study it. Jonathan and I look smitten. Dread circulates through me when another notification banner shows two missed calls from **EC**. I immediately hit it, dialing him back while I glance around, thankful no one is in clear earshot. He answers on the first ring. The call seconds start to tick by without a word spoken from him as I jump right in.

"Easton," I breathe. "I'm sorry I didn't answer. I thought you were getting ready to go on stage." I swallow as fear threatens to steal my words. "If you saw that picture—"

"Are you with him?" The accusation in his voice rips through my chest. His simmering anger last night has now turned to fury. "Answer me!" he growls.

"No, Easton…no," I whisper. "How could you possibly believe that?"

"Have you forgotten, jealousy is new for me, and me and the green guy are not fucking getting along well at all."

"Please don't believe it," I rasp.

"Looks pretty fucking believable," he fires off, voice loaded.

"You know better than to play into headlines. I'll admit, it's a damning picture—"

"He's touching you, and you're fucking smiling at him. Is that part not true?"

"Yes, but not in the way you think." I hear the distinct swish of liquid in a bottle and pause. "Are you drunk?"

"Working on it," he snaps.

"Well, it's not going to help anything and will only add to your paranoia. I'm not with him, or anyone else for that matter. You know that. You're just angry and have every right to be, but the only man I want is berating me on the phone right now. I miss you every minute of every day. I was upset and trying to gather my wits in the limo, and Jonathan spotted me hiding. He lured me out and cracked a joke to comfort me before escorting me in. That's all that was."

"You're *mine* to comfort! Those are my goddamn lips, lips meant to smile for *me* in that way. That's my body, a body *not meant for anyone else* to touch!"

"Stop it," I defend. "I shouldn't even have to say this, but Easton, he's gay."

"How convenient."

"We promised we wouldn't let this happen."

"We promised a fucking lot, Natalie, but I seem to be the only one keeping them."

"Easton, I know I haven't been fair to you." I manage to keep my voice even as I glance into the ballroom, thankful both my parents are distracted. "I was also tearful in that limo because Dad and I...we're finally talking again. He apologized to me on the way here."

Silence.

In the ballroom, Dad cracks a megawatt grin, Mom at his side as they chat with a crowd of people. It's the first genuine smile I've glimpsed from him since before Sedona. With the sight of that, I see the possibility of renewed normalcy.

"There's a plane touching down in twenty minutes. I want you on it."

"What?"

"Come to me, Beauty. I'm asking you to come to me."

"That sounded more like an order," I fire.

"So, I guess we're only taking them from Daddy, then?"

"Stop it. Stop it. You know I can't come to you tonight. If I do, it will ruin every bit of progress we just made."

He barks out a laugh full of sarcasm. "You can't be fucking serious."

"Easton, you know full well my future rests at the paper and in my relationship with my father. I thought you might be happy about the fact we're talking, just a little, for my sake."

"You altered your future when you took my ring and my fucking last name."

"I know that. You think I don't know that? Easton, I'm fucking exhausted. My life has been a literal circus since we've been apart because I'm trying so hard to get back to you. You might not see it, but that's what I'm doing."

"You're exhausted because you're living two lives. But while you're fixing your place with him, we're breaking. You're breaking me. Come to me, right now."

"I can't."

Another long damning silence.

"Then I know my place. *Nowhere*."

"That's not true. You promised me I wouldn't have to—"

"Don't act like it's *me* who's made it otherwise," he retorts unforgivingly.

"It is right now," I say. "I just told you. He's coming around."

"For *you*, Natalie, not *me*."

"I know you're upset, but it can't be tonight. This night is monumental for him."

"For him. For him. *For him.* Where is my fucking wife in all this?"

"I'm here, Easton."

"Exactly. You're *there* and playing right into his agenda and letting him win."

"This isn't a competition."

"Tell that to your fucking father!"

The price for my parents' momentary peace fumes on the end of the line, his patience gone, an ultimatum currently taking its place. The longer the silence lingers, the harsher the exhales sound between us. "I don't want to fight."

"That's the fucking problem," he scoffs. "I'm in this alone."

"That's not true. We agreed to give it some time. We've done this before."

"Circumstances are a little fucking different now, don't you think?"

"Of course. You think I haven't agonized every second we've been apart?"

"Yet I'm sitting here forty-four fucking days later, a wifeless man. *Actions,* Natalie, get on the plane."

"I can't. Tonight, I can't. I'll come to you—"

"This is a joke," he declares. "We've become the joke the media is fucking making us out to be. A shotgun wedding, yet no marriage to speak of. Very rock and roll and so fucking cliché. I can't keep defending what doesn't exist!"

"Since when do you give a shit about what the media says or even read headlines?" I retort, my heartbeat pounding in my ears.

"Since I was forced to see my wife being comforted by another man!"

"You're not fighting fair. Maybe I didn't explain the importance of tonight, but it's the—"

"You were saying goodbye to me at the villa, weren't you?" He rasps out.

"No, Easton, God, no—"

"Then get on that plane."

"If I do it this way, he'll never accept us."

"I don't give a fuck anymore."

"But I do. Easton, please don't do this," I beg. "You're the love of my life, and I don't want to lose you, but I don't know how to make it work other than to see this through. Just give me—"

"You're fucking backpedaling. Taking the easy way out. Catering to him isn't working. Can't you see that by now?" His tone goes acidic as my stomach roils.

"You're being unreasonable."

"Didn't I love you the way you needed me to?" His voice cracks on the words, his pained breaths cutting through me. "It was so effortless for me…"

"I'm coming to you, I swear. Please just give me a little more—"

"Please don't choose him," he rasps out just as a pounding on a door sounds from his side of the line.

"I won't choose, ever, so please don't make me," I beg. "He hasn't even given his toast yet."

"We never even lived in the same fucking place," he whispers as his name is muffled in a shout from the other side of the door, "not even one day." It's then I know he's not listening to me anymore because he's stopped believing me. That knowledge sets the first nail against our coffin as I scramble to figure out a way to keep him from hammering it in. It's his next words that have my heart thrashing wildly.

"You came to Seattle for *me*. You found *me*, married me, you meant it," he utters brokenly as I crack wide open.

"I'm not denying that. Easton, our fathers nearly came to blows. Your mother could have had a stroke… Jesus, my father's face, I can never forget the devastation. I'm so close—"

"No, Beauty, no, you aren't," his tortured voice rips me to shreds. "You're ending us. We're everything that matters. Please," he begs hoarsely, "come to me."

My tears fall rapidly as I search for the right words to stop the bleeding. I can't blame him for his anger or his thin patience, but I can blame him for the timing.

"Easton. When I got home, things were much worse than I led you to believe. I lost my des—"

"The fuck?!" His outburst breaks through my confession, his hoarse voice incredulous when he speaks again. "You fucking drew up divorce papers?"

"What?"

A ping sounds on my phone, and I eye it to see an email notification from my father's law firm. "Eas—"

A guttural roar sounds along with a crash before the line goes dead.

FIFTY-NINE

November Rain

Guns N' Roses

Natalie

Sweat instantly breaks out on my forehead as I brace myself on the cement staircase while battling a wave of nausea. Gaping at my phone in shock, dread courses through me as I open the email to see a petition for divorce, listing me as the one who filed. Opening the document to read the verbiage, I hit the first page, and an instant notification pops up relaying the document is now live. Thanks to modern technology, we can end our marriage with two signatures, one from each of us and another from someone who witnessed it.

"No, no, no," I choke out as my vision blurs and panic zings through me as realization sets in.

Easton can divorce me *right now* with the swipe of his finger.

Frantically, I try to dial him back, and it continually goes to his full voicemail box. My heart hammers in my chest and vision blurs while my calls continue to go unanswered. Hysterical, I dial Joel, who doesn't answer me either, deducing he's probably attempting to get to Easton himself. I leave a message for Joel, begging him to call me back before frantically searching my contacts and dialing again.

"Natalie, what the fuck?" Benji answers without greeting, his voice filled with clear animosity.

"Benji," I croak, "please tell me you're with Easton."

"What the fuck are you doing, Natalie?"

"Benji, please, are you with him?" I ask, shooting off a text to Easton, begging him to call me back.

"No," he snaps, "I'm in North Carolina, but he called me after he took off from sound check due to a picture of his bride smiling at another man like he was up next. Joel lost him. Reid's searching for him now."

"I think Reid found him. Someone did. Benji, please get ahold of someone. I have to know if he's okay."

He lets out a long exhale. "I'll call you back."

"Don't hang up, *please*!" I screech, pulling a few eyes in my direction before I turn and rush down the stairs into the sidewalk-lined courtyard. "Please don't hang up!"

"Fine. Let me send out some texts."

"Thank you." I pace the length of the courtyard in seconds, spotting some blooming miniature pink roses as images of my honeymoon flash through my mind. Easton's hair whipping around him in the convertible while flashing me a serene smile. The look in his eyes as he slipped on my ring. His profile as he gazed up at the blanket of stars on the roof of the villa.

"I love you, my beautiful wife."

"Benji? Anything?"

"Still texting."

"Okay." More memories begin to blur in—Easton singing for me at the piano of my hotel. His reflection in the glass at the Needle. The way he looked leaning against his truck, waiting for me.

"Benji, please talk to me," I plead with him, "just talk to me, tell me something. Anything."

A long exhale releases over the line, and I imagine him pacing and smoking wherever he is in North Carolina. Another few seconds of agonizing silence stretch out before he finally speaks up. "All right, when East was ten or eleven, he brought a kid home from school and let him live in his closet for three days."

"Why?"

"Apparently, the kid told East his father hit him, and East couldn't handle it, so he stowed him away in his closet. He fed him, let him wear his clothes, the whole nine yards. There was an Amber alert. The boy's disappearance was covered by local news and quickly went national. They did a community-wide search and rescue. East finally went to Reid on the third day after stashing the kid elsewhere and told him he would only tell him where the kid was if Reid agreed to be his new dad. When Reid explained that wasn't how the world worked and that he had to go back to his parents' house, Easton broke the fuck down and refused to tell Reid where he was. Reid called the kid's parents over, and only the mother came along with the police. Reid threatened him with everything under the sun, and even with as much trouble as he was in, Easton refused to give him up. Because that's East. He's always called bullshit on everyone, even on intimidating grownups or any authority figure he felt was in the wrong, no matter how much trouble he got himself into. He never backed down from a fight. And because he wouldn't then, Reid offered the kid's mother a huge sum of money to help her leave her husband and start a new life."

"Did she do it?" I ask, a tear sliding down my cheek.

"Yeah, she did. East changed that kid's life by standing his ground, and he was only in grade school. The way Reid tells it, East still wasn't satisfied and read the mother the riot act as the kid was ushered out of the house. His entire life, he's been that way. That's the man you married."

"I know," I sniff.

"No, you don't, because the only time he's ever backed out of a fight is *for you*. He's kept himself from flying to Austin every day to confront your father because he knows how detrimental it will be for you. He is altering himself for *you*, Natalie, and it's fucking him up. I've never seen him so wrung out."

"I don't want that. You have to know I don't want that. I love Easton the way he is. I wouldn't change a single thing about him. But our parents can't handle this, Benji. Not just mine, Reid and Stella, too. Easton's at odds with them, blaming them for our separation. It's too much."

"So that picture he went off about, is that your fucked up way of—"

"No, hell no. He's a coworker, and you're more his type."

"But you're letting him believe it?"

"No, I told him the truth right away, but he demanded I come to him. He's being unreasonable."

"Yeah, what, six weeks apart after getting married, and *he's* being unreasonable?" He scoffs.

"I meant tonight. Easton's giving me an ultimatum, but my dad and I just got on speaking terms a little over an *hour* ago. I want to go to him, but I can't. I don't know what else to do."

"Yes, you fucking do."

"We've nearly destroyed our families. My future is here, by my father's side. Inheriting his paper, continuing his legacy. It's my dream."

"So, you're going to destroy your own family before it even has a chance to start?"

"No matter what I fucking do, I can't seem to make the right choice. Easton's furious with me. My father's just now speaking to me. I can't please either to save my sanity. We made a mistake, and we have to—"

"No, *you* did, a major one, but not the mistake you think you made. He's figured it out already. If you don't come fix this right the fuck now, you're going to damage your relationship in a way that's irreparable. His love for you has made him too weak to fucking fight for himself. It's never going to be right, Natalie, you know that. You'll never have a fair shot together, but not because of your baggage—and it might not ever be okay, but neither of your lives are going to be bearable if you throw this away. We all know it. Even your fucking selfish parents know it. Yet they go to sleep at night, content with their own fucking choices. Don't forget, after they successfully separate you, they'll have *each other*."

More tears slide down my cheeks. I feel the truth of his statement weighing on my heart.

"I love him, Benji. He means everything to me."

"Then it should be crystal clear. Jesus, I'm so goddamn sick of witnessing this over and over again. If that's the truth, Natalie, then make a choice, make him the priority he deserves to be—give him his rightful fucking place as your husband and partner, which is number fucking *one*. Stop denying his significance in your life. The box is open now. It can't be closed."

"It's not that simple."

"It *is* that simple if you cut everything but what matters most out.

I've watched my parents tear each other apart due to pride, insecurity, and selfish shit for years. I won't watch this happen to my brother. You need to figure your shit out *now*."

"I'm trying."

"You're *failing* miserably."

"I would never ask him to give up his relationship with his father or his career for me!"

"That's the difference between you and him because he would do it without you asking."

"But he's not the one in that position to give it up, is he? He doesn't have to. This is all on me, isn't it?" I grip the phone. "I warned him, over and over. I told him this would happen, and I seem to be the one paying for it the most!"

Silence.

"Benji?"

"Just got a text from Reid," he clips out. "He's with him."

"Okay," I nod furiously as my vision blurs. "Okay. Benji…listen to me, please. Easton's not answering for me because he thinks I filed for divorce, so he hung up on me, but I didn't. My father did it without my knowledge, and the law firm sent the email while we were arguing. He thinks I filed," I croak. "Benji, are you there?"

Silence greets me for several seconds before, "Then let him think it."

"What? No! I can't—"

"The fuck you can't. Look at what you've done to him already! You're ruining his goddamn life, and he deserves better! You know he does. If you refuse to be the wife he deserves, then at least have the fucking decency to let him go."

"Benji, please—"

"It seems like you've made your decision, Natalie, so stick to it. He made his decision the day you met, and he can't comprehend, even after this shitshow, how it wasn't the right one. He chose you, and he'll never call it a mistake. It's the hill he'll die on. I know that much is fucking fact, so if you can't choose him now, that's your decision, and make it final. Don't lead him on any longer, don't answer his fucking calls, you stop existing for him. I have to go."

The line goes dead as I lower my phone, my racing mind coming to a dead stop at the truth of the matter as I lose my grip on it. My lifeline slides down my dress and cracks somewhere on the sidewalk, the sound pairing perfectly with my inner destruction.

No matter what I decide to do now, there will be no victor in the war between Butler and Crowne, and there wasn't in the last, either. The end of our stolen love story was always going to be as I predicted—disastrous. Reason being, Stella had a choice, but I *never* have.

Even if Easton thinks I do, and Benji thinks I do, even if my father still believes I do—for me, a choice never existed.

Twenty minutes after my father's toast, when the cake is cut and pictures are taken, I sit across the eight top studying the man I've deemed my hero for the entirety of my life. Catching my eye, he stares back at me before tilting his head with a curious look, a grin forming on his lips. Slowly, I lift my cracked phone to him and shake it in prompt. Grin growing, he pulls his own phone from his pocket, playing along. Grabbing my clutch, I walk over to where he sits and reach him just as he opens the email. I press a kiss to his cheek as he curses under his breath and softly whispers my name. Ignoring his attempt to gain my audience for any sort of explanation, I pull back to look him right in the eye. "Congratulations, Daddy. The paper is *all yours*."

SIXTY

Again
Sasha Alex Sloan

Natalie

Damon and Holly sit on the other side of the booth gawking at me as I suck copious amounts of frozen tequila through a straw.

"You really quit the paper?" Damon asks.

I nod.

"Even though the law firm admitted to the mix-up in sending that email out?" Holly questions next.

Another nod as I slurp back a healthy dose of strawberry-flavored Cuervo.

"And you're not speaking to Uncle Nate at all?" Holly prompts again.

I shake my head and continue to wet my dry throat as Damon shifts in the booth and Holly rests her forearms on the table.

"You never told Easton you didn't file?" She asks.

I reluctantly release my straw. "No."

"So, you married the most beautiful rock star on the planet—who would basically die for you—and then walked away?"

"If that's how you see it, then sure," I spout dryly.

"No," Damon says, keeping my gaze, "she chose herself."

Releasing my straw, I nod. "No matter what I did, I was damned. It was like being caught between two immovable boulders while constantly dodging a wrecking ball. I finally just had to let it take me out."

"Jesus," Holly says. "But he had a right to be angry."

"Which one?" I ask as Damon poses the same question simultaneously.

"Tell Easton you didn't file," Holly says.

"That's your solution? Tell my husband that the man he was starting to hate *filed for me*?"

"See, baby, that's the whole point," Damon cuts in, his explanation for Holly. "Fathers typically give their daughters *away* at a wedding for a reason, which might seem misogynistic in this day and age, but it's the blessing Nat needs. That was never going to happen, and she couldn't thrive in her marriage or career because one or the other or both would eventually make her choose. They were already punishing her for it." Damon shakes his head. "God, that's so fucked." He grabs my hand over the table like he did a few weeks ago. "I'm so sorry, Natalie."

"Technically, your dad wins by default, anyway," Holly says. "It's not like you can divorce a parent." She pauses. "Is that why you quit? To hurt him?"

"No," my tears threaten and I tamp them down, doing what I have the past week to keep them at bay—letting my anger chase them away.

Anger at the two men who proclaimed to unconditionally love me, but failed to protect me from *themselves.*

"Nobody's really right or wrong. That's the most fucked up part," Damon concludes after a few minutes. I nod as he keeps my hand while his eyes soften.

"So," I say, directing my question at Holly. "Will you look after my apartment until I come back? You can squat if you want."

While Holly's right in that I can't divorce a parent, I can distance myself. One day in the future, I'll forgive my father—but that day isn't today. Until I do, I'll be working in Hearst Media's Chicago office, which I plan on fleeing to with a tequila buzz in a few hours.

Her chin wobbles. "For how long?"

"A month," I shrug. "Maybe two, maybe more."

"You're really leaving?" She asks, sniffling. Memories of the three of us circulate through my mind, running the fields, camping in the stables, sneaking Dad's beer out, and building bonfires. Family vacations, birthdays, Christmases, graduations, every imaginable milestone, and the less memorable days in between. Sadly, as grownups, we're supposed to be starting lives and families of our own. I'm just not sure now what that looks like for me anymore.

"I have to, Holly. I have to stand on my own for a while, even if I'm still working under my family's umbrella and collecting a paycheck. It's still where I feel I belong. For now, anyway."

"And your mom is okay with this?" Holly asks.

"See, this is exactly why she's leaving," Damon speaks up. "She shouldn't have to worry about everyone else having a say in her life decisions."

"Thank you," I sip my drink. "Thank you for getting it."

"Well then, I guess I'm sorry I don't," Holly huffs indignantly. Damon throws a suit-clad arm around her and pulling her to him, begins whispering rapidly in her ear. Her eyes continually water until she finally speaks up.

"What I meant to say," she sniffs, looking over to Damon for silent encouragement—which he freely gives—before glancing back to me. "Is that I'm being selfish right now, but only because I'll miss you. I'll look after your apartment temporarily, but please don't stay gone long."

"Good girl," Damon admonishes, pressing a kiss to her temple.

"But I don't have to fucking like it," Holly pouts.

Damon and I share a smile before he speaks up. "We'll fly to you in a few weeks."

"Really?" Holly's spirits lift instantly. "Like a real trip, *together*, promise?"

"Swear," he assures her as she turns to me and smiles.

"Finally. I'm just pissed it took a disaster to get us together."

Not a disaster, but a decision *not* to make a decision and walk away from the battle of past and present. A battle I couldn't keep from happening no matter how hard I tried, which left us all casualties.

Now it's just a matter of living with it.

As much as I longed to know what it was like to be in Stella's shoes—as much as I romanticized about having this type of love—I feel cursed now for having known it only to lose it.

My story is going to end far differently than hers.

There's no white knight in my future that will ever compare, or smooth-talking aristocrat with good table manners derived from *any* universe that will ever hold a candle to him. No gentleman nor scholar with the right words will ever pierce my soul or penetrate my mind and heart as profoundly as Easton has.

All of this was set into motion by me, so it's only fair I am the one who puts a stop to it. As a result, my punishment for the foreseeable future is that I have to live with the knowledge that once upon a time—for a glimpse of it anyway—I found the perfect love with Easton Crowne.

PART II

"Every song has a memory; every song has the ability to make or break your heart, shut down the heart, and open the eyes. But I'm afraid if you look at a thing long enough; it loses all of its meaning. And your own life while it's happening to you never has any atmosphere until it's a memory."

Andy Warhol

SIXTY-ONE

Dead Man Walking
Jelly Roll

Easton
Five months later...

Faded black boots propped and crossed on one of the dressing room tables, Dad expertly twirls his sticks before tapping them on his thighs. His restless energy is palpable from across the room as he stares blankly through the blurred motions of his expert hands. I have no doubt he's running through music none of us can hear, as I often do while tapping out the beats in perfect synchronization. While he's too much of a professional to be nervous, there's an energy surrounding him. Pacing, cellphone in hand, Mom's eyes lift and remain fixed on him where he rattles. Sensing her stare, he pauses and looks over at her, his mouth twisting up in a half-grin. "Something on your mind, Grenade?"

"I'm so proud of you," she declares, her voice shaking with sentiment as the decades they've spent between them shine in their eyes. Dad lifts his chin in summons, and Mom immediately walks over to him. Dropping his legs as she reaches him, he pulls her into his lap. After a few exchanged whispers, he brackets her face before pressing a gentle kiss to her lips.

Averting my gaze to give them the privacy they clearly don't give a shit about, I catch Rye talking to his daughter where she's propped against the wall. Rian is Rye's only child, resulting from his first marriage to her mother, Angel. Their divorce ended up being the first of Rye's *three* failed marriages. Rian smiles at her father, tossing her hands into the conversation for emphasis as he grins down at her with affection and pride, no doubt not retaining a single word.

My thoughts drift to Natalie and the times I just stared at her as she chatted me up post-orgasm. Far too exhausted for conversation, I kissed her quiet until she fell asleep.

Fuck, I miss that.

I haven't spoken a word to my wife since the night of the gala, since the night I got the email. Firm on keeping a promise to myself not to be the first to reach out because of how it went down, I have no intention of remedying that anytime soon. When our silent standoff lasted past New Year's, it only confirmed what I already felt—my wife left me to swing alone in the dark before leaving me altogether. There's only one universe for us to exist in now, but even in this one, she remains *my wife*. I rest in that fact, though it's little-to-no consolation anymore.

My focus shifts back to Rian as I note what a knock-out she's grown into. Benji is going to lose his shit when he lays eyes on her. Even so, he'll do no more than burn the looks of her into memory. At one point, I know she returned his affections, but he walked away from the opportunity, closing the door purposefully. The two have barely spoken since. He didn't even give himself the time to love her.

Maybe he is the smart one, even if he's the world's biggest fucking hypocrite when it comes to matters of the heart. Fact is, when it comes to Rian, there's no denying her significance with him.

Adam sits comfortably a couch over, plucking at his unplugged bass as he chats with his wife, Lucia—the most gentle and generous woman on the planet. Adam was the last of the Sergeants to marry, save Ben, and lucked out in his choice for *all* of us. Lucia has a gift in the way she's aware of everything going on with the band, both personally and professionally, at *all times* and guards us all ferociously and protectively.

Ben sits solo in a chair adjacent to Dad, a table over. Dressed to impress by Lexi in vintage corduroy, suspenders fastened and hanging loosely at his sides, he methodically rolls up the sleeves of his linen button-down, probably by her strict instructions. Fidgeting with the collar, he anxiously flits his gaze back to the door.

True to her ambitious nature and stellar reputation, Aunt Lexi took a last-minute job styling high-profile client and family friend,

Mila, who is Hollywood legend Lucas Walker's wife. The last-minute job was commissioned because of an unexpected pre-premiere event. Just after, Lexi and Benji met up in LA to board their flight, but it was delayed. It's apparent that they're cutting it much too close for Ben's comfort with the way he's fidgeting. Over the years, and on certain occasions, I know Lexi's presence has played a major part in Ben's performances. Her absence, especially when painfully missed, led to some of his most guttural shows. For Ben, it seems as if he uses their tumultuous relationship as a fuel source. Right now, in that respect, I can relate.

Though a rock and roll family, we've been through it all and continue to spend our lives together despite the Dead Sergeants' long-standing hiatus in recording and touring. Holidays, birthdays, Grammy wins and other award shows, vacations, and sadly, one too many funerals, we've been there and through it *together*. Blood or not, we are family in every sense of the word, which would make Benji and Rian's coupling a little taboo and predictably disastrous. Just as forbidden as, say…falling madly in love with your mother's ex-fiancé's daughter and eloping with her.

Even as pride fills me for the fact that we're celebrating another milestone tonight, I can't help but wonder what my family will look like five or even ten years from now, and more so, what it would have looked like if Natalie had accepted her place at the table.

She never even got to meet them.

Ben's attention whips back to the dressing room door as it bursts open, and a perplexed Aunt Lexi stalks through, Benji on her heels as he steps in behind her before he subtly begins searching the room.

"Thank fuck, get over here," Ben rushes out, relief taking over his anxiety-filled expression as he pulls Benji into his arms. When Ben's eyes meet Lexi's over Benji's shoulder, I feel it the second they connect.

The grudge on Ben's part is noticeably absent today, as it has been for some time. He used to be the first to look away, purposefully rejecting her and breaking their connection.

Ben's long-standing *go-to* punishment.

It seems he's done penalizing her now as their eyes hold before Mom pulls Aunt Lexi into a hug. They embrace the other like they haven't seen each other in years, not days, but their state is understandable.

Truth be told, they're the ones with the most history together.

Their friendship and bond sparked the start of our family, and the two of them combined became the backbone. That fact is further emphasized as an undeniable sense of relief fills the room.

We're all here.

Save one Crowne.

A place I'm still holding for her, probably in vain.

Shaking the thought away, I focus back on our reunion. Ben's smile lifts marginally when Lexi transitions out of Mom's arms and into his. It's so clear he needs her. It's so clear she wants to be needed by him.

Similarly distracted, Benji stands frozen in place a foot from his parents, his eyes sweeping Rian as she catches his gaze and gives him a small wave before resuming her conversation with Rye.

Ouch.

Clearly stung, Benji quickly schools his features before spotting me, stalking over, and collapsing with a sigh on my right.

"How was your flight?" I jab, grinning.

"Fucking hilarious, bro," he growls as I keep my gaze focused on his parents' exchange. Benji follows my line of sight.

"Don't ever try to figure them out. Their ignorance when it comes to the other is mind-boggling."

"Yeah, I agree. It's moronic to ignore the way you feel about someone."

His reply is a cold, dead stare.

"You're a hypocrite, and you know it." I press in.

"Jesus, man. I just got here." Even as he protests, his eyes drift over to Rian, who's inching her way toward the dressing room door. His shoulders lift and tighten, and I know he's fighting the urge to go after her.

"She stopped waiting for you, Benji," I inform him. "A long time ago."

He shrugs. "So, when the time comes, I'll shake her fiancé's hand, have my dance with her at their wedding and then spoil her kids."

"I'm calling bullshit on that right now," I say, knowing he's incapable.

"I made choices I can't unmake," he confesses thoughtfully. "So, it's the only way I'll be able to remain in her life. I'm too tainted for her at this point anyway. She's a fantasy, and if I touch it," he admits, his voice raw as his eyes roll over her, "I'll destroy it for both of us. The fantasy is always better than the reality anyway."

"That's some jaded, not to mention *recycled* bullshit."

"Think so?" He turns unforgiving eyes on me. "You hit concrete not too long ago. How's that working out for you?"

"Fuck you," I grit out. "You're right. She deserves better because you're fucking poison."

"And you're filled with it," he bites out, eyeing his parents, who are now wrapped up in conversation. "Haven't you gotten it yet, East? Nothing is revered anymore. It's all talk, all words made meaningless by actions."

"Actions, Natalie, get on the plane."

The truth of his declaration hits too close to home, I move to leave him in his tainted state, and he grips my arm and yanks me back down.

"Sorry, man, it's just my perception. Doesn't mean you have to buy into it."

"Also doesn't mean I have to keep listening to it. Your headspace isn't anywhere I want to be right now."

"Sorry." He ruffles my hair, and I slap his hand away. He ignores the blatant animosity I'm displaying and questions me. "Seriously, how are you?"

"Not feeling the warm and fucking fuzzies at the moment," I clip as the dark cloud he brought with him lingers overhead.

"Have you talked to her?"

"No, and I'm trying not to think about it."

He sighs and stands. "I'm going to grab a beer. Want anything?"

"I'm good, thanks," I manage in an even tone, his presence grating.

"Brought my kit. Up for some ink therapy later?"

"Yeah…maybe."

Dad's focus flits between Benji and me before he stalks over to me. "Come on, I need a smoke." He eyes Benji's retreating back, "Let's take a walk."

Knowing he's full of restless energy, I stand as he informs our crew we'll be back. Exiting the dressing room, we start the long trek to the parking lot. A few steps in, I roll my eyes down his frame. His own look, though spruced up by Lexi, remains true to his roots and typical stage appearance. Dressed in all black, I note just how much justice she did him. "Nervous?"

“Not really, just ready. The wait is what’s killing me. It really doesn’t get much better than this,” he grins. “It’s a good send-off, right?”

“Send-off?” I stop my footing altogether and turn to him. “This is it?”

He nods. “We decided this morning. We waited for everyone to get here to let you all know. Ben, Rye, and Adam are telling the rest of them now. A farewell tour would just be a formality anyway, and none of us want it.”

“Seriously?” A ball lodges in my throat as I avert my eyes, gutted by the fact that his music career is ending in mere hours. No wonder Mom’s been so emotional today.

“We stopped touring years ago, East. We’re done.”

“Jesus,” I rasp out, my eyes stinging. Lowering them, I go to resume our walk, and Dad stops me by gripping my arm.

“Look at me, son.”

I do and see my own eyes staring back at me, his filled with calm serenity, something I so desperately wish I had.

“I’m ready, Easton.” He shrugs. “Not all of us have a son with enough talent to create their own musical legacy,” he relays with pride. “I lucked out in *that* department, and I’d rather kick back and watch you make your mark. I’m so proud I had a hand in it, no matter how small the part I played.”

“It wasn’t small. Not at all.”

“Don’t bullshit me. You’re already surpassing me in a lot of ways.”

I shake my head, incredulous. “You’re wrong if you think any part of what I’m doing doesn’t have *everything* to do with you and Mom.”

My chest tightens as he clamps a hand on my shoulder. “All I’m saying is if this is it, I’m cool with it. So, you be okay with it, too.”

“Shit,” I reply hoarsely, reeling, “I’m good if you are. Just give me a minute to process.”

He nods, and we start walking again. A few steps in, he glances over at me. “It’s been a heavy couple of months.”

“Yeah, it has,” I say, keeping my focus ahead.

“You want to talk about it?”

“No. Not today.”

“You haven’t talked about it *at all*, son, since I peeled you from the floor of that hotel room.”

"That's because there's nothing to talk about. I'm at where I'm at, and I'm dealing with it."

"Just so you know, you come first." The last part he quietly delivers in a guilt-ridden tone he's used a couple times since our standoff. The morning after Mom bitch-slapped her logic into me, literally and figuratively, Dad and I came together like we hadn't missed a second. When he opened their hotel door in New Orleans the following morning, I didn't have to say a word. He pulled me to him, and after I choked out my apology, our fight was over. We've been inseparable since. I *did* move out into a one-bedroom I treat like a hotel room and as Mom predicted, a storage room, unsure if I'll ever pass out the second key.

"I know I come first without you ever having to tell me." I relay with conviction, determined to keep my focus on my family despite the underlying gnawing in my gut, which must be apparent to everyone with the way I'm being goaded and gawked at today. "We're good, Dad. I know you're there if I need you."

"That's all that matters to me," he asserts, his voice thick.

Needing a shift in energy, I nudge his shoulder and flash him a grin. "You know, you're getting to be a sentimental old man."

"Yeah, well, so fucking be it," he quips back with a grin while patting his jean pockets in search of his cigarettes.

My spirits continue to war as we round the corner, and Dad comes to an abrupt halt, slapping a protective hand on my stomach just as I look up.

SIXTY-TWO

Impaled
Skylar Grey

Natalie

In and out, Natalie.

"Don't be too hard on yourself. It can get pretty confusing," the man who introduced himself to me as Donald says while whizzing the golf cart around another curve. Brisk wind lashes my cheeks just as my phone buzzes in my hand.

Tye: Where are you?

Got turned around and retrieved. I'll be there in a few. I'm so sorry.

Tye: No worries, beautiful. Hurry up!

It's only been three weeks since Tye approached me at my mother's annual media party in Dallas and charmed me into giving him my number. Tye was one of a few sought-after Texas-based celebrities invited to attend. It took the better part of two weeks for me to take his advances seriously and consider them, despite his insane schedule. After a lot of thought, I agreed to dinner—a dinner which the paparazzi was made privy to fifteen minutes after we were seated at the restaurant.

They stalked us for the rest of the night, making it impossible for us to retain any semblance of intimacy. Even worse, the media twisted our *maybe something* first date into some sort of whirlwind fairytale romance. The truth is, I hardly know him. Though I admit, if I'm being forced to try and move on—as my husband seems to be doing—Tye wouldn't be the worst way to go.

Not only is he easy on the eyes, but he's also taking his place as one of the most legendary quarterbacks in the NFL. In addition, he's a businessman, an entrepreneur of sorts, who has big plans beyond leaving a mark in football history. His disarming charisma made it impossible for me to turn him away completely. I battled between head and heart endlessly when he presented himself as a prospect after deciding to entertain the thought of dating again. Reason being? Easton's headlines.

The hardest-hitting report circulating a month ago with photos of him with a rock goddess named Misty Long, whom he's collaborated with on a song yet to be released. While Misty's reps denied they are dating, the pictures the paparazzi managed to get are just as damning as my shots with Jonathan, which were splashed everywhere for weeks after the gala.

The image that haunts me most is a candid of them huddled closely on the beach in Malibu just outside her home. He was smiling at her, the kind of smile that's hard to earn from him, and the sight of it damn near killed me.

Though Easton's allowed the media to paint a picture on his behalf, I remain indecisive, thankful Tye has taken the reins. He's been aggressive and decisive enough for the both of us, a burden I allow him to have as I try to come up with some clarity for a new vision of my future. Not the future my heart remains set on, which I'm mentally trying to dismantle daily.

My parents are, of course, thrilled with the possibility of me dating an NFL player, Dad especially, which is no surprise. While it's been an out-of-body experience for me, our courting mostly consists of scattered texts and a few late phone calls because dating hasn't *been possible* for us yet. For that, I've been thankful.

Ironically, our second "date" just so happens to be the day Tye plays for his second Super Bowl ring. If they win, it will be his first as the Cowboys' quarterback. He earned the last ring when he played for Tampa two years ago. In the short time we've had to get to know each other, the media has been relentless, camping out at my parents' house, my apartment, and at the doors of *Austin Speak*. The pressure is even more grueling now as I'm whisked toward Tye, knowing a hundred million pairs of eyes might be directed toward me in a few hours for more reasons than one.

"Almost there," Donald assures, three different lanyards tangled around his neck as I marvel at my idiocy. I got lost within minutes of being ushered inside the stadium. My racing mind turned simple instructions complicated as some panic slithered in. To be fair, it's not like I've ever been inside the massive, multi-billion-dollar sports arena. The state-of-the-art stadium I'm being escorted through now is a Goliath compared to the David-sized field in Austin.

Even as I fly toward the man of the hour with the support of everyone in my life—including the media who labeled me the abandoning villainess just after our trip to the altar—I feel the crushing weight of today's expectations. Though the media seems to have forgiven me recently. My guess is because there has been speculation that Easton has moved on with his goddess, which led to questions about his fidelity and the reason for me filing.

All of it bullshit.

Following Easton's lead, I've kept my 'no comment' stance as firm as he has. Positive he hasn't worried himself over the headlines produced from our corners and remained oblivious to the trash talk we've both been subjects of. It's my job to watch both our futures, speculated or not, unfold in the press. Even if I try to avoid it at this point, I can't because his rising stardom parallels any other sensational performer in history. The more his star shines, as it's sure to, the more Easton's name will become synonymous with others like Prince, Madonna, and the likes. As it is, he's constantly being compared to Elvis, his media-donned nickname, 'The New King,' which I'm certain he loathes—if he's aware of it. His music is getting more play than any other artist. As I predicted, the world is fascinated by him and more blood-thirsty than ever, thanks to his aversion to media. False Image got the Diamond award *twice* in recent months selling over twenty million copies, sales climbing daily. With the growing demand for added tour dates, the band is set for a European tour which kicks off in six weeks.

While I'm proud of him, it's been a living hell watching him resume his life and being aware of his every move and staggering success. No doubt no less grueling than what my father endured when he covered Stella and Reid's engagement, wedding, and the birth of their only child—my husband.

Easton's been on my mind more than usual. In a horrendous twist of fate—today, of all days—the powers that be saw fit to throw a gigantic wrench into my first and only attempt at moving on.

What's even more damning is that legally, I'm still married to Easton Crowne. Though we've been separated for nearly six months, neither of us has signed the papers, the live document still resting in our idle hands.

The second time I opened the document, I breathed a sigh of relief when I saw his signature was absent. What I didn't realize was that when I did, Easton would be notified by email each time I opened it, and vice versa.

Stupidly and repeatedly, I still check anyway, praying I haven't accidentally missed the notification email. All my hopes clinging to the absence of his signature until recently.

When Easton's headline with Misty was blasted into the stratosphere, my jealousy boiled over. Grapevine news reported from every major paper stated they were recording together, but TMZ was the source that reported a blacked-out SUV hadn't moved from her Malibu mansion in days.

Seconds after hearing those details and studying the photos while trying to interpret Easton's body language, I allowed suspicion and anger to take over. That day I opened the document, fully intent on signing. I scribbled my name, my finger hovering over the accept button. But no matter how angry I was, I couldn't go through with it.

Just as I cleared my signature, Easton's name lit up as active on the left-hand side of the screen. We engaged in a virtual standoff, and I knew he was there watching, knowing I'd read the news and was waiting just to see if I'd sign.

Though I assumed he'd eventually leave, he stayed with me as more time ticked by. Every minute he lingered caused another tear to fall. Ten minutes came and went, as did twenty, and at the hour mark, I was sobbing at my desk, furious with him—all the while relieved no signature appeared. His continued presence gave me every indication that he didn't want it either.

Or maybe I'm just the delusional ex who still wants to believe he cares more than he does. As the details of the picture ate me alive, and I broke down behind my office desk in Chicago, the sincerity in his words from our honeymoon hit me like a sledgehammer to the chest.

"We're as close as two people could ever be."

Feeling those words to my marrow while reliving that memory had me closing the document without signing, giving Easton the victory. Just after, I stared at my phone, praying for any word from him, but it never rang—and I knew why.

While he's blaming me, I'm blaming *us both* and *my father*. His determination to keep the ball in my court and remain silent only magnifies the fact that he feels I should shoulder *all the blame* for our marriage imploding. And for that, I'm still furious he was so damned impatient he didn't even give us the time to sort out the nuclear bomb we set off by eloping. He gave me six weeks to clean up the destruction we left in our wake, my life having the most debris to sort through, before doling out his impossible and unfair ultimatum.

Five hours after that headline broke, Nate Butler was standing in the doorway of my Chicago office. Though we spoke briefly during the months of my absence—mostly through Mom, curt check-in texts, and emails—our dynamic had drastically changed, and it was painfully apparent.

Not long after his unexpected arrival, Dad whisked me to a small, screen-littered sports bar he frequented when he came to Chicago, which sits a few city blocks from Hearst's high rise.

Half a beer in, the silence lingered as I glanced over at my father, who felt more of a stranger to me than he ever had in my entire adult life. Sipping my beer, I'd allowed him the floor to start the conversation until he finally took his cue.

"I hate that I don't know what you're thinking right now and that it's my fault," he admits, opening a line of honest conversation.

"I do too."

"Tell me what to do, Natalie. I can't do my part to repair our relationship if you continue to give me vague replies while remaining in Chicago."

"I'm trying to figure out what I want," I tell him honestly.

"You want Speak,*" he fires back. "Or you did, and I feel like I've tainted that. No, I know I have," he exhales harshly, clear fatigue in his posture.*

Guilt threatens as I bat it away, having declared it an enemy of self-preservation.

"The truth is," Dad continues as I keep my gaze fixed on my beer,

"more than anything, I still want to hand it over to you when we're both ready."

He says my name with a fair amount of authority—in a request for my full attention—and I oblige, lifting my eyes to his. "But not because it's some birthright. It's what you've been working toward for a large part of your life. That chair is yours, if you still feel like it's where you belong, Natalie."

*"It's easier for me to work at Hearst," I relay, "*Speak *would be a circus if I came back now."*

"Not necessarily. The traffic has cleared out for the most part. It thinned out a lot when I hired security."

"Jesus," I palm my forehead. "I'm sorry you had to do that."

He waves his hand in dismissal.

"You know as well as I do, Dad, they'll just come running back to the doors if and when our divorce is final." I see no satisfaction in his eyes with that admission.

"I don't give a damn about that…the media part," he clarifies, knowing the hard line still exists where I refuse to discuss my relationship status with Easton. I'm still protective of my husband, even if I'm shifting from one emotion to another regarding him on the daily.

"You have employees that will care. It's not fair to them."

"Already thinking like a chief," he says with immense pride, "but tough shit if they can't handle it. It's our chosen arena, so they can deal with it or find the door." He pauses, his beer halfway to his mouth, "but that's not why you won't come home."

Pushing up the sleeves of my thick sweater, I turn and face him fully. "I'm still in Chicago because I've realized I've let the people in my life—especially the men I trusted—have too much sway over me and say in my decisions. A flaw I didn't realize I desperately needed to correct—if only for my sanity's sake. I've set new boundaries because of it, and I refuse to go back to that."

"I'm proud of you, and I'm not trying to lure you back with the promise of inheriting a position you've already earned. It's your decision, okay?"

Dipping my chin, I take another long sip of beer. Unable to help myself, I finally speak up.

"How in the hell did you endure it?"

Fiddling with the cocktail napkin, he returns my gaze point-blank.

"Sometimes, love, no matter how real it feels and is, isn't always the right love, and you don't figure that part out until you've lost it and put some time between your feelings and reality. I got that perspective after my split with Stella. In my case, time helped, Natalie, and it's been a very, very long time."

I shake my head. "But you still had so much animosity."

"Yeah, well, I'm not proud of myself," he says, looking down at the napkin he's shredding. "But that had far more to do with you. Between finding out the way I did and being in the same room with Reid and his son—knowing your last name was theirs—it was too much at once. Though I'll forever be sorry for how I behaved that day and the ones after." His next admission is full of remorse. "I had Brad draw up those papers in my worst hour."

"I'll always be sorry, too, especially for the way you found out. I never thought it would go as far as it has."

Silence lingers until he tilts his head back up to me. "Do you still want to know?"

I dip my chin.

"Okay…the honest to God truth about my relationship with Stella is that I realized in retrospect that I held her back with my own aspirations for the paper and expectations for my own future." He shifts back on his stool, his eyes glazing over with thoughts of the past. "She tried to talk to me about it more than once, but I was selfish because I was perfectly content with the way things were. At times it felt as if she was waiting for something to happen, for her life to begin, and I couldn't figure out why. As much as I wanted to be the man for her, I wasn't right for the future she envisioned for herself and was working so tirelessly for. When I saw how much she wanted her idea of her future and with whom, I broke off our engagement immediately."

"So, you broke up with her?"

"Yeah, I did," he sighs. "But she loved me, Natalie, truly. I still believe she loved me enough to go through with marrying me. If I hadn't broken it off so abruptly, I think she might have because we were good together. But some of that choice would have been made from loyalty, and I fucking hated that. I hated it so much that I kept my distance from her for months after we broke up. That was after being together for almost four years, living together for half of that time. Talk about hell on earth. It was hard." He sips his beer.

"So, you didn't know about Reid?"

"She told me she got hurt before we got together but hid the depth of her relationship and feelings for Reid from me. The night I found out was one of the most painful nights of my life. Seeing how much she loved him and how drawn she was to him fucking gutted me. I broke it off right then."

"Is that when she quit the paper?"

"Yes, and it was brutal," he confesses. "Despite making her aware he wanted her back, Reid kept his distance. He respected her choice to stay with me if that's what she wanted—and I did the same. Selfishly, I entertained getting back with her when she didn't go running to him, but it would never have been right. Because though we were very much in love, we never fit the way we needed to in order to last. So, I let her go, and she set out on her own and started a future without either of us. You read the emails."

I nod.

"They found each other again by crazy coincidence, and the rest is their history, Natalie—not mine."

"The headlines, though," I whisper. "How did you handle it?"

"It stung pretty badly," he says honestly. "But it wasn't news to me. We'd been apart so long I made peace with it. The truth for me is, if I had stayed with Stella, married Stella knowing what I did, I would have been the one settling."

I mull over his revelation, his truth flipping so many of my theories on their head. "So, after…when you met Mom—"

"I love your mother," he cuts in sharply, "On an unparalleled level. No other love I have ever had compares to what I feel for her. I fell for her because she is beautiful, strong, independent, brave, ridiculously intelligent, loved football, and did not put up with my shit for one second. If you want the truth, she terrorized me from day one, swear to God." He grins down at the foam on his beer. "I married Addie because we fit together in a way we would work long term, because I learned how vitally important that was. The rest of that love stems from the history we made spending so much of our lives together." He turns to me. "So, I didn't tell you about my history with Stella, because frankly, it was a history I'd outgrown, living out my future with the woman I was meant to marry—and it was none of your damned business."

"I know, and I'm sorry," I let out a harsh exhale. "To be fair, Dad,

I knowingly committed every single crime you called me out for when we got back from Arizona." Taking a large sip of beer, I settle in, intent on finally explaining myself.

"It started small, shocking but a minor enough offense. I read an email I wasn't supposed to see. But it was that small shock that had me reading the second email, which led to the third. But when I realized my source was the one hurt in the love story I was becoming so invested in—and probably wouldn't be forthcoming with the whole of it—I took my father's advice and sought out another source, but in the wrong way."

I look at him pointedly, allowing my admission to flow freely. "I was utterly fascinated by it because I'd never experienced those feelings for myself." A lump begins to build in my throat. "I figured out soon after—with the help of my alternate source—that what I truly was, was envious. But in digging, I incriminated myself to the point I knew it would damage us *badly…and I was terrified. At first, the solution was just a short walk to your office. An answer to a question, a brief communication between us to put all the mystery to rest." Forcing my eyes to remain on his despite my guilt, I continue. "The next thing I knew, the tables were turned, and I was existing in a different world that you knew nothing about."*

We both sit for several minutes in silent contemplation of our reciprocal admissions before I speak up. "Now I'm in limbo between them."

"You don't have to be," he rasps out hoarsely. "I can handle a lot, but knowing your absence is my fault… It's my biggest regret as a father." He turns to me, eyes misting, "Come home, and if you do, Natalie, I promise you I won't ever abuse the paper or my relationship with you like that again."

Dad left me at the bar that night with a standing invitation to return home, along with a promise to allow me space to live my life. That conversation left the door wide open for more reconciliation. The following week, I flew back to Austin and into my mother's waiting arms, my future still uncertain but determined to restore some semblance of order.

Keeping that decision in mind this morning, I drew up a simple game plan for today—to wish Tye a good game, hide in the back of the owner's box, away from the cameras and speculation, and remain undetected.

My escort takes another curve jerking me out of my thoughts as I yelp and grip the side of the cart.

"Sorry," he chuckles. Though an older man, Donald seems to be having the time of his life, as he should be, because it is game day, and this is arguably the best sporting event in the world. My phone rattles in my hand again, and I open the text.

Dad: Where are you?

I'll be up shortly.

Dad: Two beers in. Devil Emoji. Go Cowboys! Football Emoji

I can't help my smile at his enthusiasm. Despite my hesitance to come, on the plus side, Dad is being treated like royalty at his first Super Bowl. Tye outdid himself, providing everything from plane tickets to transportation to the stadium. He's deserving of a thank you at the very least. If Easton can sleep at a rock goddess's house for three days, I'm allowed to accept an invitation to the Super Bowl. Case closed.

Even if it's too late to back out, I'm already in the thick of it, so I might as well enjoy myself.

"There he is," Donald chirps happily as Tye appears, all six-feet-four of him. His dark brown hair is mostly concealed by his NFC championship ball cap. Beneath the brim, dark blue eyes find mine. His stark white grin widens from where he stands in pinstriped ball pants, a starched towel hanging from his waist, and a matching NFC championship hoodie finishes off his pre-game look.

In and out, Natalie.

The game starts in less than ninety minutes, and due to the time wasted in getting to him, I've got just enough time to say a quick hello so he can rally and warm up with the rest of the team.

Donald stops the cart abruptly, and I bounce forward as Tye stalks toward us, chuckling through his scold. "Easy, man, that's precious cargo."

Donald reddens slightly. "Sorry about that, Tye."

"All good." Tye's eyes rake me, obvious satisfaction in them over the way I'm dressed—or the way he dressed me.

"Come here, beautiful." Tye pulls me from the seat flush to him, grinning down at me with his hundred-and-sixty-million-dollar smile. "You good?"

"Am *I* good?" I ask. *Not at all.* "You're the one about to play the game of a lifetime, so you can turn that question around."

He lifts a brow, the act making him boyishly adorable. Though he's not outspoken in the media, he can be a bit of a bad boy with his delivery when taunted. I love that aspect about him, and it's no mystery why. Our conversations are light and easy. Tye's been hesitant to broach the subject of how he knew of me at the party. I saw the recognition on his face just before he placed me. My face has been splashed across the media since the news of our elopement broke. Hence, Tye dodges the subject we've both been careful to avoid.

"I thought I was feeling pretty good until I saw you, and I have to say, I'm feeling pretty damn lucky." His eyes fixate on my jersey, a gift he had delivered to *Speak* with his invitation to the Super Bowl. Putting it to use, I'm dressed in the tightest pair of dark denim jeans and killer heels. I altered the pink jersey to mold to my frame by tying the material in a knot at my back. In turn, it now accentuates my hips over the form-fitting long-sleeved white tee that exposes a little midriff. From the look in Tye's eyes, he approves. "Gotta say, I love the way my number looks on you," he compliments with a pride-filled smirk.

"Head in the game, sir," I playfully tug on the brim of his hat.

He keeps me close, his voice suggestive. "I'm all fucking over it."

"Seriously," I ask, putting some space between us to get a better look at him. "Are you feeling good?"

"Never better," he assures confidently. "Slept well last night."

"Oh? Good."

One side of his mouth lifts. "Off-season starts tomorrow."

"Going to kill it, Tye!" A man shouts, making me jump as he passes in the bustling hall. We haven't exactly been alone since our convo started. There's a ton going on behind the scenes, and everyone seems to be traveling at breakneck speed. Tye lifts his chin in acknowledgment to the supportive passersby before his eyes flit back to me, where I'm curled into his body protectively.

"Where was I?"

"Off-season," I remind him, studying his square, clean-shaven jaw as he glances at a nearby digital clock hanging on the wall, eyes seeming to dim with regret.

"Shit, I have to go. But yeah," his voice heats. "Post season. We should talk about it..."

"If you earn another ring, I'll consider it."

"More motivation," he utters softly, cupping the back of my head before he dips, pausing for a second before pressing a tentative kiss to my lips. He pulls away before I get a chance to register the feel of it. Licking his lower lip, he goes to speak, but whatever words he was about to say are cut off when he's approached in every direction—one by a teammate just coming out of a closed door behind him, the other a staff member. Tye eyes me apologetically as I give him the out that I, myself, am becoming desperate for.

"Go. Go win the Super Bowl." With my order, I flash him a smile and do an about-face, ready to seek refuge in my getaway cart. Instead, I'm met by one of life's cruelest moments when I see two sets of hazel eyes fixed on me. Easton stands in the middle of the bustling hall with Reid by his side, Reid's palm flattened on Easton's stomach as if to protect him from *me*.

SIXTY-THREE

The Kill
Thirty Seconds to Mars

Natalie

My smile dissolves as the wrecking ball that is my husband crashes into me full force. I have no idea how many seconds pass, but it's not nearly enough for me as Easton averts his blistering gaze and resumes his footing. Reid follows his lead, his cutting eyes damning me a few seconds longer. Both Crowne men breeze past me, and I turn to follow their progress just as Reid stops and introduces himself to Tye. Seemingly unphased, Easton does the same. The cordial handshake between Easton and Tye feels a lot like lighter fluid dumped on the flames raging inside my chest. Easton goes so far as to wish Tye luck before he stalks away in the opposite direction of me. Tye's eyes start to drift my way as I quickly turn, bypassing the golf cart altogether before stalking forward, directionless.

Screw you, life.

It was a fool's plan. I knew better.

What are the odds I'd start a flirtation of dating an NFC championship-winning quarterback weeks before the Super Bowl?

Slim to none.

But I knew going in they were stacking consistently against me when he asked for this particular second date, because tonight, the Dead Sergeants are performing the Super Bowl halftime show.

Despite my attempt to keep my presence completely under wraps, my plan, like all recent others I've made, just exploded in my face.

I tempted fate, and it delivered in spades.

Which brings me back to the question that's been haunting me daily for the past week.

Sitting at the intersection of 'Fuck My Life Avenue' and 'Devastation Road' sits the Crownes and the Butlers, who have been the butt of the galaxy's jokes for three decades…but *why?*

My feet ache as I glance up at the time clock in the hall, of which there seems to be no shortage of. It's fifteen minutes until game time, and I'm not where I need to be. I'm supposed to be in the box with my dad, and I know it's him texting now as my phone vibrates in my jeans pocket. While Dad's prompt for my ETA rushes my steps, Tye's jersey number burns a hole in my back—a reminder that I'm not displaying supportive new girlfriend behavior.

But I'm not his, nor will I ever be.

"To your right, miss!" The whirr of another golf cart motor whizzes by just after I plaster myself against the wall allowing it to pass. Feeling paralyzed and knowing I'm nowhere near ready to put on the airs needed to get through the rest of the night, I close my eyes and suck in a steadying breath.

Before today I was breathing a little easier because I was back home, with my family, my friends, and at my desk at the paper. At the very least, I'd resumed my role as a contributing member of society and was growing motivated to reclaim some semblance of my old future.

Now?

I can't see a second past the one I'm living in.

The roar in the stadium has me pausing briefly before I wipe the sweat beading on my forehead. I continue my walk in search of the nearest restroom to assess my appearance for the possibility of pulling myself back to presentable. The second I spot a restroom door, I recognize Benji's outline where he lingers just outside of it. He stands with his back to me opposite Easton, who's currently shoulder to shoulder with one of the most beautiful women I've ever laid eyes on.

She's tall, her body the perfect mix of thin and curvy, her long, long, dark hair thick and wavy. It takes me a second to realize it's not Misty and a second longer not to care as I drink in their cozy posture. Feet from where they congregate, I contemplate my next step, as a landmine is sure to go off the instant I make a decision. Easton spots me over Benji's shoulder just before he also looks over to see me standing frozen in the hall. Heart thundering, I shift my focus from Benji to the woman who lifts an inquisitive brow Easton's way when she recognizes me. With a parting whisper I'm deprived of hearing, the woman kisses Easton's cheek, and he nods his head in reply.

Instead of cowering away, I force myself to walk the eight or so feet toward the door as Benji ushers the woman away without so much as glancing back at me.

Stopping at the threshold of the door where Easton leans against the jamb, I turn my head as the landmine goes off.

Boom.

Even if the scenario's imagined, this pain is the worst I've ever felt in my twenty-three years on earth.

His gaze travels from the tip of my sweaty forehead to my throbbing pinched toes before he turns and begins striding away.

"You're not going to say a word to me?" I call to his back.

Easton stops before whipping his head back in my direction. "Seems like a nice guy. Good for you, Beauty. I'm sure *Daddy* approves."

"Go to hell," I snap with a shaking voice as he reaches Benji, who's standing outside a closed door, his eyes flicking between us before opening it for Easton. Inside, I catch a flash of the Crownes' camp, spotting Ben and Lexi before it's forced shut with Easton and Benji safely on the other side.

Slapping the bathroom door open with my palms, I walk over to the sink before bracing my hands on either side of it. Studying my reflection, I'm surprised to see that, for the most part, I'm still well put together. Though slightly fuzzy around my hairline, my ringlets are still intact, my makeup artfully in place with glam team magic. A go get 'em gift from Mom in support over her purposeful absence. She decided not to come, refusing to let any of Dad's leaking past into their present. A decision I will forever respect her for. When we left her, she didn't at all look concerned. Addison Butler is a much stronger woman than me, but unlike me, she's confident in her marriage.

Pandemonium erupts in the stadium as I gaze into the mirror while my phone rattles in my pocket.

Dad: Everything okay? I'm three beers in and trying to pace myself. Hurry up.

I shoot a quick text to him before giving my reflection a pep talk.

"Get it together, Butler," I say, the name a reminder my father survived a similar fate, his strength during that time spurring me on as I mentally prepare myself for the hours to come while still reeling from the one prior.

The door swings open as I run my fingers through a few tangled curls, resigned to complete today's lie and bury myself in work the second I get back to Austin. It's when I catch the dark and deadly reflection of Easton Crowne standing behind me that my heart plummets. Refusing to look away, I brace myself for more impact.

"Go to hell?" He repeats, his velvet tone replaced with a mix of irony and feigned amusement.

"It's only fair. I've been there since Arizona, and you sure helped to pave the way."

"Seems to me you've bounced back," he quips, the change in his tone caustic. It's then I prepare for war, though I can't bring myself to fully face him because of the lingering explosion ringing throughout my being.

"Yeah, well. You've got refuge in Malibu, right?"

Nothing. Not a single tell. My thirsty eyes drink him in, his reflection like a desert mirage. He looks every bit the man I met and married, yet…different, edgier maybe, his presence more menacing.

With no way to escape it, I face the consequences of my decision to be here head-on.

"Say it," I bite out, my tone much sharper than intended. The jagged edges of the pain I've felt since we unraveled forcing the words out. He wants to hurt me. It's so evident. "Just say it."

He's never been immature when we've fought, not really. All he's ever truly done is allow his emotions to flow as they came. He's been unyielding in that respect, and he's not going to do it any differently now to spare me. But there isn't a trace of the vulnerability I fell for in his eyes. Not a single hint of softness to be found inside the edges of his fury.

"I didn't plan on being seen. I would never want to dampen this monumental night for you or your family. I don't want us to hurt each other anymore."

"Well, there's a *first*," he fronts, "you're not really good at knowing what you want and keeping firm in your decisions. Then again, you say one thing and *do* another."

"I've never changed my mind about you. I think about you, us, all the time."

"*Us* doesn't exist anymore. You made it so," he says, closing in behind me, his warmth unbearably absent. Lifting his hand, he slowly slides his fingers along the number on my spine. My heart lurches against my ribcage, begging to be released. Swallowing, I free myself to love him without abandon in these seconds.

"Easton, I can't go on like this, if you won't talk—"

"You were a temporary high…and now you're a stain." He palms his chest, "That's what you are to me now, Natalie, a fucking stain."

I turn and grip his wrist, glaring up at him.

"You don't get to take it back, not any of it," I shake my head. "You don't get to will your past with me away."

"No, no, Beauty," he grips my shoulders and turns me back toward the mirror. "You're the one who put us back here. This is our reality now. You can tell yourself you *can't* tonight before you fuck your superhero."

I scoff. "And you've been faithful?"

"I'm a married man," he declares, his tone acidic. I clutch the counter as he steps forward, caging me further while engulfing me in his wrath.

"We don't have to hate each other," I plea.

He tilts his head. "This truly was inevitable, wasn't it? I just didn't realize why it was. But now I see it. I see you."

Fed up, I lash out. "You've done an amazing job painting me the villain in all this, Easton, but you're so damned selfish and adamant on blaming me that you'll never claim your part, will you? Even when I begged you to see how badly we would hurt everyone. Even after you assured me you wouldn't force me to choose, or give up my career, that my relationships wouldn't suffer—"

"So, this is you justifying divorcing me, then? Such a beautiful martyr," he whispers darkly.

"You know, walking away would have been more convincing. Or have you forgotten I know you just as well. I see *everything* you're not saying."

"I know what I'm in for, Beauty. I've always known, and that's why

I fought so hard for you. But you're still confused, just like you were the day we met, so let me help save you the mystery of your future reality," he whispers, his tone unforgiving.

"Maybe you fuck him for the first time tonight, and while you do, you think of me the whole time. You'll smile as he pulls out and make your way to the bathroom, feeling sick because you believed for a few minutes you could do it, you could escape me. While you scrub his cum from your body, maybe you resign yourself and entertain his idea of what you could be like as a couple because you need something, anything. So, you'll play along because you don't have a choice. Months will go by as you drown in delusion. Maybe you'll adopt a puppy together and pose for the cameras to keep it going. They love you together, so you should too. Eventually, he'll get down on one knee, and you'll say yes because you feel obligated to, and you'll think to yourself, 'Why not?' because you've come this far. You'll plan an elaborate wedding and invite everyone who knows you to watch you lie your way through 'I do,' remembering the first time you said it and actually fucking meant it—but you threw that husband away. Before you know it, you're making little superheroes to fill the void and later crying your way through the carpool, realizing you're not living the life you wanted. The worst part? You won't be confused as to why you're empty. You'll know why the whole time."

He turns me to him and cups my face with a reverent palm as he presses in.

"See, Beauty, *you're* part *villain* now." Hot tears glide down my cheeks as he brushes one away with a soothing thumb. "That's my stain on you. I'm in your skin, in the blood that flows through your veins… and we all know a villain *can't* make it with a superhero."

"And your future?" I rasp out, his gentle touch driving the dagger further into my heart.

"I've got all this sickness running through me to use to my advantage," he says softly, "feels like fuel for a long fucking career. At least I have that, right?"

"Well then, I guess I feel sorry for the women you bed."

"Don't. You know how generous I can be."

My palm itches to slap him as I glare back up at him while his eyes batter me with deep-seated resentment. I lift my chin.

"I didn't throw you away, Easton. You stopped listening to me. You gave up on me."

"You gave me every reason to."

Hurt leaks into his timbre as he runs a gentle thumb down the side of my face. "You see, you got the vows *twisted,* my beautiful wife. You were supposed to forsake *all others* for *me*," his voice cracks with his admission, and I die at the sound of it.

"I've been faithful." I grip his T-shirt in my fist, hot agony sliding down my face as his warmth surrounds me. "Easton, I—"

"Shhhh, Beauty, go back to sleep," he whispers, completely dismissing my every word while lowering his thumb and aggressively smearing the lipstick across my jaw, a blatant attempt to erase Tye's kiss. As he does it, I see his eyes flit with a thousand emotions. With one last swipe of his thumb, he leans in, his kiss feeling every bit the kiss of death he intends it to be. A pained grunt leaves him as he releases my hands from his T-shirt before ripping away from me abruptly.

I keep my eyes closed, voice breaking as I repeat the truth. "I've been faithful."

SIXTY-FOUR

Drive

Sixx:AM

Natalie

Twelve to fifteen minutes. That's the length of the average halftime show. Though my hopes are that the Sergeants will take the former as the Cowboys retreat from the field with a fourteen-point lead.

Twelve minutes of hell is what awaits my father and me as the stadium staff scrambles below to set the stage for the halftime show. Thankful for the Dutch courage flowing through me and the slight ease it brings, I decline to sip my newly refilled beer. Though buzzed, I'm still painfully present. There's no remedy for the grief currently running through me in any form.

"You were a temporary high."

If Easton hadn't annihilated me with his vicious retaliation in that bathroom—if we hadn't run into each other, I'd be somewhere near the vicinity of okay. But as the teams disappear from the field and the stadium begins to shake with renewed energy for what's to come, I know the true test of the night lies in the grueling minutes ahead.

Twelve to fifteen minutes.

Please, God, let it be twelve minutes because a minute more might break me. Dad and I sit in unspoken agreement to stand our ground, glancing over at the other every few seconds as historic friction fills the air.

It's while the stadium crew begins to set up the stage and the spectators start to roar with excitement that Dad wordlessly takes my hand in silent support. My concern isn't so much for myself anymore as I'm a lost cause, but for how he might be feeling.

He's here because of me—for me, and I want to be just as much a silent strength for him. Dad catches me studying his profile and quickly tries to quash my rapidly building anxiety.

"I'm fine," he assures, and I nod, doing my best to believe him—hoping that his current state and relaxed posture will be an eventual possibility for me. "We can leave if you want to. I'm fine with that, too."

"Maybe we should, but we aren't going to," I declare vehemently. "We have just as much of a right to be here as anyone else. We aren't second-class citizens, Dad."

His reply gets drowned out as the stadium goes dark, and the first notes of "Tyrant"—an early Sergeants' hit—begin to fill the air. Sparks of light fly stage-side toward the open roof as I settle in.

Within minutes of the Sergeants taking the stage, the roar of the crowd nearly overpowers the volume of the music. The buzz they're creating consumes every inch of space as Ben bellows out every lyric with expertise—the rest of the band in sync, a clear demonstration of the legendary band they are. Relentless in their execution, they play a mind-blowing compilation of their greatest hits, spanning decades of a legacy they've built together—easily blowing away the expectations of everyone present, including me.

Despite his reassurances, every few minutes, I turn to weigh Dad's expression. Not once has he wavered. As he confessed in Chicago, he's had decades to get over any hurt regarding their breakup and has years of memories he made with my mother to wash away the sting of those he had with Stella Emerson Crowne. Even without the recognition of shaping Stella into the powerful journalist she became, my father humbly and gracefully took a back seat to any claim of his part. He selflessly loved her enough to want her to thrive—to want her happiness.

Only the six of us know the details of the more complex story behind the woman who put the legendary band ruling the stage on the map, but only *three* people *lived* it.

Dad let Stella go to finish the rest of her chapters with another man and, in turn, found his unwritten chapters with my mother—showering the two of us with all the love in his heart. A fact that only reiterates why my father remains my hero. In embracing that, I look over at him with all the love I hold.

As I do, I sense a little tension building as the AT&T stadium is blanketed in darkness while Rye's guitar screeches out, ending the last song. I look up to see Stella on the jumbotron, wiping a tear away before gripping Lexi's hand that rests on her shoulder. Seconds later, a lone spotlight shines on Reid behind his drumkit.

It's when a second spotlight appears, beaming down on a grand piano, and Easton takes the bench that what strength I've mustered starts to drain. The deafening roar of the crowd with his surprise arrival has instant tears threatening. Dad looks up at the jumbotron to see Easton smiling as the crowd's roar reaches a thunderous level.

Behind the glass partition that separates us, the whole arena buzzes with electricity as Easton gets comfortable, adjusting the mic before looking over at his father with a grin. Reid smiles back at him, his face filling the jumbotron as he scans the stadium with reverence, giving himself a moment—clear appreciation in his expression for those screaming for the band, for his son.

"Thank you," Reid speaks into the mic floating above his drum kit. "Thirty years ago… A Latina grenade stomped her way into my life and saved me seven minutes, so I promised her I would make the best of them." Pandemonium ensues as the camera focuses for several seconds on all four members of the Dead Sergeants. Reflection and emotion flits on each of their faces as they stand in contemplation on the biggest stage in the world. As the noise dies down, the camera pans back in on Reid. "She's the reason we're here tonight, so I think it's only fair we give our *last* seven minutes to her."

Easton leans into the mic with a grin, his whisper low. "For you, Mom." Easton begins to tease the stadium by repeating the opening notes of "Drive" on his piano keys. The uproar in response earns them one of Easton's most genuine smiles. The song's significance to fans and expected encore is no surprise considering the adoration and success of the movie.

Dad tightens his hold on my hand, and I glance over to see his shoulders have gone rigid, my whisper of his name getting lost in the noise of the crowd just below us.

Feeling his unease, I rack my brain for the reasoning behind his shift in demeanor. I thoroughly search my mental inventory. Well after the Sergeants' rise to stardom, Stella stumbled into Emo's and discovered Reid playing with the Sergeants at the end of one of their tours. They'd taken to the stage of the club to pay homage to their roots. Unbeknownst to Reid, Stella was at the foot of the stage, crying hysterically as Reid bellowed out the song in memory of her. As Easton continues to tease the stadium with the melodic opening, Dad's words from the bar come back to me, stinging like a thousand needles.

"The night I found out was one of the most painful nights of my life. Seeing how much she loved him, how drawn she was to him, it fucking gutted me. I broke it off right then."

Oh. My. God.

I turn to my father as the gravity of it hits me, his current reaction a byproduct of that monumental moment between Stella and Reid.

"You were there," I whisper hoarsely, eyes filling as he keeps his focus trained on the field, on the stage. "You were there. You were there when he sang for her, that's why—"

"Don't let go," he replies hoarsely, his grip on my hand tightening as I realize he's being forced to relive one of the most painful moments of his life.

"Never," I say softly, clutching his large hand in both of mine, apologies on the tip of my tongue as Easton's voice breaks through and he begins to sing as my hopes of making it through the rest of this night intact are utterly obliterated.

Even as the revelation stuns me, I'm inevitably drawn back to the man who seized my heart so many moons ago, and the lyrics of the song begin to pummel me. Easton continues to play the haunting melody as scattered neon purple lights go up one by one throughout the stadium. Synthesizers sound off along with Easton as the camera closes in on him, capturing the details of his face while he poses intimate questions filled with longing.

He continues a slow build as my throat begins to burn. I'm drawn into Easton's expression as he keeps his eyes down while the weight of our mistakes debilitates me. In these seconds, I become a firm believer that music *is* timeless. The proof of that almost tangible as years evaporate while my father and I are mutually bruised by a melody, in a front-row seat with a clear view, with history painfully repeating itself.

Even as I rebuke the circumstances against the injustice of what we're feeling—and the consequences—I grudgingly identify with Stella in the minutes she watched the love of her life sing for her, thinking she was lost to him.

The burn of that truth sears into me further as Easton slowly lifts his head and stares directly into the camera, into me.

The world in its entirety disappears in the background as my supernova sings his parents' love song, a song from one soulmate to another. The momentum continues to build as Easton casts his spell, enthralling us all just before Reid's drums kick in and the rest of the Sergeants' instruments ring out. The song draws heavy as an explosion of fireworks goes off into the night air. Reid detonates on the drums as Ben joins Easton in the chorus. Chills snake their way up my spine as every hair on my body lifts on end with the knowledge that I'm witnessing music history, and the man I've been breathing for is making it.

Easton's soul-filled melody and vocals and the Sergeants' hard-hitting sound create the perfect compilation of future and past.

Fireworks continue to explode overhead, shooting up to the top of the stadium and light the world in purple and blue. Reid's drums puncture the night as Rye walks forward, bringing the song to its crescendo with a guitar solo to rival all others—elevating it to the next level—before drawing it all back to the melody.

The lights again dim, Easton front and center in the spotlight, taking the reins naturally as he softly presses the beginning notes, dragging the melody back gently to where it started. He repeats the opening lyrics, the lilt in his voice wrapping mournfully around each word as he pours his soul into them. Just as he draws us all back in with the caress of his voice, the band again explodes into motion, singing the last of the chorus. The cameras pan in on a close-up of each of the Sergeants and Easton as they end the song on the most spectacular high before the lights go dark.

Every soul in the stadium is already on their feet. I lower my head and cough, setting my tears free. The band gathers at the edge of the stage, and Easton steps back, clapping for them in praise as the Dead Sergeants take their final bow, clear sentiment flitting over each of their faces on the jumbotron as endless applause for their performance pierces the sky.

As soon as they exit the stage, the stadium lights kick up as clouds of lingering smoke rise steadily toward the roof, the field already bustling with a whir of activity.

Knowing the performance wasn't a blatant display to hurt us—but how much it did anyway—is enough to fully resign me.

"You're a stain."

It's when I turn and see the lingering hurt in my father's expression that I allow some of my love for Easton to turn acidic. Revolted by the pain our brief love story caused us all—and the curse that came with it—I defy it all.

Fuck love.

Fuck fate.

Fuck destiny and timing and the chaotic methods of the cosmos that brought us together only to tear us apart in much the same way.

I no longer want any part of it. The cost is too high.

It's Dad's next words that briefly stun me.

"Go to him," he says softly, releasing the hand I'm still holding, his eyes filled with rare defeat, his expression urgent. "Go to him, Natalie."

I shake my head adamantly. "No, Daddy. It's over," I choke out, "It's so over."

"Natalie—"

"I'm certain," I condemn as the last of the smoke drifts up out of the stadium and into the night sky, allowing more resentment in. Even if it feels wrong, I allow the poison to seep into me because it feels a hell of a lot better than continuing to cling to hope for a future with a remedy no longer within reach.

"You're a stain."

"Fuck the Crownes," I declare, full of venom. "Every single one of them, *including me*," I let out a self-deprecating laugh as I fight and win the battle with the sting in my eyes.

No more tears, and one day, no more pain.

"Natalie," my father's eyes command mine, "Is this really what you want?"

"Doesn't matter. It's over." Feeling the finality of it, I hear Easton's venomous whisper repeat in my head.

"You're a stain."

I elbow Dad as I pull up my cellphone. "Let's drive home and surprise Mom."

"You sure?" He asks.

"Yeah, Daddy. Let's go home."

SIXTY-FIVE

From Can to Can't

Corey Taylor, Dave Grohl, Rick Nielsen, Scott Reeder

Easton

Mom begins to run full throttle toward Dad just as our golf cart rounds the curve that leads back to our dressing room. I don't miss the reddening of his eyes just before he exits and stalks towards her. She jumps into his waiting arms and showers him with kisses, tears lining her cheeks as he lifts her from her feet, arms locked around her possessively. Their murmurs echo throughout the hall as they console each other with shaky words and devotion-soaked expressions.

My own eyes burn and sting with the knowledge my father's career has just ended. The finality is sealed with a kiss by the woman who jumpstarted it and spent her life watching it unfold by his side.

Briefly, I see a glimpse of them, younger, colliding the same way all those years ago, and in a cruel twist, an image of Natalie wrapped around me takes its place.

"I've been faithful."

I had a chance of having that. Of what they have. With her.

I can now say that I loved a woman with every fiber of my being, heart and soul, and always will. I can claim that. I wonder how many souls can't.

Knowing that—the gift and rarity of it—all I want right now is the ability to stop the oxygen flow, to cease the reminder pumping in my chest, because the beat feels unnatural now.

The high of playing for an audience that size rapidly dissipates as I stand back, watching those around me embrace in melancholic-laced celebration. Emotions riding high, pieces of me rattle and begin to dismantle inside my skin. For the first time in a very long time, I feel underlying darkness threaten to overtake me.

"I've been faithful."

Knowing she might be here today, even knowing *who for* had amped my anticipation in coming and revived some lingering hope. Every bit of that hope evaporated when I saw her wearing his number—literally wrapped in his fucking name—in his arms and kissing him. That image continually resurfaces, stoking the notion I might have given so much of my love—of myself in vain. I should be riding one of the greatest highs of my life, but it feels more like a white-hot burn raging inside of me during a moment I need to be present. A moment my dad's been working toward most of his life.

"I know you're upset, but it can't be tonight. This night is monumental for him."

"Jesus Christ," I breathe, knuckling my chest, fully absorbing the depth of her plea to me the night we split. Nothing could have kept me away from being here for my parents tonight. *Nothing.*

Dad gently sets Mom on her feet, her beaming smile lighting up the hall before she turns, eyes searching for and finding me before she makes a beeline my way. It's all I can do to maintain my grin as she rushes me and pulls me to her. My insides start to come apart as she murmurs her praises. "No words, baby. No adequate words will do. You just made history. That was the best surprise of my life."

"It was Dad's idea."

"You both got me good." She pulls away and palms my jaw. "There's not a soul alive who can deny your talent now. Get ready, son. There's no stopping this train," she says with surety.

"Thanks, Mom," I utter softly as my ability to keep the burn at bay falters while pieces of me begin to ignite—Natalie's parting shot setting each one of them alight.

"I've been faithful."

My wife should have been *here.* She should be here now, finally taking full claim to the name I gave her, along with her rightful place by my side.

I've given her no reason to be here, not after what I said. I pushed her too far. Even as she confessed that she was miserable, I'd laid into her with all the anger I felt—that I still feel. She did forsake me, *us*. She allowed her guilt to overrule what we had. I put us first, and she martyred us.

Because of that, I let the monster take over and speak on my behalf, making it clear I would never forgive her. I made the notion of there being a future for us an impossibility and slammed the door. I probably just pushed her into the decision of moving on, whether it be with the fucking quarterback I shook hands with or someone else.

Even with some of my animosity justified, the burn doesn't lessen.

I told her she was a fucking stain because I couldn't see anything other than another man's kiss fresh on her lips. So, why *would* she be here?

"Motherfucker," I wheeze as I try to grapple with the fallout, finding no relief in any of my justifications.

I love her. Justifiable anymore or not, I *love* her.

Desperate to douse the overpowering and debilitating loss, I search for distraction and spot Ben, Rye, Adam, and Lucia pulling up in the cart behind ours.

Benji appears and yanks me into his embrace with Lexi on his heels.

"That was fucking…just incredible, brother," Benji claps me on the back, rare emotion heavy in his voice before Lexi pulls me to her, her face littered by mascara streaks when she pulls away. The chatter in the hall continues as the moment is celebrated by all with heartfelt sentiments and long embraces.

"I'm not a rock star anymore." The emotional declaration cuts through the chatter.

A palpable stillness fills the air as every head turns to the source of the disruption where Ben sits in the cart, his eyes zeroed in on Lexi. Mom releases Lexi from her hold as she turns to face Ben while he slowly exits the cart, eyes shimmering but intent. "Do you hear me, Lexi?" He rasps out hoarsely. "I'm not a rock star anymore…"

We all wait with bated breath as Ben stills, lowering his head as if pulling together the words he's waited a lifetime to say. When he lifts his eyes, his emotions spill over. "Now all I am," he swallows, "is the boy you fell in love with, who turned into the man you had a baby with."

Lexi's lips part in shock as the two face off. We all inch back as Ben rings out another declaration. "The man who's loved you with the whole of his heart, year after year, through Every. Single. Thing. Even when you broke it, even when I begged it to stop, tried to force it, willed it to, ignored it. It never failed you, it never stopped loving you, and it never will. I think it's past time I let it, and you let *me* love you with it, *for good.*"

"Ben," Lexi gasps as her eyes flood, and Ben stalks toward her before cupping her face. "It's just us now, baby. You and me. It's our time, Lexi. It's time."

"I love you, too," Lexi confesses, gripping his wrists as he searches her eyes, "so much. Always will." A strangled noise sounds from next to me, and I look over to see Benji utterly entranced by his parents' interaction, a tear coasting down his jaw, hands fisted at his sides.

Ben continues to gaze down at Lexi with unguarded affection, the world around him forgotten as he swipes every tear she's shedding with gentle thumbs. "Come home with me?"

Elated, Lexi replies with a repeated, "Yes, yes, yes," before Ben kisses her soundly. Next to me, I feel the second Benji cracks as a sledgehammer is taken to his impenetrable wall of beliefs. His incredulous eyes follow their every movement as Ben turns back to Benji, telling him they'll be back. With the slight dip of Benji's chin, they disappear down the hall, plastered to each other's sides.

Rye and Adam trail their escape before looking back toward the rest of us with astonished faces. True to his nature, Adam speaks up, tossing a thumb over his shoulder. "Someone, *please tell me* that just happened, and the mushrooms haven't kicked in yet."

Everyone bursts into raucous laughter, aside from Benji and me. Unable to take another second, I head toward the dressing room for a moment to myself. Rian stalks past me toward Benji, concern marring her features. Closing the door, I stand in utter disarray before heading straight toward a dark bottle. Uncapping it, I toss back a few shots, thankful for the short time I stole for myself to try and get my shit together. Visions of my wifeless future flit before my eyes as I tip more of the bottle back in an attempt to blur them out.

Not long after the liquor begins to circulate, I hear the click of the dressing room door and feel his presence behind me as I rummage through my duffle and speak up. "I need a minute alone, G."

"She didn't file, Easton. I told you that months ago."

His statement stokes the fire which begins to consume me wholly.

"And I told you I already knew that," I snarl before taking another swallow of Jack.

"How?"

"Because I know my wife," I say.

"What happened in that bathroom?" he asks, circling the couch to get a read on me. "What did you say to her?"

"I just shared a career-high many don't get," I grit out, pulling off my shirt and wiping the sweat off. "So, back the fuck off."

"It's been months, and you're still bleeding out. I told you not to go after her that amped up. What did you do, Easton?"

"What any man would do when he sees his wife put her lips on another man…I behaved *badly*."

"Jesus," he drags his hands through his hair. "You're destroying yourself."

"What the fuck do you care?" I pull on another shirt, still holding tight to the bottle. "I thought you'd be relieved."

I glance over to see a rare streak of fear in his eyes.

"What, Benji, *what*?"

"The night of the gala, I told you I told her to fuck off and leave you alone."

Bottle already halfway to my mouth, I draw my brows. "Yeah, you told me, so?"

"I was vicious. She called me for help, and I was in a bad place. I told her to make up her mind, and if it wasn't you—if she couldn't choose you, then and there, if she couldn't be what you needed, what you deserved, to stop answering your calls, to let you go."

"Exactly, G, and where is she?" I tilt my head. "Beauty, *you here*?" I scoff, lifting the bottle. Benji snatches the Jack from my hand and blatantly drops it at our feet. The shattered bottle leaks my temporary salvation between us as I glare at him. "I'm about two seconds from throwing another right, the same way I did the *first time* you came clean."

"As much good as it did. Fucking listen to me," Benji barks. "I was *vicious* with her to the point I might have pushed her into ending it with you."

"Don't credit yourself so much, asshole. She's got a mind of her own and a bite much harsher than yours. Case in point, she showed up here on a fucking *date*. You're off the hook." The truth of that is the hardest part to swallow. "We're over. That's what happened in the bathroom. Your dad just ended his career. Go be there for *him*."

"He's not the one that needs me," Benji declares.

Every cell in my body aches as I finally allow myself to acknowledge how much love ricocheted between us in that bathroom, even as my fury overshadowed it. It is still there, just as powerful—the draw, the need, the goddamn breath-stealing ache.

"I've been faithful."

"She's probably still here," Benji tries to encourage.

"It doesn't matter." I shake my head. Because I just tarnished something beautiful, and she stepped back helplessly and watched me do it. "I told you to stay the hell out of my personal life. I remember *that part* of the conversation *well*."

"Listen to me, man. Just try and get your bearings. She's still here, and you can catch her before this goes any further."

"And do what, exactly? Pledge my love and loyalty? I did when I married her. Try to be the husband she needs? She hid herself, her struggles from me. Beg her to see what we stand to lose, if we continue on that way? Did that, too." I glare at him, spitting all the venom I feel. "What the fuck is this? Because your parents are *finally* on the same page, after decades of being at odds, now you're a love enthusiast? I don't want that fucking fate, and that's exactly why we're over. No, thank you."

"You saw what I saw," he digs in further. "Step back, please, East, and take a good look at what you're doing. That's all I'm asking."

Panic seizes me, and even as I fight it, realization overtakes me that if I had a chance in hell of reclaiming the other half of my soul, I just sabotaged it with jealousy and pushed her into another man's arms. Fully aware that even if it doesn't happen tonight, it probably will in the future—which is the most excruciating kind of hell.

"I was unimaginably cruel," I whisper in broken admission.

"I'm so sorry, man. But if there's a chance to fix it, then you should try."

"Yeah, well, how about I take your advice when you apply it *yourself*."

He shakes his head in frustration as Joel walks in, no doubt leaving the seats we secured for his family to congratulate me. The grin on his face dims considerably as he reads the tension in the room. Benji lifts his chin to Joel in acknowledgment as I pull my cell from my duffle to see endless notifications coming in. One notification in particular has my boiling blood turning to ice in my veins. I look up to Benji before opening it and know without a shadow of a doubt what I'll find when I do. "Doesn't matter who filed," I lift the phone for Benji to see. "She just signed the papers."

Turning it back toward me, it's when I note the witness signature, signed by Nate himself, that I allow the darkness to consume me.

SIXTY-SIX

Stinkfist
Tool

Easton

Ambling through the party buzzed, bottle in hand, throat sore despite the numbness taking over, I glance around to see several sets of feminine eyes homing in on me. Nowhere near interested in dipping my toe into that arena, I lower my head and make my way to my suite. On the way, I spot Tack and Syd standing together, surrounded by a group of admirers, and I salute them as I pass. It's been a night to remember for all, and sadly, I've done my best to drink away every minute of it. After doling out strict instructions to security guarding the hallway that I want privacy, I slam myself inside my suite with an exhale.

Relieved I made it through enough of tonight's celebration without overshadowing it with my personal shit, I head toward my balcony. Stepping out, I find LL leaning against the railing, sipping a Coke. His drink selection is laughable because I have no doubt his drug of choice is running through him. He turns to me, confirming it, in his normal state, shaking, skin clammy, and needing a shower.

"The fuck you doing in my suite?" I slur.

"Just admiring the view," condescension ripe in his words, while rolling his eyes down my frame, "both of them."

"Yeah, enjoying this?" I point to myself in my inebriated state. "Well, take a good look, asshole. I won't be down much longer…and heads up, you're the next catastrophic mistake I'm erasing from my future."

"Now, now, don't go getting your knickers in a twist, Easton. You really don't know a good thing when you have it."

"That so?" I say, stumbling slightly, my bottle clanking on a nearby table. "You're such a prize?"

He shakes his head warily before he drains his Coke and wipes his mouth as though the act drained all of his strength. "No, mate, I'm the *bad guy*. But..." he smirks, "sometimes my misdeeds have a way of paying off. All along, I'm the man you should have been *thanking*." He sighs. "Doubt you'll see it that way now."

I toss back more Jack. "This should be good. Thanking you *for*?"

"For jumpstarting your career. For meeting your wife. I knew making that call was a risky move. But you can't lose anything you don't have, am I right?" He pins me briefly with his glacier stare. "Who knew it would actually work in getting you to pull your head out of your arse."

"The fuck?" I drop my bottle, stalking toward him, and fist his shirt.

He laughs in my face before shaking his head. "Temper, temper, young *King*," he bites out. "You're a bloody idiot, you know that?"

"Your opinion means nothing to me, or anyone else for that matter, but go ahead and enlighten me," I grit out.

"Or what, Easton? You'll beat me into submission? How has that been working out for you?"

Finding strength I never imagined I have, I release him.

Amused, he straightens his shirt. "As I was saying, I'm the one who tipped off Rosie. *Rosie*, not *Natalie,* because she was the one with the national gossip broadcast. I always wondered why that story never aired but ironically, a week later, your dad calls us in."

I gape at him as he grips the railing behind him, his knuckles turning white.

"It took me a second to figure out why you suddenly pulled the trigger." He smiles, his eyes glossing over, "and it was because a *different journalist* pursued my lead. Didn't see that one coming."

"Why?" I ask, feeling like I'm having an out-of-body experience as I glare at him, doing everything in my power to keep myself in check.

"Why else, man? To play. Always for the chance to play. You've been such a fumbling idiot with the gifts you've been given. Leaving us hanging for months without knowing our future. Every musician alive would kill for talent like yours, and you were wasting it. So, I did what I had to do to try and force your hand." He sweeps me with a look of clear disdain. "Look at you now. A real *rock star*."

"You're fucking fired."

"No surprise," he snaps. "Nor thanks," he sighs again as if bored, "not that I expected it."

"Jesus Christ, I should end you," I seethe. "Did you out our relationship?"

"No," he slurs. "As much of a bastard as I am, I didn't because I would kill to have a bird look at me the way she looked at you. But you fucked that up well, didn't you?"

"You're disgusting."

"And you're missing my point. Your life, right now, is made up of so many musician's aspirations, and you're squandering it on *senseless* emotions. Not the kind that matter. Anger is not fueled by the heart—bitterness isn't either. Pride? Please, it's annoying. You're annoying, and you'll lose it all by paying attention to the wrong things. The gigs, the women, you're blowing all of it. You owe it to everyone dreaming on a rock star who wishes they had your advantages not to toss it for stupidity. You can start by going to get your bird back."

"She's just divorced me, you fucking imbecile."

"And things aren't going your way anymore because you're all *heart*," he taunts as if my answers are obvious.

On the verge of snapping, I turn my back, heeding Dad's warning. I've already cost myself with my rage, and if I assault LL a second time, he could rob me of some of my net worth, or worse, cost me my career. Maybe that's his intention.

"So why tell me now?"

"Because my dream has played out, and I'll be honest, I'm disappointed, probably because I don't have the drive or energy I used to."

"Just get out," I whisper, the need to hurt him surging through my veins. "Please, man. Just get the fuck out."

"I have just *one ask* before you decide whether or not to bloody me up, mate."

"Fuck you," I spit, my back to him as I text Joel to come for him before I black out on him in a rage.

"Call a medic."

LL's words register as I turn back just as his expression blanks, and he falls, face down, landing in a motionless heap at my feet.

"Somebody help!" I scream, the music drowns me out as I dial 911 and turn LL over to see blood pouring out of his nose and mouth. A few of his teeth are broken, probably due to the dead weight of his fall.

I'm on the phone with the operator, hysterically relaying our location, when Joel and Dad fly onto the balcony. I put the phone on speaker as Joel checks LL's breathing, and Dad curses, frantically trying to get him to respond. When the operator prompts us for a possible cause, I look over to Dad.

"Dad, I don't know what happened. One minute, he was talking his usual shit, the next, he was face down at my feet. I didn't touch him, I swear."

"He's not on anything," Dad says with a grim shake of his head.

"Well, he's not unconscious for no fucking reason!" I say in a panic.

"He's a type 2 diabetic with severe insulin resistance," Dad imparts to the operator. I gape at my father as he works with Joel to try and revive him. Unsure of how much time passes, I avert my attention to LL's lifeless body until two paramedics burst onto the balcony.

Sitting at LL's bedside at the hospital, I stare up at the tiny holes in the ceiling tiles, blindsided by the fact that LL's selfish decision—a decision he disguised as faith in my talent, mixed with his jealousy—is part of the reason behind everything that's happened this past year.

Unreal.

If he ever wakes up, I'm going to kill him. At the same time, should I thank him? The odds are unlikely that will happen since the crazy bastard went kamikaze with my life choices to fulfill dreams he couldn't accomplish on his own.

But if LL hadn't made that call, Natalie would still have found those emails. Rosie's story was Natalie's *excuse* to come to Seattle—to me. Knowing Natalie, she might have come anyway.

That tip-off was the only decision in LL's hands. The result after, completely and utterly a result of my own decisions—of Natalie's decisions.

Is fate real?

The universe starts to feel small as I sort through the domino effect. I wonder if LL even knew his call to the paper in Austin, Texas, held such a history for my mother or if it was a coincidence.

He's an observant fuck, so chances are, maybe he did his research. Perhaps the reason he placed the call was that he was aware of my mother's history at the paper. It's a well-known fact she started her career there.

"What the fuck, man?" I watch LL from the plastic-covered chair at his bedside, the monitors steadily beeping.

Syd and Tack held out for as long as they could, regretting their overindulgence at the party before heading back to the hotel to sleep it off. For some reason when we arrived, I lied to the hospital staff and told them I was LL's next of kin. Oddly enough, Dad was listed as his emergency contact, so my lie would have been believable enough, though it was clear they knew who we were. Dad and I haven't had a chance to talk about his huge fucking omission regarding my lead guitarist yet due to his mission to cover us with PR and get the hotel situation under control while the doctors stabilized LL. I cradle my neck, both hangover and fatigue setting in as the question of how long Dad's known about LL's condition begins to grate on me. As if sensing my need for answers, Dad appears by my side. Eyes on LL, he breaks the silence first. "You should go back to the hotel. Shower, eat. Get some sleep."

"Dad, why didn't you tell me?"

He sighs. "You want to do this now, son?"

"Considering what this bastard confessed, yeah."

"He didn't want any special treatment, and he knew his time was limited. That his disease wouldn't let him play permanently with the band, and I felt for him."

"Who the fuck is this guy?"

"A kid who grew up dirt poor, neglected by shitty parents, and wandered around totally fucked up until he found a guitar. That's his summary, and it's not even the worst of it."

"What is?"

"Ask him yourself when he wakes up."

"Dad, we don't lie to each other. Or at least, I thought we didn't. Not anymore."

"I'm sorry, son, I am. This is the only thing I've been keeping from you, and it was for selfish reasons. I always knew I'd have to come clean, and this would probably be why. I was hoping you two would bond, so he would tell you himself." He chuckles dryly. "That didn't work out."

"Selfish how?"

He looks down at me. "Try not to take offense, but you're such a perfectionist, and I hate saying this, but I think his condition would have clouded your judgment and you would have missed touring with a great guitarist, and...in turn, LL would have missed fulfilling his dream. This was his last chance." He exhales harshly. "I've been in his shoes, been as desperate as he was, and I noticed it right away." Dad's expression darkens, as it does when he talks about that time in his life, years before he and Mom got married. "He wanted it so badly, so much more than anyone else that auditioned, and he's more talented than over half the guitar players I know. I'm sorry if that pisses you off, but I wanted him to have it."

"You're kind of making it hard to stay pissed off," I say, glancing up at him.

Dad doesn't answer, his eyes back on LL as I study him, nothing but empathy rolling off him as I spot my messenger bag dangling from his hand. Dad seems to realize he's blanked out and lifts it within my reach.

"I brought this, just in case you decided to stay. There's some grub in there too."

I grab the offered bag. "Thanks. They're bringing me a cot, though I'm completely clueless why I am staying. I damn near threw him off the balcony tonight."

"Kindred spirits don't always get along. In fact, they often butt heads. I've learned that over the years. Try to understand, son, the hand he was dealt was brutal. He may have proven to be a shifty asshole, but for some reason, he had a part to play in our lives."

"You believe that 11:11 cosmic crap, Dad? Truly?"

"Fuck yeah, I do. There have been times that I tried to reason my way out of it, and even when I'm successful, there has to be a reason *behind that reason*. I gave up trying to figure it out years ago."

"I get exactly what you're saying. I wouldn't have ten minutes ago, but trust me, I'm reeling."

He shakes his head, eyes wary. "Facts are facts, and what's happened over the years—especially in our family—most would consider a series of coincidences, but I deem small miracles." He blows out a harsh breath. "I'm fucking beat. I'm going back to the hotel. Text me when he wakes up."

"What if he doesn't?" I ask, and we share a long, loaded silence.

"Then it will be a tragedy," he replies, eyeing LL before pulling his gaze away.

"I don't hate him, and I'm really not even that pissed anymore, but I can't figure out why," I confess.

"He looks pretty harmless on life support, and maybe because you finally recognize beneath his bullshit, he's a human being that's suffering, and I raised a good man."

I swallow as I focus back on LL. "What the hell are we going to do about our tour? I don't want to leave him in a hospital. I don't think I could even get on stage if he's…here like this."

"One thing at a time," he says, "and that's a ways away. We'll figure it all out."

"Yeah?" I manage a grin. "You going to come out of retirement?"

"Fuck no," he chuckles. "And I'm a drummer."

"The best alive," I add.

He cuffs my shoulder in goodbye. "Love you."

"You, too," I say as he leaves me in the room with LL, who's only breathing right now, due to a machine.

Opening my messenger bag, I retrieve the toothpaste and brush, a clean T-shirt, and a travel-sized bar of Dad's Irish Spring. I can't help my grin at the sight of it and I head to LL's pint-sized bathroom to shower. Tonight most definitely took a turn I wasn't expecting. Distracted by the past four hours, it's when I line my toothbrush that I realize I've propped my cell up against the sink out of old habit. Something I haven't done in months. The difference is, on the other side, the screen remains dark. Gut-wrenching pain crashes into me as I replay every detail of the hours prior.

She *signed*.

Aching and raw, my thoughts stray back to where they have been the last year. I situate myself on the newly delivered bed that was set adjacent to LL's, the quality far better than I had imagined it would be. Thankful for the comfort, I sit atop it and adjust the pillows before pulling my messenger bag into my lap.

Popping the Tylenol and downing the water Dad provided, I glance over to LL. According to the specialist, he's nowhere close to out of the woods yet, his prognosis uncertain, but his comatose state says enough for now.

LL has been neglecting his disease in order to play rock star and keep up with the band and the lifestyle. He wants it so badly that he's risked his life for it and holds a grudge against me for not stepping up. He's been worn out the entire tour. Guilt sets in from the way I've categorized and dismissed him so easily. I'd pegged him as a functioning druggie of sorts. All the while, his body was betraying him. Even if his fucked-up behaviors warranted certain reactions from me, it was his envy to be in my shoes, with my opportunities and my advantages, that put us at odds. He wants what I have—my health, my career, my stage presence, and the love of a worthy woman.

Since my split with Natalie, I realize—to a degree, he's right—I've been slowly imploding. As long as this goes on, the closer I get to becoming the musician I swore I wouldn't be.

It ends now. Tonight.

I can't let any more of my life slip through my fingers, no matter how bad my heart is aching. Broken I may be for the moment, I would do it all over again, just to feel what I did when I had that time to love her. As disastrously as it's ending, I know without a doubt that I would do it all over again.

Running my hands through my hair, I dig for the bag of food Dad stashed, my hand hitting the edge of the manuscript that's been sitting in it for months. Glancing back over at LL, I table the sub and flip to the plastic cover.

Drive
A memoir of a love story through music
by
Stella Emerson Crowne

As I flip through the first few preliminary pages, a small envelope addressed to my mother slides to the edge of the script and into my lap. Opening it, I immediately notice my dad's handwriting.

Stella,

I've been sitting in this hotel for two days, waiting to marry you.

It's irony at its finest. I've been waiting for you so long that sometimes my mind treks back to when we weren't together. When I felt helpless, hopeless, and that life would never give me a chance, no matter how hard I fought back. You became that chance and losing you was agony.

The only thing that kept me going was the possibility that this day would come and the hope there would be no hesitation from either of us to claim what's always been ours.

I missed you to the point my soul bled.

I missed you when I didn't have to.

I miss you now.

I'm okay with how it fucking stings because it's a reminder of how hard that part of my life was without you. The silver lining is that in a few hours, you'll claim my name. Nothing has ever meant so much to me, and nothing will ever mean more.

This day is about us. But it's still tainted with my regret.

I got us lost.

I should have fought harder for you. I thought being selfless and letting you go made me the bigger man. I should have been a little more selfish and heavy-handed. I wish I had done more to ensure you knew your place was with me. I would give anything to erase the years we missed, but I can't help but to thank those years...and as much as I fucking hate it, thank him for being there when I couldn't—encouraging you to become the woman you are now, the woman I was meant to be with, no matter how we grew.

Thank Christ we grew back together. And fuck me that I didn't have more of a hand in it.

But if fate can bring us back full circle and gift us a new life where I don't have to miss you, I can only try to forgive.

My expectation is this, us, nothing more. It's so simple but a means to an end to the most complicated journey I've ever taken. Forgive me for being blind to the fact that your love was bottomless, and I'll forgive fate and the hard road we had to travel.

You are my destination, my life. I don't need anything else.

Take those steps toward me today and put your hand in mine, and with a stinging soul, I promise never to get us lost again.

I love you, and I'm waiting.

Reid

Chest burning, I turn the page.

SIXTY-SEVEN

I Still Love You

NIGHT TRAVELER

Natalie

Quarterback Sneaks Out On Media Princess.

"Well, this is just fucking embarrassing," I admit, handing my father's tablet back to him as he eyes me with concern across my desk. "Gotta admit, the headline is pretty clever and a nice play on words."

His eyes flare with a fury that I know he's trying his best to temper. "Do you want to take the day?"

"Hell no. I'm not cowering away from this."

The lines begin to light up more aggressively on my phone console, no doubt another nightmare for the paper. I've gone and done it again—making *Austin Speak* a media target. Dad has probably already hired the same security he commissioned months ago, at the end of my last disastrous relationship. I wince when every line goes red. "Crap, Dad, I'm sorry."

"It will die down," he assures me with the wave of his hand. "There'll be something within a day or two to take the place of this."

"I will *never* date a public figure again. Scout's honor." I grin, giving him a playful salute.

His expression remains impenetrably one of parental concern.

"Trust me, Mr. Butler, this is hurting *you* far more than it is me. Sorry about the season tickets."

"Natalie," he sighs.

"Daddd," I draw out. Am I embarrassed? Yes. Is my pride stinging, of course. Tye turned out to be more of a super *whore* than a superhero. Though we didn't need a paternity test to end our relationship. Apparently, Tye fathered a child *during* our short stint as the media's new 'it' couple. A relationship the media drew out far longer than it lasted. Ironically, the reason for our breakup is as much news to me as it is to the rest of the world.

Sadly, my future didn't go quite to plan as Easton predicted.

No puppy.

No ring.

No future carpool full of internal self-loathing.

Take *that*, rock star.

Stifling the threat of lingering on any more of Easton's predictions, a little laugh escapes me as Dad looks at me like I'm growing an extra head.

"Just another embarrassing media bookmark of my crappy streak with men. Awesome." Dad winces at my candor. "Come on, Daddy, we are *press*. It's ironic."

Dad fumes, and for a hot second, I fear for Tye if they ever again come face to face. "Don't you even think about calling a favor in to smear him, young man," I jest. "It's poor form."

He presses his lips together as I nail his line of thinking.

Guilty.

"No-no, Daddy," I scold playfully. "You're not allowed to punish my exes with a rolled-up newspaper." Nate Butler has far too much integrity to carry out one of the dozen revenge scenarios forming in his mind, which only makes me smile.

He crosses his arms, fatigue in his posture as I do my best to ease his worries. Since the Super Bowl, we've become a lot closer to where we used to be, in a time I now define as B.E.C.—Before Easton Crowne.

"If it's any consolation, I've decided to give dating a rest for a while."

I get nothing but a sad, blue stare in return.

"Tough room. Dad, I'm okay, better than okay," I say honestly. "Tye was an attempt at a rebound, reigning Super Bowl champ or not."

"You liked him."

"I did, from what I knew of him, but love was never in the cards. I think he knew it, and that's probably why he dipped out—or *into* someone else."

Dad cringes at my frankness, and I join him. "Sorry, too far."

"Don't blame yourself for another man's poor fucking choices."

"I'm not. Trust me, and I won't."

"Okay, but if you change your mind, just take off. The building will probably be surrounded within the hour."

"God bless Texas," I say. Paparazzi are nowhere near as prominent in Austin as they are in other cities, though in this age if you're recognizable enough, *everyone's* a pap. We're lucky that people still rely on the news at this point with so many rogue reporters out there. Sadly, being Easton Crowne's ex and now Tye's, I am highly recognizable, but in the *worst* possible way.

Regardless, I have no doubt whoever is in the vicinity is making a beeline for *Speak*. "If it gets to be too much, I'll jet. Promise."

Seeming satisfied, Dad stands and heads toward my office door. My courtship with Tye made headlines for the five weeks we 'dated,' which did nothing to aid my belief that we had some sort of fairytale future. Easton did his part to taint the idea the day of the Super Bowl, but Tye and our reality as a couple—which was nonexistent—finished it off.

There were few sparks without a single trace of fire. I've had fire, and even if I lost it, I refuse to settle for anything less. I also refuse to believe that my chances of ever having it again are as slim as my ex claims. Case in point, my father celebrated his twenty-fourth wedding anniversary after losing who he thought was the love of his life.

Even if a large part of me believes Easton, I'm determined to die on my stance to keep my eyes open in search for smoke. Otherwise, well…fuck the alternative. I'm too young to consider myself damned and believe it's already a curtain call for me in the love department.

I'm not aiding Easton's ridiculous belief that I have no hope of any real romantic future or buying into 'the one and only' notion anymore, no matter how true it feels at times and especially on days like today.

Screw Easton Crowne and the awareness that loving him brought me.

Screw men in general, aside from the *one* man I've almost always been able to count on.

Dad lingers at my office door as I do my best to relieve him of the burden of being a concerned parent. "Please tell Mom just how *fine* I am and be gone, good media king," I wave him away, "this *princess* has a deadline. Find someone else to hover over and terrorize."

Dad lingers a bit longer when my intercom buzzes, and I snatch the cradled phone like the lifeline it is, willing to talk to *anyone* who will get the overprotective guardian out of my office.

"Line one—"

"Got it," I say, with the phone already to my ear, continuously shooing my father away. When he's out of earshot, I hit the button with a 'no comment' ready on my tongue. "This is Natalie Hearst."

"Beauty..."

Stunned, I focus on the blooming flowers of my screensaver and school my expression.

"Are you okay?" His voice is void of sarcasm, but that does nothing to curb my contempt.

"About the puppy? I'm good. I'm not much of an animal person anyway, a fun fact you didn't know about your ex-wife."

"I didn't fucking mean that," he rasps out, his voice scratchy as though he just woke up.

"Well, you were right about some of it, so feel free to congratulate yourself."

"Natalie...I'm sorry."

"I've already forgiven you, and I did it for *me*. Anything else?"

"I'm in Austin."

"Yeah? Good for you. Go to Sam's on 12th street, amazing barbecue."

"Can I see you?"

"No thanks. I barely survived the last scathing interaction." Heart pounding, I tilt my head and type gibberish on my board to make myself look busy while feeling the prodding blue eyes across the pit.

Not again. Nope. Nope. Nope.

"You're a stain."

Easton made every imaginable headline professionally for weeks following the Super Bowl. His sales skyrocketed along with the simultaneous hunger for his picture and any personal information. His half-time performance blasted him into the stratosphere, quadrupling his already impressive sales and putting all twelve of his singles on the Billboard, numbering one through twelve. Personally, he disappeared, not a single picture of him surfacing. Not only has Easton's success become ceaseless in media chatter, but the Sergeants' performance was rated by many as one of the top ten half-time shows in NFL history. Even so, Easton seems to have exiled himself from the spotlight.

"Let me come to you," he says. "I want to apologize in person."

"No!" I blurt as several sets of eyes fly my way. "No," I repeat, lowering my voice. "It's not a good idea, and you know it's not. Listen to me…you're okay, you're better than okay, and I'm going to be okay, and I need you to respect that. I'm happy for you, I really am, and I'll accept your apology now, but please don't call me again. There's nothing more to say. I wish you well."

I hang up the phone and stare at it, just as the line instantly lights up with another incoming call. The gravity of what I just did begins to hit as I try not to let the burn singe too much of me.

He didn't call. You imagined it.

The lines continue to explode, and my phone texts tick up in numbers—no doubt Holly and Damon attempting to check on me.

I send them a group text to assure them I'm okay, and they both instantly start an emotional welfare check interrogation.

"Damnit," I mutter, hanging my head. Dad's right. I need to try to avoid this circus for at least a few days until some of the storm blows over. Grabbing my laptop, I walk across the pit. Employees eyes follow me as I command my heart to slow.

He didn't just call. You imagined it. He's not in Austin.

I knock on Dad's doorframe, and he immediately puts his call on hold, kicking back in his leather chair while squeezing his stress ball.

"What's up?" He eyes my laptop.

"You're right. I'm going to go. I'll work from home for the next few days. I'm so sorry, Daddy."

"Look at me," he commands, and I do. "Do I look upset? This isn't on you." I can feel his aggravation for me in his posture, but see nothing but love in his eyes.

"Thank you. Love you."

"You too. Come home if you want."

"I may ride Percy later on. I'll let you know."

With that, I hurriedly make my way to the back exit of the building. The minute I step out, I'm blinded by the Texas sun while my name is shouted from a block away by a voice I don't recognize. They're already here.

"Shit."

Digging in my purse, hand on my stun gun, I round the building and stop briefly as I spot the few who've gathered in front of the main entrance. Turning, I start a sprint as they catch sight of me fleeing toward the coffee shop where I parked this morning in anticipation. The second I turn the corner, a black SUV cuts me off in the alley, just as I'm spotted by a few more photographers. I shield my face with my laptop as a window lowers, expectant of camera flashes. "No comment for the rest of my fucking life!"

"Think that will work for me?" an amused voice replies, followed by an accompanying chuckle. Lowering my laptop, I meet the jade eyes that haunt me in the waking hours when my guard is lowered.

"What in the hell are you doing?!" I snap, realizing Joel is in the driver's seat, grinning at me, seemingly just as amused. "I told you I didn't want to see you!"

"Damn, Beauty, you're foul today," Easton's smooth voice reaches my ears, and I shake off the chill, knowing it has nothing to do with the lingering spring temperature.

"Might want to get in," Easton urges as I glance back and see paparazzi closing in, less than a block away.

"Damnit!" I open the door, Joel rolls the windows up and I manage to slam myself inside just as they surround the car.

"This is just fucking perfect!" I shield my face again with my laptop as we're engulfed, and flashes go off. Joel lays on the horn before slamming on the gas, giving us a wider berth while tearing out of the alley in reverse.

"Good to see you, Nat," he chimes in obvious amusement before throwing the SUV into drive and speeding away from the swarming bodies chasing us.

Stare lingering back through the rear windshield, I unload a slew of curses as Joel maneuvers us through traffic while breaking every imaginable law.

Turning my glare toward Easton, I'm struck stupid by the sight of him smiling, his green eyes glittering as he drinks in my appearance. I close my eyes and tilt my head back on the rest as his chuckle fills the cabin.

"This isn't funny. *At fucking all*," I grit out.

"Depends on the perspective, I guess."

I slink back in the buttery soft seat, my laptop and purse clutched to my chest, my leather skirt riding high on my thighs. Why am I wearing a leather miniskirt, heels, and a thin V-neck sweater that highlights my cleavage on a frosty spring day? Because I'm determined to send a message that I will not cower away from the perception of being cheated on, nor will I play the martyr by dressing like a nun. The outfit is borderline office inappropriate, but I didn't want to be caught in the crosshairs of the blood-thirsty media looking my worst on a day where they're conspiring to paint me the victim. Thank God Dad got the heads up on the story breaking last night, so we were better prepared. I have zero doubts that after today I'll be the woman notorious for being unable to keep a rock star and one of the world's greatest athletes within my grasp.

The attention to the details I put into my appearance are blatant as Easton's gaze lights up my skin. I keep my own averted while the downtown buildings pass us in a blur.

After a few wordless seconds, Easton closes in and gently pries my whitening fingers from my laptop before setting it on the seat between us.

Ignoring Easton's play for attention, I speak up. "Joel, will you please drop me home?"

"They'll be there waiting," Easton reminds me.

"I can handle it, and I said I didn't want to see you."

"You've barely looked at me since you got in the SUV, so you're safe in that respect."

"Glad you find this so amusing, but I'm not in need of saving today."

"You never really have been, have you?"

"I wouldn't go that far. I was damn near *delusional* when we met."

"You had grandiose dreams of finding true love."

"Yeah," I retort, "we both see how that worked out."

Silence.

"Joel," Easton summons softly. Joel pulls over a minute later in a busy shopping center, exiting the SUV. I sit silently in anticipation and don't wait long.

"You can continue to feed me bullshit, or you can really talk to me. Either way, I see what you're not saying, Beauty."

Do not look at your beautiful ex-husband, Natalie. Do not look at your beautiful ex-husband.

"It's called self-preservation," I snark. "You should try it sometime. Though I doubt the tortured artist that dwells inside you will allow it for your *long prosperous* career."

"I know what's real."

"Yeah, so you've told me." I turn to see his eyes heating. "Stop looking at me like that."

"Like what?"

"Like I'm some sort of answer," I bite cynically. "Clearly I'm not."

"Aren't you?"

"No. I'm a *fucking stain*, remember?"

The silence drags on until I finally brave a glance over to see Easton staring out the window. So many questions rest on my tongue, but I can't ask them. I go for diplomatic instead.

"LL…is he okay? I read that he's recovering, but how is he now?"

"He's good, but it was close. Much to his complete and utter dismay, he's going to be under strict medical care the entire time we're overseas, and we're going to go from there."

"Are you two…getting along?"

"Yeah," Easton nods. "There's a lot more to him than I originally thought. But then again, he's still LL," his chest bounces with a silent chuckle.

"I knew it wasn't drugs," I relay happily.

"He wanted the dream," Easton says softly, "so much that he risked his life for it."

More questions spring to mind, but I can't ask them. I can't, because if I do, I know I'll want to dive deeper. There's nothing about this man I don't want to know. Do I still know him? The awareness trying to awaken inside me says I do, and I'm still probably one of the closest people to him.

Do I still *want* to know him?

Six weeks ago, the old me would have jumped at the chance

to remain in his life, but our last exchange broke something inside me—mostly hope. Our relationship felt toxic when he left me in that bathroom.

Even with all his allure, and the things his presence does to me, I feel stronger, even if I'm still bleeding.

"What are you thinking?" He asks softly without looking my way.

I sigh. "That I'm too damned young to feel this tired," I glance at my smartwatch, "at eight twenty-seven a.m. Easton, what are you doing in Austin?"

"We'll get to that."

Turning, he reads my real question.

"Yeah, Beauty, I was already here before I found out your boyfriend cheated on you."

I nod. "So, are you kidnapping me?"

"Do you really want to go home and search the web for bullshit?"

"No, but spending time with you could be just as catastrophic."

"I'm not here to hurt you, Natalie."

"Thank God for small favors," my reply is barely audible.

He pulls my hand from the seat, and I shake my head adamantly, denying his touch. "Please don't."

His shoulders slump forward as he pulls his hand away. "All right. Part of why I'm here is that I wanted to apologize in person. I didn't mean it, what I said about your future. I had a little growing up to do and still do. But I didn't mean what I said. You're too fucking smart to settle for less than what you deserve, and you didn't."

"So was my father," I clarify. "If I would have realized that before I went off on a wild goose chase, then we—"

"Never would have happened," he finishes, my conclusion paining him *and me*. "And I know."

"Know what?"

"We'll get to it," he assures again.

I decide to give him honesty. "I've spent the last six weeks pulling myself together, Easton. Part of that was forgiving you. I'm still working on me."

"But you haven't," he whispers softly. "Not really."

"I haven't heard a word from you since I divorced you and really never expected to again. What is with you fucking Crownes anyway? Is it our surname? Butlers to serve the Crowne? Is that why you people think you can barge into our lives, take what you need from us, and tear us apart before you take off again?"

He runs his hands through his hair. "Is that what you think I'm doing?"

"I think…that I remember every second of what I felt from the minute we met and the days, weeks, and months leading up to the last time I saw you and after. So no, I don't truly believe that it's intentional. But letting my heart rule my head, I'm fucking done with that, and I have to be for a while. We were idiots," I whisper in an attempt to keep my voice even. "You know that, right? Both of us. We eloped after a handful of months together and really expected to be some sort of rare exception." I bite my lip, withholding the comment that I believed we were.

"I still have the same heart I did then, Beauty. It beats the same fucking way. You're still angry, so stop lying about that."

"Why do you think that? Because I'm trying to use good judgment?" I retort. "Something you've never bothered to try and understand."

Resting his face against the seat, his eyes float over and sweep me wholly. "Give me the words."

"The words?"

"A way to get to *her*," he says softly. "Something, anything to get back to her. Point me there. Because I really need to talk to *her* today."

I return his earnest gaze with a frown before I realize what he's asking. He wants the woman who was open with him, who didn't hide behind the hurt, the woman who trusted him and handed over her heart. The woman he married. The version of the woman he nicknamed 'Beauty' because of his attraction to the raw, unguarded state he drew from within her that had nothing to do with her appearance. The version he left in shambles with his parting words in that bathroom. "Easton—"

"Fuck," he sighs, "okay, Natalie, just tell me where you want to go, wherever that may be."

He knocks on the window, and within seconds, we're being chauffeured through Austin streets.

Knowing I'm being unreasonable and childish, I entertain the idea of hearing him out as I scan his face. This may be our chance to fix what we jaded and sullied and leave each other amicably. Flashes of my life in Austin flit through my mind, of places I've felt safe, of places where I know we might be able to make peace with all that's transpired. Glancing in the rearview, I project my directions to Joel. "Get on 35 South."

"The middle of fucking nowhere," Easton muses as I start to walk through the lifeless pasture toward a cluster of oak trees. The sun mildly warms the morning as I turn back to Easton with my explanation.

"My father's best friend, Marcus, Damon's dad, owns this land. These are some of my old childhood stomping grounds." I scour the field and sigh. "I haven't been here in years. It seemed so much bigger back then. Must admit, it's lost some of its magic."

Easton steps up next to me and sweeps the large pasture before I feel his eyes on my profile for long seconds. "Can't have that."

He turns on a dime and walks over to the SUV, conversing briefly with Joel. In less than a minute, the SUV is speeding away from us, leaving us alone in the frost-tipped field.

"What the hell are you doing?"

Easton walks toward me with confident strides. "Trust me?"

"Sadly…maybe a little."

"Okay then," he says, walking further into the field toward a twin cluster of oak trees as I follow, my heels sinking into the dirt.

"Shit, this was a bad idea," I say, inspecting the bottom of one of my soiled heels, "these are expensive—"

In a blink, I'm swept into Easton's arms honeymoon-style. Inhaling his intoxicating scent, I glare at him while being forced to wrap around him for support. I don't miss his satisfied smile.

"You're going to fuck this place up for me," I mumble.

"Not intentionally," he replies, biting away the rest of his smile as he carries me over to the trees. When we get to his designated destination, he gently sets me onto my feet on brownish-green grass. A cool breeze freezes me where I stand just as the smell of cow shit hits us both. Our eyes meet as the putrid stench overtakes us, and we burst into laughter.

"Yeah," he chuckles, "I can smell why you thought this place is *magical*."

"Shut up."

"Just admit it, out of the two of us, you're the shittier tour guide."

"Whatever. I was forced to think on my toes, and this is what I came up with. You're welcome to summon Joel back." I wave my hand dismissively and sit on the cool grass, staring up at the cloudless early morning sky.

"Nah, this is the perfect place," he twists a piece of plucked grass between his fingers after taking a seat next to me.

"Okay, I'm here, and I'm freezing. Out with it."

"I'm getting to it," he says, "just talk to me for a little while."

"What's the point?"

"Because you're the only one I find I want to talk to anymore, and I fucked that up. So please, Natalie, humor me."

His eyes search mine briefly, and I nod. Ten minutes of small talk later, Joel pulls up and pops the back hatch of the SUV.

"What's going on?"

Easton stands. "Sit tight."

In minutes, Easton's stalking back towards me, arms loaded. A bag hangs from one of his wrists as he hauls a Styrofoam cooler covered with thick, folded blankets, a bound manuscript sitting atop them. Standing, I help him spread a blanket and wrap myself in another as he unloads a bag full of snacks and a thermos full of coffee. Popping the top off the cooler, I discover a mix of juices, water, and beer. "Seriously, Joel is a miracle worker," I say, pulling out a water.

"Yeah, he is," Easton agrees. "Is it weird that my best friend is twenty years older than me?"

"No. Not at all. Why? Did someone tell you that?"

"Yeah. But you know I don't care about anyone else's opinions." He stares at me pointedly, and I read between the lines. *But yours.*

Refuting the new chill up my spine, I eye the script.

"Time to come clean, Easton."

"When we split, I struggled with it so badly. It never felt right. Not once. I couldn't understand why the most beautiful, intelligent creature to ever come into my life wasn't for me..." he shakes his head and swallows.

Please, God, be merciful.

"I went a little rogue, and then I ignored it, but I decided I had to figure it out, or I wouldn't be able to find any peace. LL's incident kind of drove me over, and it was that night I realized the answer to everything plaguing me had been sitting in my messenger bag for months."

He flips the cover of the manuscript.

"I've seen the movie."

He shakes his head. "This is the *book* my mom wrote, the *whole* story."

I pick it up and weigh its thickness. "With my father?"

"Yeah. It's all in there. All of it."

"Where did you get it?"

"Mom gave it to me when we were all at odds—before the night of the gala, before we broke up—but I was too pissed at them to bother opening it."

For the first time since Easton pulled up, I feel real fear snake through me.

"Easton, I don't know if I can go back there," I shiver, tightening the blanket more firmly around me. "I don't see the point."

"Whatever trust you have left for me," he whispers, "use it now, okay?"

Biting my lip, I stare back at him before my fear finally speaks for me. "I don't see how this—"

"Beauty," he murmurs, and in that second, our eyes connect, and all the space between us disappears.

We're just raw hearts who completely recognize the other. It's the best I've felt since before we separated on our honeymoon. Blowing out a breath, I slowly nod my head and turn the first page.

SIXTY-EIGHT

The Dance
Fist of Five

Natalie

On a plush blanket in the middle of nowhere, I pull on a dark beer as I continue to read. Morning became afternoon, and as the story progressed, I traded in coffee for something a little stronger to take the hard edge off Stella's bared bones story about falling for two men—our *fathers*. Every so often, I glance up at Easton where he lays propped on his side. He's dressed in jeans, solid red high tops, and a thick hoodie—a hoodie no doubt covered in his scent, which he's offered more than once, and I've repeatedly declined. Earbuds in, he's posted next to me like he has all the time in the world. More than once, I've found his eyes trailing down my exposed skin, denying myself the rush it brings as I became more immersed.

Flipping a page, I feel the heat rush to my cheeks as Stella sneaks over to Reid's apartment for the first time. Throat drying, my pulse kicks up.

"She blushes." I look up to see Easton smirking.

"You *read* this?"

"The whole thing," he says softly, "but *you* might be skimming soon."

"This feels..."

"Invasive? Yeah, I thought so too, at first, but it's the story she wanted to share with the world. Keep going," he urges, moving to lay on his back, his hoodie riding up to expose some of the tattoo on his side. Ignoring the urge to trace the skin with my gaze, I divert my focus back to the page, continue reading, and become lost.

Hours later, sitting with the script propped on my thighs, tears streaming down my cheeks, I read Stella's tearful goodbye to my father as they locked eyes across the stage at the music festival. Swallowing repeatedly, Easton gently scrapes away a tear with the pad of his finger as I soak in the true ending of their relationship while marveling at what an incredible man my father was and *is*. Of how Stella truly loved him. The words blur until I manage to make it through the last few pages, understanding the context of their final emails more clearly.

Reeling from what I have just experienced, I lay the manuscript on the blanket, staring at the rapidly darkening sky. We lay there for a few silent minutes as I absorb what I just read, a vortex of feelings. Turning my head, I look over to see Easton's eyes on me.

"Say something," he whispers.

"It's pretty obvious now why we were born so close together," I manage a watery smile. "My parents were on their honeymoon, and your mother was...reaffirming their relationship." I shake my head. "This is all so crazy. Our stories are so different and so similar too. It's like...I don't know what to do with all of this," I pull in a shaky inhale, my heart raw as my emotions get the best of me, and I let my words fly.

"My dad tried at the Super Bowl. He really did. For the most part, he was okay, but that song forced him to relive that night, and it didn't matter. It didn't matter how much time had passed—he felt it. Watching him relive it...it was hell on earth. I was so angry with your mother, with you, with our circumstances, with what became of *us*, that's how I was able to—"

"Sign the papers," he finishes for me. "I can't blame him, Natalie. I just can't anymore." Easton blows out a harsh breath. "I was fool enough to believe that time mattered. But love is like music for so many in the fact that it's—"

"Timeless," I finish for him. "That's how I felt about their emails, like it was happening *as* I read them." Another tear escapes as I shake my head. "I don't know what to say. I'm just..."

"You don't have to explain it to me," he assures. "But I've been fucking blind to how much you *could* see. I always was. You saw how much it was destroying your father and our families, and I was too consumed in what I felt for you to see you were right in many respects. I'm sorry for that."

"Yeah. But I see too. I see how she truly loved him. I-I—"

"Clarity, insight, remorse," he finishes for me. "That's why I'm here. I wanted you to have this, so you could get some much-needed, much-deserved perspective, if you still wanted it. You paid for it dearly. We both did. Fuck knows I needed it and found it in there." He moves to sit. "I tried to hate him, but the more I read, the more I understood who Nate is, it evaporated. Somewhere deep down, I knew if I read it, I couldn't hold him responsible."

"God, what we put them through," I say. "I feel so bad for all of them."

"There was no winner," he says.

"I came to that conclusion months ago."

Easton nods. "At least we know why they reacted the way they did and were initially so fucking adamant about keeping us apart."

"It's so weird, but I'm not angry anymore."

"Me neither," he croons softly, lifting his eyes to the purpling sky.

"I'm just...sad." I press against my aching chest with both hands. "Jesus, this hurts so much."

"There's more," he says, pulling an envelope from his pocket, "but I have to take this back with me."

I open it to see it is a letter addressed to Stella. More tears emerge as I read Reid's letter to Stella on their wedding day and finish it with an exhale bordering a sob. "God, it's so beautiful. Thank you for sharing it with me."

"I probably shouldn't have, and I don't think Mom realized she left it in there. But we've come this far...and there's more."

"Um, Easton, look at me," I wave my hand around my stinging cheeks. "Do you really think I'm up for it?"

"Not like that," he lifts his chin toward the paper. "Look at the bottom of the stationery."

I lift it, and even with dusk setting in, I manage to catch the logo.

"The Edgewater," I gasp, utterly stunned. "That's just…wow."

"I wonder which room it was," he says thoughtfully. "I wonder if Dad remembers."

"I bet he does, but please don't tell me, because I have a feeling it will totally freak me out."

"But it's cool, right?"

Biting my lip to hide the tremble, I nod in agreement.

"We were asking too much, weren't we?" I wipe my eyes with my sweater sleeve. "Doomed from the start."

"That's not my take away. Mine is a lot like my father's now," he exhales, "I have a grudge-filled respect for Nate Butler that I couldn't have ever managed before."

"He's a good man."

"Yeah. I wish…fuck…," he exhales, "what I wish. And as much as I fucking hate to admit it, they all had every right to their initial reaction. When they were trying to get over it—"

"We screwed the rest up ourselves," I finish for him.

He gives me a subdued nod.

"Thank you for this," I say, hugging the manuscript to my chest. "I wonder if my father has read it."

"He *lived* it," Easton says, "but I don't think so. Mom says her agent and lawyer reached out with the original, and he denied having any part in it."

"He did?" I shake my head as dozens of answers to questions I never thought to ask circle in my mind. Silence lingers as I start to plug some of the pieces into place.

"You're going to have a lot to unpack," Easton supplies, "it will take a little time, but you'll get through it."

"My dad was a badass," I grin, hugging the manuscript a little harder.

"Mine was an *asshole*," he says, "*and* a badass."

"How do you feel about the part where he…almost—"

"Killed himself?" Easton shakes his head while brushing off his jeans. "I never would have thought him capable of that, but the way I feel sometimes when I get really low, I understand the thoughts… Honestly, I can barely imagine that version of him. Living on a mattress, starving, on a fucking floor."

"Your mother saved him by washing his hair," a fast tear forms and falls, and he catches it with his thumb, seeming briefly fascinated by it.

"Jesus, Crowne. You know, you *always* do this to me. One minute I'm emotionally stable and somewhat put together, and the next, with you, I'm a damn mess."

"Such a beautiful mess," he fires back.

I glance around as the sun disappears. "What have *you* been doing all day?"

"Staring at my beautiful wife."

"*Ex*-wife."

"Right," he says as he stands and holds out his hand. "Come on, Beauty. I'll take you home."

The ride back to my apartment is silent as I mull over what I just read, which felt more like what I *lived*. Our parents' love story in its entirety. Emotions swirl in my chest as my mind races with the knowledge we *both* have now.

Joel pulls the SUV to a stop two buildings away from mine and parks between two cars to keep us hidden. When he exits, a strange energy rolls off Easton, who sits next to me, his gaze trained out his passenger window. I can't get a clear read on him as I soak in his profile—as much as I can in the dark cabin of the SUV.

"So, now we both know," I state the obvious, my perception shifting by the second. "Do you…feel like it was a mistake…like we were a mistake?"

"Never, and I never fucking will," his declaration strikes deep. "So yeah, now we both know," he says, his voice hoarse. "It's funny though."

"What?"

"Their story doesn't change the significance of ours." I manage to catch him licking the corner of his mouth as he keeps his gaze on the car parked next to him.

"So, do we try to forgive each other now?" I ask.

"I want to… See, the thing is, I will never regret us, Beauty, because…" he seems to sort through his words, choosing each carefully—which I hate because it's new, and I know it's because of post-apocalyptic Easton and Natalie.

"Because?"

He turns to face me, eyes shimmering. "I can't recall any other time in my life where I was so blissfully happy." A tear slowly rolls down his cheek, "Can you?"

The burn starts in my throat, and I choke out my answer while letting my own tears free. "No."

"If that's not a sign of something fucking real, something worth fighting for, something worth *keeping*, then I don't know fucking anything at all."

"We tried," I sniff, my own tears cascading down my cheeks, "didn't we?"

"We succeeded," he says, plucking one away, "we really did when we kept everyone else out of it."

"Until we tore each other apart," I say. "We…." I shake my head. "We *really hurt* each other."

"I'm sorry," he whispers. "I still think the world of you. I still think you're the most beautiful creature I've ever laid eyes on. I will never regret us."

"Jesus, Easton, can't you, just for once, be a less authentic human being? Just once?"

"You know I fucking can't," he replies with a shaky breath.

"So, what's your future now?" I ask, just as Joel raps on the hood and Easton eases away from me.

"New York," he answers. "We're kicking off the tour at the Garden in five hours."

"That's right," I say. "A European tour. That's so incredible. Are you excited?" He gives me a small dip of his chin.

The air of the SUV thickens with emotion as I blurt my truth. "Easton, I don't want to not know you. You became my best friend. I miss that so much, outside of everything else. Can we at least try to be what we couldn't be before? I don't want to not know you," I repeat. "It's too hard. I miss you." He remains quiet as I grab his hand, and he turns back to face me. "Maybe, one day, when it doesn't feel…so much like entering the seventh circle of hell?"

He lowers his eyes to our clasped hands, and I'm not sure he's going to answer, but he speaks up, his voice ragged. "Yeah, maybe then."

Joel knocks again on the hood in warning.

"I've got to go. I've got a plane to catch," Easton sighs.

"But this, right now, this isn't goodbye, right?" My pulse picks up as panic sets in.

"Not for me. I really need to go," he repeats.

"But we will talk again?" I ask, unrestrained tears flowing down as I gather my purse and laptop and clutch them to me.

He focuses on me, his expression pained. "If you ever…need me," he utters softly, "I'll be right where you left me, okay?" He turns back toward the window as the roar in my chest intensifies.

"Okay," I agree easily. "You, too." I pause with my hand on the door. "Easton?"

"Yeah, Beauty?"

"Did you just *lie to me* for the first time?"

"I don't know," he utters weakly as Joel knocks again. "I don't want it to be."

"Okay," I say, opening my door. "Okay," I whisper, "well, I won't say goodbye then. H-h-have a good show tonight."

He nods as I open the door and step out of the SUV. Joel gazes at me, reading my expression, before pulling me into him—my laptop smashed between our chests as we hug.

"Take care of him, please, Joel."

"I'm trying," he presses a kiss against my temple.

"I love you," I sniffle, "you know that, right?"

"You too, sweetheart. I'm here for you always."

"Same."

A sob escapes me before I rip myself away from his warm embrace and turn, starting at a dead run toward my apartment.

Standing in Easton's jacket on my balcony that night, holding my Edgewater teddy bear, wind whipping around me, I blur out the downtown noise as I replay our parents' love story—clicking in the last pieces of the puzzle that has plagued me since I began my search a year ago. It's on the wind, in an urgent whisper that Stella's words come to me.

"Look up."

And I do. Straining against the restraints of my balcony, I search for and fail to find a single star while standing in the haze of the bustling city below. Sniffing the collar of Easton's jacket, I note the absence of a scent that used to be so present. He was just with me, his warmth within reach, but I couldn't allow myself to get intimate or reacquainted with it. I wouldn't have survived it. The only thing I regret now is everything left unsaid. So many things I wished I would've told him, knowing that we may never speak on that sort of unguarded, intimate level again. Remorse riddles me until I decide for what it's worth to relay some of it by text, in hopes to open a window, even if the door feels closed. Just as I go to compose a message, a video attachment comes in from Joel. I open it to see Easton paused on screen, on stage behind his piano, a lone spotlight shining down on him.

Joel sent me tonight's encore.

Heart speeding, I click play, and Easton begins to play the opening of "The Dance," an old favorite of my father's I'm oddly familiar with. But within the first few bars, I realize Easton's playing a very *different* version than the one I know. When the words begin to pour from his lips, he sings about love found and lost. About being thankful for the ignorance of the cost of the toll that love would take. The music takes a haunting, drastic turn, and Easton goes heavy, gutturally screaming along with LL's heavy guitar riffs. My entire body lights on fire, every hair standing on end with the knowledge that he's singing of our demise. Every word burns through to my core as he plays expertly along the keys before tilting his head back and screaming, coming apart on stage. I see and *feel* it all, the bitterness and rage in his posture, the agony in his expression, the loss of us. Hysterical sobs leave me as Easton brutally echoes the most defining moments of my life. He leads the song through a heart-stopping crescendo…and then it's just him and his piano, the final notes ringing in clearly as he whispers the last lyric into the mic before slamming it closed.

The meaning of this act is not at all lost on me.

Gaping at the screen as the stage goes black and the video stops, a notification lowers for a new email.

An email I haven't thought to look for since the Super Bowl. An email I've been too immersed in my own pain to realize was never sent.

Opening the document, I watch in real-time as Easton signs our divorce papers. Bracing myself on the thin rail of my balcony, all the hope I've been harboring disintegrates to ashes and begins to scatter away from me. Remnants of who I was a few minutes before, I again look up to the starless night sky, knowing I'll find no solace there—or anywhere else.

My supernova just passed me by.

SIXTY-NINE

Adrift
Jesse Marchant

Natalie
Seven months later...

"This. Is. Living!" Holly exclaims as she plucks sunscreen from her bag sitting between our loungers in our beachside cabana. "Like *really* living," she cries joyously, shimmying further into her chair as I scan the tranquil, tropical water and those frolicking in the surf.

"I can't disagree." I manage to summon another smile as I sit back in the luxurious chair while the gnawing continues in my gut. The gnawing that's been eating away at me since we touched down two days ago.

Holly looks over to me, beaming while drawing her long brown locks into a messy bun on her head. "Girl, your dad is the *shit*. Not only does he hand over the keys to the kingdom, but he also sends you on a Mexication to celebrate! Seriously, you won the parent lottery."

I turn to her and quirk a brow, and she ducks beneath the implication.

"I mean, aside from that…thing he did, but no parent is perfect." She lathers her rapidly browning skin. "But way to make it up, Uncle Nate, right?"

I've broken my back most of my life to earn his chair, but I don't bring that to her attention. Instead, I just nod in agreement. In the last seven months, I've done the layout on every issue with little-to-no help. When I walked into the paper Monday, the entire staff was waiting, Mom standing at Dad's side, champagne in hand, and a congratulations sign strung across the pit, and I'd been in an utter state of disbelief.

Editor in Chief is mine.

I hadn't expected it so soon, but it feels earned, warranted, and in no way premature. I just hadn't expected to feel what I did, which was…so much less than I thought.

After handing over the key, Dad only had a few conditions—that he stays on a part-time basis until he's ready to fully retire. Not only did I wholeheartedly agree, but I was also slightly relieved.

That anxiety eased further when he showed up like clockwork the day after passing the baton with his second condition—that I take a five-day vacation he booked for me, Holly, and Damon in this little paradise.

Apparently, Dad has been making future plans of his own, and as soon as I get back to Austin, he's whisking my mother away to Greece for a well-earned hiatus.

All of this I expected—eventually—in the future.

The future turned out to be *now.*

What was *unexpected* was the screeching halt of my thousand-mile-an-hour mind. At the time, my happy tears had been genuine, if only a little forced—the feeling of accomplishment real, but the after… the after has been *debilitating.*

The future is now.

I'm living it, and it's done absolutely nothing but drag me into a place I wasn't at all prepared for after hitting such a sought-after milestone.

For the last two days and nights, I've been staring aimlessly at the ocean as a face, and expression, flit to mind—along with the words that *should have fit* my feelings that day.

"I can't recall a time in my life where I was so blissfully happy… can you?"

Holly chimes in again as I cover my telling eyes by adjusting my sunglasses.

"Seriously, no complaints, Nat, but—"

"Here it comes," I grumble around my straw.

"I'm just saying, we've been here two days and have gone to bed before midnight. It wouldn't hurt to mix it up, maybe grab a nice big—"

"Margarita? I agree." I thrust my frozen concoction her way, the mini-inverted Corona bottle clinking against the rim of the schooner. "Have at it."

"Whatever," she says, taking a long drink. "Ohhhh, that's too damned good."

"Good enough to shut you up? This isn't Cabo. Act like a lady and find a *gentleman*."

"I'm just asking for a wing woman tonight. We haven't prowled together," her beautiful features pinch before she places a hand on my arm for added drama, "girl, since *college!*"

"If you want a hookup, there are apps for that, but I'll be damned if you get catfished here, and Damon won't let it happen, either. Besides, the last time I played *wing woman* for you, I ended up drunk and deserted in some techie's living room as you screamed through the walls, faking orgasms. So, that's a hard pass."

"You're never going to let me live that down, are you? Men *like* that."

"Not if it's fake, and you shouldn't be encouraging men who aren't getting the job done. It's an injustice to women. Especially like *that*, Jesus. You sounded ridiculous."

"Shut up," she says, slurping back a good amount of my margarita just as Damon emerges from the ocean. He's looking absolutely gorgeous in light blue swimming trunks, his mocha skin glittering with cascading water and late-day sun as he saunters through the sand. I drink him in fully because there are beautiful men, and then there's Damon, in a class of his own.

Completely aware of it, his Spidey-dick senses kick in as heads begin to turn. Looking like a man capable of satisfying every nearby mermaid, he subtly shifts his radar toward a woman in a barely-there bikini. She looks up at him biting her lip, and in return, he flashes her his signature megawatt grin, hooking her instantly. I can practically see the hearts in her eyes as they trail him while he glides by, swagger in full effect.

"What makes you the expert on orgasms anyway?" Holly prods, her back to the spectacle Damon's making.

Within earshot now, Damon quirks a brow. Devising a quick

plan, he moves to shield himself behind the thick curtains of our cabana. I take my margarita back from Holly and sip it to hide my grin.

"I know real, and I know fake. A man who can work it right can also tell the difference, so you should tone down the enthusiasm and make him earn it." Damon lifts his chin in an urge to keep me going as I make the split decision to bait her. "If you want to stop faking it, why not hook up with Damon?"

"Are you fucking kidding me? God, no."

Damon scowls at her back as she draws some polish from her bag while frowning at a chipped nail.

"Why not? You two have had a vibe going for years that's well over the border of flirtatious." Damon crosses his arms over his sculpted chest, apparently thoroughly enjoying our conversation. Sadly, Holly's not the only one I'm attempting to lure in.

"Damon vibes with *everyone*," she protests. "I'm not special. Besides, it would screw us up."

I weigh Damon's reaction as he stands waiting and interpret mild irritation.

"So, you've thought about it?"

She glares at me and quickly glances behind her, missing Damon, who's now concealed behind the curtain.

"I mean *recently*," I add, covering myself.

"You didn't pick up on that in the hundred or more conversations I've had with you over the *years*?"

Just as Damon comes back into view, he stills, lifting his eyes to mine, his expression turning to shock.

That's right, bestie, it's time you know the truth.

"I've had more *real* orgasms *solo* calling his name than with any other man," she admits.

Whoops, she's going to fucking kill me.

Seeing this convo going into far more dangerous territory than anticipated, Damon fully perks up, his grin unmistakable as I try to shut it down.

"Tell me about the last guy."

Damon's eyes drill into me as I frantically wave him away from the cabana while Holly begins to touch up her polish. He jerks his chin in determination to get answers, eyes challenging as I narrow mine, and he narrows his right back.

Beautiful bastard.

Damon and I continue our wordless argument as Holly cluelessly runs polish along her flawed nail. I lift my sunglasses to telepathically wage war.

Get out, Damon. You're crossing a line!

I give no fucks.

She'll never forgive me!

He lifts his chin in prompt. *Ask her something else.*

This has already gone too far!

A jerk of his chin. *Ask her!*

"I love him so damned much," Holly offers as my chest seizes. "He's the only man other than our dads that I *truly respect* in this world, and that's so hard to come by. He's also the only man I'm brutally honest with—about everything *but* my feelings for him. Even if he was game, I can't gamble our lifelong friendship for an easy O."

"That's if he's even capable," I taunt as his honey eyes flare.

"True. God, what if he can't carry his weight? What if I risk us for nothing because he's horrible in bed?"

Damon's indignant shift in posture and matching glare has me pressing my lips together.

"*Nightmare*, and all the more reason to stay away. Besides, even if he felt something for me, which he clearly doesn't..." she pauses thoughtfully. "I mean, I've always loved him, and I've been in love with him for more years than I haven't, I think. But lately, I've been thinking it's time to let that dream go." She pauses again, pushing the top of her polish in the uncorked bottle to look up at me. "Nat, I don't think he's capable of being faithful. He hasn't grown out of the fuck-boy phase yet, and we're getting older."

I lift a brow as Damon's expression shifts again. This time it's anxiety.

"But you're still in love with him?"

"Six months ago, yeah, now? I'm not sure anymore."

I decipher his reaction to her words clear as day—*panic*.

"Can we please change the subject? I don't want to go down this road if I'm going to be forced to watch him hook up with every *bonita señorita* that looks his way for the next three days. I have to block that shit out." She stands suddenly as Damon leaps back to conceal himself from view. "I'm going to get another margarita." Holly glances around as my heart explodes into a panicked rhythm.

"Where is that man, anyway? Days are supposed to be ours, *together*."

"It's almost sunset, but I'm sure he's around here somewhere."

"Exactly, he's probably already snuck in a nooner. Like how could I ever take him seriously? I'll get him a drink, just in case. Be right back."

She saunters off toward the bar as I whisper-yell, "Get your *ass* in *here*!"

Damon steps in and rakes a hand down his face, eyes cast down.

"Why the hell would you do that? We don't shank each other and watch the other bleed out. You just forced me into the *worst imaginable situation*. If I don't tell her, she'll hate me."

"Don't tell her," he implores. "I'm fucking begging you, Nat."

"You asked for it," I snap.

"I know."

"Then look at me," I command, "and be honest with me."

He dips his chin, his eyes flitting with emotion as he lifts them. Damon doesn't hide from me, ever. He's one of the rare men who won't, but I sense him trying now.

"She knows exactly who you are and everything about you. There's always been something there between you, and it's been there for *years*. She's ready for something real, and if you aren't, you don't go *anywhere* near that. I've watched you two dance around your true feelings since you were teenagers, and I almost reconsidered inviting you on this trip because I'm starting to fear for her."

"The fuck, Nat?"

"I love you, Damon, but you're reckless," I swallow as the hypocrite in me speaks up to save her friends from a similar fate. "And if you think you can quench your curiosity for her and come out unscathed, you're so fucking wrong."

"I know that. Why do you think I haven't gone there?"

"Well, you better make up your mind and do it fast. But, Damon," I warn, "if she means as much to you as I think she does, you have no idea how much it will hurt if you lose her." My voice goes chalky, my warning full of venom. "You won't recover, so you better damned well make sure she's not the woman you see in your future." I let out a heavy breath. "If you don't..." I try to come up with better words because the wrong decision could tear the three of us apart.

"If I what?"

"If you don't give her everything she deserves—all of it, not the bullshit façade we both can see through, that you've used to fuck your way through half of Austin, then do not go there with her."

"I need to think—"

"Then you aren't ready," I boil over. "You've had half your lifetime to decide, and we're family, so you need to prepare yourself to regret it." The image of Easton splashed all over the headlines, coffee in one hand, his new girlfriend in tow in the other, instantly comes to mind. The hand holding hers, the one that used to reach for mine. Agony sears through me as I speak my truth. "Because *that pain* is indescribable."

"Natalie—"

"Damon, you have to love with your whole being and make sacrifices. If you can't—Do. Not. Enter."

"I just," he crushes his eyes closed, his expression pained.

"You do love her."

"Always have," he says. "Always, I knew when we were fourteen."

"Are you in love with her now?"

"I'm trying not to be."

"So, you can live without her?"

"Fuck no, but—"

"Can you watch her stare at another man like he is her whole world? Can you watch her pledge her life to another man as she marries him?"

"Jesus Christ, Nat," he says. "What the hell is happening?"

"The reckoning of too many years of denial," I take another long sip of my drink, the words coming easier. "You've suspected it for years. You wanted to know, and now you do. If you can't pull the trigger… then bury the gun in a place you'll never find it again."

"Nat," he slides closer to me, patting my knee as the stupid tequila gets my voice shaking.

"Look, Damon, you might think I'm projecting my own shit, and maybe I am, but I have to live with my decision every day." I grip his jaw firmly in my hand. "I love you too much not to warn you in a *scary* way."

"A little help here," Holly calls as she approaches, hands full of margaritas she's struggling to keep upright. "We have a soldier about to go down."

"I'll say," I smirk as Damon gives me the stink eye before leaping to his feet to help her.

Holly looks up at him and smiles with her whole being, and I physically feel it when it strikes Damon. "Where did you go off to? Practicing impregnation?"

"Funny," he mutters, his tone giving his inner struggle away.

She frowns. "What's wrong? You get some sand in your junk, you look..." she tilts her head. "Constipated."

Jesus, Holly.

I slap my forehead as he considers her as his life's purpose, and she all but offers him Ex-Lax.

A girl can only do so much.

Holly steps into the cabana, tossing her wrap off as Damon's eyes cover her bikini-clad body in one longing and completely conflicted sweep. It's then I know I've gotten through to him.

I take my fresh margarita and decide to stir the pot just a little more.

"Good news, Holly. Damon said he'll be your wingman tonight."

Damon's eyes strangle me in a slow, agonizing death over her shoulder as she situates herself on the chair.

"Really?" She glances over to him, and he gives her a very, *very* unconvincing nod. Frowning, Holly grips his hand. "You sure you're okay?"

"Yeah, just wiped from swimping."

"Swimping?" She laughs. "You must be tired. Well, hey, if you aren't up to tonight," she says, nodding toward me, "I'll twist Sister Mary Butler's arm." She shifts her focus my way, tossing me into the fire. "How long has it been since you've seen action, Nat?"

"I'm good," Damon interjects. "Just need a power nap." *Time to think.* "I'm going to go," he tosses a thumb over his shoulder, "get some of that...nap."

He follows that up with the most awkward delivery ever.

"Twatu," he shakes his head, "to...stay and that," he gestures toward her drink. "...mmm looks good. I wake up you t-to just text me when you're ready."

"Oh my God, *Natalie!*" Holly's jaw goes slack as she furiously thumps my arm, fear in her voice, "He's having a sunstroke!"

"No!" Damon booms and we both jump out of our skin. "I'm fine, baby, see?" He flashes the scariest grin ever. "I promise."

A burst of hysterical laughter escapes me, but my empathy silences it shortly after. Damon rarely ever lets his guard down *this* low, nor does he drop the ball. He's reeling, his struggle at present, painfully palpable.

Was I so obvious with Easton?

Were Easton and I fools to think we hid our attraction, our affection, so well? Joel saw it, and he really didn't hide that he did. Thinking back, I can remember Joel staring between us a dozen or so times, probably tempted to bang our heads together more than once. Maybe it takes finding a soul-stealing love to truly recognize it—and losing it—to realize it's worth having, no matter what you have to invest or the total cost.

I'm still waiting on that final sum, but it seems to be the gift that keeps on giving.

"Let's do dinner first?" Holly asks between the both of us.

"I'm ordering room service tonight," I say, ignoring Damon's pleading gaze. He opened this box. It's his chore to unpack it. "I'm positive I'll be hungover by dinner."

"Isn't day drinking the best?" Holly pipes cheerfully between us.

As the tension thickens, she grips Damon's hand and presses a chaste kiss to his knuckles. "Nap in here. I haven't seen you in like three weeks. You've been working too hard. I'll keep my voice down."

He grins down at her with genuine adoration. "Impossible."

"You love my mouth," she quips.

"Yeah, I do," he says before placing a brief kiss on her temple.

"I love you," she says easily.

"I love you, too," he says softly, his eyes lingering, as she turns to me and Damon does too. "Love you," he says, in afterthought.

"Love you," I reply, my tone more like *yeah, bestie, take a minute.* "Text me, if you need me."

"For what? He's got me," she boasts proudly. Damon starts to walk away as I debate whether to come clean when she speaks up.

"Do you think he heard us?" She whisper-yells, eyes wide as Damon stops, lingering just outside the cabana again. He's pushing it too far, so I decide to, as well.

"Would that be the worst thing?"

"Absolutely," she says, her expression panicked. "Oh my God, what if he did?"

"I don't know, babe. Maybe he did."

"I would die. Jesus, full-blown denial starts now."

"Haven't you been there long enough?"

"I'm on vacation. You don't go to Mexico to get your fucking heart broken."

"He probably didn't hear anything. I would have seen him."

The ball is yours, Damon. Please don't drop it.

"Thank God," she sighs. Everything in me wants to scream at her to pay attention and that her life is about to drastically change. Damon finally takes his leave, and I again lower my glasses, my happiness for her turning envious as my eyes water.

Last week, I was fine, well, fine-*ish*, and the week before, and the week before that. As of a month ago, I was starting to come to grips with life as I know it post-divorce from the love of my life.

It's been months. If I'm honest, just over a year of grieving since that blissful time in Sedona. I've been grieving three times as long as I got to love him.

Last week, I was moving, keeping up while burying myself in other's stories, other's lives, in headlines. Now I'm on a dream vacation with my best friends after hitting a career achievement I've been working toward my entire adult life.

My vision blurs as it comes to me.

The future I fought so hard for feels a lot like settling. And if that's really the truth, then I have no purpose past getting back to my desk. But that should be enough for me, at least until I can manage to fall in love again.

It *should be* enough.

I still love being a journalist. That much is a fact. I love writing. I love being editor. I love working with my father. That much hasn't changed.

"You got quiet," Holly says as I press my towel to my face.

You're only having a moment because of what you just witnessed. This is their time, soldier the fuck up!

"I'm just relaxing," I say. "It's hot."

"You asked Damon to be my wingman? Seriously?"

I look over to my best friend as years of their history flits through my mind. The time Max Sutton broke her heart when she was sixteen. Damon showed up as I was comforting her, a pizza and her favorite cupcakes from a local bakery in hand. Damon carrying her across our pasture when she hyperextended her knee after dismounting Percy. Damon's eyes dimming as she proclaimed she was in love during our first year at UT. He pulled the same move six months later with the pizza and twice the cupcakes when it ended—*badly.* Holly holding Damon's hand during his grandmother's funeral. Not letting go for *one second* as he openly grieved her in the rawest state he's ever been in.

"Holly," I say softly.

"Yeah, babe?"

"I love you," I tell her with a watery smile as my chest continues to burn. "I'm so glad you're here."

"Are you kidding? I wouldn't miss this. All your dreams came true. I'm so proud of you. It might have been a given eventually, but we all know, Uncle Nate included, that you *earned* that paper."

"Thank you, I needed you to acknowledge that."

"Babe, you worked so hard for it. You're going to kick so much ass!"

We clink glasses as I force myself back into the present, trying to remember the quote that I've sort of adopted as my motto—'Don't seek happiness in the place you lost it.'

But I didn't lose my happiness in Easton Crowne. I lost my happiness when I *lost* Easton Crowne. Still, it's memories of loving him that push me back from progressing. Ironically, as I sit back now, celebrating my accomplishments, I know my progress is severely lacking because I still haven't budged *personally.*

Because I can't. Because I divorced a man who loved me so fiercely, so completely, that I might have destroyed a part of him that trusted enough to allow himself to love that way again. If so, I did a disservice to the women who will love him in the future, because I doubt he will ever open himself as deeply.

Sadly, neither will I.

Then again, it's Easton. He won't settle.

Even with our fate sealed, I have to try to live in the moment and every moment after. I have to look around, count my blessings, and be thankful. I've paved my way. This is my life and reality, and I'm determined to live it.

As the tequila glides down my throat, I decide to replace my motto with all the others I can summon with the ever-present sting in my chest.

Carpe Diem. Seize this day—Natalie!

Today is the first day of the rest of your life—Natalie!

You are your own captain—Natalie!

SEVENTY

like i never even loved you
Today Kid, EL ROMA

Natalie

I'm drunk. And not in the giggly, cute, adorably passable type of way. As it is, I'm close to sloppy, and gauging from the looks being slung my way by my unimpressed bartender Jerry, in danger of possible arrest.

Little does *Jerry know* I'm already locked in a Mexican prison, even if it is five-star.

No matter how many bumper sticker slogans I've recited to myself today, I lost the battle. So, I dove headfirst into the top-shelf tequila that I've been swimming in since Holly left our cabana to prep for the night out.

All thoughts of my victory in becoming Editor in Chief of *Speak* tarnish as my past and present—which pales in comparison—collide. It all brings me back to the same damning conclusion—the future is now.

After endless months of burying my head in the sand at work, and hiding my raging heartache behind my career, it's reared its ugly head. Remorse has its wicked way with me and the itch to go back and seek refuge in a packed schedule has me looking up early flights home.

You cannot live to work, Natalie.

It's the remembrance of Easton's headlines that keep me parked on my stool at the poolside lounge, adjacent to the resort lobby.

At least in Mexico, I'm safe from continuous updates regarding the new love interest of the world's most promising new rock star. Here, I don't have to avoid them as if they don't exist and press through the rest of my day, pretending I didn't soak in every line like the rest of his starry-eyed fans. Because that's all I am now, a spectator, a fan. His past, and maybe for him, still considered a stain.

Even though, *technically*, I was his *first* fan and his first *wife*. No one but me will ever get to claim that title, even if he's intent on replacing me sometime in the future.

It's an immature thought, but a valid claim and win, nevertheless.

"AHA!" I shout, and Jerry jumps back in fright, managing to keep a grip on the glass before it slips from his hand. "Whaddaya know, Jerry," I muse, twirling my colorful drink umbrella between pinched fingers. "I just caught a glimpse of the bright side. Things may be looking up for me."

He gives me a dead stare as he continues drying his glass. "Congratulations."

"Thank you," I mumble, sucking on the ice from my last drained margarita, attempting to ingest more tequila.

The downside of not catching an early plane home? Watching my best friends fall in love at a time when it's the most heart-wrenching to witness.

"I have *so much* to be thankful for, a lot, really," I reiterate to myself and to Jerry, who motions to my untouched *complimentary* appetizer in blatant suggestion.

Ironically, even as I continually try to count my blessings, I can't find one fuck to give about the future that awaits me back in Austin. Not since the tranquil Mexican waters and Señor Tequila smacked me with a good dose of vitamin truth.

I knew what was expected of me, so I stepped up, took control of my emotions, myself, and my life, and let it fuel me. I did what I do best, I compartmentalized my pain and made and attained new goals. A faint, but new set of abs included.

I've since met those goals, and now…my future will consist of more of the same, and it's blindsiding.

"Jerrryyy," I drag out his name, a clear solicitation for a pinch more of the numbing juice.

"No," he belts in reply without so much as a glance my way, the *hospitality* portion of his demeanor long gone.

"Fine," I slouch into my stool and close my eyes, listening to the sounds around me—the fountain gurgling in the nearby pool, and just beyond, the faint but distinct lapping of ocean waves which lulls me into a happier place.

"I, Elliot Easton Crowne…Take you, Natalie Renee Butler…To be my lawfully wedded wife…" he declares reverently, a glimmer of love resting on his lash line as he takes the ring from Joel and turns back to me. His warmth engulfs me wholly as he pushes the promise onto my finger.

"Love is patient," I recite. "Love is kind."

"Love is not boastful," he murmurs, "nor does it insist on its own way."

"Love is not self-seeking," I say, voice shaking with the love I feel as I push the band on his finger.

"Or easily angered," he squeezes my fingers, and I feel the implication of it—a second promise.

"Love keeps no records of wrongdoings," I recite back when prompted. Just as we're pronounced, he whispers my name in awe.

"Natalie…"

"Ha!" I exclaim at the faint sound of my name, an echo of the most defining moment of my life by the velvet voice that continually haunts me. Jerry glances over at me, brows lifting to his hairline to let me know I'm still cut off. Feeling the impact of that whisper, I briefly wonder how I managed such a clear audible memory and giggle maniacally as I squint at my empty margarita schooner. It's apparent I need to steer clear of tequila…and maybe Jerry until the end of my Mexication.

When I feel the prickling sensation of a presence behind me, I begin to rattle on my barstool and realize both sets of Jerry's eyes are still on me as the silky voice repeats my name.

"Humor me, okay, Jerry?" I straighten on my stool as much as possible as the hairs on the back of my neck start to rise at an alarming rate. "Just for shits and giggles. Is it the tequila, or is there someone behind me? Say…yea tall," I position my hand well above my head, "resembling a criminally good-looking, but very *broody* rock star?"

"It's *Jerod*," he says, "and yes."

"Yes, it's the tequila?"

"Yes, there's a rock star behind you."

Turning sideways on my stool, I'm met with widening hazel eyes and get lost in them as easily as I did when I first became acquainted with them so many moons ago. Easton Crowne gapes back at me, sporting a deep tan, wearing board shorts and a form-fitting V-neck. Wayfarers rest on top of his thick, black hair, which now hangs a few inches from his shoulders. He's grown even more into his impressive physique than the last time I saw him. Looking impossibly fit, he stands before me every bit the rock god he's become.

In my tequila haze, I reach out and poke his chest as he gawks back at me, seemingly just as confused as I am before I finally speak up.

"Easton," I croak out, vision blurring as elation slams into me. "You're in…M-Mex…you're really *here*?" I reach out to cup his jaw, and his eyes close at the contact before he utters a low curse.

"Jesus, Natalie. You're fucking wasted."

"Meixcation," I start to tequila-splain. "Dad sent me here for the paper."

"You're fucking kidding me, right?" He snaps, shaking his head while simultaneously freeing himself of my touch.

"No. I mean, yes. He gave me the paper and sent me here to celebrate! Been here a few, t-two days… Doyouwanna m-margarita?" I stumble over my words. "Jerry makes them so good you can conjure a *daydream* into reality *poolside*."

"Jerod," Jerry corrects behind me.

"You overserved a little, didn't you, man?" Easton scolds Jerry as I greedily take him in, hands moving on their own accord, palming his chest.

"She was cut off an hour ago," Jerry explains, "I've been trying to get her to eat or call someone. I even offered to have a bellman escort her to her room, but she says it's haunted by *Prince Phillip*."

"The fuck?" Easton frowns. "Natalie, what—"

"Damon will come," I tell the apparition I'm pawing.

Easton's eyes lower as he edges further away to skirt my touch.

"So, you're here with *Damon*?"

"Yes. God, yes. It's wonderful. He's so in love," I explain. "Both of them, Holly too."

Easton tilts his head, eyes assessing. "Let's get you to your room."

"Are you...you come...for...to see *me*?"

He pauses at my question before shaking his head. "My girlfriend is checking us in while I scope out the place." He scratches the back of his neck, raking his lower lip before speaking. "Do you want to meet her?"

A sobering lightning bolt shoots straight into my chest, frying my hopeful insides as I realize just how fucking drunk and delusional I currently am. This is no apparition standing in front of me. It's my ex-husband, who is here with another woman. A woman who knows what it feels like to take his offered hand, who gets to soak in his warmth, who might even be lucky enough to gain the rare looks in his eyes I once thought solely belonged to me.

Another woman who gets to know him intimately, in the way I was just with him mere minutes ago while wrapped in my blissful memory. Lightning threatens again, hovering, lingering—as does Easton's question.

"Do I want to—," I manage to stand on shaky legs and end up chest to chest with Easton. His nostrils flare as I try not to inhale and fail. He takes a step back as I grip the bar blindly behind me to correct my balance before jutting my chin. "Do I want to meet your girlfriend?" I force myself to choke out. "No, thank you, Easton. Honestly, I'd rather go for a slow dive to the bottom of the fucking sea."

Confident I got my message across, I march straight through the patio bar and down the walkway toward the ocean, dead set on seeing my declaration through.

SEVENTY-ONE

Crazy Love
Poco

Easton

"Are you fucking kidding me?" I grit through clenched teeth, watching Natalie wobble along the long dock that edges the patio leading to the beach.

The bartender speaks up. "I take it this was not a good coincidence?"

Reeling, I pull some cash from my pocket and tap the bar. "No, Jerod, it's not. Line them up, top-shelf, please." He immediately starts pouring, and I slam two shots back in rapid succession. Tossing another bill onto the bar, I keep my eyes glued to Natalie, who continues her drunken trek toward the water. I damn near ran headfirst into a fucking tropical plant when I saw her profile. The same reaction I've had the half dozen or so other times when I've searched for her in a crowd and found a likeness to her. But her doppelganger always pales in comparison the closer I get.

This time, no such luck.

No. This time, when I have the strength, an inkling I can grow differently, and finally have some of the needed mindset that life might have a better trajectory than me bleeding out on the stage—*this* is when she appears out of thin air.

"Jerod…humor me," I toss more liquid fire down my throat, monitoring Natalie's slow, drunken progress.

"I'm listening."

"What are the odds of taking your new girlfriend on a short

getaway to Mexico and running into your ex-wife, who's vacationing at the same resort?"

Jerod barks out a sympathetic laugh and pours another shot. "So slim those odds probably don't exist. Damn, man," he mutters, pushing the brimming glass forward. "This one is on me."

"Appreciate it, but help me think this through," I toss another bill on the bar as Natalie stalls in the middle of the sand, halfway to the beach. "Mexico is a popular vacation spot."

"Agreed," he says quickly.

"This resort is one of the highest-rated."

"True, probably first to pop up in the search engine."

"That's how I found it," I fire back, clinging to that lifeline.

"Narrows it down a lot," Jerod agrees.

"So, we're getting warmer?" I ask.

He doesn't at all look convinced as he pours one more shot. "Possibly."

Chuckling dryly, I lift my brimming glass. "To the inherited luck of my *mother*."

He pours his own and taps it with mine, and we both drink.

Taking my eyes off Natalie for a second, I meet his amused gaze as he lifts the bottle in offering. I cut my hand through the air to stop him from pouring another, my mother's voice screaming in my head about signs and fate and magical nonsense I never believed for myself, until I met the woman currently stumbling through the sand. A woman who landed into my life, seemingly as lost now, as she was then. A woman I heavily pursued—and married—that eventually led me down the narrow path of self-destruction and premature aging.

"Since we're being honest," Jerod speaks up. "I'm having a bit of a moment, man. I'm a huge fan."

"Thanks for that, but my question for you right now is, are you an *honorable* man?" I ask him, not taking my eyes off Natalie as fear starts to circulate. She's headed toward the dark, unlit part of the beach. "Because that's all I care about right now, and I'm willing to do just about anything for you, if you'll keep what I just told you in confidence."

"We all signed NDAs before you got here, and I swear to you, I won't utter a word."

"You will eventually," I say, knowing it to be the truth. "Eventually, you'll tell someone, but can you do me a solid and wait until I leave?"

"Swear it, man."

"Thank you. Can I ask one more favor?"

"Anything."

"Can you please dial my room and let my girlfriend know I'll meet her at the restaurant in an hour, because I'm going to have to go keep my ex-wife from drowning?"

"Is that how you want it worded?"

"Fuck no, throw a shitload of finesse into that and completely leave out the ex-wife part. I'll break that to her myself, *later*." With that, I start stalking after Natalie as she heads straight toward the water.

"Wait, man," Jerry speaks up, stopping me. "The restaurant closed ten minutes ago, but you can still order room service."

Knowing it in my gut, I force myself to search for and find an inch-tall digital clock next to Jerry's register, just as the minutes on the hour tick over.

11:11.

I make it to Natalie just as her toes reach the water. Her skin sun-kissed despite her pale complexion, her wild curls blowing in the breeze. Aside from the lights of the resort a fair distance away, we're shadowed in darkness by the night sky. A blanket of stars hovers above us, the moon absent. Even so, I can make out her profile, her light blue sarong coverup outlining her frame as the ocean breeze whips it against her.

"I haven't seen stars like this since our honeymoon. These look so much further out of reach," she whispers softly over the sounds of the harsh breeze.

While Mom would undoubtedly call this collision an act of fate, I decide the time stamp Stella Crowne deems such a cosmic sign is insignificant when it comes to me. As of tonight, I'm relabeling fate's definition—hell.

The mere sight of Natalie on this beach already has faint anger simmering beneath while my heart simultaneously threatens to swell familiarly in my chest. With every second that passes, a memory threatens both good and bad. Mostly good, of her, of us. Throat dry, buzz kicking in, I take a long, much-needed drink of her before I stow it away, leaving myself only one thought.

Why?

Why is life so fucking cruel to let me see her like this, if she can't be mine? If I can no longer be hers. If we weren't meant for one another in the way I once so adamantly believed—to the point it made me sick.

Fucking *why*?

"Make plans, and God laughs," Natalie recites from feet away, answering my question without being aware of it. "I've been talking to myself in bumper stickers, memes, slogans, and mottos all day. I'd say it's appropriate for the present moment, don't you think?" She glances over at me, her eyes glassy. "God's probably laughing his ass off right now."

"You know I'm not going to be able to leave you here. You know that, right?"

"I don't want to ruin your night, but I don't want to go to my room—yet. I'm not…I'm not your responsibility, Easton."

"I'm not leaving you here," I state firmly.

"Then I'll text Damon." She pats down her dress as if her phone will appear. "No phone. Shit, I don't even have my room key."

I pull my phone out and unlock it before extending it towards her.

"I don't know his number," she frowns, "I've known him my whole life. Is that bad?"

"Does anyone know anyone's number?" I manage a hint of a smile, not feeling an ounce of it.

"206-792-5959," she recites, her eyes boring into mine before darting them away.

"It hasn't changed," I tell her because the number she just sounded off is *mine*. So, why didn't she ever fucking use it?

Don't go there, East. Dead and buried horse.

"But we have. We've changed, haven't we?" She grins over at me. "Happy birthday, by the way."

"Thanks. You too."

"We're close to grownups by now, aren't we? We don't get to use our age as an excuse for stupid and reckless anymore," she says in a mournful tone. "I think maybe it's no longer allowed at twenty-four."

"Is that so?"

Our eyes connect and hold.

Goddamnit.

"Easton," she sighs. "I'm okay. Really. I don't need Damon to get back to my room. Please go," she swallows, "to *her*."

"And what? Pretend I didn't see you trashed on the fucking beach at the same resort?"

"Precisely," she answers with a firm dip of her chin.

"I'm going to tell her."

"As you should," she says as I try and fail not to memorize the way she looks wrapped in silk, tan skin, her bare feet and polished toes washed in white foam.

"We can switch hotels," I offer.

She crosses her arms, grips her biceps, and doesn't respond.

"It's not a problem," I try again.

"I'm just..." she smiles, but it's distant. "Sorry, I'm having a Seattle moment in Mexico." She turns and stares through me. "In more ways than one."

Feeling the tequila start to circulate, I bite my tongue and hold it. I'm not giving her an inch. She's done nothing but pummel me since I gave her permission to.

"My best friends are about to admit they love each other. I don't want to get in the way of that."

"Holly and Damon?"

"Yeah. I said they were in so...much love," she sighs wistfully. "I think I witnessed the true beginning of them today. It was so beautiful to observe." Her speech is improving slightly. It's obvious she's trying hard to sober up. "I got sentimental and drunk, and that's why I was thinking of us." She laughs lightly. "I'm still drunk and sentimental. I can't seem to stop it today, so can you please save me some humiliation and just go back to her?"

"Not yet."

"Fine," she sighs and looks right at me, her blue eyes invoking more of the familiar energy.

"I thought I imagined you. Dreamed you up, but you're really here, aren't you?"

I nod. "I needed a break."

"Yeah, me too...as it turns out, I hate breaks. Jesus, Easton...just give me a minute, okay?" She bends and cups water over her bare feet and arms to wake herself up.

Running my fingers through my hair, I scoff at the fact that she thinks this is the only one this is happening to. "You're not alone in this, you know? It's fucking uncomfortable for me, too."

"Really?" She asks, disbelieving. "I would say your particular circumstances give you the upper hand."

"What's that supposed to mean?"

"It means I'm alone, and you're here with *Malibu*."

The simmer beneath threatens to boil with her accusation, and I can't help the bite in my reply. "She's been a good friend to me, and not that I owe you any explanation, but we met up at one of her gigs when I got back from Europe last month. I didn't touch her when we were married, nor did I want to. So yeah, we're together *now*, but it's *new*. And considering I've traveled the *globe* recently and landed *here* for a break, it's pretty fucking mind-blowing that *you're* standing in front of *me* in Mexico."

"Which means you still can't kiss me, fuck me, or love me," she utters brokenly between us on the breeze, her eyes closing.

Stunned and feeling stung, I recover quickly. She's drunk. This is Natalie drunk.

"We were friends once. Best friends…we talked for hours every night. I miss that so much…I *miss you*."

"Natalie," I start as she whips her head toward me.

"Do you get so lost in her, when you fuck her, that you lose all sense of time?"

"What are you doing?" I whisper hoarsely, her words wringing me out as she takes a step toward me, pressing in.

"I'm asking you questions, Easton," she fires back as if she was ready for this, her violet-blue gaze tearing into me. "Tell me, Easton," her voice shakes as she poses her next heartrending question. "Are you as *close as two people could ever be*?"

Soul charred, anger rapidly surfacing, I bite my tongue to the point it hurts.

Her features twist in pain as she grips her dress. "Because we were. We were *so close*." A pained sound escapes her as I fight myself to bridge the distance. I'm barely able to process her last words before she digs in again.

"I know how I got to Seattle, Easton. But how the hell are you in Mexico right now?"

Anger replaces some of the devastation in her tone, but it's not directed at me. It's because of the fucked-up circumstances we can't seem to escape when we collide in every universe. "I'm getting so tired of repeating their history."

"Well, it's not ours," I say, dead set on the same stance I've kept since I signed the papers.

"No, it's not," she agrees easily, wiping her tears. "Not at all, and the way Stella romanticized these run-ins is fucking cruel, no matter how many times I hoped for it to happen. But the way this feels...Jesus," her voice cracks. "I would give anything to make it stop."

Her words strike deeper as I fight myself again and win, *again.*

She steps toward me, her scent floating through the breeze—orchids with a hint of something spicy mixed in. A minute ticks by, maybe two, as I get lost in the sight of her, my weakness threatening. But I keep my distance because I know a sip of her is lethally addicting for me. I refuse to go down this path again, *alone.*

"You're a supernova," she murmurs. "I thought it the first time you sang for me in Seattle, and it's what I thought the night we locked ourselves in that Dallas hotel while we were falling in love, making love. I knew I caught one and told myself to hold onto you with everything in me. I told myself to hold on, even back then, because I knew it was going to be impossible. I was right." She looks up to the sky as if searching for an alternate star, a tear traveling a slow path down her cheek. "You should know—you need to know—you were just as sacred to me, even if I didn't prove it when you demanded it of me." Her confessions slap me, as does the wind, while the bolts keeping my heart on lockdown threaten to come loose.

Fuck no.

"If you weren't wasted," I reply dryly, unable to stop the acid from seeping into my tone. "This would probably mean a lot to me."

"It's the truth," she pierces me with her damning violet blues. "But too little, too late, right?"

"Something like that."

"Something *like* that?"

"Exactly like that," I slide my fists into my shorts.

"Well then, we best tuck me away, right?" She clears her throat, seeming to gather herself. "You know I've been watching your progress, Easton. Of course I have, and I'm so unbelievably happy for you. You deserve all your success. Truly. It's been incredible to witness."

"Thank you, and you got your paper," I say.

Her eyes dim, and she nods, going quiet for a few seconds.

"I earned it," she states without a hint of offense before sweeping me from head to feet. "Okay," she nods in some sort of affirmation before clearing her cheeks with the sides of her palms. "Well, fuck today, and fuck Mexico," she laughs, but it's full of pain, and I see the trail of her tears clearly as she stops in front of me. More tears than I realized she was shedding.

"Natalie—" I start again, unsure of what the hell I'll finish with. I'm still reeling from words I prayed to hear for months and months and never got. Nothing close to the guttural admissions she's been spewing at me since I got here.

And what the fuck exactly *is this*?

Another crossroads she's going to stomp on my heart to step through?

Fuck that.

Stay done, Easton.

"It's okay, Easton. I'll make myself scarce."

"You don't have to do that," I say, trailing her as she heads toward the resort, far steadier on her feet.

"Oh, yes, I do," she replies before turning back and stalking forward until she's inches from me. "But I'll be damned if I waste another chance to say the things I didn't say to you the night you divorced me."

"Don't. What's the point? We've already had this talk."

"I'm sorry I didn't call or keep the promise to try and be in each other's lives, but it was always going to feel like a lie for me because *this* feels every bit like reentering hell. Maybe..." she exhales, "maybe I just need to get used to the temperature."

I scoff. "This is unbelievable. You sure have a lot to fucking say for someone who's memorized my number and never once used it."

"You didn't call, either," she fires back. "Shit, I'm sorry, I don't want to fight." Gripping her wrap, she brushes past me.

"Of course, you don't. So, is that it? That's where we're leaving this?"

She shrugs with her back to me. "Pretty sure we've covered the 'What the fuck is my ex doing in Mexico?' Relationship statuses, the bullshit pleasantries, which is surprising considering the company," she fires over her shoulder.

"Yeah, well, maybe I've finally learned my lesson on that front. At least when it comes to you."

She tosses her hands up. "I was just trying to have an honest conversation with you, Easton."

"No, you're trying to drunkenly confess your regrets, a tactic I've always refused to allow you."

"Of course. Brutal honesty is the best policy."

"Yeah, it really fucking is," I spout to her retreating back.

"Damned if I do or don't with you anyway," she utters, already a few strides toward the hotel.

I catch myself and stop my footing, calling at her back. "There's no need to run anymore, Beauty. *No one* is chasing you."

She turns on a dime, her eyes glimmering with pain as she sees me standing a good distance away.

"It was good to see you, Natalie. Congratulations."

Nothing about the hurt shining in her eyes feels like a victory. *Nothing*, and I wish like hell it did. She swallows the last of a harsh exhale before she turns back toward the hotel. As the distance grows, her words threaten to brand their way into my psyche as I try to rebuke each one.

That's all they are. *Words.*

As she enters the bar, Jerod produces the purse she left behind and waves it toward her from where he stands. Without missing a step, she claims it and stalks forward. As she disappears into the lobby, so do my expectations that this vacation—along with the strides I've taken in the last few months—are salvageable.

Damn this woman.

"Another shot?" Jerod asks as I plant myself at the bar while trying to get my heart to obey my fucking mind. "Just a beer."

SEVENTY-TWO

Always Remember Us This Way
Lady Gaga

Natalie

Holly paces in front of me as I sip my Bloody Mary, deciding it's as close to drinking tequila as I'm ever going to get again. The last time I drank tequila, my ex-husband showed up on my Mexication with his beautiful new girlfriend waiting for him—probably naked—when he got back to his hotel room. And by last time, I mean—*last night*. I woke up today in full-fledged denial, praying I dreamt it, until Damon came to me with a fistful of options. In one hand, a coffee, in the other, a Bloody Mary. Option two has been good to me.

"What are the odds, Nat? What are the fucking odds!?" Holly says as I mentally plot my next few days in paradise.

"Chill out. I'm working on a new itinerary. Today is vodka, tomorrow rum. Oh," I exclaim, "let's have a schnapps day!"

"This isn't funny."

"I'm painfully aware of that. Please stop pacing. You're making me dizzy," I whine as I take a hard pull of the cocktail. Holly kneels in front of me, placing her hands on my terry cloth-covered knees. At least my wardrobe is sorted. It will remain my staple uniform as I live in my hotel room for the next three days charging away my sobriety drink by drink. Thankfully with my new salary, I can afford it.

"You can't hide in here," Holly reasons.

"Watch me make a liar out of you. Let's change the subject. Can we talk about last night?" I beg. "Please. What happened with Damon?"

"Nothing to report. We had a quiet dinner, followed closely by quiet drinks. His wingman skills are *nonexistent*. He's in a weird headspace. The bars were scarce, so sadly, I danced by myself for an hour until I managed to hook a hottie on the floor. The cockblocker immediately claimed I was drunk and whisked me back to my room. Something's wrong with him, and he won't tell me what." Her eyes implore mine. "Do you know what's wrong?"

"No idea," I lie.

"Well, he's going to come clean to me, or we're going to fight."

I have a feeling it's going to be a damn good one. I fish my bacon olive breakfast off my shiny, yellow cocktail sword and begin devouring it as she snatches the drink away from me.

"Get dressed immediately. Poolside, *now*."

"No."

Ignoring me, she tosses a glittering, emerald bikini my way. "You've finally got six abs. The world deserves to know."

"No."

She plucks the golden chain I brought off my dresser full of accessories and tosses it on the bed next to the bikini, completely unaware of the piece of the past she just added to her demands. "Put it on."

Staring at the chain, a clear memory surfaces of Easton running a worshipful finger along it as I slowly rode him. Lush red lips parted, he looked up at me with a loved-soaked expression. He loved me, even then. In hindsight, I think he loved me before I left Seattle, as I did him.

"Natalie, this is something you can't pass on—an opportunity."

"To watch my ex-husband frolic with his new girlfriend on a Mexican beach? I'm good here."

"Jesus, you know I don't say this often, but you disappoint me. He married you. Married *you*, Natalie. If you've got anything, you've got that. Now find your pride somewhere in the self-pity closet you're hiding in and get dressed."

When I don't budge, Holly digs her heels in, arms crossed. "You still love him. This could be your last chance."

"My last chance was the day he signed the divorce papers."

"What?"

"Hindsight is a bitch, my friend—and I *hate* her. Loathe her," I say, swiping my drink back. "Despise, detest—dislike very strongly," I giggle. "See? I'm perfectly capable of speaking. Easton's always been the reason behind my damn impediment."

"Get up!" She orders, prying the drink from my hand before walking over to the toilet and dumping it.

"No good can come of this," I grumble, grabbing the bikini and chain before pushing her out of the bathroom and slamming the door in her smiling face.

"You're going to burn in hell for this," I grit out to Holly when Easton appears with Misty at his side, who looks ravishing in a gold bikini. Holly's eyes bulge as she tries and fails to school her expression.

"Jesus, that bikini is so tacky," she lies through her teeth.

"Please don't," I say. "I'll hate you more for lying."

She shrugs, mimosa in hand. "I mean, she's not ugly."

I lower my shades so Holly can clearly read my warning. Easton scouts the pool while Misty lays a towel on an oversized lounger. I sense it the minute his eyes find me and push my glasses back up. I made a fool out of myself last night—and I was okay with that—but he wasn't at all receptive, and that's the hardest pill to swallow. The imprint on that particular pill—*he's moved on.*

"He's looking."

"Shut up and don't look back."

In a gift of divine intervention, Damon appears, blocking my view before taking a seat on the edge of my lounger. My small victory is cut short when he speaks up. "Oh, damn, I see I've arrived in time for the show."

"Shut up," I snap. "Both of you, this *isn't funny*. At all."

"Well, you've got us," Damon offers, "and because you do, I've taken the liberty of signing us up for an outing."

"Thank God," I exhale. "I don't give a shit what it is. Sign us up for *every* damned excursion."

"*Don't* do that," Holly warns Damon. "And where are we going?"

He grins wickedly. “It’s a surprise.”

“But this is a *touristy thing*, right?” Holly wrinkles her nose. “It’s going to be boring.”

“So what, is there a bar?” I ask, my only condition.

“Don’t worry, you’ll be hooked up, lush,” Damon assures.

“Hey,” I hear uttered in a soft greeting. My body jerks to attention when Easton appears over Damon’s shoulder. Holly bolts upright in her lounger as Damon turns to look up at Easton. They both stare at him, temporarily starstruck, and I vow to disown them both as soon as we touch back down on Texas soil.

“I didn’t mean to interrupt, but I just came over to check on you, see how your head’s doing.” Easton stands there, glowing beneath the sun that only highlights his perfection, his board shorts hanging on for dear life below the deep muscles of his hips. Holly’s tongue begins to roll out of her mouth as Damon and I speak up simultaneously.

“She’s a shit drunk—” Damon starts.

“—it’s still attached,” I fake a smile, tapping my temple.

“Sure about that?” Easton replies with a smirk.

“Well, today’s only Thursday, and the wind is blowing, so we’ll keep you updated,” Damon digs as I resist clawing at his flawless skin.

Easton’s gaze lingers on me before he lowers it to address Damon. “Easton,” he says, extending his hand to Damon, who accepts it. “Heard a lot of good things about you, man.”

“Same,” Damon replies, enthusiastically pumping Easton’s hand. “Nice to finally meet my best friend’s ex-husband,” he jokes as I implore God to grant me the ability to laser Damon’s face off with nothing but a pointed stare.

“Would have met you a lot sooner if you, you know, hadn’t secretly *met, dated*,” Holly draws out bitterly, “eloped and *divorced*,” she finishes before shifting personalities. “I’m Holly,” she extends her hand to Easton, who takes it with a full-fledged grin. The recognition in his eyes implies he likes them both.

“Heard a lot about *you, too*, Holly,” Easton delivers expertly before Holly’s pupils begin to heart like a damned cartoon character. I can’t blame her. The sight of him, and with as disarming as he is, it’s easy to see the shiny. For me, he’s all shine.

“Well, you know our girl,” Damon chuckles, playing diplomat, “go big or go home.”

"Go home," I mutter under my breath during a few words of mixed chatter. "Now, there's a fine idea."

Easton turns his attention back to me, his eyes signifying he didn't miss it. "So, you good?"

"Perfect, thanks for checking on me. I was *really* drunk." I lift my sunglasses as his return stare hardens, keeping me from going further in trying to play off a single word I said. Because he's still Easton, and he'll never settle for anything less than brutal honesty. Nostrils flaring in irritation, his words from our honeymoon ring through as they have for endless months.

"Don't ever hide from me. We're as close as two people could ever be."

My lungs decide in that moment that breath is no longer necessary as another bolt of lightning sears my chest. Desperate, I grapple with the feel, refuting the threatening sting in my eyes which are no longer concealed.

I. Hate. Mexico!

I couldn't forget a single minute of him if I wanted to, and I'm almost positive I can remember every word we've ever exchanged. My cursed brain can't even seem to short circuit a single recollection of my time with him, even after drinking my weight in tequila. Holly and Damon chat Easton up, and he converses with an easy timbre. When Easton goes still mid-chatter, I pause, shielding my eyes with my hand to see he's focused on the gold chain secured around my waist. His flaring jades remain fixed on the glittering reminder for a few soul-stealing seconds before darting away. Freshly charred, I avert my own gaze, smoke no one else can see billowing from me as Damon speaks up. Tuning them out, I peruse Easton's ribs, littered with more tattoos I don't recognize, before finding the one I do. My heart swells as I visually trace the Chihuly design, which stands out easily amongst the others as I summarize our short love story with my thoughts.

Once upon a time, Elliot Easton Crowne was mine. He was mine, and we were as close as two people could ever be.

"Sorry, where?" Easton asks, diving back into the conversation as a splash sounds nearby in the pool.

"We're going on one of the excursions the hotel offered. I had to reserve the whole thing, and it's for six. You're welcome to join us," Damon offers, flashing me a subtle smirk that screams *payback is a bitch.* Instead of clawing his eyes out, I turn in my lounger and slap my bottle of sunblock in his hand. "Get my back, would you? My shoulders are burning."

"I'll have to check with Misty," Easton hedges, "but I think we're—"

"We're what, babe?" Her voice chimes in, just as I turn my back, saving myself a few more seconds from the meet and greet, which is inevitable.

Damon leans in, massaging the lotion into my shoulders exaggeratedly. While he's within earshot and as Holly introduces herself, I take my window to utter my threat. "Make sure to take a good look at the view today, Damon, because it's your last," I hiss from between my teeth, "I'm going to fucking kill you."

The widening of his eyes, followed by his swallow, has me convinced he's taking my threat seriously as I give him crazy eyes to relay the rest.

Thanks for volunteering, bestie. I'll be taking every bit of this jacked situation out on you.

"Sounds fun," Misty says with a notable amount of hesitation in her tone.

Pulling up my big girl panties, I turn and get my first look at my replacement. A dazzling, dripping wet replacement who's got her hands folded on Easton's shoulder. I mentally note her posture is natural—intimate—before I flick my eyes to hers.

"Hi," I say, proud of myself for getting the greeting out without a trace of malice or a hint of the jealousy I feel.

"Hi, Natalie. Nice to meet you."

"You too, Misty," I reply, doing my best not to acknowledge she's built like a supermodel and has the face and hair to match the body. Even her voice is attractive. I'm not allowed to hate her or her hand placement. My bare ring finger is a reminder of that.

"Okay, then, let's do it," Easton concedes, his eyes filled with apology for me, the pity in them pushing me closer to DEFCON 1.

We said we would try to be in each other's lives, even if we were lying, because we both knew it would be hard. If we have any chance of that happening, this is what that chance looks like.

"Yeah, let's do it," I say with a shrug. "Why not?"

Misty's eyes flit between Easton and me as I find myself speaking up to try and ease the crease of worry in her brow. "It really is nice to meet you, Misty," I manage as a sign of good faith. "It'll be fun," I add as Holly and Damon whip their heads between the three of us.

A hint of a smile lifts Easton's lips, and it's not the good kind, but a recognizable call of bullshit.

I blame my emboldened speech on the lingering vodka because right now, I'm surprising the hell out of myself. Easton pulls his glasses down between pinched fingers. "Meet you in the lobby in two hours?"

"Perfect."

Just after we exchange parting words, Easton and Misty retreat, and I lay back into the chair, feeling Holly and Damon's gazes collide on me. Damon is the first to speak.

"Nat—"

"Listen to me," I speak up. "Please listen to me," I beg of them both. "He shut me down last night. I tried, and he cut me to the quick. I know," my voice quakes with lingering emotion at the remembrance of our exchange and his ice-cold shoulder before I attempt to shove it in a box to unpack back in Texas. "I know what you're trying to do, but if you really want to be *there for me*," I lower my glasses. "Do nothing. No plotting, no scheming, no more crazy best friend Hail Mary's," I direct the last part to Damon, "okay?"

They nod in sync, as if they're watching a lit fuse drawing closer to a bomb.

"I'm okay, I think," I inhale a calming breath. "It's weird, but right now, I'm okay. I can handle this."

"It's going to be good," Holly lies, and I dip my chin.

"She's fucking smoking, Natalie, but she's *not you*," Damon says in an effort to comfort me.

"Yeah, well, I'm not *her*," I say, wishing on a shooting star as he guides her by the hand, *my hand*, back to the other side of the pool.

SEVENTY-THREE

One

U2

Natalie

"You look beautiful," Damon says, "really, Nat," he assures before turning to Holly. "And you, especially."

"Oh? Why am I special?" Holly asks, pinching her flowing sundress between her fingers, looking like she may curtsy.

This is just getting weird.

"You've always been special," he presses a lingering kiss to her temple. Her eyes fly to mine as he turns toward the lobby, and I give her a wink.

"You really okay with this?" She asks me as Damon offers each of us an elbow, and we take it.

"I mean, my head's been scrambling to catch up since last night, but yeah, I'm finally evening out. Enough to be civil. But Damon, you're still going down."

"You seem okay," Holly offers, completely unconvinced before gesturing to my sundress. "And you really do look incredible."

"Thank you." I glance down at my powder blue halter dress, loving the look of the form-fitting bodice that accentuates my waist before it flows over my hips. My favorite part are the slits, which run clear up to the top of both my thighs. The silky material stops just short of my sandal laces which are tied in a crisscross pattern around my calves.

"If you want to bail," Holly offers, "I'm game."

"Holly," Damon sighs as he pauses in the middle of the corridor, which stops us all. She releases Damon's elbow and adamantly shakes her head.

"No, this feels wrong, this *is* wrong. You royally fucked up." She glances over at me with concern. "Not that you would know anything about it," she focuses accusing eyes on Damon, "but it really hurts to be in love with someone while forced to watch them hook up with someone else."

"I would know," he snaps in defense.

"Right," she huffs dismissively. "Well then, you should know damn good and well that she shouldn't have to spend a night hanging out with her gorgeous, world-famous ex-husband and his new girlfriend. What in the hell were you thinking?"

"Jesus," Damon curses before looking between us apologetically. "I'm sorry, Nat. It was a stupid move. Say the word, and this ends right here."

I think of my father in that moment and feel the full weight of the burden he's had to endure himself, and I know a lot of his strength resides within me.

"I'll be okay. Maybe they'll make an excuse."

Ironically, we find Easton and Misty waiting for us in the lobby. From the look on Easton's face when he greets Holly and Damon, I expect an excuse to come, but I am surprised when he gives none. Just after successfully avoiding direct eye contact with Easton and Misty—while managing a cordial greeting—we file out of the hotel into a waiting SUV. An SUV with *just* enough room to accommodate all of us.

Once inside the car, I focus on Damon, or rather his hands, as he worries about the placement of them sitting next to Holly. My lips lift in amusement as our Casanova's nerves get the best of him. He's going to go for it.

"Okay, Damon, time to fess up. Where are we going?" Holly asks.

"Where else? A tequila distillery," he replies, just before I leap for the SUV's handle. Laughing, Damon wrestles me back into my seat as

Holly's dam bursts. I glare between them both after catching Easton pressing his lips together to stifle his own laugh.

"Worst best friends *ever*," I grit out as Damon winks.

"Oh no, what's the tequila story?" Misty asks, looking between us all and apparently clueless as to exactly what went down last night.

"Funny you should ask," Damon speaks up just as a demonic threat escapes me.

"Say another word, Damon. I love you, but you're a man child, and if you continue down this path, I'm not above making you disappear—*here*. Plenty of unexplainable things happen past the border."

"That bad, huh?" Misty says as Holly lets out a nervous bubble of laughter, looking between all of us.

"Not to add insult to injury," Holly spouts, opening her luggage-sized drawstring vacation purse and pulling out a bottle of tequila. She braves a look my way as she passes out some plastic-wrapped cups. "Sorry, babe," she winces adorably as Damon takes and opens the bottle, "it's the only liquor they had in a plus-sized bottle in the gift shop."

"It's fine. When in Rome, right?" I hold my cup out, dazed and defeated by the past twenty-four hours as Holly free pours, while a full circle Mexican fiesta dances in my head. I just want it to stop. I want this to be over with. With that in mind, I can't help but glance around, reading the expressions of all who've agreed to this disastrous waste of a day while inhaling and exhaling the uncomfortable air circulating throughout the cabin.

It's then I have a small epiphany.

Oh, life, you funny, inconsiderate, untimely motherfucker.

Full circle is right.

In the midst of this nightmarish situation, I realize it's how our parents must have felt when we were just as reckless with their history, discarding it like it didn't matter as we selfishly basked in our happiness. What's worse is that at some point, we expected them to be okay with it.

Even if they found their happily ever afters, I can't imagine *ever* being okay watching Easton happily move on with another woman—as I'm forcing myself to do now.

This is exactly what we would have pressured them into doing—putting on airs, trying their hardest to put their past away as they toasted us. This is the hell we would have subjected them to on every special occasion. Though our stories and endings—well, *my* ending—is far different from theirs, the dynamic is still the same, and frankly, it fucking sucks.

"I get it," I spout ironically as everyone brings their cups up to toast.

"Get what, babe?" Holly asks as all eyes pin me quizzically.

"All of it," I manage through a laugh, "but fuck it, Viva La Vida!" I tap glasses with all of them, looking them directly in the eyes as I was taught, in order to avoid bad luck. I make a point to do it, knowing I can't possibly survive any more. We all toss the spicy liquor back right after toasting, save one jade-eyed man. A man who returns my lingering eye contact with a rapidly hardening gaze of his own before slowly lifting his cup and tossing back his shot. Breaking eye contact when Holly prompts me for my cup to refill it, I decline. I opt to stare out of the window at the landscape. I'll be serving the rest of my time, my *sentence*, in Mexico—*sober*.

After walking through endless oversized barrels, and spending hours learning about a liquor I now despise, I lift my camera and take a panoramic view of my surroundings. While everyone else seems sufficiently buzzed from the tasting, I've just eaten my weight in tacos. Damon, being the generous bastard he is, added a romantic sunset buffet for the five of us at the end of our tour.

Because slaughtered hearts have to eat too, right?

The distillery provided the most spectacular view to dine at with its cliffside location. The patio is surrounded by similar rocky cliffs, and in the distance, an ample view of the ocean to watch the descent of the sun. Our candle-lit round top sits on a beautifully paved deck full of empty tables. We seem to be the only group who opted for the top-notch buffet and romantic atmosphere tonight—which pairs perfectly with the irony bouncing around us.

The vibe is surprisingly chill, with Spanish guitar music crooning softly out of nearby speakers. Our overly attentive catering staff continues to change out the buffet trays with fresh eats every few minutes as though they're serving royals. I, myself, dined like a queen eating her feelings while keeping my focus averted from the man sitting across the table. Feeling somewhat safe in my chair now, Damon serves as our buffer while Misty vapes, chatting with Holly next to the waist-high brick wall encasing the patio. I tune out of Easton and Damon's exchange while praying for the minutes of this sentence to tick out. Feeling somewhat confident that I'm going to get through the last of it unscathed, my safety is abruptly ripped from me when Damon excuses himself to answer a call. Ignoring my pleading eyes, holding a finger up to the two of us, he leaves Easton and me alone at the table.

As he walks back toward the distillery for privacy, I decide Damon is an Olympic-level Judas in the best friend department. I will be informing him of his update in status *as soon as* I have the opportunity. Having already spent most of my day facing as much of this reality as I can withstand, I look over to Easton to engage him, instead of shying away from conversation. I find his eyes already focused curiously on me as the sun begins its descent, tinting the sky in various hues of pink and red.

"Not so horrible, right?" I speak up while snapping another photo. "This view is—"

"What do you get?" Easton cuts me off abruptly, his tone biting.

"Pardon?" I ask, texting a picture of our view to Dad.

"Don't play ignorant. You know exactly what I'm asking. Put the phone down and tell me what you *get*, Natalie."

My eyes widen as he kicks back in his seat, his delivery far too hostile for casual conversation. Though his posture is relaxed, the look in his eyes tells me he's anything but.

"Fine. I *get* that we *married* our parents into this very type of situation."

"I fucking knew it," he scoffs.

"Knew what?"

"That you were justifying our divorce."

"Never that," I sip my water.

"No? Sure seems like it. *Newsflash*, Natalie. Plenty of people get along with their exes for the sake of their children." He tosses his napkin on his plate, the leather cuff fastened around his wrist keeping the majority of my focus before I take him in fully—something I've deprived myself of since we met up hours ago. His thick hair, which is definitely a few inches longer, hangs just above the collar of his dark blue linen button-down.

"I would say ours was a much different situation, but I'm not entirely disagreeing with you. Even so, there's no point in arguing about it since it's been put to bed, right?"

He scoffs. "Sure has, *Sleeping Beauty*."

"Hey, *hey*," I speak up in defense, "I'm just as uncomfortable as you are, but we don't have to turn on each other."

"That's always been your angle, hasn't it, Natalie? Putting everyone else's feelings first."

"Don't," I warn in a harsh whisper. "I was just trying to find some meaning in the situation. It's ironic and probably a little deserved, considering. You don't have to be such a jerk about it."

"Yeah, well, maybe tequila brings out the worst in me," he snaps, grabbing his rocks glass and tossing some back. "Or maybe it's *you*."

"Easton, please put your weapons away. We're leaving soon." I glance around uneasily to see our rapidly heating exchange unnoticed. "I fly home in two days, but I can make an early exit, if that's what you've decided you want."

"Maybe you should," his expertly thrown dagger lands squarely in my chest. "Yeah, Natalie, that's what I want."

A three-alarm fire begins to roar in my throat as he presses in.

"Oh, sorry, did that hurt?"

"Like hell," I admit. *"Happy?"*

"Sure," he spouts dryly.

"Well, that's all I want for you."

"Jesus," he rakes an impatient hand through his hair, hazel eyes drilling unforgivingly. "You really just talk *at people*, don't you?"

"You loved that about me once."

"No, that's the one thing I couldn't take about you. You've got immaculate perception about everyone that comes into your life, but play completely fucking blind on the perception to help yourself."

"I'm wide awake, Easton, and bullseye accurate on my perceptions of you. I don't need help knowing what's good for me."

"No, you're beyond that," he fires back before projecting his voice. "Come on, Misty. We're leaving."

"Five more minutes," she replies, oblivious, before diving back into conversation with Holly.

I can't help my snort. "She seems really *attuned* to *you*. Congratulations."

"Don't be petty."

"Then don't be a prick!" I whisper-yell, before tempering myself. "Look, I'm sorry if this situation is upsetting you. I don't want this to get ugly."

"Of course, you're sorry. God forbid, you have one selfish fucking moment where the whole of your sentiments can ring true."

"I'm all too painfully aware of the mistakes I've made, Easton. I wanted to tell you last night, but you didn't want to hear me."

He tosses back the rest of his drink and pushes his chair back to stand.

"You didn't want a divorce."

His eyes snap to mine.

"The day you came to me with the book, you wanted me to stop it. I didn't ask why you hadn't signed because I was too wrapped up in my pain and residual anger to realize we were *still married*, but you knew that. You wanted me to stop you. Tell me I'm wrong."

Slowly easing back down into his chair, he hooks an elbow over the back of it. "What's the point?"

"The point is that I'm not asleep, not playing immune, or ignorant—but you are, and have been since you saw me last night. You don't want my truth, and I know why. You're scared of it, and trust me, the more we confirm it, it scares me too."

His nostrils flare in annoyance, but I press in, my aching chest rattling with awareness that I may never get this chance again.

"I get why you're doing it, and I know it's my fault, and that hurts like hell." I swallow. "I know my own apology is long overdue, but hey," I shrug. "I'm just taking a page from your ruthless and blunt playbook because let's face it, you're still *you,* and I'm still *me.* You're being a hypocrite right now, because you still seem to think being brutally honest is the best damned way to handle every situation, but you don't want *mine* anymore. Tell me why, Easton."

His expression turns to stone. "You were drunk."

"I haven't had a drop in five hours, so let's test your theory, shall we?"

He searches my expression, his own wary. "Natalie—"

"Call me *Beauty*," I snap, eyes watering, "I prefer it because that's who you're talking to, or rather who you're *refusing* to listen to."

His shifts uncomfortably as I resign myself.

"Here's a newsflash for *you*, Easton. Despite your beliefs, brutal honesty is *not* the best way to conduct yourself in *every* situation. It's not the *bravest* way, either. There's a difference between being *brave*—ready to face and endure danger or pain, and *inappropriate*—which means not suitable or proper in the *circumstances*." I lift my chin defiantly. "But I'm trying to be *brave* in lieu of inappropriate because inappropriate would be confessing that I'm still wholly, unconditionally, and definitively *in love with you* while you're on a romantic getaway in Mexico with your girlfriend!"

Easton's nostrils flare as all heads start to turn our way. Battered heart spurring me on, I mentally glove up.

"You want truth? You want brutal honesty? The truth is, for the last two days, I've been sitting on the beach drowning in the realization that while loving you helped me *recognize* my worst fear, losing you left me *living* in it. Any life I live without you now will feel like settling." Fear for what I'm doing threatens, but I push through it as Easton stares back at me, his stoic expression unforgiving. In the past it would have intimidated me, but I know better.

"Do you think I didn't know what I was giving up when I let you go? I've been *brave*, Easton. Brave enough to *face* and *endure* the pain and the knowledge that I lost the thing with you that made me feel the most alive. I've *braved* every day knowing I should never have let you drive away that night without telling you that I *love* you, that I'm *sorry*, and that I wish I would have done so many things differently. And I'll regret it tomorrow, the day after, and after that for the rest of my fucking life—that's *bravery*!"

Holly harshly whispers my name from beside me, tugging on my arm before I rip it free. Twin tears spill from my eyes which remain bolted on Easton.

"*Inappropriate* would be confessing I never slept with that quarterback because you were the last man to touch me intimately and are the only man I'll ever want to again...because despite everything that's happened, I've remained *faithful!*"

Easton's eyes widen slightly as I smack the table and lean forward.

"So, you can keep on pretending that it's no longer there between us, but you and I both know the love we feel—that we've always felt—isn't going anywhere. As you've said all along, our parents' story isn't ours. But in one major way *it is*—because like theirs, our love is *timeless*," my voice cracks on that truth because it's the hardest to bear. "So, if you want my silence, you're going to have to earn it with your first lie to me and tell me that I've got it all wrong."

Unbearably thick tension brews as silence hangs in the air until a muffled cry cuts through it. Easton's eyes hold me hostage as Misty races toward the building, a hand clamped over her mouth.

"Oh, look," I jerk my head in her direction, and Easton's guilt-ridden eyes follow. "There goes another casualty of Easton's brutal honesty policy. I just hurt her with it. Is that selfish enough for you?"

Easton lowers his eyes, a curse leaving him as he cups his jaw.

"Natalie, you're making a scene," Damon hisses next to me as I palm the table to keep myself upright.

"Oh, but he deserves it," I rasp out with sincerity as Easton's eyes slam back into mine, a thousand emotions running through them as I allow him to see every crack in my exterior. "He deserves it, Damon, because he deserves a woman who's just as protective of him and of his heart. A woman who will fight just as hard for him as he did for her." My tears blind me briefly before I blink them free to see Easton devouring every word of the revelations pouring freely from my lips. I choke on a sob before I go completely blind to my surroundings. "I'm so sorry," I croak. "I'm sorry if I ever made you feel like anything less to me than my supernova…and you should know the only thing I've ever despised about you, Elliot Easton Crowne, is your last fucking name."

"That's enough, Nat!" Damon hooks his arm around my waist in an attempt to drag me away.

Overcome with emotion, I turn and crumble in Damon's arms. He sweeps me firmly into his grip as I bury my head into his neck, sobbing while he carries me away. Within seconds, I'm whisked into the SUV as Damon barks at the driver to go. Cradled in his hold, I unleash my hurt as we speed away while Damon begs me to forgive him.

SEVENTY-FOUR

Always Been You
Jessie Murph

Natalie

Sitting at the edge of the surf wrapped in Easton's jacket, I watch the violet sky darken further, giving way to the moon's beam as it begins to light up the water. All too tempted to flee after the spectacle I made, I only retreated to gather myself together. Though mortified by what I did, I'm finding it hard to regret it, and I refuse to back down now. I hadn't planned on having that fight with him the way it happened, but some part of me knew I was already gloving up this morning.

The way I knew I would seek him out when I left Mexico, face to face, and finally come clean with him about everything I didn't the night he divorced me. No matter what happens, I'm not hiding my hurts, my feelings, or my own needs anymore. Sometimes saving face while displaying quiet strength isn't worth the cost.

I might hate hindsight for the bitch she is, but I have her to thank for giving me clarity on exactly what my worst crimes are when it comes to my ex-husband.

It isn't the promises we've broken but the vows we both failed to uphold. Patience, kindness, understanding, protection, preservation, all of them. They're the chosen vows countless others have spoken in ceremony for good reason. I didn't fully comprehend how keeping them close could have kept us united, nor did I understand the importance of each one of them, until we fell apart.

Either way, intertwined between my melancholy and heartbreak, is a relief that, at least now, he knows. If he decides to walk away, I'll force myself to watch him with a peace I didn't have before I voiced my regrets to him. That is, if he hasn't already fled himself.

Even knowing my rejection may be inevitable, like Easton, I have to swing anyway. There are high stakes to truly loving another human being, and you have to hand your heart to them with all the trust you have without knowing the outcome. These are the things that loving Easton has taught me.

But in order for it to be a fair fight, I have to put myself wholly on the line the way he did for me, time and again.

Intent on seeing it through, I power up my cellphone and press send as the raw ache in my chest reignites. He answers on the second ring.

"Hey," he speaks up in alarm, hearing my sniffle. "Are you okay?"

"N-no," I croak as my voice breaks. "No, I'm not," I confess. "And I haven't been okay for a long time."

"You can tell me anything," he urges in a tone that has my tears spilling over. I falter, briefly holding the phone away as I choke on another wave of pain before gathering the strength and breath I need.

"I'm glad, Daddy, because I want to tell you about the man I fell in love with in Seattle."

SEVENTY-FIVE

One More Try
George Michael

Easton

Once Misty is loaded into her waiting car, I watch it pull away. As I do, a sudden but familiar anger surges through me. The feeling only intensifies as I turn and stalk back into the lobby.

Guilt-ridden, pissed about my current circumstances, fed the fuck up with fate and the havoc it's wreaked on me, along with my ex-wife—who's determined to make me dismantle my freshly constructed system for self-preservation—I prowl back into the resort lobby on a mission. Walking up to the reception desk, I grit out my request. "Can you please dial Natalie Butler's room?"

The man behind the counter clicks his mouse to look her up and dials. "Sorry, Mr. Crowne, she's not answering."

"Of course she isn't, because that would make this much less difficult," I grit out.

"Pardon?"

"Nothing, sorry," I say, raking my hands through my hair. Heart pumping with fear that she left before I got a chance to thank her for her belated birthday present—I wonder if she's already headed toward a plane bound for Texas.

Wouldn't surprise me. After all, it's her MO—intoxicate, devastate, and dash.

Fuming, I decide to have the front desk call her again, taking note of the room number when he dials. "Sorry, Mr. Crowne, she's still—"

"It's fine," I wave him off. "Thank you."

Sweat gathering on my brow, I bang on her hotel door minutes later as my heart begins thrashing wildly in my chest. "Open the fucking door, Natalie!"

My knock goes unanswered as the door adjacent clicks open, and Holly and Damon's heads pop out, one atop the other. Both their heads slowly turn my way, eyes widening as they take in my state.

"Where is she?" I bark in demand.

Holly speaks up first. "Um, with all due respect, Easton, I'm not telling you *shit* with that intent to *murder* look in your eyes."

"I would never hurt her," I hear myself say. "And you both fucking know it."

"But haven't you?" Holly asks as I fist my hands at my sides before stalking toward them.

Both of them jerk back behind the door, leaving only a fraction open as Damon tosses a progress report from the other side of it. "She's not in good shape."

"No shit," I snap sarcastically, trying to get a handle on my anger. "I just want to talk to her."

"Is Misty okay?" Holly asks as muffled commotion breaks out behind the door.

"My newest ex?" I belt to them both. "Well, right now, she's on her way to a different hotel to wipe her memory free of any remnants of me," I practically shout as Damon's head reappears. "Probably with someone who looks a lot like *you*."

Damon winces. "Shit, man, I'm sorry. That's on me. That tequila tour was my bad."

"Yeah, well, what did *I* ever do to you?" I ask him.

"Believe it or not, you're getting me back pretty good right now." He widens his eyes.

I furrow my brows. "What?"

"Nothing," he sighs. "Look, man. I've never seen her that distraught, and I've known her since we were babies."

Panic threatens, the devastation on her face all I can see. "Just tell me where she is."

"I really don't know. When she got out of the SUV, she begged me not to follow. We've called her a dozen times, and her phone is going straight to voicemail. She turned off her locator, too."

"Of course, she did," I palm my face in frustration.

"I can help you look for her," he offers.

"I'll find her," I inch forward. "Can you at least give me a general direction? This resort is three fucking miles wide."

"East." Damon offers in fast response.

"East? You're joking, right?"

He cocks his head. "Unfortunately...*no*?"

"Just...," I exhale harshly, "...if you see her, tell her I'm looking for her, all right?"

"I will."

I back a step away from the door just as he closes it. Not ten seconds later, Holly calls to my retreating back just after I push the button for the elevator. "Easton Crowne!" She booms with protective authority, forcing me to turn and address her as she secures a bedsheet around her.

Oh. Ohhh.

The last few awkward minutes begin to make sense as Holly reads my state—heartbeat erratic, mind in overdrive, worry overtaking me, anger due to Natalie's disappearance the front runner. Dressed in an impromptu toga, Holly squares her shoulders before issuing her threat. "Rock star or not, I'll put my foot up your ass, if you hurt my girl!"

"Tell 'im, baby," Damon sounds from behind the door.

"I don't see *you* telling him," she fires back to the crack of space.

"It's implied," he grits out.

"It's *unnecessary*," I inform them, denying my smile and dismissing them both, turning to repeatedly jab the elevator button.

"Just...please, Easton," Holly reasons at my back. "She's been through enough."

All I can do is nod before I step into the elevator turning to briefly meet Holly's pleading gaze as the doors close.

Less than twenty-four hours in, my ex-wife is putting me through my paces as my ex-girlfriend literally runs for the hills.

I shouldn't have expected any less.

Same woman.

Same result.

Stay pissed, Easton.

But I don't stay pissed. Panic takes the lead and runs rampant after endless minutes of fruitlessly combing the resort and coming up empty. Muscles aching, heart racing, her pained cries echoing throughout my mind, I start my search along the beach, seeing no signs of her. Fear snatches me in a chokehold as I stop briefly, panting heavily, gut churning. In an attempt to calm myself, I brace my hands on my thighs.

Fuck, Beauty, where are you?

Sweat dripping from every inch of my body, I spot a dune a short distance away and stalk toward it. It's when I reach the top of it that her voice carries to me on the wind. Relieved, I let the anger seep back in as I lose my footing on the other side of the dune, all but tumbling down, before barely managing to catch myself in time to land on my feet. Feeling crazed and possessed, emotions in overdrive, I slap at the sand covering me in irritation as I stalk toward her where she sits, her back to me, phone lifted to her ear.

"No, I'm not," she sniffs. "And I haven't been okay for a long time." Hunched over in my jacket, her wedding dress, I bat the sentimental thought away, ready to lay into her but am stopped dead in my tracks when she speaks again.

"I'm glad, Daddy, because I want to tell you about the man I fell in love with in Seattle."

Her tearful admission grips my seizing heart like a vise as I'm frozen where I stand, waiting on bated breath for Nate's reply. During those short seconds, I toss up a prayer, if only for her sake, for him to finally hear her out. It's when she begins her tearful confession that I stop breathing altogether.

"He's perceptive. He can read people easily and usually judge people's character within minutes. He speaks the way he lives—with *intent,* and it's fascinating to me because I've never met anyone so brave. He's brilliant, magnetic, and…magical, and I'm drawn to him more than I have ever been to any other soul in my life. He listens to my passion like it's his favorite pastime and treats me like I'm the most precious thing on earth—with the utmost respect and care. He's fiercely protective and has a temper. Still, it's mostly directed towards those who endanger the ones he loves, who purposefully play ignorant, or treat others unfairly, but would never, ever hurt me."

She runs my jacket sleeve along her face as my heart stalls out altogether.

"Like me, he's close to his parents and mildly superstitious because of his mother. He habitually practices a few of her quirks, though he'll be hard-pressed to admit it. He idolizes his father, too," her voice cracks painfully with that admission, as does my chest. "He's insanely talented and can memorize songs in mere minutes, the notes, the lyrics, all of it, though he'll never call himself a prodigy or a genius, he's too humble... He's famous and hates it, but only because he's an empath to his core and doesn't want to be idolized or held responsible for other people's life choices." She cups her mouth briefly to stifle her cries before continuing. "He's my supernova, the only star in my sky, and oh...how he shines. Every time I look at him, my insides light fire, and I am every bit a moth to his flame. But I don't care if I burn because...because I would rather burn with him in any capacity, than exist safely anywhere else without him."

Raking my hand through my hair, I stand back helplessly, unraveling with every word she speaks.

Damn this woman.

"I'm in love with Easton Crowne, Daddy, and I'm never going to fall out of love with him, and I t-think..." she hangs her head, her cries carrying over to me and breaking me down completely, piece by piece as does her next declaration. "I think it's way too late. I think...I think I've lost him for good, but I'm going to try like hell to get him back, and if I do...I'm going to put him *first*."

Every ounce of my anger dissipates as my frustration also threatens to shake free. Gutted by her admissions, by what I still feel for her, emotions strangle me as the words I thought I would never hear in my lifetime continue to pour from her lips.

"I just wanted to tell you why I have to break your heart again, Daddy. Despite it being the worst twist of fate imaginable, Easton is the man who fills my heart and soul, and with me, he comes first."

I send up another quick prayer as brief silence lingers before she speaks again. "I l-l-love you, t-too, thank y-you, Daddy. I'm g-getting t-too upset to talk. I need to go now, okay? I'll c-call you when I've c-calmed down."

A pause, a sniff, another muffled cry into the sleeve of my jacket. “O-kay. B-bye, Daddy.” She ends the call, bends her head, and sobs into her hands.

Destroyed by the sight of it and unable to handle another second, I move to go to her just as she snaps her shoulders back, stands, dusts herself off, and turns. Eyes lowered, she begins charging toward the resort, toward *me* with determination.

I’ve never in my life loved the sight of anything more.

A few steps in, she pauses as if sensing me, lifts her head, eyes widening when she sees me standing there. Posture faltering, she croaks my name in defeat before again dropping her face in her palms.

SEVENTY-SIX

I Don't Want to Talk About It
Rod Stewart

Natalie

"This feels familiar," Easton's coarse voice cuts through the whirring breeze filling my ears as I allow myself a few more seconds of reprieve in my hands. I look over at him where he stands, soaked by the light of the moon, head tilted back, eyes brimming with unshed tears.

I notice he's covered in sweat, and there's sand coating his right side, his jeans and boots dusted with it, chest heaving, as though he's just run a marathon.

"What's going on. What happened?"

"What happened?" He croaks incredulously. "You can't be serious." He stares back at me, bewildered. "Jesus, I thought *I* was supposed to be the showstopper," he relays in a gruff whisper, "but you definitely upstaged me tonight."

"Easton," I swallow, "I'm—"

"You're right. You're still *you,* and I'm still *me,*" he continues, tears spilling over and gliding down his cheeks. "And you're still a nightmare…but you should know…" his voice shakes, "you've become a master at arguing your point."

"Is Misty…"

"Oh, you drilled your point into her very well and sent her packing, *literally.*"

"I'm sorry for what I did, for the way I did it—hurting her. But I'm," I lift my chin, "but I'm not at all sorry for what I said."

"Oh, I believe you, Beauty," his shoulders slump as he steps forward. "Now tell me what you were going to say when you found me."

Itching to go to him where he stands feet away, rattling with emotion and residual hurt, unchecked tears gliding down his face, I drop my hands to my sides.

"We broke a lot of promises being young, reckless, and naïve—but I think I figured out where we went wrong—at least, where I went wrong." Taking a steadying breath, I keep swinging. "Love *is* patient, Easton—it has to be, and we both needed it. Love is kind. We had that in abundance and lost it along the way. We both needed to remember that, we...I," I run the sleeve of his jacket over my face. "Those promises we made, they mattered, but it was the *vows* that would have kept us together—the vows I wish I would have paid more attention to. You were always protective, but I wasn't the only one that needed protecting, and I didn't do my part, and for that, I'll forever be sorry."

Mustering the strength I have left, I continue to swing.

"I left you alone in it—I didn't mean to, but I did. I let their past and my guilt tear us apart. I allowed my relationship with my father to overrule the most important love of my life—*you*. I took your patience and love for granted, Easton, because I believed in you—in everything you said, in the way you viewed and felt about us, because I felt and believed it too. But I didn't nurture us the way I should have, when you needed me most, because I was too terrified to lose my future. But I lost it anyway when I lost you...and I miss you so much. I miss *us*. I regret more than anything, not apologizing for my mistakes when I had the chance." I step closer to him, and he remains where he stands. "Married or not, I want the chance back to uphold those vows. I want the chance to be the partner you deserve. I w-want you t-to take me back." An involuntary hiccup interrupts me as I shudder with it. Easton's chest rises and falls. "I-if y-you can find it in your heart to forgive me for that mistake. If you c-can give me a chance—"

"You're unbelievable, you know that?" He admonishes as I lower my guilty gaze. "Look at me, Beauty," the hint of command in his words kicks my heart into overdrive. He finally steps forward, trapping my face in his hands, eyes searching. "What took you so fucking long?"

"I'm sorry," I lick the salt from my lips. "I got lost."

"But I told you where to find me. I told you I'd be right here where you left me," he reminds me as I shake in his hold, hope lighting up my being. "It's not too late, Beauty," he murmurs, "and with you, it was never going to be."

He jerks me to him, diminishing all space between us as I wrap myself around him, relieved cries leaving me as I soak in his scent. Pressing kisses from his throat to his lips, they urgently meet and mold as we get lost in our kiss. My breaths continue to hitch as he sweeps his urgent tongue along mine, a pained groan leaving him as we cry our relief into each other's mouths. We drag it out for several blissful minutes, our connection a balm to our stinging souls. Easton gently pulls away, eyes full of concern as he furiously begins to wipe my tears with gentle thumbs.

"Please don't cry anymore, baby. I'm sorry for being such a bastard," he whispers, "I let the bitter asshole take over, but I'm giving his self-righteous ass the boot because I hate seeing you like this."

Running gentle knuckles along my face, I lean into his touch. "So...I was right...you didn't want a divorce that day."

He shakes his head. "God, no."

"But you signed," I sniffle.

"You didn't stop me," he croaks as he continually soothes me with gentle thumbs. "How I was hoping you would stop me, Natalie. I couldn't take it when you asked for friendship, and I felt like I'd lost you for good then. I was fucking breaking apart because I knew I had to set you free and that you may never come back."

"Why?"

"I was so fucking selfish in my pain. I didn't care who else it was hurting. I knew if we had a chance, I had to let you come to me. Reading my mother's book changed a lot of my perception. The answer rang clear for me from what I derived from our parents' story. After we fell apart, I took a page from my father's book and decided to give you the time to choose your path, whether it included me or not—like he did for my mom. I practically forced you into a relationship the first time."

"That's not true. I wanted it too."

"I know that...but I went about it the wrong way. I didn't heed your constant warnings because I wanted us to happen too much. Even when you begged me, I didn't listen. I'm at fault, too, Natalie. This isn't solely on you."

"So, you've been waiting on me?"

"At first, yes…until waiting became unhealthy for me. I was…it made me sick. Physically and mentally, so, I would say, more like *hoping*. That day in Austin, even six weeks later, we were still so raw after what we went through, what we put our parents through. Because of the things I said, the way I hurt you, I knew I couldn't force us back together. I just didn't know how long it would take, or…" another tear falls, and I hate the sight of his pain, "or if it would ever happen at all. I spent my trip to Europe holding out hope I would spot you in the crowd, that you would come to me. When I got home, I made the decision I couldn't do it anymore. So, I forced myself to try to move on. I already knew it was a fool's errand, but last night, the second I saw you," he shakes his head. "You're right. I went into full-blown denial, bitter because I'd finally taken steps to try and move on, and there you were."

"I don't blame you, Easton. I don't. You're right. I knew your number, but I didn't use it. But when I got here, actually long before I got here, I knew without a doubt I was coming for you—"

"That isn't all," he interjects. "As selfish as it may be to say," he exhales harshly, "I think I really needed to see you fight for us."

I cock my hip and palm it. "Well, did I make enough of a stink for you?"

He grins and pushes my curls away from my splotched cheeks. "I think half of Mexico heard you missed my cock."

"It's a cock worthy of missing," I sniff.

"God, I've missed you so much," he murmurs, keeping my face in his palm. "You really haven't been with anyone?"

"No, I couldn't, and I don't care if you can't say the same." I declare and immediately backtrack. "I mean, I do care, *a lot*, but I won't let it come between us. You had every right to—"

"I love you," he whispers, a tear gliding along his jaw. "Wholly, unconditionally, and definitively, Natalie. There's no other woman in the world that could replace you either, Beauty. I'm the fucking fool for trying."

"I'll never let you go without a fight," I promise.

"Jesus," he chuckles, "after what you just did, you won't ever have to. I'm good for the foreseeable future."

"I needed my soul back," I declare. Relief floods me as I slide my arms around his waist. "And from now until forever, I'm holding onto my life-changing man with *both hands*."

"Can I...," he swallows, anxiety flitting through his features. "Can I ask what Nate said before he hung up?"

"How much of that did you hear?"

"All of it," he replies unapologetically.

"Wow," I sniff, "I bet your head is about to explode."

"I'm so glad I did hear it. I was so pissed at you for sucker-punching my heart and disappearing. I was coming to read you the riot act, but hearing that...Jesus, baby, it meant *everything* to me."

"I'm so—"

"No more apologies," he says. "I swear to God, Beauty, I'm letting all of it go, right fucking now, and I hope you do too. I'm yours," he buries his head in my neck, nudging me to answer, "please tell me what he said."

I beam up at him. "He said he would really like to meet the man I fell in love with in Seattle."

SEVENTY-SEVEN

This Love
Taylor Swift

Natalie

"I'm never letting you go," Easton murmurs against my mouth as he carries me through the bar, past Jerry, who flashes us a smile along with the lift of his chin. Easton bypasses the lobby, heading straight toward the elevator.

Raw and emotional, his heart pounds against mine from the way I'm wrapped around him—we wait for what seems like an eternity as the floors slowly tick off.

"This is the slowest elevator ever," I groan. "You can let me down," I press a kiss to his neck.

"Fuck that, you're not leaving my arms," he growls when the doors finally open. My back meets the side of the elevator as he uses his keycard to access his floor before crushing me against him, cradling my face, his eyes intent as he gazes at me. "I need inside you, Beauty, right fucking now."

My body instantly responds, tightening with urgency as we begin to ascend. I clutch him as he makes more declarations, his hand gripping my bare thigh beneath my dress. "From now until fucking forever," he whispers vehemently, "we pay attention to *our* story, not theirs."

Getting lost in sensation, in his touch, in him, I flick my tongue against his neck with my reply. "*Bet.*"

Relief sweeps his features as I press kisses along his jaw, repeating the word between each. As if my sentiments break the last of his control, he plunges into my mouth with a possessive tongue, feeding it to me first before I latch onto it and suck as he hoists me up further against the elevator wall. All at once, we burst into motion, his kiss sending me straight into orbit. The time and space between us continually diminish as the elevator doors open, and I remain wrapped around him, pulling my phone out of my pocket in an attempt to type out quick texts with my lips still latched to his neck.

With Easton. Presidential Suite. Never leaving. Go home without me.

Holly: All good. Eggplant emoji

Confused by her reply and easy permission, I frown at my phone. "Huh? That's weird."

"What?"

"Holly just let me off the hook without demanding an explanation, no sign of mama bear in sight."

"I can't believe you're fucking texting right now," he growls, walking us down the corridor.

I lick along his neck before sweeping up the wet trail with the brush of my lips. "I'm clearing my schedule for my number one priority." I pull his lobe into my mouth and bite.

"Well, when you put it that way, fine, but make it snappy," he orders in heated demand.

"Snappy?" I laugh as he bursts through the door of his suite with me still firmly in his hold.

"That's from my mom," he admits with a smirk before setting me on my feet, his eyes pooling rapidly with desire before he pins me with his hips to the wall. He begins his wicked assault as I attempt to compose one last short text.

"I just have to," *Kiss.* "Text." *Kiss.* "My dad," I finish as he pushes the jacket off my shoulders before he trails a tongue-filled kiss from the hollow of my throat to my lips. I adjust my arms to accommodate him as I try to type behind his back.

Groaning in frustration, he further nails me to the wall, fisting my dress at my thigh and gathering the material into his hand while using the other to dip in the back of my panties. Gripping my bare ass, he jerks my lower half forward, grinding the swollen length of his jean-covered cock against the thin material of my panties.

"Ah," I gasp out, shooting off the only text I'm able to manage before releasing my phone. It clatters somewhere on the floor beneath us. I lick along his Adam's apple just as he pushes my panties to the side and thrusts thick fingers into me. Shuddering around him, I cry out in pleasure.

"Maybe I should punish you," he utters in a lust-filled threat.

"Absolutely...*not*," I protest while he runs a featherlight fingertip along my clit, leaving me needy.

"You looked so fucking beautiful last night it hurt," he pants, "but you meant to hurt me in that fucking bikini today. I almost had a goddamned heart attack when I saw that chain around your waist. It took every bit of my willpower not to get hard. That was cruel, baby."

"I'm sorry."

"I don't think you are," he taunts, pumping his fingers faster. I hear my own arousal as his touch brings me straight to the brink. "Jesus...Easton, I'm going to come."

"Not without me inside you." He withdraws his fingers as I grip his wrist with one hand, bringing it back to where it was, and use the other to clutch his jaw firmly. "Easton, I love you, and if you want to punish me later, I'm all for it, but it's been way too long, so I'm going to need you to skip the preliminaries and *punch the hell in* to get to *work*."

A short pause before a burst of laughter follows, and I glare at him. "Please, Easton," I whimper, "I need you."

"I've got you, Beauty," he murmurs before kneeling and untying my sandals. Standing, he brings the hem of my dress up and over my head, leaving me in nothing but a white thong.

Raking his lip with his teeth, he steps back and scans me as I grip the back of his neck. "*Buttons*, I need you to concentrate on my buttons. Easton, focus," I grit out, clit thrumming, body blazing with need.

"Okay, Beauty, okay," he murmurs in amusement, sweeping me into his arms and gently depositing me on my feet next to the bed.

As he discards his boots, I glance back at the oversized king to see it's freshly made. I swallow down the jealous sting the sight of it brings while biting the question away. Standing, Easton begins to unbutton his shirt and pauses when he reads my hesitation. "No, baby, fuck no. I couldn't," he admits earnestly. "Especially after I saw you last night. I couldn't, Natalie. You're safe with me."

Relieved, I nod, "We hurt her, Easton."

"We hurt a lot of people, but the only two we need to be worrying about right now are in *this room*."

"Right," I agree, temporarily letting that guilt go and clasping my hands around his neck. "I love you."

"I love you, too, Beauty," his eyes glitter down on me, "so fucking much. Now," he says, sliding a palm down my stomach and into my panties, slipping a few fingers inside me, just as his thumb begins to slowly massage my clit, "about these buttons."

He kisses me, and all outside thoughts melt away, as do the rest of our clothes. The second Easton has me ready, he turns me to lay on my stomach and drags me to the edge of the bed. One hand gripping the back of my neck, he lifts my leg, propping my bent knee on the mattress. His breath hits my ear as his words set my body alight. "Just so you know, I missed this pussy so much. I plan on working a lot of overtime." With that, he buries himself to the hilt. Stretched in a mix of pain and pleasure, I call out to him as a groan bursts from his own lips. Wasting no time, he angles his hips, pushing in impossibly further. He drives his point home as he squeezes the back of my neck, claiming words pouring from his lips, "For *me*."

"Forever," I pant out as he leaves us locked. Tilting his pelvis, he grinds into me with expert precision, hitting me *just so*. Not long after, I'm convulsing around him, ecstasy-laced words and praises pouring from me. He milks my orgasm until I go boneless, whispering my love. Withholding his own release, he slowly turns me over, lust taking up his expression as he rears his hips back and slowly pushes in, eyes hooding as he watches the stretch he's creating. Rapt, his focus remains on where we connect before his eyes light a trail of fire up my body, seeking and holding mine. We get lost in our stare, and it's there we hurdle over the rest of our separation in the last year, our struggle to get to this point, so painful, so heart-wrenching but so incredibly—

"Worth it," he finishes because he's thinking the same thing.

My best friend.
My lover.
My forever.

Covered in a sheen of sweat, Easton keeps my leg hooked on his hip with his palm as he thrusts into me with abandon, shifting his angle to hit me exactly where I need him to. Within seconds, I'm coiled and ready.

"Give it up, Beauty," he pants, just before my body obeys, heart thundering in my ears as pleasure pulses through me. Groaning through his own release, he pulses inside while kissing me breathless.

Collapsing onto his back, he pulls me to cover his upper half and turns to catch the light filtering in behind the curtain. His lips lift in a grin.

"What?" I ask.

"Is it sunrise or sunset?"

"Morning…definitely morning."

The truth is, neither of us has any clue at this point. We haven't left our room or opened the thick curtains to gauge time, but instead spent it all making up for what we lost before losing track of it altogether.

What I am sure of is that I don't want to return to the world yet, nor do I want to share the man I'm holding hostage just as much as he is me.

The difference now is that I'm not dreading the return, not at all—just prolonging it. Easton traces my skin before running a finger over the faint pink scar along my breast.

"What happened here?"

Lifting, I gaze down at him apprehensively, not wanting to alter the calm in his expression. Sitting, I pull a pillow onto my naked lap. "If I tell you, you can't freak out and get all…well, *you*—or use it against me in the future to fuel your paranoia."

"That's a lot of demands," his grin disappears, and his stare hardens slightly. "Did someone hurt you? If so, all fucking bets are off."

I shake my head. "There he is, the paleolithic man I married."

"And will be marrying again in the very near future."

"Just give me the date and time."

He again runs the pad of his finger across my scar. "Answer me. Did someone hurt you?"

"Just the opposite, someone *saved me.*" I caress his jaw as he draws his brows. "Actually, it was the damn *ding, ding, ding* from my Prince Phillip."

"Baby, you good?" He scrutinizes me, "Did I fuck you too hard? Did you hit your head on the board?"

Hello, Easton's sexy as fuck half-grin. God, how I've missed you.

"And who the hell is Prince Phillip?" He bites out. "The English Queen's deceased husband is haunting you?"

"No, you *dope.* Prince Phillip is the Disney prince who kissed Sleeping Beauty awake." Unable to help myself, I bend down and kiss his twisted lips. "It was *you*, Easton. It was *you* who saved me with your constant reminders to buckle up. Your droning eventually led me to a state where every time it went off, all I heard was you bickering with me to put on my seatbelt." I grab his hand and turn it over on the pillow on my lap, running my fingers along his palm. "That day, you won the argument that saved my life."

All traces of his smile disappear. "You were in a wreck?"

I nod. "My Prius didn't make it, but the State Trooper said I wouldn't have either, if I didn't have my seatbelt on. It was raining pretty hard, and I was in a hurry."

"To get to where?"

"That's the worst part."

"Out with it, Natalie."

"Well, I was rushing toward the airport because I had just maxed out my AmEx again. I was on my way to Stockholm."

He gapes at me. "To my last concert?"

I nod.

"Baby," he hangs his head, his tone both mournful and irritated. "Why, why, fucking *why* didn't you call me?"

"Because it was *my turn* for a grand gesture. Jesus, Easton. After all we'd been through, I wanted to do what you'd done for me every single time. You deserved it. I had no idea what the reception would be, but when I finally convinced myself to just fucking do it, to show up and go for broke, I decided I didn't want to wait for your tour to end. On the way, I got in the wreck, and it stalled me from getting to you. And then you were home and—"

"And dating Misty," he adds. "Fuck."

"I hate that part of it," I whisper as I trace his lips. "I'd already wasted too much time, and I knew it, but I was always, always coming to you. You should know by now, even when we were apart, you've *always* been with me." His eyes shine with emotion. "You're so much a part of me—it's unreal."

He grips my hand and presses a delicate kiss to the back of it. "I know exactly what you mean. You asked me once when I knew I loved you." He takes my finger and runs it along the loop in his Chihuly tattoo. "Well, this loop represents *you*, literally, figuratively, and poetically, but crazier than that, *predictively*—because fuck, reckless and naïve—we're the definition of insanity. But I'll take insanity any day. I'll relive it with you on loop."

"You're turning me on with that witty word usage, Crowne."

"Do you want your answer or not?"

"Of course."

He smirks, "I still don't know."

"Seriously?" I grumble. "That's not an answer."

"But I can tell you it was somewhere between you stalking into that bar dressed in your entire suitcase and my decision to alter the tattoo. So, when did I know I loved you? Somewhere in the first few days. But I *can* tell you for certain when I knew I wanted to marry you…and it was when your plane taxied away from me in Dallas." He lifts my empty left hand, his expression darkening. "We never should have gotten divorced."

Expression turning thoughtful, he stands in naked glory and stalks over to a dresser pulling out the ring he proposed to me with on stage before slipping back in bed.

"Beauty…" he says softly.

"It's not even a question you need to ask again, Easton," I say as he lifts his jade gaze and slides the ring back on my finger. Eyes watering, I gaze down at it with reverence. "Easton, I swear—"

"No, baby, no more promises," he says, gripping the back of my neck.

I frown. "You don't think we're capable of keeping them?"

"I think we wasted too much time worrying about them to just be," he murmurs. "We'll make more on our next wedding day."

I can't help my smile. "So, we're doing it again?"

"Hell yes, we are. This time, you're planning it."

"Our first one was perfect," I sigh.

"It was. You have your work cut out for you," he boasts as he dips to kiss me and jerks back suddenly. "Oh, and just so you fucking know, the second we leave Mexico, our life starts together. I don't care if all four of our parents show up with the fucking cartel behind them for backup. We're leaving on a plane—together."

"Fine by me, Mr. Crowne, but I sincerely hope you're okay with the destination and being covered in sweat three steps outside your front door while inhaling a good whiff of steamed-up cow shit."

"Really?" He curls his lip at the idea, and I giggle at his reaction before he shrugs. Kissing my ring first, he begins to wordlessly express his love for me with his lips. Just as we start to lose ourselves, my phone vibrates on the nightstand, drawing our attention to it as we both turn our heads. I glance down at Easton, who's kept us both unplugged since we entered the suite.

"Let me check it, Easton."

"Just…wait," he says, running the pad of his finger along my scar.

"We have to eventually acknowledge them," I say, reaching over to grab my phone. "The last text I sent my dad was a heart eyes emoji and a thumbs up. It's a pretty asshole move, considering the state I was in on the phone."

"'K, baby," he whispers, releasing me as I turn and lift my phone, seeing a missed text notification from my father.

"Is it Nate?" He asks from where he lays, his focus trained on the ceiling, voice laced with a tinge of apprehension.

"Yeah, it is. But I told you what he said."

He nods, that reminder doing little to ease his mind as he turns on his side, propping his head in his hand while I open the message and scan the text. "What is he saying?"

Beaming, I turn to him, lowering the cell to his line of sight so he can read it for himself.

> **Daddy: All your mother and I ask is that you please not marry him again before leaving Mexico. We'd like to attend at least ONE of your weddings.**

It's the first time my dad makes Easton laugh.

EPILOGUE

Memory Lane
Haley Joelle

Nate

Six months later...

The door opens to the bathroom as I secure my cufflinks and pull my jacket down.

"Can you zip me?" Addie asks as I turn to see my wife holding the top of her long, navy silk gown to her chest. It flows over her porcelain skin, perfectly accentuating her figure. With her glossy dark hair secured on top of her head, tendrils of flyaway curls already coming loose—just the way I like them. The floating diamond I gave her on our tenth-anniversary sparkles on her chest, next to the diamond on her left hand, which glints against the material. A diamond I gifted her on our twenty-fifth wedding anniversary. She lifts a brow at my reaction to her half-dressed, half-accessible body and does her best to hide her smile.

"Not bad for an old lady?" She asks, wrinkling her nose.

"Jesus, you're so fucking perfect," I murmur, taking long strides toward her as she turns and offers her bare back to me. Taking the opportunity, I press a kiss to her nape and feel her involuntary shiver.

"You're anything but an old lady," I assure her. "Apparently, I did a shit job of reminding you last night."

"That was two nights ago, *old man*."

I slowly pull the zipper up to secure her dress. "You're fucking breathtaking, Addie, always have been," I tell her as she glances at me over her shoulder, her pink-painted lips curling up.

"You don't look so bad, yourself," she murmurs, "but get *that look* out of your eyes, Butler. We have an appointment to keep."

"What look?" I taunt, playing the long game we started with years ago as a flash of Addie the first time I saw her at the party flits through my mind. She looked like a living dream, despite the scowl on her face as she chugged champagne. Stunned by the sight of her, I stood waiting until she spotted me standing between the tables, zeroed in on her. The second our eyes met, she stopped her glass halfway to her mouth, her lips lifting up in much the same way as they are now, her expression looking a lot like 'okay, now who in the hell are you?'

Like me, she was a little bit jaded, a little bit over it, but just as hopeful she was wrong about being both those things. I didn't have the answer that night of who I was to her, but it hit me like a freight train a few months later.

Hers.

"What are you thinking about?" she asks. "You okay?"

Turning her toward the mirror, I circle her waist and dip my chin to rest in the curve of her neck as I study our reflection. "Better than okay…thinking about the night I saw the most beautiful pissed-off woman at a party and immediately wanted her naked."

She grips my hands resting on her stomach. "Good thing to think about," she says as we soak each other in. "This is going to be one of those days, isn't it?"

The slight shake in her voice tells me none of us are getting out of this without our emotions getting the best of us. Though my wife is tougher than nails—tougher than me—I can't help but feel the same burn of what she's feeling as her eyes mist. "We've still got a ton to look forward to as well, Addie."

"I wish we'd have had more kids," she sighs. "At least so we wouldn't lose our shit on her every time she hits a milestone. That's a lot of pressure for her," she says through a laugh.

"I wouldn't change anything."

She runs a hand up to catch a tear from beneath her eyes. "Me neither. Now get away from me before you ruin my makeup."

Refusing to budge, I hold her tightly to me a little bit longer. "I love you, Addison Butler."

"What did I just say, you jackass?" She snaps playfully as I turn her and gently lift her tears away with my thumbs.

"Not my fault you're a cry baby."

She smooths her palms over my shoulders before gliding them down the arms of my jacket, eyes flaring with familiar heat. "Don't drink too much," she orders huskily, the promise of a good night shining in her eyes if I obey.

I run my nose along hers. "Yes, ma'am."

Ignoring her protest, I kiss her, ruining her lipstick, and she resists for just a second before she allows it. It deepens, and I rip myself free before I make good on what's brewing between us.

"I'm going to go check on the bride."

"Okay," she says, wiping my lips free of the color before turning back toward the mirror. "I'll be there in a bit."

"Take your time, baby. We've still got a few hours."

"Go," she waves me off, "stop worrying about me and go take care of our little girl."

The humidity covers me as soon as I close the door to our bungalow. Sweat gathering on my brow, I follow the walkway past the lush tropical landscape and take it all in. Aside from the heat, it's the perfect day. Fragrance drifts from a cluster of some exotic flowers I can't identify a few feet away, and I inhale it deeply, deciding to burn every detail of this day into memory. This is definitely one of those days to pay attention to, to take detailed notes of, to cherish.

Addie and I have had hundreds of them over our years together, and adding today to the collection is bittersweet. The burn in my throat threatens as they continue to trickle in, and I pause on the rolling memory of Addie in the back of my Tahoe—hovering over our newly occupied car seat the day we brought our baby home from the hospital. Terrified, I drove home going ten miles an hour as every asshole in Austin sped around us, cursing us and laying on their horn. The mortification I felt that day knowing I had a big job to do, the pressure continually mounting as the world revealed its ugly side while I fought to safely get my wife and newborn home. Addie had laughed at me for driving too slowly, but I could see the slight fear in her own expression just before she shakily whispered, "We've got this."

We didn't always have it, but at least it didn't feel that way until we had weathered through some of our trials. It was only after when we came out stronger, wiser—if not a bit tattered, that those words rang true. Years of trials and triumphs continue to replay in my mind as I travel down the well-marked path of the tiny island resort toward Natalie's bungalow. Turning the corner, back already covered in a sheen of humidity-induced sweat, I'm stopped short when I see Stella stepping out and pulling the door closed, a close-lipped smile on her face. She takes the few steps down and stops. As if sensing me, she looks up, and our eyes meet for the first time in nearly three decades.

"Nate," she rushes out, watering eyes sweeping me from head to freshly polished wingtips.

"Hi, Stella. Fancy meeting you here," I quip, sliding my hands into the pockets of my tailored tuxedo slacks. Reid and Stella's flight got delayed due to a tropical storm, so they missed the rehearsal dinner. They arrived late last night, and we haven't had a chance to greet each other yet.

"Oh my God," she proclaims, "we got old."

"Hey, speak for yourself. I'm feeling every bit the handsome motherfucker today," I grin, exaggeratedly adjusting my bowtie.

"Well, most definitely that," she compliments as her eyes trail over me. I take her in as well, her flowing pale pink dress. Her long, black hair curled and draped over her shoulders.

"You look beautiful." I take a step forward. "It's good to see you. Ready for this?"

She immediately lifts a palm. "Stay back!"

I flinch at her outburst and stop my approach.

"Sorry," she sniffs and laughs. "But I'm warning you, I'm an emotional, sentimental wreck today. If you come any closer, I *will* cry."

"Well," I say, stalking toward her, "tough shit."

I make it to her in two more strides, and she grips me tightly to her as I lift her off her feet. We hug for several seconds, and I keep her suspended as she pulls away, her palms on my shoulders, beaming as a tear skates down her cheek. "I warned you," she says. "Wow...Nate." She shakes her head in disbelief.

"I know...but you should know you aren't alone," I say, easing her back to her feet. "You should go introduce yourself to Addie. Bungalow 12. She's anxious to meet you and hasn't been able to leave the room yet, because she's in the same state. Though she'll be hard-pressed to admit it."

"Really?"

"Yeah, really," I grin. "Believe it or not, I married a woman more ornery than you."

"Ohhhh, in that case," she playfully rubs her hands together. "Then I definitely will. Maybe I'll grab a bottle of something strong we can share."

I chuckle. "That's a *very good* idea, and at the same time, fucking *terrifying*."

She laughs, and the sound hits me with a shot of nostalgia. We take a few seconds to soak in the moment, lost in our individual recollections.

"See you in a little while?" She asks, giving us both an out.

"See you there," I say with a wink before turning and taking the stairs up to the bungalow.

"Nate?"

Glancing over my shoulder, I see Stella's already at the foot of the stairs, her eyes lowered. Her fearful expression has me walking back down to stand in front of her.

"Yeah?"

"I can't believe this happened—this is happening, has been happening." She lifts her grey eyes to mine, and in them, I see a glimpse of the girl who kicked open my office door with sharpie lyric scribbled Converse before roller-skating her way into my heart.

"Yeah, it's pretty surreal," I agree.

"Fate really did its thing, didn't it?"

"Sure," I say, rolling my eyes up.

"Oh, please," she scolds playfully. "*Fate* is why you became a writer. I'll always remember the story of how you got started."

"I know. I read your book."

Mouth parting, eyes wide, she gapes at me.

"Stella…speechless," I buff my nails on the breast of my tux. "I've definitely still got it."

"You read it?"

"Yeah, I did," I say, as our own memories continue to trickle in. Memories of a different life. "A copy materialized on my desk last year."

"Oh," she says, her expression clouding with anxiety.

"I'm glad I read it," I admit.

"Yeah?" She prompts, hope lighting her eyes.

"Yeah, I am," I say sincerely. "Kind of hard to hold onto any grudge when your ex-fiancée introduces you as a *sex* God someone forgot about."

"Pretty sure *sex* wasn't the preface—"

"You have your interpretation. I have mine. But…to be honest, I loved your interpretation."

"Really?"

"Really. It fit."

"Well, that's…shit…Nate." Her eyes water over again as she inhales a deep breath, her voice shaking when she speaks. "Even if this was hard to accept at first, it's…kind of beautiful, isn't it? That *our* love story led to theirs?"

"Yeah, it is, truly," I agree as we fully relax our guards. "You raised a good man, Stella."

"I think so, too," she says with pride. "And Natalie is…she's absolutely beautiful, Nate. The spitting image of *you*, too, in every imaginable way."

"I know," I smile with my own parental pride as she playfully slaps my chest.

"Ughhh, still an egomaniac."

"Some things never change," I muse.

"Good," she whispers, "and I hope some things never will."

"They won't," I assure, bending and pressing a quick kiss to her temple.

Relief relaxes her features as we silently exchange that we're both at peace with the place we have in each other's lives. I don't want Stella feeling guilty because I meant the words I spoke to my wife. I wouldn't change a thing. I wouldn't go back. I wouldn't alter a minute of my life, not a fucking second.

"Now, go fetch my wife from the closet I'm sure she's hiding in, and please do your best not to corrupt her."

"No promises," she quips, her grin growing as she begins to back away, beaming a smile at me before turning. I do the same as she disappears and I reclimb the steps before knocking on the door.

"Uncle Nate, you look so handsome," Holly says with a smile, ushering me inside.

Before I get a chance to reply, I spot Natalie standing on a step-stool in front of a floor-to-ceiling mirror in her wedding gown, a bouquet of pale pink roses in hand. Eyes already stinging, it's when ours meet in the reflection, and she gasps out an elated but tearful, "Daddy," that I'm a goner.

Sleep Walk
Deftones

Shaking my hands free of excess water, I grab a fresh towel and wipe them dry as the bass filters through the walls from the reception. Exiting the restroom, I retrieve Addie's empty champagne flute where I left it. Headed towards the bar, I stop dead in my tracks as a familiar voice sounds up from the other side of a closed door.

"Oh my God…stop! We're going to get busted."

"It's all right, baby. No one can hear us. The music is too loud." I know *that voice*, too.

"We…have…to…stop. Jesus, Damon, what in the hell was in that Mexican beach water?!"

"I love you, Holly, that's what was in the damned water, now less talking and less pant—"

I rap firmly on the door *twice*. "I'm going to stop you right there and tell you that anyone, and I mean *anyone*, who walks past this door, will be able to both hear and identify you, *clearly*."

A long pause.

Holly is the first to speak up. "Uncle Nate?"

"Yes, sweetheart, it's me."

"Ummm, I…we…thank you for…this…see, the truth is, we really haven't come—"

"Out of the closet?" I finish, because it can't be helped. "That's apparent. Tell you what, I'll do you both and *myself* a favor and pretend like I didn't hear anything."

Because you've changed both their damned diapers.

The thought of that has me cringing as they speak up in unison. "Thank you."

I take two steps away, hearing the click of my wingtips on the floor and their relieved sighs just before Holly whispers a scolding, "I told you!"

"And guys..." I speak up again, only to be met by another pregnant pause.

"Yes, Uncle Nate?" Holly asks. The squeak in her tone has my smile cracking wider.

"It's about damned time."

I walk away in fast strides, thankful that I didn't exit the bathroom a minute later. I might not have survived it. Entering the reception, I walk up to the bar and hand over the empty champagne glass to the bartender requesting a fresh one.

"Hey, man."

I turn to see Reid standing next to me, dressed in a matching tux, his hair still slicked back presentably.

"Hey," I chuckle as he adjusts his jacket, looking uncomfortable before patting down his pockets.

"Fuck," he closes his eyes briefly before shaking his head in irritation. "Leave it to me to quit smoking on an overseas trip where my wife assured me some witch doctor's herbs will help curb it."

"Careful, Crowne, you almost passed for a gentleman." I grin as he scowls at me, fidgeting with the collar of his fitted tux.

"Let's get you some old-fashioned therapy," I suggest. "What are you drinking?"

He tilts his empty rocks glass my way. "Whiskey."

"I'll join you," I say, nodding toward the bartender to add to my order before tossing a bill in his tip jar. Drinks in hand, we both sip our whiskey as our wives—who are standing on opposite sides of the reception hall—spot us at the bar, their expressions a mix of fear and intrigue. I stifle my grin by taking a long sip of my drink.

"They're nervous as hell right now," Reid mutters, his tone just as amused as he keeps a straight face.

"This is too good. It's like they're expecting a full-on brawl," I agree, trying like hell to keep my cool as Stella watches us carefully like we're zoo animals.

"It's amazing how helpless they think we are," Reid says.

"Little do they know," I say, turning back toward the bar, no longer able to hide my smile. Reid follows suit as we both let them slip. Under the radar, I clink my glass to his. "Should we keep them guessing?"

"Maybe a little longer," he says. "This is too good."

The bartender flits his attention behind us, and we take the cue and step aside to allow the guests their turn at the bar. Though the wedding is on the smaller scale, the hall is filled to the brim with friends and family from both sides—some of whom I have yet to meet. My eyes drift toward familiar when I spot Lexi and Ben, who are slow dancing on the floor.

"Are they ever going to get it together?" I ask. Reid follows my line of sight and the lift of my chin. I'm all too aware of Lexi and Ben's drama, having firsthand witnessed Lexi's state in the aftermath of her and Ben's initial breakup, along with following the headlines they've made over the years.

"Ben has had a diamond in his pocket since the day after we played at the Super Bowl," Reid chuckles. "I have no doubt it will be on her finger one day soon. And she'll marry him and throw it back at him a hundred times before we finally toss them in the grave *together*. To be honest, right now, they're the least of my worries. I'm seeing a lot more drama unfolding than those two can toss at us tonight."

"Do tell," I say, circling the whiskey in my glass before taking a sip.

"Benji," he prompts, and I follow his line of sight to see Ben and Lexi's tuxedo-clad son standing on the side of the dance floor, his posture relaxed, his expression *livid*.

"Oh, I see him, and he's foaming at the mouth at—"

"Easton's bodyguard."

"Joel," I toss in. "Yeah, I've met him. Good man, oh shit, I *see*," I reiterate, spotting Joel on the dance floor with Rye's daughter, Rian, their body language making it clear they're sharing more than a friendly dance.

Reid exhales harshly, "We should fucking pop some popcorn and wait this out because we've got the best seats in the house."

"It's never easy, is it?" I shake my head as our eyes focus on Easton and Natalie, who are in the middle of the dance floor nose to nose, swaying to the guitar-fueled melody of "Sleep Walk," completely oblivious of the world around them.

"They have no idea what they're in for," Reid says, a father's concern in his voice.

"They have *some* idea," I remind him.

"Yeah, that's true." He glances over at me. "We did a good thing, man."

"More than one," I say as Easton dips and whispers to Natalie, and she beams up at him in response before her smile grows impossibly brighter. "I'm pretty sure we can thank Stella's cosmic influence on both of them. Otherwise, we couldn't have pulled it off."

"Still," he says, "it was a stroke of genius to throw them in the blender in Mexico."

"Yes, it was," I say with a chuckle. "Stella can replace the *F* in fate with an *N*," I muse, tossing back more whiskey.

"Still no way to make sense of how they ended up together in the first place," Reid states with a bewildered tone.

"I can't deny that—At. Fucking. All. Can't say it didn't play a part, either."

Reid glances over at me. "What if it hadn't worked out?"

"We can only do so much, right? God knows we made our own mistakes."

"Truth," he says, slowly lifting his chin to Stella to ease her worry just before I catch Addie's eye and give her a slow wink.

"Nate." Reid's change of tone has me glancing over at him. "Can we keep this to—"

I nod, sharply cutting him off. "It stays solely between us. It's the secret we can take to our *separate* graves."

He nods, seeming satisfied as I retire my rocks glass and exchange it before lifting the flute in my hand. "I'm going to bring my wife her champagne."

"See you around, Butler."

"Yeah, you will," I circle my face with my free hand while sporting a shit- eating grin. "So, you might want to get used to this pretty face."

"Careful, Butler. You almost dodged pretentious prick." Reid full-on smiles at me before sipping his whiskey.

"Touché, Crowne."

THE END

Well, maybe one more for the road.

DRIVE—SYMPHONIC VERSION THE CARS

ABOUT THE AUTHOR

USA Today bestselling author and Texas native, Kate Stewart, lives in North Carolina with her husband, Nick. Nestled within the Blue Ridge Mountains, Kate pens messy, sexy, angst-filled contemporary romance, as well as romantic comedy and erotic suspense.

Kate's title, *Drive*, was named one of the best romances of 2017 by The New York Daily News and Huffington Post. *Drive* was also a finalist in the Goodreads Choice awards for best contemporary romance of 2017. The Ravenhood Trilogy, consisting of *Flock, Exodus,* and *The Finish Line*, has become an international bestseller and reader favorite. Her holiday release, *The Plight Before Christmas,* ranked #6 on Amazon's Top 100. Kate's works have been featured in *USA TODAY, BuzzFeed, The New York Daily News, Huffington Post* and translated into a dozen languages.

Kate is a lover of all things '80s and '90s, especially John Hughes films and rap. She dabbles a little in photography, can knit a simple stitch scarf for necessity, and on occasion, does very well at whiskey.

OTHER TITLES AVAILABLE NOW BY KATE

Romantic Suspense

THE RAVENHOOD SERIES
Flock
Exodus
The Finish Line
SEXUAL AWAKENINGS
Excess
Predator and Prey
Lust & Lies Box Set

Contemporary Romance
Room 212
Never Me
Loving the White Liar
The Fall
The Mind
The Heart
The Brave Line
Drive
The Real
Someone Else's Ocean
Heartbreak Warfare
Method

Romantic Dramedy

BALLS IN PLAY SERIES
Anything but Minor
Major Love
Sweeping the Series
Balls in Play Box Set: Anything but Minor, Major Love, Sweeping the Series, The Golden Sombrero

THE UNDERDOGS SERIES
The Guy on the Right
The Guy on the Left
The Guy in the Middle

THANK YOU

First and foremost, thank you, dear reader, for trusting me enough to give another of my literal indulgences a chance. As with every book I write, I poured my heart and soul into every page of *Reverse* with the intent that you get the most of it—and I so hope you enjoyed Easton and Natalie's journey. For those who enjoyed the book, it would mean the world to me if you composed a sentence or two and leave a review. From the bottom to the top of my heart, thank you for continuing to gift me the ability to work my favorite ever day job.

There is a family I've been blessed to be a part of for the last thirty-three years. A family who I can attribute a lot of my inspiration for scenes in Drive, and particularly, Stella's character to. In meeting my best friend, Irene Garza, I, in turn, gained an entire second family. A family who took me in as one of their own, immersed me in their culture, and gave me shelter during some of the hardest times of my life. I don't, for one second, think these books would be what they are, nor would I be who I am, without the love and support of my Mexican American family. Licha and Roman Garza, thank you for being my second parents, for the unconditional love and support you've given to me over the years. Oh, and you too, Irene. Love you endlessly, C.C.

Feesh!

It's no exaggeration that it takes a village to get a novel published, and none of this would have been possible without mine. So, I must thank every house it's composed of in its entirety for being individual pillars of strengths in helping me finish this massive novel. So, without further ado…

Thank you to my chief editor and gatekeeper, Donna Cooksley Sanderson, for being the most incredible and loyal companion during this quest. Across the seven thousand miles and time zones that separate us, you've remained steadfast and dedicated. Your attention to detail has liberated me from so much of the hardship. From four a.m. phone calls just for welfare checks on both ends after back-breaking days behind the keyboard, to spending endless hours bouncing ideas and polishing sentences, you made the massive undertaking bearable. 'They' say no one cares as much as the creator, but with you, that's never been the case. Because of your care, and along with the rest of the village you help run with an iron fist, I never felt alone in this. Our friendship remains one of my most cherished and forever will be. I'm so lucky to have you in my life.

Thank you to my editor Grey, for being such a huge support, for the check-ins, for the music suggests to help spark my creativity, and for reminders to breathe during times my writer brain makes it feel like a hard feat. Your dedication to this project and belief in me make it all worthwhile. I adore you.

A huge thank you to Autumn Gantz for whom this book is dedicated. This full-circle book is for you, my dear friend. Even if the circle is completed, we still have *so much* journey left to venture on together and to navigate—which wouldn't be possible without your expertise and gentle guidance. I can't wait to see what the next part of it entails, especially with you by my side.

A massive, massive thank you to my as*sister*, Angela Scott, whom I was introduced to, due to relation, brought on in the last year as a much-needed right hand. Without you these past months, I can honestly say I would have fumbled the ball—badly. Your dedication to the job and our collective passions have created some absolutely incredible results. I couldn't be happier about that. You're an amazing extra hand, but more so, human being, and I'm excited for our future together, both personally and professionally. I love you.

A huge thank you to my sister, Kristan, for keeping me sorted, literally, and easing my worries. For checking in on me even when and *especially* when you have a full plate of your own.

Thank you as well to Amanda Lenz for being Kris's right hand and helping her with the chore that is me. You're amazing, and I adore you.

Thanks to my dear PA, Bex Kettner, who continues to love me unconditionally, anticipate my needs, and goes above and beyond despite all the crazy twists that go along with being my PA. You're a mighty hand, madam, and one I refuse to go without. Thank you for six years of dedication and unconditional love.

Christy Baldwin- you continue to remain one of the blessings I'm most thankful for. Your love and loyalty knows no bounds, and I'm forever grateful for the gift of your friendship. Your selfless heart and beaming presence play a large part of the foundation of our village, and we are so lucky because of it. I love you.

Thank you to my darling niece, Allison Samples, for the insight on motocross and to her fiancé, Jedidiah, for the inspiration.

A huge thank you to my incredible betas and proofers—Angie Maroni, Rita Roman, Maria Black, Christy Baldwin, Autumn Gantz, Stacey Hahn, Rhonda Bobbitt Love, Kathy Sheffler, Malene Diech, Maiween Bizien, Bethany Lynn, and Marissa D'Onofrio. Most of whom have been with me for every book and continue to show up when called upon without fail. Thank you so much for your endless patience, and despite the wait, cheering me on from the sidelines, especially when it was hard to see the finish line. There's no way I could have crossed this one without you. Thank you, thank you, thank you, beauties, with all my heart, thank you.

Once again, I must thank Amy Q of Q Design for plucking another rough vision for a cover from my racing mind and bringing it to life in the best imaginable way. Between our collective imaginations and because of your patience and expertise, you continue to astound me with your limitless talent. I love you, dear friend.

Thank you, Stacey Ryan Blake, for continuing to beautify the polished results of our village's collective efforts in such a breathtaking way. I'm forever grateful for the incomparable artist you are and for our longstanding friendship.

Thank you to my husband, family, and dear friends who continue to support me despite my notable absence when I get lost in words. For your bottomless understanding from the beginning of the rough, through the rocky road between, until the end—when all that's left of me is the frazzled remnants of the wife, sister, aunt, daughter, and friend I resembled before I begin. Thank you for nursing that girl back to health with your love and acceptance, time and time again. But mostly, thank you for allowing me the space I need to keep doing what I love without fear of losing your affections. It's a gift I do not take for granted.

A special thank you to DJ and Fist of Five for permission to use your hauntingly beautiful rendition of "The Dance." As music is the backbone and underlying hero in this series, your reimagined and heart-stopping cover of a classic aided in the word flow and gave shape to a vital chapter in this book.

Thank you to my darling Amy Halter, who made true magic in doing the trailer video for *Reverse*. Not only have we created some magic together, but we've also managed to start and cultivate a friendship I've come to rely on and adore. I adore you, lady, and can't wait to see what's next for us.